Everyman, I will go with thee,
and be thy guide

Maria Edgeworth

BELINDA

"A prudence undeceiving, undeceived,
That not too little, nor too much believed;
That scorned unjust Suspicion's coward fear,
And without weakness knew to be sincere."

Lord Lyttleton's "Monody on his Wife"

———

Edited by
EILÉAN NÍ CHUILLEANÁIN

Trinity College, Dublin

EVERYMAN
J. M. DENT · LONDON
CHARLES E. TUTTLE
VERMONT

Introduction and critical apparatus
© J. M. Dent 1993

This edition first published in Everyman by J. M. Dent 1993

Reprinted 1994

J. M. Dent
Orion Publishing Group
Orion House
5 Upper St Martin's Lane, London WC2H 9EA
and
Charles E. Tuttle Co. Inc.
28 South Main Street, Rutland, Vermont
05701, USA

Typeset at The Spartan Press Ltd,
Lymington, Hants
Printed in Great Britain by
The Guernsey Press Co. Ltd,
Guernsey, C.I.

British Library Cataloguing-in-Publication Data
is available upon request

ISBN 0 460 87228 1

CONTENTS

NOTE ON THE AUTHOR AND EDITOR

MARIA EDGEWORTH was born on 1 January 1768, at Black Bourton in Oxfordshire. She was the third daughter of Richard Lovell Edgeworth (1744–1817), the son of an Anglo-Irish landlord family established at Edgeworthstown, Co. Longford since the early seventeenth century. Edgeworth had been married at nineteen and was only twenty-three at Maria's birth; he was to develop into one of the most noted intellectuals of his day, an educational theorist, inventor, enlightened landlord and politician, now mainly remembered because of his great and lifelong influence on his daughter. His *Autobiography*, partly written by her, is full of entertaining portraits of contemporaries.

Maria's mother died when she was five, and Edgeworth married Honora Sneyd a few months later. The family moved from England to Edgeworthstown, which was to remain, with a break of five years when she was at boarding-school in England, Maria's home until her death. Honora died and was succeeded by two more stepmothers; with all of them but especially with the last, Frances Beaufort, their stepdaughter enjoyed affectionate relationships.

Her father began Maria's literary career by giving her the task of translating Mme de Genlis' *Adèle and Theodore* in 1782; her first published work was *Letters for Literary Ladies*, in 1795, containing a spirited defence of women's education. After a collection of stories for children and a theoretical treatise, *Practical Education*, written with her father, she produced her first successful work, still her most popular, *Castle Rackrent* in 1800. It was followed the next year by *Belinda*, and the combination made their author a celebrity.

For the remainder of her long life she lived in Edgeworthstown, occasionally travelling abroad, and producing many more novels.

Of these, *Ennui* (1809), *The Absentee* (1812) and *Ormond* (1817) are the best known, probably because of their Irish interest; *Patronage* (1814) and *Helen* (1834), her last novel, both set in England, have been reprinted in recent years. She was hardworking and successful both as novelist and as manager of the Edgeworthstown estate on behalf of her brother Lovell.

Maria Edgeworth died in 1849. Her letters, mostly to members of her family, show that her strength of mind, wit and affection for humanity remained with her. Her last work, *Orlandino* (1848), was written to raise money for the victims of the Irish Famine.

EILÉAN NÍ CHUILLEANÁIN, born 1942, has been a lecturer in English at Trinity College, Dublin since 1966. She has published five volumes of poetry as well as essays on Renaissance and on Irish literature, and in 1985 edited a collection of essays, *Irish Women: Image and Achievement*. The Irish–American Cultural Institute awarded her the O'Shaughnessy Prize for poetry in 1992. She is married to the poet Macdara Woods and they have a son, Niall.

NOTE ON THE TEXT

The text of *Belinda* used here is that of the first edition of 1801. Obvious mistakes and misprints, usually corrected by the author herself in later editions, have been rectified. The spelling and capitalisation, and occasionally punctuation, have been somewhat modernised. The revisions to the plot of the novel and some of its language, which Maria Edgeworth undertook under pressure from her critics, and which appear in all of the editions after 1810, are described in the Introduction.

CHRONOLOGY OF MARIA EDGEWORTH'S LIFE

Year	Key Events
1744	Richard Lovell Edgeworth born
1763	RLE married in Scotland to Anna Maria Elers
1764	*February* remarried under English law with parental consent; *May* eldest son Richard born
1768	*1 January* Maria Edgeworth born (Three more children of this marriage)
1771	RLE set out for France with Thomas Day
1773	*March* death of Anna Maria Edgeworth; *July* RLE marries Honora Sneyd; family moves to Edgeworthstown (Honora bears two children)
1775	Maria sent to Mrs Latuffière's school at Derby
1777	Family moves back to England, settles in Hertfordshire
1779	RLE and Honora start writing for children – plan for the first version of *Practical Education*

Year	Literary Context	Historical Events
1766	Adam Ferguson, *Essay on Civil Society*	
		Octennial Act (Irish parliament's life limited to eight years)
1771	Henry Mackenzie, *The Man of Feeling*	
1773	Oliver Goldsmith, *She Stoops to Conquer*; Chesterfield dies	Boston tea party
1775	Jane Austen born	Battles of Lexington, Concord and Bunker Hill in the USA
1776	Adam Smith, *Wealth of Nations*; Jeremy Bentham, *A Fragment on Government; or, a Comment on the Commentaries*; Edward Gibbon, *Decline and Fall of the Roman Empire* (−1788); Charles Burney, *History of Music*; David Hume born	American Declaration of Independence
1777	Henry Mackenzie, *Julia de Roubigné*	American Congress adopts Confederation Articles of perpetual Union of United States
1778	Frances Burney, *Evelina*; Richard Brinsley Sheridan, *The School for Scandal*; Jean Jacques Rousseau dies	Catholic Relief Act grants rights of leasing and inheritance

1780   *May* death of Honora; *December* RLE marries her sister
         Elizabeth after much family opposition (Elizabeth to bear
         him nine children)
1781   Maria at school in London

1782   Leaves school; family moves back to Edgeworthstown; RLE
         starts Maria's literary career by giving her the task of
         translating Mme de Genlis' *Adèle et Theodore*

1783   RLE attends Volunteer conference in Dublin

1792–3   Family in London and Clifton

1795   *Letters for Literary Ladies*, Maria's first published work

1796   RLE defeated in Longford election; *The Parent's Assistant*
         published
1797   Death of Elizabeth

1798   *February* RLE elected to parliament; *Practical Education* by
         Maria and RLE published; *May* RLE marries Frances
         Beaufort (she is to bear him six children); *September*
         French invading force defeated at Granard; Edgeworth
         family takes refuge in Longford and RLE is nearly
         lynched by a crowd who believe him to be a French spy
1800   Act of Union between the Parliaments of Great Britain and
         Ireland. RLE twice speaks in favour of the motion, and
         twice votes against it; *Castle Rackrent* published

1780	Arthur Young, *Tour in Ireland*; Immanuel Kant, *Critique of Pure Reason*	Act opening colonial trade to Irish goods
1781	Jean Jacques Rousseau, *Confessions*	Cornwallis capitulates to American forces at Yorktown
1782	Frances Burney, *Cecilia*; Dugald Steward, *Elements of the Philosophy of the Human Mind*	Ireland achieves legislative independence
1783	Thomas Day, *Sandford and Merton* (–1789); Jean d'Alembert dies	Peace of Versailles agreed between Britain, France, Spain and USA; Britain officially recognises USA
1791	Elizabeth Inchbald, *A Simple Story*; Thomas Paine, *The Rights of Man, I*	Theobald Wolfe Tone founds the Society of United Irishmen
1792	Mary Wollstonecraft, *A Vindication of the Rights of Woman*; Thomas Paine, *The Rights of Man, II*	Catholic Relief Act allows Catholics to practise law
1793		Further Relief Act grants Catholics parliamentary franchise and some civil and military rights
1795	Samuel Taylor Coleridge, *Conciones ad Populum*; John Keats born	Act providing for establishment of Catholic seminary, opened as Royal College of St Patrick at Maynooth; the Directory in France; Napoleon Bonaparte made commander of the army
1796	Frances Burney, *Camilla*	Insurrection Act in Ireland; Habeas Corpus suspended
1797	Samuel Coleridge, *Kubla Khan*; Edmund Burke dies; Mary Wollstonecraft dies	Irish Whigs invite the Prince of Wales to become Lord Lieutenant of Ireland
1798	Mary Hays, *Memoirs of Emma Courtney; An Appeal to the Men of Great Britain on Behalf of the Women*	Rebellion in Wexford defeated; General Humbert's French forces land in Co. Mayo, move almost as far as Co. Longford before defeat
1800	Humphry Davy, *Researches, Chemical and Philosophical, Chiefly Concerning Nitrous Oxide*	Act of Union passed in Irish parliament

1801   *Early Lessons, Moral Tales* and *Belinda* published

1802   Trip to England and France with father and stepmother; the
        Chevalier Edelcrantz proposes to Maria in Paris in
        December and she refuses him; *Essay on Irish Bulls* by
        Maria and RLE published

1805   *The Modern Griselda* published

1806   *Leonora* published

1809   *Essays on Professional Education* published; also *Tales of
        Fashionable Life* vols 1–3 (*Ennui, Almeria, Madame de
        Fleury, The Dun, Manoevring*)

1812   *Tales of Fashionable Life*, vols 4–6 (*Vivian, Emilie de
        Coulanges, The Absentee*) published

1813   In London with father and stepmother

1814   *Patronage* published

1817   *Harrington* and *Ormond* published; *13 June* death of RLE

1818–19   In London to arrange publication of her father's *Memoirs*

1820   *Memoirs of Richard Lovell Edgeworth* (second volume by
        Maria Edgeworth) published; Maria in France and
        Switzerland with her half-sisters Fanny and Harriet

Year		
1801	Robert Southey, *Thalaba the Destroyer*	Union takes effect; Pitt resigns over royal veto on Catholic emancipation
1802	Mme de Staël, *Delphine*	Britain signs Peace of Amiens with France
1803	Erasmus Darwin, *Temple of Nature*	Failed rising of Robert Emmet
1804	Amelia Opie, *Adeline Mowbray*	Napoleon becomes Emperor
1805	Walter Scott, *The Lay of the Last Minstrel*	Battles of Trafalgar and Austerlitz
1806	Sydney Owenson (Lady Morgan), *The Wild Irish Girl*	Pitt dies; "Ministry of all the Talents", with Grenvile as PM
1809	Quarterly Review founded by Scott and others; Walter Scott, *Marmion*; Johann Wolfgang von Goethe, *The Elective Affinities*	Napoleon imprisons Pope Pius VII
1812	Lord Byron, *Childe Harold's Pilgrimage*; Percy Bysshe Shelley, *Address to the Irish People*; Charles Dickens born	War with USA; Napoleon invades Russia
1813	Jane Austen, *Pride and Prejudice*; Walter Scott, *Waverley*; Lady Morgan, *O'Donnel*	Wellington defeats the French at Vittoria
1814	Jane Austen, *Mansfield Park*	Fall of Paris; Napoleon abdicates
1817	Thomas Moore, *Lallah Rookh*; David Ricardo, *Principles of Political Economy and Taxation*; Jane Austen dies	Habeas Corpus suspended in Britain
1819	Walter Scott, *Tales of My Landlord*; George Eliot born	Peterloo Massacre
1820	Walter Scott, *Ivanhoe*; Percy Bysshe Shelley, *Prometheus Unbound*; Thomas Malthus, *Principles of Political Economy*	Accession of George IV

1821	Thomas de Quincey, *Confessions of an English Opium Eater*; Walter Scott, *Kenilworth*; Keats dies	Death of Napoleon
1822	John Galt, *The Provost*; Shelley dies	Irish Constabulary Act
1823	Walter Scott, *Quentin Durward*; Mary Shelley, *Valperga*	Catholic Association founded; war between France and Spain
1825	Thomas Crofton Croker, *Fairy Legends and Traditions of the South of Ireland*; James Stuart Mill, *Essays on Government*; Anna Laetitia Barbauld dies	Lords reject Catholic Emancipation Bill
1827	Lady Morgan, *The O'Briens and the O'Flahertys*	
1830		Accession of William IV
1833	Thomas Carlyle, *Sartor Resartus*;	British Factory Act passed
1834	Honoré de Balzac, *La Recherche de l'Absolu*	O'Connell introduces debate on Repeal of Union; slavery abolished in the British Empire
1837		Accession of Victoria
1840		Repeal Association founded
1843		First "monster" Repeal meeting
1845		Irish famine begins
1846		Repeal of the Corn Laws
1847		Death of Daniel O'Connell
1848		John Mitchel's journal, *United Irishman* began and ceased publication. Young Ireland rising failed.

INTRODUCTION

Maria Edgeworth's *Belinda* appeared in 1801, with the author's name on the title page. Although she had already written a successful novel, *Castle Rackrent*, published anonymously, and although her name was known as a writer of moral fiction and (with her father) of an innovative treatise, *Practical Education*, *Belinda* really inaugurates her career as novelist and moralist combined. Like her other major novels *Ennui, Ormond, The Absentee, Patronage, Helen*, it is conceived on a large scale and has a complex plot; like them it focuses on the happiness of private life as the supreme human good, with which characters who have been educated by misfortune and vicissitude are rewarded. But unlike her great contemporary Jane Austen, who notoriously limits her range, excluding world affairs as well as sexual passion, Edgeworth carries into these novels all the breadth of those interests represented by her work up to 1800, and more. *Belinda*'s material belongs to the mainstream English novel of manners – there are the dilemmas of lovers, the misunderstandings and rivalries which delay or endanger consummation, as comic relief the satiric picture of what marriage may bring for those who make ill-considered choices. This drama of personal decision takes place in a world aware of other dramas. The characters are reminded by the elegant refugees from the Reign of Terror, by the talk of slavery, of religious persecution and of the Methodist movement, even of Benjamin Franklin's views on swimming, that there are upheavals in the public world in Britain and abroad. The books they read and quote – and this is a novel full of allusion and parody – the catchphrases of their conversation, reflect the philosophical ferment which preceded the French Revolution and the later debate of the rights of woman which was so firmly excluded from the agenda of the proponents of the Rights of Man. Even the children who point the moral of the importance of domestic concerns simultaneously illustrate the Edgeworths' educational theories.

But *Belinda* like *Helen*, Maria Edgeworth's last novel, turns especially on a relationship between two women, so that its politics are predominantly the politics of private life. The "Advertisement" which precedes the novel defines it as a "moral tale" in contradistinction to common novels which are full of "folly, error and vice", while praising the works of novelists such as Frances Burney and Dr John Moore. It thus declares adherence to a tradition in fiction which rejects romance and examines social realities and ethical problems of a kind especially likely to confront women readers.

The opening situation is the classic one of "a young lady's entrance into the world". Belinda is young, beautiful and accomplished but has only a modest fortune; her visit to the fashionable Lady Delacour is intended to promote her "establishment" in society through a suitable marriage to a man with a large income. Lady Delacour confides to her young friend her secret: she believes herself to be suffering from cancer of the breast and is terrified lest anybody should find this out. From Lady Delacour's character and history as a dissipated fine lady with a private obsession, from her vanity, fear and suspicions, most of the book's central action flows. Belinda is compromised in society by the expectations of the men in her circle, that she will sell herself to the highest bidder, but she is in constant danger of being even more compromised by Lady Delacour's confiding in her, by the fits of jealousy Lady Delacour falls into when Belinda tries to persuade her to let her husband know of her condition and by Lady Delacour's indiscreet promotion of the love affair between her friend and the young man she is eventually to marry, Clarence Hervey. Here Lady Delacour is allowed to triumph at last, disposing of a rival claimant to Clarence's love with a comic *coup de théâtre*.

Lady Delacour's secret is an explosive one because it draws attention to her body which is conventionally supposed to be desirable – she is suspected of more than one adulterous love affair, she is "courted by the gay, the witty and the gallant". Like Queen Elizabeth, in whose character she appears at one point, she sustains the fiction of her beauty by the use of cosmetics long after its reality has decayed. But her own experience of her body is one of pain and failure; one of her children whom she breast-fed has died, and her remaining daughter makes her scream with pain when she embraces her. She is elated and depressed in turn by the laudanum she takes; she treats friends and society, too, as drugs. She transforms sexual into medical flirtation, defining herself as a patient but avoiding medical scrutiny; at a memorable moment in the novel the beating of her pulse, the vibrations charted by the motion of the large Elizabethan ruff she is wearing and magnified by the shadow cast on a wall, is secretly watched by Clarence Hervey and the novel's benevolent philosopher, Dr X —. But just as there is no adultery, there is no cancer, there is only the tension generated by an uneasy woman who has never recovered from the sexual and emotional disaster of a foolish marriage.

Lady Delacour's body is legally the possession of her husband, which is why she is afraid to consult a physician; a reputable practitioner would refuse to amputate a breast for a married woman without her husband's knowledge and consent. And her husband is a rather stupid, often drunk man who is dismayed by his wife's intelligence and not inclined to give up his claim to marital authority. He has actually cheated her of her dowry so that she is financially dependent on him. Yet Maria Edgeworth has succeeded in making him not only a comic success but a pathetic and in the end a sympathetic figure, whose ignorance of his wife's bodily condition complicates the plot but also symbolizes the general puzzlement of a foolish and prejudiced man to whom the whole world is a mystery once he strays from the safe masculine haven of drink and gambling. Another success is the couple's daughter Helena, whose painful position is unsentimentally conveyed and who appears, in spite of her youth, as an individual acting independently rather than as a pathetic pendant to her parents' vices.

Secrecy and mysteries generate the action of a novel in which the declared ethical ideal is one of openness and ingenuousness. Secrets may be necessary because the world is inquisitive and censorious; on the other hand those who seem most open and simple may be the greatest deceivers because they deceive themselves. This is true of Belinda's second lover Mr Vincent, who believes himself to have conquered a passion for gambling and then finds himself concealing from her, on the eve of their marriage, the near loss at play of his entire estate. It is true of Virginia, the girl whom Clarence Hervey finds in the New Forest and educates to be his wife until, having met Belinda, he finds her simplicity boring. He is convinced by her governess Mrs Ormond that Virginia is in love with him and thus feels bound to marry her.

But Virginia has in fact fallen in love with a picture – the first masculine image she ever saw in her life – and simply lacks the words and the experience of life to explain her state of mind.

The Virginia plot is based on the true story of Thomas Day, a friend of Maria Edgeworth's father Richard Lovell Edgeworth, who began to educate an orphan girl, Sabrina Sidney, as an ideal wife for himself. Then in 1771 he met Honora Sneyd, a beautiful and intelligent woman whom he courted but who refused him; the relationship with Sabrina came to an end. Day and Sabrina were both to make happy marriages with others. But Day was not alone in falling in love with Honora Sneyd in 1771. Richard Lovell Edgeworth not only did so, he did so while still married to his first wife, Maria's mother. Two years later in 1773, her death freed him and he married Honora.

The scruples which attack Clarence Hervey have then an acute significance for his creator; the dilemma of a man caught between a simple, passive woman to whom he feels a moral obligation, and an educated and energetic one who demands a high moral standard of behaviour – such a one as Honora Sneyd, Maria Edgeworth's first stepmother certainly was – lay at the origins not of her physical existence but of the whole pattern of her life in a family she never left, presided over by a succession of three intellectual stepmothers, from the age of five. The fiction of the hero's liberation by the fortunate discovery of a substitute love-object for Virginia (the picture she fell in love with has a living and willing original, who puts in a brief, wordless appearance in the last scene of the novel) provides a perfectly satisfactory conclusion to an *impasse* which in reality had not been so painless for either Edgeworth or Day.

Or, presumably, for the rejected Sabrina. Maria Edgeworth, while letting Clarence Hervey discover the folly of his romantic project, is far from blind to the sufferings of the girl who is the guinea pig for his experiment. Virginia has a revealing dream in which Hervey is killed by the hero of her fantasies. While this may express her unconscious wish to be rid of him and his designs for her, it is also an atrocious nightmare; Virginia is a gentle, grateful girl who really possesses the ideal feminine virtues of modesty, simplicity and generosity. But her whole life has been a nightmare; from her birth the subject of other people's obsessions, she is brought up by a grandmother who never wishes her to see or speak to a man, read a newspaper or learn to write in case she might write love letters. The grandmother dies and she passes into the hands of Clarence Hervey who changes her name and attempts to turn her into an illustration of the theories of Jean-Jacques Rousseau. Her nice ordinary governess has a more ordinary fantasy; she assumes Virginia must be in love with Hervey and oppresses her with assurances that this is quite in order whereas both she and he wish to escape, Hervey to marry Belinda and Virginia back to her imaginary lover. The Virginia story mocks philosophical theorizing and romantic exaltation, but not by suggesting that people in real life never have philosophical or romantic motives or that when these motives lead them into absurdity they do not suffer.

The indebtedness of this part of *Belinda* to the friendship between her father and Thomas Day has been noticed; it has even been suggested that Richard Lovell Edgeworth, often disliked by his daughter's admirers in her lifetime and since, actually interfered in the writing of the work and may have written this part himself. Marylin Butler has shown[1] that there is no evidence for this view, and that the nature of the collaboration between father and daughter in the books bearing her name has been misunderstood. It is true that the first sketch of the novel does not contain the Virginia subplot; instead, Clarence Hervey almost kills himself with dissipation, reforms and goes into Parliament. But that first sketch too shows the influence of Edgeworth's youthful friendships; the important figure here is Sir Francis Delaval, a notorious rake who is in part the model for Lady Delacour. Maria Edgeworth, in all her work, not only makes use of the actual experiences of herself and her acquaintances and family, especially her father; she draws attention to the fact in her letters and in occasional footnotes, even in trivial matters. Her writing shows her pleasure in the transcription of actuality: scenes, sayings and events are identified as factually based. The range and confidence of her work, her willingness to describe male as well as female experience, to discuss public issues, would not be possible without this quasi-journalistic talent. The reader, too, is offered the pleasure of facts; there is a particular relish in reading the account of the duel between Lady Delacour and Mrs Luttridge when we hear that Mr Edgeworth could give "chapter and verse for the female duel and the pigs and the turkeys".[2] His influence on his daughter is in part a matter of sensibility – pushing her towards the odd and extraordinary rather than the acceptably normal – and in part a philosophical bias in favour of the intrinsic interest of what has really happened. She never escapes from fact into art, rather constantly returns to living facts.

Returns, through the interstices of a complex, ingenious plot which gathers speed as it goes, to end in a parody of both novel and romance. The plot of *Belinda* had from the first appeared resistant to definition. As the history of a young lady, who is described at the outset as having been "but a puppet in the hands of others", and who must learn to think and act for herself, it promises an ethical novel of character. As the story of Lady Delacour it promises a tragic melodrama, such as the author had in fact projected at first. But in the published version the reader is teased, from the second chapter, "Masks", onward, by the alteration of tragic and comic modes – just as Lady Delacour, in spite of literary decorum, insists on changing from the costume of the tragic to that of the comic muse.

The Virginia plot is appropriately constructed as a romance, full of coincidences and revealing tokens. The girl brought up in the forest is also the abandoned daughter of a rich man who identifies her by a mole on her forehead. His life has been saved by Captain Sunderland, the original of the picture his daughter fell in love with; coincidentally he has fallen in love with her through a telescope, and traces her through a bullfinch which he had left as an anonymous gift to her; it is lost, found by Lady Delacour's maid and returned to Virginia in circumstances of great complexity and misunderstanding.

The conclusion of the novel, in which the last complications of the Virginia plot are briskly disposed of by Lady Delacour as comic narrator, should clear the way for the marriage of Belinda with Clarence Hervey. But Belinda protests, "there is nothing in which novelists are so apt to err, as in hurrying things toward the conclusion. In not allowing *time* enough for that change of feeling, which change of situation cannot instantly produce." Lady Delacour offers "to draw out the story to five volumes more", with the help of "blushes, and sighs, and doubts, and fears, and misunderstandings, and jealousies without end or common sense, to fill up the necessary space", but settles for a final tableau in which Belinda and Virginia are both posed as brides but neither has agreed to marry. Doubts about the appropriateness of telling formally constructed stories about life, about the usefulness of such traditional labels as tragedy, comedy, romance, reassert the ambiguous feelings Maria Edgeworth had expressed in her opening remarks about calling her narrative a novel.

The debate in the closing pages is about life and marriage as well as art. Belinda's belief in custom, as opposed to passion, as a basis for marriage choice is harshly antiromantic but is of a piece with her earlier conduct in the novel. It made her an unpopular heroine; the critics objected to her unsentimental determination to marry Vincent without being in love with him, after curing herself of her first love for Clarence Hervey; her behaviour in breaking off with Vincent when she discovers his gambling propensities on the eve of marriage was found indelicate. Hostile criticism made Maria Edgeworth begin a process of revision which, extended over several reprintings – for *Belinda*, in spite of critical blame, was a popular book – changed it a good deal. The major revision was undertaken for Mrs Barbauld's series of "British Novelists" in which *Belinda* appeared in 1810. Here Belinda does not agree to marry Vincent, so that her breach with him is made less offensive to the feelings of readers who, in a world where marriage was indissoluble in all cases except the unthinkable one of the wife's adultery, objected to her caution in refusing to bind herself for life to a gambler. The exchanges in the debate on passion and custom between Belinda and Lady Delacour are toned down, and an event which Maria Edgeworth was told "gave the gentlemen the horrors" was excised – the marriage of Vincent's black West Indian servant Juba to an English girl.

The effect of these changes is to take away some of the strangeness of reality as the Edgeworth family had known it, and to circumscribe Belinda, to make her a more conventional heroine rather than one who has indeed learned to think for herself – for example about the limitations of delicacy as a female virtue. The character of Juba, carefully though conventionally drawn, loses much of its point as an illustration of the folly of prejudice, when he is silently robbed of the reward of his virtues and talents by critical squeamishness. More squeamishness is evident in later revisions; some of the free expressions in the debate between the radical feminist Mrs Freke and the philosophical Mr Percival disappear.

EILÉAN NÍ CHUILLEANÁIN

1. Marylin Butler, *Maria Edgeworth*; *A Literary Biography*, pp. 282–5.
2. Butler, p. 243.

ACKNOWLEDGEMENTS

I am grateful to the staff of the Library of Trinity College, Dublin, The National Library, Dublin, the British Library, London, the Bibliotheca Augusta, Perugia and the Bibliotheca dell' Universita degli Studi, Perugia, and to my niece Léan Ní Chuilleanáin, for their assistance.

AUTHOR'S ADVERTISEMENT
FOR *Belinda*

Every author has a right to give what appellation he may think proper to his works. The public have also a right to accept or refuse the classification that is presented.

The following work is offered to the public as a Moral Tale – the author not wishing to acknowledge a Novel. Were all novels like those of madame de Crousaz, Mrs Inchbald, Miss Burney, or Dr Moore, she would adopt the name of novel with delight: But so much folly, error, and vice are disseminated in books classed under this denomination, that it is hoped the wish to assume another title will be attributed to feelings that are laudable, and not fastidious.

April 20, 1801

VOLUME I

CHAPTER I

Characters

_____

Mrs Stanhope, a well-bred woman, accomplished in that branch of knowledge, which is called the art of rising in the world, had, with but a small fortune, contrived to live in the highest company. She prided herself upon having established half a dozen nieces most happily; that is to say, upon having married them to men of fortunes far superior to their own. One niece still remained unmarried – Belinda Portman, of whom she was determined to get rid with all convenient expedition. Belinda was handsome, graceful, sprightly, and highly accomplished; her aunt had endeavoured to teach her, that a young lady's chief business is to please in society, that all her charms and accomplishments should be invariably subservient to one grand object – the establishing herself in the world.

> "For this, hands, lips, and eyes were put to school,
> "And each instructed feature had its rule."

Mrs Stanhope did not find Belinda such a docile pupil as her other nieces, for she had been educated chiefly in the country; she had early been inspired with a taste for domestic pleasures; she was fond of reading, and disposed to conduct herself with prudence and integrity. Her character, however, was yet to be developed by circumstances.

Mrs Stanhope lived at Bath, where she had opportunities of showing her niece off, as she thought, to advantage; but as her health began to decline, she could not go out with her as much as she wished. After manoeuvering with more than her usual art, she succeeded in fastening Belinda upon the fashionable Lady Delacour for the season. Her ladyship was so much pleased by Miss Portman's accomplishments and vivacity, as to invite her to spend the winter with her in London. Soon after her arrival in town, Belinda received the following letter from her aunt Stanhope.

Crescent, Bath.

"After searching every place I could think of, Anne found your bracelet in your dressing table, amongst a heap of odd things, which you left behind you to be thrown away – I have sent it to you by a young gentleman, who came to Bath (unluckily) the very day you left me – Mr Clarence Hervey – an acquaintance, and great admirer of my Lady Delacour's. He is really an uncommonly pleasant young man, is highly connected, and has a fine independent fortune. Besides, he is a man of wit and gallantry, quite a connoisseur in female grace and beauty – just the man to bring a new face into fashion – So my dear Belinda, I make it a point – look well when he is introduced to you, and remember, what I have told you, that nobody *can* look well without taking some pains to please.

"I see –, or at least when I went out more than my health will at present permit – I used to see multitudes of silly girls, seemingly all cut out upon the same pattern, who frequented public places day after day, and year after year, without any idea further than that of diverting themselves, or of obtaining transient admiration – How I have pitied and despised the giddy creatures, whilst I have observed them playing off their unmeaning airs, vying with one another in the most *obvious*, and consequently the most ridiculous manner, so as to expose themselves before the very men they would attract; chattering, tittering, and flirting; full of the present moment, never reflecting upon the future; quite satisfied if they got a partner at a ball, without ever thinking of a partner for life. I have often asked myself, what is to become of such girls, when they grow old or ugly, or when the public eye grows tired of them? If they have large fortunes, it is all very well; they can afford to divert themselves for a season or two without doubt; they are sure to be sought after and followed, not by mere danglers, but by men of suitable views and pretensions – But nothing to my mind can be more miserable than the situation of a poor girl, who, after spending not only the interest, but the solid capital of her small fortune in dress, and frivolous extravagance, fails in her matrimonial expectations, (as many do merely from not beginning to speculate in time). She finds herself at five or six and thirty a burden to her friends, destitute of the means of rendering herself independent (for the girls I speak of never think of *learning* to play cards), *de trop* in society, yet obliged to hang upon all her acquaintance, who wish her in Heaven, because she is unqualified to make the *expected* return for civilities, having no home, I mean no establishment, no house, &c. fit for the reception of company of a certain rank. – My dearest Belinda, may this never be your case! – You have every possible advantage, my love: no pains have been spared in your education, and (which is the essential point) I have taken care that this should be known – So that you have *the name* of being perfectly accomplished – You will also have the name of being very fashionable, if you go much into public, as doubtless you will with Lady Delacour. – Your own good sense must make you aware, my dear, that from her ladyship's situation and knowledge of the world, it will always be proper, upon all subjects of conversation, for her to lead and you to follow – It would be very unfit for a young girl like you, to suffer yourself to stand in competition with Lady Delacour, whose high pretentions to wit and beauty are *indisputable*. I need say no more to you upon this subject, my dear. Even with your limited experience, you must have observed how foolish young people offend those who are the most necessary to their interests, by an imprudent indulgence of their vanity.

"Lady Delacour has an incomparable taste in dress – Consult her, my dear, and do not, by an ill-judged economy, counteract my views – Apropos – I have no object to your being presented at court. You will, of course, have credit with all her ladyship's trades-people, if you manage properly. To know how and when to lay out money, is highly commendable, for in some situations people judge of what one can afford by what one actually spends. – I know of no law, which compels a young lady, to tell what her age or her fortune may be – You have no occasion for caution yet on one of these points.

"I have covered my old carpet with a handsome green baize, and every stranger, who comes to see me, I observe, takes it for granted, that I have a rich carpet under it. Say every thing that is proper, in your best manner for me to Lady Delacour. –

Adieu, my dear Belinda,
    Yours very sincerely,
        SELINA STANHOPE."

It is sometimes fortunate, that the means, which are taken to produce certain effects upon the mind, have a tendency directly opposite to what is expected. Mrs Stanhope's perpetual anxiety about her niece's appearance, manners, and establishment had completely worn out Belinda's patience; she had become more insensible to the praises of her personal charms and accomplishments, than young women of her age usually are, because she had been so much flattered and *shown off*, as it is called, by her match-making aunt. – Yet Belinda was fond of amusement, and had imbibed some of Mrs Stanhope's prejudices in favour of rank and fashion. Her taste for literature declined in proportion to her intercourse with the fashionable world, as she did not in this society perceive the least use in the knowledge that she had acquired. Her mind had never been roused to much reflection; she had in general acted but as a puppet in the hands of others. To her aunt Stanhope she had hitherto paid unlimited, habitual, blind obedience; but she was more undesigning, and more free from affectation and coquetry, than could have been expected, after the course of documenting, which she had gone through. She was charmed with the idea of her visit to Lady Delacour, whom she thought the most agreeable – no, that is too feeble an expression – the most fascinating person she had ever beheld. Such was the light in which her ladyship appeared, not only to Belinda, but to all the world – that is to say, all the world of fashion, and she knew of no other. – The newspapers were full of Lady Delacour's parties, and Lady Delacour's dresses, and Lady Delacour's bon mots: every thing, that her ladyship said, was repeated as witty; every thing, that her ladyship wore, was imitated as fashionable. Female wit sometimes depends on the beauty of its possessor, for its reputation; and the reign of beauty is proverbially short. Fashion often capriciously deserts her favourites, even before nature withers their charms. Lady Delacour seemed to be a fortunate exception to these general rules; long after she had lost the bloom of youth, she continued to be admired as a fashionable *bel esprit*; and long after she had ceased to be a novelty in society, her company was courted by all the gay, the witty, and the gallant. To be seen in public with Lady Delacour, to be a visitor at her house, were privileges, of which numbers were vehemently ambitious; and Belinda Portman was congratulated and envied by all her acquaintance, for being admitted as an inmate. How could she avoid thinking herself singularly fortunate?

A short time after her arrival at Lady Delacour's, Belinda began to see through the thin veil, with which politeness covers domestic misery. – Abroad, and at home, Lady Delacour was two different persons. Abroad she appeared all life, spirit, and good humour – at home, listless, fretful, and melancholy; she seemed like a spoiled actress off the stage, over stimulated by applause, and exhausted by the exertions of supporting a fictitious character. – When her house was filled with well-dressed crowds, when it blazed with lights, and resounded with music and dancing, Lady Delacour, in the character of the mistress of the revels, shone the soul and spirit of pleasure and frolic – But the moment the company retired, when the music ceased, and the lights were extinguishing, the spell was dissolved.

She would sometimes walk up and down the empty magnificent saloon, absorbed in thoughts seemingly of the most painful nature.

For some days after Belinda's arrival in town, she heard nothing of Lord Delacour; his lady never mentioned his name, except once accidentally, as she was showing Miss Portman the house, she said — "Don't open that door – those are only Lord Delacour's apartments." – The first time Belinda ever saw his lordship, he was dead drunk in the arms of two footmen, who were carrying him up stairs to his bedchamber; his lady, who was just returned from Ranelagh, passed by him on the landing place with a look of sovereign contempt.

"What is the matter? – Who is this?" said Belinda.

"Only the body of my Lord Delacour," said her ladyship – "his bearers have brought it up the wrong staircase – take it down again, my good friends – let his lordship go his *own way* – don't look so shocked and amazed, Belinda – don't look so *new*, child – this funeral of my lord's intellects is to me a nightly, or," added her ladyship, looking at her watch and yawning – "I believe I should say a *daily* ceremony. – Six o'clock I protest!"

The next morning, as her ladyship and Miss Portman were sitting at the breakfast table, after a very late breakfast, Lord Delacour entered the room.

"Lord Delacour – sober, my dear," – said her ladyship to Miss Portman, by way of introducing him. Lord Delacour, sober, did not appear to Belinda more agreeable or more rational, than Lord Delacour drunk. His haggard yet bloated countenance was expressive of sullen discontent, and inveterate obstinacy. "How old do you take my lord to be?" whispered her ladyship, as she saw Belinda's eye fixed upon the trembling hand, which carried his teacup to his lips – "I'll lay you a wager," continued she, aloud – "I'll lay your birthnight* dress, gold fringe, and yellow laurel wreaths into the bargain, that you don't guess right." –

"I hope you don't think of going to this birthnight, Lady Delacour?" said his lordship.

"I'll give you six guesses, and I'll bet you don't come within sixteen years," – pursued her ladyship, still looking at Belinda.

"You cannot have the new carriage you have bespoke," – said his lordship. "Will you do me the honour to attend to me, Lady Delacour."

"Then you won't venture to guess, Belinda," said her ladyship, (without honouring her lord with the smallest portion of her attention) – "Well, I believe you are right – for certainly you would guess him to be six and sixty, instead of six and thirty – but then he can drink more than any two legged animal in his majesty's dominions; and you know that is an advantage, which is well worth twenty or thirty years of a man's life – especially to persons, who have no other chance of distinguishing themselves."

"If some people had distinguished themselves a little less in the world," – retorted his lordship, "it would have been as well!"

"As well! – how flat?" –

"Flatly then I have to inform you, Lady Delacour, that I will neither be contradicted, nor laughed at – You understand me. – It would be as well, flat or not flat, my Lady Delacour, if your ladyship would attend more to your own conduct, and less to others!"

"To *that* of others – his lordship means, if he means anything – Apropos – Belinda – did not you tell me Clarence Hervey is coming to town? – You have never seen him? – Well, I'll describe him to you by negatives. He is not a man, who ever says any thing *flat* – He is *not* a man who must be wound up with half a dozen bottles of champagne, before he can *go* – He is *not* a man, who, when he does go, goes wrong, and won't be set right – He is *not* a man, whose whole consequence, if he were married, would depend on his wife – He is *not* a man, who, if he were married, would be so desperately afraid of being governed by his wife, that he would turn gambler, jockey, or sot; merely to show, that he could govern himself." –

"Go on, Lady Delacour," said his lordship, who had been in vain attempting to balance a spoon on the edge of his teacup, during the whole of this speech, which was delivered with the most animated desire to provoke – "Go on, Lady Delacour – all I desire is, that you should go on – Clarence Hervey will be much obliged to you, and I am sure so shall I, – go on, my Lady Delacour – go on, and you'll oblige me."

"I never will oblige you, my lord, that you may depend upon," cried her ladyship, with a look of indignant contempt.

His lordship whistled, rang for his horses, and looked at his nails with a smile. Belinda shocked, and in a great confusion, rose to leave the room, dreading the gross continuance of this matrimonial dialogue.

"Mr Hervey, my lady," said a footman, opening the door; and he was scarcely announced, when her ladyship went forward to receive him with an air of easy familiarity – "Where have you buried yourself, Hervey, this age past?" cried she, shaking hands with him – "There's absolutely no living in this most stupid of all worlds, without you, Mr Hervey – Miss Portman – but don't look as if you were half asleep, man – What are you dreaming of Clarence? – Why looks your grace so heavily to day?"

"Oh I have passed a miserable night," replied Clarence, throwing himself into an actor's attitude, and speaking in a fine tone of stage declamation.

"What was your dream, my lord, I pray you tell me?"

said her ladyship in a similar tone – Clarence went on –

> "O lord, methought what pain it was to dance!
> "What dreadful noise of fiddles in my ears!
> "What sights of ugly *belles* within my eyes!
> — "Then came wandering by,
> "A shadow like a devil, with red hair,
> "Dizened with flow'rs; and she bawl'd out aloud,
> "Clarence is come, false, fleeting, perjur'd Clarence!"

"O, Mrs Luttridge to the life!" cried Lady Delacour. "I know where you have been now, and I pity you – But sit down," said she, making room for him between Belinda and herself upon the sofa – "Sit down here, and tell me what could take you to that odious Mrs Luttridge's."

Mr Hervey threw himself on the sofa, Lord Delacour whistled as before, and left the room without uttering a syllable.

"But my dream has made me forget myself, strangely," said Mr Hervey, turning to Belinda, and producing her bracelet, "Mrs Stanhope promised me, that if I delivered it safely, I should be rewarded by the honour of putting it on the owner's fair arm." A conversation now took place on the nature of ladies' promises – on fashionable bracelets – on the size of the arm of the Venus de Medicis – on Lady Delacour's, and Miss Portman's – on the thick legs of ancient statues – and on the various defects and absurdities of Mrs Luttridge and her wig. – On all these topics Mr Hervey displayed much wit, gallantry, and satire, with so happy an effect, that Belinda, when he took leave, was precisely of her aunt's opinion, that he was a most uncommonly pleasant young man.

Clarence Hervey might have been more than a pleasant young man, if he had not been smitten with the desire of being thought superior in every thing, and of being the most admired person in all companies. He had been early flattered with the idea, that he was a man of genius; and he imagined, that, as such, he was entitled to be imprudent, wild, and eccentric. He affected singularity, in order to establish his claims to genius. He had considerable literary talents, by which he was distinguished at Oxford; but he was so dreadfully afraid of passing for a pedant, that when he came into the company of the idle and the ignorant, he pretended to disdain every species of knowledge. His chameleon character seemed to vary in different lights, and according to the different situations, in which he happened to be placed. He could be all things to all men – and to all women – He was supposed to be a favourite with the fair sex; and of all his various excellencies and defects, there was none, on which he valued himself so much as on his gallantry. He was not profligate; he had a strong sense of honour, and quick feelings of humanity; but he was so easily led, or rather so easily excited by his companions, and his companions were now of such a sort, that it was probable he would soon become vicious. As to his connexion with Lady Delacour, he would have started with horror at the idea of disturbing the peace of a family; but in her family, he said, there was no peace to disturb: he was vain of having it seen by the world, that he was distinguished by a lady of her wit and fashion, and he did not think it incumbent on him to be more scrupulous, or more attentive to appearance, than her ladyship. By Lord Delacour's jealousy he was sometimes provoked, sometimes amused, and sometimes flattered. He was constantly of all her ladyship's parties, in public and private; consequently he saw Belinda almost every day, and every day he saw her with increasing admiration of her beauty, and with increasing dread of being *taken in*, to marry a niece of *"the catch-match-maker"*; the name by which Mrs Stanhope was known among the men of his acquaintance. Young ladies, who have the misfortune to be *conducted* by these artful dames, are always supposed to be partners in all the speculations, though their names may not appear in the firm of the house. If he had not been prejudiced by the character of her aunt, Mr Hervey would have thought Belinda an undesigning, unaffected girl; but now he suspected her of artifice in every word, look, and motion; and even when he felt himself most charmed by her powers of pleasing, he was most inclined to despise her for what he thought such premature proficiency in scientific coquetry. He had not sufficient resolution, to keep beyond the sphere of her attraction; but frequently, when he found himself within it, he cursed his folly, and drew back with sudden terror. His manner towards her was so variable and inconsistent, that she knew not how to interpret its language. Sometimes she fancied, that with all the eloquence of eyes he said, "*I adore you*, Belinda"; at other times she imagined, that his guarded silence meant to warn her, that he was so entangled by Lady Delacour, that he could not extricate himself from her snares. Whenever this last idea struck her, it excited, in the most edifying manner, her indignation against coquetry in general, and against her ladyship's in particular; she became wonderfully clear sighted to all the improprieties of her ladyship's conduct. Belinda's newly acquired moral sense was so much shocked, that she actually wrote a full statement of her observations, and her scruples, to her aunt Stanhope, concluding by a request, that she might not remain under the protection of a lady, whose character she could not approve, and whose intimacy might perhaps be injurious to her reputation, if not to her principles.

Mrs Stanhope answered Belinda's letter in a very guarded style; she rebuked her niece severely for her imprudence in mentioning *names* in such a manner, in a letter sent by the common post; assured her, that her reputation was in no danger; that she hoped no niece of hers would set up for a prude; a character more suspected by men of the world, than even that of a coquette; that the person alluded to was a perfectly fit chaperon for any young lady to appear with in public, as long as she was visited by the first people in town; that as to any thing in the *private* conduct of that person, and as to any *private brouilleries* between her and her lord, Belinda should observe, on these dangerous topics, a profound silence, both in her letters, and her conversation; that as long as the lady continued under the protection of her husband, the world might whisper, but would not speak out; that as to Belinda's own principles, she would be utterly inexcusable, if, after the education she had received, they could be hurt by any bad examples; that she could not be too cautious in her management of a man of — 's character; that she could have no *serious* cause for jealousy in the quarter she apprehended, as marriage there could not be the object; and there was such a difference of age, that no permanent influence could probably be obtained by the lady; that the most certain method for Miss Portman to expose herself to the ridicule of one of the parties, and to the total neglect of the other, would be to betray anxiety or jealousy: that, in short, if she were fool enough to lose her own heart, there would be little chance of her being wise enough to win that of — , who was evidently a man of gallantry rather than of sentiment, and who was known to play his cards well, and to have good luck, whenever *hearts* were trumps.

Belinda's fears of Lady Delacour, as a dangerous rival, were much quieted by the artful insinuations of Mrs Stanhope, with respect to her age, &c. and in proportion, as her fears subsided, she blamed herself for her having written too harshly of her ladyship's conduct. The idea, that whilst she appeared as Lady Delacour's friend, she ought not to propagate any stories to her disadvantage, operated powerfully upon Belinda's mind, and she reproached herself for having told, even her aunt, what she had seen in private. She thought that she had been guilty of treachery, and she wrote again immediately to Mrs Stanhope, to conjure her to burn her last letter, to forget, if possible, its contents, and to believe, that not a syllable of a similar nature should ever more be heard from her: she was just concluding with the words — "I hope my dear aunt will consider all this as an error of my judgment, and not of my heart," — when Lady Delacour burst into the room, exclaiming, in a tone of gaiety — "Tragedy or comedy, Belinda? The masquerade dresses are come. But how's this?" added she, looking full in Belinda's face — "tears in the eyes! blushes in the cheeks! tremors in the joints! and letters shuffling away! But you novice of novices, how awkwardly shuffled! — A niece of Mrs Stanhope's, and so unpractised a shuffler! — And is it credible she should tremble in this ridiculous way about a love-letter or two?"

"No love-letters, indeed, Lady Delacour," said Belinda, holding the paper fast, as her ladyship, half in play, half in earnest, attempted to snatch it from her.

"No love-letters! then it must be treason, and see it I must, by all that's good, or by all that's bad – I see the name of Delacour!" – and her ladyship absolutely seized the letters by force, in spite of all Belinda's struggles and entreaties.

"I beg, I request, I conjure you not to read it!" cried Miss Portman, clasping her hands. "Read mine, read mine, if you *must*, but don't read my aunt Stanhope's. – Oh! I beg, I entreat, I conjure you!" and she threw herself upon her knees.

"You beg! you entreat! you conjure! Why, this is like the Duchesse de Brinvilliers,* who wrote on her paper of poisons, Whoever finds this, I entreat, I conjure them, in the name of more saints than I can remember, not to open the paper any farther. – What a simpleton, to know so little of the nature of curiosity.

As she spoke, Lady Delacour opened Mrs Stanhope's letter, read it from beginning to end, folded it up coolly when she had finished it, and simply said, "the *person alluded to* is almost as bad as her name at full length: does Mrs Stanhope think no one can make out an innuendo in a libel, or fill up a blank, but an attorney general?" pointing to a blank in Mrs Stanhope's letter, left for the name of Clarence Hervey.

Belinda was in too much confusion, either to speak or think.

"You were right to swear they were not love-lettrs," pursued her ladyship, laying down the papers. "I protest I snatched them by way of frolic – I beg pardon. All I can do now is not to read the rest."

"Nay – I beg – I wish – I insist upon your reading mine," said Belinda.

When Lady Delacour had read it, her countenance suddenly changed – "Worth a hundred of your aunt's, I declare," said she, patting Belinda's cheek. "What a treasure, to meet with any thing like a *new* heart – all hearts, nowadays, are secondhand at best."

Lady Delacour spoke with a tone of feeling which Belinda had never heard from her before, and which at this moment touched her so much, that she took her ladyship's hand and kissed it.

CHAPTER II

Masks

———————

"Where were we when all this began?" cried Lady Delacour, forcing herself to resume an air of gaiety — "O, masquerade was the order of the day – tragedy or comedy? which suits your genius best, my dear?"

"Whichever suits your ladyship's taste least."

"Why, my woman, Marriott, says, I ought to be tragedy; and, upon the notion that people always succeed best when they take characters diametrically opposite to their own – Clarence Hervey's principle – Perhaps you don't think that he has any principles; but there you are wrong; I do assure you, he has sound principles – of taste."

"Of that," said Belinda, with a constrained smile, "he gives the most convincing proof, by his admiring your ladyship so much."

"And by his admiring Miss Portman so much more. But whilst we are making speeches to one another, poor Marriott is standing in distress like Garrick, between tragedy and comedy."*

Lady Delacour opened her dressing-room door, and pointed to her as she stood with the dress of the comic muse on one arm, and the tragic muse on the other.

"I am afraid I have not spirits enough to undertake the comic muse," said Miss Portman.

Marriott, who was a personage of prodigious consequence, and the judge in the last resort at her mistress's toilette, looked extremely out of humour at having been kept waiting so long; and yet more so, at the idea that her appellant's jurisdiction could be disputed.

"Your ladyship's taller than Miss Portman by half a head," said Marriott, "and to be sure will best become tragedy, with this long train; besides, I'd settled all the rest of your ladyship's dress. Tragedy, they say, is always tall, and, no offence, your ladyship's taller than Miss Portman by half a head."

"For head read inch," said Lady Delacour, "if you please."

"When things are settled, one can't bear to have them unsettled

– but your ladyship must have your own way, to be sure – I'll say no more," cried she, throwing down the dresses.

"Stay, Marriott," said Lady Delacour, and she placed herself between the angry waiting-maid and the door.

"Why will you, who are the best creature in the world, put yourself into these *furies* about nothing – have patience with us, and you shall be satisfied."

"That's another affair," said Marriott.

"Miss Portman," continued her ladyship, "don't talk of not having spirits – you that are all life and spirits! – What say you, Belinda? – O yes, you must be the comic muse; and I, it seems, must be tragedy, because Marriott has a passion for seeing me 'come sweeping by'. And because Marriott must have her own way in every thing – she rules me with a rod of iron, my dear – so tragedy I needs must be – *Marriott knows her power.*"

There was an air of extreme vexation in Lady Delacour's countenance, as she pronounced these last words, in which evidently more was meant than met the ear. Upon many occasions Miss Portman had observed, that Marriott exercised despotic authority over her mistress; and she had seen, with surprise, that a lady, who would not yield an iota of power to her husband, submitted herself to every caprice of the most insolent of waiting-women. For some time, Belinda imagined that this submission was merely an air, as she had seen some other fine ladies proud of appearing to be governed by a favourite maid; but she was soon convinced, that Marriott was no favourite with Lady Delacour; that her ladyship's was not *proud humility*, but fear. It seemed certain, that a woman, extravagantly fond of her own *will*, would never have given it up without some very substantial reason. It seemed as if Marriott was in possession of some secret, which should for ever remain unknown. This idea had occurred to Miss Portman more than once; but never so forcibly as upon the present occasion. There had always been some mystery about her ladyship's toilette; at certain hours doors were bolted, and it was impossible for any body but Marriott to obtain admission. Miss Portman at first imagined that Lady Delacour dreaded the discovery of her cosmetic secrets, but her ladyship's rouge was so glaring, and her pearl powder was so obvious, that Belinda was convinced there must be some other cause for this toilette secrecy. There was a little cabinet beyond her bedchamber, which Lady Delacour called her boudoir, to which there was an entrance by a back stair-case; but no one ever entered there but Marriott. One night, Lady Delacour, after dancing with great spirit at a ball, at her own house, fainted suddenly; Miss Portman attended her to her bedchamber, but Marriott begged that her lady might be left alone with *her*, and she would by no means suffer Belinda to follow her into the boudoir. – All these things Belinda recollected in the space of a few seconds, as she stood contemplating Marriott and the dresses. The hurry of getting ready for the masquerade, however, dispelled these thoughts, and by the time she was dressed, the idea of what Clarence Hervey would think of her appearance was uppermost in her mind. She was anxious to know, whether he would discover her in the character of the comic muse. Lady Delacour was discontented with her tragic attire, and she grew still more out of humour with herself, when she saw Belinda.

"I protest Marriott has made a perfect fright of me," said her ladyship, as she got into her carriage, "and I'm positive my dress would become you a million of times better than your own."

Miss Portman regretted that it was too late to change.

"Not at all too late, my dear," said Lady Delacour; "never too late for women to change their minds, their dress, or their lovers. Seriously, you know we are to call at my friend Lady Singleton's – she sees masks to night – I'm quite intimate there; I'll make her let me step up to her own room, where no soul can interrupt us, and there we can change our dresses, and Marriott will know nothing of the matter. Marriott's a faithful creature, and very fond of me; fond of power too – but who is not? – we must all have our faults – one would not quarrel with such a good creature as Marriott for a trifle." Then suddenly changing her tone, she said, "not a human being will find us out at the masquerade; for no one but Mrs Freke knows that we are two muses. Clarence Hervey swears he should know me in any disguise – but I defy him – I shall take special delight in puzzling him. Harriet Freke has told him, in confidence, that I'm to be the widow Brady, in man's clothes; now that's to be Harriet's own character, so Hervey will make fine confusion."

As soon as they got to Lady Singleton's, Lady Delacour and Miss Portman immediately went up stairs to exchange dresses. Poor Belinda, now that she felt herself in spirits to undertake the comic muse, was rather vexed to be obliged to give up her becoming character; but there was no resisting the polite energy of Lady Delacour's vanity. Her ladyship ran as quick as lightning into a closet within the bedchamber, saying to Lady Singleton's woman, who attempted to follow with – "Can I do any thing for your ladyship." – "No, no, no – nothing, nothing – thank ye, thank ye, – I want no assistance – I never let any body do any thing for me but Marriott"; and she bolted herself in the closet. In a few minutes she half opened the door, threw out her tragic robes, and cried, "Here, Miss Portman, give me yours – quick – and let's see whether comedy or tragedy will be ready first."

"Lord bless and forgive me," said Lady Singleton's woman, when Lady Delacour at last threw open the door, when she was completely dressed – "but, if your la'ship has not been dressing all this time in that den, without any thing in the shape of a looking-glass – and not to let me help! I that should have been so proud."

Lady Delacour put half a guinea into the waiting-maid's hand, laughed affectedly at her own *whimsicalities*, and declared, that she could always dress herself better without a glass than with one. All this went off admirably well with everybody but Miss Portman; she could not help thinking it extraordinary, that a person who was obviously fond of being waited upon, would never suffer any person to assist her at her toilette except Marriott, a woman of whom she was evidently afraid. Lady Delacour's quick eye saw curiosity painted in Belinda's countenance, and for a moment she was embarrassed; but she soon recovered herself, and endeavoured to turn the course of Miss Portman's thoughts, by whispering to her some nonsense about Clarence Hervey – A cabalistical name, which she knew had the power, when pronounced in a certain tone, of throwing Belinda into confusion.

The first person they saw, when they went into the drawing-room at Lady Singleton's, was this very Clarence Hervey, who was not in a domino. He had laid a wager with one of his acquaintance, that he could perform the part of the serpent, such as he is seen in Fuseli's* well-known picture. For this purpose he had exerted much ingenuity in the invention and execution of a length of coiled skin, which he manoeuvered with great dexterity, by means of internal wires; his grand difficulty had been to manufacture the rays that were to come from his eyes. He had contrived a set of phosphoric rays, which he was certain would charm all the fair daughters of Eve. He forgot, it seems, that phosphorus could not well be seen by candle light. When he was just equipped as a serpent, his rays set fire to part of his *envelope*, and it was with the greatest difficulty that he was extricated. He escaped unhurt, but his serpent's skin was utterly consumed; nothing remained, but the melancholy spectacle of its skeleton. He was obliged to give up the hopes of shining at the masquerade, but he resolved to be at Lady Singleton's, that he might meet Lady Delacour and Miss Portman. The moment that the tragic and comic muse appeared, he invoked them with much humour and mock pathos, declaring that he knew not which of them could best sing his adventure. After a recital of his misfortune had entertained the company, and after the muses had performed their parts to the satisfaction of the audience, and their own, the conversation ceased to be supported in masquerade character; muses and harlequins, gipsies and Cleopatras, began to talk of their private affairs, and of the news and the scandal of the day.

A group of gentlemen, amongst whom was Clarence Hervey, gathered round the tragic muse; as Mr Hervey had hinted that he knew she was a person of distinction, though he would not tell her name. He thought that he could not flatter her ladyship more than by abusing Miss Portman. After he had exercised his wit for some time, without obtaining from the tragic muse one single syllable, he whispered, "Lady Delacour, why this unnatural reserve? do you imagine, that through this tragical disguise I have not found you out?"

The tragic muse, apparently absorbed in meditation, vouch-safed no reply.

"The devil a word can you get for your pains, Hervey," said a gentleman of his acquaintance, who joined the party at this instant. "Why didn't you stick to t'other muse, who, to do her justice, is as errant a flirt as your heart could wish for."

"There's a danger in flirting," said Clarence, "with an errant flirt of Mrs Stanhope's training. There's a kind of electricity about that girl. I have a sort of cobweb feeling, an imaginary net coming all over me."

"Fore-warned is fore-armed," replied his companion – "a man must be a novice indeed, that could be taken in at this time of day by a niece of Mrs Stanhope's."

"That Mrs Stanhope must be a good clever dame, faith," said a third gentleman, – "There's no less than six of her nieces, whom she has *got off* within these four winters – Not one of 'em now, that has not made a catch-match – There's the eldest of the set, Mrs Tollemache, what had she, in the devil's name, to set up with in the world, but a pair of good eyes – Her aunt, to be sure, taught her the use of them early enough – They might have rolled to all eternity, before they would have rolled me out of my senses; but you see, they did Tollemache's business – However, they are going to part now, I hear – Tollemache was tired of her, before the honey-moon was over, as I foretold. Then there's the musical girl – Joddrell, who has no more ear than a post, went and married her, because he had a mind to set up for a connoisseur in music, and Mrs Stanhope flattered him that he was one."

The gentlemen joined in the general laugh – The tragic muse sighed –

"Even were she at the School for Scandal,* the tragic muse dare not laugh, except behind her mask," said Clarence Hervey.

"Far be it from her, to laugh at those follies which she must for ever deplore!" said Belinda, in a feigned voice – "What miseries spring from these ill-suited marriages! – The victims are sacrificed, before they have sense enough to avoid their fate."

Clarence Hervey imagined, that this speech alluded to Lady Delacour's own marriage.

"Damn me, if I know any woman, young or old, that would *avoid* being married, if she could, though, damn me": cried Sir Philip Baddely, a gentleman who always supplied "each vacuity of sense" with an oath – "But damn me, Rochfort, didn't Valleton marry one of those nieces?"

"Yes: she was a mighty fine dancer, and had good legs enough: Mrs Stanhope got poor Valleton to fight a duel about her place in a country dance, and then he was so pleased with himself for his prowess, that he married the girl."

Belinda made an effort to change her seat, but she was encompassed so, that she could not retreat.

"As to Jenny Mason, the fifth of *the nieces*," continued the witty gentleman, "she was as brown as mahogany, and had neither eyes, nose, mouth, nor legs: what Mrs Stanhope could do with her, I often wondered; but she took courage, *rouged* her up, set her a going as a *dasher*, and she dashed herself into Tom Levit's curricle, and Tom couldn't get her out again, till she was the honourable Mrs Levit – She then took the reins into her own hands, and I hear, she's driving him and herself *the road to ruin*, as fast as they can gallop. As for this Belinda Portman, 'twas a good hit to send her to Lady Delacour's; but I take it, she hangs upon hands; for last winter, when I was at Bath, she was hawked about every where, and the aunt was puffing her with might and main. You heard of nothing, wherever you went, but of Belinda Portman, and Belinda Portman's accomplishments – Belinda Portman, and her accomplishments, I'll swear, were as well advertised, as Packwood's razor strops."

"Mrs Stanhope overdid the business, I think," resumed the gentleman who began the conversation – "Girls brought to the hammer this way don't go off well. It's true, Christie himself is no match for dame Stanhope – many of my acquaintance were tempted to go and look at the premises, but not one, you may be sure, had a thought of becoming a tenant for life."

"That's an honour reserved for you, Clarence Hervey," said another, tapping him upon the shoulder – "Give ye joy, Hervey, – Give ye joy!"

"Me!" said Clarence, starting.

"I'll be hanged if he didn't change colour," said his facetious companion; and all the young men again joined in a laugh.

"Laugh on, my merry men all!" cried Clarence, "but the devil's in it if I don't know my own mind better than any of you – you don't imagine I go to Lady Delacour to look for a *wife*? – Belinda Portman's a good pretty girl, but what then? Do you think I'm an idiot – do you think I could be taken in by one of the Stanhope school? Do you think I don't see as plainly as any of you, that Belinda Portman's a composition of art and affectation?"

"Hush – not so loud, Clarence; here she comes," said his companion. "The comic muse, is not she?" –

Lady Delacour, at this moment, came lightly tripping towards them, and addressing herself in the character of the comic muse, to Hervey, exclaimed,

"Hervey! *my* Hervey! most favoured of my votaries, why do you forsake me?

"Why mourns my friend, why weeps his down-cast eye?
"That eye where mirth and fancy used to shine."

"Though you have lost your serpent's form, your own may please any of the fair daughters of Eve."

Mr Hervey bowed; all the gentlemen, who stood near him, smiled; the tragic muse gave an involuntary sigh.

"Could I borrow a sigh, or a tear, from my tragic sister," pursued Lady Delacour, "however unbecoming to my character, I would, if only sighs or tears can win the heart of Clarence Hervey

– Let me practise" – and her ladyship practised sighing with much comic effect.

"Persuasive words, and more persuasive sighs,"

said Clarence Hervey.

"A good bold Stanhope cast of the net, faith," whispered one of his companions – "Melpomene, hast thou forgot thyself to marble?" pursued Lady Delacour – "I am not very well," whispered Miss Portman to her ladyship – "could we get away?"

"Get away from Clarence Hervey, do you mean?" replied her ladyship, in a whisper – "'tis not easy, but we'll try what can be done, if it is necessary." –

Belinda had no power to reply to this raillery, indeed she scarcely heard the words that were said to her; but she put her arm within Lady Delacour's, who, to her great relief, had the good nature to leave the room with her immediately. – Her ladyship, though she would sacrifice the feelings of others, without compunction, to her vanity, whenever the power of her wit was disputed; yet towards those by whom it was acknowledged, she showed some mercy.

"What is the matter with the child?" said she, as she went down the staircase.

"Nothing, if I could have air," said Belinda. There was a crowd of servants in the hall.

"Why does Lady Delacour avoid me so pertinaciously? What crime have I committed, that I was not favoured with one word," said Clarence Hervey, who had followed them down stairs, and overtook them in the hall.

"Do see, if you can find any of my people," cried Lady Delacour.

"Lady Delacour the comic muse!" exclaimed Mr Hervey – "I thought," –

"No matter what you thought," interrupted her ladyship – "Let my carriage draw up, for here's a young friend of yours trembling so about *nothing*, that I am half afraid she will faint; and you know it would not be so pleasant to faint here amongst footmen – Stay! this supper room is empty – O, I did not mean to tell *you* to stay," said she to Hervey, who involuntarily followed her in the utmost consternation.

"I'm perfectly well, now – perfectly well," said Belinda.

"Perfectly a simpleton, I think," said Lady Delacour – "Nay, my dear, you must be ruled, your mask must come off; didn't you tell me you wanted air – What now! This is not the first time Clarence Hervey has ever seen your face without a mask, is it? It's the first time indeed he, or any body else, ever saw it of such a colour, I believe."

When Lady Delacour pulled off Belinda's mask, her face was, during the first instant, pale; the next moment, crimsoned over with a burning blush. –

"What is the matter with ye both? – How he stands!" said Lady Delacour, turning to Mr Hervey – "Did you never see a woman blush before? – or did you never say or do any thing to make a woman blush before? – Will you give Miss Portman a glass of water? – there's some behind you on that sideboard, man! – but he has neither eyes, ears, nor understanding – Do go about your business," said her ladyship, pushing him towards the door – "Do go about your business, for I haven't common patience with you – on my conscience, I believe the man's in love – and not with me! – There's sal-volatile for you, child," continued she to Belinda. "O, you can walk now – but remember you're on slippery ground – remember Clarence Hervey is not a marrying man, and you are not a married woman."

"It is perfectly indifferent to me, madam," Belinda said, with a voice and look of proud indignation.

"Lady Delacour, your carriage has drawn up," said Clarence Hervey, returning to the door, but without entering.

"Then put this 'perfectly well,' and 'perfectly indifferent' lady into it," said Lady Delacour.

He obeyed without uttering a syllable.

"Dumb! Absolutely dumb: I protest," said her ladyship, as he handed her in afterward. "Why Clarence, the casting of your serpent's skin seems to have quite changed your nature – nothing but the simplicity of the dove left; and I expect to hear you cooing presently – don't you, Miss Portman?" She ordered the coachman to drive to the Pantheon.

"To the Pantheon! I was in hopes your ladyship would have the goodness to set me down at home; for indeed I shall be a burden to you, and every body else at the masquerade."

"If you have made any appointment for the rest of the evening in Berkeley square, I'll set you down certainly, if you insist upon it, my dear; for punctuality is a virtue – but prudence is a virtue too, in a young lady; who, as your aunt Stanhope would say, has to *establish* herself in the world. – Why these tears, Belinda? – Or are they tears? for by the light of the lamps I can scarcely tell; tho' I'll swear I saw the handkerchief at the eyes. – What is the meaning of all this? You'd best trust me; for I know as much of men and manners, as your aunt Stanhope at least; and in one word, you have nothing to fear from me, and every thing to hope from yourself; if you will only dry up your tears, *keep on your mask*, and take my advice; you'll find it as good as your aunt Stanhope's."

"My aunt Stanhope's! O," cried Belinda, "never, never more will I take such advice – never more will I expose myself to be insulted as a female adventurer – Little did I know in what a light I appeared – Little did I know what *gentlemen* thought of my aunt Stanhope – of my cousins – of myself."

"*Gentlemen*! I presume Clarence Hervey stands at this instant, in your imagination, as the representative of all the gentlemen upon earth; and he, instead of Anacharsis Cloots,* is now to be sure l'orateur du genre humain* – Pray let me have a specimen of the eloquence, which, to judge by its effects, must be powerful indeed."

Miss Portman, not without some reluctance, repeated the conversation which she had heard – "And is this all?" cried Lady Delacour – "Lord, my dear, you must either give up living in the world, or expect to hear yourself, and your aunts, and your cousins, and your friends, from generation to generation, abused every hour in the day, by their friends, and your friends – 'tis the common course of things. Now you know what a multitude of obedient humble servants, dear creatures, and very sincere and most affectionate friends, I have, in my writing desk, and on my mantle-piece, not to mention the cards which crowd the common rack from intimate acquaintance; who cannot live without the honour, or favour, or pleasure, of seeing Lady Delacour twice a week – do you think I'm fool enough to imagine that they would care the hundredth part of a straw, if I were this minute thrown into the Red, or the Black sea! – No, I have not one *real* friend in the world, except Harriet Freke – yet, you see, I am the comic muse, and mean to keep it up – keep it up to the last – on purpose to provoke those, who would give their eyes to be able to pity me – I humbly thank them, no pity for Lady Delacour – Follow my example, Belinda; elbow your way through the crowd; if you stop to be civil and beg pardon, and 'hope I didn't hurt ye,' you will be trod under foot. – Now you'll meet those young men continually, who took the liberty of laughing at your aunt, and your cousins, and yourself; they are men of fashion – Show them you've no feeling, and they'll acknowledge you for a woman of fashion – you'll marry better than any of your cousins, Clarence Hervey if you can; and then it will be your turn to laugh about nets and cages – As to love and all that – "

The carriage stopped at the Pantheon, just as her ladyship came to the words "love and all that," – her thoughts took a different turn, and during the remainder of the night she exhibited, in such a manner as to attract universal admiration, all the ease, and grace, and gaiety of Euphrosyne.

To Belinda the night appeared long and dull; the common place wit of chimney-sweepers and gipsies; the antics of harlequins; the graces of flower-girls and Cleopatras, had not power to amuse her; for her thoughts still recurred to that conversation, which had given her so much pain – pain which Lady Delacour's raillery had failed to obliterate.

"How happy you are, Lady Delacour," said she, when they got into the carriage to go home – "How happy you are to have such an amazing flow of spirits!" –

"Amazing you might well say, if you knew all," said Lady Delacour – and she heaved a deep sigh, threw herself back in the carriage, let fall her mask, and was silent. – It was broad daylight, and Belinda had a full view of her countenance, which was the picture of despair – She uttered not one syllable more, nor had Miss Portman the courage to interrupt her meditations, till they came within sight of Lady Singleton's; when Belinda ventured to remind her, that she had resolved to stop there, and change dresses, before Marriott saw them.

"No, it's no matter," said Lady Delacour – "Marriott will leave me at the last, like all the rest – 'tis no matter." – Her ladyship sunk back into her former attitude; but after she had remained silent for some moments, she started up and exclaimed –

"If I had served myself, with half the zeal that I have served the world, I should not now be thus forsaken! – I have sacrificed reputation, happiness – every thing, to the love of frolic – All frolic will soon be at an end with me – I am dying – and I shall die unlamented by any human being. – If I were to live my life over again, what a different life it should be! – What a different person *I would be!*[1] – But it is all over now – I am dying."

Belinda's astonishment at these words, and at the solemn manner in which they were pronounced, was inexpressible; she gazed at Lady Delacour, and then repeated the word – "dying!" – "Yes, dying," said Lady Delacour.

"But you seem to me, and to all the world, in perfect health; and but half an hour ago in perfect spirits," said Belinda.

"I seem to you, and to all the world, what I am not – I tell you I am dying," said her ladyship, in a more emphatic tone.

Not a word more passed, till they got home. Lady Delacour hurried up stairs, bidding Belinda follow her, to her dressing-room. Marriott was lighting the six wax candles on the dressing-table – "As I live, they have changed dresses after all," said Marriott to herself, as she fixed her eyes upon Lady Delacour and Miss Portman. "I'll be burnt, if I don't make my lady remember this."

"Marriott, you need not wait; I'll ring when I want you," said Lady Delacour, and taking one of the candles from the table, she passed on hastily with Miss Portman, through her dressing-room, through her bedchamber, and to the door of the mysterious cabinet.

"Marriott, the key of this door," cried she, impatiently, after she had, in vain, attempted to open it.

"Heavenly graciousness!" cried Marriott, "is my lady out of her senses?"

"The key – the key – quick, the key," repeated Lady Delacour, in a peremptory tone. She seized it as soon as Marriott drew it from her pocket, and unlocked the door.

"Had not I best put *the things* to rights, my lady?" said Marriott, catching fast hold of the opening door.

"I'll ring when you are wanted, Marriott," said Lady Delacour; and pushing open the door with violence, she rushed forward to the middle of the room, and turning back, she beckoned to Belinda to follow her – "Come in, what is it you are afraid of?" said she. – Belinda went on, and the moment she was in the room, Lady Delacour shut and locked the door. The room was rather dark, as there was no light in it, except what came from one candle, which Lady Delacour held in her hand, and which burned but dimly. – Belinda, as she looked round, saw

---

[1]   This declaration was taken from the lips of a celebrated character.*

nothing but a confusion of linen rags – vials, some empty, some full – and she perceived that there was a strong smell of medicines.

Lady Delacour, whose motions were all precipitate, like those of a person whose mind is in great agitation, looked from side to side of the room, without seeming to know what she was in search of. – She then, with a species of fury, wiped the paint from her face, and returning to Belinda, held the candle so as to throw the light full upon her livid features. – Her eyes were sunk, her cheeks hollow – no trace of youth or beauty remained on her death-like countenance, which formed a horrid contrast with her gay fantastic dress.

"You are shocked, Belinda," said she, "but as yet you have seen nothing – look here," – and baring one half of her bosom, she revealed a hideous spectacle.

Belinda sunk back into a chair – Lady Delacour flung herself on her knees before her.

"Am I humbled, am I wretched enough?" cried she, her voice trembling with agony – "Yes, pity me, for what you have seen; and a thousand times more, for that which you cannot see – my mind is eaten away like my body, by incurable disease – inveterate remorse – remorse for a life of folly – of folly which has brought on me all the punishments of guilt."

"My husband," continued she, and her voice suddenly altered, from the tone of grief to that of anger – "My husband hates me – no matter – I despise him – His relations hate me – no matter – I despise them – My own relations hate me – no matter, I never wish to see them more – never shall they see my sorrow – never shall they hear a complaint, a sigh from me. There is no torture which I could not more easily endure than their insulting pity. I will die, as I have lived, the envy and admiration of the world. When I am gone, let them find out their mistake; and moralise, if they will, over my grave." – She paused – Belinda had no power to speak.

"Promise, swear to me," resumed Lady Delacour vehemently, seizing Belinda's hand, "that you will never reveal to any mortal what you have seen and heard this night. No living creature suspects that Lady Delacour is dying by inches, except Marriott, and that woman, whom but a few hours ago I thought my *real friend*, to whom I trusted every secret of my life, every thought of my heart. – Fool! idiot! Dupe that I was to trust to the friendship of a woman, whom I knew to be without principle – but I thought she had honour; I thought she could never betray *me* – O Harriet!

Harriet! you to desert me! – Any thing else I could have borne – but you, who I thought would have supported me in the tortures of mind and body which I am to go through – you, that I thought would receive my last breath – you to desert me! – Now I am alone in the world – left to the mercy of an insolent waiting-woman.

Lady Delacour hid her face on Belinda's lap, and almost stifled by the violence of contending emotions, she at last gave vent to them, and sobbed aloud.

"Trust to one," said Belinda, pressing her hand with all the tenderness which humanity could dictate, "who will never leave you at the mercy of an insolent waiting-woman – trust to me."

"Trust to you," said Lady Delacour, looking up eagerly in Belinda's face; "yes – I think – I may trust to you – for though a niece of Mrs Stanhope's, I have seen this day, and have seen with surprise, symptoms of artless feeling about you. This was what tempted me to open my mind to you, when I found that I had lost the only friend – but I will think no more of that – if you have a heart, you must feel for me – Leave me now – tomorrow you shall hear my whole history – now I am quite exhausted – ring for Marriott." – Marriott appeared with a face of constrained civility, and latent rage. – "Put me to bed, Marriott," said Lady Delacour, with a subdued voice – "but first light Miss Portman to her room – she need not – yet – see the horrid business of my toilette."

Belinda, when she was left alone, immediately opened her shutters, and threw up the sash to refresh herself with the morning air. She felt excessively fatigued, and in the hurry of her mind, she could not think of any thing distinctly. She took off her masquerade dress, and went to bed, in hopes of forgetting, for a few hours, what she felt indelibly impressed upon her imagination. But it was in vain that she endeavoured to compose herself to sleep; her ideas were in too great and painful confusion. For some time, whenever she closed her eyes, the face and form of Lady Delacour, such as she had just beheld them, seemed to haunt her; afterward, the idea of Clarence Hervey, and the painful recollection of the conversation she had overheard, recurred to her; the words, "do you think I don't know that Belinda Portman is a composition of artifice and affectation," were fixed in her memory. She recollected with the utmost minuteness every look of contempt, which she had seen in the faces of the young gentlemen, whilst they spoke of Mrs Stanhope the match-maker.

Belinda's mind, however, was not yet sufficiently calm to reflect: she seemed only to live over again the preceding night. At last the strange motley figures which she had seen at the masquerade flitted before her eyes, and she sunk into an uneasy slumber.

CHAPTER III

Lady Delacour's History

Miss Portman was awakened by the ringing of Lady Delacour's bedchamber bell. She opened her eyes with the confused idea that something disagreeable had happened; and before she had distinctly recollected herself, Marriott came to her bedside, with a note from Lady Delacour – It was written with a pencil.

"Delacour – *my* lord!!!! is to have today what Garrick used to call a *gander feast* – will you dine with me tête-a-tête, and I'll write an *excuse*, alias a lie, to Lady Singleton in the form of a charming note. I pique myself *sur l'éloquence du billet** – then we shall have the evening to ourselves – I have much to say, as people usually have when they begin to talk of themselves.

"I have taken a double dose of opium, and am not so horridly out of spirits as I was last night – so you need not be afraid of another *scene*.

"Let me see you in my dressing-room, dear Belinda, as soon as you have adored

"With head uncover'd, the cosmetic powers."

"But you don't paint – no matter – you will – you must – every body must, sooner or later. In the mean time, whenever you want to send a note that shall not be opened by *the bearer*, put your trust neither in wafer nor wax, but twist it as I twist mine. You see I wish to put you in possession of some valuable secrets before I leave this world – this, by the by, I don't, upon second thoughts, which are always best, mean to do yet. – There certainly were such people as Amazons* – I hope you admire them – for who could live without the admiration of Belinda Portman! – not Clarence Hervey, assuredly – nor yet

T. C. H. DELACOUR."

Belinda obeyed the summons to her ladyship's dressing-room: she found Lady Delacour with her face completely repaired with paint, and her spirits with opium. She was in high consultation with Marriott and Mrs Franks, the milliner, about the crape petticoat of her birthnight dress, which was extended over a large hoop in full state. Mrs Franks descanted long and learnedly upon festoons and loops, knots and fringes, submitting all the time every thing to her ladyship's better judgment.

Marriott was sulky and silent. She opened her lips but once upon the question of laburnum, or no laburnum flowers. Against them she quoted the memoirs and authority of the celebrated Mrs Bellamy,* who has a case in point to prove, that "straw colour must ever look like dirty white by candlelight." Mrs Franks, to compromise the matter, proposed gold laburnums, "because nothing can look better by candlelight, or any light, than gold"; and Lady Delacour, who was afraid that the milliner's imagination, now that it had once touched upon gold, might be led to the vulgar idea of *ready money*, suddenly broke up the conference, by exclaiming,

"We shall be late at Phillips's exhibition of French china. Mrs Franks must let us see her again to-morrow, to take into consideration your court dress, my dear Belinda – "Miss Portman presented by Lady Delacour" – Mrs Franks, let her dress, for Heaven's sake, be something that will make a fine paragraph – I give you four and twenty hours to think of it. – I have done a horrid act this day," continued she, after Mrs Franks had left the room – "absolutely written a *twisted* note to Clarence Hervey, my dear – but why did I tell you that? Now your head will run upon the twisted note all day, instead of upon 'The Life and Opinions of a Lady of Quality, related by herself'."

After dinner, Lady Delacour, having made Belinda protest and blush, and blush and protest, that her head was not running upon the twisted note, began the history of her life and opinions in the following manner:

"I do nothing by halves, my dear – I shall not tell you my adventures, as Gil Blas* told his to the archbishop of Grenada – skipping over the *useful* passages – because you are not an archbishop, and I should not have the grace to put on a sanctified face, if you were. – I am no hypocrite, and have nothing worse than folly to conceal – That's bad enough – for a woman who is known to play the fool, is always suspected of playing the devil – But I begin where I ought to end, with my moral, which I dare say you are not impatient to anticipate – I never read or listened to a moral at the end of a story in my life – manners for me, and morals

for those that like them. – My dear, you will be woefully
disappointed, if in my story you expect any thing like a novel. I
once heard a general say, that nothing was less like a review than a
battle; and I can tell you, that nothing is more unlike a novel than
real life. Of all lives, mine has been the least romantic. No love in
it, but a great deal of hate. I was a rich heiress – I had, I believe, a
hundred thousand pounds, or more; and twice as many caprices –
I was handsome and witty – or, to speak with that kind of
circumlocution which is called humility, the world, the partial
world, thought me a beauty, and a bel-esprit. – Having told you
my fortune, need I add, that I, or it, had lovers in abundance – of
all sorts and degrees – not to reckon those, it may be presumed,
who died of concealed passions for me. I had sixteen declarations
and proposals in form – then what in the name of wonder, or of
common sense, which by the by is the greatest of wonders – what
in the name of common sense made me marry Lord Delacour? –
Why, my dear, you – no, not *you*, but any girl who is not used to
have a parcel of admirers, would think it the easiest thing in the
world to make her choice; but let her judge by what she feels when
a dexterous mercer or linen-draper produces pretty thing after
pretty thing – and this is so becoming, and this will wear for ever –
as he swears; but then that's so fashionable – the novice stands in
a charming perplexity, and after examining, and doubting, and
tossing over half the goods in the shop, it's ten to one, when it
begins to get late, the young lady, in a hurry, pitches upon the very
ugliest and worst thing that she has seen. Just so it was with me
and my lovers, and just so –

"Sad was the hour, and luckless was the day"

I pitched upon Viscount Delacour, for my lord and judge. He had
just at that time lost at Newmarket more than he was worth, in
every sense of the word; and my fortune was the most convenient
thing in the world to a man in his condition. – Lozenges are of
sovereign use in some complaints. The heiress lozenge is a specific
in some consumptions. You are surprised that I can laugh and jest
about such a melancholy thing as my marriage with Lord
Delacour; and so am I, especially when I recollect all the
circumstances – for though I bragged of there being no love in my
history, there was when I was a goose or a gosling of about
eighteen – just your age, Belinda, I think – something very like
love playing about my heart, or my head – There was a certain

Henry Percival, a Clarence Hervey of a man – no, he had ten times
the sense, begging your pardon, of Clarence Hervey – his
misfortune, or mine, was that he had too much sense – he was in
love with me but not with my faults; now I, wisely considering,
that my faults were the greatest part of me, insisted upon his being
in love with my faults. – He wouldn't or couldn't – I said wouldn't
– he said couldn't. I had been used to see the men about me lick the
dust – for it was gold dust. – Percival made wry faces – Lord
Delacour made none. – I pointed him out to Percival as an
example – it was an example he would not follow. – I was
provoked, and I married, in hopes of provoking the man I loved. –
The worst of it was, I did not provoke him as much as I expected. –
Six months afterward, I heard of his marriage with a very amiable
woman. – I hate those *very amiable women*. – Poor Percival! – I
should have been a very happy woman, I fancy, if I had married
you – for I believe you were the only man who ever really loved me
– but all that is over now! – Where were we? – O, I married my
Lord Delacour, knowing him to be a fool, and believing that, for
this reason, I should find no trouble in governing him. – But what
a fatal mistake! – a fool, of all animals in the creation, is the most
difficult to govern. – We set out in the fashionable world, with a
mutual desire to be as extravagant as possible. – Strange, that
with this similarity of taste we could never agree! – Strange, that
this similarity of taste was the cause of our perpetual quarrels! –
During the first year of our marriage, I had always the upper hand
in these disputes, and the last word; and I was content – Stubborn
as the brute was, I thought I should in time break him in. – From
the specimens you have seen, you may guess that I was even then a
tolerable proficient in the dear art of *self-justification* – I had
almost gained my point, just broken my lord's heart, when one
fair morning, I unluckily told his man Champfort, that he knew
no more how to cut hair than a sheepshearer. – Champfort, who is
conceit personified, took mortal offence at this; and the devil,
who is always at hand to turn anger into malice, put it into
Champfort's head, to put it into my lord's head, that the world
thought – '*My lady governed him.*' – My lord took fire – They say
the torpedo,* the coldest of cold creatures, sometimes gives out a
spark – I suppose, when electrified with anger. – The next time
that innocent I insisted upon my Lord Delacour's doing, or not
doing – I forget which – the most reasonable thing in the world,
my lord turns short round, and answers – 'My Lady Delacour, I

am not a man to be governed by a wife.' – And from that time to this, the words 'I am not a man to be governed by a wife' – have been written in his obstinate face, as all the world who can read the human countenance may see. – My dear, I laugh, but even in the midst of laughter, there is sadness. – But you don't know what it is – I hope you never may – to have an obstinate fool for a bosom friend.

"I at first flattered myself, that my lord's was not an inveterate, incurable malady, but from his obvious weakness, I might have seen that there was no hope; for cases of obstinacy are always dangerous in proportion to the weakness of the patient. – My lord's case was desperate. – Kill or cure, was my humane, or prudent maxim. – I determined to try the poison of jealousy, by way of an alternative. – I had long kept it in petto* as my ultimate remedy. I fixed upon a proper subject – a man with whom I thought that I could coquette to all eternity, without any danger to myself – a certain Colonel Lawless – as empty a coxcomb as you would wish to see. – The world, said I to myself, can never be so absurd as to suspect Lady Delacour with such a man as this, though her lord may, and will, for nothing is too absurd for him to believe. – Half my theory proved just – that is saying a great deal for any theory. – My lord swallowed the remedy that I had prepared for him, with an avidity, and a bonhommie, which it did me good to behold – my remedy operated beyond my most sanguine expectations. – The poor man was cured of his obstinacy, and became stark mad with jealousy. – Then indeed I had some hopes of him; for a madman can be managed, a fool cannot. In a month's time, I made him quite docile. With a face longer than the weeping philosopher's, he came to me one morning, and assured me, 'he would do every thing I pleased, provided I would consult my own honour and his, and give up Colonel Lawless.'

"'Give up!' – I could hardly forbear laughing at the expression. – I replied, 'that as long as my lord treated me with becoming respect, I had never, in thought or deed, given him just cause of complaint; but that I was not a woman to be insulted, or to be kept, as I had hitherto been, in leading-strings, by a husband.' – My lord, flattered, as I meant he should be, with the idea, that it was possible he should be suspected of keeping a wife in leading-strings, fell to making protestations – 'he hoped his future conduct would prove, &c.' – Upon this hint, I gave the reins to my imagination, and full drive I went into a fresh career of extravagance; if I were checked, it was *an insult*, and I began directly to talk of *leading-strings*. This ridiculous game I played, successfully enough, for some time, till at length, though naturally rather slow at calculation, he actually discovered, that if we lived at the rate of twenty thousand a year, and had only ten thousand a year to spend, we should, in due time, have nothing left. This notable discovery he communicated to me one morning, after a long preamble. When he had finished prosing, I agreed, that it was demonstrably just, that he should retrench his expenses; but that it was equally unjust and impossible, that I could make any reformation in my civil list. – That economy was a word which I had never heard of in my life, till I married his lordship; that, upon second recollection, it was true, I had heard of such a thing as national economy; and that it would be a very pretty, though rather hackneyed topic of declamation for a maiden speech in the house of lords. I therefore advised him to reserve all he had to say upon this subject for the noble lord upon the woolsack; nay, I very graciously added, that upon this condition, I would go to the house myself, to give his arguments and eloquence a fair hearing, and that I would do my best to keep myself awake. – This was all mighty playful and witty; but it happened that my Lord Delacour, who never had any great taste for wit, could not this unlucky morning at all relish it. Of course I grew angry, and reminded him, with an indelicacy which his want of generosity justified, that an heiress, who had brought a hundred thousand pounds into his family, had some right to amuse herself, and that it was not my fault if elegant amusements were more expensive than others.

"Then came a long criminating and recriminating chapter. – It was 'My lord, your Newmarket blunders.' – 'My lady, your cursed *theatricals*.' – 'My lord, I have surely a right' – 'and my lady, I have surely as good a right.'

"But my dear, Belinda, however we might pay one another, we could not pay all the world with words. In short, after running through thousands, and tens of thousands, we were actually in distress for money. – Then came selling of lands, and I don't know what devices, for raising money, according to the mode of lawyers and attorneys. It was quite indifferent to me, how they got money, provided that they got it for us. – By what art these gentlemen raised money, I never troubled myself to inquire; it might have been the black art, for any thing I know to the contrary. I know nothing of business. So I signed all the papers they brought to me; and I was mighty well pleased to find, that by so easy an expedient as writing, 'T. C. H. Delacour,' I could command money at will. – I signed, and signed, till at last I was with all due civility informed, that my signature was no longer worth a farthing; and when I came to inquire into the cause of this phenomenon, I could nowise understand what my Lord Delacour's lawyer said to me. He was a prig, and I had not patience either to listen to him, or to look at him. I sent for an old uncle of mine, who used to manage all my money matters before I was married: I put the uncle and the lawyer into a room together with their parchments, to fight the matter out, or to come to a right understanding if they could. – The last it seems was quite impossible. – In the course of half an hour, out comes my uncle in such a rage! I never shall forget his face – all the bile in his body had gotten into it – he had literally no whites in his eyes. 'My dear uncle,' said I, 'what is the matter? – Why you are absolutely gold stick in waiting.'

"'No matter what I am, child,' said the uncle, 'I'll tell you what you are with all your wit – a dupe – 'tis a shame for a woman of your sense to be such a fool, and to know nothing of business – and if you knew nothing yourself, could not you send for me?'

"'I was too ignorant to know that I knew nothing,' said I; but I will not trouble you with all the said Is and said hes. I was made to understand, that if Lord Delacour were to die the next day, I should live a beggar. – Upon this I grew serious, as you may imagine. My uncle assured me that I had been grossly imposed upon by my lord and his lawyer, and that I had been swindled out of my senses, and out of my dower. I repeated all that my uncle said, very faithfully, to Lord Delacour; and all that either he or his lawyer could furbish out by way of answer was, that 'necessity had no law.' Necessity, it must be allowed, though it might be the mother of law, was never with my lord the mother of invention. Having now found out that I had a good right to complain, I indulged myself in it most gloriously. In short, my dear, we had a comfortable family quarrel – love quarrels are easily made up – but of money quarrels there is no end. – From the moment these money quarrels commenced, I began to hate Lord Delacour – before, I had only despised him. – You can have no notion to what meanness extravagance reduces men. – I have known Lord Delacour shirk, and look so shabby, and tell so many lies to people about a hundred guineas – a hundred guineas! What do I say? About twenty, ten, five! – O, my dear, I cannot bear the thoughts of it! – But I was going on to tell you that my good uncle, and all my relations, quarrelled with me for having ruined myself, as they said – but I said, they quarrelled with me for fear I should ask them for some of their 'VILE TRASH'. – Accordingly I abused and ridiculed them, one and all; and for my pains, all my acquaintance said that 'Lady Delacour was a woman of a vast deal of spirit.'

"We were relieved from our money embarrassments by the timely death of a rich nobleman; to whose large estate my Lord Delacour was heir at law. I was intoxicated with the idle compliments of all my acquaintance, and I endeavoured to console myself for misery at home, by gaiety abroad. Ambitious of pleasing universally, I became the worst of slaves – a slave to the world. – Not a moment of my time was at my own disposal – not one of my actions; I may say, not one of my thoughts, was my own – I was obliged to find things 'charming' every hour, which tired me to death; and every day it was the same dull round of hypocrisy and dissipation. You wonder to hear me speak in this manner, Belinda, but one must speak the truth sometimes; and this is what I have been saying to Harriet Freke continually – continually, for these ten years past. Then why persist in the same kind of life, you say? – Why, my dear, because I could not stop – I was fit for this kind of life, and for no other – I could not be happy at *home*, for what sort of a companion could I have made of Lord Delacour? By this time he was tired of his horse Potatoes, and his horse Highflier, and his horse Eclipse, and Goliah, and Jenny Gray, &c. and he had taken to hard drinking, which soon turned him, as you see, quite into a beast. – I forgot to tell you, that I had three children during the first five years of my marriage. The first was a boy; he was born dead; and my lord, and all his odious relations, laid the blame upon me; because I would not be kept prisoner half a year by an old mother of his, a vile Cassandra, who was always prophesying that my child would not be born alive. – My second child was a girl, but a poor diminutive, sickly thing. – It was the fashion at this time for fine mothers to suckle their own children – so much the worse for the poor brats. – Fine nurses never made fine children. There was a prodigious rout made about the matter; a vast deal of sentiment and sympathy, and compliments and inquiries; but after the novelty was over, I became heartily sick of the business; and at the end of about three months my poor child was sick too – I don't much like to think of it – it died. – If I had put it out to nurse, I should have been thought by my friends an unnatural mother – but I should have saved its life. I should have bewailed the loss of the infant more, if Lord Delacour's relations and my own had not made such lamentations upon the occasion, that I was stunned. – I couldn't or wouldn't shed a tear, and I left it to the old dowager to perform in public, as she wished, the part of chief mourner, and to comfort herself in private, by lifting up her hands and eyes, and railing at me as the most insensible of mothers. All this time I suffered more than she did; but that is what she shall never have the satisfaction of knowing. I determined, that if ever I had another child I would not have the barbarity to nurse it myself. Accordingly, when my third child, a girl, was born, I sent it off immediately to the country, to a stout, healthy, broad-faced nurse, under whose care it grew and flourished; so that at three years old, when it was brought back to me, I could scarcely believe the chubby little thing was my own child. The same reasons which convinced me I ought not to nurse my own child, determined me, *à plus forte raison*,* not to undertake its education. Lord Delacour could not bear the child because it was not a boy. The girl was put under the care of a governess, who plagued my heart out with her airs and tracasseries* for three or four years; at the end of which time, as she turned out to be Lord Delacour's mistress in form, I was obliged – in form – to beg she would leave my house, and I put her pupil into better hands, I hope, at a celebrated academy for young ladies. There she will, at any rate, be better instructed than she could be at home. – I beg your pardon, my dear, for this digression on nursing and schooling, but I wanted only to explain to you why it was, that when I was weary of the business, I still went on in a course of dissipation. You see I had nothing at home, either in the shape of husband or children, to engage my affections. I believe it was this 'aching void' in my heart which made me, after looking abroad some time for a bosom friend, take such a prodigious fancy to Mrs Freke. She was just then coming into fashion – she struck me the first time I met her, as being downright ugly; but there was a wild oddity in her countenance which made one stare at her, and she was delighted to be stared at – especially by me – so we were mutually agreeable to each other – I as starer, and she as staree. Harriet Freke had, without comparison, more assurance than any man or woman I ever saw. She was downright brass –

but of the finest kind – Corinthian brass – She was one of the first who brought what I call *harum scarum* manners into fashion. I told you that she had assurance – *impudence* I should have called it, for no other word is strong enough. – Such things as I have heard Harriet Freke say! – You will not believe it; but her conversation at first absolutely made me, like an old fashioned fool, wish I had a fan to play with. But to my astonishment, all this *took* surprisingly with a set of fashionable young men. I found it necessary to reform my manners. If I had not taken heart of grace, and publicly abjured the heresies of *false delicacy*, I should have been excommunicated – Lady Delacour's sprightly elegance – allow me to speak of myself in the style in which the newspaper writers talk of me – Lady Delacour's sprightly elegance was but pale – not to say *faded* pink, compared with the scarlet of Mrs Freke's dashing audacity. As my rival, she would on certain ground have beaten me hollow; it was therefore good policy to make her my friend. We joined forces, and nothing could stand against us. But I have no right to give myself credit for good policy in forming this intimacy; I really followed the dictates of my heart, or my imagination. There was a frankness in Harriet's manner, which I mistook for artlessness of character. She spoke with such unbounded freedom on certain subjects, that I gave her credit for unbounded sincerity on all subjects. She had the talent of making the world believe *that* virtue to be invulnerable by nature, which disdained the common outworks of art for its defence. I, amongst others, took it for granted, that the woman who could make it her sport to 'touch the brink of all we hate,' must have a stronger head than other people. – I have since been convinced, however, of my mistake. – I am persuaded that few can touch the brink without tumbling headlong down the precipice – Don't apply this, my dear, *literally*, to the person of whom we were speaking. I am not base enough to betray her secrets, however I may have been provoked by her treachery. Of her character and history you shall hear nothing, but what is necessary for my own justification. The league of amity between us was scarcely ratified, before my Lord Delacour came with his wise remonstrating face, to beg me 'to consider what was due to my own honour and his.' – Like the cosmogony-man in the Vicar of Wakefield, he came out over and over with this cant phrase, which had once stood him in stead. – 'Do you think my lord,' said I, 'that because I give up poor Lawless to oblige you, I shall give up all common sense, to suit myself to your taste? – Harriet Freke is visited by every body but old dowagers and old maids. – I am neither an old dowager nor an old maid – The consequence is obvious, my lord.' – Pertness in dialogue, my dear, often succeeds better with my lord than wit. – I therefore saved the sterling gold, and bestowed upon him nothing but counters – I tell you this to save the credit of my taste and judgment. – But to return to my friendship for Harriet Freke. I, of course, repeated to her every word which had passed between my husband and me. She out-Heroded Herod upon the occasion; and laughed so much at what she called my folly in *pleading guilty* in the Lawless cause, that I was downright ashamed of myself, and purely to prove my innocence, I determined, upon the first convenient opportunity, to renew my intimacy with the colonel. The opportunity which I so ardently desired of redeeming my independence, was not long wanting. – Lawless, as my stars (which you know are always more in fault than ourselves) would have it, returned just at this time from the continent, where he had been with his regiment; he returned with a wound across his forehead, and a black fillet; which made him look something more like a hero, and ten times more like a coxcomb, than ever. – He was in fashion at all events, and amongst other ladies, Mrs Luttridge – odious Mrs Luttridge! smiled upon him. – The colonel, however, had taste enough to know the difference between smile and smile; he laid himself and his laurels at my feet, and I carried him and them about in triumph. Wherever I went, especially to Mrs Luttridge's, envy and scandal joined hands to attack me, and I heard wondering and whispering wherever I went. I had no object in view but to provoke my husband, therefore, conscious of the purity of my intentions, it was my delight to brave the opinion of the wondering world. I gave myself no concern about the effect my coquetry might have upon the object of this flirtation – poor Lawless! – heart – I took it for granted he had none. – How should a coxcomb come by a heart – vanity I knew he had in abundance, but this gave me no alarm, as I thought that if it should ever make him forget himself – I mean, forget what was due to me – I could, by one flash of my wit, strike him to the earth, or blast him for ever. One night we had been together at Mrs Luttridge's, – she, amongst other good things, kept a faro bank – and I am convinced, cheated – Be that as it may, I lost an immensity of money, and it was my pride to lose with as much gaiety as any body else could win; so I was, or appeared to

be, in uncommonly high spirits, and Lawless had his share of my
good humour. We left Mrs Luttridge's together early; about half
past one. As the colonel was going to hand me to my carriage, a
smart-looking young man, as I thought, came up close to the
coach door, and stared me full in the face: I was not a woman to be
disconcerted at such a thing as this, but I really was startled when
the young fellow jumped into the carriage after me: I thought he
was mad: I had only courage enough to scream. – Lawless seized
hold of the intruder to drag him out, and out he dragged the
youth, exclaiming in a high tone – 'What is the meaning of all this,
sir? – Who the devil are you?' – 'My name's Lawless: – who the
devil are you?' The answer to this was a convulsion of laughter. By
the laugh, I knew it to be Harriet Freke. – 'Who am I! only a
Freke!' cried she – 'shake hands.' I gave her my hand, into the
carriage she sprang, and desired the colonel to follow her: Lawless
laughed, we all laughed, and drove away. 'Where do you think
I've been?' said Harriet, 'in the gallery of the House of Commons;
almost squeezed to death these four hours; but I swore I'd hear
Sheridan's speech* to night, and I did – Betted fifty guineas I
would, with Mrs Luttridge, and have won. – Fun and Freke for
ever, huzza!' Harriet was mad with spirits, and so noisy and
unmanageable that, as I told her, I was sure she was drunk. –
Lawless, in his silly way, laughed incessantly, and I was so taken
up with her oddities, that, for some time, I did not perceive we
were going the Lord knows where; till, at last, when the 'larum of
Harriet's voice ceased for an instant, I was struck with the strange
sound of the carriage. 'Where are we? Not upon the stones, I'm
sure;' said I; and putting my head out of the window, I saw we
were beyond the turnpike. – 'The coachman's drunk as well as
you, Harriet,' said I; and I was going to pull the string to stop him,
but Harriet had hold of it. – 'The man is going very right,' said she,
'I've told him where to go. – Now don't fancy that Lawless and I
am going to run away with you. – All that is unnecessary now-a-
days, thank God!' – To this I agreed, and laughed for fear of being
ridiculous. – 'Guess where you are going,' said Harriet, – I
guessed and guessed, but could not guess right; and my merry
companions were infinitely diverted with my perplexity and
impatience, more especially, as I believe, in spite of all my efforts, I
grew rather graver than usual. We went on to the end of Sloane-
street, and quite out of town; at last we stopped. – It was dark, the
footman's flambeau was out, I could only just see by the lamps,

that we were at the door of a lone, odd looking house. – The house door opened, and an old woman appeared with a lantern in her hand.

" 'Where is this farce or freak, or whatever you call it, to end?' said I, as Harriet pulled me into the dark passage along with her.

"Alas! my dear Belinda," said Lady Delacour, pausing; "I little foresaw where or how it was to end: but I am not come yet to the tragical part of my story, and as long as I can laugh, I will. – As the old woman and her miserable blue light went on before us, I could almost have thought of Sir Bertrand,* or of some German *horrifications*, but I heard Lawless, who never could help laughing at the wrong time, bursting behind me, with a sense of his own superiority.

" 'Now you will learn your destiny, Lady Delacour!' said Harriet, in a solemn tone.

" 'Yes! from the celebrated Mrs W —', the modern dealer in art magic,' said I, laughing, 'for now I guess whereabouts I am.' – Colonel Lawless's laugh broke the spell – 'Harriet Freke, never whilst you live expect to succeed in *the sublime*.' – Harriet swore at the colonel, for the veriest *spoil-sport* she had ever seen, and she whispered to me – 'the reason he laughs is, because he is afraid of our suspecting the truth of him, that he believes *tout de bon* in conjuration, and the devil, and all that.' – The old woman, whose cue I found was to be dumb, opened a door at the top of a narrow staircase, and pointing to a tall figure, completely enveloped in fur, left us to our fate. I will not trouble you with a pompous description of all the mummery of the scene, my dear, as I despair of being able to frighten you out of your wits. I should have been downright angry with Harriet Freke for bringing me to such a place, but that I knew women of the first fashion had been with Mrs W — before us – some in sober sadness – some by way of frolic. – So as there was no fear of being ridiculous, there was no shame, you know, and my conscience was quite at ease. Harriet had no conscience, so she was always at ease; and never more so than in male attire, which she had been told became her particularly. She supported the character of a young rake with such spirit and *truth*, that I am sure no common conjurer could have discovered any thing feminine about her. She rattled on with a set of nonsensical questions; and among other things, she asked, 'How soon will Lady Delacour marry again after her lord's death?'

"'She will never marry after her lord's death,' answered the oracle. – 'Then she will marry during his life time,' said Harriet. – 'True,' answered the oracle. – Colonel Lawless laughed; I was angry; and the colonel would have been quiet, for he was a gentleman, but there was no such thing as managing Mrs Freke, who, though she had laid aside the modesty of her own sex, had not acquired the decency of the other. – 'Who is to be Lady Delacour's second husband?' cried she. 'You'll not offend any of the present company by naming the man.' – 'Her second husband I cannot name,' replied the oracle, 'but let her beware of a Lawless lover.' Mrs Freke and Colonel Lawless, encouraged by her, triumphed over me without mercy; I may say, without shame! – Well, my dear, I am in a hurry to have done with all this: though I 'doated upon folly,' yet I was terrified at the thoughts of any thing worse. The idea of a divorce, the public brand of shameful life, shocked me, in spite of all my real and all my assumed levity. O that I had, at this instant, dared to be myself! But my fear of ridicule was greater than my fear of vice. – 'Bless me, my dear Lady Delacour,' whispered Harriet, as we left this house, 'what can make you in such a desperate hurry to get home? – You gape and fidget – one would think you had never sat up a night before in your life. – I verily believe you are afraid to trust yourself with us. – Which of us are you afraid of; Lawless, or me, or yourself?' – There was a tone of contempt in the last words, which piqued me to the quick, and, however strange it may seem, I was now anxious only to convince Harriet that I was not afraid of myself. – False shame made me act, as if I had no shame. – You would not suspect me of knowing any thing of false shame, but depend upon it, my dear, many, who appear to have as much assurance as I have, are secretly its slaves. – I moralise, because I am come to a part of my story, which I should almost be glad to omit – but I promised you, that there should be no sins of omission. It was light, but not broad daylight, when we got to Knightsbridge. Lawless encouraged, for I cannot deny it, by the levity of my manner, as well as of Harriet's, was in higher and more familiar spirits than I ever saw him. – Mrs Freke desired me to set her down at her sister's, who lived in Grosvenor place – I did so, and I beg you to believe, that I was in an agony to get rid of my colonel at the same time; but you know, I could not, before Harriet Freke, absolutely say to him – 'Get out!' – Indeed, to tell things as they were, it was scarcely possible to guess by my manner, that I was under any anxiety – I acted my part so well, or so ill. – As Harriet Freke jumped out of the coach, a cock crowed in the area of her sister's house. 'There!' cried Harriet, 'do you hear the cock crow, Lady Delacour?' – Now it's to be hoped your fear of goblins is over – else I would not be so cruel, as to leave the pretty dear all alone – 'All alone,' answered I – 'your friend the colonel is much obliged to you for making nobody of him.' – 'My friend the colonel,' whispered Harriet, leaning with her bold masculine arms folded upon the coach door – 'My friend the colonel is much obliged to me, I'm sure, for remembering what the cunning, or the knowing woman told us just now, that you and he are – or are to be – one and the same person. So when I said I left you alone, I was not guilty of a bull, was I?' – I had the grace to be heartily ashamed of this speech, and called out in utter confusion – 'to Berkeley square. – But where shall I set you down, colonel? – Harriet, good morning – don't forget you are in man's clothes.' – I did not dare to repeat the question of 'where shall I set you down, colonel?' at this instant, because Harriet gave me such an arch sneering look, as much as to say – still afraid of yourself! – We drove on – I'm persuaded that the confusion which, in spite of all my efforts, broke through my affected levity, encouraged Lawless, who was naturally a coxcomb and a fool, to believe that I was actually his – else he never could have been so insolent. – In short, my dear, before we had got through the turnpike-gate, I was downright obliged to say to him – 'Get out!' – which I did with a degree of indignation, that quite astonished him. – He muttered something about ladies knowing their minds – and I own, though I went off with flying colours, I secretly blamed myself as much as I did him, and I blamed Harriet more than I did either. – I sent for her the next day as soon as I could, to consult her. She expressed such astonishment, and so much concern, at this catastrophe of our night's frolic, and blamed herself with so many oaths, and execrated Lawless for a coxcomb so much to the ease and satisfaction of my conscience, that I was confirmed in my good opinion of her, and indeed felt for her the most lively affection and esteem – for observe, with me esteem ever followed affection, instead of affection following esteem. – Woe be to all, who in morals preposterously put the cart before the horse! – But to proceed with my history – all fashionable historians stop to make reflections, supposing that no one else can have the sense to make any. My *esteemed* friend agreed with me, that it would be best for

all the parties concerned to hush up this business; that as Lawless
was going out of town in a few days, to be elected for a borough,
we should get rid of him in the best way possible, without 'more
last words' – that he had been punished sufficiently on the spot,
and that to punish twice for the same offence, once in private and
once in public, would be contrary to the laws of English men and
English women, and in my case would be contrary to the evident
dictates of prudence – because I could not complain, without
calling up Lord Delacour, to call Lawless out – This I could not do
without acknowledging that his lordship had been in the right, in
warning me about *his honour and my own*, which old phrase I
dreaded to hear for the ninety-ninth time; besides, Lord Delacour
was the last man in the world I should have chosen for my knight –
though unluckily he was my lord. – Besides, all things considered,
I thought the whole story might not tell so well in the world for
me, tell it which way I would – We therefore agreed, that it would
be most expedient to hold our tongues. We took it for granted,
that Lawless would hold his, and as for my people, they knew
nothing, I thought, or if they did, I was sure of them. How the
thing got abroad, I could not at the time conceive, though now I
am well acquainted with the baseness and treachery of the woman
I called my friend. – The affair was known, and talked of every
where the next day, and the story was told especially at odious
Mrs Luttridge's, with such exaggerations as drove me almost
mad. – I was enraged, inconceivably enraged with Lawless, from
whom I imagined the reports originated.

"I was venting my indignation against him in a room full of
company, where I had just made my story good, when a
gentleman, to whom I was a stranger, came in breathless, with the
news that Colonel Lawless was killed in a duel by Lord Delacour –
that they were carrying him home to his mother's, and that the
body was just going by the door. – The company all crowded to
the windows immediately, and I was left standing alone, till I
could stand no longer. – What was said or done after this, I do not
remember – I only know, that when I came to myself, the most
dreadful sensation I ever experienced was, the certainty that I had
the blood of a fellow creature to answer for – I wonder," said
Lady Delacour, breaking off at this part of her history, and rising
suddenly – "I wonder what is become of Marriott? – surely it is
time for me to have my drops. – Miss Portman, have the goodness
to ring, for I *must* have something immediately." – Belinda was

terrified at the wildness of her manner. – Lady Delacour became more composed, or put more constraint upon herself, at the sight of Marriott – Marriott brought from the closet in her lady's room the drops, which Lady Delacour swallowed with precipitation. – Then she ordered coffee, and afterwards chasse-café, and at last, turning to Belinda with a forced smile, she said –

"Now shall the princess Scheherazade go on with her story?"

CHAPTER IV

Lady Delacour's History Continued

"I left off with the true skill of a good storyteller, at the most interesting part – a duel – and yet, duels are so common now, that they are really vulgar incidents.

"But we think that a duel concerning ourselves must be more extraordinary than any other. – We hear of men being shot in duels about nothing every day, so it is really a weakness in me to think so much about poor Lawless's death, as Harriet Freke said to me at the time. – She expected to see me show sorrow in public – but very fortunately for me, she roused my pride – which was always stronger than my reason; and I behaved myself upon the occasion as became a fine lady. – There were some things, however, I could hardly stand. – You must know that Lawless, fool and coxcomb as he was, had some magnanimity, and showed it – as some people do from whom it is least expected – on his deathbed. The last words he said, were – 'Lady Delacour is innocent – I charge you don't prosecute Lord Delacour.' – This he said to his mother – who – to complete my misery – is one of the most respectable women in England, and was most desperately fond of Lawless, who was an only son. – She never has recovered his loss. – Do you remember asking me who a tall elderly lady in mourning was, that you saw getting into her carriage one day, in South-Audley street chapel, as we passed by in our way to the park? – That was Lady Lawless – I believe I didn't answer you at the time. – I meet her every now and then – to me a spectre of dismay. – But as Harriet Freke said, certainly such a man as poor Lawless was a useless being in society, however he may be regretted by a doating mother. – We should see things in a philosophical light if we can. – I should not have suffered half as much as I did, if he had been a man of a stronger understanding; but he was a poor, vain, weak creature, that I actually drew on and duped with my own coquetry, whilst all the time I was endeavouring only to plague Lord Delacour. – I was punished enough by the airs his lordship doubly gave himself, upon the

strength of his valour and his judgment – they roused me
completely – and I blamed him with all my might, and got an
enormous party of my friends, I mean my acquaintance, to run
him down full cry, for having fought for me – It was absurd – It
was rash – It was want of proper confidence in his wife; *thus we*
said: – Lord Delacour had his partisans, it is true, amongst whom
the loudest was odious Mrs Luttridge. I embraced the first
opportunity I met with of retaliation. – You must know that Mrs
Luttridge, beside being a great faro-player, was a great dabbler in
politics; for she was almost as fond of power as of money: she
talked loud and fluently, and had, somehow or other, partly by
intriguing, partly by relationship, connected herself with some of
the leading men in parliament. – There was to be a contested
election in our county; Mr Luttridge had a good estate there next
to Lord Delacour's, and being of an ancient family, and keeping a
good table, the Luttridges were popular enough. – At the first
news of an election, out comes a flaming advertisement from Mr
Luttridge; away posted Mrs Luttridge to begin her canvass, and
away posted Lady Delacour after her, to canvass for a cousin of
Harriet Freke's. – This was a new scene for me; but I piqued
myself on the versatility of my talents, and I laid myself out to
please all the squires, and, what was more difficult, all the squires'
ladies in *****shire. I was ambitious to have it said of me, 'that I
was the finest figure that ever appeared upon canvass.' – O ye
*****shireians, how hard did I work to obtain your praise! – All
that the combined force of vanity and hatred could inspire, I
performed, and with success. You have but little curiosity, I
presume, to know how many hogsheads of port went down the
throat of John Bull, or how many hecatombs were offered up to
the genius of English liberty. My hatred to Mrs Luttridge was, of
course, called love of my country. Lady Delacour was deified by
all *true* patriots – and, luckily, a handsome legacy left me for my
spirit, by an uncle who died six weeks before the election, enabled
us to sustain the expense of my apotheosis. – The day of election
came – Harriet Freke and I made our appearance on the hustings,
dressed in splendid party uniforms; and before us, our knights
and squires held two enormous panniers full of ribands and
cockades; which we distributed with a grace that won all hearts, if
not all votes. – Mrs Luttridge thought the panniers would carry
the election; and forthwith she sent off an express for a pair of
panniers twice as large as ours. I took out my pencil, and drew a

caricature of *the ass and her panniers*; wrote an epigram at the bottom of it; and the epigram and the caricature were soon in the hands of half *****shire. The verses were as bad as impromptus usually are, and the drawing was not much better than the writing, but the *good will* of the critics supplied all my deficiencies; and never was more praise bestowed upon the pen of Burke, or the pencil of Reynolds, than was lavished upon me by my honest friends. – My dear Belinda, if you will not quarrel with the quality, you may have what quantity of praise you please. – Mrs Luttridge, as I hoped and expected, was beyond measure enraged at the sight of the caricature and epigram. – She was, beside being a gamester and a politician – what do you think? – an excellent shot! – She wished, she said, to be a man, that she might be qualified to take proper notice of my conduct – The same kind friends who showed her my epigram, repeated to me her observation upon it. Harriet Freke was at my elbow, and offered to take any *message* I might think proper to Mrs Luttridge. I scarcely thought her in earnest, till she added, that the only way left, nowadays, for a woman to distinguish herself, was by spirit; as every thing else was grown 'cheap and vulgar in the eyes of men.' – That she knew one of the cleverest young men in England, and a man of fashion into the bargain, who was just going to publish a treatise 'upon the Propriety and Necessity of Female Duelling'; and that he had demonstrated beyond a possibility of doubt, that civilised society could not exist half a century longer without this necessary improvement. I had prodigious deference for the masculine superiority, as I thought it, of Harriet's understanding. She was a philosopher, and a fine lady – I was only a fine lady – I had never fired a pistol in my life; and I was a little inclined to cowardice; but Harriet offered to bet any wager upon the steadiness of my hand, and assured me that I should charm all beholders in male attire – In short, as my second, if I would furnish her with proper credentials, she swore she would undertake to furnish me with clothes, and pistols, and courage, and every thing I wanted. – I sat down to pen my challenge. When I was writing it, my hand did not tremble *much* – not more than my Lord Delacour's always does. The challenge was very prettily worded – I believe I can repeat it.

'Lady Delacour presents her compliments to Mrs Luttridge – she is informed that Mrs L —— wishes she were a man, that she might be qualified to take *proper* notice of Lady D —— 's conduct.

Lady Delacour begs leave to assure Mrs Luttridge, that though she has the misfortune to be a woman, she is willing to account for her conduct, in any manner Mrs L — may think proper – and at any hour and place she may appoint. Lady D — leaves the choice of the weapons to Mrs L —. Mrs H. Freke, who has the honour of presenting this note, is Lady Delacour's *friend* upon this occasion.'

"I cannot repeat Mrs Luttridge's answer; all I know is, it was not half as neatly worded as my note; but the essential part of it was, that she accepted my challenge *with pleasure*, and should do herself the honour of meeting me at six o'clock the next morning – that Miss Honour O'Grady would be her *friend* upon the occasion – and that pistols were the weapons she preferred. The place of appointment was behind an old barn, about two miles from the town of ****. The hour was fixed to be early in the morning, to prevent all probability of interruption. In the evening, Harriet and I rode to the ground. There were several bullets sticking in the posts of the barn: – this was the place where Mrs Luttridge had been accustomed to exercise herself in firing at a mark. I own my courage 'oozed out' a little at this sight. – The Duc de Rochefoucault, I believe, said truly, that 'many would be cowards if they dared.' There seemed to me to be no physical, and less moral necessity for my fighting this duel, but I did not venture to reason on a point of honour with my spirited second. I bravadoed to Harriet most magnanimously, but at night, when Marriott was undressing me, I could not forbear giving her a hint, which I thought might tend to preserve the king's peace, and the peace of the county. I went to the ground in the morning, in good spirits and with a safe conscience. Harriet was in admiration of my 'lion-port:' to do her justice, she conducted herself with great coolness upon the occasion; but then it may be observed, that it was I who was to stand fire, and not she. I thought of poor Lawless a billion of times at least, as we were going to the ground; and I had my presentiments, and my confused notions of poetic justice – but poetic justice, and all other sorts of justice, went clear out of my head, when I saw my antagonist and her friend actually pistol in hand, waiting for us: they were both in men's clothes. – I secretly called upon the name of Marriott with fervency, and I looked round with more anxiety than ever Bluebeard's wife, or 'Anne, sister Anne!' looked to see if any body was coming: nothing was to be seen, but the grass blown by the wind – No

Marriott to throw herself *toute éplorée** between the combatants
– no peace-officers to bind us over to our good behaviour – no
deliverance at hand – and Mrs Luttridge, by all the laws of
honour, as challenged, was to have the first shot – O, those laws of
honour! – I was upon the point of making an apology, in spite of
them all, when, to my inexpressible joy, I was relieved from the
dreadful alternative of being shot through the head, or of
becoming a laughing-stock for life, by an incident, less heroic, I'll
grant ye, than opportune. – But you shall have the whole scene, as
well as I can recollect it – *as well* – for those who, for the first time,
go to a field of battle, do not, as I am credibly informed, and
internally persuaded, always find the clearness of their memories
improved by the novelty of their situation. Mrs Luttridge, when
we came up, was leaning, with a truly martial negligence, against
the wall of the barn, with her pistol, as I told you, in her hand. She
spoke not a word, but her second, Miss Honour O'Grady,
advanced towards us immediately, and taking off her hat very
manfully, addressed herself to my second. – 'Mistress Harriet
Freke, I presume, if I mistake not.' – Harriet bowed slightly, and
answered – 'Miss Honour O'Grady, I presume, if I mistake not.' –
'The same, at your service,' replied Miss Honour. – 'I have a few
words to suggest, that may save a great deal of noise, and
bloodshed, and ill will.' – 'As to noise,' said Harriet, 'it is a thing in
which I delight, therefore, I beg that mayn't be spared on my
account; as to bloodshed, I beg that may not be spared on Lady
Delacour's account, for her honour, I am sure, is dearer to her
than her blood; and as to ill will, I should be concerned to have
that saved on Mrs Luttridge's account, as we all know it is the
thing in which she delights, even more than I do in noise, or Lady
Delacour in blood: – but pray proceed, Miss Honour O'Grady;
you have a few words to suggest.' – 'Yes, I would willingly
observe, as it is my duty to my *principal*,' said Honour, 'that one,
who is compelled to fire a pistol with her left hand, though ever so
good a shot *naturally*, is by no means on a footing with one who
has the advantage of her right hand.' Harriet rubbed my pistol
with the sleeve of her coat, and I, recovering my wit with my hopes
of being witty with impunity, answered – 'Unquestionably! –
left-handed wisdom and left-handed courage are neither of them
the very best of their kinds but we must content ourselves with
them, *if* we can have no other.' 'That *if*,' cried Honour O'Grady,
'is not, like most of the family of the *ifs*, a peace-maker. My Lady

Delacour, I was going to observe, that my principal has met with an unfortunate accident in the shape of a whitlow on the fore-finger of her right hand, which incapacitates her from drawing a trigger; but I am at your service, ladies, either of you, that can't put up with a disappointment with good humour.' – I never, during the whole course of my existence, was more disposed to bear a disappointment with good humour, to prove that I was incapable of bearing malice; and, to oblige the seconds, for form sake, I agreed that we should take our ground, and fire our pistols into the air – Mrs Luttridge, with her left-handed wisdom, fired first – and I, with great magnanimity, followed her example. – I must do my adversary's second, Miss Honour O'Grady, the justice to observe, that in this whole affair she conducted herself not only with the spirit, but with the good nature and generosity characteristic of her nation – We met enemies and parted friends.

"Life is a tragicomedy! – Though the critics will allow of no such thing in their books, it is a true representation of what passes in the world; and of all lives, mine has been the most grotesque mixture, or alternation I should say, of tragedy and comedy. – All this is à-propos to something I have not told you yet. – This comic duel ended tragically for me – 'How?' – you say – Why, 'tis clear that I was not shot through the head; but it would have been better, a hundred times better for me, if I had; I should have been spared, in this life at least, the torments of the damned – I was not used to priming and loading – my pistol was overcharged – when I fired, it recoiled, and I received a blow on my breast, the consequences of which you have seen – or are to see.

"The pain was nothing at the moment compared with what I have since experienced – But I will not complain till I cannot avoid it – I had not, at the time I received the blow, much leisure for lamentation; for I had scarcely discharged my pistol, when we heard a loud shout on the other side of the barn, and a crowd of town's people, country people, and hay makers, came pouring down the lane towards us with rakes and pitch forks in their hands. – An English mob is really a formidable thing. – Marriott had mismanaged her business most strangely – she had, indeed, spread a report of a duel – a female duel – but the untutored sense of propriety amongst these rusticks was so shocked at the idea of a duel fought by women in *men's clothes*, that I verily believe they would have thrown us into the river with all their hearts – Stupid blockheads! I am convinced that they would not have been half so much scandalised if we had boxed in petticoats – The want of these petticoats had nearly proved our destruction, or at least our disgrace – a peeress, after being ducked, could never have held her head above water again with any grace. – The mob had just closed round us, crying 'shame! shame! shame! – duck 'em, duck 'em – gentle or simple – duck 'em – duck 'em' – when their attention was suddenly turned towards a person, who was driving up the lane a large herd of squeaking, grunting pigs. – The person was clad in splendid regimentals, and he was armed with a long pole, to the end of which hung a bladder, and his pigs were frightened, and they ran squeaking from one side of the road to the other; and the pig-driver in regimentals, in the midst of the noise, could not without difficulty make his voice heard; but at last he was understood to say, that a bet of a hundred guineas depended upon his being able to keep these pigs ahead of a flock of turkeys that were following them, and he begged the mob to give him and his pigs fair play. – At the news of this wager, and at the sight of the gentleman turned pig-driver, the mob were in raptures, and, at the sound of his voice, Harriet Freke immediately exclaimed – 'Clarence Hervey! – By all that's lucky!'

"Clarence Hervey!" interrupted Belinda. – "Clarence Hervey, my dear," said Lady Delacour, coolly – "he can do every thing you know! even drive pigs better than any body else" – but let me go on.

"Harriet Freke shouted in a Stentorean voice, which actually made your pig-driver start: she explained to him in French our distress, and the cause of it. Clarence was, as I suppose you have discovered long ago, 'that cleverest young man in England, who had written on the propriety and necessity of female duelling.' – He answered Harriet in French – 'To attempt your rescue by force would be vain – but I will do better, I will make a diversion in your favour.' – Immediately our hero, addressing himself to the sturdy fellow who held me in custody, exclaimed – 'Huzza, my boys! Old England for ever! Yonder comes a Frenchman with a flock of turkeys. My pigs will beat them for a hundred guineas. – Old England for ever, huzza!'

"As he spoke, the French officer, with whom Clarence Hervey had laid the wager, appeared at the turn of the lane – his turkeys half flying, half hobbling up the road before him. – The Frenchman waved a red streamer over the heads of his flock – Clarence shook a pole, from the top of which hung a bladder full of beans. The pigs grunted – the turkeys gobbled, and the mob shouted – eager for the fame of old England, the crowd followed Clarence with loud acclamations. – The French officer was followed with groans and hisses. – So great was the confusion, and so great the zeal of the patriots, that even the pleasure of ducking the female duellists was forgotten in the general enthusiasm. – All eyes and all hearts were intent upon the race – and now the turkeys got foremost – and now the pigs. – But when we came within sight of the horsepond, I heard one man cry – 'don't forget the ducking.' – How I trembled! but our knight shouted to his followers – 'For the love of old England, my brave boys, keep between my pigs and the pond – if our pigs see the water they'll run to it, and England's undone.'

"The whole attention of the mob was by this speech conducted away from us – 'On, on my boys into town, to the market-place; whoever gains the market place first, wins the day.' – Our general shook the rattling bladder in triumph, over the heads of 'the swinish multitude,' as we followed in perfect security in his train into the town.

"Men, women, and children, crowded to the windows and doors. – 'Retreat into the first place you can,' whispered Clarence to us; we were close to him. – Harriet Freke pushed her way into a milliner's shop – I could not get in after her, for a frightened pig turned back suddenly, and almost threw me down. Clarence Hervey caught me, and favoured my retreat into the shop. But poor Clarence lost his bet by his gallantry. Whilst he was manoeuvering in my favour, the turkeys got several yards ahead of the pigs, and reaching the market-place first, won the race.

"The French officer found great difficulty in getting safe out of the town; but Clarence represented to the mob, that he was a prisoner on his parole, and that it would be unlike Englishmen, to insult a prisoner. – So he got off without being pelted, and they both returned in safety to the house of General Y —, where they were to dine, and where they entertained a large party of officers with the account of this adventure.

"Mrs Freke and I rejoiced in our escape, and we thought that the whole business was now over – but in this we were mistaken. The news of our duel, which had spread in the town, raised such an uproar as had never been heard, even at the noisiest election. – Would you believe it? The fate of the election turned upon this duel. – The common people, one and all, declared, that they would not vote either for Mr Luttridge or Mr Freke, because *as how* – But I need not repeat all the *platitudes* that they said. – In short, neither ribands nor brandy could bring them to reason. With true English pig-headedness, they went every man of them and polled for an independent candidate of their own choosing, whose wife, forsooth, was a proper behaved woman.

"The only thing I had to console me for all this, was Clarence Hervey's opinion, that I looked better in man's clothes, than my friend Harriet Freke. – Clarence was charmed with my spirit and grace, but he had not leisure at that time to attach himself seriously to me, or to any thing. – He was then, I guess, about nineteen or twenty; he was all vivacity, presumption, and paradox; he was enthusiastic in support of his opinions, but he was at the same time the most candid man in the world; for there was no set of tenets which could be called exclusively his; he adopted in liberal rotation every possible absurdity, and to do him justice, defended each in its turn with the most ingenious arguments that could be devised, and with a flow of words which charmed the ear if not the sense. – His essay on female duelling was a most extraordinary performance; it was handed about in manuscript till it was worn out, he talked of publishing it, and dedicating it to me. However, this scheme, amongst a million of others, he *talked of*, but never put into execution. – Luckily for him, many of his follies evaporated in words. – I saw but little either of him or his follies at this time. – All I know about him is, that after he had lost his bet of a hundred guineas, as a pig-driver, by his knight-errantry in rescuing the female duellists from a mob, he wrote a very charming copy of verses upon the occasion; and that he was so much provoked by the stupidity of some of his brother officers, who could not understand the verses, that he took a disgust to the army, and sold his commission. He set out upon a tour to the continent, and I returned with Harriet Freke to London, and forgot the existence of such a person as Clarence Hervey for three or four years. – Unless people can be of some use, or unless they are actually present, let them be ever so agreeable or meritorious, we are very apt to forget them. – One grows strangely selfish by living in the world. – 'Tis a perfect cure for romantic notions of gratitude, and love, and so forth. – If I had lived in the country, in an old manor house, Clarence Hervey would have doubtless reigned paramount in my imagination, as the deliverer of my life, &c. But in London one has no time for thinking of deliverers. And yet what I did with my time I cannot tell you — 'Tis gone, and no trace left — One day after another went, I know not how. — Had I wept for every day I lost, I'm sure I should have cried my eyes out before this time. — If I had enjoyed any amusement in the midst of this dissipation, it would all have been very well; but I declare to you in confidence, I have been tired to death. — Nothing can be more monotonous than the life of a hackneyed fine lady. — I question whether a drayhorse, or a horse in a mill, would willingly exchange places with one — if they could know as much of the matter as I do. — You are surprised at hearing all this from me. — My dear Belinda, how I envy you! — You are not yet tired of every thing. — *The world* has still the gloss of novelty for you — But don't expect that can last above a season. — My first winter was certainly entertaining enough. — One begins with being charmed with the bustle and glare, and what the French call *spectacle*; this is over, I think, in six months. — I can but just recollect having been amused at the Theatres, and the Opera, and the Pantheon, and Ranelagh, and all those places, for their own sakes. — Soon, very soon we go out to see people, not things. — Then we grow tired of seeing people — then we grow tired of being seen by people — and then we go out, merely because we can't stay at home — A dismal story, and a true one. — Excuse me for showing you the simple truth; well dressed falsehood is a personage much more *presentable*. — I am now come to an epoch in my history, in which there is a dearth of extraordinary events — What shall I do? — Shall I invent — I would if I could — but I cannot — Then I must confess to you, that during these last four years I should have died of ennui if I had not been kept alive by my hatred of Mrs Luttridge, and of my husband — I don't know which I hate most — O, yes I do — I certainly hate Mrs Luttridge the most — for a woman can always hate a woman more than she can hate a man, unless she has been in love with him — which I never was with poor Lord Delacour. — Yes! I certainly hate Mrs Luttridge the most — I cannot count the number of extravagant things I have done on purpose to eclipse her. — We have had rival routs, rival concerts, rival galas, rival theatres — she has cost me more than *she's* worth — But then I certainly have mortified her once a month at least. — My hatred to Mrs Luttridge, my dear, is the remote cause of my love for you — for it was the cause of my intimacy with your aunt Stanhope — Mrs Stanhope is really a clever woman, she knows how to turn the hatred of all her friends and acquaintance to her own advantage. – To serve lovers, is a thankless office, compared with that of serving *haters* – polite haters I mean. – It may be dangerous, for aught I know, to interpose in the quarrels of those who hate their neighbours, not only with all their souls, but with all their strength – the barbarians fight it out, kiss, and are friends. – The quarrels which never come to blows are safer for a go-between; but even these are not to be compared to such as never come to words – Your true silent hatred is that which lasts for ever. – The moment it was known that Mrs Luttridge and I had come to the resolution never to speak to one another, your aunt Stanhope began to minister to my hatred so, that she made herself quite agreeable. She, one winter, gave me notice that my adversary had set her heart upon having a magnificent entertainment, on a particular day. On that day, I determined, of course, to have a rival gala. – Mrs Stanhope's maid had a lover, a gardener, who lived at Chelsea; and the gardener had an aloe, which was expected soon to blow. Now, a plant that blows but once in a hundred years is worth having. The gardener intended to make a public exhibition of it; by which he expected to gain about a hundred guineas. – Your aunt Stanhope's maid got it from him, for me, for fifty; and I had it whispered about, that an aloe in full blow, would stand in the middle of one of Lady Delacour's supper tables. – The difficulty was to make Mrs Luttridge fix upon the very day we wanted; for you know we could not possibly put off the blowing of our aloe. – Your aunt Stanhope managed the thing admirably, by means of a *common friend*, who was not a suspected person with the Luttridges – in short, my dear, I gained my point – every body came from Mrs Luttridge's to me, or to my aloe – She had a prodigiously fine supper, but scarcely a soul staid with her; they all came to see, what could be seen but once in a hundred years. – Now, the aloe, you know, is of a cumbersome height for a supper ornament. – My saloon luckily has a dome, and under the dome we placed it. – Round the huge china vase in which it was planted, we placed the most beautiful, or rather the most expensive hot-house plants we could procure. – After all, the aloe was an ugly thing – but it answered my purpose – it made Mrs Luttridge, as I am credibly informed, absolutely weep with vexation. – I was excessively obliged to your aunt Stanhope, and I assured her, that if ever it were in my power, she might depend upon my gratitude. – Pray, when you write, repeat the same thing to her, and tell her, that since she has introduced Belinda Portman to me, I am a hundred times more obliged to her than ever I was before. – But to proceed with my important history. – I will not tire you, with fighting over again all my battles, in my seven years war with Mrs Luttridge. – I believe love is more to your taste than hatred; therefore I will go on as fast as possible to Clarence Hervey's return from his travels. – He was much improved by them; or at least I thought so, for he was heard to declare, that after all he had seen in France and Italy, Lady Delacour appeared to him the most charming woman *of her age*, in Europe. – The words, *of her age*, piqued me, and I spared no pains to make him forget them – a stupid man cannot readily be persuaded out of his senses – what he sees, he sees, and neither more nor less – but 'tis the easiest thing in the world to catch hold of a man of genius –you have nothing to do but to appeal from his senses to his imagination; and then he sees with the eyes of his imagination, and hears with the ears of his imagination; and then no matter what the age, beauty, or wit of the charmer may be – no matter whether it be Lady Delacour, or Belinda Portman – I think I know Clarence Hervey's character *au fin fond*,* and I could lead him where I pleased – but don't be alarmed, my dear, you know I can't lead him into matrimony. – You look at me, and from me – and you don't well know which way to look – You are surprised perhaps, after all that passed, all that I felt, and all that I still feel about poor Lawless, I should not be cured of coquetry – So am I surprised – but habit, fashion, the devil, I believe, leads us on – and then, Lord Delacour is so obstinate and jealous – you can't have forgotten the *polite conversation* that passed one morning at breakfast between his lordship and me, about Clarence Hervey – but neither does his lordship know, nor does Clarence Hervey suspect, that my object with him is to conceal from the world, what I cannot conceal from myself, that I am a dying woman. – I am, and I see you think me, a strange, weak, inconsistent creature – I was intended for something better – but now it is too late – a coquette I have lived, and a coquette I shall die – I speak frankly to you – let me have the glory of leading Clarence Hervey about with me in public for a few months longer, then I must quit the stage. – As to love, you know with me, that is out of the question; all I ask or wish for is admiration."

Lady Delacour paused, and leaned back on the sofa – she appeared in great pain.

"O! – I am, sometimes," resumed she, "as you see, in terrible pain. – For two years after I gave myself that blow with the pistol, I neglected the warning twinges that I felt from time to time – at last I was terrified. – Marriott was the only person to whom I mentioned my fears, and she was profoundly ignorant. – She flattered me with false hopes, till, alas! it was in vain to doubt of the nature of my complaint. – Then she urged me to consult a physician – that I would not do – I could not – I never will consult a physician – I would not for the universe have my situation known. – You stare – you cannot enter into my feelings. – Why, my dear, if I lose admiration, what have I left? – Would you have me live upon pity? – Consider, what a dreadful thing it must be to me, who have no friends, no family, to be confined to a sick room – a sick bed – 'tis what I must come to at last – but not yet – not yet – I have fortitude – I should despise myself if I had no species of merit – besides, it is still some occupation to me, to act my part in public – and bustle, noise, nonsense, if they do not amuse, or interest me, yet they stifle reflection – may you never know what it is to feel remorse! – The idea of that poor wretch, Lawless, whom I actually murdered, as much as if I had shot him, haunts me whenever I am alone – It is now between eight and nine years since he died, and I have lived ever since in a constant course of dissipation – but it won't do – Conscience! conscience will be heard. – Since my health has been weakened, I believe I have acquired more conscience – I really think that my stupid lord, who has neither ideas nor sensations, except when he is intoxicated, is a hundred times happier than I am. – But I will spare you, Belinda – I promised that you should not have a *scene*, and I will keep my word – It is, however, a great relief to open my mind to one who has some feeling – Harriet Freke has none – I am convinced that she has no more feeling than this table. – I have not yet told you how she has used me. – You know that it was she who led, or rather dragged me into that scrape with Lawless – For that I never reproached her. – You know it was she who frightened me into fighting that duel with Mrs Luttridge – For this I never reproached her – She has cost me my peace of mind – my health – my life – She knows it, and she forsakes, betrays, insults, and leaves me to die – I cannot command my temper sufficiently to be coherent when I speak of her – I cannot express in words what I feel – How could that most treacherous of beings, for ten years, make me believe that she was my friend? – Whilst I thought she really loved me, I pardoned her all her faults – *All* – what a comprehensive word! – All, all I forgave, and continually said – *but* she has a good heart – A good heart! – She has no heart! She has no feeling for any living creature but herself – I always thought that she cared for no one but for me – but now I find she can throw me off as easily as she would her glove – And this too I suppose she calls a frolic – or, in her own vulgar language, fun. – Can you believe it? – What do you think she has done, my dear? She has gone over at last to odious Mrs Luttridge – actually she is gone down with the Luttridges to — shire – The independent member has taken the Chiltern Hundreds, vacates his seat, a new election comes on directly – the Luttridges are to bring in Freke – not Harriet's cousin, they have cut him – but her husband, who is now to commence senator – he is to come in for the county, upon condition that Luttridge shall have Freke's borough. – Lord Delacour, without saying one syllable, has gone and promised his interest to this precious junto, and Lady Delacour is left a miserable cipher – My lord's motives I can clearly understand; he lost a thousand guineas to Mrs Luttridge this winter, and this is a convenient way of paying her – why Harriet should be so anxious to serve a husband whom she hates – bitterly hates – might surprise any body who did not know *les dessous des cartes** as well as I do. – You are but just come into the world, Belinda – the world of wickedness I mean, my dear, or you would have heard what a piece of work there was, a few years ago, about Harriet Freke, and this cousin of hers. – Without betraying her confidence, I may just tell you what is known to every body, that she went so far, that if it had not been for me, not a soul would have visited her – she swam in the sea of folly out of her depth – the tide of fashion ebbed, and then was she left sticking knee deep in the mud; a ridiculous, scandalous figure; I had the courage and foolish good nature to hazard myself for her, and actually dragged her to terra firma – how she has gone on since I *cannot* tell you – precisely, because I am in the secret – but the catastrophe is public – to make her peace with her husband, she gives up her friend. – Well! that I could have pardoned, if she had not been so base as to go over to Mrs Luttridge. – Mrs Luttridge offered (I've seen the letter and Harriet's answer) to bring in Freke, the husband, and to make both a county and *a family peace*, on condition that Harriet should give up all connexion with Lady Delacour. – Mrs Luttridge knew this would provoke me beyond measure, and there is nothing she would not do to gratify her mean, malevolent passion – she has succeeded for once in her life – the blame of the duel, of course, is all thrown upon me – and, would you believe it, Harriet Freke, I am credibly informed, throws all the blame of Lawless's business on me – nay, hints that Lawless's deathbed declaration of my innocence was *very generous*. – O, the treachery, the baseness of this woman! – and it was my fate to hear all this last night, at the masquerade – I waited, and waited, and looked every where for Harriet – she was to be the widow Brady, I knew – At last the widow Brady made her apperance, and I accosted her with all my usual familiarity – The widow was dumb – I insisted upon knowing the cause of this sudden loss of speech – The widow took me into another apartment, unmasked, and there I beheld Mr Freke, the husband. – I was astonished, had no idea of the truth – 'Where is Harriet?' I believe were the first words I said – 'Gone to the country.' – 'To the country!' – 'Yes; to — shire, with Mrs Luttridge.' – Mrs Luttridge, odious Mrs Luttridge! I could scarcely believe my senses – but Freke, who always hated me, believing that I led his wife, instead of her leading me into mischief, would have enjoyed my astonishment and my rage – so I concealed both, with all possible presence of mind. – He went on overwhelming me with explanations and copies of letters; and declared it was at Mrs Freke's request he did and said all this; and that he was to follow her early the next morning to — shire. – I broke from him, simply wishing him a good journey, and as much family peace as his patience merited. – He knows that I know his wife's history, and though *she* has no shame, he has some. – I had the satisfaction to leave him blushing with anger, and I supported the character of the comic muse a full hour afterward, to convince him, that all their combined malice would fail to break my spirit – in public – what I suffer in private, is known only to my own heart."

As she finished these words, Lady Delacour rose abruptly, and hummed a new opera air. Then she retired to her boudoir, saying, with an air of levity, to Belinda, as she left the room —

"Good bye, my dear Belinda; I leave you to ruminate sweet and bitter thoughts – to think of the last speech and confession of Lady Delacour, or, what will interest you much more, the first speech and confession of – Clarence Hervey."

CHAPTER V

Birthday Dresses

Lady Delacour's history, and the manner in which it was related, excited in Belinda's mind astonishment – pity – admiration – and contempt. – Astonishment at her inconsistency – pity for her misfortunes – admiration of her talents – and contempt for her conduct. – To these emotions succeeded the recollection of the promise which she had made, not to leave her in her last illness, at the mercy of an insolent attendant. This promise Belinda thought of with terror – she dreaded the sight of sufferings, which she knew must end in death – she dreaded the sight of that affected gaiety, and of that real levity, which so ill became the condition of a dying woman. – She trembled at the idea of being under the guidance of one, who was so little able to conduct herself; and she could not help blaming her aunt Stanhope severely, for placing her in such a perilous situation. It was obvious, that some of Lady Delacour's history must have been known to Mrs Stanhope; and Belinda, the more she reflected, the more she was surprised at her aunt's having chosen such a chaperon for a young woman just entering the world. When the understanding is suddenly roused and forced to exert itself, what a multitude of deductions it makes in a short time. – Belinda saw things in a new light; and for the first time in her life she reasoned for herself upon what she saw and felt. – It is sometimes safer for young people to see, than to hear of certain characters. – At a distance, Lady Delacour had appeared to Miss Portman the happiest person in the world; upon a nearer view, she discovered that her ladyship was one of the most miserable of human beings. – To have married her niece to such a man as Lord Delacour, Mrs Stanhope would have thought the most fortunate thing imaginable; but it was now obvious to Belinda, that neither the title of viscountess, nor the pleasure of spending three fortunes, could ensure felicity. Lady Delacour confessed, that in the midst of the utmost luxury and dissipation, she had been a constant prey to ennui; that the want of domestic happiness could never be supplied by that public admiration, of which she was so ambitious; and that the immoderate indulgence of her vanity had led her, by inevitable steps, into follies and inprudence, which had ruined her health, and destroyed her peace of mind. "If Lady Delacour, with all the advantages of wealth, rank, wit and beauty, has not been able to make herself happy in this life of fashionable dissipation," said Belinda to herself, "why should I follow the same course, and expect to be more fortunate?"

It is singular that the very means, which Mrs Stanhope had taken to make a fine lady of her niece, tended to produce an effect diametrically opposite to what might have been expected. – The result of Belinda's reflections upon Lady Delacour's history was a resolution to profit by her bad example; but this resolution it was more easy to form than to keep. – Her ladyship, where she wished to please or to govern, had fascinating manners, and could alternately use the sarcastic powers of wit, and the fond tone of persuasion, to accomplish her purposes. – It was Belinda's intention, in pursuance of her new plans of life, to spend, whilst she remained in London, as little money as possible upon superfluities and dress. – She had, at her own disposal, only 100l. per annum, the interest of her fortune; but beside this, her aunt, who was desirous that she should go to court, and make a splendid figure there, had sent her a draft on her banker for two hundred guineas. "You will, I trust," said her aunt, at the conclusion of her letter, "repay me when you are established in the world, as I hope and believe, from what I hear from Lady Delacour of the power of your charms, you will soon be, to the entire satisfaction of all your friends. – Pray do not neglect to mention my friend Clarence Hervey particularly, when you write next. – I understand from one who is well acquainted with him, and who has actually seen his rent-roll, that he has a clear 10,000l. year.

Belinda resolved neither to go to court, nor to touch her aunt's two hundred guineas; and she wrote a long letter to her, in which she explained her feelings and views at large. In this letter she meant to have returned Mrs Stanhope's draft, but her feelings and views changed between the writing of this epistle, and the going out of the post. – Mrs Franks, the milliner, came in the interim, and brought home Lady Delacour's beautiful dress; it was not the sight of this, however, which changed Belinda's mind, but she could not resist Lady Delacour's raillery.

"Why, my dear," said her ladyship, after having listened to all Miss Portman could say about her love of independence, and the necessity of economy to preserve that independence – "all this is prodigiously fine – but shall I translate it into plain English – You were mortally wounded the other night by some random reflections of a set of foolish young men – Clarence Hervey amongst the number – and instead of punishing them, you sagely and generously determined to punish yourself. Then, to convince this youth that you have not a thought of those odious nets and cages, that you have no design whatever upon his heart, and that he has no manner of influence on yours; you very judiciously determine, at the first hint from him, to change your dress, your manners, and your character; and thus to say to him, in as plain terms as possible – 'You see, sir, a word to the wise is enough – I understand you disapprove of showy dress, and coquetry, and therefore, as I dressed and coquetted only to please you, now I shall lay aside dress and coquetry, since I find that they are not to your taste – and I hope, sir, you like my simplicity!' – Depend upon it, my dear, Clarence Hervey understands simplicity as well as you or I do. – All this would be vastly well, if he did not know that you overheard that conversation; but as he does know it, trust me he will attribute any sudden change in your manners and appearance, right or wrong, to the motives I have mentioned. – So don't, novice as you are! set about to manoeuvre for yourself. Leave all that to your aunt Stanhope, or to me, and then you know your conscience will be all the time as white as – your hands – which, by the by, Clarence Hervey, the other day, said were the whitest hands he had ever seen. – Perhaps all this time you have taken it into your head, that full dress will not become you; but I assure you that it will – you look well in any thing –

'But from the hoop's bewitching round,
'The very shoe has power to wound.'

So come down to Mrs Franks, and order your birthnight dress like a reasonable creature."

Like a reasonable creature, Miss Portman followed Lady Delacour, and bespoke, or rather let her ladyship bespeak for her, fifty guineas worth of elegance and fashion. – "You must go to the drawing-room with me next week, and be presented," said Lady Delacour, "and then, as it is the first time, you must be elegantly dressed – and you must not wear the same dress on the birthnight.

– So Mrs Franks let this be finished first, as fast as you can, and by that time perhaps, we shall think of something superlatively charming for the night of nights."

Mrs Franks departed, and Belinda sighed. – "A silver penny for your thoughts!" cried Lady Delacour – "You are thinking that you are like Camilla,* and I like Mrs Mitten – novel reading, as I dare say you have been told by your governess, as I was told by mine, and she by hers, I suppose – novel reading for young ladies is the most dangerous –

"O, Clarence Hervey, I protest!" cried Lady Delacour, as he at this instant entered the room. – "Do, pray Clarence, help me out, for the sake of this young lady with a moral sentence against novel reading: but that might go against your conscience – or your interest, so we'll spare you. – How I regret that we had not the charming serpent at the masquerade the other night!"

The moment her ladyship mentioned the masquerade, the conversation which had passed at Lady Singleton's, came full into Clarence Hervey's recollection, and his embarrassment was evident – not indeed to Belinda, who had turned away to look over some new music that lay upon a stand at the farthest end of the room, and she found this such a wonderfully interesting occupation, that she did not for some minutes hear, or appear to hear, one word of the conversation which was going on between Mr Hervey and Lady Delacour. – At last her ladyship tapped her upon the shoulder, saying in a playful tone – "Miss Portman, I arrest your attention at the suit of Clarence Hervey – this gentleman is passionately fond of music – to my curse – for he never sees my harp, but he worries me with reproaches for having left off playing upon it. – Now he has just given me his word, that he will not reproach me again for a month to come, if you will favour us with one air. – I assure you Clarence, that Belinda touches a harp divinely – she would absolutely charm." – "Your ladyship should not waste such valuable praise," interrupted Belinda. – "Do you forget, that Belinda Portman and her accomplishments have already been as well advertised as Packwood's razor strops?"

The manner in which these words were pronounced, made a great impression upon Clarence Hervey, and he began to believe it was possible, that a niece of the match-making Mrs Stanhope might not be "a compound of art and affectation" – "Though her aunt has advertised her," said he to himself, "she seems to have too much dignity to advertise herself, and it would be very unjust to blame her for the faults of another person. – I will see more of her."

Some morning visitors were announced, who for the time suspended Clarence Hervey's reflexions; the effect of them, however, immediately appeared, for as his good opinion of Belinda increased, his ambition to please her was strongly excited. – He displayed all his powers of wit and humour; and not only Lady Delacour, but every body present observed, "that Mr Hervey, who was always the most entertaining man in the world, this morning surpassed himself, and was absolutely the most entertaining man in the universe." He was mortified notwithstanding, for he distinctly perceived, that whilst Belinda joined with ease and dignity in the general conversation, her manner towards him was grave and reserved. – The next morning he called earlier than usual, but though Lady Delacour was always at home to him, she was then unluckily dressing to go to court; he inquired whether Miss Portman would accompany her ladyship, and he learnt from his friend Marriott, that she was not to be presented this day, because Mrs Franks had not brought home her dress. – Mr Hervey called again two hours afterwards – Lady Delacour was gone to court – He asked for Miss Portman – "Not at home" – was the mortifying answer, though as he had passed by the windows, he had heard the delightful sound of her harp. - He walked up and down in the square impatiently, till he saw Lady Delacour's carriage appear.

"The drawing-room has lasted an unconscionable time this morning," said he, as he handed her ladyship out of her coach. – "Am not I the most virtuous of virtuous women," said Lady Delacour, "to go to court such a day as this?" – But whispered she, as she went up stairs, "like all other amazingly good people, I have amazingly good reasons for being good. – The queen is soon to give a charming breakfast at Frogmore, and I am paying my court with all my might, in hopes of being asked, for Belinda must see one of their galas before we leave town, *that* I'm determined upon. – But where is she?" – "Not at home," said Clarence, smiling. – "O, not at home is nonsense, you know. – Shine out, appear, be found, my lovely Zara!"* cried Lady Delacour, opening the library door. – "Here she is – what doing I know not – studying Hervey's Meditations* on the Tombs I should guess, by the sanctification of her looks – If you be not totally above all sublunary considerations, admire my lilies of the valley – and let me give you a lecture, not upon heads – or upon hearts – but on what is of much more consequence, upon hoops. – Every body wears hoops, but how few – 'tis a melancholy consideration! – how very few can manage them. There's my friend lady C — in an elegant undress; she passes for very genteel, but put her into a hoop and she looks as pitiable a figure – as much a prisoner – and as little able to walk as a child in a go-cart. – She gets on, I grant you, and so does the poor child, but getting on you know is not walking. – O, Clarence, I wish you had seen the two lady Rs, sticking close to one another; their father pushing them on together, like two decanters in a bottle-coaster – with such magnificent diamond labels round their necks!"

Encouraged by Clarence Hervey's laughter, Lady Delacour went on to mimic what she called the hoop awkwardnesses of all her acquaintance, and if these could have failed to divert Belinda, it was impossible for her to be serious, when she heard Clarence Hervey declare, that he was convinced he could manage a hoop as well as any woman in England, except Lady Delacour.

"Now here," said he, "is the purblind dowager Lady Boucher, just at the door, Lady Delacour; she would not know my face, she would not see my beard, and I will bet fifty guineas, that I come into a room in a hoop, and that she does not find me out by my air – that I do not betray myself, in short, by my masculine awkwardness."

"I hold you to your word, Clarence," cried Lady Delacour. – "They have let the purblind dowager in, I hear her on the stairs. – Here – through this way you can go – as you do every thing quicker than any body else in the world, you will certainly be full-dressed in a quarter of an hour, I'll engage to keep the dowager in scandal for that time. – Go! – Marriott has old hoops and old finery of mine, and you have all powerful influence, I know, with Marriott – So go and use it, and let us see you in all your glory – though I vow I tremble for my fifty guineas."

Lady Delacour kept the dowager in scandal, according to her engagement, for a good quarter of an hour; then the dresses at the drawing-room took up another quarter; and, at last, the dowager began to give an account of sundry wonderful cures that had been performed to her certain knowledge, by her favourite concentrated extract or anima of quassia, – She entered into the history of the Negro slave named Quassi, who discovered this medical wood, which he kept a close secret till Mr Daghlberg, a magistrate of Surinam, wormed it out of him, brought a branch of the tree to Europe, and communicated it to the great Linnæus* – when Clarence Hervey was announced, by the title of – "The Comtesse de Pomenars".

"An émigrée* – a charming woman!" whispered Lady Delacour – "she was to have been at the drawing-room to day, but for a blunder of mine; ready dressed she was and I didn't call for her! – Ah, Madame de Pomenars, I am actually ashamed to see you," continued her ladyship, and she went forward to meet Clarence Hervey, who really made his entrée with very composed assurance and grace – He managed his hoop with such skill and dexterity, that he well deserved the praise of being a universal genius. The Comtesse de Pomenars spoke French, and broken English incomparably well; and she made out that she was descended from the Pomenars of the time of Madame de Sevigné:* she said that she had in her possession several original letters of Madame de Sevigné's, and a lock of Madame de Grignan's fine hair.

"I have sometimes fancied – but I believe it is only my fancy," said Lady Delacour, "that this young lady," turning to Belinda, "is not unlike your Madame de Grignan – I have seen a picture of her at Strawberry-hill."

Madame de Pomenars acknowledged that there was a resemblance – but added, that it was flattery in the extreme to Madame de Grignon to say so.

"It would be a sin, undoubtedly, to waste flattery upon the dead, my dear comtesse," said Lady Delacour. – "But here, without flattery to the living, as you have a lock of Madame de Grignan's hair, you can tell us whether *la belle chevelure,** of which Madame de Sevigné talked so much, was any thing to be compared to my Belinda's." – As she spoke, Lady Delacour, before Belinda was aware of her intentions, dextrously let down her beautiful tresses – and the Comtesse de Pomenars was so much struck at the sight, that she was incapable of paying the necessary compliments – "Nay, touch it," said Lady Delacour – "it is so fine and so soft." –

At this dangerous moment her ladyship artfully let drop the comb; Clarence Hervey suddenly stooped to pick it up, totally forgetting his hoop and his character. – He threw down the music stand with his hoop – Lady Delacour exclaimed, "bravissima!"

and burst out a laughing. – Clarence Hervey acknowledged he had lost his bet – joined in the laugh, and declared that fifty guineas was too little to pay for the sight of the finest hair that he had ever beheld. – "I declare he deserves a lock of *la belle chevelure* for that speech, Miss Portman," cried Lady Delacour, "I'll appeal to all the world – Madame de Pomenars must have a lock to measure with Madame de Grignan's? – Come, a second rape of the lock,* Belinda."

Fortunately for Belinda, "the glittering forfex" was not immediately produced, as fine ladies do not now, as in former times, carry any such useless implements about with them. –

Such was the modest, graceful dignity of Miss Portman's manners, that she escaped without even the charge of prudery – She retired to her own apartment as soon as she could.

"She passes on in unblenched majesty" – said Lady Delacour.

"She is really a charming woman," said Clarence Hervey, in a low voice, to Lady Delacour, drawing her into a recessed window; he in the same low voice continued – "Could I obtain a private audience of a few minutes when your ladyship is at leisure? – I have" – "I am never at leisure," interrupted Lady Delacour, "but if you have any thing particular to say to me, as I guess you have, by – my skill in human nature – come here to my concert, to night, before the rest of the world – wait patiently in the music room, and perhaps I may grant you a private audience. – As you had the grace not to call it a *tête-a-tête*. – In the mean time, my dear Comtesse de Pomenars, had not we better take off our hoops."

In the evening, Clarence Hervey was in the music room a considerable time before Lady Delacour appeared; how patiently he waited is not known to any one but himself. –

"Have not I given you time to compose a charming speech," said Lady Delacour as she entered the room – "but make it as short as you can, unless you wish that Miss Portman should hear it, for she will be down stairs in three minutes."

"In one word then, my dear Lady Delacour, can you, and will you, make my peace with Miss Portman – I am much concerned about that foolish razor-strop dialogue, which she overheard at Lady Singleton's." –

"You are concerned that she overheard it – no doubt."

"No," said Clarence Hervey, "I am rejoiced that she overheard it, since it has been the means of convincing me of my mistake; but I am concerned that I had the presumption and injustice to judge of Miss Portman so hastily. – I am convinced, that though she is a niece of Mrs Stanhope's, she has dignity of mind, and simplicity of character. – Will you, my dear Lady Delacour, tell her so?"

"Stay," interrupted Lady Delacour, "let me get it by heart – I should have made a terrible bad messenger of the gods and goddesses, for I never in my life could, like Iris, repeat a message in the same words in which it was delivered to me – Let me see – 'Dignity of mind, and simplicity of character,' was not it? May not I say at once, 'my dear Belinda, Clarence Hervey desires me to tell you, that he is convinced you are an angel?' – That single word *angel* is so expressive, so comprehensive, so comprehensible, it contains, believe me, all that can be said or imagined on these occasions, *de part et d'autre*."*

"But," said Mr Hervey, "perhaps Miss Portman has heard the song of –

'What know we of angels,
'I meant it in joke.'

"Then you are not in jest, but in downright sober earnest? – "Ha!" said Lady Delacour with an arch look, "I did not know it was already come to *this* with you."

And her ladyship, turning to her piano forte, played –

'There was a young man in Ballinacrasy
'Who wanted a wife to make him un*as*y,
'And thus in gentle strains he spoke her,
'Arrah, vill you marry me, my dear Ally Croker.'

"No, no," exclaimed Clarence, laughing, "it is not come to *that* with me yet, Lady Delacour, I promise you; but is not it possible to say, that a young lady has dignity of mind, and simplicity of character, without having or suggesting any thoughts of marriage."

"You make a most proper, but not sufficiently emphatic difference between having, or suggesting such thoughts," said Lady Delacour. – "A gentleman sometimes finds it for his interest, his honour, or his pleasure, to suggest what he would not for the world promise – I mean perform."

"A scoundrel," cried Clarence Hervey, "not a gentleman, may find it for his honour, or his interest, or his pleasure, to promise what he would not perform – but I am not a scoundrel – I never made any promise to man or woman, that I did not keep faithfully – I am not a swindler in love."

"And yet," said Lady Delacour, "you would have no scruple to trifle or flatter a woman out of her heart."

"*Cela est selon*!"* said Clarence smiling, "a fair exchange you know is no robbery. – When a fine woman robs me of my heart, surely Lady Delacour could not expect, that I should make no attempt upon hers." – "Is this part of my message to Miss Portman," said Lady Delacour? – "As your ladyship pleases," said Clarence. "I trust entirely to your ladyship's discretion."

"Why I really have a great deal of discretion," said Lady Delacour, "but you trust too much to it, when you expect that I should execute, both with propriety and success, the delicate commission of telling a young lady who is under my protection, that a young gentleman who is a professed admirer of mine, is in love with her, but has no thoughts, and wishes to suggest no thoughts of marriage."

"In love!" exclaimed Clarence Hervey, "but when did I ever use the expression? In speaking of Miss Portman, I simply expressed esteem and ad — O, no *and* — "

"No additions," said Lady Delacour, "content yourself with esteem – simply – and Miss Portman is safe, and you too – I presume. – Apropos; pray, Clarence, how do your esteem and *admiration* – (I may go as far as that, may not I?) of Miss Portman agree with your admiration of Lady Delacour."

"Perfectly well," replied Clarence, "for all the world must be sensible, that Clarence Hervey is a man of too much taste to compare a country novice in wit and accomplishments, to Lady Delacour. – He might, as men of genius sometimes do, look forward to the idea of forming a country novice* for a wife. – A man must marry some time or other – but my hour, thank Heaven, is not come yet."

"Thank Heaven!" said Lady Delacour, "for you know, a married man is lost to the world of fashion and gallantry."

"Not more so, I should hope, than a married woman," said Clarence Hervey. – Here a loud knocking at the door announced the arrival of company to the concert. – "You will make my peace, you promise me, with Miss Portman," cried Clarence, eagerly.

"Yes, I will make your peace, and you shall see Belinda smile upon you once more, upon condition," continued Lady

Delacour, speaking very quickly, as if she was hurried by the sound of people coming up stairs – "but we'll talk of that another time."

"Nay, nay, my dear Lady Delacour, now, now," said Clarence, seizing her hand. – Upon condition! upon what condition?"

"Upon condition that you do a little job for me – indeed for Belinda. – She is to go with me to the birthnight – and she has often hinted to me, that our horses are shockingly shabby for people of our condition. – I know she wishes, that upon such an occasion – her first appearance at court, you know – we should go in style. – Now my dear positive lord has *said*, he will not let us have a pair of the handsomest horses I ever saw, which are at Tattersal's, and on which Belinda, I know, has secretly set her heart, as I have openly in vain."

"Your ladyship and Miss Portman cannot possibly set your hearts on any thing in vain – especially on any thing that it is in the power of Clarence Hervey to procure. Then," added he gallantly, kissing her hand, "may I thus seal my treaty of peace?"

"What audacity! – don't you see these people coming in?" cried Lady Delacour, and she withdrew her hand, but with no great precipitation: she was evidently "at this moment, as in all the past," neither afraid nor ashamed, that Mr Hervey's devotions to her should be paid in public. With much address she had satisfied herself as to his views, with respect to Belinda. She was convinced that he had no immediate thoughts of matrimony; but that if he were condemned to marry, Miss Portman would be his wife. – As this did not interfere with her plans, Lady Delacour was content.

CHAPTER VI

Ways and Means

When Lady Delacour repeated to Miss Portman the message about "simplicity of mind, and dignity of character," she frankly said –

"Belinda, notwithstanding all this, observe, I'm determined to retain Clarence Hervey among the number of my public worshippers during my life – which you know cannot last long. – After I am gone, my dear, he'll be all your own, and of that I give you joy. – Posthumous fame is a silly thing, but posthumous jealousy is detestable."

There was one part of the conversation between Mr Hervey and her ladyship, which she, in her great discretion, did not immediately repeat to Miss Portman – that part which related to the horses. – In this transaction Belinda had no farther share, than having once, when her ladyship had the handsome horses brought for her to look at, assented to the opinion, that they were the handsomest horses she ever beheld. – Mr Hervey, however gallantly he replied to her ladyship, was secretly vexed to find that Belinda had so little delicacy, as to permit her name to be employed in such a manner. He repented having used the improper expression of *dignity of mind*, and he relapsed into his former opinion of Mrs Stanhope's niece. – A relapse is always more dangerous than the first disease. – He sent home the horses to Lady Delacour, the next day, and addressed Belinda, when he met her, with the air of a man of gallantry, who thought that his peace had been cheaply made. – But in proportion as his manners became more familiar, hers grew more reserved. – Lady Delacour rallied her upon *her prudery*, but in vain. – Clarence Hervey seemed to think, that her ladyship had not fulfilled her part of the bargain. – "Is not *smiling*" said he, "the epithet always applied to peace – yet I have not been able to obtain one smile from Miss Portman since I have been promised peace." – Embarrassed by Mr Hervey's reproaches, and provoked to find that Belinda was proof against all her raillery, Lady Delacour grew quite ill-humoured towards her. Belinda, unconscious of having given any just cause of offence, was unmoved; and her ladyship's embarrassment increased. – At last, resuming all her former appearance of friendship and confidence, she suddenly exclaimed, one night after she had flattered Belinda into high spirits –

"Do you know, my dear, that I have been so ashamed of myself for this week past, that I have hardly dared to look you in the face. – I am sensible I was downright rude and cross to you one day – and ever since I have been penitent; and as all penitents are, very stupid and disagreeable, I am sure – but tell me you forgive my caprice, and Lady Delacour will be herself again."

It was not difficult to obtain Belinda's forgiveness.

"Indeed," continued Lady Delacour, "you are too good – but then, in my own justification I must say, that I have more things to make me ill-humoured than most people have. – Now, my dear, that most obstinate of human beings, Lord Delacour, has reduced me to the most terrible situation – I have made Clarence Hervey buy a pair of horses for me, and I cannot make my Lord Delacour pay for them – but I forgot to tell you, that I took your name – not in vain indeed – in this business. – I told Clarence, that upon condition he would do this *job* for me, you would forgive him for all his sins, and – nay, my dear, why do you look as if I had stabbed you to the heart – after all, I only drew upon your pretty mouth for a few smiles – Pray let me see whether it has actually forgotten *how* to smile."

Belinda was too much vexed at this instant to understand raillery. – She was inspired by anger with unwonted courage, and losing all fear of Lady Delacour's wit, she very seriously expostulated with her ladyship upon having thus used her name, without her consent or knowledge. Belinda felt she was now in danger of being led into a situation, which might be fatal to her reputation and her happiness; and she was the more surprised at her ladyship, when she recollected the history she had so lately heard of Harriet Freke and Colonel Lawless.

"You cannot but be sensible, Lady Delacour," said Belinda, "that after the contempt I have heard Mr Hervey express for match-making Mrs Stanhope's nieces, I should degrade myself by any attempts to attract his attention. – No wit, no eloquence, can change my opinion upon this subject – I cannot endure contempt."

"Very likely – no doubt" – interrupted Lady Delacour, "but if you would only open your eyes, which heroines make it a principle never to do – or else there would be an end of the novel – if you would only open your eyes, you would see that this man is in love with you; and whilst you are afraid of his contempt, he is a hundred times more afraid of yours; and as long as you are each of you in such fear of you know not what – you must excuse me if I indulge myself in a little wholesome raillery." – Belinda smiled – "There now, one such smile as that for Clarence Hervey, and I am out of debt and danger," said Lady Delacour.

"O, Lady Delacour, why, why will you try your power over me, in this manner?" said Belinda. – "You know that I ought not to be persuaded to do what I am conscious is wrong. – But a few days ago you told me yourself, that Mr Hervey is – is not a marrying man; and a woman of your penetration must see that – that he only means to flirt with me. – I am not a match for Mr Hervey in any respect. – He is a man of wit and gallantry – I am unpractised in the ways of the world. – I was not educated by my aunt Stanhope – I have only been with her a few years – I wish I had never been with her in my life."

"I'll take care Mr Hervey shall know that," said Lady Delacour, "but in the mean time, I do think any fair appraiser of delicate distresses would decide, that I am, all the circumstances considered, more to be pitied at this present moment than you are. – For the catastrophe of the business evidently is, that I must pay two hundred guineas for the horses some how or other."

"I can pay for them," exclaimed Belinda, "and will with the greatest pleasure. – I will not go to the birthnight – my dress is not bespoke. – Will two hundred guineas pay for the horses? – O, take the money – pay Mr Hervey, dear Lady Delacour, and it will all be all right."

"You are a charming girl," said Lady Delacour, embracing her, "but how can I answer for it to my conscience, or to your aunt Stanhope, if you don't appear on the birthnight. – That cannot be, my dear; besides, you know Mrs Franks will send home your drawing-room dress to-day, and it would be so foolish to be presented for nothing – not to go to the birthnight afterwards. – If you say *a* you must say *b*."

"Then," said Belinda, "I will not go to the drawing-room." – "Not go, my dear! What, throw away fifty guineas for nothing! Really I never saw any one so lavish of her money, and so economic of her smiles."

"Surely," said Miss Portman, "it is better for me to throw away fifty guineas, poor as I am, than to hazard the happiness of my life. – Your ladyship knows that if I say *a* to Mr Hervey, I must say *b*. – No, no, my dear Lady Delacour – here is the draft for two hundred guineas – pay Mr Hervey, for Heaven's sake, and there is an end of the business."

"What a positive child it is! – Well, then it shall not be forced to say the a, b, c, of Cupid's alphabet, to that terrible pedagogue Clarence Hervey, till it pleases – but seriously, Miss Portman, I'm concerned that you will make me take this draft. – It is absolutely robbing you. – But Lord Delacour's the person you must blame – it is all his obstinacy – having once said he would not pay for the horses, he would see them and me and the whole human race expire, before he would change his silly mind. – Next month I shall have it in my power, my dear, to repay you with a thousand thanks – and in a few months more we shall have another birthday, and a new star shall appear in the firmament of fashion, and it shall be called Belinda. – In the mean time, my dear, upon second thoughts, perhaps we can get Mrs Franks to dispose of your drawing-room dress to some person of taste, and you may keep your fifty guineas for the next occasion. – I'll see what can be done – adieu – a thousand thanks, silly child as you are."

Mrs Franks at first declared, that it would be an impossibility to dispose of Miss Portman's dress, though she would do any thing upon earth to oblige Lady Delacour – however, ten guineas made every thing possible. Belinda rejoiced, at having, as she thought, extricated herself at so cheap a rate; and well pleased with her own conduct, she wrote to her aunt Stanhope, to inform her of as much of the transaction as she could disclose, without betraying Lady Delacour. "Her ladyship," she said, "had immediate occasion for two hundred guineas, and to accommodate her with this sum, she had given up the idea of going to court."

The tenor of Miss Portman's letter will be sufficiently apparent from Mrs Stanhope's answer.

MRS STANHOPE TO MISS PORTMAN

Bath, June 2d

"I cannot but feel some astonishment, Belinda, at your very extraordinary conduct, and more extraordinary letter. – What you can mean by principles and delicacy, I own I don't pretend to understand, when I see you not only forget the respect that is due to the opinions and advice of the aunt, to whom you owe every thing; but you take upon yourself to lavish her money, without common honesty. – I send you 200 guineas, and desire you to go to court – you lend my 200 guineas to Lady Delacour, and inform me that as you think yourself bound in honour to her ladyship, you cannot explain all the particulars to me, otherwise, you are sure I should approve of the reasons which have influenced you. – Mighty satisfactory, truly! – And then to mend the matter, you tell me that you do not think, that in your situation in life it is necessary that you should go to court. Your opinions and mine, you add, differ in many points. – Then I must say that you are as ungrateful, as you are presumptuous – for I am not such a novice in the affairs of this world, as to be ignorant that when a young lady professes to be of a different opinion from her friends, it is only a prelude to something worse. – She begins by saying, that she is determined to think for herself, and she is determined to act for herself – and then it is all over with her – and all the money, &c. that has been spent upon her education, is so much dead loss to her friends.

"Now I look upon it, that a young girl who has been brought up, and brought forward in the world as you have been by connexions, is bound to be guided implicitly by them in all her conduct. – What should you think of a man, who, after he had been brought into parliament by a friend, would go and vote against that friend's opinions. – You do not want sense, Belinda – you perfectly understand me – and consequently, your errors I must impute to the defect of your heart, and not of your judgment. – I see, that on account of the illness of the princess – the king's birthday is put off for a fortnight. If you manage properly, and if (unknown to Lady — , who certainly has not used you well in this business, and to whom therefore you owe no peculiar delicacy) you make Lord — sensible how much your aunt Stanhope is disappointed and displeased (as I most truly am) at your intention of missing this opportunity of appearing at court; it is ten to one but his lordship, who has not made it a point to refuse your request, I suppose, will pay you your two hundred guineas. – You of course will make proper acknowledgments; but at the same time, entreat that his lordship will not *commit* you with his lady, as she might be offended at your application to him. – I understand from an intimate acquaintance of his, that you are a great favourite of his lordship's, and though an obstinate, he is a good-natured man, and can have no fear of being governed by you; consequently he will do just as you would have him.

"Then you have an opportunity of representing the thing, in the prettiest manner imaginable, to Lady — as an instance of her lord's consideration for her – So you will oblige all parties (a very desirable thing) without costing yourself one penny, and go to the birthnight after all. – And this only by using a little address – without which nothing is to be done in this world.

"Yours *affectionately*, (if you follow my advice,)

SELINA STANHOPE."

Belinda, though she could not, consistently with what she thought right, follow the advice so artfully given to her in this epistle, was yet extremely concerned to find, that she had incurred the displeasure of an aunt to whom she thought herself under obligations. She resolved to lay by as much as she possibly could, from the interest of her fortune, and to repay the two hundred guineas to Mrs Stanhope: she was conscious that she had no right to lend this money to Lady Delacour, if her aunt had expressly desired that she should spend it only on her court dress; but this had not distinctly been expressed, when Mrs Stanhope sent her niece the drafts. That lady was in the habit of speaking and writing ambiguously, so that even those who knew her best, were frequently in doubt how to interpret her words. – Yet she was extremely displeased when her hints, and her half expressed wishes were not understood. – Beside the concern she felt from the thoughts of having displeased her aunt, Belinda was both vexed and mortified, to perceive that in Clarence Hervey's manner towards her there was not the change, which she had expected that her conduct would naturally produce.

One day she was surprised by his reproaching her for caprice in having given up her intentions of going to court. Lady Delacour's embarrassment whilst Mr Hervey spoke, Belinda attributed to her ladyship's desire that Clarence should not know, that she had been obliged to borrow the money to pay him for the horses. Belinda thought that this was a species of mean pride, but she made it a point to keep her ladyship's secret: she therefore slightly answered Mr Hervey, "that she wondered that a man, who is so well acquainted with the female sex, should be surprised at any instance of caprice from a woman." – The conversation then took another turn, and whilst they were talking on indifferent subjects, in came Lord Delacour's man, Champfort, with Mrs Stanhope's draft for two hundred guineas, which the coachmaker's man had just brought back, because Belinda had forgotten to endorse it. – Belinda's astonishment was almost as great at this instant, as Lady Delacour's confusion – "Come this way, my dear, and we'll find you a pen and ink – you need not wait, Champfort – but tell the man to wait for the draft – Miss Portman will endorse it immediately." – And she took Belinda into another room.

"Good Heavens! Has not this money been paid to Mr Hervey?" exclaimed Belinda.

"No, my dear, but I will take all the blame upon myself; or, which will do just as well for you, throw it all upon my better half – my Lord Delacour would not pay for my new carriage. – The coach maker, insolent animal, would not let it out of his yard without two hundred guineas in ready money. – Now you know I had the horses, and what could I do with the horses without the carriage. Clarence Hervey, I knew, could wait for his money better than a poor devil of a coach-maker, so I paid the coach-maker, and a few months sooner or later can make no difference to Clarence, who rolls in gold, my dear – if that will be any comfort to you, as I hope it will."

"O, what will he think of me!" said Belinda.

"Nay, what will he think of *me*, child?"

– "Lady Delacour," said Belinda, in a firmer tone than she had ever before spoken – "I must insist upon this draft's being given to Mr Hervey."

"Absolutely impossible, my dear. – I cannot take it from the coach-maker – he has sent home the carriage – the thing's done, and cannot be undone. – But come, since I know nothing else will make you easy, I will take this mighty favour from Mr Hervey entirely upon my own conscience. – You cannot object to that, for you are not the keeper of my conscience – I will tell Clarence the whole business, and do you honour due, my dear – so endorse the note, whilst I go and sound both the praises of your dignity of mind, and simplicity of character, &c. &c. &c. &c. &c." – And her ladyship broke away from Belinda, returned to Clarence Hervey, and told the whole affair with that peculiar grace with which she knew how to make a good story of a bad one. – Clarence was as favourable an auditor at this time as she could possibly have found, for no human being could value money less than he did, and all sense of her ladyship's meanness was lost in his joy at discovering that Belinda was worthy of his esteem. — Now he felt in its fullest extent all the power she had over his heart, and he was upon the point of declaring his attachment to her, when — "*malheureusement*," * — Sir Philip Baddely and Mr Rochfort announced themselves by the noise they made on the staircase. These were the young men who had spoken in such a contemptuous manner at Lady Singleton's of the match-making Mrs Stanhope and her nieces. — Mr Hervey was anxious that they should not penetrate into the state of his heart, and he concealed his emotion by instantly assuming that kind of rattling gaiety, which always delighted his companions, who were ever in want of some one to set their stagnant ideas in motion. At last they insisted upon carrying Clarence away with them to taste some wines for Sir Philip Baddely.

CHAPTER VII

The Serpentine River

In his way to St James's street, where the wine merchant lived, Sir Philip Baddely picked up several young men of his acquaintance, who were all eager to see a trial of *taste*, of epicurean taste – between the baronet and Clarence Hervey. Amongst his other accomplishments our hero piqued himself upon the exquisite accuracy of his organs of taste. He neither loved wine, nor was he fond of eating; but at fine dinners, with young men who were real epicures, Hervey gave himself the airs of a connoisseur, and asserted superiority even in judging of wine and sauces. – Having gained immortal honour at an entertainment, by gravely protesting that some turtle would have been excellent if it had not been done *a bubble too much*, he presumed, elate as he was with the applauses of the company, to assert, that no man in England had a more correct taste than himself. – Sir Philip Baddely could not passively submit to this arrogance; he loudly proclaimed, that though he would not dispute Mr Hervey's judgment as far as eating was concerned, yet he would defy him as a connoisseur in wines, and he offered to submit the competition to any eminent wine-merchant in London, and to some common friend of acknowledged taste and experience. – Mr Rochfort was chosen as the common friend of acknowledged taste and experience; and a fashionable wine-merchant was pitched upon, to decide with him the merits of these candidates for bacchanalian fame. Sir Philip, who was just going to furnish his cellars, was a person of importance to the wine-merchant, who produced accordingly his choicest treasures. – Sir Philip and Clarence tasted of all in their turns; Sir Philip with real, and Clarence with affected gravity; and they delivered their opinions of the positive and comparative merits of each. The wine-merchant evidently, as Mr Hervey thought, leaned towards Sir Philip. – "Upon my word, Sir Philip, you are right – that wine is the best I have – you certainly have a most discriminating taste," said the complaisant wine-merchant. – "I'll tell you what," cried Sir Philip, "the thing is this – by G –

now there's no possibility now – no possibility now by G – of imposing upon me." – "Then," said Clarence Hervey, "would you engage to tell the difference between these two wines ten times running, blindfold?" – "Ten times, that's nothing," replied Sir Philip; "yes, fifty times, I would, by G –."

But when it came to the trial, Sir Philip had nothing left but oaths in his own favour. Clarence Hervey was victorious, and his sense of the importance of this victory was much increased by the fumes of the wine, which began to operate upon his brain. – His triumph was, as he said it ought to be, bacchanalian – he laughed and sang with Anacreontic spirit, and finished by declaring, that he deserved to be crowned with vine-leaves. – "Dine with me, Clarence," said Rochfort, "and we'll crown you with three times three – and," whispered he to Sir Philip – "we'll have another trial after dinner."

"But as it's not near dinner time yet – only half past six by me – what shall we do with ourselves till dinner time?" said Sir Philip, yawning pathetically.

Clarence, not being used to drink in a morning, though all his companions were, was much affected by the wine, and Rochfort proposed that they should take a turn in the park to cool Hervey's head. – To Hyde-park they repaired; Sir Philip boasting all the way they walked, of the superior strength of his head.

Clarence protested that his own was stronger than any man's in England, and observed, that at this instant he walked better than any person in company, Sir Philip Baddely not excepted. Now, Sir Philip Baddely was a noted pedestrian, and he immediately challenged our hero to walk with him for any money he pleased. – "Done," said Clarence, "for ten guineas – for any money you please" – and instantly they set out to walk, as Rochfort cried "one, two, three, and away; keep the path, and whichever reaches that elm tree first has it."

They were exactly even for some yards, then Clarence got ahead of Sir Philip, and he reached the elm tree first; but as he waved his hat, exclaiming, "Clarence has won the day," Sir Philip came up with his companions, and coolly informed him that he had lost his wager – "lost! lost! lost! Clarence; fairly lost."

"Didn't I reach the tree first," said Clarence.

"Yes," answered his companions, "but you didn't keep the path. – You turned out of the way when you met that crowd of children, yonder. – Now *I*, said Sir Philip, dashed fairly through them – kept the path, and won my bet."

"But," said Hervey, "would you have had me run over that little child, who was stooping down just in my way?"

"*I*, not I," said Sir Philip, "but I would have you go through with your civility – If a man will be polite, he must pay for his politeness sometimes. – You said you'd lay me *any money* I pleased, recollect – now I'm very moderate – and as you are a particular friend, Clarence, I'll only take your ten guineas."

A loud laugh from his companions provoked Clarence; they were glad "to have a laugh against him," because he excited universal envy, by the real superiority of his talents, and by his perpetually taking the lead in those trifles which were beneath his ambition, and exactly suited to engage the attention of his associates.

"Be it so – and welcome – I'll pay ten guineas for having better manners than any of you," cried Hervey, laughing; "but remember, though I've lost this bet, I don't give up my pedestrian fame. – Sir Philip, there are no women to throw golden apples in my way now, and no children for me to stumble over; I dare you to another trial – double or quit."

"I'm off by G–," said Sir Philip – "I'm too hot, damme, to walk with you any more – but I'm your man if you've a mind for a swim – damme, here's the Serpentine river, Clarence. – Hey? damn it! – Hey?"

Sir Philip and all his companions knew that Clarence had never learned to swim.

"You may wink at one another, as wisely as you please," said Clarence, "but come on my boys – I *am* your man for a swim – a hundred guineas upon it" –

———— 'Darest thou, Rochfort, now,
'Leap in with me into this weedy flood,
'And swim to yonder point.'

and instantly Hervey, who had in his confused head some recollection of an essay of Dr Franklin's* on swimming, by which he fancied that he could ensure at once his safety and his fame, threw off his coat and jumped into the river – luckily he was not in boots. – Rochfort began coolly to undress himself under the trees, and all the other young men stood laughing by the river side. – "Who the devil are these two that seem to be making up to us," said Sir Philip, looking at two gentlemen who were coming towards them. – "St George, hey, you know every body?" – "The foremost is Percival of Oakly Park, I think, 'pon my honour," replied Mr St George – and he then began to settle how many thousands a year Mr Percival was worth; this point was not decided when the gentlemen came up to the spot where Sir Philip was standing.

The child for whose sake Clarence Hervey had lost his bet was Mr Percival's, and he came to thank him for his civility. – The gentleman who accompanied Mr Percival was an old friend of Clarence Hervey's, he had met him abroad, but had not seen him for some years.

"Pray gentlemen," said he to Sir Philip and his party – "is Mr Clarence Hervey amongst you? I think I saw him pass by me just now."

"Damn it, yes, where is Clary though?" exclaimed Sir Philip, suddenly recollecting himself. – Clarence Hervey at this instant was drowning, he had got out of his depth, and had struggled in vain to recover himself.

"Curse me, if it's not all over with Clary," continued Sir Philip. – "Do any of you see his head any where? Damn you, Rochfort, yonder it is."

'Damme, so it is," said Rochfort – "but he's so heavy in his clothes, he'd pull me down along with him to Davy's Locker – damme if I'll go after him."

"Damn it, though, can't some of ye swim? – Can't some of ye jump in?" cried Sir Philip, turning to his companion – "Damn it, Clarence will go to the bottom."

And so he inevitably would have done, had not Mr Percival at this instant leaped into the river, and seized hold of the drowning Clarence. It was with great difficulty that he dragged him to shore. – Sir Philip's party, as soon as the danger was over, officiously offered their assistance. Clarence Hervey was absolutely senseless. – "Damn it, what shall we do with him now," said Sir Philip – "Damn it, we must call some of the people from the boat-house, he's as heavy as lead – damn me if I know what to do with him."

Whilst Sir Philip was damning himself, Mr Percival ran to the boat-house for assistance, and they carried the body into the house: the elderly gentleman who had accompanied Mr Percival now made his way through the midst of the noisy crowd, and directed what should be done to restore Mr Hervey's suspended animation. Whilst he was employed in this benevolent manner, Clarence's worthy friends were sneering at him, and whispering to one another — "Ecod he talks as if he was a doctor," said Rochfort.

"'Pon honour I do believe," said St George, "he is the famous Dr X — *; I met him at a circulating library t'other day."

"Dr X — the writer, do you mean," said Sir Philip — "then damn me we'd better get out of his way as fast as we can, or he'll have some of us down in black and white, and curse me if I should choose to meet with myself in a book." — "No danger of that," said Rochfort, "for how can one meet with oneself in a book, Sir Philip, if one never opens one. — By G — that's the true way!"

"But 'pon my honour," said St George, "I should like of all things to see myself in print; 'twould make one famously famous."

"Damn me if I don't flatter myself, though, one can make oneself famous enough to all intents and purposes, without having any thing to say to these author geniuses. — You're a famous fellow, faith, to want to see yourself in print — I'll publish this in Bond street — damn it, in point of famousness, I'd sport my Random against all the books that ever were read or written, damn me — but what are we doing here?" "Hervey's in good hands," said Sir Philip — "and this here's a cursed stupid lounge for us — besides, it's getting towards dinner time, so my voice is, let's be off, and we can leave St George (who has such a famous mind to be in the doctor's books) to bring Clary after us, when he's ready for dinner and good company again, you know, ha! ha! ha!"

Away the faithful friends went to the important business of their day.

When Clarence Hervey came to his senses, he started up, rubbed his eyes, and looked about, exclaiming — "What's all this? — Where am I? — Where's Baddely? — Where's Rochfort? — Where are they all?"

"Gone home to dinner," answered Mr St George, who was a hanger on of Sir Philip's. — "But they left me to bring you after them. — Faith, Clary, you've had a squeak for your life — 'pon my honour, we thought at one time it was all over with you — but you're a tough one — We shan't have to 'pour over your grave a full bottle of red,' as yet my boy — you'll *do* as well as ever. — So I'll step and call a coach for you Clary, and we shall be at dinner as

soon as the best of 'em after all, by jingo. – I leave you in good
hands with the doctor here, that brought you to life, and the
gentleman that dragged you out of the water. – Here's a note for
you," whispered Mr St George, as he leaned over Clarence
Hervey – "Here's a note for you from Sir Philip and Rochfort –
read it, do you mind, *to yourself.*"

"If I can," said Clarence – "but Sir Philip writes a bloody bad
hand."*

"O, he's a *baronet,*" said St George, "ha! ha! ha!" – and
charmed with his own wit, he left the room.

Clarence with some difficulty deciphered the note, which
contained these words:

> "Quiz the doctor, Clary, as soon as you are up to it – he's an author
> – so fair game – quiz the doctor, and we'll drink your health with three
> times three in Rochfort's Burgundy.
>
> Yours, &c.
> PHIL BADDELY.

"P.S. Burn this when read."

With the request contained in the postcript Clarence immediately
complied; he threw the note into the fire with indignation, the
moment that he had read it, and turning towards the gentleman to
whom it alluded, he began to express in the strongest terms his
gratitude for their benevolence. – But he stopped short in the
midst of his acknowledgements, when he discovered to whom he
was speaking.

"Dr X — !" cried he, "is it possible? – how rejoiced I am to see
you – and how rejoiced I am to be obliged to you – there is not a
man in England to whom I would rather be obliged."

"You are not acquainted with Mr Percival, I believe," said
Dr X —, "give me leave, Mr Percival, to introduce to you the
young gentleman whose life you have saved, and whose life –
though by the company in which you found him, you might not
think so – is worth saving. – This sir, is no less a man than Mr
Clarence Hervey – of whose universal genius you have just had a
specimen; for which he was crowned, as he well deserved, by the
God of the Serpentine river with sedges. – Do not be so unjust as
to imagine, that he has any of the presumption which is sometimes
the chief characteristic of a man of universal genius. – Mr
Clarence Hervey is, without exception, the most humble man of

my acquaintance, for whilst all good judges would think him fit
company for Mr Percival, he has the humility to think himself
upon a level with Mr Rochfort, and Sir Philip Baddely."

"You have lost as little of your satirical wit, Dr X——, as of your
active benevolence, I perceive," said Clarence Hervey, "since I
met you abroad. – But as I cannot submit to your unjust charge of
humility, will you tell me where you are to be found in town, and
to morrow" – "to morrow – and to morrow – and to morrow,"
said Dr X——, "why not to day?" – "I am engaged," said Clarence,
hesitating and laughing – "I am unfortunately engaged to day to
dine with Mr Rochfort, and Sir Philip Baddely – and in the
evening I am to be at Lady Delacour's."

"Lady Delacour! – not the same Lady Delacour whom four
years ago, when we met at Florence, you compared to the Venus
de Medicis – no, no, it cannot be the same, a goddess of four years
standing! incredible!"

"Incredible as it seems," said Clarence, "it is true – I admire her
ladyship more than ever I did."

"Like a true connoisseur," said Dr X——, "you admire a fine
picture, the older it grows – I hear that her ladyship's face is really
one of the finest pieces of painting extant, with the advantage of

'Every grace which time alone can grant.' "

"Come, come, Doctor X——," cried Mr Percival, "no more wit at
Lady Delacour's expense – I have a fellow feeling for Mr Hervey.

"Why you are not in love with her ladyship, are you?" said Dr
X——. "I am not in love with Lady Delacour's picture of herself,"
replied Mr Percival, "but I was once in love with the original."

"How? – When? – Where?" cried Clarence Hervey, in a tone
totally different from that in which he had first addressed Mr
Percival.

"To morrow you shall know the how, the when, and the
where," said Mr Percival, "here's your friend, Mr St George, and
his coach." – "The deuce take him," said Clarence – "but tell me,
is it possible that you are not in love with her still? – and why?" –
"Why!" said Mr Percival – "why – come to morrow, as you have
promised, to Upper Grosvenor street, and let me introduce you to
Lady Anne Percival – she can answer your question better than I
can – if not entirely to your satisfaction, at least entirely to mine,
which is more surprising, as the lady is my wife."

By this time, Clarence Hervey was equipped in a dry suit of clothes – and by the strength of an excellent constitution, which he had never injured, even amongst his dissipated associates, he had recovered from the effects of his late imprudence. – "Clary, let's away, here's the coach," said Mr St George – "Why my boy! that's a famous fellow, faith! Why you look the better for being drowned – 'pon honour, if I was you, I would jump into the Serpentine river once a day." – "If I could always be sure of such good friends to pull me out," said Hervey. – "Pray St George, by the by, what where you, and Rochfort, and Sir Philip, and all the rest of my friends doing, whilst I was drowning?"

"I can't say particularly, upon my soul," replied Mr St George, "for my own part, I was in boots, so you know I was out of the question. – But what signifies all that now? – Come, come, we had best think of looking after our dinners."

Clarence Hervey, who had very quick feelings, was extremely hurt by the indifference which his dear friends had shown, when his life was in danger; he was apt to believe that he was really an object of affection and admiration amongst his companions, and that though they were neither very wise, nor very witty, they were certainly very good natured. When they had forfeited by their late conduct these claims to his regard, his partiality for them was changed into contempt.

"You had better come home and dine with me, Mr Hervey," said Mr Percival, "if you be not absolutely engaged, for here is your physician, who tells me that temperance is necessary for a man just recovered from drowning, and Mr Rochfort keeps too good a table, I am told, for one in your condition."

Clarence accepted of this invitation with a degree of pleasure which perfectly astonished Mr St George.

"Every man knows his own affairs best," said he to Clarence, as he stepped into his hackney coach – "but for my share, I will do my friend Rochfort the justice to say, that no one lives as well as he does." –

"If to live well means nothing but to eat,"

said Clarence.

"Now," said Dr X — , looking at his watch, "it will be eight o'clock by the time we get to Upper Grosvenor street, and Lady Anne will have probably waited dinner for us about two hours, which I apprehend is sufficient to try the patience of any woman but Griselda.* – Do not," continued he, turning to Clarence Hervey, "expect to see an old fashioned, spiritless, patient Griselda, in Lady Anne Percival – I can assure you that she is – but I will neither tell you what she is, nor what she is not. – Every man, who has any abilities, likes to have the pleasure and honour of finding out a character by his own penetration, instead of having it forced upon him at full length in capital letters of gold, finely emblazoned and illuminated by the hand of some injudicious friend. – Every child thinks the violet of his own finding the sweetest. – I spare you any farther allusions and illustrations," concluded Dr X — , "for here we are, thank God, in Upper Grosvenor street."

CHAPTER VIII

A Family Party

They found Lady Anne Percival in the midst of her children; who all turned their healthy, rosy, intelligent faces towards the door the moment that they heard their father's voice. Clarence Hervey was so much struck with the expression of happiness in Lady Anne's countenance, that he absolutely forgot to compare her beauty with Lady Delacour's. Whether her eyes were large or small, blue or hazel, he could not tell; nay, he might have been puzzled if he had been asked the colour of her hair – Whether she were handsome by the rules of art, he knew not; but he felt that she had the essential charm of beauty, the power of prepossessing the heart immediately in her favour. The effect of her manners, like that of her beauty, was rather to be felt than described. Every body was at ease in her company, and none thought themselves called upon to admire her. – To Clarence Hervey, who had been used to the brilliant and *exigeante** Lady Delacour, this respite from the fatigue of admiration was peculiarly agreeable. The unconstrained cheerfulness of Lady Anne Percival spoke a mind at ease, and immediately imparted happiness by exciting sympathy; but in Lady Delacour's wit and gaiety there was an appearance of art and effort, which often destroyed the pleasure that she wished to communicate. – Some people may admire, but none can sympathise with affectation. – Mr Hervey was, perhaps, unusually disposed to reflection, by having just escaped from drowning; for he made all these comparisons, and came to this conclusion with the accuracy of a metaphysician, who has been accustomed to study cause and effect – indeed there was no species of knowledge for which he had not taste and talents, though, to please fools, he too often affected "the bliss of ignorance."

The children at Lady Anne Percival's happened to be looking at some gold fish, which were in a glass globe, and Dr X —, who was a general favourite with the younger, as well as with the elder part of the family, was seized upon the moment he entered the room: a pretty little girl of five years old took him prisoner by the flap of the coat, whilst two of her brothers assailed him with questions about the ears, eyes, and fins of fishes. One of the little boys flipped the glass globe, and observed, that the fish immediately came to the surface of the water, and seemed to hear the noise very quickly; but his brother doubted, whether the fish heard the noise, and remarked, that they might be disturbed by seeing or feeling the motion of the water, when the glass was struck.

Dr X — observed, that this was a very learned dispute, and that the question had been discussed by no less a person than the abbé Nollet;* and he related some of the ingenious experiments tried by that gentleman to decide, whether fishes can or cannot hear. — Whilst the doctor was speaking, Clarence Hervey was struck with the intelligent countenance of one of the little auditors – a girl of about ten or twelve years old; he was surprised to discover in her features, though not in their expression, a singular resemblance to Lady Delacour. He remarked this to Mr Percival, and the child, who overheard him, blushed as red as scarlet. – Dinner was announced at this instant, and Clarence Hervey thought no more of the circumstance, attributing the girl's blush to confusion at being looked at so earnestly. – One of the little boys whispered as they were going down to dinner, "Helena, I do believe that this is the good natured gentleman, who went out of the path to make room for us, instead of running over us as the other man did." – The children agreed that Clarence Hervey certainly was *the good natured gentleman*, and upon the strength of this observation, one of the boys posted himself next to Clarence at dinner, and by all the little playful manoeuvres in his power endeavoured to show his gratitude, and to cultivate a friendship which had been thus auspiciously commenced. – Mr Hervey, who piqued himself upon being able always to suit his conversation to his companions, distinguished himself at dinner by an account of the Chinese fishing-bird, from which he passed to the various ingenious methods of fishing practised by the Russian Cossacks. He asked Dr X — what he thought could be the cause of the prejudice, which prevents the Russian peasants from eating the chad, which is so plentiful in their fisheries. – Then from modern he went to ancient fish, and he talked of that which was so much admired by the Roman epicures for exhibiting a succession of beautiful colours whilst it is dying; and which was, upon that account, always suffered to die in the presence of the guests, as part of the entertainment. – Clarence was led on by the questions of the children from fishes to birds; he spoke of the Roman aviaries, which were so constructed, as to keep from the sight of the prisoners that they contained, "the fields, woods, and every object which might remind them of their former liberty." – From birds Clarence Hervey was going on to beasts, when he was nearly struck dumb by the forbidding severity, with which an elderly lady, who sat opposite to him, fixed her eyes upon him. – He had not, till this instant, paid the smallest attention to her; but her stern countenance was now so strongly contrasted with the approving looks of the children, who sat next to her, that Clarence could not help remarking it. – He asked her to do him the honour to drink a glass of wine with him. – She declined doing him that honour; observing that she never drank more than one glass of wine at dinner, and that she had just taken one with Mr Percival. – Her manner was well-bred, but haughty in the extreme; and she was so passionate, that her anger sometimes conquered even her politeness. Her dislike to Clarence Hervey was apparent, even in her silence. – "If the old gentlewoman have taken an antipathy to me at first sight, I cannot help it," thought he, and he went on to the beasts. The boy, who sat next him, had asked some questions about the proboscis of the elephant, and Mr Hervey mentioned Ives's account of the elephants in India, who have been set to watch young children, and who draw them back gently with their trunks, when they go out of bounds. He talked next of the unicorn; and addressing himself to Dr X — and Mr Percival, he declared, that in his opinion Herodotus did not deserve to be called the father of lies; he cited the mammoth to prove, that the apocryphal chapter in the history of beasts should not be condemned – that it would in all probability be soon established as true history. – The dessert was on the table before Clarence had done with the mammoth.

As the butler put a fine dish of cherries upon the table, he said, "My lady, these cherries are a present from the old gardener to Miss Delacour."

"Set them before Miss Delacour then," said Lady Anne. "Helena, my dear, distribute your own cherries."

At the name of Delacour, Clarence Hervey, though his head was still half full of the mammoth, looked around in astonishment, and when he saw the cherries placed before the young lady, whose resemblance to Lady Delacour he had before observed, he could not help exclaiming,

"That young lady then is not a daughter of your ladyship's?"

"No; but I love her as well as if she were," replied Lady Anne. – "What were you saying about the mammoth?"

"That the mammoth is supposed to be — " but interrupting himself, Clarence said, in an inquiring tone – "A *niece* of Lady Delacour's?"

"Her ladyship's *daughter*, sir," said the severe old lady, in a voice more terrific than her looks.

"Shall I give you some strawberries, Mr Hervey," said Lady Anne, "or will you let Helena help you to some cherries?"

"Her ladyship's *daughter*!" exclaimed Clarence Hervey, in a tone of surprise.

"Some cherries, sir?" said Helena, but her voice faltered so much, that she could hardly utter the word.

Clarence perceived that he had been the cause of her agitation, though he knew not precisely by what means, and he now applied himself in silence to the picking of his strawberries with great diligence.

The ladies soon afterward withdrew, and as Mr Percival did not touch upon the subject again, Clarence forbore to ask any farther questions, though he was considerably surprised by this sudden discovery. – When he went into the drawing-room to tea, he found his friend, the stern old lady, speaking in a high declamatory tone. – The words which he heard as he came into the room were –

"If there were no Clarence Herveys, there would be no Lady Delacours." – Clarence bowed, as if he had received a high compliment – the old lady walked away to an antichamber, fanning herself with great energy.

"Mrs Margaret Delacour," said Lady Anne, in a low voice to Hervey, "is an aunt of Lord Delacour's. – A woman whose heart is warmer than her temper."

"And that is never *cool*," said a young lady, who sat next to Lady Anne – "I call Mrs Margaret Delacour the volcano; I'm sure I am never in her company without dreading an explosion. – Every now and then out comes, with a tremendous noise, fire, and smoke, and rubbish."

"And precious minerals," said Lady Anne, "amongst the rubbish."

"But the best of it is," continued the young lady, "that she is seldom in a passion without making a hundred mistakes, for which she is usually obliged afterward to ask a thousand pardons."

"By that account," said Lady Anne, "which I believe to be just, her contrition is always ten times as great as her offences."

"Now you talk of contrition, Lady Anne," said Mr Hervey, "I should think of my own offences; I am very sorry that my indiscreet questions gave Miss Delacour any pain – my head was so full of the mammoth, that I blundered on without seeing what I was about, till it was too late."

"Pray sir," said Mrs Margaret Delacour, who now returned, and took her seat upon a sofa, with the solemnity of a person who was going to sit in judgment upon a criminal – "pray sir, may I ask how long you have been acquainted with my Lady Delacour?"

Clarence Hervey took up a book, and with great gravity kissed it, as if he had been upon his oath in a court of justice, and answered,

"To the best of my recollection, madam, it is now four years since I had first the pleasure and honour of seeing Lady Delacour."

"And in that time, intimately as you have had the pleasure of being acquainted with her ladyship, you have never discovered that she had a daughter?"

"Never," said Mr Hervey.

"There, Lady Anne! – There!" cried Mrs Delacour, "will you tell me after this, that Lady Delacour is not a monster."

"Every body says, that she's a prodigy," said Lady Anne, "and prodigies and monsters are sometimes thought synonymous terms."

"Such a mother was never heard of," continued Mrs Delacour, "since the days of Savage and Lady Macclesfield.* – I am convinced that she *hates* her daughter. – Why she never speaks of her – she never sees her – she never thinks of her!"

"Some mothers speak more than they think of their children, and others think more than they speak of them," said Lady Anne.

"I always thought," said Mr Hervey, "that Lady Delacour was a woman of great sensibility."

"Sensibility!" exclaimed the indignant old lady – "She has no sensibility, sir – none – none. – She who lives in a constant round of dissipation; who performs no one duty; who exists only for herself; how does she show her sensibility? – Has she sensibility for her husband – for her daughter – for any one useful purpose upon earth? – Oh, how I hate the cambrick-handkerchief sensibility, that is brought out only to weep at a tragedy! – Yes; Lady Delacour has sensibility enough, I grant ye, when sensibility is the fashion. – I remember well her performing the part of a nurse with vast applause; and I remember, too, the *sensibility* she showed, when the child that she nursed fell a sacrifice to her dissipation. – The second of her children, that she killed – "

"Killed! – O, surely my dear Mrs Delacour, that is too strong a word," said Lady Anne – "You would not make a Medea of Lady Delacour."

"It would have been better if I had," cried Mrs Delacour – "I can understand that there may be such a thing in nature as a jealous wife, but an unfeeling mother I cannot comprehend – That passes my powers of imagination."

"And mine, so much," said Lady Anne, "that I cannot believe such a being to exist in the world – notwithstanding all the descriptions I have heard of it, as you say, my dear Mrs Delacour, it passes my powers of imagination. – Let us leave it in Mr Hervey's apocryphal chapter of animals, and he will excuse us if I never admit it into true history – at least without some better evidence than I have yet heard."

"Why, my dear, dear Lady Anne," cried Mrs Delacour – "bless me, I've made this coffee so sweet, there's no drinking it – what evidence would you have?"

"None," said Lady Anne, smiling, "I would have none."

"That is to say, you will take none," said Mrs Delacour, "but can any thing be stronger evidence than her ladyship's conduct to *my* poor Helena – to *your* Helena I should say – for you have educated, you have protected her, you have been a mother to her. – I am an infirm, weak, ignorant, passionate old woman – I could not have been what you have been to that child – God will bless you! – God will bless you!"

She rose as she spoke, to set down her coffee cup on the table. Clarence Hervey took it from her with a look which said much, and which she was perfectly capable of understanding.

"Young man," said she, "it is very unfashionable to treat age and infirmity with politeness. – I wish that your friend, Lady Delacour, may at my time of life meet with as much respect, as she has met with admiration and gallantry in her youth. – Poor

woman, her head has absolutely been turned with admiration –
and if fame say true, Mr Clarence Hervey has had his share in
turning that head by his flattery."

"I am sure her ladyship has turned mine by her charms," said
Clarence, "and I certainly am not to be blamed for admiring what
all the world admires."

"I wish," said the old lady, "for her own sake, for the sake of
her family, and for the sake of her reputation, that my Lady
Delacour had fewer admirers, and more friends."

"Women, who have met with so many admirers, seldom meet
with many friends," said Lady Anne.

"No," said Mrs Delacour, "for they seldom are wise enough to
know their value."

"We learn the value of all things, but especially of friends, by
experience," said Lady Anne, "and it is no wonder, therefore, that
those who have little experience of the pleasures of friendship
should not be wise enough to know their value."

"This is very good natured sophistry – but Lady Delacour is too
vain ever to have a friend," said Mrs Delacour. – "My dear Lady
Anne, you don't know her as well as I do – she has more vanity
than ever woman had."

"That is certainly saying a great deal," said Lady Anne, "but
then we must consider, that Lady Delacour, as an heiress, a
beauty, and a wit, has a right to a triple share of vanity at least."

"Both her fortune and her beauty are gone; and if she have any
wit left, it is time it should teach her how to conduct herself, I
think," said Mrs Delacour, "but I give her up – I give her up."

"O, no," said Lady Anne, "you must not give her up yet. – I
have been informed, and upon *the best authority*, that Lady
Delacour was not always the unfeeling dissipated fine lady that
she now appears to be. – This is only one of the transformations of
fashion – the period of her enchantment will soon be at an end,
and she will return to her natural character. – I should not be at all
surprised, if Lady Delacour were to appear at once, '*la femme
comme il y en a peu.*"*

"Or '*la bonne mère?*"* said Mrs Delacour, sarcastically, "after
leaving her daughter."

"*Pour bonne bouche*,"* interrupted Lady Anne, "when she is
tired of the insipid taste of other pleasures, she will have a higher
relish for those of domestic life, which will be new and fresh to
her."

"And so you really think, my dear Lady Anne, that my Lady Delacour will end by being a domestic woman – Well," said Mrs Margaret, after taking two pinches of snuff; "some people believe in the millennium – but I confess I am not one of them – are you, Mr Hervey?"

"If it were foretold to me by a good angel," said Clarence, smiling, as his eye glanced at Lady Anne – "If it were foretold to me by a good angel, how could I doubt it?"

Here the conversation was interrupted by the entrance of one of Lady Anne's little boys, who came running eagerly up to his mother, to ask whether he might have "the sulphurs* to show to Helena Delacour. – I want to show her Vertumnus and Pomona,* mamma," said he. – "Were not the cherries, that the old gardener sent, very good?"

"What is this about the cherries and the old gardener, Charles?" said the young lady who sat beside Lady Anne: "come here and tell me the whole story."

"I will but I should tell it to you a great deal better another time," said the boy, "because now Helena's waiting for Vertumnus and Pomona."

"Go your ways then to Helena," said Lady Anne, "and I will tell the story for you."

Then turning to the young lady, she began – "Once upon a time there lived an old gardener at Kensington; and this old gardener had an aloe, which was older than himself; for it was very near a hundred years of age, and it was just going to blossom, and the old gardener calculated how much he might make by showing his aloe, when it should be in full blow, to the generous public – and he calculated that he might make a hundred pounds; and with this hundred pounds he determined to do more than ever was done with a hundred pounds before; but, unluckily, as he was thus reckoning his blossoms before they were blown, he chanced to meet a fair damsel, who ruined all his calculations."

"Ay, Mrs Stanhope's maid, was not it?" interrupted Mrs Margaret Delacour. "A pretty damsel she was, and almost as good a politician as her mistress. – Think of that jilt's tricking this poor old fellow out of his aloe – and – O, the meanness of Lady Delacour, to accept of that aloe for one of her extravagant entertainments!"

"But I always understood, that she paid fifty guineas for it," said Lady Anne.

"Whether she did or not," said Mrs Delacour, "her ladyship and Mrs Stanhope between them were the ruin of this poor old man. – He was taken in to marry that jade of a waiting maid; she turned out just as you might expect from a pupil of Mrs Stanhope's – the match-making Mrs Stanhope – you know, sir." (Clarence Hervey changed colour.) – "She turned out," continued Mrs Delacour, "every thing that was bad – ruined her husband – ran away from him – and left him a beggar."

"Poor man!" said Clarence Hervey.

"But now," said Lady Anne, "let's come to the best part of the story – mark how good comes out of evil. – If this poor man had not lost his aloe and his wife, I probably should never have been acquainted with Mrs Delacour, or with my little Helena. – About the time that the old gardener was left a beggar, as I happened to be walking one fine evening in Sloane street, I met a procession of school girls – an old man begged from them in a most moving voice; and as they passed, several of the young ladies threw halfpence to him. – One little girl, who observed that the old man could not stoop without great difficulty, staid behind the rest of her companions, and collected the halfpence which they had thrown to the old man, and put them into his hat. – He began to tell his story over again to her, and she stayed so long listening to it, that her companions had turned the corner of the street, and were out of sight. – She looked about in great distress; and I never shall forget the pathetic voice with which she said, 'O, what will become of me? every body will be angry with me!' – I assured her that nobody should be angry with her, and she gave me her little hand with the most innocent confidence. – I took her home to her schoolmistress, and I was so pleased with the beginning of this acquaintance, that I was determined to cultivate it. – One good acquaintance I have heard always leads to another. – Helena introduced me to her aunt Delacour, as her best friend. – Mrs Margaret Delacour has had the goodness to let her little niece spend the holidays, and all her leisure time with me, so that our acquaintance has grown into friendship. – Helena has become quite one of my family."

"And I am sure she has become quite a different creature, since she has been so much with you," cried Mrs Delacour, "her spirits were quite broken by her mother's neglect of her – young as she is, she has a great deal of real sensibility – but as to her mother's sensibility — ."

At the recollection of Lady Delacour's neglect of her child, Mrs Delacour was going again to launch forth into indignant invective, but Lady Anne stopped her, by whispering –

"Take care what you say of the mother, for here is the daughter coming, and she has, indeed, a great deal of real sensibility."

Helena and her young companions now came into the room, bringing with them the sulphurs at which they had been looking.

"Mamma," said little Charles Percival, "we have brought the sulphurs to you, because there are some of them that *I* don't know."

"Wonderful!" said Lady Anne, "and what is not quite so wonderful, there are some of them that *I* don't know."

The children spread the sulphurs upon a little table, and all the company gathered round it.

"Here are all the nine muses for you!" said the least of the boys, who had taken his seat by Clarence Hervey at dinner – "Here are all the muses for you, Mr Hervey; which do you like best? – O, that's the tragic muse that you have chosen! – You don't like the tragic better than the comic muse do you?"

Clarence Hervey made no answer, for he was at that instant recollecting how Belinda looked in the character of the tragic muse.

"Has your ladyship ever happened to meet with the young lady, who has spent this winter with Lady Delacour?" said Clarence to Lady Anne.

"I sat near her one night at the opera," said Lady Anne, "she has a charming countenance."

"Who! – Belinda Portman do you mean?" said Mrs Delacour – "I am sure if I were a young man, I would not trust to the charming countenance of a young lady, who is a pupil of Mrs Stanhope's and a friend of — Helena, my dear, shut the door – the most dissipated woman in London."

"Indeed," said Lady Anne, "Miss Portman is in a dangerous situation – but some young people learn prudence by being placed in dangerous situations, as some young horses, as I have heard Mr Percival say, learn to be sure footed, by being left to pick their own way on bad roads."

Here Mr Percival, Dr X—, and some other gentlemen, came up stairs to tea, and the conversation took another turn. – Clarence Hervey endeavoured to take his share in it with his usual vivacity, but he was thinking of Belinda Portman, dangerous situations, stumbling horses, &c. and he made several blunders, which showed his absence of mind.

"What have you there, Mr Hervey?" said Dr X — , looking over his shoulder – "The tragic muse? – this tragic muse seems to rival Lady Delacour in your admiration."

"O," said Clarence, smiling, "you know I was always a votary of the muses."

"And a favoured votary," said Dr X —. "I wish for the interests of literature, that poets may always be lovers, though I cannot say that I desire lovers should always be poets. – But Mr Hervey, you must never marry, remember," continued Dr X — , "never – for your true poet must always be miserable. – You know, Petrarch tells us, he would not have been happy if he could; he would not have married his mistress if it had been in his power; because, then there would have been an end of his beautiful sonnets."

"Every one to his taste," said Clarence; "for my part, I have even less ambition to imitate the heroism, than hope of being inspired with the poetic genius of Petrarch. – I have no wish to pass whole nights composing sonnets. – I would (am not I right, Mr Percival?) infinitely rather be a slave of the ring, than a slave of the lamp."

Here the conversation ended – Clarence took his leave, and Mrs Margaret Delacour said, the moment he had left the room –

"Quite a different sort of young man from what I expected to see!"

CHAPTER IX

Advice

The next morning Mr Hervey called on Dr X —, and begged that he would accompany him to Lady Delacour's.

"To be introduced to your tragic muse?" said the doctor.

"Yes," said Hervey, "I must have your opinion of her before I devote myself."

"My opinion! but of whom? – Of Lady Delacour?"

"No; but of a young lady whom you will see with her."

"Is she handsome?"

"Beautiful!"

"And young?"

"And young."

"And graceful?"

"The most graceful person you ever beheld."

"Young, beautiful, graceful; then the deuce take me," said Dr X —, "if I give you my opinion of her; for the odds are, that she has a thousand faults, at least, to balance these perfections."

"A thousand faults! a charitable allowance," said Clarence, smiling.

"There now," said Dr X —

'Touch him, and no minister's so sore.'

To punish you for wincing at my first setting out, I promise you, that if the lady have a million faults, each of them as high as huge Olympus, I will see them with the eye of a flatterer – not of a friend."

"I defy you to be so good, or so bad as your word, doctor," said Hervey. – "You have too much wit to make a good flatterer."

"And perhaps you think too much to make a good friend," said Dr X —.

"Not so," said Clarence, "I would at any time rather be cut by a sharp knife than by a blunt one. – But, my dear doctor, I hope you will not be prejudiced against Belinda, merely because she is with Lady Delacour; for, to my certain knowledge, she is not under her ladyship's influence. – She judges and acts for herself, of which I have had an instance."

"Very possibly," interrupted Dr X — , "but before we go any farther, will you please to tell me of what Belinda you are talking?"

"Belinda Portman. – I forgot that I had not told you."

"Miss Portman, a niece of Mrs Stanhope's?"

"Yes, but do not be prejudiced against her on that account," said Clarence, eagerly, "though I was at first myself."

"Then you will excuse my following your example instead of your precepts."

"No," said Clarence, "for my precepts are far better than my example."

Lady Delacour received Dr X — most courteously, and thanked Mr Hervey for introducing to her a gentleman with whom she had long desired to converse. – Dr X — had a great literary reputation, and she saw that he was a perfectly well-bred man; consequently she was ambitious of winning his admiration. – She perceived also, that he had considerable influence with Clarence Hervey, and this was a sufficient reason to make her wish for his good opinion. – Belinda was particularly pleased with his manners and conversation; she saw that he paid her much attention, and she was desirous that he should think favourably of her; but she had the good sense and good taste to avoid a display of her abilities and accomplishments. – A sensible man, who has any knowledge of the world, and talents for converstion, can easily draw out the knowledge of those with whom he converses. – Dr X — possessed this power in a superior degree.

"Well," cried Clarence, when their visit was over, "what is your opinion of Lady Delacour?"

"I am 'blasted with excess of light'," said the doctor.

"Her ladyship is certainly very brilliant," said Clarence, "but I hope that Miss Portman did not overpower you."

"No – I turned my eyes from Lady Delacour upon Miss Portman, as a painter turns his eyes upon mild green, to rest them, when they have been dazzled by glaring colours.

'She yields her charms of mind with sweet delay.' "

"I was afraid," said Hervey, "that you might think her manners too reserved and cold – they are certainly become more so than they used to be. — But so much the better; by and by we shall find beautiful flowers spring up from beneath the snow."

"A very poetical hope," said Dr X — ; "but in judging of the human character, we must not entirely trust to analogies and allusions taken from the vegetable creation."

"What!" cried Clarence Hervey, looking eagerly in the doctor's eyes — "What do you mean? — I am afraid you do not approve of Belinda."

"Your fears are almost as precipitate as your hopes, my good sir — but to put you out of pain, I will tell you, that I approve of all I have seen of this young lady, but that it is absolutely out of my power, to form a decisive judgment of a woman's temper and character in the course of a single morning visit. — Women, you know, as well as men, often speak with one species of enthusiasm, and act with another. — I must see your Belinda act — I must study her, before I can give you my final judgment. — Lady Delacour has honoured me with her commands to go to her as often as possible. — For your sake, my dear Hervey, I shall obey her ladyship most punctually, that I may have frequent opportunities of seeing your Miss Portman."

Clarence expressed his gratitude with much energy, for this instance of the doctor's friendship. — Belinda, who had been entertained by Dr X — 's conversation during this visit, was more and more delighted with his company, as she became more acquainted with his understanding and character. She felt that he unfolded her powers, and that with the greatest politeness and address he raised her confidence in herself, without ever descending to flattery. — By degrees, she learned to look upon him as her friend; she imparted to him with great ingenuousness her opinions on various subjects, and she was both amused and instructed by his observations on the characters and manners of the company, who frequented Lady Delacour's assemblies. — She did not judge of the doctor's sincerity merely by the kindness he showed her, but by his conduct towards others.

One night, at a select party at Lady Delacour's, a Spanish gentleman was amusing the company with some anecdotes, to prove the extraordinary passion which some of his countrymen formerly showed for the game of chess. — He mentioned families, in which unfinished games, bequeathed by will, had descended from father to son, and where victory was doubtful for upwards of a century.

Mr Hervey observed, that gaining a battle was, at that time, so common to the court of Spain, that a victory at chess seemed to confer more eclat; for that an abbé, by losing adroitly a game at chess to the Spanish minister, obtained a cardinal's hat.

The foreigner was flattered by the manner in which Hervey introduced this slight circumstance, and he directed to him his conversation, speaking in French and Italian successively; he was sufficiently skilled in both languages, but Clarence spoke them better. Till he appeared, the foreigner was the principal object of attention, but he was soon eclipsed by Mr Hervey. – Nothing amusing or instructive that could be said upon the game of chess escaped him, and the literary ground, which the slow don would have taken some hours to go regularly over, our hero traversed in a few minutes. – From Twiss* to Vida,* from Irwin* to Sir William Jones,* from Spain to India, he passed with admirable celerity, and seized all that could adorn his course from Indian antiquities or Asiatic researches.

By this display of knowledge he surprised even his friend Dr X — . The ladies admired his taste as a poet, the gentlemen his accuracy as a critic; Lady Delacour loudly applauded, and Belinda silently approved. – Clarence was elated. – The Spanish gentleman, to whom he had just quoted a case in point from Vida's Scacchia, asked him if he were as perfect in the practice as in the theory of the game of chess. – Clarence was too proud of excelling in every thing to decline the Spaniard's challenge. – They sat down to chess. – Lady Delacour, as they ranged the pieces on the board, cried –

"Whoever wins shall be my knight; and this silver chess-man shall be his prize. – Was it not Queen Elizabeth, who gave a silver chess-man to one of her courtiers as a mark of her royal favour? – I am ashamed to imitate such a pedantic coquette – but since I have said it, how can I retract!"

"Impossible, impossible!" cried Clarence Hervey – "This silver chess-man be our prize; and if I win it, like the gallant Raleigh, I'll wear it in my cap; and what proud Essex shall dare to challenge it!"

The combat now began – the spectators were silent. – Clarence made an error in his first move, for his attention was distracted by seeing Belinda behind his adversary's chair. – The Spaniard was deceived by this mistake into a contemptuous opinion of his opponent – Belinda changed her place – Clarence recovered his presence of mind, and convinced him that he was not a man to be despised. The combat was long doubtful, but at length, to the surprise of all present, Clarence Hervey was victorious.

Exulting in his success he looked round for Lady Delacour, from whom he expected the honours of his triumph. – She had left the room, but soon she returned, dressed in the character of Queen Elizabeth, in which she had once appeared at a masquerade, with a large ruff, and all the costume of the times.

Clarence Hervey, throwing himself at her feet, addressed her in that high flown style, which her majesty was wont to hear from the gallant Raleigh, or the accomplished Essex.

Soon the coquetry of the queen entirely conquered her prudery; and the favoured courtier, evidently elated by his situation, was as enthusiastic as her majesty's most insatiable vanity could desire. –The characters were well supported; both the actor and actress were highly animated, and seemed so fully possessed by their parts, as to be insensible to the comments that were made upon the scene. – Clarence Hervey was first recalled to himself by the deep blush which he saw on Belinda's cheek, when Queen Elizabeth addressed her as one of her maids of honour, of whom she affected to be jealous. – He was conscious that he had been hurried by the enthusiasm of the moment farther than he either wished or intended. It was difficult to recede, when her majesty seemed disposed to advance; but Sir Walter Raleigh, with much presence of mind, turned to the foreigner, whom he accosted as the Spanish ambassador.

"Your Excellency sees," said he, "how this great queen turns the heads of her faithful subjects, and afterward has the art of paying them with nothing but words. – Has the new world afforded you any coin half so valuable?"

The Spanish ambassador's grave replies to this playful question gave a new turn to the conversation, and relieved Clarence Hervey from his embarrassment. Lady Delacour, though still in high spirits, was easily diverted to other objects. She took the ambassador with her to the next room, to show him a picture of Mary, queen of Scots. The company followed her – Clarence Hervey remained with Dr X — and Belinda, who had just asked the doctor to teach her the moves at chess.

"Lady Delacour has charming spirits," said Clarence Hervey, "they inspire every body with gaiety."

"Every body! They incline me more to melancholy than mirth," said Dr X — . "These high spirits do not seem quite natural. The vivacity of youth and of health, Miss Portman, always charms me; but this gaiety of Lady Delacour's does not appear to me that of a sound mind in a sound body."

The doctor's penetration went so near the truth, that Belinda, afraid of betraying her friend's secret, never raised her eyes from the chess-board whilst he spoke, but went on setting up the fallen castles, and bishops, and kings, with expeditious diligence.

"You are putting the bishop into the place of the knight," said Clarence.

"Lady Delacour," continued the doctor, "seems to be in a perpetual fever, either of mind or body – I cannot tell which – and as a professional man, I really have some curiosity to determine the question. If I could feel her pulse, I could instantly decide; but I have heard her say, that she has a horror against having her pulse felt – and a lady's horror is invincible – by reason — "

"But not by address," said Clarence, "I can tell you a method of counting her pulse, without her knowing it – without her seeing you – without your seeing her."

"Indeed!" said Dr X — , smiling, "that may be a useful secret in my profession; pray impart it to me – you who excel in every thing."

"Are you in earnest, Mr Hervey?" said Belinda.

"Perfectly in earnest – my secret is quite simple. – Look through the door at the shadow of Queen Elizabeth's ruff – observe how it vibrates; the motion as well as the figure is magnified in the shadow. – Cannot you count every pulsation distinctly?"

"I can," said Dr X — , "and I give you credit for making an ingenious use of a trifling observation." – The doctor paused, and looked round. "Those people cannot hear what we are saying, I believe?"

"O, no," said Belinda, "they are intent upon themselves."

Doctor X — fixed his eyes mildly upon Clarence Hervey, and exclaimed in an earnest friendly tone – "What a pity, Mr Hervey, that a young man of your talents and acquirements, a man who might be any thing, should – pardon the expression – choose to be – nothing – should waste upon petty objects powers suited to the greatest – should lend his soul to every contest for frivolous superiority, when the same energy concentrated might ensure honourable preeminence among the first men in his country. – Shall he, who might not only distinguish himself in any science or situation, who might not only acquire personal fame, but, O, far more noble motive! – who might be permanently useful to his fellow creatures, content himself with being the evanescent amusement of a drawing-room? – Shall one, who might be great in public, or happy in private life, waste in this deplorable manner the best years of his existence – time that never can be recalled?" –" This is declamation!" –"No: it is truth put into the strongest language that I have power to use, in the hope of making some impression: I speak from my heart, for I have a sincere regard for you, Mr Hervey, and if I have been impertinent, you must forgive me."

"Forgive you!" cried Clarence Hervey, taking Dr X — by the hand, I think you are a real friend – you shall have the best thanks, not in words, but in actions – you have roused my ambition, and I will pursue noble ends by noble means. – A few years have been sacrificed – but the lessons that they have taught me remain. – I cannot, presumptuous as I am, flatter myself that my exertions can be of any material utility to my fellow-creatures, but what I can do I will. – My excellent friend! If I be hereafter either successful in public, or happy in private life, it is to you I shall owe it."

Belinda was touched by the candour and good sense with which Clarence Hervey spoke. – His character appeared in a new light – she was proud of her own judgment, in having discerned his merit, and for a moment she permitted herself to feel "unreproved pleasure in his company."

The next morning, Sir Philip Baddely and Mr Rochfort called at Lady Delacour's – Mr Hervey was present – Her ladyship was summoned to Mrs Franks, and Belinda was left with these gentlemen.

"Why, damme, Clary! you have been a lost man," cried Sir Philip, "ever since you were drowned. – Damme, why did not you come to dine with us that day, now I recollect it? – We were all famously merry – but for your comfort, Clarence, we missed you cursedly, and were damned sorry you ever took that damned unlucky jump into the Serpentine river – damned sorry – were not we Rochfort?"

"O," said Clarence, in an ironical tone, "you need no vouchers to convince me of the reality of your sorrow. – You know I can never forget your jumping so courageously into the river, to save the life of your friend."

"Oh, pooh! damn it," said Sir Philip, "what signifies who pulled you out, now you are safe and sound? By the by, Clary, did you ever quiz that doctor, as I desired you? – No, that I'm sure you didn't; but I think he has made a quiz of you; for damme, I believe you have taken such a fancy to the old quizzical fellow, that you can't live without him. – Miss Portman, don't you admire Hervey's taste?"

"In this instance I certainly do admire Mr Hervey's taste," said Belinda, "for the best of all possible reasons, because it entirely agrees with my own."

"Very extraordinary, faith," said Sir Philip.

"And what the devil can you find to like in him, Clary?" continued Mr Rochfort, "for one wouldn't be so rude to put that question to a lady. – Ladies you know are never to be questioned about their likings and dislikings. – Some have pet dogs, some have pet cats; then why not a *pet quiz.*"

"Ha! ha! ha! that's a good one, Rochfort – a pet quiz – Ha! ha! ha! Dr X — shall be Miss Portman's pet quiz. – Put it about – put it about, Rochfort," continued the witty baronet, and he and his facetious companion continued to laugh as long as they possibly could, at this happy hit.

Belinda, without being in the least discomposed by their insolent folly, as soon as they had finished laughing, very coolly observed, that she could have no objection to give her reasons for preferring Dr X — 's company, but for fear they might give offence to Sir Philip and his friends. She then defended the doctor with so much firmness, and yet with so much propriety, that Clarence Hervey was absolutely enchanted with her, and with his own penetration in having discovered her real character, notwithstanding she was Mrs Stanhope's niece.

"I never argue, for my part," cried Mr Rochfort, "'pon honour 'tis a deal too much trouble. – A lady, a handsome lady I mean, is always in the right with me."

"But as to you, Hervey," said Sir Philip, "damme, do you know, my boy, that our club has come to a determination to black-ball you, if you keep company with this famous doctor?"

"Your club, Sir Philip, will do me honour by such an ostracism."

"Ostracism!" repeated Sir Philip – "In plain English, does that mean that you choose to be black-balled by us? – Why damn it, Clary, you'll be nobody – But follow your own genius – damn me if I take it upon me to understand your men of genius – they are in the Serpentine river one day, – and in the clouds the next – so fare ye well, Clary. – I expect to see you a doctor of physic, or a methodist parson soon, damn me if I don't – so fare ye well, Clary – Is black-ball your last word? or will you think better on't, and give up the doctor?"

"I can never give up Dr X — 's friendship – I would sooner be black-balled by every club in London. – The good lesson you gave me, Sir Philip, the day I was fool enough to jump into the Serpentine river, has made me wiser for life. – I know, for I have felt, the difference between real friends and fashionable acquaintance. – Give up Dr X — ! Never! never!"

"Then fare ye well, Clary," said Sir Philip, "you're no longer one of us."

"Then, fare ye well, Clary, you're no longer the man for me," said Rochfort."

"*Tant pis* and *tant mieux*,"* said Clarence, and so they parted.

As they left the room, Clarence Hervey involuntarily turned to Belinda, and he thought that he read in her ingenuous, animated countenance, full approbation of his conduct.

"Hist! are they gone? Quite gone?" said Lady Delacour, entering the room from an adjoining apartment, "they have staid an unconscionable time – how much I am obliged to Mrs Franks for detaining me! I have escaped their vapid impertinence; and in truth, this morning, I have such a multiplicity of business, that I have scarcely a moment even for wit and Clarence Hervey. – Belinda, my dear, will you have the charity to look over some of these letters for me, which, as Marriott tells me, have been lying in my writing table this week – expecting most unreasonably, that I should have the grace to open them. – We are always punished for our indolence – as your friend Dr X — said the other day – if we suffer business to accumulate, it drifts with every ill wind like snow, till at last an avalanche of it comes down at once, and quite overwhelms us. – Excuse me, Clarence," continued her ladyship, as she opened her letters – "This is very rude – but I know I have secured my pardon from you by remembering your friend's wit – wisdom, I should say – How seldom are wit and wisdom joined! – They might have been joined in Lady Delacour, perhaps – there's vanity! – if she had early met with such a friend as Dr X — but it's too late now," said she, with a deep sigh.

Clarence Hervey heard it, and it made a great impression upon his benevolent imagination. – "Why too late?" said he to himself – "Mrs Margaret Delacour is mistaken, if she think this woman wants sensibility."

"What have you there, Miss Portman?" said Lady Delacour, taking from Belinda's hand one of the letters which she had begged her to look over – "Something wondrous pathetic, I should guess, by your countenance. – '*Helena Delacour*.' – O, read it to yourself, my dear – a school-girl's letter is a thing I abominate – I make it a rule never to read Helena's epistles."

"Let me prevail upon your ladyship to make an exception to the general rule then," said Belinda, "I can assure you this is not a common school-girl's letter; Miss Delacour seems to inherit her mother's '*éloquence de billet*.'"

"Miss Portman seems to possess, by inheritance, by instinct, by magic, or otherwise, powers of persuasion, which no one can resist. – There's compliment for compliment, my dear. – Is there any thing half so well turned in Helena's letter? – Really 'tis vastly well," continued her ladyship, as she read the letter – "where did the little gipsy learn to write so charmingly – I protest I should like of all things to have her at home with me this summer – the 21st of June – well, after the birthday, I shall have time to think about it. – But then, we shall be going out of town, and at Harrowgate I should not know what to do with her – she had better, much better go to her humdrum aunt Margaret's, as she always does – she is a fixture in Grosvenor square – these stationary good people – these zoophite friends are sometimes very convenient – and Mrs Margaret Delacour is the most unexceptionable zoophite in the creation. – She has, it is true, an antipathy to me, because I'm of such a different nature from herself; but then her antipathy does not extend to my offspring – she is kind, beyond measure, to Helena, on purpose, I believe, to provoke me. Now I provoke her in my turn, by never being provoked – and she saves me a vast deal of trouble, for which she is overpaid by the pleasure of abusing me. – This is the way of the world, Clarence. – Don't look so serious – you are not come yet to daughters and sons, and schools, and holidays, and all the evils of domestic life."

"Evils!" repeated Clarence Hervey, in a tone which surprised her ladyship. She looked immediately with a significant smile at Belinda. – "Why do not you echo *evils*, Miss Portman?"

"Pray Lady Delacour," interrupted Clarence Hervey, "when do you go to Harrowgate?"

"What a sudden transition!" said Lady Delacour – "What association of ideas could just at that instant take you to Harrowgate?

"When do I go to Harrowgate? Immediately after the birth-day, I believe we shall – I advise you to be of the party."

"Your ladyship does me a great deal of honour," said Hervey, "I shall, if it be possible, do myself the pleasure of attending you."

And soon after this arrangement was made, Mr Hervey took his leave.

"Well, my dear, are you still poring over that letter of Helena's," said Lady Delacour to Miss Portman.

"I fancy your ladyship did not quite finish it," said Belinda.

"No; I saw something about the Leverian Museum, and a swallow's nest in a pair of garden shears; and I was afraid I was to have a catalogue of curiosities for which I have little taste, and less time."

"You did not see, then, what Miss Delacour says of the lady who took her to that Museum?"

"Not I – What lady? her aunt Margaret?"

"No; Mrs Margaret Delacour, she says, has been so ill for some time past, that she goes no where, but to Lady Anne Percival's."

"Poor woman," said Lady Delacour, "she will die soon, and then I shall have Helena upon my hands, unless some other kind friend takes a fancy to her. – Who is this lady that has carried her to the Leverian Museum?"

"Lady Anne Percival; of whom she speaks with so much gratitude and affection, that I quite long — "

"Lord bless me!" interrupted Lady Delacour, "Lady Anne Percival! Helena has mentioned this Lady Anne Percival to me before, I recollect, in some of her letters."

"Then you did read some of her letters."

"Half! – I never read more than half, upon my word," said Lady Delacour, laughing.

"Why will you delight in making yourself appear worse than you are, my dear Lady Delacour," said Belinda, taking her hand.

"Because I hate to be like other people," said her ladyship, "who delight in making themselves appear better than what they are – but I was going to tell you, that I do believe I did provoke Percival by marrying Lord Delacour. – I cannot tell you how much this idea delights me – I am sure that the man has a lively remembrance of me, or else he would never make his wife take so much notice of my daughter."

"Surely your ladyship does not think," said Belinda, "that a wife is a being whose actions are necessarily governed by a husband."

"Not necessarily – but accidentally. – When a lady accidentally sets up for being a good wife, she must of course love, honour, and obey. Now, you understand, I am not in the least obliged to Lady Anne for her kindness to Helena; because it all goes under the head of obedience, in my imagination – and her ladyship is paid for it by an accession of character – she has the reward of having it said – 'O, Lady Anne Percival is the best wife in the world' – 'O, Lady Anne Percival is quite a pattern woman!' – I hate pattern women – I hope I may never see Lady Anne, for I'm sure I should detest her beyond all things living – Mrs Luttridge not excepted."

Belinda was surprised, and shocked at the malignant vehemence with which her ladyship uttered those words; it was in vain, however, that she remonstrated on the injustice of predetermining to detest Lady Anne; merely because she had shown kindness to Helena, and because she bore a high character. – Lady Delacour was a woman who never listened to reason; or listened to it only that she might parry it by wit. Upon this occasion, her wit had not its usual effect upon Miss Portman; instead of entertaining, it disgusted her.

"You have called me your friend, Lady Delacour," said she, "I should but ill deserve that name, if I had not the courage to speak the truth to you – if I had not the courage to tell you when I think you are wrong."

"But I have not the courage to hear you, my dear," said Lady Delacour, stopping her ears. – "So your conscience may be at ease; you may suppose that you have said every thing that is wise, and good, and proper, and sublime, and that you deserve to be called the best of friends – you shall enjoy the office of censor to Lady Delacour, and welcome; but remember, it is a sinecure place, though I will pay you with my love and esteem to any extent you please. – You sigh – for my folly. – Alas, my dear, 'tis hardly worth while – my follies will soon be at an end. – Of what use could even the wisdom of Solomon be to me now? – If you have any humanity, you will not force me to reflect – whilst I yet live I must *keep it up* with incessant dissipation – the teetotum keeps upright only while it spins – so let us talk of the birthnight, or the new play that we are to see to night, or the ridiculous figure Lady H — made at the concert, or let us talk of Harrowgate, or what you will."

Pity succeeded to disgust and displeasure in Belinda's mind, and she could hardly refrain from tears, whilst she saw this unhappy creature, with forced smiles, endeavour to hide the real anguish of her soul – she could only say –

"But, my dear Lady Delacour, do not you think that your little Helena, who seems to have a most affectionate disposition, would add to your happiness at home?"

"Her affectionate disposition can be nothing to me," said Lady Delacour.

Belinda felt a hot tear drop upon her hand, which lay upon Lady Delacour's lap.

"Can you wonder," continued her ladyship, hastily wiping away the tear which she had let fall; "can you wonder that I should talk of detesting Lady Anne Percival! – You see she has robbed me of the affections of my child. – Helena asks to come home – yes – but how does she ask it? coldly; formally; as a duty – but look at the end of her letter – I have read it all – every bitter word of it I have tasted. – How differently she writes – look even at the flowing hand – the moment she begins to speak of Lady Anne Percival – then her soul breaks out – 'Lady Anne has offered to take her to Oakly-park – she should be extremely happy to go, if I please.' – Yes, let her go – let her go as far from me as possible – let her never, never, see her wretched mother more. – Write," said Lady Delacour, turning hastily to Belinda, "write in my name, and tell her to go to Oakly-park, and to be happy."

"But why should you take it for granted that she cannot be happy with you?" said Belinda. "Let us see her – let us try the experiment?"

"No;" said Lady Delacour, "no – it is too late – I will never condescend in my last moments to beg for that affection to which it may be thought I have forfeited my natural claim."

Pride, anger, and sorrow, struggled in her countenance as she spoke. – She turned her face from Belinda, and walked out of the room with dignity.

Nothing remains for me to do, thought Belinda, but to sooth this haughty spirit – all other hope I see is in vain.

At this moment Clarence Hervey, who had no suspicion that the gay, brilliant Lady Delacour was sinking into the grave, had formed a design worthy of his ardent and benevolent character. – The manner in which her ladyship had spoken of his friend Dr X—, the sigh which she gave at the reflection that she might have been a very different character, if she had early had a sensible friend, made a great impression upon Mr Hervey. Till then, he had merely considered her ladyship as an object of amusement, and an introduction to high life; but he now felt so much interested for her, that he determined to exert all his influence to promote her happiness. – He knew *that* influence to be considerable – not that he was either coxcomb, or dupe enough, to imagine that Lady Delacour was in love with him; he was perfectly sensible that her only wish was to obtain his admiration, and he resolved to show her, that it could no longer be secured without deserving his esteem. – Clarence Hervey was a thoroughly generous young man: capable of making the greatest sacrifices, when encouraged by the hope of doing good, he determined to postpone the declaration of his attachment to Belinda, that he might devote himself entirely to his new project. His plan was to wean Lady Delacour, by degrees, from dissipation, by attaching her to her daughter, and to Lady Anne Percival. He was sanguine in all his hopes, and rapid, but not unthinking, in all his decisions. – From Lady Delacour he went immediately to Dr X —, to whom he communicated his designs.

"I applaud your benevolent intentions," said the doctor, "but have you really the presumption to hope, that an ingenuous young man of eight and twenty can reform a veteran coquette of eight and thirty?"

"Lady Delacour is not yet six and thirty," said Clarence; "but the older she is, the better the chance of her giving up a losing game. – She has an admirable understanding, and she will soon – I mean as soon as she is acquainted with Lady Anne Percival – discover that she has mistaken the road to happiness. – All the difficulty will be to make them fairly acquainted with each other – for this, my dear doctor, I must trust to you. – Do you prepare Lady Anne to tolerate Lady Delacour's faults, and I will prepare Lady Delacour to tolerate Lady Anne's virtues."

"You have generously taken the more difficult task of the two," replied Dr X —. "Well, we shall see what can be done. – After the birthday, Lady Delacour talks of going to Harrowgate – you know, Oakly-park is not far from Harrowgate, so they will have frequent opportunities of meeting. But, take my word for it, nothing can be done till after the birthday; for Lady Delacour's head is at present full of crape petticoats, and horses, and carriages, and a certain Mrs Luttridge, whom she hates with a hatred passing that of women."

CHAPTER X

The Mysterious Boudoir

Accustomed to study human nature, Dr X — had acquired peculiar sagacity in judging of character. Notwithstanding the address, with which Lady Delacour concealed the real motives for her apparently thoughtless conduct, he quickly discovered that the hatred of Mrs Luttridge was her ruling passion. Above nine years of continual warfare had exasperated the tempers of both parties, and no opportunities of manifesting their mutual antipathy were ever neglected. Extravagantly as Lady Delacour loved admiration, the highest possible degree of positive praise was insipid to her taste, if it did not imply some superiority over the woman whom she considered as her perpetual rival.

Now, it had been said by the coach-maker, that Mrs Luttridge would sport a most elegant new vis-à-vis, on the King's birthday. Lady Delacour was immediately ambitious to outshine her in equipage; and it was this paltry ambition, that made her condescend to all the meanness of the transaction, by which she obtained Miss Portman's draft, and Clarence Hervey's two hundred guineas. – The great, the important day at length arrived. – Her ladyship's triumph in the morning, at the drawing-room, was complete. – Mrs Luttridge's dress, Mrs Luttridge's vis-à-vis, Mrs Luttridge's horses, were nothing – absolutely nothing in comparison with Lady Delacour's – her ladyship enjoyed the full exultation of vanity; and at night she went in high spirits to the birthnight ball.

"O, my dearest Belinda," said she, as she left her dressing-room, how terrible a thing it is, that you cannot go with me! – None of the joys of this life are without alloy! – 'Twould be too much to see in one night Mrs Luttridge's mortification, and my Belinda's triumph. – Adieu! my love – we shall live to see another birthday, it is to be hoped. – Marriott, my drops. – O, I have taken them."

Belinda, after her ladyship's departure, retired to the library. – Her time passed so agreeably during Lady Delacour's absence, that she was surprised when she heard the clock strike twelve.

"Is it possible," thought she, "that I have spent three hours by myself in a library, without being tired of my existence! – How different are my feelings now, to what they would have been in the same circumstances six months ago! – I should then have thought the loss of a birthnight ball a mighty trial of temper. – It is singular, that my having spent a winter with one of the most dissipated women in England should have sobered my mind so completely. If I had never seen the utmost extent of the pleasures of the world, as they are called, my imagination might have misled me to the end of my life; but now I can judge from my own experience, and I am convinced that the life of a fine lady would never make me happy. – Dr X — told me, the other day, that he thinks me formed for something better, and he is incapable of flattery."

The idea of Clarence Hervey was so intimately connected with that of his friend, that Miss Portman could seldom separate them in her imagination – and she was just beginning to reflect upon the manner in which Clarence looked, whilst he declared to Sir Philip Baddely, that he would never give up Dr X — , when she was startled by the entrance of Marriott.

"O, Miss Portman, what shall we do! – What shall we do? – My lady! my poor lady!" cried she.

"What is the matter?" said Belinda.

"The horses – the young horses! – O I wish my lady had never seen them. O my lady, my poor lady, what will become of her!"

It was some minutes before Belinda could obtain from Marriott any intelligible account of what had happened.

"All I know, ma'am, is what James has just told me," said Marriott. – "My lady gave the coachman orders upon no account to let Mrs Luttridge's carriage get before hers. – Mrs Luttridge's coachman would not give up the point either. – My lady's horses were young and ill broke, they tell me, and there was no managing of them no ways. – The carriages got some how across one another, and my lady was overturned, and all smashed to atoms. – O ma'am!" continued Marriott, "if it had not been for Mr Hervey, they say, my lady would never have been got out of the crowd alive. – He's bringing her home in his own carriage – God bless him!"

"But is Lady Delacour hurt?" cried Belinda.

"She *must* – to be sure she must, ma'am," cried Marriott, putting her hand to her bosom. – "But let her be ever so much hurt, my lady will keep it to herself – the footmen swear she did not give a scream, not a single scream; so it's their opinion she was no ways hurt – But that I know can't be – And indeed, they are thinking so much about the carriage, that they can't give one any rational account of any thing – and as for myself, I'm sure I'm in such a flutter. – Lord knows, I advised my lady not to go with the young horses, no later than" –

"Hark!" cried Belinda, "here they are." She ran down stairs instantly. The first object that she saw was Lady Delacour in convulsions – the street-door was open – the hall was crowded with servants. Belinda made her way through them, and in a calm voice, requested that Lady Delacour might immediately be brought to her own dressing-room, and that she should there be left to Marriott's care and hers. Mr Hervey assisted in carrying Lady Delacour – she came to her senses as they were taking her up stairs. "Set me down – set me down," she exclaimed. "I am not hurt – I am quite well. – Where's Marriott? Where's Miss Portman?"

"Here we are – you shall be carried quite safely – trust to me," said Belinda, in a firm tone, "and do not struggle."

Lady Delacour submitted – she was in agonising pain; but her fortitude was so great that she never uttered a groan. It was the constraint which she had put upon herself, by endeavouring not to scream, which threw her into convulsions. "She is hurt, I am sure she is hurt, though she will not acknowledge it," cried Clarence Hervey. "My ankle is sprained, that's all," said Lady Delacour – "lay me on this sofa, and leave me to Belinda."

"What's all this?" cried Lord Delacour, staggering into the room: he was much intoxicated, and in this condition had just come home, as they were carrying Lady Delacour up stairs: he could not be made to understand the truth, but as soon as he heard Clarence Hervey's voice, he insisted upon going up to *his wife*'s dressing-room. It was a very unusual thing, but neither Champfort nor any one else could restrain him, the moment that he had formed this idea; he forced his way into the room.

"What's all this? – Colonel Lawless!" said he, addressing himself to Clarence Hervey, whom, in the confusion of his mind, he mistook for the colonel, the first object of his jealousy. "Colonel Lawless," cried his lordship, "you are a villain – I always knew it.

"Softly! – she's in great pain, my lord," said Belinda, catching

Lord Delacour's arm, just as he was going to strike Clarence Hervey. She led him to the sofa where Lady Delacour lay, and uncovering her ankle, which was much swelled, showed it to him. His lordship, who was a humane man, was somewhat moved by this appeal to his remaining senses, and he began roaring as loud as he possibly could for arquebusade.

Lady Delacour rested her head upon the back of the sofa, her hands moved with convulsive twitches – she was perfectly silent. Marriott was in a great bustle, running backwards and forwards for she knew not what, and continually repeating, "I wish nobody would come in here but Miss Portman and me. – My lady says nobody must come in. – Lord bless me! – my lord here too!"

"Have you any arquebusade, Marriott? Arquebusade, for your lady directly!" cried his lordship, following her to the door of the boudoir, where she was going for some drops.

"O my lord, you can't come in, I assure you, my lord, there's nothing here, my lord, nothing of the sort," said Marriott, setting her back against the door. – Her terror and embarrassment instantly recalled all the jealous suspicions of Lord Delacour. "Woman!" cried he, "I *will* see whom you have in this room! – You have some one concealed there, and I *will* go in." – Then with brutal oaths he dragged Marriott from the door, and snatched the key from her struggling hand.

Lady Delacour started up, and gave a scream of agony. "My lord! – Lord Delacour," cried Belinda, springing forward, "hear me."

Lord Delacour stopped short. – "Tell me then," cried Lord Delacour, "is not a lover of Lady Delacour's concealed there?" "No! – No! – No!" answered Belinda. "Then a lover of Miss Portman's," said Lord Delacour – "Gad! we have hit it now, I believe."

"Believe whatever you please, my lord," said Belinda hastily – "but give me the key."

Clarence Hervey drew the key from Lord Delacour's hand, gave it to Miss Portman without looking at her, and immediately withdrew. – Lord Delacour followed him with a sort of drunken laugh; and no one remained in the room but Marriott, Belinda, and Lady Delacour. – Marriott was so much *fluttered*, as she said, that she could do nothing. – Miss Portman locked the room door, and began to undress Lady Delacour, who lay motionless. "Are we by ourselves," said Lady Delacour, opening her eyes.

"Yes — are you much hurt?" said Belinda. "O, you are a charming girl!" said Lady Delacour. — "Who would have thought you had so much presence of mind and courage — have you the key safe?" "Here it is," said Belinda, producing it; and she repeated her question — "are you much hurt?" "I am not in pain now," said Lady Delacour, "but I *have* suffered terribly. — If I could get rid of all this finery — if you could put me to bed I could sleep perhaps."

Whilst Belinda was undressing Lady Delacour, she shrieked several times; but between every interval of pain she repeated, "I shall be better to morrow." As soon as she was in bed, she desired Marriott to give her double her usual quantity of laudanum; for that all the inclination which she had felt to sleep was gone, and that she could not endure the shooting pains that she felt in her breast.

"Leave me alone with your lady, Marriott, said Miss Portman, taking the bottle of laudanum from her trembling hand, "and go to bed; for I am sure you are not able to sit up any longer."

As she spoke, she took Marriott into the adjoining dressing-room. — "Oh dear Miss Portman," said Marriott, who was sincerely attached to her lady, and who at this instant forgot all her jealousies, and all her love of power — "I'll do any thing you ask me — but pray let me stay in the room, though I know I'm quite helpless. — It will be too much for you to be here all night by yourself. — The convulsions may take my lady. — What shrieks she gives every now and then! — and nobody knows what's the matter but ourselves; and every body in the house is asking me why a surgeon is not sent for, if my lady is so much hurt. O I can't answer for it to my conscience, to have kept the matter secret so long; for to be sure a physician, if had in time, might have saved my lady — but now nothing can save her!" — And here Marriott burst into tears.

"Why don't you give me the laudanum?" cried Lady Delacour, in a loud peremptory voice — "Give it to me instantly." — "No," said Miss Portman firmly. — "Hear me, Lady Delacour — you must allow me to judge, for you know that you are not in a condition to judge for yourself — or rather you must allow me to send for a physician, who may judge for us both."

"A physician!" cried Lady Delacour, — "Never — never. — I charge you let no physician be sent for. — Remember your promise — you *cannot* betray me — you *will* not betray me."

"No," said Belinda, "of that I have given sufficient proof – but you will betray yourself – it is already known by your servants that you have been hurt by the overturn of your carriage – if you do not let either a surgeon or physician see you, it will excite surprise and suspicion. – It is not in your power when violent pain seizes you to refrain from" – "It is," interrupted Lady Delacour, "not another scream shall you hear – only do not, do not, my dear Belinda, send for a physician."

"You will throw yourself again into convulsions," said Belinda – "Marriott you see, has lost all command of herself – I shall not have strength to manage you – perhaps I may lose my presence of mind, I cannot answer for myself – your husband may desire to see you."

"No danger of that," said Lady Delacour, "tell him my ankle is sprained – tell him I am bruised all over – tell him any thing you will – he will not trouble himself any more about me – he will forget all that passed to night by the time he is sober – O! – give me the laudanum, dearest Belinda – and say no more about physicians."

It was in vain to reason with Lady Delacour. Belinda attempted to persuade her – "for my sake, dear Lady Delacour," said she, "let me send for Dr X — , he is a man of honour, your secret will be perfectly safe with him."

"He will tell it to Clarence Hervey," said Lady Delacour – "of all men living I would not send for Dr X — , I will not see him if he comes."

"Then," said Belinda, calmly, but with a fixed determination of countenance, "I must leave you to morrow morning – I must return to Bath."

"Leave me! Remember your promise."

"Circumstances have occurred, about which I have made no promise," said Belinda – "I must leave you, unless you will now give me your permission to send for Dr X—."

Lady Delacour hesitated. "You see," continued Belinda, "that I am in earnest, when I am gone you will have no friend left – when I am gone your secret will inevitably be discovered, for without me Marriott will not have sufficient strength of mind to keep it."

"Do you think we might trust Dr X — ?" said Lady Delacour.

"I am sure you may trust him," said Belinda with energy: "I will pledge my life upon his honour."

"Then send for him, since it must be so," said Lady Delacour.

No sooner had the words passed Lady Delacour's lips, than Belinda flew to execute her orders. – Marriott recovered her senses, when she heard that her ladyship had consented to send for a physician, but she declared, that she could not conceive how any thing less than the power of magic could have brought her lady to such a determination.

Belinda had scarcely dispatched a servant for Dr X —, when Lady Delacour repented of the permission she had given, and all that could be said to pacify, only irritated her temper. – She became delirious, Belinda's presence of mind never forsook her, she remained quietly beside the bed waiting for the arrival of Dr X—, and she absolutely refused admittance to the servants, who, drawn by their lady's outrageous cries, continually came to her door with offers of assistance.

About four o'clock the doctor arrived, and Miss Portman was relieved from some of her anxiety. He assured her that there was no immediate danger, and he promised that the secret which she had entrusted to him should be faithfully kept. – He remained with her some hours, till Lady Delacour became more quiet and fell asleep, exhausted with delirious exertions. – "I think I may now leave you," said Dr X—, but as he was going through the dressing-room, Belinda stopped him. – "Now that I have time to think of myself," said she – "let me consult you as my friend – I am not used to act entirely for myself, and I shall be most grateful if you will assist me with your advice. – I hate all mysteries, but I feel myself bound in honour to keep the secret, with which Lady Delacour has entrusted me. – Last night I was so circumstanced, that I could not extricate her ladyship without exposing myself to – to suspicion."

Miss Portman then related all that had passed about the mysterious door, which Lord Delacour, in his fit of drunken jealousy, had insisted upon breaking open.

"Mr Hervey," continued Belinda, "was present when all this happened – he seemed much surprised – I should be sorry that – he should remain in an error which might be fatal to my reputation – you know a woman ought not even to be suspected – yet how to remove this suspicion I know not, because I cannot enter into any explanation without betraying Lady Delacour – she has, I know, a peculiar dread of Mr Hervey's discovering the truth."

"And is it possible," cried Dr X —, "that any woman should be so meanly selfish, as thus to expose the reputation of her friend, merely to preserve her own vanity from mortification."

"Hush – don't speak so loud," said Belinda, "you will awaken her – and at present she is certainly more an object of pity than of indignation. – If you will have the goodness to come with me, I will take you by a back-staircase up to the *mysterious boudoir*. – I am not too proud to give positive proofs of my speaking truth; the key of that room now lies on Lady Delacour's bed – it was that which she grasped in her hand during her delirium – she has now let it fall – it opens both the doors of the boudoir – you shall see," added Miss Portman, with a smile, "that I am not afraid to let you unlock either of them."

"As a polite man," said Dr X — , "I believe that I should absolutely refuse to take any external evidence of a lady's truth; but demonstration is unanswerable even by enemies, and I will not sacrifice your interests to the foppery of my politeness – so I am ready to follow you. The curiosity of the servants may have been excited by last night's disturbance, and I see no method so certain as that which you propose of preventing busy Rumour. That goddess (let Ovid say what he pleases) was born and bred in a kitchen, or a servant's hall. – But," continued Dr X — , "my dear Miss Portman, you will put a stop to a number of charming stories by this prudence of yours – a romance called the Mysterious Boudoir, of nine volumes at least, might be written on this subject, if you would only condescend to act like almost all other heroines, that is to say, without common sense."

The doctor now followed Belinda, and satisfied himself by ocular demonstration, that this cabinet was the retirement of disease, and not of pleasure.

It was about eight o'clock in the morning when Dr X — got home; he found Clarence Hervey waiting for him. Clarence seemed to be in great agitation, though he endeavoured, with all the power which he possessed over himself, to suppress his emotion.

"You have been to see Lady Delacour," said he, calmly – "Is she much hurt? – It was a terrible accident."

"She has been much hurt," said Dr X — , "and she has been for some hours delirious – but ask me no more questions now, for I am asleep and must go to bed – unless you have any thing to say that can waken me – you look as if some great misfortune had befallen you, what is the matter?"

"O, my dear friend," said Hervey, taking his hand – "do not jest with me, I am not able to bear your raillery in my present

temper – in one word, I fear that Belinda is unworthy of my esteem –
I can tell you no more – except that I am more miserable than I
thought any woman could make me."

"You are in a prodigious hurry to be miserable," said Dr X — ;
"upon my word, I think you would make a mighty pretty hero in a
novel; you take things very properly for granted, and stretched out
upon that sofa, you act the distracted lover vastly well – and to
complete the matter, you cannot tell me why you are more
miserable than ever man or hero was before. – I must tell you then,
that you have still more cause for jealousy than you suspect. – Ay,
start – every jealous man starts at the sound of the word jealousy – a
certain sympton this of the disease."

"You mistake me," cried Clarence Hervey, "no man is less
disposed to jealousy than I am – but – "

"But your mistress – no, not your mistress, for you have never yet
declared to her your attachment – but the lady you admire will not
let a drunken man unlock a door, and you immediately suppose – "

"She has mentioned the circumstance to you!" exclaimed
Hervey, in a joyful tone – "then she *must* be innocent."

"Admirable reasoning! – I was going to have told you just now, if
you would have suffered me to speak connectedly, that you have
more reason for jealousy than you suspect, for Miss Portman has
actually unlocked for me – for me! look at me – the door, the
mysterious door – and whilst I live, and whilst she lives, we can
neither of us ever tell you the cause of the mystery. – All I can tell you
is, that no lover is in the case, upon my honour – and now, if you
should ever mistake curiosity in your own mind for jealousy,
expect no pity from me."

"I should deserve none," said Clarence Hervey, "you have made
me the happiest of men."

"The happiest of men! – No, no; keep that superlative
exclamation for a future occasion. – But now you behave like a
reasonable creature, you deserve to hear the praises of your Belinda
– I am so much charmed with her, that I wish — "

"When can I see her," interrupted Hervey, "I'll go to her this
instant."

"Gently," said Dr X — , "you forget what time of the day it is –
you forget that Miss Portman has been up all night – that Lady
Delacour is extremely ill – and that this would be the most
unseasonble opportunity you could possibly choose for your
visit."

To this observation Clarence Hervey assented; but he immediately seized a pen from the doctor's writing-table, and began a letter to Belinda. – The doctor threw himself upon his sofa, saying – "Waken me when you want me" – and in a few minutes he was fast asleep.

"Doctor, upon second thoughts," said Clarence, rising suddenly, and tearing his letter down the middle, "I cannot write to her yet – I forgot the reformation of Lady Delacour – how soon do you think she will be well? – Besides, I have another reason for not writing to Belinda – at present you must know, my dear doctor, that I have, or had, another mistress."

"Another mistress indeed!" cried Doctor X —, trying to waken himself.

"Good God! I do believe you've been asleep."

"I do believe I have."

"But is it possible that you could fall sound asleep in that time?"

"Very possible," said the doctor, "what is there so extraordinary in a man's falling asleep? – Men are apt to sleep some time within the four and twenty hours – unless they have half a dozen mistresses to keep them awake, as you seem to have, my good friend."

A servant now came into the room with a letter, that had just arrived express from the country for Dr X —."

"This is another affair," cried he, rousing himself.

The letter required the doctor's immediate attendance. He shook hands with Clarence Hervey –

"My dear friend, I am really concerned that I cannot stay to hear the history of your six mistresses; but you see that this is an affair of life and death."

"Farewell," said Clarence, "I have not six, I have only three goddesses; even if you count Lady Delacour for one. – But I really wanted your advice, in good earnest."

"If your case be desperate, you can write, cannot you? – Direct to me at Horton-hall, Cambridge. – In the mean time, as far as general rules go, I can give you my advice gratis, in the formula of an old Scotch song –

> 'Tis good to be merry and wise,
> 'Tis good to be honest and true,
> 'Tis good to be off with the old love,
> Before you be on with the new.'"

CHAPTER XI

Difficulties

Before he left town, Dr X — called in Berkeley square, to see Lady Delacour; he found that she was out of all immediate danger. — Miss Portman was sorry that he was obliged to quit her at this time, but she felt the necessity for his going; he was sent for to attend Mr Horton, an intimate friend of his, a gentleman of great talents, and of the most active benevolence, who had just been seized with a violent fever, in consequence of his exertions in saving the poor inhabitants of a village in his neighbourhood from the effects of a dreadful fire, which broke out in the middle of the night.

Lady Delacour, who heard Dr X — giving this account to Belinda, drew back her curtain, and said —

"Be gone this instant, doctor — I am out of all immediate danger, you say — but if I were not — I must die in the course of a few months, you know — and what is my life or death, compared with the chance of saving your excellent friend! — He is of some use in this world — I am of none — begone, this instant, doctor."

"What a pity," said Dr X — , as he left the room, "that a woman who is capable of so much magnanimity should have wasted her life on petty objects."

"Her life is not yet at an end — O, sir, if you *could* save her!" cried Belinda.

Doctor X — shook his head — but returning to Belinda, after going half way down stairs, he added, "when you read this paper, you will know all that I can tell you upon the subject."

Belinda, the moment the doctor was gone, shut herself up in her own room, to read the paper which he had given to her. Dr X — first stated all that he thought would be most efficacious in mitigating the pain that Lady Delacour might feel, and all that could be done, with the greatest probability of prolonging her life. — Then he concluded with the following words:

"These are all temporising expedients: according to the usual progress of the disease, Lady Delacour may live a year or perhaps two.

"It is possible that her life might be saved by a *skilful* surgeon. — By a few words that dropped from her ladyship last night, I apprehend that she has some thoughts of submitting to an operation, which will be attended with much pain and danger, even if she employ the most experienced surgeon in London; but if she put herself, from a vain hope of secrecy, into ignorant hands, she will inevitably destroy herself."

After reading this paper, Belinda had some faint hopes that Lady Delacour's life might be saved; but she determined to wait till Doctor X — should return to town, before she mentioned his opinion to his patient; and she earnestly hoped that no idea of putting herself into ignorant hands would recur to her ladyship.

Lord Delacour, in the morning, when he was sober, retained but a confused idea of the events of the preceding night; but he made an awkwardly good natured apology to Miss Portman for his intrusion, and for the disturbance he had occasioned, which he said must be laid to the blame of Lord Studley's admirable Burgundy. — He expressed much concern for Lady Delacour's terrible accident, but he could not help observing, that if his advice had been taken the thing could not have happened — that it was the consequence of her ladyship's self-willedness about the young horses.

"How she got the horses without paying for them, or how she got money to pay for them, I know not," said his lordship; "for I said I would have nothing to do with the business, and I have kept to my resolution."

His lordship finished his morning visit to Miss Portman, by observing that "the house would now be very dull for her; that the office of a nurse was ill-suited to so young and beautiful a lady, but that her undertaking it with so much cheerfulness was a proof of a degree of good nature, that was not always to be met with in the young and handsome.

The manner in which Lord Delacour spoke convinced Belinda, that he was in reality attached to his wife, however the fear of being, or of appearing to be governed by her ladyship might have estranged him from her, and from home. — She now saw in him much more good sense, and symptoms of a more amiable character than his lady had described, or than she ever would allow that he possessed.

The reflections however, which Miss Portman made upon the miserable life this ill-matched couple led together did not incline her in favour of marriage in general; great talents on one side, and good nature on the other, had, in this instance, tended only to make each party unhappy. Matches of interest, convenience, and vanity, she was convinced diminished, instead of increasing happiness. – Of domestic felicity she had never, except during her childhood, seen examples – she had, indeed, heard from Dr X — descriptions of the happy family of Lady Anne Percival, but she feared to indulge the romantic hope of ever being loved by a man of superior genius and virtue, with a temper and manners suited to her taste. – The only person she had seen, who at all answered this description, was Mr Hervey, and it was firmly fixed in her mind, that he was not a marrying man, and consequently not a man of whom any prudent woman would suffer herself to think with partiality. She could not doubt that he liked her society and conversation; his manner had sometimes expressed more than cold esteem. – Lady Delacour had assured her that it expressed love; but Lady Delacour was an imprudent woman in her own conduct, and not scrupulous as to that of others. – Belinda was not guided by her opinions of propriety, and now that her ladyship was confined to her bed, and not in a condition to give her either advice or protection, she felt that it was peculiarly incumbent on her to guard, not only her conduct from reproach, but her heart from the hopeless misery of an ill-placed attachment. – She examined herself with firm impartiality – she recollected the excessive pain that she had endured, when she first heard Clarence Hervey say, that Belinda Portman was a compound of art and affectation; but this she thought was only the pain of offended pride – of proper pride – She recollected the extreme anxiety she had felt, even within the last four and twenty hours, concerning the opinion which he might form of the transaction about the key of the boudoir – but this anxiety she justified to herself; it was due, she thought, to her reputation; it would have been inconsistent with female delicacy, to have been indifferent about the suspicions that necessarily arose from the circumstances in which she was placed. – Before Belinda had completed her self-examination, Clarence Hervey called to inquire after Lady Delacour. – Whilst he spoke of her ladyship, and of his concern for the dreadful accident, of which he believed himself to be in a great measure the cause, his manner and language were animated and unaffected; but the moment that this subject was exhausted, he became embarrassed; though he distinctly expressed perfect confidence and esteem for her, he seemed to wish, and yet to be unable to support the character of a friend, contradistinguished to an admirer. He seemed conscious that he could not, with propriety, advert to the suspicions and jealousy which he had felt the preceding night; for a man who has never declared love would be absurd and impertinent, were he to betray jealousy. – Clarence was destitute neither of address nor presence of mind, but an accident happened, when he was just taking leave of Miss Portman, which threw him into utter confusion. – It surprised, if it did not confound Belinda. – She had forgotten to ask Dr X — for his direction; and as she thought it might be necessary to write to him concerning Lady Delacour's health, she begged of Mr Hervey to give it to her. – He took a letter out of his pocket, and wrote the direction with a pencil, but as he opened the paper, to tear off the outside, on which he had been writing, a lock of hair dropped out of the letter; he hastily stooped for it, and as he took it up from the ground the lock unfolded. – Belinda, though she cast but one involuntary, hasty glance at it, was struck with the beauty of its colour, and its uncommon length. – The confusion of Clarence Hervey convinced her, that he was extremely interested about the person to whom the hair belonged, and the species of alarm which she had felt at this discovery, opened her eyes effectually to the state of her own heart. – She was sensible that the sight of a lock of hair, however long, or however beautiful, in the hands of any man but Clarence Hervey, could not possibly have excited any emotion in her mind. "Fortunately," thought she, "I have discovered that he is attached to another, whilst it is yet in my power to command my affections, and he shall see that I am not so weak as to form any false expectations from what I must now consider as mere common-place flattery." Belinda was glad that Lady Delacour was not present at the discovery of the lock of hair, as she was aware that she would have rallied her unmercifully upon the occasion; and she rejoiced that she had not been prevailed upon to give *Madame la Comtesse de Pomenars* a lock of her *belle chevelure*. She could not help thinking, from the recollection of several minute circumstances, that Clarence Hervey had endeavoured to gain an interest in her affections, and she felt that there would be great impropriety in receiving his ambiguous visits during Lady

Delacour's confinement to her room. – She therefore gave orders, that Mr Hervey should not in future be admitted, till her ladyship should again see company. This precaution proved totally superfluous, for Mr Hervey never called again, during the whole course of Lady Delacour's confinement; though his servant regularly came every morning with inquiries after her ladyship's health. – She kept her room for about ten days: a confinement to which she submitted with extreme impatience: bodily pain she bore with fortitude, but constraint and ennui she could not endure.

One morning as she was sitting up in bed, looking over a large collection of her notes, and cards of inquiry after her health, she exclaimed –

"These people will soon be tired of bidding their footmen put in their heads to inquire whether I am alive or dead – I must appear amongst them again, if it be only for a few minutes, or they will forget me. – When I am fatigued, I will retire, and you, my dear Belinda, shall represent me – so tell them to open my doors, and unmuffle the knocker – let me hear the sound of music and dancing, and let the house be filled again, for Heaven's sake. – Dr Zimmermann* should never have been my physician, for he would have prescribed solitude. – Now solitude and silence are worse for me than poppy and mandragora. – It is impossible to tell how much silence tires the ears of those who have not been used to it. – For mercy's sake, Marriott," continued her ladyship, turning to Marriott, who just then came softly into the room. – "For mercy's sake, don't walk to all eternity on tiptoes – to see people gliding about

'Would Chloe know if you're alive or dead,
She bids her footman put it in her head.'*

like ghosts makes me absolutely fancy myself amongst the shades below. – I would rather be stunned by the loudest peal, that ever thundering footman gave at my door, than hear Marriott lock that boudoir, as if my life depended on my not hearing the key turned."

"Dear me! I never knew any lady that was ill, except my lady, complain of one's not making a noise to disturb her," said Marriott.

"Then, to please you, Marriott, I will complain of the only noise that does, or ever did disturb me – the screaming of your odious macaw."

Now Marriott had a prodigious affection for this macaw, and she defended it with as much eagerness as if it had been her child.

"Odious! O dear, my lady! to call my poor macaw odious! – I didn't expect it would ever have come to this – I am sure I don't deserve it – I'm sure I don't deserve, that my lady should have taken such a dislike to me."

And here Marriott actually burst into tears. – "But my dear Marriott," said Lady Delacour, "I only object to your macaw – may not I dislike your macaw without disliking you? – I have heard of 'love me, love my dog' – but I never heard of 'love me, love my bird.' – Did you, Miss Portman."

Marriott turned sharply round upon Miss Portman, and darted a fiery look at her through the midst of her tears. – "Then 'tis plain," said she, "who I'm to thank for this," and as she left the room her lady could not complain of her shutting the door after her too gently.

"Give her three minutes grace, and she will come to her senses," said Lady Delacour – "for she is not a bankrupt in sense. – O, three minutes won't do, I must allow her three days grace, I perceive," said Lady Delacour, when Marriott half an hour afterward reappeared, with a face which might have sat for the picture of ill humour. Her ill humour, however, did not prevent her from attending her lady as usual; she performed all her customary offices with the most officious zeal, but in profound silence, except every now and then she would utter a sigh, which seemed to say, "See how much I'm attached to my lady, and yet my lady hates my macaw!" Her lady, who perfectly understood the language of sighs, and felt the force of Marriott's, forbore to touch again on the tender subject of the macaw, hoping that when her house was once more filled with company, she should be relieved by more agreeable noises from continually hearing this pertinacious tormentor.

As soon as it was known that Lady Delacour was sufficiently recovered to receive company, her door was crowded with carriages; and as soon as it was understood that balls and concerts were to go on as usual at her house, her "troops of friends" appeared to congratulate her, and to amuse themselves.

"How stupid it is," said Lady Delacour to Belinda, "to hear congratulatory speeches from people, who would not care if I were in the black hole at Calcutta this minute; but we must take the world as it goes – dirt and precious stones mixed together.

Clarence Hervey, however, *n'a pas une ame de boue*;* he I am
sure has been really concerned for me; he thinks that his young
horses were the sole cause of the whole evil, and he blames himself
so sincerely, and so unjustly, that I really was half tempted to
undeceive him; but that would have been doing him an injury; for
you know great philosophers tell us, that there is no pleasure in
the world equal to that of being well deceived, especially by the
fair sex. – Seriously, Belinda, is it my fancy, or is not Clarence
wonderfully changed? – Is not he grown pale, and thin, and
serious, not to say melancholy? What have you done to him since I
have been ill?"

"Nothing – I have never seen him."

"No! then the thing is accounted for very naturally – he is in
despair, because he has been banished from your divine
presence."

"More likely because he has been in anxiety about your
ladyship," said Belinda.

"I will find out the cause, let it be what it may," said Lady
Delacour – "luckily my address is equal to my curiosity, and that
is saying a great deal."

Notwithstanding all her ladyship's address, her curiosity was
baffled; she could not discover Clarence Hervey's secret, and she
began to believe, that the change which she had noticed in his
looks and manner was imaginary or accidental. Had she seen
more of him, at this time she would not have so easily given up her
suspicions; but she saw him only for a few minutes every day, and
during that time he talked to her with all his former gaiety;
besides, Lady Delacour had herself a daily part to perform, which
occupied almost her whole attention. Notwithstanding the
vivacity which she affected, Belinda perceived that she was now
more seriously alarmed than she had ever been about her health. It
was all that her utmost exertions could accomplish, to appear for
a short time in the day – some evenings she came into company
only for half an hour, on other days only for a few minutes, just
walked through the rooms, paid her compliments to every body,
complained of a nervous head ache, left Belinda to do the honours
for her, and retired.

Miss Portman was now really placed in a difficult and
dangerous situation, and she had ample opportunities of learning
and practising prudence. – All the fashionable dissipated young
men in London frequented Lady Delacour's house, and it was

said, that they were drawn thither by the attractions of her fair
representative. The gentlemen considered a niece of Mrs Stanhope's as their lawful prize. The ladies wondered that the men
could think Belinda Portman a beauty; but whilst they affected to
scorn, they sincerely feared her charms. – Thus, left entirely to her
own discretion, she was exposed at once to the malignant eye of
envy, and the insidious voice of flattery – she had no friend, no
guide, and scarcely a protector: her aunt Stanhope's letters,
indeed, continually supplied her with advice, but with advice
which she could not follow consistently with her own feelings and
principles. – Lady Delacour, even if she had been well, was not a
person on whose counsels she could rely: our heroine was not one
of those daring spirits, who are ambitious of acting for themselves; she felt the utmost diffidence of her own powers, yet at the
same time a firm resolution not to be led even by timidity into
follies, which the example of Lady Delacour had taught her to
despise. Belinda's prudence seemed to increase with the necessity
for its exertion. It was not the mercenary wily prudence of a young
lady, who has been taught to think it virtue to sacrifice the
affections of her heart to the interests of her fortune – it was not
the prudence of a cold and selfish, but of a modest and generous
woman. – She found it most difficult to satisfy herself in her
conduct towards Clarence Hervey: he seemed mortified and
miserable if she treated him merely as a common acquaintance,
yet she felt the danger of admitting him to the familiarity of
friendship: had she been thoroughly convinced that he was
attached to some other woman, she hoped that she could freely
converse with him, and look upon him as a married man; but
notwithstanding the lock of beautiful hair, she could not entirely
divest herself of the idea that she was beloved, when she observed
the extreme eagerness with which Clarence Hervey watched all
her motions, and followed her with his eye as if his fate depended
upon her. She remarked that he endeavoured as much as posisble
to prevent this species of attention from being noticed, either by
the public or by herself: his manner towards her every day became
more distant and respectful, more constrained and embarrassed;
but now and then a different look and expression escaped. She
had often heard of Mr Hervey's great *address* in affairs of
gallantry, and she was sometimes inclined to believe that he was
trifling with her, merely for the glory of a conquest over her heart;
at other times she suspected him of deeper designs upon her, such

as would deserve contempt and detestation; but upon the whole she was disposed to believe, that he was entangled by some former attachment from which he could not extricate himself with honour; upon this supposition she thought him worthy of her esteem, and of her pity.

About this time Sir Philip Baddely began to pay a sort of lounging attention to Belinda – he knew that Clarence Hervey liked her, and this was the principal cause of his desire to attract her attention. – "Belinda Portman," became his favourite toast, and amongst his companions he gave himself the air of talking of her with rapture.

"Rochfort," said he, one day to his friend – "damme, if I was to think of Belinda Portman in *any way*, you take me – Clary would look damned blue – hey? damned blue, and devilish small, and cursed silly too – hey?"

"'Pon honour, I should like to see him," said Rochfort – "'pon honour he deserves it from us, Sir Phil, and I'll stand your friend with the girl, and it will do no harm to give her a hint of Clary's Windsor flame – as a dead secret – 'pon honour he deserves it from us."

Now it seems that Sir Philip Baddely and Mr Rochfort, during the time of Clarence Hervey's intimacy with them, observed that he paid frequent visits at Windsor, and they took it into their heads that he kept a mistress there. They were very curious to see her, and unknown to Clarence, they made several attempts for this purpose; at last, one evening, when they were certain that he was not at Windsor, they scaled the high garden wall of the house which he frequented, and actually obtained a sight of a beautiful young girl and an elderly lady, whom they took for her gouvernante.* This adventure they kept a profound secret from Clarence, because they knew that he would have quarrelled with them immediately, and would have called them to account for their intrusion. They now determined to avail themselves of their knowledge, and of his ignorance of this circumstance; but they were sensible that it was necessary to go warily to work, lest they should betray themselves. Accordingly they began by dropping distant mysterious hints about Clarence Hervey, to Lady Delacour and Miss Portman. – Such for instance as –

"Damme, we all know Clary's a perfect connoisseur in beauty – hey, Rochfort – one beauty at a time is not enough for him – hey, damme? And it is not fashion, nor wit, nor elegance, and all that – that he looks for *always*."

These observations were accompanied with the most significant looks. – Belinda heard and saw all this in painful silence, but Lady Delacour often used her address to draw some farther explanation from Sir Philip – his regular answer was – "No, no, your ladyship, must excuse me there, I can't peach, damme – hey, Rochfort?"

He was in hopes from the reserve with which Miss Portman began to treat Clarence, that he should, without making any distinct charge, succeed in disgusting her with his rival. – Mr Hervey was about this time less assiduous than formerly in his visits at Lady Delacour's; Sir Philip was there every day, and often for Miss Portman's entertainment exerted himself so far as to tell the news of the town. – One morning, when Clarence Hervey happened to be present, the baronet thought it incumbent upon him to eclipse his rival in conversation, and he began to talk of the last fête champêtre, at Frogmore.

"What a cursed unlucky overturn that was of yours, Lady Delacour, with those famous young horses – why – what with this sprain, and this nervous business, you've not been able to stir out since the birthday, and you've missed the breakfast, and all that, at Frogmore – why all the world staid broiling in town on purpose for it, and you that had a card too – how damned provoking."

"I regret extremely that my illness prevented me from being at this charming fête. – I regret it more on Miss Portman's account than on my own," said her ladyship. – Belinda assured her that she felt no mortification from the disappointment.

"O, damme! but I would have driven you in my curricle," said Sir Philip – "It was the finest sight and best conducted I ever saw, and only wanted Miss Portman to make it complete. – We had gipsies, and Mrs Mills the actress for the queen of the gipsies; and she gave us a famous good song, Rochfort, you know – and then there *was* two children upon an *ass*, damme, I don't know how they came there, for they're things one sees every day – and belonged only to two of the soldiers wives – for we had the whole band of the Staffordshire playing at dinner, and we had some famous glees – and Fawcett gave us his laughing song, and then we had the launching of the ship, and only it was a boat, it would have been well enough – but damme, the song of Polly Oliver was worth the whole – except the Flemish Hercules – du Crow, you know, dressed in light blue and silver – and Miss Portman! I wish you had seen this! three great coach wheels on his chin, and a ladder and two chairs and two children on them – and after that, he sported a musquet and bayonet with the point of the bayonet on his chin – faith! that was really famous! – but I forgot the Pyrrhic dance, Miss Portman, which was damned fine too – danced in boots and spurs by those Hungarian fellows – they jump and turn about, and clap their knees with their hands, and put themselves in all sorts of ways – and then we had that song of Polly Oliver, as I told you before, and Mrs Mills gave us – no, no – it was a drummer of the Staffordshire dressed as a gipsy girl, gave us *the cottage on the moor*, the most charming thing, and would suit your voice, Miss Portman – damme you'd sing it like an angel – but where was I? – O, then they had tea – and fire places built of brick, out in the air – and then the entrance to the ball room was all a colonnade done with lamps and flowers, and that sort of thing – and there was some bon mot (but that was in the morning) amongst the gipsies about an orange, and the stadtholder* – and then there was a Turkish dance, and a Polonese dance, all very fine, but nothing to come up to the Pyrrhic touch, which was a great deal the most knowing, in boots and spurs – damme, now I can't describe the thing to you, 'tis a cursed pity you weren't there, damme."

Lady Delacour assured Sir Philip that she had been more entertained by the description, than she could have been by the reality. – "Clarence, was not it the best description you ever heard? – But pray favour us with *a touch* of the Pyrrhic dance, Sir Philip?"

Lady Delacour spoke with such polite earnestness, and the baronet had so little penetration and so much conceit, that he did not suspect her of irony: he eagerly began to exhibit the Pyrrhic dance, but in such a manner, that it was impossible for human gravity to withstand the sight. – Rochfort laughed first, Lady Delacour followed him, and Clarence Hervey and Belinda could no longer restrain themselves.

"Damme, now I believe you've all been quizzing me, damme," – cried the baronet, and he fell into a sulky silence, eyeing Clarence Hervey and Miss Portman from time to time with what he meant for a *knowing* look. His silence and sulkiness lasted till Clarence took his leave. Soon afterward Belinda retired to the music room. Sir Philip then begged to speak a few words to Lady

Delacour, with a face of much importance; and after a preamble of nonsensical expletives, he said that his regard for her ladyship and Miss Portman made him wish to explain hints which had been dropped from him at times, and which he could not explain to her satisfaction, without a promise of inviolable secrecy – "As Hervey is, or was a sort of a friend, I can't, damme, mention this sort of thing without such a preliminary." – Lady Delacour gave the preliminary promise, and Sir Philip informed her, that people began to take notice that Hervey was an admirer of Miss Portman's, and that it might be a disadvantage to the young lady, as Mr Hervey could have no serious intentions, because he had an attachment, to his certain knowledge, elsewhere.

"A matrimonial attachment?" said Lady Delacour.

"Why damme, as to matrimony, I can't say, but the girl's so famously beautiful, and Clary has been constant to her so many years" –

"Many years – then she is not young?"

"O, damme, yes, she is not more than seventeen – and let her be what else she will, she's a famous fine girl – I had a sight of her once at Windsor, by stealth.'

And then the baronet described her after his manner. – "Where Clary keeps her now I can't make out, but he has taken her away from Windsor. – She was then with a gouvernante, and is as proud as the devil, which smells like matrimony for Clary."

"And do you know this peerless damsel's name?"

"Damme, I think the old jezabel called her Miss St Pierre – ay, damme – it was Virginia too – Virginia St Pierre." *

"Virginia St Pierre, a pretty romantic name," said Lady Delacour – "Miss Portman and I are extremely obliged by your attention to the preservation of our hearts – and I promise you we shall keep your counsel, and our own."

Sir Philip then, with more than his usual complement of oaths, pronounced Miss Portman to be the finest girl he had ever seen, and took his leave.

When Lady Delacour repeated this story to Belinda, she concluded by saying – "Now my dear, you know Sir Philip Baddely has his own views in telling us all this – in telling *you* all this – for evidently he admires you, and consequently hates Clarence. – So I believe only half the man says, and the other half, though it has made you turn so horribly pale, my love, I consider as a thing of no manner of consequence to you."

"Of no manner of consequence to me, I assure your ladyship," said Belinda, "I have always considered Mr Hervey as – "

"O, as a common acquaintance, no doubt – but we'll pass over all those pretty speeches – I was going to say that this 'mistress of the wood' can be of no consequence to your happiness, because whatever that fool Sir Philip may think, Clarence Hervey is not a man to go and marry a girl who has been his mistress for half a dozen years – do not look so shocked my dear, I really cannot help laughing – I congratulate you, however, that the thing is no worse – it is all in rule and in course – when a man marries he sets up new equipages, and casts off old mistresses – or if you like to see the thing as a woman of sentiment, rather than as a woman of the world, here is the prettiest opportunity for your lover's making a sacrifice. – I am sorry I cannot make you smile, my dear – but consider, as nobody knows this naughty thing but ourselves, we are not called upon to bristle up our morality, and the most moral ladies in the world do not expect men to be as moral as themselves – so we may suit the measure of our external indignation to our real feelings – Sir Philip cannot stir in the business – for he knows Clarence would call him out, if his secret viz to Virginia was to come to light – I advise you *d'aller votre train** with Clarence, without seeming to suspect him in the least – there is nothing like innocence in these cases, my dear – but I know by the Spanish haughtiness of your air at this instant, that you would sooner die the death of the sentimental – than follow my advice."

Belinda without any haughtiness, but with firm gentleness, replied, "that she had no designs whatever upon Mr Hervey, and that therefore there could be no necessity for any manoeuvring on her part. – That the ambiguity of his conduct towards her had determined her long since to guard her affections, and that she had the satisfaction to feel, that they were entirely under her command."

"That is a great satisfaction indeed, my dear," said Lady Delacour – "It is a pity that your countenance, which is usually expressive enough, should not at this instant obey your wishes and express perfect felicity – But though you feel no pain from disappointed affection, doubtless the concern that you show arises from the necessity you are under of withdrawing a portion of your esteem from Mr Hervey – this is the style for you, is it not? – After all, my dear, the whole may be a quizzification of Sir Philip's – and yet he gave me such a minute description of her person – I am sure the man has not invention or taste enough to produce such a fancy piece."

"Did he mention," said Belinda, in a low voice – "the colour of her hair?"

"Yes – light brown – but the colour of this hair seems to affect you more than all the rest."

Here, to Belinda's great relief, the conversation was interrupted by the entrance of Marriott. – From all she had heard, but especially from the agreement between the colour of the hair which dropped from Hervey's letter with Sir Philip's description of Virginia's, Miss Portman was convinced that Clarence had some secret attachment; and she could not help blaming him in her own mind, for having, as she thought, endeavoured to gain her affections, whilst he knew that his heart was engaged to another. – Mr Hervey, however, gave her no farther reason to suspect him of any design to win her love; for about this time his manner towards her changed, he obviously endeavoured to avoid her; his visits were short, and his attention was principally directed to Lady Delacour; when she retired, he took his leave, and Sir Philp Baddely had the field to himself. – The baronet, who thought that he had succeeded in producing a coldness between Belinda and his rival, was surprised to find, that he could not gain any advantage for himself; for some time he had not the slightest thoughts of any serious connexion with the lady, but at last he was piqued by her indifference, and by the raillery of his friend Rochfort.

"'Pon honour," said Rochfort, "the girl must be in love with Clary, for she minds you no more than if you were nobody."

"Damme, I could make her sing to another tune, if I pleased," said Sir Philip; "but damme, it would cost me too much – a wife's too expensive a thing, damme, nowadays. – Why, a man could have twenty curricles, and a fine stud, and a pack of hounds, and as many mistresses as he chooses into the bargain, for what it would cost him to take a wife. – O, damme, Belinda Portman's a fine girl, but not worth so much as that comes to – and yet, confound me, if I should not like to see how blue Clary would look, if I were to propose for her in good earnest – hey, Rochfort! – I should like to pay him for the way he served us about that quiz of a doctor, hey?"

"Ay," said Rochfort, "you know he told us there was a *tant pis* and a *tant mieux* in every thing – he's not come to the *tant pis* yet. – 'Pon honour, Sir Philip, the thing rests with you."

The baronet vibrated for some time, between the fear of being taken in by one of Mrs Stanhope's nieces, and the hope of triumphing over Clarence Hervey. – At last, what he called love prevailed over prudence, and he was resolved, cost him what it would, to have Belinda Portman. He had not the least doubt of being accepted, if he made a proposal of marriage; consequently, the moment that he came to this determination, he could not help assuming *d'avance** the tone of a favoured lover.

"Damme," cried Sir Philip, one night at Lady Delacour's concert, "I think that Mr Hervey has taken out a patent for talking to Miss Portman – but damme if I give up this place, now I have got it," cried the baronet, seating himself beside Belinda.

Mr Hervey did not contest his seat, and Sir Philip kept his post during the remainder of the concert, but though he had the field entirely to himself, he could not think of any thing more interesting, more amusing to whisper in Belinda's ear, than – "Don't you think the candles want snuffing famously?"[1]

1.   Taken from real life.

CHAPTER XII

The Macaw

———

The baronet determined the next day upon the grand attack. He waited upon Miss Portman, with a certainty of being favourably received; but he was, nevertheless, somewhat embarrassed to know how to begin the conversation, when he found himself alone with the lady.

He twirled and twisted a short stick that he held in his hand, and put it in and out of his boot twenty times, and at last he began with –

"Lady Delacour's not gone to Harrowgate yet?"

"No – her ladyship has not yet felt herself well enough to undertake the journey."

"That was a cursed unlucky overturn – she may thank Clarence Hervey for that – it's like him – he thinks he's a better judge of horses, and wine, and every thing else, than any body in the world. – Damme now if I don't believe he thinks nobody else but himself has eyes enough to see that a fine woman's a fine woman – but I'd have him to know, that Miss Belinda Portman has been Sir Philip Baddely's toast these two months."

As this intelligence did not seem to make the expected impression upon Miss Belinda Portman, Sir Philip had recourse again to his little stick, with which he went through the sword exercise – after a silence of some minutes, and after walking to the window, and back again, as if to look for sense, he exclaimed –

"How is Mrs Stanhope now, pray, Miss Portman? – and your sister, Mrs Tollemache – she was the finest woman, I thought, the first winter she came out, that ever I saw, damme. – Have you ever been told that you're like her?"

"Never, sir."

"O, damn it then, but you are, only ten times handsomer."

"Ten times handsomer than the finest woman you ever saw, Sir Philip?" said Belinda, smiling.

"Than the finest woman I had ever seen *then*," said Sir Philip, "for damme I did not know what it was to be in love *then*," (here the baronet heaved an audible sigh) "I always laughed at love, and all that, *then*, and marriage particularly – I'll trouble you for Mrs Stanhope's direction, Miss Portman; I believe, to do the thing in style, I ought to write to her before I speak to you."

Belinda looked at him with astonishment, and laying down the pencil, with which she had just begun to write a direction to Mrs Stanhope, she said –

"Perhaps, Sir Philip, *to do the thing in style*, I ought to pretend at this instant not to understand you – but such false delicacy might mislead you – permit me therefore to say, that if I have any concern in the letter which you are going to write to my aunt Stanhope — "

"Well guessed!" interrupted Sir Philip, "to be sure you have, and you're a charming girl, damn me if you aren't, for meeting my ideas in this way – which will save a cursed deal of trouble," added the polite lover, seating himself on the sofa, beside Belinda.

"To prevent your giving yourself any farther trouble then, sir, on my account," said Miss Portman –

"Nay, damme, don't catch at that unlucky word, trouble, nor look so cursed angry; though it becomes you too, uncommonly, and I like pride in a handsome woman, if it was only for variety's sake, for it's not what one meets with often, nowadays. – As to trouble, all I meant was, the trouble of writing to Mrs Stanhope, which of course I thank you for saving me; for to be sure, damn it, I'd rather (and you can't blame me for that) have my answer from your own charming lips, if it was only for the pleasure of seeing you blush in this heavenly sort of style."

"To put an end to this heavenly sort of style, sir," said Belinda, withdrawing her hand, which the baronet took, as if he was confident of its being his willing prize – "I must explicitly assure you, that it is not in my power to encourage your addresses. – I am fully sensible," added Miss Portman, "of the honour Sir Philip Baddely has done me, and I hope he will not be offended by the frankness of my answer."

"You can't be in earnest, Miss Portman!" exclaimed the astonished baronet.

"Perfectly in earnest, Sir Philip."

"Confusion seize me!" cried he, starting up, "if this isn't the most extraordinary thing I ever heard! – Will you do me the honour, madam, to let me know your particular objections to Sir Philip Baddely."

"My objections," said Belinda, "cannot be obviated, and therefore it would be useless to state them."

"Nay – pray – ma'am – do me the favour – I only ask for information sake – is it to Sir Philip Baddely's fortune, 15,000l. a year, you object, or to his family, or to his person. – O, curse it!" said he, changing his tone, you're only quizzing me to see how I should look – damn me you did it too well, you little coquette."

Belinda again assured him that she was entirely in earnest, and that she was incapable of the sort of coquetry which he ascribed to her.

"O, damme, ma'am, then I've no more to say – a coquette is a thing I understand as well as another, and if we had been only talking in the air, it would have been another thing; but when I come at once to a proposal in form, and a woman seriously tells me she has objections that cannot be obviated, damme, what must I, or what must the world conclude, but that she's very unaccountable, or that she's engaged – which last I presume to be the case, and it would have been a satisfaction to me to have known it sooner – at any rate, it is a satisfaction to me to know it now."

"I am sorry to deprive you of so much satisfaction," said Miss Portman, "by assuring you, that I am not engaged to any one."

Here the conversation was interrupted by the entrance of Lord Delacour, who came to inquire from Miss Portman how his lady did. The baronet, after twisting his little black stick into all manner of shapes, finished by breaking it, and then having no other resource, suddenly wished Miss Portman a good morning, and decamped with a look of silly ill humour. – He was determined to write to Mrs Stanhope, whose influence over her niece he had no doubt would be decisive in his favour. "Sir Philip seems to be a little out of sorts this morning," said Lord Delacour, "I am afraid he's angry with me for interrupting his conversation; but really I did not know he was here, and I wanted to catch you a moment alone, that I might, in the first place, thank you for all your goodness to Lady Delacour – she has had a tedius sprain of it; these nervous fevers and convulsions – I don't understand them, but I think Dr X — 's prescriptions seem to have done her good, for she is certainly better of late, and I am glad to hear music and people again in the house, because I know all this is what my Lady Delacour likes, and there is no reasonable indulgence that I would not willingly allow a wife; but I think there is a medium in all things. – I am not a man to be governed by a wife, and when I have once said a thing, I like to be steady, and always shall. And I am sure Miss Portman has too much good sense to think me wrong; for now Miss Portman, in that quarrel about the coach and horses, which you heard part of one morning at breakfast – I must tell you the beginning of that quarrel."

"Excuse me, my lord, but I would rather hear of the end than of the beginning of quarrels."

"That shows your good sense as well as your good nature. I wish you could make my Lady Delacour of your taste – she does not want sense – but then (I speak to you freely of all that lies upon my mind, Miss Portman, for I know – I *know* you have no delight in making mischief in a house) – between you and me, her sense is not of the right kind. – A woman may have too much wit – now too much is as bad as too little, and in a woman, worse; and when two people come to quarrel, then wit on either side, but more especially on the wife's, you know, is very provoking – 'tis like concealed weapons, which are wisely forbidden by law. – If a person kill another in a fray with a concealed weapon, ma'am, by a sword in a cane for instance, 'tis murder by the law. Now even if it were not contrary to law, I would never have such a thing in my cane to carry about with me; for when a man's in a passion he forgets every thing, and would as soon lay about him with a sword as with a cane – so it is better such a thing should not be in his power. – And it is the same with wit, which would be safest and best out of the power of some people."

"But is it fair, my lord, to make use of wit yourself to abuse wit in others?" said Belinda with a smile, which put his lordship into perfect good humour with both himself and his lady. "Why really," said he, "there would be no living with Lady Delacour, if I did not come out with a little fly bit of wit now and then; but it is what I am not in the habit of doing, I assure you, except when very hard pushed. – But Miss Portman, as you like so much to hear the end of quarrels, here's the end of one which you have a particular right to hear something of," continued his lordship, taking out his pocketbook and producing some bank notes – "you should have received this before, madam, if I had known of the transaction sooner – of your part of it, I mean."

"Milord, de man call to speak about de burgundy you order, milord," said Champfort, who came into the room with a sly inquisitive face.

"Tell him I'll see him immediately – show him into the parlour, and give him a newspaper to read."

"Yes, milord – milord has it in his pocket since he dress."

"Here it is," said his lordship, and as Champfort came forward to receive the newspaper, his eye glanced at the banknotes, and then at Miss Portman.

"Here," continued Lord Delacour, as Champfort had left the room – "here are your two hundred guineas, Miss Portman, and as I am going to this man about my burgundy, and shall be out all the rest of the day, let me trouble you the next time you see Lady Delacour to give her this pocketbook from me. – I should be sorry Miss Portman, from any thing that has passed, should run away with the idea that I am a niggardly husband, or a tyrant, though I certainly like to be master in my own house. – What are you doing, madam? – that is your note, that does not go into the pocketbook, you know.

"Permit me to put it in, my lord," said Belinda, returning the pocketbook to him, "and to beg you will give Lady Delacour the pleasure of seeing you: she has inquired several times whether your lordship were at home. I will run up to her dressing-room and tell her that you are here."

"How lightly she goes, on the wings of good nature!" said Lord Delacour, "I can do no less than follow her; for though I like to be treated with respect in my own house, there is a time for every thing. – I would not give Lady Delacour the trouble of coming down here to me with her sprained ankle, especially as she has inquired for me several times."

His lordship's visit was not of unseasonable length; for he recollected that the man who came about the burgundy was waiting for him. But, perhaps, the shortness of the visit rendered it the more pleasing, for Lady Delacour afterward said to Belinda –

"My dear, would you believe it, my Lord Delacour was absolutely a perfect example of the useful and agreeable this morning – who knows but he may become the sublime and beautiful in time – *en attendant*.* Here are your two hundred guineas, my dear Belinda – a thousand thanks for the thing, and a million for the manner – manner is all in all in conferring favours. My lord, who, to do him justice, has too much honesty to pretend to more delicacy than he really possesses, told me that he had been taking a lesson from Miss Portman this morning in the art of obliging; and really, for a grown gentleman, and for the first lesson, he comes on surprisingly. I do think, that by the time he is a widower, his lordship will be quite another thing – quite an agreeable man – not a genius, not a Clarence Hervey, that you cannot expect. – Apropos, what is the reason that we have seen so little of Clarence Hervey lately? He has certainly some secret attraction elsewhere. – It cannot be that girl Sir Philip mentioned. – No – she's nothing new. Can it be at Lady Anne Percival's? – or where can it be? Whenever he sees me I think he asks, when we go to Harrowgate. – Now Oakly-park is within a few miles of Harrowgate. I will not go there, that's decided. Lady Anne is an exemplary matron, so she is out of the case; but I hope she has no *sister excellence*, no niece, no cousin, to entangle our hero."

"*Ours!*" said Belinda.

"Well, *yours*, then," said Lady Delacour.

"*Mine!*"

"Yes, yours: I never in my life saw a better struggle between a sigh and a smile. But what have you done to poor Sir Philip Baddely? – My Lord Delacour told me – you know all people who have nothing else to say tell news quicker than others – my Lord Delacour told me, that he saw Sir Philip part from you this morning in a terrible bad humour. – Come, whilst you tell your story, help me to string these pearls; that will save you from the necessity of looking at me, and will conceal your blushes. – You need not be afraid of betraying Sir Philip's secrets; for I could have told you long ago, that he would inevitably propose for you – the fact is nothing new or surprising to me, but I should really like to hear how ridiculous the man made himself."

"And that," said Belinda, "is the only thing which I do not wish to tell your ladyship."

"Lord, my dear, surely it is no secret that Sir Philip Baddely is ridiculous – but you are so good natured that I can't be out of humour with you. – If you won't gratify my curiosity, will you gratify my taste, and sing for me once more that charming song which none but you *can* sing to please me – I must learn it from you absolutely."

Just as Belinda was beginning to sing, Marriott's macaw began to scream, so that Lady Delacour could not hear any thing else.

"O, that odious macaw!" cried her ladyship, "I can endure it no longer" – and she rang her bell violently – "It kept me from sleeping all last night – Marriott must give up this bird. – Marriott, I cannot endure that macaw – you must part with it for my sake Marriott. – It cost you four guineas, I am sure I would give five with the greatest pleasure to get rid of it, for it is the torment of my life."

"Dear my lady! I can assure you it is only because they will not shut the doors after them below as I desire – I am certain Mr Champfort never shut a door after him in his life, nor never will if he was to live to the days of Methusalon."

"That is very little satisfaction to me, Marriott," said Lady Delacour.

"And indeed, my lady, it is very little satisfaction to me, to hear my macaw abused as it is every day of my life, for Mr Champfort's fault."

"But it cannot be Champfort's fault that I have ears."

"But if the doors were shut, my lady, you wouldn't or couldn't hear – as I'll prove immediately," said Marriott, and she ran directly and shut, according to her own account, "eleven doors which were stark staring wide open." – "Now, my lady, you can't hear a single syllable of the macaw."

"No, but one of the eleven doors will open presently," said Lady Delacour – "you will observe it is always more than ten to one against me."

A door opened, and the macaw was heard to scream.

"The macaw must go, Marriott, that is certain," said her ladyship – firmly –

"Then *I* must go, my lady," said Marriott – angrily – "that is certain – for to part with my macaw is a thing I cannot do to please *any* body." – Her eyes turned with indignation upon Belinda – from association merely; because the last time that she had been angry about her macaw, she had also been angry with Miss Portman, whom she imagined to be the secret enemy of her favourite.

"To stay another week in the house, after my macaw's discarded in disgrace, is a thing nothing shall prevail upon me to do." – She flung out of the room in a fury.

"Good Heavens! am I reduced to this?" said Lady Delacour – "she thinks that she has me in her power – No – I can die without her – I have but a short time to live, I will not live a slave – let the woman betray me if she will – follow her this moment, my dear – generous friend! – tell her never to come into this room again – take this pocketbook – pay her whatever is due to her in the first place, and give her fifty guineas – observe! – not as a bribe, but as a reward."

It was a delicate and difficult commission – Belinda found Marriott at first incapable of listening to reason – "I am sure there is nobody in the world, that would treat me and my macaw in this manner, except my lady!" cried she, "and some body must have set her against me, for it is not natural to her – but since she can't bear me about her any longer, 'tis time I should be gone."

"The only thing of which Lady Delacour complained, was the noise of this macaw," said Belinda; "it was a pretty bird – how long have you had it?"

"Scarcely a month," said Marriott, sobbing.

"And how long have you lived with your lady?"

"Six years! – And to part with her after all! – "

"And for the sake of a macaw! And at a time when your lady is so much in want of you, Marriott! – You know she cannot live long, and she has much to suffer before she dies, and if you leave her, and if in a fit of passion you betray the confidence she has placed in you, you will reproach yourself for it ever afterward. – This bird – no, nor all the birds in the world, will not be able to console you – for you are of an affectionate disposition, I know, and sincerely attached to your poor lady."

"That I am! – and to betray her! – O, Miss Portman, I would sooner cut off my hand than do it. – And I have been tried more than my lady knows of, or you either (for Mr Champfort, who is the greatest mischief-maker in the world, and is the cause, by not shutting the door, of all this dilemma – for now, ma'am, I'm convinced, by the tenderness of your speaking, that you are not the enemy to me I supposed – and I beg your pardon) but I was going to say that Mr Champfort, who saw the *frecas* between my lord and me, about the key and the door, the night of my lady's accident, has whispered it about at Lady Singleton's, and every where – Mrs Luttridge's maid, ma'am, who is my cousin, has pestered me with so many questions and offers, from Mrs Luttridge and Mrs Freke, of any money, if I would only tell who was in the boudoir – and I have always answered, no body – and I defy them to get any thing out of me. – Betray my lady! I'd sooner cut my tongue out this minute – can she have such a base opinion of me, or can you, ma'am?"

"No, indeed, I am convinced that you are incapable of betraying her, Marriott, but in all probability after you have left her – "

"If my lady would let me keep my macaw," interrupted Marriott, "I should never think of leaving her."

"The macaw she will not suffer to remain in the house – and is it reasonable that she should? – it deprives her of sleep – it kept her awake three hours this morning."

Marriott was beginning the history of Champfort and the doors again, but Miss Portman stopped her by saying –

"All this is past now. – How much is due to you, Mrs Marriott? Lady Delacour has commissioned me to pay you every thing that is due to you."

"Due to me! – Lord bless me, ma'am – am I to go?"

"Certainly – it was your own desire – it is consequently your lady's – she is perfectly sensible of your attachment to her, and of your services, but she cannot suffer herself to be treated with disrespect – here is a fifty guinea note, which she gives you as a reward for your past fidelity – not as a bribe to secure your future secrecy. – You are at liberty, she desires me to say, to tell her secret to the whole world, if you choose to do so."

"O, Miss Portman, take my macaw – do what you will with it – only make my peace with my lady," cried Marriott, clasping her hands in an agony of grief – "here are the fifty guineas, ma'am, don't leave it with me – I will never be disrespectful again – take my macaw and all! – No, I'll carry it myself to my lady."

Lady Delacour was surprised by the sudden entrance of Marriott, and her macaw; the chain which held the bird Marriott put into her ladyship's hand without being able to say any thing more than – "Do what you please, my lady, with it – and with me."

Pacified by this submission, Lady Delacour granted Marriott's pardon, and she most sincerely rejoiced at this reconciliation.

The next day Belinda asked the dowager Lady Boucher, who was going to a bird fancier's, to take her with her, in hopes that she might be able to meet with some bird more musical than a macaw, to console Marriott for the loss of her screaming favourite. – Lady Delacour commissioned Miss Portman to go to any price she pleased. – "If I were able, I would accompany you myself, my dear, for poor Marriott's sake, though I would almost as soon go to the Augean stable."

There was a bird fancier in High-Holborn, who had bought several of the hundred and eighty beautiful birds, which, as the newspapers of the day advertised, had been "collected after great labour and expense, by Mons. Marten, and Co. for the Republican Museum at Paris; and lately landed out of the French brig Urselle, taken on her voyage from Cayenne to Brest, by his Majesty's ship Unicorn."

When Lady Boucher and Belinda arrived at this bird fancier's, they were long in doubt to which of the feathered beauties they should give the preference. Whilst the dowager was descanting upon their various perfections, a lady and three children came in; she immediately attracted Belinda's attention, by her likeness to Clarence Hervey's decription of Lady Anne Percival. – It was Lady Anne, as Lady Boucher, who was slightly acquainted with her, informed Belinda in a whisper.

The children were soon eagerly engaged looking at the birds.

"Miss Portman," said Lady Boucher, "as Lady Delacour is so far from well, and wishes to have a bird that will not make any noise in the house, suppose you were to buy for Mrs Marriott this beautiful pair of green paroquets – or stay – a goldfinch is not very noisy, and here is one that can play a thousand pretty tricks. – Pray sir, make it draw up water in its little bucket for us?"

"O! mamma," said one of the little boys, "this is the very thing that is mentioned in Bewick's History of Birds. Pray look at this goldfinch, Helena – now it is drawing up its little bucket – but where is Helena? – here's room for you, Helena."

Whilst the little boys were looking at the goldfinch, Belinda felt somebody touch her gently. – It was Helena Delacour.

"Can I speak a few words to you?" said Helena.

Belinda walked to the farthest end of the shop with her.

"Is my mamma better?" said she, in a timid tone, "I have some gold fish, which you know cannot make the least noise; may I send them to her? – I heard that lady call you Miss Portman; I believe you are the lady who wrote such a kind postscript to me in mamma's last letter – that is the reason I speak so freely to you now. – Perhaps you would write to tell me, if mamma will see me; and Lady Anne Percival would take me at any time, I am sure – but she goes to Oakly-park in a few days – I wish I might be with mamma, whilst she is ill, I would not make the least noise. – But don't ask her if you think it will be troublesome – only let me send the gold fish."

Belinda was touched by the manner in which this affectionate little girl spoke to her. She assured her that she would say all she wished to her mother, and she begged Helena to send the gold fish whenever she pleased.

"Then," said Helena, "I will send them as soon as I go *home* – as soon as I go back to Lady Anne Percival's, I mean."

Belinda, when she had finished speaking to Helena, heard the man, who was showing the birds, lament that he had not a blue macaw, which Lady Anne Percival was commissioned to procure for Mrs Margaret Delacour.

"Red macaws, my lady, I have in abundance; but unfortunately a blue macaw I really have not, at present; nor have I been able to get one, though I have inquired amongst all the bird fanciers in town; and I went to the auction at Haydon square, on purpose, but could not get one."

Belinda requested Lady Boucher would tell her servants to bring in the cage that contained Marriott's blue macaw; and as soon as it was brought, she gave it to Helena, and begged that she would carry it to her aunt Delacour.

"Lord, my dear Miss Portman," said Lady Boucher, drawing her aside, "I am afraid you will get yourself into a scrape, for Lady Delacour is not upon speaking terms with this Mrs Margaret Delacour; she cannot endure her; you know she is my Lord Delacour's aunt."

Belinda persisted in sending the macaw, for she was in hopes that these terrible family quarrels might be made up, if either party would condescend to show any disposition to oblige the other.

Lady Anne Percival understood Miss Portman's civility as it was meant.

"This is a bird of good omen," said she, "it augurs family peace."

"I wish you would do me the favour, Lady Boucher, to introduce me to Miss Portman," continued Lady Anne.

"The very thing I wished!" cried Helena.

A few minutes conversation passed afterward upon different subjects, and Lady Anne Percival and Belinda parted with a mutual desire to see more of each other.

VOLUME II

CHAPTER XIII

Sortes Virgilianæ

When Belinda got home, Lady Delacour was busy in the library, looking over a collection of French plays with the *ci-devant**
Comte de N — ; a gentleman who possessed such singular talents for reading dramatic compositions, that many people declared that they would rather hear him read a play, than see it performed at the theatre. Even those who were not judges of his merit, and who had little taste for literature, crowded to hear him because it was the fashion. — Lady Delacour engaged him for a reading party at her house, and he was consulting with her what play would be most amusing to his audience. — "My dear Belinda! I am glad you are come to give us your opinion," said her ladyship, "no one has a better taste: but first I should ask you what you have done at your bird fancier's; I hope you have brought home some *horned cock*,[1] or some *monstrously* beautiful creature for Marriott. If it has not a voice like the macaw I shall be satisfied; but even if it be the bird of paradise, I question whether Marriott will like it as well as its screaming predecessor."

"I am sure she will like what is coming for her," said Belinda, "and so will your ladyship; but do not let me interrupt you and Monsieur le Comte." And, as she spoke, she took up a volume of plays which lay upon the table.

"Nanine, or La Prude? which shall we have?" said Lady Delacour: "or what do you think of L'Ecossaise?"

"The scene of L'Ecossaise is laid in London," said Belinda; "I should think with an English audience it would therefore be popular."

"Yes! so it will," said Lady Delacour: "then let it be L'Ecoissaise. M. le Comte I am sure will do justice to the character of *Friport* the Englishman, 'qui sait donner, mais qui ne sait pas vivre.'* My dear, I forgot to tell you that Clarence Hervey has been here: it is a pity you did not come a little sooner, you would

1. See Adventures of a Guinea, vol. I, chap 16.*

have heard a charming scene of the School for Scandal read by him. — M. le Comte was quite delighted — but Clarence was in a great hurry, he would only give us one scene, he was going to Mr Percival's on business. — I am sure what I told you the other day is true: — but, however, he has promised to come back to dine with me — M. le Comte, you will dine with us, I hope?"

The count was extremely sorry that it was impossible — he was engaged. — Belinda suddenly recollected that it was time to dress for dinner; but just as the count took his leave, and as she was going up stairs, a footman met her, and told her that Mr Hervey was in the drawing-room, and wished to speak to her. Many conjectures were formed in Belinda's mind as she passed on to the drawing-room; but the moment that she opened the door, she knew the nature of Mr Hervey's business, for she saw the glass globe containing Helena Delacour's gold fishes standing on the table beside him. "I have been commissioned to present these to you for Lady Delacour," said Mr Hervey; "and I have seldom received a commission that has given me so much pleasure — I perceive that Miss Portman is indeed a real friend to Lady Delacour — How happy she is to have such a friend!"

After a pause Mr Hervey went on speaking of Lady Delacour, and of his earnest desire to see her as happy in domestic life as she *appeared* to be in public. He frankly confessed, that when he was first acquainted with her ladyship, he had looked upon her merely as a dissipated woman of fashion, and he had considered only his own amusement in cultivating her society — "But," continued he, "of late I have formed a different opinion of her character; and I think, from what I have observed, that Miss Portman's ideas on this subject agree with mine. I had laid a plan for bringing her ladyship acquainted with Lady Anne Percival, who appears to me one of the most amiable and one of the happiest of women. Oakly-park is but a few miles from Harrowgate — But I am disappointed in this scheme; Lady Delacour has changed her mind, she says, and will not go there. Lady Anne, however, has just told me, that, though it is July, and though she loves the country, she will most willingly stay in town a month longer, as she thinks that, with your assistance, there is some probability of her effecting a reconciliation between Lady Delacour and her husband's relations, with some of whom Lady Anne is intimately acquainted. To begin with my friend Mrs Margaret Delacour: the macaw was most graciously received, and I flatter myself that I have prepared Mrs Delacour to think somewhat more favorably of her niece than she was wont to do. All now depends upon Lady Delacour's conduct towards her daughter – If she continues to treat her with neglect, I shall be convinced that I have been mistaken in her character."

Belinda was much pleased by the openness and the unaffected good nature with which Clarence Hervey spoke, and she certainly was not sorry to hear from his own lips a distinct explanation of his views and sentiments. She assured him that no effort that she could make with propriety should be wanting, to effect the desirable reconciliation between her ladyship and her family; as she perfectly agreed with him in thinking, that Lady Delacour's character had been generally misunderstood by the world.

"Yes," said Mr Hervey, "her connexion with that Mrs Freke hurt her more in the eyes of the world, than she was aware of. It is tacitly understood by the public, that every lady goes bail for the character of her female friends. If Lady Delacour had been so fortunate, as to meet with such a friend as Miss Portman in her early life, what a different woman she would have been! – She once said some such thing to me herself, and she never appeared to me so amiable as at that moment."

Mr Hervey pronounced these last words in a manner more than usually animated; and whilst he spoke, Belinda stooped to gather a sprig from a myrtle, which stood on the hearth. She perceived that the myrtle, which was planted in a large china vase, was propped up on one side with the broken bits of Sir Philip Baddely's little stick: she took them up, and threw them out of the window. – "Lady Delacour stuck those fragments there this morning," said Clarence, smiling, "as trophies. She told me of Miss Portman's victory over the heart of Sir Philip Baddely; and Miss Portman should certainly have allowed them to remain there, as indisputable evidence in favour of the baronet's taste and judgment."

Clarence Hervey appeared under some embarrassment, and seemed to be restrained by some secret cause from laying open his real feelings: his manner varied continually. – Belinda could not avoid seeing his perplexity – she had recourse again to the gold fishes, and to Helena: upon these subjects they could both speak very fluently. Lady Delacour made her appearance by the time that Clarence had finished repeating the abbé Nollet's experiments, which he had heard from his friend Dr X —.

"Now, Miss Portman, the transmission of sound in water,"

said Clarence —

"Deep in philosophy, I protest!" said Lady Delacour, as she came in: "What is this about the transmission of sound in water? – Ha! whence come these pretty gold fishes?"

"These gold fishes," said Belinda, "are come to console Marriott for the loss of her macaw."

"Thank you, my dear Belinda! for these mute comforters," said her ladyship – "The very best things you could have chosen!"

"I have not the merit of the choice," said Belinda, "but I am heartily glad that you approve of it."

"Pretty creatures!" said Lady Delacour: "no fish were ever so pretty since the days of the prince of the Black Islands in the Arabian Tales. And am I obliged to you, Clarence, for these subjects?"

"No; I have only had the honour of bringing them to your ladyship from — "

"From whom? – Amongst all my numerous acquaintance, have I one in the world who cares a gold fish about me? – Stay – don't tell me, let me guess — Lady Newland? — No. You shake your heads – I guessed her ladyship merely because I know she wants to bribe me some way or other to go to one of her stupid entertainments; she wants to pick out of me taste enough to spend a fortune. But, you say it was not Lady Newland? – Mrs Hunt, then, perhaps; for she has two daughters whom she wants to ask to my concerts? – It was not Mrs Hunt? – Well, then, it was Mrs Masterson; for she has a mind to go with me to Harrowgate, where, by the by, I shall not go – so I won't cheat her out of her gold fishes – It was Mrs Masterson, ay?"

"No. But these little gold fishes came from a person, who would be very glad to go with you to Harrowgate," said Clarence Hervey – "or who would be very glad to stay with you in town," said Belinda – "from a person who wants nothing from you but – your love."

"Male or female?" said Lady Delacour.

"Female."

"Female? I have not a female friend in the world but yourself, my dear Belinda! nor do I know another female in the world, whose love I should think about for half an instant. But pray tell me the name of this unknown friend of mine, who wants nothing from me but love?"

"Excuse me," said Belinda; "I cannot tell her name, unless you will promise to see her."

"You have really made me impatient to see her," said Lady Delacour; "but I am not able to go out, you know, yet; and with a new acquaintance one must go through the ceremony of a morning visit &c. – Now, *en conscience*,* is it worth while?"

"Very well worth while," cried Belinda and Clarence Hervey eagerly.

"Ah pardi!" as M. le Comte exclaims continually – "Ah pardi! You are both wonderfully interested in this business. – It is some sister, niece, or cousin, of Lady Anne Percival's – or – No; Belinda looks as if I were wrong. – Then, perhaps, it is Lady Anne herself? – Well, take me where you please, my dear Belinda! and introduce me where you please; I depend on your taste and judgment in all things; but I really am not yet able to pay morning visits."

"The ceremony of a morning visit is quite unnecessary here," said Belinda: "I will introduce the unknown friend to you to morrow, if you will let me invite her to your reading party."

"With pleasure. She is some charming émigrée of Clarence Hervey's acquaintance. But where did you meet with her this morning? – You have both of you conspired to puzzle me. – Take it upon yourselves, then, if this new acquaintance should not, as Ninon de l'Enclos* used to say, *quit cost*. – If she be half as agreeable and *graceful*, Clarence, as Madame la Comtesse de Pomenars, I should not think her acquaintance too dearly purchased by a dozen morning visits."

Here the conversation was interrupted by a thundering knock at the door.

"Whose carriage is it?" said Lady Delacour – "O! Lady Newland's ostentatious livery; and here is her ladyship getting out of her carriage as awkwardly, as if she had never been in one before. – Overdressed like a true city dame! – Pray, Clarence, look at her, entangled in her bale of gold muslin, and conscious of her bulse of diamonds! – 'Worth, if I'm worth a farthing, five hundred thousand pounds Bank currency!' she says, or seems to say, whenever she comes into a room. – Now let us see her entrée.

"But, my dear!" cried Lady Delacour, starting at the sight of Belinda, who was still in her morning dress – "Absolutely below par! – Make your escape to Marriott, I conjure you; by all your fears of the contempt of a lady, who will at the first look estimate you, *au juste*,* to a farthing a yard."

As she left the room, Belinda heard Clarence Hervey repeat to Lady Delacour –

"Give me a look, give me a face,
"That makes simplicity a grace;
"Robes loosely flowing, hair as free — "

he paused — but Belinda recollected the remainder of the stanza —

"Such sweet neglect more taketh me
"Than all th' adulteries of art,
"That strike mine eyes, but not mine heart."

It was observed, that Miss Portman dressed herself this day with the most perfect simplicity.

Lady Delacour's curiosity was raised by the description which Belinda and Clarence Hervey had given of the new acquaintance who sent her the gold fishes, and who wanted nothing from her but love.

Miss Portman told her, that the *unknown* would probably come half an hour earlier to the reading party than any of the rest of the company. Her ladyship was alone in the library, when Lady Anne Percival brought Helena, in consequence of a note from Belinda.

Miss Portman ran down stairs to the hall to receive her: the little girl took her hand in silence. — "Your mother was much pleased with the pretty gold fishes," said Belinda, "and she will be still more pleased, when she knows that they came from you: — she does not know *that* yet."

"I hope she is better to day? I will not make the least noise," whispered Helena, as she went up stairs on tiptoe.

"You need not be afraid to make a noise — you need not walk on tiptoe, nor shut the doors softly; for Lady Delacour seems to like all noises except the screaming of the macaw. — This way, my dear."

"O, I forgot — it is so long since! — Is mamma up and dressed?"

"Yes. She has had concerts and balls since her illness. — You will hear a play read to night," said Belinda, "by that French gentleman whom Lady Anne Percival mentioned to me yesterday."

"But is there a great deal of company, then, with mamma?"

"Nobody is with her now: so come into the library with me," said Belinda. — "Lady Delacour, here is the young lady who sent you the gold fishes."

"Helena!" cried Lady Delacour.

"You must, I am sure, acknowledge that Mr Hervey was in the right, when he said that the lady was a striking resemblance of your ladyship."

"Mr Hervey knows how to flatter. I never had that ingenuous countenance, even in my best days – But certainly the air of her head is like mine – and her hands and arms – But why do you tremble, Helena? Is there any thing so very terrible in the looks of your mother?"

"No, only — "

"Only what, my dear?"

"Only – I was afraid – you might not like me."

"Who has filled your little foolish head with these vain fears? – Come, simpleton, kiss me – and tell me how comes it that you are not at Oakly-hall; – or – what's the name of the place? – Oakly-park?"

"Lady Anne Percival would not take me out of town, she said, whilst you were ill; because she thought that you might wish – I mean she thought that I should like, to see you – if you pleased."

"Lady Anne is very good – very obliging – very considerate."

"She is *very* good natured," said Helena.

"You love this Lady Anne Percival, I perceive."

"O yes, that I do. She has been so kind to me! I love her as if she were — "

"As if she *were* – What? – Finish your sentence."

"My mother," – said Helena, in a low voice, and she blushed.

"You love her as well as if she were your mother," – repeated Lady Delacour: "that is intelligible: speak intelligibly whatever you say, and never leave a sentence unfinished."

"No, ma'am."

"Nothing can be more ill-bred, nor more absurd; for it shows that you have the wish without the power to conceal your sentiments. – Pray, my dear!" continued Lady Delacour, "go to Oakly-park immediately – all further ceremony towards me may be spared."

"Ceremony, mamma!" said the little girl, and the tears came into her eyes – Belinda sighed; and for some moments there was a dead silence.

"I mean only to say, Miss Portman," resumed Lady Delacour, "that I hate ceremony: but I know that there are people in the world who love it, who think all virtue, and all affection, depend on ceremony – who are

'Content to dwell in *decencies* for ever.'

"I shall not dispute their merits. Verily, they have their reward in the good opinion and good word of all little minds; that is to say, of above half the world. I envy them not their hard-earned fame. Let ceremony curtsy to ceremony with Chinese decorum; but, when ceremony expects to be paid with affection, I beg to be excused."

"Ceremony sets no value upon affection, and therefore would not desire to be paid with it," said Belinda.

"Never yet," continued Lady Delacour, pursuing the train of her own thoughts without attending to Belinda, – "never yet was any thing like real affection won by any of these ceremonious people."

"Never," said Miss Portman, looking at Helena; who, having quickness enough to perceive, that her mother aimed this *tirade* against ceremony at Lady Anne Percival, sat in the most painful embarrassment, her eyes cast down, and her face and neck colouring all over. – "Never yet," said Miss Portman, "did a mere ceremonious person win any thing like real affection; especially from children, who are often excellent, because unprejudiced, judges of character."

"We are all apt to think, that an opinion that differs from our own is a prejudice," said Lady Delacour – "What is to decide?"

"Facts, I should think," said Belinda.

"But it is so difficult to get at facts, even about the merest trifles," said Lady Delacour. – "Actions we see, but their causes we seldom see – An aphorism worthy of Confucius himself – Now to apply: – Pray, my dear Helena! how came you by the pretty gold fishes, that you were so good as to send to me yesterday?"

"Lady Anne Percival gave them to me, ma'am."

"And how came her ladyship to give them to you, ma'am?"

"She gave them to me," said Helena hesitating.

"You need not blush, nor repeat to me that she gave them to you; that I have heard already – that is the fact – now for the cause: unless it be a secret. – If it be a secret, which you have been desired to keep, you are quite right to keep it. – I make no doubt of it's being necessary, according to some systems of education, that children should be taught to keep secrets; and I am convinced (for Lady Anne Percival is, I have heard, a perfect judge of propriety) that it is peculiarly proper that a daughter should know how to keep secrets from her mother: – therefore, my dear! you need not trouble yourself to blush or hesitate any more – I shall ask no farther questions. – I was not aware, that there was any secret in the case."

"There is no secret in the world in the case, mamma," said Helena; "I only hesitated because — "

"You hesitated *only* because, I suppose, you mean. – I presume Lady Anne Percival will have no objection to your speaking good English?"

"I hesitated only because I was afraid it would not be right to praise myself. Lady Anne Percival one day asked us all – "

"Us all?"

"I mean Charles, and Edward, and me, to give her an account of some experiments on the hearing of fishes, which Dr X — had told to us; she promised to give the gold fishes, of which we were all very fond, to whichever of us should give the best account of them – Lady Anne gave the fishes to me."

"And is this all the secret? – So, it was real modesty made her hesitate, Belinda? I beg your pardon, my dear – and Lady Anne's – You see how candid I am, Belinda. But one question more, Helena: Who put it into your head to send me your gold fishes?"

"Nobody, mamma; no one put it into my head – But I was at the bird fancier's yesterday, when Miss Portman was trying to get some bird for Mrs Marriott, that could not make any noise to disturb you: so I thought my fishes would be the nicest things for you in the world; because they cannot make the least noise, and they are as pretty as any birds in the world – prettier, I think – and I hope Mrs Marriott thinks so too."

"I don't know what Marriott thinks about the matter, but I can tell you what I think," said Lady Delacour, "that you are one of the sweetest little girls in the world, and that you would make me love you if I had a heart of stone – which I have not, whatever some people may think – Kiss me, my child!"

The little girl sprang forwards, and threw her arms round her mother, exclaiming – "Oh, mamma! are you in earnest?" and she pressed close to her mother's bosom, clasping her with all her force.

Lady Delacour screamed, and pushed her daughter away.

"She is not angry with you, my love!" said Belinda, "she is in sudden and violent pain – Don't be alarmed – she will be better soon. No – don't ring the bell, but try whether you can open these window-shutters, and throw up the sash."

Whilst Belinda was supporting Lady Delacour, and whilst Helena was trying to open the window, a servant came into the room, to announce the Comte de N — .

"Show him into the drawing-room," said Belinda. – Lady Delacour, though in great pain, rose and retired to her dressing-room. – "I shall not be able to go down to these people yet," said she; "you must make my excuses to the count and every body; and tell poor Helena I was not angry, though I pushed her away. Keep her below stairs, I will come as soon I am able – Send Marriott – Do not forget, my dear! to tell Helena I was not angry."

The reading party went on, and Lady Delacour made her appearance as the company were drinking orgeat, between the fourth and fifth act. "Helena, *my dear*!" said she, "will you bring me a glass of orgeat?" – Clarence Hervey looked at Belinda with a congratulatory smile: – "Do not you think," whispered he, "that we shall succeed? Did you see that look of Lady Delacour's?"

Nothing tends more to increase the esteem and affection of two people for each other, than their having one and the same benevolent object. Clarence Hervey and Belinda seemed to know one another's thoughts and feelings this evening, better than they had ever done before during the whole course of their acquaintance.

After the play was over, most of the company went away; only a select party of *beaux esprits* staid to supper; they were standing at the table at which the count had been reading: several volumes of French plays and novels were lying there, and Clarence Hervey, taking up one of them, cried: "Come, let us try our fate by the Sortes Virgilianæ."*

Lady Delacour opened the book, which was a volume of Marmontel's* Tales.

"La femme comme il y en a peu!" exclaimed Hervey.

"Who will ever more have faith in the Sortes Virgilianæ?" said Lady Delacour laughing: but whilst she laughed she went closer to a candle, to read the page which she had opened. Belinda and Clarence Hervey followed her. "Really, it is somewhat singular, Belinda, that I should have opened upon this passage," continued she in a low voice, pointing it out to Miss Portman.

It was a description of the manner in which la femme comme il y en a peu managed a husband, who was excessively afraid of being thought to be governed by his wife. As her ladyship turned over the page, she saw a leaf of myrtle which Belinda, who had been reading the story the preceding day, had put into the book for a mark.

"Whose mark is this? Yours, Belinda, I am sure, by its elegance," said Lady Delacour. "So! this is a concerted plan between you two, I see," continued her ladyship with an air of pique – "you have contrived prettily de me dire des vérités!* One says, 'Let us try our fate by the Sortes Virgilianæ': – the other has dexterously put a mark in the book, to make it open upon a lesson for the naughty child."

Belinda and Mr Hervey assured her, that they had used no such mean arts – that nothing had been concerted between them.

"How came this leaf of myrtle here, then?" said Lady Delacour.

"I was reading that story yesterday, and I left it as my mark."

"I cannot help believing you, because you never yet deceived me, even in the merest trifle: – you are truth itself, Belinda. – Well, you see that *you* were the cause of my drawing such an extraordinary lot; the book would not have opened here but for your mark. My fate, I find, is in your hands: if Lady Delacour is ever to be la femme comme il y en a peu, which is the most *improbable* thing in the world, Miss Portman will be the cause of it."

"Which is the most probable thing in the world," said Clarence Hervey. "This myrtle has a delightful perfume," added he, rubbing the leaf between his fingers.

"But, after all," said Lady Delacour, throwing aside the book, "this heroine of Marmontel's is not la femme comme il y en a peu, – but la femme comme il n'y en a *point*."*

"Mrs Margaret Delacour's carriage, my lady, for Miss Delacour!" – said a footman to her ladyship.

"Helena stays with me to night, – my compliments," – said Lady Delacour. – "How pleased the little gipsy looks!" added she, turning to Helena, who heard the message, "and how handsome she looks when she is pleased! – Do these auburn locks of yours, Helena, curl naturally or artificially?"

"Naturally, mamma."

"Naturally? – So much the better. So did mine at your age."

Some of the company now took notice of the astonishing resemblance between Helena and her mother; and the more Lady Delacour considered her daughter as a part of herself, the more she was inclined to be pleased with her. The glass globe containing the gold fishes was put in the middle of the table at supper; and Clarence Hervey never paid her ladyship such respectful attention in his life, as he did this evening.

The conversation at supper turned upon a magnificent and elegant entertainment which had lately been given by a fashionable duchess, and some of the company spoke in high terms of the beauty and accomplishments of her grace's daughter, who had for the first time appeared in public on that occasion.

"The daughter will eclipse, totally eclipse, the mother," said Lady Delacour. "That total eclipse has been foretold by many knowing people," said Clarence Hervey; "but how can there be an eclipse between two bodies which never cross one another? — And that I understand to be the case between the duchess and her daughter."

This observation seemed to make a great impression upon Lady Delacour. Clarence Hervey went on, and with much eloquence expressed his admiration of the mother, who had stopped short in the career of dissipation to employ her inimitable talents in the education of her children; who had absolutely brought virtue into fashion by the irresistible powers of wit and beauty.

"Really, Clarence," said Lady Delacour, rising from table, "vous parlez avec beaucoup d'onction.* I advise you to write a sentimental comedy, a comédie larmoyante,* or a drama on the German model, and call it The School for Mothers, and beg her grace of — to sit for your heroine."

"Your ladyship, surely, would not be so cruel as to send a faithful servant a begging for a heroine?" said Clarence Hervey.

Lady Delacour smiled at first at the compliment, but a few minutes afterward she sighed bitterly. "It is too late for me to think of being a heroine," said she.

"Too late?" cried Hervey, following her eagerly as she walked out of the supper-room — "Too late? — Her grace of — is *some* years older than your ladyship."

"Well, — I did not mean to say *too late*," said Lady Delacour: "but let us go on to something else — Why were not you at the fête champêtre the other day? and where were you all this

morning? – And pray can you tell me when your friend Dr X —
returns to town?"

"Mr Horton is getting better," said Clarence, "and I hope that
we shall have Dr X — soon amongst us again. I hear that he is to
be in town in the course of a few days."

"Did he inquire for me? – Did he ask how I did?"

"No. I fancy he took it for granted that your ladyship was quite
well; for I told him you were getting better every day, and that you
were in charming spirits."

"Yes," said Lady Delacour, "but I wear myself out with these
charming spirits. I am very nervous still, I assure you, and sitting
up late is not good for me. So I shall wish you and all the world a
good night – You see I am absolutely a reformed rake."

CHAPTER XIV

The Exhibition

Two hours after her ladyship had retired to her own room, as Belinda was passing by the door to go to her own bedchamber, she heard Lady Delacour call to her.

"Belinda, you need not walk so softly, I am not asleep. Come in, will you, my dear? I have something of consequence to say to you. Is all the world gone?"

"Yes; and I thought that you were asleep. I hope you are not in pain?"

"Not just at present, thank you; but that was a terrible embrace of poor little Helena's. You see to what accidents I should be continually exposed, if I had that child always about me; and yet she seems of such an affectionate disposition, that I wish it were possible to keep her at home. Sit down by my bedside, my dear Belinda! and I will tell you what I have resolved upon."

Belinda sat down, and Lady Delacour was silent for some minutes.

"I am resolved," said she, "to make one desperate effort for my life. New plans, new hopes of happiness, have opened to my imagination, and, with my hopes of being happy, my courage rises. I am determined to submit to the dreadful operation, which alone can radically cure me; – you understand me. But it must be kept a profound secret. I know of a person who could be got to perform this operation with the utmost secrecy."

"But surely," said Belinda, "safety must be your first object?"

"No; secrecy is my first object. Nay, do not reason with me; it is a subject on which I cannot, will not, reason. Hear me – I will keep Helena with me for a few days; she was surprised by what passed in the library this evening; I must remove all suspicion from her mind."

"There is no suspicion in her mind," said Belinda.

"So much the better; she shall go immediately to school, or to Oakly-park. – I will then stand my trial for life or death; and if I live, I will be, what I have never yet been, a mother to Helena. If I die, you and Clarence Hervey will take care of her; – I know you will. That young man is worthy of you, Belinda. If I die, I charge you to tell him that I knew his value; that I had a soul capable of being touched by the eloquence of virtue." Lady Delacour, after a pause, said, in an altered tone,

"Do you think, Belinda, that I shall survive this operation?"

"The opinion of Dr X — ," said Belinda, "must certainly be more satisfactory than mine;" and she repeated what the doctor had left with her in writing upon this subject.

"So it is the doctor's opinion that I shall inevitably destroy myself, if, from a vain hope of secrecy, I put myself into ignorant hands? These are his own words, are they? – Very strong – and he is prudent to leave that opinion in writing. Now, whatever happens, he cannot be answerable for 'measures which he does not guide'. Nor you either, my dear! – you have all done what is prudent and proper. – But I must beg you to recollect that I am neither a child nor a fool; that I am come to years of discretion, and that I am not now in the delirium of a fever; consequently there can be no pretence for *managing* me. In this particular I must insist upon managing myself. I have confidence in the skill of the person whom I shall employ. Dr X — , very likely, would have none, because the man may not have a diploma for killing or curing in form. That is nothing to the purpose. It is I that am to undergo the operation. It is *my* health, *my* life, that is risked; and if I am satisfied, that is enough. – Secrecy, as I told you before, is my first object."

"And cannot you," said Belinda, "depend with more security upon the honour of a surgeon who is at the head of his profession, and who has a high reputation at stake, than upon a vague promise of secrecy from some obscure quack, who has no reputation to lose?"

"No," said Lady Delacour: "I tell you, my dear! that I cannot depend upon any of these 'honourable men'. I have taken means to satisfy myself on this point; their honour and foolish delicacy would not allow them to perform such an operation for a wife, without the knowledge, privity, consent, &c. &c. &c. of her husband. Now Lord Delacour's knowing the thing is quite out of the question."

"Why, my dear Lady Delacour! why?" said Belinda with great earnestness. "Surely a husband has the strongest claim to be consulted upon such an occasion! Let me entreat you to tell Lord

Delacour your intentions, and then all will be right. Say *Yes*; my dear friend! let me previal upon you," said Belinda, taking her ladyship's hand, and pressing it between both of hers with the most affectionate eagerness.

Lady Delacour made no answer, but fixed her eyes upon Belinda's.

"Lord Delacour," continued Miss Portman, "deserves this from you, by the great interest, the increasing interest, that he has shown of late about your health: his kindness and handsome conduct the other morning certainly pleased you; and you have now an opportunity of showing that confidence in him, which his affection and constant attachment to you merit."

"I trouble myself very little about the constancy of Lord Delacour's attachment to me," said her ladyship, coldly withdrawing her hand from Belinda. "Whether his lordship's affection for me have of late increased, or diminished, is an object of perfect indifference to me. But if I were inclined to reward him for his late attentions, I should apprehend that we might hit upon some better reward than you have pitched upon. Unless you imagine that Lord Delacour has a peculiar taste for surgical operations, I cannot conceive how his becoming my confidant upon this occasion could have an immediate tendency to increase his affection for me – about which affection I don't care a straw; as you, better than any one else, must know. For I am no hypocrite; I have laid open my whole heart to you, Belinda."

"For that very reason," said Miss Portman, "I am eager to use the influence which I know I have in your heart, for your happiness. I am convinced that it will be absolutely impossible, that you should carry on this scheme in the house with your husband, without its being discovered. If he *discover* it by accident, he will feel very differently from what he would do, if he were trusted by you."

"For Heaven's sake, my dear!" cried Lady Delacour, "let me hear no more about Lord Delacour's feelings."

"But allow me then to speak of my own," said Belinda; "I cannot be concerned in this affair, if it is to be concealed from your husband."

"You will do about that as you think proper," said Lady Delacour haughtily. "Your sense of propriety towards Lord Delacour is, I observe, stronger than your sense of honour towards me. But I make no doubt that you act upon principle –

just principle. You promised never to abandon me; – but when I most want your assistance you refuse it, from consideration for Lord Delacour. A scruple of delicacy absolves a person of nice feelings, I find, from a positive promise! – A new and convenient code of morality!"

Belinda, though much hurt by the sarcastic tone in which her ladyship spoke, mildly answered, "That the promise she had made to stay with her ladyship during her illness was very different from an engagement to assist her in such a scheme as she had now in contemplation."

Lady Delacour suddenly drew the curtain between her and Belinda, saying, "Well, my dear! at all events I am glad to hear you don't forget your promise of *staying* with me. You are, perhaps, prudent to refuse me your assistance – all circumstances considered. Good night! I have kept you up too long. Good night!"

"Good night!" said Belinda, drawing aside the curtain. "You will not be displeased with me, when you reflect coolly."

"The light blinds me," said Lady Delacour; and she turned her face away from Miss Portman, and added, in a drowsy voice, "I will *think of what has been said*, some time or other: but just now I would rather go to sleep, than say or hear any more; for I am more than half asleep already."

Belinda closed the curtains, and left the room. But Lady Delacour, notwithstanding the drowsy tone in which she pronounced these last words, was not in the least inclined to sleep. A passion had taken possession of her mind, which kept her broad awake the remainder of the night, – the passion of jealousy. The extreme eagerness with which Belinda had urged her to consult Lord Delacour, and to trust him with her secret, displeased her; not merely as an opposition to her will and an undue attention to his lordship's feelings, but as "confirmation strong" of a hint which had been dropped by Sir Philip Baddely, but which never till now had appeared to her worthy of a moment's consideration. Sir Philip had observed, that "if a young lady had any hopes of being a viscountess, it was no wonder she thought a baronet beneath her notice." – "Now," thought Lady Delacour, "this is not impossible. In the first place, Belinda Portman is niece to Mrs Stanhope; she may have all her aunt's art, and the still greater art to conceal it under the mask of openness and simplicity: *Volto sciolto, pensieri stretti,* * is the grand maxim of the Stanhope school." The moment Lady Delacour's mind turned to suspicion, her ingenuity rapidly supplied her with circumstances and arguments to confirm and justify her doubts.

"Miss Portman fears that my husband is growing too fond of me: she says, he has been very attentive to me of late. Yes, so he has, and on purpose to disgust him with me, she immediately urges me to tell him that I have a loathsome disease, and that I am about to undergo a horrid operation. How my eyes have been blinded by her artifice! This last stroke was rather too bold, and has opened them effectually, and now I see a thousand things that escaped me before. Even to night, the Sortes Virgilianæ, the myrtle leaf, Miss Portman's mark, left in the book exactly at the place where Marmontel gives a receipt for managing a husband of Lord Delacour's character. Ah, ha! By her own confession, she had been reading this; studying it. Yes, and she has studied it to some purpose; she has made that poor weak lord of mine think her an angel. How he ran on in her praise the other day, when he honoured me with a morning visit! That morning visit, too, was of her suggestion; and the bank notes, as he, like a simpleton, let out in the course of the conversation, had been offered to her first. She, with a delicacy that charmed my short-sighted folly, begged that they might go through my hands. How artfully managed! Mrs Stanhope herself could not have done better. So, she can make Lord Delacour do whatever she pleases; and she condescends to make him behave *prettily* to me, and desires him to bring me peace-offerings of bank notes! She is, in fact, become my banker; mistress of my house, my husband, and myself. Ten days I have been confined to my room. Truly, she has made a good use of her time; and I, fool that I am, have been thanking her for all her disinterested kindness!

"Then her kindness to my daughter! disinterested, too, as I thought! – But, Good Heavens, what an idiot I have been! She looks forward to be the mother-in-law of Helena; she would win the simple child's affections even before my face, and show Lord Delacour what a charming wife and mother she would make! He said some such thing to me, as well as I remember, the other day. Then her extreme prudence! She never coquettes, not she, with any of the young men who come here on purpose to see her. Is this natural? Absolutely unnatural; artifice! artifice! To contrast herself with me in Lord Delacour's opinion, is certainly her object. Even to Clarence Hervey, with whom she was, or pretended to be, smitten, how cold and reserved she is grown of late! And how haughtily she rejected my advice, when I hinted that she was not taking the way to win him! I could not comprehend her; she had no designs on Clarence Hervey, she assured me. Immaculate purity! I believe you.

"Then her refusal of Sir Philip Baddely! – A baronet with fifteen thousand a year to be refused by a girl who has nothing, and merely because he is a fool! How could *I* be such a fool as to believe it? Worthy niece of Mrs Stanhope, I know you now! And now I recollect that extraordinary letter of Mrs Stanhope's, which I snatched out of Miss Portman's hands some months ago, full of blanks, and inuendoes, and references to some letter which Belinda had written about my disputes with my husband! From that moment to this, Miss Portman has never let me see another of her aunt's letters. So I may conclude they are all in the same style; and I make no doubt that she has instructed her niece, all this time, how to proceed. Now I know why she always puts Mrs Stanhope's letters into her pocket the moment she receives them, and never opens them in my presence. And I have been laying open my whole heart, telling my whole history, confessing all my faults and follies, to this girl! And I have told her that I am dying; I have taught her to look forward, with joy and certainty, to the coronet on which she has fixed her heart.

"On my knees I conjured her to stay with me to receive my last breath. Oh, dupe, miserable dupe, that I am! could nothing warn me? In the moment that I discovered the treachery of one friend, I went and prostrated myself to the artifices of another – of another a thousand times more dangerous – ten thousand times more beloved! For what was Harriet Freke in comparison with Belinda Portman? Harriet Freke, even whilst she diverted me most, I half despised. But Belinda! – Oh, Belinda! how entirely have I loved! trusted! admired! adored! respected! revered you!"

Exhausted by the emotions to which she had worked herself up by the force of her powerful imagination, Lady Delacour, after passing several restless hours in bed, fell asleep late in the morning; and when she awaked, Belinda was standing by her bed-side. "What could you be dreaming of?" said Belinda smiling. "You started, and looked at me with such horror, when you opened your eyes, as if I had been your evil genius."

It is not in human nature, thought Lady Delacour, suddenly overcome by the sweet smile and friendly tone of Belinda, – it is not in human nature to be so treacherous; and she stretched out both her arms to Belinda, saying, "You my evil genius? No. My guardian angel, my dearest Belinda! kiss me, and forgive me."

"Forgive you for what?" said Belinda; "I believe you are dreaming still and I am sorry to awaken you; but I am come to tell you a wonderful thing – that Lord Delacour is up, and dressed, and actually in the breakfast room; and that he has been talking to me this half hour – of what do you think? – of Helena. He was quite surprised, he said, to see her grown such a fine girl, and he declares that he no longer regrets that she was not a boy; and he says that he will dine at home to day, on purpose to drink Helena's health in his new burgundy; and, in short, I never saw him in such good spirits, or so agreeable – I always thought he was one of the best natured men I had ever seen. Will not you get up to breakfast? Lord Delacour has asked for you ten times within these five minutes."

"Indeed!" said Lady Delacour, rubbing her eyes. "All this is vastly wonderful; but I wish you had not awakened me so soon."

"Nay, nay," said Belinda, "I know, by the tone of your voice, that you do not mean what you say; I know you will get up, and come down to us directly – so I will send Marriott."

Lady Delacour got up, and went down to breakfast, in much uncertainty what to think of Miss Portman; but ashamed to let her into her mind, and still more afraid that Lord Delacour should suspect her of doing him the honour to be jealous. – Belinda had not the least guess at what was really passing in her ladyship's heart; she implicitly believed her expressions of complete indifference to her lord; and jealousy was the last feeling which Miss Portman would have attributed to Lady Delacour, because she unfortunately was not sufficiently aware that jealousy can exist without love. The idea of Lord Delacour, as an object of attachment; or of a coronet, as an object of ambition; or of her friend's death, as an object of joy, were so foreign to Belinda's innocent mind, that it was scarcely possible she could decipher Lady Delacour's thoughts. Her ladyship affected to be in "remarkably good spirits this morning," declared that she had never felt so well since her illness, ordered her carriage as soon as breakfast was over, and said she would take Helena to Maillardet's, to see the wonders of his little conjurer and his singing bird. "Nothing equal to Maillardet's singing bird has ever been seen or heard of, my dear Helena! since the days of

Aboulcasem's peacock in the Persian Tales. – Since Lady Anne Percival has not shown you these charming things, I must."

"But I hope you won't tire yourself, mamma," said the little girl.

"I am afraid you will," said Belinda. "And you know, my dear!" added Lord Delacour, "that Miss Portman, who is so very obliging and good natured, *could* go just as well with Helena; and, I am sure, *would*, rather than that you should tire yourself, or give yourself any unnecessary trouble."

"Miss Portman is very good," answered Lady Delacour, hastily; "but I think it no unnecessary trouble to give my daughter any pleasure in my power – As to its tiring me, I am neither dead, nor dying, *yet* – For the rest, Miss Portman, who understands what is proper, blushes for you, as you see, my lord, when you propose that she, who is not yet a married woman, should *chaperon* a young lady. It is quite out of rule; and Mrs Stanhope would be shocked if her niece could, or would, do such a thing to oblige any body."

Lord Delacour was too much in the habit of hearing sarcastic, and to him incomprehensible speeches from her ladyship, to take any extraordinary notice of this, – and if Belinda blushed, it was merely from the confusion into which she was thrown by the piercing glance of Lady Delacour's black eyes – a glance, which neither guilt nor innocence could withstand. Belinda imagined, that her ladyship still retained some displeasure from the conversation that had passed the preceding night; and the first time that she was alone with Lady Delacour, she again touched upon the subject, in hopes of softening or convincing her. "At all events, my dear friend!" said she, "you will not, I hope, be offended by the sincerity with which I speak– I *can* have no object but your safety and happiness."

"Sincerity never offends me," was her ladyship's cold answer. And all the time that they were out together, she was unusually ceremonious to Miss Portman; and there would have been but little conversation, if Helena had not been present, to whom her mother talked with fluent gaiety. When they got to Spring-gardens, Helena exclaimed, "O! there's Lady Anne Percival's carriage, and Charles and Edward with her – They are going to the same place that we are, I dare say, for I heard Charles ask Lady Anne to take him to see Maillardet's little bird – Mr Hervey mentioned it to us, and he said it was a curious piece of machinery."

"I wish you had told me sooner that Lady Anne was likely to be there, I don't wish to meet her so awkwardly – I am not well enough yet, indeed, to go to these odious, hot, close places; and, besides, I hate seeing sights."

Helena, with much good humour, said, that she would rather give up seeing the sight than be troublesome to her mother. – When they came to Maillardet's, however, Lady Delacour saw Mrs — getting out of her carriage, and to her she consigned Helena and Miss Portman, saying, that she would take a turn or two in the park, and call for them in half an hour. When the half hour was over, and her ladyship returned, she carelessly asked, as they were going home, whether they had been pleased with their visit to the bird and the conjurer. "O, yes, mamma!" said Helena: "and do you know, that one of the questions that the people ask the conjurer is, "*Where is the happiest family to be found?*" And Charles and Edward immediately said, if he is a good conjurer, if he tells truth, he'll answer, '*At Oakly-park.*'"

"Miss Portman, had you any conversation with Lady Anne Percival?" said Lady Delacour, coldly.

"A great deal," said Belinda, "and such as I am sure you would have liked: and so far from being a ceremonious person, I think I never saw any body who had such easy engaging manners."

"And did she ask you, Helena, again to go with her to that place where the happiest family in the world is to be found?"

"Oakly-park? – No, mamma; she said that she was very glad that I was with you; but she asked Miss Portman to come to see her whenever it was in her power."

"And could Miss Portman withstand such a temptation?"

"You know that I am engaged to your ladyship," said Belinda.

Lady Delacour bowed. "But from what passed last night," said she, "I was afraid that you might repent your engagement to me; and if so, I give up my bond. I should be miserable if I apprehended that any one, but more especially Miss Portman, felt herself a prisoner in my house."

"Dear Lady Delacour! I do not feel myself a prisoner; I have always, till now, felt myself a friend in your house: but we'll talk of this another time. Do not look at me with so much coldness; do not speak to me with so much politeness. I will not let you forget that I am your friend."

"I do not wish to forget it, Belinda," said Lady Delacour, with emotion; "I am not ungrateful, though I may seem capricious – bear with me."

"There now, you look like yourself again, and I am satisfied," cried Belinda. "As to going to Oakly-park, I give you my word I have not the most distant thoughts of it. I stay with you from choice, and not from compulsion, believe me."

"I *do* believe you," said Lady Delacour, and for a moment she was convinced, that Belinda staid with her for her own sake alone; but the next minute she suspected, that Lord Delacour was the secret cause of her refusing to go to Oakly-park. His lordship dined at home this day, and two or three succeeding days, and he was not intoxicated from Monday till Thursday. These circumstances appeared to his lady very extraordinary. In fact, he was pleased and amused with his little daughter, Helena; and whilst she was yet almost a stranger to him, he wished to appear to her in the most agreeable and respectable light possible. One day after dinner Lord Delacour, who was in remarkably good humour, said to her ladyship – "My dear! you know that your new carriage was broken almost to pieces the night when you were overturned. Well, I have had it all set to rights again, and new painted, and it is all complete, except the hammer-cloth,* which must have new fringe. What colour will you have the fringe?"

"What do you say, Miss Portman?" said her ladyship.

"Black and orange would look well, I think," said Belinda, "and would suit the lace of your liveries – would not it?"

"Certainly – Black and orange then," said Lord Delacour, "it shall be."

"If you ask my opinion," said Lady Delacour, "I am for blue and white, to match the cloth of the liveries."

"Blue and white then it shall be," said Lord Delacour.

"Nay, Miss Portman has a better taste than I have; and she says black and orange, my lord."

"Then you'll have it black and orange, will you?" said Lord Delacour.

"Just as you please," said Lady Delacour, and no more passed.

Soon afterward a note came from Lady Anne Percival, with some trifles belonging to Helena, for which her mother had sent. The note was for Belinda – another pressing invitation to Oakly-park – and a very civil message from Mrs Margaret Delacour, and thanks to Lady Delacour for the macaw. Ay, thought Lady Delacour, Miss Portman wants to ingratiate herself in time with all my husband's relations. "Mrs Margaret Delacour should have addressed these thanks to you, Miss Portman, for I had not the grace to think of sending her the macaw." Lord Delacour, who was very fond of his aunt, immediately joined his thanks, and observed, that Miss Portman was always considerate – always obliging – always kind. Then he drank her health in a bumper of burgundy, and insisted upon his little Helena's drinking her health. "I am sure you ought, my dear! for Miss Portman is very good – too good to you, child."

"Very good – not too good, I hope," said Lady Delacour. "Miss Portman, your health."

"And I hope," continued his lordship, after swallowing his bumper, "that my Lady Anne Percival does not mean to inveigle you away from us, Miss Portman. You don't think of leaving us, Miss Portman, I hope? Here's Helena would break her little heart; – I say nothing for my Lady Delacour, because she can say every thing so much better for herself; and I say nothing for myself, because I am the worst man in the world at making speeches, when I really have a thing at heart – as I have your staying with us, Miss Portman."

Belinda assured him, that there was no occasion to press her to do what was perfectly agreeable to her, and said that she had no thoughts of leaving Lady Delacour. Her ladyship, with some embarrassment, expressed herself "extremely obliged, and gratified, and happy". Helena, with artless joy, threw her arms about Belinda, and exclaimed, "I am glad you are not going – for I never liked any body so much, of whom I knew so little."

"The more you know of Miss Portman, the more you will like her, child – at least, I have found it so," said Lord Delacour.

"Clarence Hervey would, I am sure, have given the Pigot diamond, if it were in his gift, for such a smile as you bestowed on Lord Delacour just now," whispered Lady Delacour. – For an instant Belinda was struck with the tone of pique and reproach, in which her ladyship spoke. "Nay, my dear! I did not mean to make you blush so piteously," pursued her ladyship: "I really did not think it a blushing matter – but you know best. Believe me, I spoke without malice; we are so apt to judge from our own feelings – and I could as soon blush about the old man of the mountains as about my Lord Delacour."

"Lord Delacour!" said Belinda, with a look of such unfeigned surprise, that her ladyship instantly changed countenance, and, taking her hand with gaiety, said, "So, my little Belinda! I have caught you – the blush belongs then to Clarence Hervey? Well, any man of common sense would rather have one blush than a thousand smiles, for his share – Now we understand one another. And will you go with me to the exhibition to morrow? I am told there are some charming pictures this year. Helena, who really has a genius for drawing, should see these things; and whilst she *is* with me, I will make her as happy as possible. You see the reformation is beginning – Clarence Hervey and Miss Portman can do wonders. If it be my fate, at last, to be *la bonne mère*, or *la femme comme il y en a peu*, how can I help it? There is no struggling against fate, my dear!"

Whenever Lady Delacour's suspicions of Belinda were suspended, all her affections returned with double force; she wondered at her own folly, she was ashamed that she could have let such ideas enter her mind, and she was beyond measure astonished that any thing relative to Lord Delacour could so far have interested her attention. "Luckily," said she to herself, "he has not the penetration of a blind beetle; and, besides, he has little snug jealousies of his own; so he will never find me out. It would be an excellent thing indeed, if he were to turn my '*master torment*' against myself – it would be a judgment upon me. The manes of poor Lawless would then be appeased. But it is impossible I should ever be a jealous wife: I am only a jealous friend, and I must satisfy myself about Belinda. To be a second time a dupe to the treachery of a friend, would be too much for me – too much for my pride – too much for my heart."

The next day, when they came to the exhibition, Lady Delacour had an opportunity of judging of Belinda's real feelings. As they went up the stairs, they heard the voices of Sir Philip Baddely and Mr Rochfort, who were standing upon the landing-place, leaning over the banisters, and running their little sticks along the iron rails, to try which would make the loudest noise.

"Have you been much pleased with the pictures, gentlemen?" said Lady Delacour, as she passed them.

"O, damme! no; 'tis a cursed bore; – and yet there are some fine pictures; one in particular, – hey, Rochfort? one damned fine picture!" said Sir Philip: and the two gentlemen, laughing significantly, followed Lady Delacour and Belinda into the rooms.

"Ay, there's one picture that's worth all the rest, 'pon honour!" repeated Rochfort; "and we'll leave it to your ladyship's and Miss Portman's taste and judgment to find it out; – Mayn't we, Sir Philip?"

"O, damme! yes," said Sir Philip, "by all means." But he was so impatient to direct her eyes, that he could not keep himself still an instant.

"O, curse it! Rochfort, we'd better tell the ladies at once, else they may be all day looking and looking."

"Nay, Sir Philip, may not I be allowed to guess? Must I be told which is your fine picture? – This is not much in favour of my taste."

"O, damn it! your ladyship has the best taste in the world, every body knows; and so has Miss Portman – and this picture will hit her taste particularly, I'm sure. It is Clarence Hervey's fancy; but this is a dead secret – dead – Clary no more thinks that we know it than the man in the moon."

"Clarence Hervey's fancy! – Then I make no doubt of its being good for something," said Lady Delacour, "if the painter have done justice to his imagination; for Clarence has really a fine imagination."

"O, damme! 'tis not amongst the history pieces," cried Sir Philip: "'Tis a portrait."

"And a history piece, too, 'pon honour!" said Rochfort: – "a family history piece, I take it, 'pon honour! it will turn out," said Rochfort; and both the gentlemen were, or affected to be, thrown into convulsions of laughter, as they repeated the words "family history piece – 'pon honour! family history piece, damme!"

"I'll take my oath as to the portrait's being a devilish good likeness," added Sir Philip; and, as he spoke, he turned to Miss Portman – "Miss Portman has it! damme! Miss Portman has him!"

Belinda hastily withdrew her eyes from the picture at which she was looking. – "A most beautiful creature!" exclaimed Lady Delacour. –

"O, faith! yes – always did Clary the justice to say, he has a damned good taste for beauty." – "But this seems to be a foreign beauty," continued Lady Delacour, "if one may judge by her air, her dress, and the scenery about her – cocoa-trees, plantains – Miss Portman, what think you?"

"I think," said Belinda (but her voice faltered so much that she could hardly speak), "that it is a scene from Paul and Virginia. I think the figure is St Pierre's Virginia."

"Virginia St Pierre! ma'am," cried Mr Rochfort, winking at Sir Philip. "No, no, damme! there you are wrong, Rochfort. Say Hervey's Virginia, and then you have it, damme! or, may be, Virginia Hervey, – who knows?"

"This is a portrait," whispered the baronet to Lady Delacour, "of Clarence's mistress." Whilst her ladyship leant her ear to this whisper, which was sufficiently audible, she fixed a seemingly careless, but most observing, inquisitive eye upon poor Belinda. Her confusion, for she heard the whisper, was excessive.

"She loves Clarence Hervey – she has no thoughts of Lord Delacour and his coronet – I have done her injustice," thought Lady Delacour, and instantly she dispatched Sir Philip out of the room, for a catalogue of the pictures, begged Mr Rochfort to get her something else, and, drawing Miss Portman's arm within hers, she said, in a low voice, "Lean upon me, my dearest Belinda! depend upon it, Clarence will never be such a fool as to marry the girl – Virginia Hervey she will never be!"

"And what will become of her? can Mr Hervey desert her? she looks like innocence itself! and so young, too! Can he leave her for ever to sorrow, and vice, and infamy?" thought Belinda, as she kept her eyes fixed, in silent anguish, upon the picture of Virginia: – No, he cannot do this; if he could, he would be unworthy of me, and I *ought* to think of him no more. No; he will marry her; and I *must* think of him no more."

She turned abruptly away from the picture, and she saw Clarence Hervey standing beside her.

"What do you think of this picture? Is it not beautiful? We are quite enchanted with it; but you do not seem to be struck with it, as we were at the first glance."

"Because," answered Clarence, gaily, "it is not the first glance I have had at that picture – I admired it yesterday, and admire it to day."

"But you are tired of admiring it, I see. Well, we shall not force you to be in raptures with it – shall we Miss Portman? A man may be tired of the most beautiful face in the world, or the most beautiful picture; but really there is so much sweetness, so much innocence, such tender melancholy in this countenance, that, if I were a man, I should inevitably be in love with it, and in love for ever! Such beauty, if it were in nature, would certainly fix the most inconstant man upon earth."

Belinda ventured to take her eyes for an instant from the picture, to see whether Clarence Hervey looked like the most inconstant man upon earth. He was intently gazing upon her; but as soon as she looked up, he suddenly exclaimed, as he turned to the picture –

"A heavenly countenance indeed! – the painter has done justice to the poet."

"Poet!" repeated Lady Delacour: "the man's in the clouds!"

"Pardon me," said Clarence; "does not M. de St Pierre deserve to be called a poet? Though he does not write in rhyme, surely he has a poetical imagination?"

"Certainly," said Belinda; – and from the composure with which Mr Hervey now spoke, she was suddenly inclined to believe, or to hope, that all Sir Philip's story was false. "M. de St Pierre undoubtedly has a great deal of imagination, and deserves to be called a poet."

"Very likely, good people!" said Lady Delacour; "but what has that to do with the present purpose?"

"Nay," cried Clarence, "your ladyship certainly sees that this is St Pierre's Virginia?"

"St Pierre's Virginia! – O, I know who it is, Clarence, as well as you do. I am not quite so blind, or so stupid, as you take me to be." Then recollecting her promise, not to betray Sir Philip's secret, she added, pointing to the landscape of the picture – "These cocoa-trees, this fountain, and the words *Fontaine de Virginie*, inscribed on the rock – I must have been stupidity itself, if I had not found it out. I absolutely *can* read, Clarence, and spell, and put together. – But here comes Sir Philip Baddely, who, I believe, cannot read, for I sent him an hour ago for a catalogue, and he pores over the book as if he had not yet made out the title."

Sir Philip had purposely delayed, because he was afraid of rejoining Lady Delacour whilst Clarence Hervey was with her, and whilst they were talking of the picture of Virginia.

"Here's the catalogue; here's the picture your ladyship wants – St Pierre's Virginia; – damme! I never heard of that fellow before; he is some new painter; damme! that is the reason I did not know the hand. – Not a word of what I told you, Lady Delacour – you won't blow us to Clary," added he *aside* to her ladyship. "Rochfort keeps aloof; and so will I, damme!"

A gentleman at this instant beckoned to Mr Hervey with an air of great eagerness. Clarence went and spoke to him; then returned with an altered countenance, and apologized to Lady Delacour for not dining with her, as he had promised. Business, he said, of great importance, required that he should leave town immediately. – Helena had just taken Miss Portman into a little room, where Westal's* drawings were hung, to show her a group of Lady Anne Percival and her children; and Belinda was alone with the little girl, when Mr Hervey came to bid her adieu. He was in much agitation.

"Miss Portman, I shall not, I am afraid, see you again for some time; – perhaps I may never have that – hem! – happiness. I had something of importance, that I wished to say to you before I left town; but I am forced to go so suddenly, I can hardly hope for any moment but the present to speak to you, madam. May I ask, whether you purpose remaining much longer with Lady Delacour?"

"Yes;" said Belinda much surprised, "I believe – I am not quite certain – but – I believe I shall stay with her ladyship some time longer."

Mr Hervey looked painfully embarrassed, and his eyes involuntarily fell upon little Helena. Helena drew her hand gently away from Belinda, left the room, and retired to her mother.

"That child, Miss Portman, is very fond of you," said Mr Hervey. Again he paused, and looked round, to see whether he could be overheard. "Pardon me for what I am going to say. This is not a proper place. I must be abrupt; for I am so circumstanced, that I have not a moment's time to spare. May I speak to you with the sincerity of a friend?"

"Yes. Speak to me with sincerity," said Belinda, "and you will deserve that I should think you my friend." She trembled excessively, but spoke and looked with all the firmness that she could command.

"I have heard a report," said Mr Hervey, "which is most injurious to you."

"To me!"

"Yes. No one can escape calumny. It is whispered, that if Lady Delacour should die — "

At the word *die*, Belinda started.

"That if Lady Delacour should die, Miss Portman would become the mother of Helena!"

"Good Heavens! what an absurd report! Surely *you* could not for an instant believe it, Mr Hervey.

"Not for an instant. But I resolved, as soon as I heard it, to mention it to you; for I believe that half the miseries of the world arise from foolish mysteries – from the want of courage to speak the truth. Now that you are upon your guard, your own prudence will defend you sufficiently. I never saw any of your sex, who appeared to me to have so much prudence, and so little art – But – farewell – I have not a moment to lose," added Clarence, suddenly checking himself; and he hurried away from Belinda, who stood fixed to the spot where he left her, till she was roused by the voices of several people who came into the room to see the drawings. She started as if from a dream, and went immediately in search of Lady Delacour.

Sir Philip Baddely was in earnest conversation with her ladyship; but he stopped speaking when Belinda came within hearing, and Lady Delacour turned to Helena, and said, "My dear, if you are satisfied, for mercy's sake let us begone, for I am absolutely overcome with heat – and with curiosity," added she in a low voice to Belinda – "I long to hear how Clarence Hervey likes Westal's drawings."

As soon as they got home, Lady Delacour sent her daughter to practise a new lesson upon the harpsichord. "And now sit down, my dear Belinda!" said she, "and satisfy my curiosity. It is the curiosity of a friend, not of an impertinent busy-body. Has Clarence declared himself? He chose an odd time and place; but that is no matter, I forgive him, and so do you, I dare say. But why do you tear that unfortunate carnation to pieces? Surely you cannot be embarrassed in speaking to me! What's the matter? I once did tell you, that I would not give up my claim to Clarence's adorations during my life – But I intend to live a few years longer after the amazonian operation is performed, you know – And I could not have the conscience to keep you waiting whole years. It is better to do things with a good grace, lest one should be forced at last to do them with an ill grace. Therefore I give up all manner of claim to every thing but – flattery! – that, of course, you will allow me from poor Clarence. So now do not begin upon another flower; but, without any further superfluous modesty, let me hear all the pretty things Clarence said or swore."

Whilst Belinda was pulling the carnation to pieces, she recollected what Mr Hervey had said to her about mysteries: his words still sounded in her ear. "*I believe that half the miseries of the world arise from foolish mysteries – from the want of courage to speak the truth*." I will have the courage to speak the truth, thought she, whatever it may cost me.

"The only pretty thing that Mr Hervey said was, that he never saw any woman who had so much prudence and so little art," said Belinda.

"A very pretty thing indeed, my dear! But it might have been said in open court by your grandfather, or your great-grand-father. I am sorry, if that was all, that Helena did not stay to hear such a charming moral compliment – *Moralité à la glace** –. The last thing I should have expected in a *tête-à-tête* with Clarence Hervey. Was it worth while to pull that poor flower to pieces for such a pretty speech as this? – And so that was all?"

"No, not all; but you overpower me with your wit; and I cannot stand the 'lightning of your *eyes*'."

"There!" said her ladyship, letting down her veil over her face, "the fire of my eyes it not too much for you now."

"Helena was showing me Westal's drawing of Lady Anne Percival and her children – "

"And Mr Hervey wished that he was the father of such a charming group of children, and you the mother? Hey! was not that it? It was not put in such plain terms, but that was the purport, I presume?"

"No, not at all; he said nothing about Lady Anne Percival's children, but — "

"But — why then did you bring in her ladyship and her children? To gain time? – Bad policy! – Never whilst you live, when you have a story to tell, bring in a parcel of people who have nothing to do with the beginning, the middle, or the end of it. How could I suspect you of such false taste? I really imagined these children were essential to the business; but I beg pardon for giving you these elements of criticism. I assure you I interrupt you, and talk on so fast, from pure good nature, to give you time to recollect yourself; for I know you've the worst of memories, especially for what Clarence Hervey says. But come, my dear, dash into the middle of things at once, in the true epic style."

"Then, to dash into the midst of things at once," said Miss Portman, speaking very quick, "Mr Hervey observed, that Miss Delacour was growing very fond of me."

"Miss Delacour, did you say?" cried her ladyship – "*Et puis?*" *

At this instant Champfort opened the door, looked in, and, seeing Lady Delacour, immediately retired.

"Champfort, whom do you want? – or what do you want?" said her ladyship.

"Miladi, c'est que – I did come from milord, to see if miladi and mademoiselle were visible. I did tink miladi was not at home."

"You see I am at home though," said her ladyship. "Has Lord Delacour any business with me?"

"No, miladi; not with miladi," said Champfort; "it was with mademoiselle."

"With me, Monsieur Champfort; Then you will be so good as to tell Lord Delacour I am here."

"And that *I* am not here, Champfort; for I must be gone to dress."

She rose hastily to leave the room, but Miss Portman caught her hand – "You won't go, I hope, Lady Delacour," said she, "till I have finished my long story?" Lady Delacour sat down again, ashamed of her own embarrassment, when she saw that Belinda was so calm and composed.

Whether this be art, innocence, or assurance, thought she, I cannot tell; but we shall see.

Lord Delacour now came in, with a half-unfolded newspaper and a packet of letters in his hand. He came to apologise to Miss Portman for having, by mistake, broken the seal of a letter to her, which had been sent under cover to him. He had simply asked Champfort whether the ladies were at home, that he might not have the trouble of going up stairs if they were out. Monsieur Champfort possessed, in an eminent degree, the mischievous art of appearing mysterious about the simplest things in the world.

"Though I was so thoughtless as to break the seal before I looked at the direction of the letter," said Lord Delacour, "I assure you I went no farther than the three first words; for I knew 'my dear niece' could not possibly mean me." He gave Miss Portman the letter, and left the room. This explanation was perfectly satisfactory to Belinda; but Lady Delacour, prejudiced by the hesitation of Champfort, could not help suspecting, that this letter was merely the ostensible cause of his lordship's visit.

"From my aunt Stanhope," said Miss Portman, as she opened her letter. She folded it up again after glancing over the first page, and put it into her pocket, colouring deeply.

All Lady Delacour's suspicions about Mrs Stanhope's epistolary counsels and secrets instantly recurred with almost the force of conviction to her mind.

"Miss Portman," said she, "I hope your politeness to me does not prevent you from reading your letter? Some ceremonious people think it vastly rude to read a letter in company; but I am not one of them: I can write whilst you read, for I have fifty notes and more to answer. So pray read your letter at your ease."

Belinda had but just unfolded her letter again, when Lord Delacour returned, followed by Champfort, who brought with him a splendid hammer-cloth.

"Here, my dear Lady Delacour!" said his lordship, "is a little surprise for you: here is a new hammer-cloth of my bespeaking and taste, which I hope that you will approve."

"Very handsome, upon my word!" said Lady Delacour coldly, and she fixed her eyes upon the fringe, which was black and orange – "Miss Portman's taste, I see!"

"Did not you say black and orange fringe, my dear?"

"No. I said blue and white, my lord."

His lordship declared he did not know how the mistake had happened; it was merely a mistake: – But her ladyship was convinced that it was done on purpose. And she said to herself, "Miss Portman will order my liveries next! I have not even the shadow of power left in my own house! I am not treated with even a decent show of respect! But this shall go on till I have full conviction of her views."

Dissembling her displeasure, she praised the hammer-cloth, and especially the fringe. Lord Delacour retired satisfied; and Miss Portman sat down to read the following letter from her aunt Stanhope.

CHAPTER XV

Jealousy

MY DEAR BELINDA

"I received safely the bank notes for my two hundred guineas, enclosed in your last. But you should never trust unnecessarily in this manner to the post – always, when you are obliged to send bank notes by post, cut them in two, and send half by one post and half by another. This is what is done by all prudent people. Prudence, whether in trifles or in matters of consequence, can be learned only by experience (which is often too dearly bought) – or by listening, which costs nothing, to the suggestions of those who have a thorough knowledge of the world.

"A report has just reached me concerning you and *a certain lord*, which gives me the most heartfelt concern. I always knew, and told you, that you were *a great favourite* with the person in question. I depended on your prudence, delicacy, and principles, to understand this hint properly, and I trusted that you would conduct yourself accordingly. It is too plain (from the report alluded to) that there has been some misconduct or mismanagement somewhere. The misconduct I cannot – the mismanagement I must attribute to you, my dear. For, let a man's admiration for any woman be ever so great, unless she suffer herself to be dazzled by vanity, or unless she be naturally of an inconsiderate temper, she can surely prevent his partiality from becoming so glaring as to excite envy. Envy is always to be dreaded by handsome young women, as being, sooner or later, infallibly followed by scandal. – Of this I fear you have not been sufficiently aware, and you see the consequences – consequences which, to a female of geniune delicacy or of real good sense, must be extremely alarming – Men of contracted minds and cold tempers, who are absolutely incapable of feeling generous passion for our sex, are often unaccountably ambitious to gain the reputation of being *well* with any woman whose beauty, accomplishments, or connexions, may have brought her into fashion. Whatever affection may be pretended, this is frequently the *ultimate* and *sole* object of these selfish creatures. Whether or not the person I have in my eye deserves to be included in this class, I will not presume positively to determine; but you, who have personal opportunities of observation, may decide this point (if you have any curiosity on the subject) by observing whether he most affects to pay his devoirs to you in public or in private. If the latter be the case, it is the most dangerous: because a man even of the most contracted understanding has always sense, or instinct, enough to feel that the slightest taint in the reputation of the woman who is, or who is to be, his wife, would affect his own private peace, or his honour, in the eyes of the world. A husband who has, in a first marriage, been, as it is said, in constant fear both of matrimonial subjugation and disgrace, would, in his choice of a second lady, be peculiarly nice, and probably *tardy*. Any degree of favour that might have been shown him, any report that may have been raised, and, above all, any restraint he might feel himself under from implied engagement, or from the discovery or reputation of superior understanding and talents in the object beloved, would operate infallibly against her, to the confusion of all her plans, and the ruin at once of her reputation, her peace of mind, and her hopes of an establishment. – Nay, supposing the best that could possibly happen – that, after playing with the utmost dexterity this desperate game, the pool were absolutely your own; yet, if there were any suspicions of unfair play buzzed about amongst the by-standers, you would not in the main be a gainer; for, my dear, without character, what is even wealth, or all that wealth can bestow? – I do not mean to trouble you with stale wise sayings, which young people hate, nor musty morality, which is seldom fit for use in the world, or which smells too much of books to be brought into good company. This is not my way of giving advice; but I only beg you to observe what actually passes before your eyes in the circle in which we live. – Ladies of the best families, with rank and fortune, and beauty and fashion, and every thing in their favour, cannot (as yet in this country) dispense with the strictest observance of the rules of virtue and decorum. Some have fancied themselves raised so high above the vulgar, as to be in no danger from the thunder and lightning of public opinion: but these ladies in the clouds have found themselves mistaken; they have been blasted, and have fallen nobody knows where! – What is become of Lady —, and the Countess of —, and others I could mention, who were as high as envy could look? – I remember seeing the Countess of —, who was then the most beautiful creature my eyes ever beheld, and the most admired that ever was heard of, come into the Opera-house, and sit the whole night in her box without any woman's speaking or curtsying to her, or taking any more notice of her than you would of a post, or a beggar woman. – And there was the ci-devant Lady —; I danced in the same set with her myself at Cheltenham about fifteen years ago, – the best dressed woman in the room she was, sparkling as I well remember with diamonds; – this same woman was seen yesterday by a gentleman on whom I can depend, at — races, in rags, absolute rags! drinking brandy in a booth with common soldiers! – I protest I tremble when I think of these things, – and you do too, I am sure, my dear! Even a coronet cannot protect a woman, you see, from disgrace: if she falls, she and it and all together are trampled under foot. – But why should I address all this to my dear niece? Whither have the terror and confusion I was thrown into by this strange report about you and Lord — led me? – And yet one cannot be too cautious – 'Ce n'est que le premier *mot* qui coute'* – Scandal never stops after the first word, unless she be instantly gagged by a dexterous hand. Nothing shall be wanting on my part, but you alone are the person who can do any thing effectual. Do not imagine that I would have you quit Lady —; that is the first idea, I know, that will come into your silly little head, but put it out directly. If you were upon this attack to quit the field of battle, you yield the victory to your enemies. To leave Lady — 's house would be folly and madness. As long as she is your friend, or *appears* such, all is safe; but any coolness on her part would, in the present circumstances, be death to your reputation. And even if you were to leave her on the best terms possible, the malicious world would say that you left her on the worst, and would assign as a reason the report alluded to. People who have not yet believed it would then conclude that it must be true; and thus, by your cowardice, you would furnish an incontrovertible argument against your innocence. I therefore desire that you will not upon any account think of coming home to me at present. Indeed, I hope your own good sense would prevent you from wishing it, after the reasons that I have given. Far from quitting Lady — from false delicacy, it is your business, from consideration for her peace as well as your own, to redouble your attentions to her in private, and, above all things, to appear as much as possible with her in public. I am glad to hear her health is so far reestablished that she *can* appear again in public – her spirits, as you may hint, will be the better for a little amusement. Luckily, you have it completely in your power to convince her and all the world of the correctness of your mind. I believe I certainly should have fainted, my dear, when I first heard this shocking report, if I had not just afterward received a letter from Sir Philip Baddely which revived me. His proposal at this crisis for you, my dear, is a charming thing. You have nothing to do but to encourage his addresses immediately, – the report dies away of itself, – and all is just as your best friends wish. Such an establishment for you, my dear, is indeed beyond their most sanguine expectations. Sir Philip hints in his letter, that my influence might be wanting with you in his favour – But this surely cannot be. As I have told him, he has merely mistaken becoming female reserve for a want of sensibility on your part, which would be equally unnatural and absurd. Do you know, my dear, that Sir Philip Baddely has an estate of fifteen thousand a year in Wiltshire? and his uncle Barton's estate in Norfolk will, in due time, pay his debts. Then, as to family – look in the list of baronets in your pocketbook; and surely, my love, an old baronetage in actual possession is worth something more than the reversion of a new coronet – supposing that such a thing could properly be thought of, which Heaven forbid! – So I see no possible objection to Sir Philip, my dear Belinda! and I am sure you have too much candour and good sense to make any childish or romantic difficulties. Sir Philip is not, I know, a man of what you call genius. So much the better, my dear! – Those men of genius are dangerous husbands; they have so many oddities and eccentricities there is no managing them, though they are mighty pleasant men in company to enliven conversation. For example, your favourite Clarence Hervey. As it is well known he is not a marrying man, you never can have thought of him. – You are not a girl, to expose yourself to the ridicule, &c. of all your female acquaintance by romance and nonsense. I cannot conceive that a niece of mine could degrade herself by a mean prepossession for a man, who has never made any declaration of his attachment to her, and who, I am sure, feels no such attachment. That you may not deceive yourself, it is fit I should tell you, what otherwise it might not be so proper to mention to a young lady, that he keeps, and has kept a mistress for some years; and those who are most intimately in his confidence have assured me, that, if ever he marries any body, he will marry this girl; which is not impossible, considering that she is, they say, the most beautiful young creature that ever was seen, and he *a man of genius*. If you have any sense or spirit, I have said enough. – So adieu! – Let me hear, by return of the post, that every thing is going on as it should do. I am impatient to write to your sister Tollemache this good news. I always foretold, that my Belinda would marry better than her sister, or any of her cousins, and take place of them all. Are not you obliged to me for sending you this winter to town to Lady — ? It was an admirable hit. Pray tell Lady Delacour, with my best compliments, that our *aloe* friend (her ladyship will understand me) cheated a gentleman of my acquaintance the other day, at casino, out of seventy guineas. He hates the sight of her odious red wig as much now as we always did. I knew, and told Lady D —, as she will do me the justice to remember, that Mrs — cheated at play. – What a contemptible character! – Pray, my dear, do not forget to tell Lady Delacour, that I have a charming anecdote for her, about another *friend* of ours who has lately gone over to the enemy. Has her ladyship seen a manuscript that is handed about as a great secret, and said to be by — , a parallel between *our friend* and the chevalier D'Eon?* It is done with infinite wit and humour, in the manner of Plutarch. I would send a copy, but am afraid my frank would be too heavy if I began upon another sheet. – So once more, adieu, my dear niece! Write to me without fail, and mention Sir Philip. I have written to him my thanks, approbation, &c.

> Yours sincerely,
> SELINA STANHOPE."

"Mrs Stanhope seems to have written you a volume instead of a letter, Miss Portman!' cried Lady Delacour as Belinda turned over the sheets of her aunt's long epistle. She did not attempt to read it regularly through: some passages here and there were sufficient to astonish and shock her extremely. "No bad news, I hope?" – said Lady Delacour, again looking up from her writing at Belinda, who sat motionless, leaning her head upon her hand as if in deep thought – Mrs Stanhope's unfolded letter hanging from her hand. In the midst of the variety of embarrassing, painful, and alarming feelings excited by this letter, she had sufficient strength of mind to adhere to her resolution of speaking the exact truth to Lady Delacour. When she was roused by her ladyship's question, "No bad news, I hope, Miss Portman?" she instantly answered, with all the firmness she could command.

"Yes. My aunt has been alarmed by a strange report which I heard myself for the first time this morning from Mr Hervey. I am sure I am much obliged to him for having the courage to speak the truth to me."

And here she repeated what Mr Hervey had said to her.

Lady Delacour never raised her eyes whilst Belinda spoke, but went on scratching out some words in what she was writing. Through the mask of paint which she wore, no change of colour could be visible; and as Belinda did not see the expression of her ladyship's eyes, she could not in the least judge of what was passing in her mind.

'Mr Hervey has acted like a man of honour and sense," said Lady Delacour; 'but it is a pity, for your sake, he did not speak sooner – before this report became so public – before it reached Bath, and your aunt. – Though it could not surprise her much – she has such a perfect knowledge of the world, – and – "

Lady Delacour uttered these broken sentences in a voice of suppressed anger; cleared her throat several times, and at last, unable to speak, stopped short – and then began with much precipitation to put wafers into several notes that she had been writing. So, it has reached Bath? – thought she – The report is public! – I never till now heard a hint of any such thing, except from Sir Philip Baddely; but it has doubtless been the common talk of the town, and I am laughed at as a dupe and an idiot, as I am. And now, when the thing can be concealed no longer, she comes to me with that face of simplicity, and, knowing my generous temper, throws herself on my mercy, and trusts that her speaking to me with this audacious plainness will convince me of her innocence. "You have acted in the most prudent manner possible, Miss Portman.," said her ladyship, as she went on sealing her notes, "by speaking at once to me of this strange, scandalous, absurd report. Do you act from your aunt Stanhope's advice, or entirely from your own judgment and knowledge of my character?"

"From my own judgment and knowledge of your character, in which I hope – I am not – I cannot be mistaken," said Belinda, looking at her with a mixture of doubt and astonishment.

"No – you calculated admirably – 'twas the best, the only thing you could do – Only," said her ladyship, falling back in her chair with an hysteric laugh, "only the blunder of Champfort, and the entrance of my Lord Delacour, and the hammer-cloth with the orange and black fringe. Forgive me, my dear! for the soul of me I can't help laughing! it was rather unlucky; so awkward, such a contre-temps! But you," added she, wiping her eyes, and recovering from laughter, "you have such admirable presence of mind, nothing disconcerts you! You are equal to all situations and stand in no need of such long letters of advice from your aunt Stanhope," pointing to the two folio sheets which lay at Belinda's feet.

The rapid, unconnected manner in which Lady Delacour spoke, the hurry of her motions, the quick, suspicious, angry glances of her eye, her laugh, her unintelligible words, all conspired at this moment to give Belinda the idea that her intellects were suddenly disordered. She was so firmly persuaded of her ladyship's utter indifference to Lord Delacour, that she never conceived the possibility of her being actuated by the passion of jealousy – by the jealousy of power – a species of jealousy which she had never felt, and could not comprehend. But she had sometimes seen Lady Delacour in starts of passion that seemed to border on insanity, and the idea of her losing all command of her reason now struck Belinda with irresistible force. She felt the necessity for preserving her own composure; and with all the calmness that she could assume she took up her aunt Stanhope's letter, and looked for the passage in which Mrs Luttridge and Harriet Freke were mentioned. If I can turn the course of Lady Delacour's mind, thought she, or catch her attention, perhaps she will recover herself. "Here is a message to you, my dear Lady Delacour!" cried she, "from my aunt Stanhope, about – about Mrs Luttridge."

Miss Portman's hands trembled as she turned over the pages of the letter. "I am all attention," said Lady Delacour with a composed voice, "only take care don't make a mistake: I am in no hurry, don't read any thing Mrs Stanhope might not wish. It is dangerous to garble letters, almost as dangerous as to snatch them out of a friend's hand, as I once did, you know – but you need not now be under the least alarm."

Conscious that this letter was not fit for her ladyship to see, Belinda neither offered to show it to her, nor attempted any apology for her reserve and embarrassment, but hastily began to read the message relative to Mrs Luttridge; her voice gaining confidence as she went on, as she observed that she had fixed Lady Delacour's attention, who now sat listening to her, calm and motionless. But when Miss Portman came to the words "Do not forget to tell Lady D — , that I have a charming anecdote for her about another *friend* of hers, who lately went over to the enemy," — her ladyship exclaimed with great vehemence,

"*Friend*! — Harriet Freke! — Yes — like all other friends — Harriet Freke! — What was she compared to? — 'Tis too much for me — too much." and she put her hand to her head.

"Compose yourself, my dear *friend*!" said Belinda, in a calm gentle tone; and she went towards her with an intention of soothing her by caresses: but, at her approach, Lady Delacour pushed the table on which she had been writing from her with violence; started up, flung back the veil which fell over her face as she rose, and darted upon Belinda a look which fixed her to the spot where she stood. It said, "Come not a step nearer, at your peril!" Belinda's blood ran cold — she had no longer any doubt that this was insanity. She shut the penknife which lay upon the table, and put it in her pocket.

"Cowardly creature!" cried Lady Delacour, and her countenance changed to the expression of ineffable contempt — "what is it you fear?"

"That you should injure yourself. — Sit down — For Heaven's sake listen to me, to your friend, to Belinda!"

"My friend! my Belinda!" cried Lady Delacour, and she turned from her, and walked away some steps in silence; then suddenly clasping her hands, she raised her eyes to Heaven with a fervent but wild expression of devotion, and exclaimed —

"Great God of Heaven! my punishment is just. The death of Lawless is avenged. — May the present agony of my soul expiate my folly! — Of guilt — deliberate guilt — of hypocrisy — treachery — I have not — O never may I have — to repent!"

She paused — her eyes involuntarily returned upon Belinda. "Oh Belinda! — You! whom I have so loved! so trusted!"

The tears rolled fast down her painted cheeks; she wiped them hastily away, and so roughly, that her face became a strange and ghastly spectacle. Unconscious of her disordered appearance, she rushed past Belinda, who vainly attempted to stop her, threw up the sash, and, stretching herself far out of the window, gasped for breath. Miss Portman drew her back, and closed the window, saying, "The rouge is all off your face, my dear Lady Delacour! – you are not fit to be seen. Sit down upon this sofa, and I will ring for Marriott, and get some fresh rouge. Look at your face in this glass – you see – "

"I see," interrupted Lady Delacour, looking full at Belinda, "that she who I thought had the noblest of souls has the meanest! – I see that she is incapable of feeling. – *Rouge!* – *not fit to be seen*! – At such a time as this, to talk to me in this manner! – O niece of Mrs Stanhope! – dupe! dupe that I am!" She flung herself upon the sofa, and struck her forehead with her hand violently several times. Belinda catching her arm, and holding it with all her force, cried in a tone of authority –

"Command yourself, Lady Delacour! I conjure you, or you will go out of your senses; and if you do, your secret will be discovered by the whole world."

"Hold me not – you have no right," cried Lady Delacour, struggling to free her hand. "All powerful as you are in this house, you have no longer any power over me! – I am not going out of my senses! – You cannot get me into Bedlam, all powerful, all artful as you are. You have done enough to drive me mad – but I am not mad. – No wonder you cannot believe me – no wonder you are astonished at the strong expression of feelings that are foreign to your nature – no wonder that you mistake the writhings of the heart, the agony of a generous soul, for madness! Look not so terrified, I will do you no injury. Do not you hear that I can lower my voice? – do not you see that I can be calm? – Could Mrs Stanhope herself – could *you*, Miss Portman, speak in a softer, milder, more polite, more proper tone than I do now? – Are you pleased, are you satisfied?"

"I am better satisfied – a little better satisfied," said Belinda.

"That's well, – but still you tremble. There's not the least occasion for apprehension – You see I can command myself, and smile upon you."

"O, do not smile in that horrid manner."

"Why not? – Horrid! – Don't you love deceit?"

"I detest it from my soul."

"Indeed!" said Lady Delacour, still speaking in the same low, soft, unnatural voice – "Then why do you practise it, my love?"

"I never practised it for a moment – I am incapable of deceit. – When you are *really* calm, when you can *really* command yourself, you will do me justice, Lady Delacour; but now it is my business, if I can, to bear with you."

"You are goodness itself, and gentleness, and prudence personified. – You know how perfectly to *manage* a friend, whom you fear you have driven just to the verge of madness. But tell me, good, gentle, prudent Miss Portman, why need you dread so much that I should go mad? You know, if I went mad, nobody would mind, nobody would believe whatever I said – I should be no evidence against you, and I should be out of your way sufficiently, shouldn't I? – And you would have all the power in your own hands, would not you? – And would not this be almost as well as if I were dead and buried? – No. Your calculations are better than mine. The poor mad wife would still be in your way, would yet stand between you and the fond object of your secret soul – a coronet!"

As she pronounced the word *coronet*, she pointed to a coronet set in diamonds on her watch-case, which lay on the table. Then suddenly seizing the watch, she dashed it upon the marble hearth with all her force – "Vile bauble!" cried she, "must I lose my only friend for such a thing as you? Oh, Belinda! do not you see that a coronet cannot confer happiness?"

"I have seen it long: – I pity you from the bottom of my soul," said Belinda, and she burst into tears.

"Pity me not. I cannot endure your pity, treacherous woman!" cried Lady Delacour, and she stamped with a look of rage – "most perfidious of women!"

"Yes, call me perfidious, treacherous, – stamp at me – say, do what you will; I can and will bear it all – all patiently; for I am innocent, and you are mistaken and unhappy," said Belinda. "You will love me when you return to your senses, then how can I be angry with you!"

"Fondle me not," said Lady Delacour, starting back from Belinda's caresses – "Do not degrade yourself to no purpose – I never more can be your dupe – Your protestations of innocence are wasted on me – I am not so blind as you imagine – Dupe as you think me, I have seen much in silence. The whole world, you find, suspects you now. – To save your reputation, you want my friendship – you want — "

"I want nothing from you, Lady Delacour," said Belinda – "*You have suspected me long in silence* – Then I have mistaken your character. I can love you no longer – Farewell for ever! Find another – a better friend."

She walked away from Lady Delacour with proud indignation; but, before she reached the door, she recollected her promise to remain with this unfortunate woman.

Is a dying woman, in the paroxysm of insane passion, a fit object of indignation? thought Belinda, and she stopped short. – "No, Lady Delacour," cried she, "I will not yield to my humour – I will not listen to my pride. A few words said in the heat of passion shall not make me forget myself or you. You have given me your confidence, I am grateful for it. I cannot – will not desert you – my promise is sacred."

"Your promise!" said Lady Delacour contemptuously, "I absolve you from your promise. Unless you find it *convenient* to yourself to remember it, pray let it be forgotten, and if I must die — "

At this instant, the door opened suddenly, and little Helena came in singing –

> "Merrily, merrily shall we live now,
> "Under the blossom that hangs on the bough."

"What comes next, Miss Portman?"

Lady Delacour dragged her veil across her face, and rushed out of the room.

"What is the matter? – Is mamma ill?"

"Yes, my dear," said Belinda. But at this instant she heard the sound of Lord Delacour's voice upon the stairs, and she broke from the little girl, and with the greatest precipitation retreated to her own room.

She had not been alone above half an hour before Marriott knocked at the door.

"Miss Portman, you don't know how late it is. Lady Singleton and the Miss Singletons are come. But, merciful Heaven!' exclaimed Marriott as she entered the room, "what is all this packing up? What is this trunk?"

"I am going to Oakly-park with Lady Anne Percival," said Belinda calmly.

"I thought there was something wrong, my mind misgave me all the time I was dressing my lady, she was in such a flutter, and never spoke to me – I'd lay my life this is, some way or other, Mr Champfort's doings. But, good dear Miss Portman, can you leave my poor lady when she wants you so much – and I'll take upon me to say, ma'am, loves you so much at the bottom of her heart? –

Dear me, how your face is flushed! – Pray let me pack up these things, if it must be. But I do hope, if it be possible, that you should stay. – However, I've no business to speak. I beg pardon for being so impertinent; I hope you won't take it ill, it is only from regard to my poor lady I ventured to speak."

"Your regard to your lady deserves the highest approbation, Marriott," said Belinda. "It is impossible that I should stay with her any longer. When I am gone, good Marriott, and when her health and strength decline, your fidelity and your services will be absolutely necessary to your mistress; and from what I have seen of the goodness of your heart, I am convinced that the more she is in want of you, the more *respectful* will be your attention."

Marriott answered only by her tears, and went on packing up in a great hurry.

Nothing could equal Lady Delacour's astonishment when she learnt from Marriott that Miss Portman was actually preparing to leave the house. After a moment's reflection, however, she persuaded herself that this was only a new artifice to work upon her affections; that Belinda did not mean to leave her; but that she would venture all lengths, in hopes of being at the last moment pressed to stay. Under this persuasion, Lady Delacour resolved to disappoint her expectations; she determined to meet her with that polite coldness, which would best become her own dignity, and which, without infringing the laws of hospitality, would effectu-ally point out to the world, that Lady Delacour was no dupe, and that Miss Portman was an unwelcome inmate in her house.

The power of assuming gaiety when her heart was a prey to the most poignant feelings, she had completely acquired by long practice. With the promptitude of an actress she could instantly appear upon the stage, and support a character totally foreign to her own. The loud knocks at the door which announced the arrival of company, were signals that operated punctually upon her associations; and to this species of conventional necessity her most violent passions submitted with magical celerity. Fresh rouged, and elegantly dressed, she was performing her part to a brilliant audience in her drawing-room, when Belinda entered. Belinda beheld her with much astonishment, but more pity.

"Miss Portman," said her ladyship, turning carelessly towards her, "where do you buy your rouge? Lady Singleton, would you rather at this moment be mistress of the philosopher's stone, or have a patent for rouge that will come and go like Miss

Portman's? – A propos, have you read St Leon?" Her ladyship was running on to a fresh train of ideas, when a footman announced the arrival of Lady Anne Percival's carriage; and Miss Portman rose to depart.

"You dine with Lady Anne, Miss Portman, I understand? – My compliments to her ladyship, and my duty to Mrs Margaret Delacour, and her macaw. – *Au revoir*! Though you talk of running away from me to Oakly-park, I am sure you will do no such cruel thing. I am, with all due humility, so confident of the irresistible attractions of this house, that I defy Oakly-park and all its charms. – So, Miss Portman, instead of adieu, I shall only say – *Au revoir*!"

"Adieu, Lady Delacour!" said Belinda with a look and tone which struck her ladyship to the heart. All her suspicions, all her pride, all her affected gaiety vanished; her presence of mind forsook her, and for some moments she stood motionless and powerless. Then recollecting herself, she flew after Miss Portman abruptly, stopped her at the head of the stairs, and exclaimed,

"My dearest Belinda, are you gone? – My best, my only friend! – Say you are not gone for ever! – Say you will return!"

"Adieu!" repeated Belinda. It was all she could say; and she broke from Lady Delacour, and hurried out of the house with the strongest feeling of compassion for this unhappy woman, but with an unaltered sense of the propriety and necessity of her own firmness.

CHAPTER XVI

Domestic Happiness

There was an air of benevolence and perfect sincerity in the politeness, with which Lady Anne Percival received Belinda, that was peculiarly agreeable to her agitated and harassed mind.

"I am afraid," said Belinda, "that your ladyship will think me capricious for coming to you at last an unbidden guest, after having so often refused your kind invitations."

"Nay," said Lady Anne, "your surrendering yourself at discretion, just when I was going to raise the siege in despair, is the most flattering thing possible to my self-complacency. And the only terms I shall impose are, that you will stay at Oakly-park with us as long as we can make it agreeable to you, and no longer. Whether those who cease to please, or those who cease to be pleased, are most to blame,[1] it may sometimes be difficult to determine − so difficult, that, when this becomes a question between two friends, they perhaps had better part than venture upon the discussion."

Lady Anne Percival could not avoid suspecting, that something disagreeable had passed between Lady Delacour and Belinda; but she was not troubled with the disease of idle curiosity, and her example prevailed upon Mrs Margaret Delacour, who dined with her, to refrain from all questions and comments.

The prejudice, which this lady had conceived against our heroine, as being a niece of Mrs Stanhope's, had lately been vanquished by the favourable representations of her conduct which she had heard from her nephew, and by the kindness that Belinda had shown to little Helena.

"Madam," said Mrs Delacour, addressing herself to Miss Portman with some formality, but much dignity, "permit me, as one of my Lord Delacour's nearest relations now living, to return you my thanks, for having, as my nephew informs me, exerted your influence over Lady Delacour for the happiness of his family. My little Helena, I am sure, feels her obligations towards you, and

1. Marmontel.

I rejoice that I have had an opportunity of expressing, in person, my sense of what our family owes to Miss Portman. As to the rest, her own heart will reward her. The praise of the world is but an inferior consideration. However, it deserves to be mentioned, as an instance of the world's candour, and for the singularity of the case, that every body agrees in speaking well even of so handsome a young lady as Miss Portman."

"She must have had extraordinary prudence," said Lady Anne; "and the world does justly to reward it with extraordinary esteem."

Belinda, with equal pleasure and surprise, observed that all this was said naturally, and that the report, which she had feared was public, had never reached Mrs Delacour, or Lady Anne Percival.

In fact, it was known and believed only by those who had been prejudiced by the malice, or folly, of Sir Philip Baddely. Piqued by the manner in which his addresses had been received by Belinda, he readily listened to the comfortable words of his valet de chambre, who assured him that he had it from the best possible authority (Lord Delacour's own gentleman, Mr Champfort), that his lordship was deeply *taken* with Miss Portman – that the young lady managed every thing in the house – that she had been very prudent, to be sure, and had refused large presents – but that there was no doubt of her becoming Lady Delacour, if ever his lordship should be at liberty. Sir Philip was the person who mentioned this to Clarence Hervey, and Sir Philip was the person who hinted it to Mrs Stanhope, in the very letter which he wrote to implore her influence in favour of his own proposal. This manouevring lady represented this report as being universally known and believed, in hopes of frightening her niece into an immediate match with the baronet. In the whole extent of Mrs Stanhope's politic imagination, she had never foreseen the possibility of her niece's speaking the simple truth to Lady Delacour, and she had never guarded against this danger. She never thought of Belinda's mentioning this report to her ladyship, because she would never have dealt so openly, had she been in the place of her niece. Thus her art and falsehood operated against her own views, and produced consequences diametrically opposite to her expectations. – It was her exaggerations that made Clarence Hervey speak to Belinda; and that made Lady Delacour believe, when Belinda repeated what he had said, that this report was universally known and credited; her own suspicions were by these means again awakened, and her jealousy and rage were raised to such a pitch, that, no longer mistress of herself, she insulted her friend and guest. Miss Portman was then obliged to do the very thing that Mrs Stanhope most dreaded; to leave Lady Delacour's house and all its advantages. As to Sir Philip Baddely, Belinda never thought of him from the moment she read her aunt's letter till after she had left her ladyship; her mind was firmly decided upon this subject; yet she could not help fearing, that her aunt would not understand her reasons, or approve her conduct. She wrote to Mrs Stanhope in the most kind and respectful manner; assured her that there had been no foundation whatever for the report, which had produced so much uneasiness; that Lord Delacour had always treated her with politeness and good nature, but that such thoughts or views as had been attributed to him, she was convinced, had never entered his lordship's mind; that hearing of the publicity of this report had, however, *much affected* Lady D — . "I have therefore," said Belinda, "thought it prudent to quit her ladyship, and to accept of an invitation from Lady Anne Percival to Oakly-park. I hope, my dear aunt, that you will not be displeased by my leaving town without seeing Sir Philip Baddely again. Our meeting could indeed answer no purpose, as it is entirely out of my power to return his partiality. Of his character, temper, and manners, I know enough to be convinced, that our union could tend only to make us both miserable. After what I have seen, nothing can ever tempt me to marry from any of the common views of interest or ambition.

On this subject Belinda, though she declared her own senti-ments with firm sincerity, touched as slightly as she could, because she anxiously wished to avoid all appearance of *braving* the opinions of an aunt, to whom she was under obligations. She was tempted to pass over in silence all that part of Mrs Stanhope's letter, which related to Clarence Hervey; but, upon reflection, she determined to conquer her repugnance to speak of him, and to make perfect sincerity the steady rule of her conduct. She therefore acknowledged to her aunt, that, of all the persons she had hitherto seen, this gentleman was the most agreeable to her; but at the same time she assured her, that the refusal of Sir Philip Baddely was totally independent of all thoughts of Mr Hervey — that, before she had received her aunt's letter, circumstances had convinced her that Mr Hervey was attached to another woman. She concluded by saying, that she had neither romantic hopes nor wishes, and that her affections were at her own command.

Belinda, just when the carriage was at the door to take her to Oakly-park, received the following angry answer from Mrs Stanhope:

"Henceforward, Belinda, you may manage your own affairs as you think proper; I shall never more interfere with my advice. Refuse whom you please — go where you please — get what friends, and what admirers, and what establishment you can — I have nothing more to do with it — I wash my hands of it — I will never more undertake the management of young people. There's your sister Tollemache has made a pretty return for all my kindness! She is going to be parted from her husband, and basely throws all the blame upon me. — But 'tis the same with all of you. — There's your cousin Joddrell refused me a hundred guineas last week, though the piano forte and harp I bought for her before she was married stood me in double that sum, and are now useless lumber on my hands; and she never could have had Joddrell without them, as she knows as well as I do. As for Mrs Levit, she never writes to me, and takes no manner of notice of me. But this is no matter, for her notice can be of no consequence now to any body. He has run out every thing he had in the world! — All Levit's fine estates advertised in to day's paper — an execution in the house, I'm told. I expect that she will have the assurance to come to me in her distress; but she shall find my doors shut, I promise her. Your cousin Valleton's match has, through her own folly, turned out like all the rest. She, her husband, and all his relations are at daggersdrawing; and Valleton will die soon, and won't leave her a farthing in his will, I foresee, and all the fine Valleton estate goes to God knows who!

"If she had taken my advice after marriage as before, it would have been all her own at this instant. But the passions run away with people, and they forget every thing — common sense, gratitude, and all — as you do, Belinda. Clarence Hervey will never think of you, and I give you up! — Now manage for yourself as you please, and as you can! I'll have nothing more to do with the affairs of young ladies, who will take no advice.

"SELINA STANHOPE.

"P.S. If you return directly to Lady Delacour's, and marry Sir Philip Baddely, I will forgive the past."

The regret which Belinda felt at having grievously offended her aunt was somewhat alleviated by the reflection that she had acted with integrity and prudence. Thrown off her guard by anger, Mrs Stanhope had inadvertently furnished her niece with the best possible reasons against following her advice with regard to Sir Philip Baddely, by stating that her sister and cousins, who had married with mercenary views, had made themselves miserable, and had shown their aunt neither gratitude nor respect.

It is scarcely necessary to say, that Belinda did not return to Lady Delacour, nor change her mind with respect to Sir Philip Baddely; but as soon as she had read this letter, she got into the carriage with Lady Anne Percival, and they pursued their journey to Oakly-park.

The tranquillity of Belinda's mind was gradually restored by the society that she enjoyed *there*. She found herself in the midst of a large and cheerful family, with whose domestic happiness she could not forbear to sympathise. There was an affectionate confidence, an unconstrained gaiety in this house, which forcibly struck her, from its contrast with what she had seen at Lady Delacour's. She perceived, that between Mr Percival and Lady Anne there was a union of interests, occupations, taste, and affection. She was at first astonished by the openness with which they talked of their affairs in her presence; that there were no family secrets, nor any of those petty mysteries which arise from a discordance of temper or struggle for power. In conversation, every person expressed without constraint their wishes and opinions; and wherever these differed, reason and the general good were the standards to which they appealed. The elder and younger part of the family were not separated from each other; even the youngest child in the house seemed to form part of the society, to have some share and interest in the general occupations or amusements. The children were treated neither as slaves nor as playthings, but as reasonable creatures; and the ease with which they were managed, and with which they managed themselves, surprised Belinda; for she heard none of that continual lecturing which goes forward in some houses, to the great fatigue and misery of all the parties concerned, and of all the spectators. Without force, or any factitious excitements, the taste for knowledge, and the habits of application, were induced by example, and confirmed by sympathy. Mr Percival was a man of science and literature, and his daily pursuits and general conversation were in the happiest manner instructive and interesting to his family. His knowledge of the world, and his natural gaiety of disposition, rendered his conversation not only useful, but in the highest degree amusing. From the merest trifles he could lead to some scientific fact, some happy literary allusion or philosophic investigation.

Lady Anne Percival had, without any pedantry or ostentation, much accurate knowledge, and a taste for literature, which made her the chosen companion of her husband's understanding, as well of his heart. He was not obliged to reserve his conversation for friends of his own sex, nor was he forced to seclude himself in the pursuit of any branch of knowledge; the partner of his warmest affections was also the partner of his most serious occupations; and her sympathy and approbation, and the daily sense of her success in the education of their children, inspired him with a degree of happy social energy, unknown to the selfish solitary votaries of avarice and ambition.

In this large and happy family there was a variety of pursuits. One of the boys was fond of chemistry, another of gardening; one of the daughters had a talent for painting, another for music; and all their acquirements and accomplishments contributed to increase their mutual happiness, for there was no envy or jealousy amongst them.

Those who unfortunately have never enjoyed domestic happiness, such as we have just described, will perhaps suppose the picture to be visionary and romantic; there are others, it is hoped many others, who will feel that it is drawn from truth and real life. Tastes that have been vitiated by the stimulus of dissipation might, perhaps, think these simple pleasures insipid.

Every body must ultimately judge of what makes them happy, from the comparison of their own feelings in different situations. Belinda was convinced by this comparison, that domestic life was that which could alone make her really and permanently happy. She missed none of the pleasures, none of the gay company, to which she had been accustomed at Lady Delacour's. She was conscious at the end of each day, that it had been agreeably spent; yet there were no extraordinary exertions made to entertain her, every thing seemed in its natural course, and so did her mind. Where there was so much happiness, no want of what is called *pleasure* was ever experienced. She had not been at Oakly-park a week, before she forgot that it was within a few miles of

Harrowgate, and she never once recollected her vicinity to this fashionable water-drinking place for a month afterward.

"Impossible!" some young ladies will exclaim. We hope others will feel, that it was perfectly natural. But to deal fairly with our readers, we must not omit to mention a certain Mr Vincent, who came to Oakly-park during the first week of Belinda's visit, and who stayed there during the whole succeeding month of felicity. Mr Vincent was a creole; he was about two and twenty; his person and manners were striking and engaging; he was tall, and remarkably handsome; he had large dark eyes, an aquiline nose, fine hair, and a sun burnt complexion, which gave him a manly appearance; his countenance was open and friendly, and when he spoke upon any interesting subject it lighted up, and became full of fire and animation. He used much gesture in conversation; he had not the common manners of young men who are, or who aim at being thought, fashionable, but he was perfectly at ease in company, and all that was uncommon about him appeared foreign. He had a frank, ardent temper, incapable of art or dissimulation, and so unsuspicious of all mankind, that he could scarcely believe falsehood existed in the world, even after he had himself been its dupe. He was in extreme astonishment at the detection of any species of baseness in a *gentleman*; for he considered honour and generosity as belonging indefeasibly, if not exclusively to the privileged orders. His notions of virtue were certainly aristocratic in the extreme, but his ambition was to entertain such only as would best support and dignify an aristocracy. His pride was magnanimous, not insolent; and his social prejudices were such as, in some degree, to supply the place of the power and habit of reasoning, in which he was totally deficient. One principle of philosophy he practically possessed in perfection; he enjoyed the present undisturbed by any unavailing regret for the past, or troublesome solicitude about the future. All the goods of life he tasted with epicurean zest; all the evils he braved with stoical indifference. The mere pleasure of existence seemed to keep him in perpetual good humour with himself and others; and his never-failing flow of animal spirits exhilarated even the most phlegmatic. To persons of a cold and reserved temper he sometimes appeared rather too much of an egotist; for he talked with fluent enthusiasm of the excellent qualities and beauties of whatever he loved, whether it were his dog, his horse, or his country: but this was not the egotism of vanity; it was the overflowing of an affectionate heart, confident of obtaining sympathy from his fellow-creatures, because conscious of feeling it for all that existed.

He was as grateful as he was generous; and, though high-spirited and impatient of restraint, he would submit with affectionate gentleness to the voice of a friend, or listen with deference to the counsel of those in whose superior judgment he had confidence. Gratitude, respect, and affection, all conspired to give Mr Percival the strongest power over his soul. Mr Percival had been a guardian and a father to him. His own father, an opulent creole, on his deathbed requested that his son, who was then about eighteen, might be immediately sent to England for the advantages of an European education. Mr Percival, who had a regard for the father, arising from circumstances which it is not here necessary to explain, accepted the charge of young Vincent, and managed so well, that his ward when he arrived at the age of twenty-one did not feel relieved from any restraint. On the contrary, his attachment to his guardian, increased from that period, when the laws gave him full command over his fortune and his actions.

Mr Vincent had been at Harrowgate for some time before Mr Percival came into the country; but as soon as he heard of Mr Percival's arrival, he left half finished a game at billiards, of which, by the by, he was extremely fond, to pay his respects at Oakly-park. At the first sight of Belinda, he did not seem much struck with her appearance; perhaps, from his thinking that there was too little languor in her eyes, and too much colour in her cheeks: he confessed that she was graceful, but her motions were not quite slow enough to please him.

It is somewhat singular, that Lady Delacour's faithful friend, Harriet Freke, should be the cause of Mr Vincent's first fixing his favourable attention on Miss Portman.

He had a black servant of the name of Juba, who was extremely attached to him; he had known Juba from a boy, and had brought him over with him, when he first came to England, because the poor fellow begged so earnestly to go with young massa. Juba had lived with him ever since, and accompanied him wherever he went. Whilst he was at Harrowgate, Mr Vincent lodged in the same house with Mrs Freke. Some dispute arose between their servants, about the right to a coach-house, which each party claimed as exclusively their own. The master of the house was appealed to by Juba, who sturdily maintained his massa's right;

he established it, and rolled his massa's curricle into the coach-house in triumph. Mrs Freke, who heard and saw the whole transaction from her window, said, or swore, that she would make Juba repent of, what she called, his insolence. The threat was loud enough to reach his ears, and he looked up in astonishment, to hear such a voice from a woman; but an instant afterward he began to sing very gaily, as he jumped into the curricle to turn the cushions, and then danced himself up and down by the springs, as if rejoicing in his victory. A second and a third time Mrs Freke repeated her threat, confirming it by an oath, and then violently shut down the window and disappeared. Mr Vincent, to whom Juba, with much simplicity, expressed his aversion of the *man-woman* who lived in the house with them, laughed at the odd manner in which the black imitated her voice and gesture, but thought no more of the matter. Some time afterward however, Juba's spirits forsook him, he was never heard to sing or to whistle, he scarcely ever spoke even to his master, who was much surprised by this sudden change from gaiety and loquacity to melancholy and taciturnity. Nothing could draw from the poor fellow any explanation of the cause of this alteration in his humour; and though he seemed excessively grateful for the concern which his master showed about his health, no kindness or amusement could restore him to his wonted cheerfulness. Mr Vincent knew that he was passionately fond of music; and having heard him once express a wish for a tambourine, he gave him one: but Juba never played upon it, and his spirits seemed every day to grow worse and worse. This melancholy lasted during the whole time that he remained at Harrowgate, but from the first day of his arrival at Oakly-park he began to mend: after he had been there a week, he was heard to sing, and whistle, and talk as he used to do, and his master congratulated him upon his recovery. One evening his master asked him to go back to Harrowgate for his tambourine, as little Charles Percival wished to hear him play upon it. This simple request had a wonderful effect upon poor Juba; he began to tremble from head to foot, his eyes became fixed, and he stood motionless; after some time he suddenly clasped his hands, fell upon his knees, and exclaimed:

"O, massa, Juba die! If Juba go back, Juba die!" and he wiped away the drops that stood upon his forehead. "But me will go, if massa bid – me will die!"

Mr Vincent began to imagine, that the poor fellow was out of his senses. He assured him, with the greatest kindness, that he would almost as soon hazard his own life, as that of such a faithful, affectionate servant; but he pressed him to explain what possible danger he dreaded from returning to Harrowgate. Juba was silent, as if afraid to speak – "Don't fear to speak to me," said Mr Vincent, "I will defend you: if any body have injured, or if you dread that any body will injure you, trust to me, I will protect you."

"Ah, massa, you no can! Me die, if me go back! Me no can say word more;" and he put his finger upon his lips, and shook his head. Mr Vincent knew that Juba was excessively superstitious; and convinced that, if his mind were not already deranged, it would certainly become so, were any secret terror thus to prey upon his imagination, he assumed a very grave countenance, and assured him, that he should be extremely displeased if he persisted in this foolish and obstinate silence. Overcome by this, Juba burst into tears, and answered,

"Den me will tell all."

This conversation passed before Miss Portman and Charles Percival, who were walking in the park with Mr Vincent, at the time he met Juba and asked him to go for the tambourine. When he came to the words "me will tell all", he made a sign that he wished to tell it to his master alone. Belinda and the little boy walked on to leave him at liberty to speak; and then, though with a sort of reluctant horror, he told that the figure of an old woman, all in flames, had appeared to him in his bedchamber at Harrowgate every night, and that he was sure she was one of the obeah-women* of his own country, who had pursued him to Europe to revenge his having once, when he was a child, trampled upon an egg shell that contained some of her poisons. The extreme absurdity of this story made Mr Vincent burst out a laughing: but his humanity the next instant made him serious; for the poor victim of superstitious terror, after having revealed what, according to the belief of his country, it is death to mention, fell senseless on the ground. When he came to himself, he calmly said, that he knew he must now die, for that the obeah-women never forgave those that talked of them or their secrets; and, with a deep groan, he added, that he wished he might die before night, that he might not see *her* again. It was in vain to attempt to reason him out of the idea, that he had actually seen this apparition: his account of it was, that it first appeared to him in the coach-house one night, when he went thither in the dark – that he never afterward went to the coach-house in the dark – but that the same figure of an old woman, all in flames, appeared at the foot of his bed every night whilst he stayed at Harrowgate; and that he was then persuaded she would never let him escape from her power, till she had killed him. That since he had left Harrowgate, however, she had not tormented him, for he had never seen her, and he was in hopes that she had forgiven him; but that now he was sure of her vengeance for having spoken of the past.

Mr Vincent knew the astonishing power, which the belief in this species of sorcery[1] has over the minds of the Jamaica negroes; they pine and actually die away, from the moment they fancy themselves under the malignant influence of these witches. He almost gave poor Juba over for lost. The first person that he happened to meet after this conversation was Belinda, to whom he eagerly related it, because he had observed, that she had listened with much attention and sympathy to the beginning of the poor fellow's story. The moment that she heard of the flaming apparition, she recollected having seen a head drawn in phosphorus, which one of the children had exhibited for her amusement, and it occurred to her that, perhaps, some imprudent or ill-natured person might have terrified the ignorant negro by similar means. When she mentioned this to Mr Vincent, he recollected the threat that had been thrown out by Mrs Freke, the day that Juba had taken possession of the disputed coach-house; and from the character of this lady, Belinda judged that she would be likely to play such a trick, and to call it as usual fun or frolic. Miss Portman proposed that a figure should be drawn with phosphorus, as nearly as possible to resemble that which Juba had described, and that it should be shown to him at night, to try whether it would excite his apprehensions. Mr Vincent drew the figure of a frightful old woman on the wall, opposite to the foot of Juba's bed. In the morning he told his master that he had been again visited by the obeah-woman, and he exhibited all the signs of extreme terror. Belinda then suggested that one of the children should show him the phosphorus, and should draw some ludicrous figure with it in his presence. This was done, and it had the effect that she expected. Juba, familiarised by degrees with the

1. See Edwards's History of the West Indies, vol. II.

object of his secret horror, and convinced that no obeah-woman was exercising over him her sorceries, recovered his health and spirits. His gratitude to Miss Portman, who was the immediate cause of his cure, was as simple and touching as it was lively and sincere. This was the circumstance which first turned Mr Vincent's attention towards Belinda. Upon examining the room in which the negro used to sleep at Harrowgate, the strong smell of phosphorus was perceived, and part of the paper was burnt on the very spot where he had always seen the figure, so that he was now perfectly convinced that this trick had been purposely played to frighten him, in revenge for his having kept possession of the coach-house.

Mrs Freke, when she found herself detected, gloried in the jest, and told the story as a good joke wherever she went – triumphing in the notion, that it was she who had driven both *master and man* from Harrowgate.

The exploit was, however, by no means agreeable in its consequences to her friend Mrs Luttridge, who was now at Harrowgate. For reasons of her own, she was very anxious to fix Mr Vincent in her society, and she was much provoked by Mrs Freke's conduct. The ladies came to high words upon the occasion, and an irreparable breach would have ensued, had not Mrs Freke, in the midst of her rage, recollected Mr Luttridge's electioneering interest: and suddenly changing her tone, she declared that "she was really sorry to have driven Mr Vincent from Harrowgate; that her only intention was to get rid of his black; she would lay any wager that, with Mrs Luttridge's assistance, they could soon get the gentleman back again;" and she proposed as a certain method of fixing Mr Vincent in Mrs Luttridge's society, to invite Belinda to Harrowgate.

"You may be sure," said Mrs Freke, "that she must by this time be cursedly tired of her visit to those stupid good people at Oakly-park, and never woman *wanted* an excuse to do any thing she liked: so trust to her own ingenuity to make some decent apology to the Percivals for running away from them. As to Vincent, you may be sure Belinda Portman is his only inducement for staying with that precious family party; and if we have her, we have him. Now, we can be sure of her, for she has just quarrelled with our dear Lady Delacour. I had the whole story from my maid, who had it from Champfort. Lady

Delacour and she are at daggersdrawing, and it will be delicious to her to hear her ladyship handsomely abused. We are the declared enemies of her enemy, so we must be her friends. Nothing unites folk so quickly, and so solidly, as hatred of some common foe."

This argument could not fail to convince Mrs Luttridge, and the next day Mrs Freke commenced her operations. She drove in her *unicorn** to Oakly-park, to pay Miss Portman a visit. She had no acquaintance either with Mr Percival or Lady Anne, and she had always treated Belinda, when she met her in town, rather cavalierly, as an humble companion of Lady Delacour. But it cost Mrs Freke nothing to change her tone: she was one of those ladies, who can remember or forget people, be perfectly familiar or strangely rude, just as it suits the convenience, fashion, or humour of the minute.

CHAPTER XVII

Rights of Woman

Belinda was alone, and reading, when Mrs Freke dashed into the room.

"How do, dear creature!" cried she, stepping up to her, and shaking hands with her boisterously – "How do? – Glad to see you, 'faith! – Been long here? Tremendously hot today!"

She flung herself upon the sofa beside Belinda, threw her hat upon the table, and then continued speaking.

"And how d'ye go on here, poor child! – 'God! I'm glad you're alone – Expected to find you encompassed by a whole host of the righteous. Give me credit for my courage in coming to deliver you out of their hands. Luttridge and I had such compassion upon you, when we heard you were close prisoner here! – I swore to set the distressed damsel free, in spite of all the dragons in Christendom – So let me carry you off in triumph in my unicorn, and leave these good people to stare when they come home from their sober walk, and find you gone. There's nothing I like so much as to make *good* people stare – I hope you're of my way o'thinking – You don't look as if you were though – but I never mind young ladies' looks – always give the lie to their thoughts. – Now we talk o'looks – Never saw you look so well in my life – as handsome as an angel! – And so much the better for me. – Do you know, I've a bet of twenty guineas on your head – on your face, I mean. There's a young bride at Harrowgate, Lady H — , they're all mad about her, the men swear she's the handsomest woman in England, and I swear I know one ten times as handsome. They've dared me to make good my word, and I've pledged myself to produce my beauty at the next ball, and to pit her against their belle for any money. – Most votes carry it. – I'm willing to double my bet since I've seen you again. – Come, had not we best be off? Now don't refuse me and make speeches – you know that's all nonsense – I'll take all the blame upon myself."

Belinda, who had not been suffered to utter a word whilst Mrs Freke ran on in this strange manner, looked in unfeigned atonishment; but when she found herself seized and dragged towards the door, she drew back with a degree of gentle firmness that equally astonished Mrs Freke. With a smiling countenance, but a steady tone, she said, "that she was sorry Mrs Freke's knight-errantry should not be exerted in a better cause, for that she was neither a prisoner, nor a distressed damsel."

"And will you make me lose my bet?" cried Mrs Freke. "O, at all events you must come to the ball! – I'm down for it. – But I'll not press it now, because you're frightened out of your poor little wits, I see, at the bare thoughts of doing any thing out of rule, by these good people. Well, well! it shall be managed for you – leave that to me. – I'm used to managing for cowards. – Pray tell me – You and Lady Delacour are off, I understand? – Give ye joy! – She and I were once great friends; that is to say, I had over her 'that power which strong minds have over weak ones'; but she was too weak for me – one of those people that have neither courage to be good, nor to be bad."

"The courage to be bad," said Belinda, "I believe, indeed, that she does not possess."

Mrs Freke stared. – "Why, I heard you had quarrelled with her!"

"If I had," said Belinda, "I hope that I should still do justice to her merits. It is said that people are apt to suffer more by their friends than their enemies. I hope that will never be the case with Lady Delacour, as I confess that I have been one of her friends."

"'Gad, I like your spirit – you don't want courage, I see, to fight even for your enemies. You are just the kind of girl I admire – I see you've been prejudiced against me by Lady Delacour. But whatever stories she may have trumped up, the truth of the matter is this; there's no living with her she's so jealous – so ridiculously jealous – of that lord of hers, for whom all the time she hasn't the impudence to pretend to care more than I do for the sole of my boot," said Mrs Freke, striking it with her whip, "but she hasn't the courage to give him tit for tat. – Now this is what I call weakness. – Pray, how do she and Clarence Hervey go on together? – Are they out o'the hornbook of platonics yet?"

"Mr Hervey was not in town when I left it," said Belinda.

"Was not he? – Ho! ho! – He's off then! – Ay, so I prophesied. She's not the thing for him – He has some strength of mind – some soul – above vulgar prejudices – So must a woman be to hold him. He was caught at first by her grace and beauty, and that sort of stuff; but I knew it could not last – knew she'd dilly dally with Clary, till he would turn upon his heel and leave her there."

"I fancy that you are entirely mistaken both with respect to Mr Hervey and Lady Delacour," Belinda very seriously began to say; but Mrs Freke interrupted her, and ran on –

"No! no! no! I'm not mistaken; Clarence has found her out. – She's a *very* woman – *that* he could forgive her, and so could I – But she's a *mere* woman – and that he can't forgive – no more can I."

There was a kind of drollery about Mrs Freke, which, with some people, made the odd things she said pass for wit. Humour she really possessed; and when she chose it, she could be diverting to those who like buffoonery in women. She had set her heart upon winning Belinda over to her party. She began by flattery of her beauty; but as she saw that this had no effect, she next tried what could be done by insinuating that she had a high opinion of her understanding, by talking to her as an esprit fort.

"For my part," said she, "I own I should like a strong devil better than a weak angel."

"You forget," said Belinda, "that it is not Milton, but Satan, who says,

'Fallen spirit, to be weak is to be miserable.'"

"You read, I see! – I did not know you were a reading girl. – So did I once! but I never read now. Books only spoil the originality of genius. Very well for those who can't think for themselves – But when one has made up one's opinions, there is no use in reading."

"But to *make* them up," replied Belinda, "may it not be useful?"

"Of no use upon earth to minds of a certain class. – You, who can think for yourself, should never read."

"But I read that I may think for myself."

"Only ruin your understanding, trust me. Books are full of trash – nonsense – Conversation is worth all the books in the world."

"And is there never any nonsense in conversation?"

"What have you here?" continued Mrs Freke, who did not choose to attend to this question; exclaiming as she reviewed each of the books on the table in their turns, in the summary language of presumptuous ignorance. 'Smith's Theory of Moral Sentiments' – Milk and water! 'Moore's Travels' – Hasty pudding! 'La

Bruyere' – Nettle porridge! This is what you were at when I came in, was it not?" said she, taking up a book in which she saw Belinda's mark, 'Essay on the Inconsistency of Human Wishes'. Poor thing! who bored you with this task?"

"Mr Percival recommended it to me, as one of the best essays in the English language."

"The devil! They seem to have put you in a course of the bitters – a course of the woods might do your business better. Do you ever hunt? – Let me take you out with me some morning – You'd be quite an angel on horseback; or let me drive you out some day in my unicorn."

Belinda declined this invitation, and Mrs Freke strode away to the window to conceal her mortification, threw up the sash, and called out to her groom,

"Walk those horses about, blockhead!" – Mr Percival and Mr Vincent at this instant came into the room.

"Hail, fellow! well met," cried Mrs Freke, stretching out her hand to Mr Vincent.

It has been remarked, that an antipathy subsists between creatures, who, without being the same, have yet a strong external resemblance. Mr Percival saw this instinct rising in Mr Vincent, and smiled.

"Hail, fellow! well met, I say – Shake hands, and be friends, man! – Though I'm not in the habit of making apologies, if it will be any satisfaction to you, I beg your pardon for frightening your poor devil of a black."

Then turning towards Mr Percival, she measured him with her eye, as a person whom she longed to attack. She thought, that if Belinda's opinion of the understanding of *these Percivals* could be lowered, she should rise in her opinion: accordingly, she determined to draw Mr Percival into an argument.

"I've been talking treason, I believe, to Miss Portman," cried she, "for I've been opposing some of your opinions, Mr Percival."

"If you opposed them all, madam, said Mr Percival, "I should not think it treason."

"Vastly polite! – But I think all our politeness hypocrisy. What d'ye say to that?"

"You know that best, madam!"

"Then I'll go a step farther; for I'm determined you shall contradict me. – I think all virtue is hypocrisy."

"I need not contradict you, madam," said Mr Percival, "for the terms which you make use of contradict themselves."

"It is my system," pursued Mrs Freke, "that shame is always the cause of the vices of women."

"It is sometimes the effect," said Mr Percival, "and, as cause and effect are reciprocal, perhaps you may, in some instances, be right."

"O! I hate qualifying arguers – Plump assertion or plump denial for me – You shan't get off so – I say, shame is the cause of all women's vices."

"False shame, I suppose you mean?" said Mr Percival.

"Mere play upon words! – All shame is false shame – We would be a great deal better without it. What say you, Miss Portman? – Silent – hey? – Silence that speaks!"

"Miss Portman's blushes," said Mr Vincent, "speak *for* her."

"*Against* her," – said Mrs Freke – "Women blush because they understand."

"And you would have them understand without blushing?" said Mr Percival. "So would I; for nothing can be more different than innocence and ignorance. Female delicacy — "

"This is just the way you men spoil women," cried Mrs Freke, "by talking to them of the *delicacy of their sex*, and such stuff. This *delicacy* enslaves the pretty delicate dears."

"No; it enslaves us," said Mr Vincent.

"I hate slavery! Vive la liberté!" cried Mrs Freke – "I'm a champion for the Rights of Women."

"I am an advocate for their happiness," said Mr Percival, "and for their delicacy, as I think it conduces to their happiness."

"I'm an enemy to their delicacy, as I am sure it conduces to their misery."

"You speak from experience?" said Mr Percival.

"No, from observation. – Your most delicate women are always the greatest hypocrites; and, in my opinion, no hypocrite can or ought to be happy."

"But you have not proved the hypocrisy," said Belinda. "Delicacy is not, I hope, an indisputable proof of it? – If you mean *false* delicacy – "

"To cut the matter short at once," cried Mrs Freke, "why, when a woman likes a man, does not she go and tell him so honestly?"

Belinda, surprised by this question from a woman, was too much abashed instantly to answer.

"Because she's a hypocrite. That is and must be the answer."

"No," said Mr Percival, "because, if she be a woman of sense, she knows that by such a step she would disgust the object of her affection."

"Cunning! – cunning! – cunning! – the arms of the weakest."

"Prudence! – prudence! – the arms of the strongest. Taking the best means to secure our own happiness without injuring that of others, is the best proof of sense and strength of mind, whether in man or woman. Fortunately for society, the same conduct in ladies which best secures their happiness most increases ours."

Mrs Freke beat the devil's tattoo for some moments, and then exclaimed –

"You may say what you will, but the present system of society is radically wrong: – whatever is, is wrong."

"How would you improve the state of society?" asked Mr Percival calmly.

"I'm not tinker general to the world," said she.

"I am glad of it," said Mr Percival; "for I have heard that tinkers often spoil more than they mend."

"But if you want to know," said Mrs Freke, "what I would do to improve the world, I'll tell you: I'd have your sex taught to say, Horns! horns! I defy you."

"This would doubtless be a great improvement," said Mr Percival; "but you would not overturn society to attain it? would you? – Should we find things much improved by tearing away what has been called the decent drapery of life?"

"Drapery, if you ask me my opinion," cried Mrs Freke, "drapery, whether wet or dry, is the most confoundedly indecent thing in the world."

"That depends on *public* opinion, I allow," said Mr Percival. "The Lacedæmonian* ladies, who were veiled only by public opinion, were better covered from profane eyes, than some English ladies are in wet drapery."

"I know nothing of the Lacedæmonian ladies, I took my leave of them when I was a schoolboy – girl – I should say. But, pray, what o'clock is it by you – I've sat till I'm cramped all over," cried Mrs Freke, getting up and stretching herself so violently that some part of her habiliments gave way. "Honi soit qui mal y pense!"* said she, bursting into a horse laugh.

Without sharing in any degree that confusion which Belinda felt for her, she strode out of the room, saying, "Miss Portman, you understand these things better than I do; come and set me to rights."

When she was in Belinda's room, she threw herself into an arm chair, and laughed immoderately.

"How I have trimmed Percival this morning!" said she.

"I am glad you think so," said Belinda; "for I really was afraid he had been too severe upon you."

"I only wish," continued Mrs Freke, "I only wish his wife had been by. Why the devil did not she make her appearance? — I suppose the prude was afraid of my demolishing and unrigging her."

"There seems to have been more danger of that for you than for any body else," said Belinda, as she assisted to set Mrs Freke's *rigging*, as she called it, to rights.

"I do, of all things, delight in hauling good people's opinions out of their musty drawers, and seeing how they look when they're all pulled to pieces before their faces. Pray, are those Lady Anne's drawers or yours?" said Mrs Freke, pointing to a chest of drawers.

"Mine."

"I'm sorry for it; for, if they were hers, to punish her for *shirking* me, by the Lord, I'd have every rag she has in the world out in the middle of the floor in ten minutes! You don't know me — I'm a terrible person when provoked — Stop at nothing!"

As Mrs Freke saw no other chance left of gaining her point with Belinda, she tried what intimidating her would do.

"I stop at nothing," repeated she, fixing her eyes upon Miss Portman, to fascinate her by terror. "Friend or foe! Peace or war! Take your choice. — Come to the ball at Harrowgate, I win my bet, and I'm your sworn friend. — Stay away, I lose my bet, and am your sworn enemy."

"It is not in my power, madam," said Belinda calmly, "to comply with your request."

"Then you'll take the consequences," cried Mrs Freke. She rushed past her, hurried down stairs, and called out,

"Bid my blockhead bring my unicorn!"

She, her unicorn, and her blockhead, were out of sight in a few minutes.

Good may be drawn from evil. Mrs Freke's conversation, though at the time it confounded Belinda, roused her, upon reflection to examine by her reason for the habits and principles which guided her conduct. She had a general feeling that they were right and necessary; but now, with the assistance of Lady Anne and Mr Percival, she established in her own understanding the exact boundaries between right and wrong. She felt a species of satisfaction and security, from seeing the demonstration of those axioms of morality, in which she had previously acquiesced. Reasoning gradually became as agreeable to her as wit; nor was her taste for wit diminished, it was only refined by this process. She now compared and judged of the value of the different species of this brilliant talent.

Mrs Freke's wit, thought she, is like a squib let off in the street by vulgar mischievous boys – The passengers start – but it is only the terror of a moment. Lady Delacour's wit is like an elegant fire work played off at a festival – The spectators applaud – but it is only the admiration of a moment. Lady Anne Percival's wit is like

"The refulgent lamp of night – "

We

"Love the mild rays, and bless the useful light."

"Miss Portman," said Mr Percival, "are not you afraid of making an enemy of Mrs Freke, by declining her invitation to Harrowgate?"

"I think her friendship more to be dreaded than her enmity," replied Belinda.

"Then you are not to be terrified by an obeah-woman?" said Mr Vincent.

"Not in the least, unless she were to come in the shape of a false friend," said Belinda.

"Till lately," said Mr Vincent, "I was deceived in the character of Mrs Freke. I thought her a dashing, free-spoken, free-hearted sort of eccentric person, who would make a staunch friend, and a jolly companion. As a mistress or a wife, no man of any taste could think of her. Compare that woman now with one of our creole ladies."

"But why with a creole?" said Mr Percival.

"For the sake of contrast in the first place – Our creole women are all softness, grace, delicacy – "

"And indolence," said Mr Percival.

"Their indolence is but a slight, and, in my judgment, an amiable defect; it keeps them out of mischief, and it attaches them to domestic life. The activity of a Mrs Freke would never excite their emulation, and so much the better."

"So much the better, no doubt," said Mr Percival. "But is there no other species of activity, that might excite their ambition with propriety? Without diminishing their grace, softness, or delicacy, might not they cultivate their minds? Do you think ignorance, as well as indolence, an amiable defect essential to the female character?"

"Not essential. You do not, I hope, imagine that I am so much prejudiced in favour of my countrywomen, that I can neither see nor feel the superiority in *some instances* of European cultivation? I speak only in general."

"And in general," said Lady Anne Percival, "does Mr Vincent wish to confine our sex to the bliss of ignorance?"

"If it be bliss," said Mr Vincent, "what reason would they have for complaint?"

"*If*," said Belinda; "but that is a question which you have not yet decided."

"And how can we decide it?" said Mr Vincent. "The taste and feelings of individuals must be the arbiters of their happiness."

"You leave reason quite out of the question, then," said Mr Percival, "and refer the whole to taste and feeling? So that, if the most ignorant person in the world assert that he is happier than you are, you are bound to believe him."

"Why should not I?" said Mr Vincent.

"Because," said Mr Percival, "though he can judge of his own pleasures, he cannot judge of yours; his are common to both, but yours are unknown to him. — Would you, at this instant, change places with that ploughman yonder, who is whistling as he goes for want of thought? or, would you choose to go a step higher in the bliss of ignorance, and turn savage?"

Mr Vincent laughed, and protested that he should be very unwilling to give up his title to civilised society; and that, instead of wishing to have less knowledge, he regretted that he had not more. "I am sensible," said he, "that I have many prejudices: — Miss Portman has made me ashamed of some of them."

There was a degree of candour in Mr Vincent's manner and conversation which interested every body in his favour; Belinda amongst the rest. She was perfectly at ease in Mr Vincent's company, because she considered him as a person who wished for her friendship, without having any design to engage her affections. From several hints that dropped from him, from Mr Percival, and from Lady Anne, she was persuaded that he was attached to some creole lady; and all that he said in favour of the elegant softness and delicacy of his countrywomen confirmed this opinion.

Miss Portman was not one of those young ladies who fancy that every gentleman who converses freely with them will inevitably fall a victim to the power of their charms, and who see in every man a lover, or nothing.

CHAPTER XVIII

A Declaration

"I've found it! – I've found it! – mamma!" cried little Charles Percival, running eagerly into the room with a plant in his hand. "Will you send this in your letter to Helena Delacour, and tell her that it is the thing that gold fishes are so fond of? – And tell her that it is called lemna, and that it may be found in any ditch or pool."

"But how can she find ditches and pools in Grosvenor square, my dear?"

"O, I forgot that. – Then, will you tell her, mamma, that I will send her a great quantity?"

"How, my dear?"

"I don't know, mamma, yet – but I will find out some way."

"Would it not be as well, my dear," said his mother, smiling, "to consider how you can perform your promises before you make them?"

"A gentleman," said Mr Vincent, "never makes a promise that he cannot perform."

"I know that very well," said the boy proudly. "Miss Portman, who is very good natured, will, I am sure, be so good, when she goes back to Lady Delacour, as to carry food for the gold fishes to Helena – You see that I have found out a way to keep my promise."

"No, I am afraid not," said Belinda; "for I am not going back to Lady Delacour's."

"Then I am *very* glad of it!" said the boy, dropping the wood and clapping his hands joyfully – "for then I hope you will always stay here. – Don't you, mamma? – Don't *you*, Mr Vincent? – Oh, *you* do, I am sure, for I heard you say to papa the other day! – But what makes you grow so red?"

His mother took him by the hand as he was going to repeat the question, and, leading him out of the room, desired him to show her the place where he found the food for gold fishes.

Belinda, to Mr Vincent's great relief, seemed not to take any notice of the child's question, nor to have any sympathy in his curiosity; she was intently copying Westal's sketch of Lady Anne Percival and her family; and she had been roused, by the first mention of Helena Delacour's name, to many painful and some pleasing recollections. – "What a charming woman! and what a charming family!" said Mr Vincent as he looked at the drawing, "and how much more interesting is this picture of domestic happiness, than all the pictures of shepherds and shepherdesses, and gods and goddesses that ever were drawn!"

"Yes," said Belinda, "and how much more interesting this picture is to us, from our knowing that it is not a fancy-piece; that the happiness is real, not imaginary; that this is the natural expression of affection in the countenance of the mother; and that these children, who crowd round her, are what they seem to be, the pride and pleasure of her life!"

"There cannot," exclaimed Mr Vincent with enthusiasm, "be a more delightful picture! O, Miss Portman! is it possible that you should not feel what you can paint so well?"

"Is it possible, sir," said Belinda, "that you should suspect me of such wretched hypocrisy, as to affect to admire what I am incapable of feeling?

"You misunderstand – you totally misunderstand me. – Hypocrisy! – No; there is not a woman upon earth whom I believe to be so far above all hypocrisy, all affectation. – But I imagined – I feared — "

As he spoke these last words he was in some confusion, and hastily turned over the prints in a portfolio which lay upon the table. Belinda's eye was caught by an engraving of Lady Delacour in the character of the comic muse. Mr Vincent did not know the intimacy that had subsisted between her ladyship and Miss Portman – She sighed from the recollection of Clarence Hervey, and of all that had passed at the masquerade.

"What a contrast!" – said Mr Vincent, placing the print of Lady Delacour beside the picture of Lady Anne Percival. "What a contrast! – Compare their pictures: – compare their characters: – compare – "

"Excuse me," interrupted Belinda; "Lady Delacour was once my friend, and I do not like to make a comparison so much to her disadvantage. I have never seen any woman who would not suffer by a comparison with Lady Anne Percival."

"I have been more fortunate, I *have* seen one – one equally worthy of esteem – admiration – love."

"Mr Vincent's voice faltered in pronouncing the word love; yet Belinda, prepossessed by the idea that he was attached to some creole lady, simply answered, without looking up from her drawing, "You are indeed very fortunate, peculiarly fortunate. Are the West-Indian ladies – "

"West-Indian ladies!" interrupted Mr Vincent. "Surely, Miss Portman cannot imagine that I am at this instant thinking of any West-Indian lady!" Belinda looked up with an air of surprise. – "Charming Miss Portman!" continued he, "I have learnt to admire *European beauty*, *European excellence* – I have acquired new ideas of the female character – ideas, feelings that must henceforward render me exquisitely happy, or exquisitely miserable."

Miss Portman had been too often called "*charming*", to be much startled or delighted by the sound; the word would have passed by unnoticed, but there was something so impassioned in Mr Vincent's manner, that she could no longer mistake it for common gallantry, and she was in evident confusion. – Now for the first time the idea of Mr Vincent as a lover came into her mind. The next instant she accused herself of vanity, and dreaded that he should read her thoughts.

"Exquisitely miserable!" said she in a tone of raillery. "I should not suppose, from what I have seen of Mr Vincent, that any thing could make him exquisitely miserable."

"Then you do not know my character – you do not know my heart. – It is in your power to make me exquisitely miserable. – Mine is not the cold hackneyed phrase of gallantry, but the fervid language of passion," cried he, seizing her hand.

At this instant one of the children came in with some flowers for Belinda; and glad of the interruption, she hastily put up her drawings and left the room, observing that she should scarcely have time to dress before dinner. – However, as soon as she found herself alone, she forgot how late it was; and though she sat down before the glass to dress, she made no progress in the business, but continued for some time motionless, endeavouring to recollect and to understand all that had passed. The result of her reflections was the conviction, that her partiality for Clarence Hervey was greater, than she had ever till this moment suspected. – I have told my aunt Stanhope, thought she, that the idea of Mr Hervey had no influence in my refusal of Sir Philip Baddely. I have said that my affections are entirely at my own command. Then why do I feel this alarm at the discovery of Mr Vincent's views? Why do I compare him with one whom I thought I had forgotten? – And yet, how are we to judge of character? How can we form any estimate of what is amiable, of what will make us happy or miserable, but by comparison? – Am I to blame for perceiving superiority? – Am I to blame if one person be more agreeable than another? – Am I to blame if I cannot love Mr Vincent?

Before Belinda had answered these questions to her satisfaction, the dinner-bell rang. There happened to dine this day at Mr Percival's a gentleman who had just arrived from Lisbon, and the conversation turned upon the sailors' practice of stilling the waves over the bar of Lisbon by throwing oil upon the water. Charles Percival's curiosity was excited by this conversation, and he wished to see the experiment. In the evening his father indulged his wishes. The children were delighted at the sight, and little Charles insisted upon Belinda's following him to a particular spot, where he was well convinced that she could see better than any where else in the world. "Take care," cried Lady Anne, "or you will lead your friend into the river, Charles." The boy paused, and soon afterward asked his father several questions about swimming and drowning, and bringing people to life after they had been drowned. "Don't you remember, papa," said he, "*that* Mr Hervey, who was almost drowned in the Serpentine river in London?" – Belinda coloured at hearing unexpectedly the name of the person of whom she was at that instant thinking, and the child continued —

"I liked that Mr Hervey very much – I liked him from the first day I saw him. What a number of entertaining things he told us at dinner! We used to call him the good natured gentleman. – I like him very much – I wish he was here this minute. Did you ever see him, Miss Portman? – O yes, you must have seen him; for it was he who carried Helena's gold fishes to her mother, and he used often to be at Lady Delacour's – was not he?"

"Yes, my dear, often."

"And did not you like him very much?" – This simple question threw Belinda into inexpressible confusion; but fortunately the crimson on her face was seen only by Lady Anne Percival. To her great satisfaction, Mr Vincent forbore this evening any attempt to renew the conversation of the morning: he endeavoured to mix with his usual animation and gaiety in the family society; and her embarrassment was much lessened, when she heard the next day

at breakfast that he was gone to Harrowgate. Lady Anne
Percival took notice that she was this morning unusually
sprightly.

After breakfast, as they were passing through the hall to take a
walk in the park, one of the little boys stopped to look at a
musical instrument which hung up against the wall.

"'What is this, mamma? – It is not a guitar, is it?"

"No, my dear, it is called a banjore; it is an African instrument, of which the negroes are particularly fond – Mr Vincent
mentioned it the other day to Miss Portman, and I believe she
expressed some curiosity to see one. Juba went to work immediately to make a banjore I find. – Poor fellow, I dare say that he
was very sorry to go to Harrowgate, and to leave his African
guitar half finished; especially as it was intended for an offering
to Miss Portman. He is the most grateful, affectionate creature I
ever saw."

"But why, mamma," said Charles Percival, "is Mr Vincent
gone away? I am sorry he is gone. I hope he will soon come back.
– In the mean time I must run and water my carnations."

"His sorrow for his friend Mr Vincent's departure does not
seem to affect his spirits much," said Lady Anne. "People who
expect sentiment from children of six years old will be disappointed, and will probably teach them affection. Surely it is
much better to let their natural affections have time to expand. If
we tear the rose-bud open, we spoil the flower for ever." Belinda
smiled at this parable of the rose-bud, which, she said, might be
applied to men and women, as well as to children; that the
growth of the affections must be spontaneous.

"And yet upon reflection," said Lady Anne, "the heart has
nothing in common with a rose-bud. Nonsensical allusions pass
off very prettily in conversation. – I mean, when we converse
with partial friends: but we should reason ill, and conduct
ourselves worse, if we were to trust implicitly to poetical analogies. Our affections," continued Lady Anne, "arise from circumstances totally independent of our will."

"That is the very thing I meant to say," interrupted Belinda
eagerly.

"They are excited by the agreeable or useful qualities that we
discover in things or in persons."

"Undoubtedly," said Belinda.

"Or by those which our fancies discover," said Lady Anne.

Belinda was silent; but after a pause she said, "That it was certainly very dangerous, especially for women, to trust to fancy in bestowing their affections. And yet," continued she, "it is a danger to which they are much exposed in society. Men have it in their power to assume the appearance of every thing that is amiable and estimable, and women have scarcely any opportunities of detecting the counterfeit. Without Ithuriel's spear,* how can they distinguish the good from the evil?" said Belinda. "This is a commonplace complaint, I know; the ready excuse that we silly young women plead, when we make mistakes for which our friends reproach us, and for which we too often reproach ourselves."

"The complaint is commonplace precisely because it is general and just," replied Lady Anne. "In the slight and frivolous intercourse, which fashionable belles usually have with those fashionable beaux who call themselves their lovers, it is surprising that they can discover any thing of each other's real character. Indeed they seldom do; and this probably is the cause why there are so many unsuitable and unhappy marriages. A woman who has an opportunity of seeing her lover in private society, in domestic life, has infinite advantages; for, if she has any sense, and he has any sincerity, the real character of both may be developed."

"True," said Belinda (who now suspected that Lady Anne alluded to Mr Vincent): "and in such a situation a woman would readily be able to decide, whether the man who addressed her would suit her taste or not; so she would be inexcusable if, either from vanity or coquetry, she disguised her real sentiments."

"And will Miss Portman, who cannot by any one to whom she is known be suspected of vanity or coquetry, permit me to speak to her with the freedom of a friend?"

Belinda, who was much touched by the kindness of Lady Anne's manner, pressed her hand, and exclaimed, "Yes, dear Lady Anne, speak to me with freedom, you cannot do me a greater favour. No thought of my mind, no secret feeling of my heart, shall be concealed from you."

"Do not imagine that I wish to encroach upon the generous openness of your temper," said Lady Anne; "tell me when I go too far, and I will be silent. One who, like Miss Portman, has lived in the world, has seen a variety of characters, and probably has had a variety of admirers, must have formed some determinate idea of the sort of companion, that would make her happy, if she were to marry – unless," said Lady Anne, "she has formed a resolution against marriage."

"I have formed no such resolution," said Belinda. "Indeed, since I have seen the happiness which you and Mr Percival enjoy in your own family, I have been much more disposed to think that a union with – that a union such as yours would increase my happiness. At the same time, my aversion to the idea of marrying from interest, or convenience, or from any motives but esteem and love, is increased almost to horror. O, Lady Anne! there is nothing that I would not do to please the friends to whom I am under obligations, except sacrificing my peace of mind, or my integrity, the happiness of my life, by – "

Lady Anne, in a gentle tone, assured her, that she was the last person in the world, who would press her to any union which would make her unhappy, "You perceive that Mr Vincent has spoken to me of what passed between you yesterday. You perceive that I am his friend, but do not forget that I am also yours. If you fear *undue influence* from any of your relations in favour of Mr Vincent's large fortune, &c., let his proposal remain a secret between ourselves, till you can decide, from further acquaintance with him, whether it will be in your power to return his affection."

"I fear, my dear Lady Anne," cried Belinda, "that it is not in my power to return his affection."

"And may I ask your objections?"

"Is not it a sufficient objection, that I am persuaded I cannot love him."

"No; for you may be mistaken in that persuasion. Remember what we said a little while ago about *fancy and spontaneous affections*. Does Mr Vincent appear to you defective in any of the qualities, which you think essential to happiness? Mr Percival has known him from the time he was a man, and can answer for his integrity and his good temper. Are not these the first points you would consider? They ought to be, I am sure, and I believe they are. Of his understanding I shall say nothing, because you have had full opportunities of judging of it from his conversation."

"Mr Vincent appears to have an excellent understanding," said Belinda.

"Then to what do you object? – Is there any thing disgusting to you in his person or manners?"

"He is remarkably handsome, he is well bred, and his manners are perfectly unaffected," said Belinda, "but – do not accuse me of caprice – altogether he does not suit my taste; and I cannot think it sufficient not to feel disgust for a husband – though I believe this is the fashionable doctrine."

"It is not mine, I assure you," said Lady Anne. "I am not one of those who think it 'safest to begin with a little aversion'; but since you acknowledge, that Mr Vincent possesses the essential good qualities that entitle him to your esteem, I am satisfied. In a mind as well regulated as yours, esteem may certainly in time be improved into love. I will tell him so, my dear."

"No, my dear Lady Anne! No; you must not, indeed you must not. You have too good an opinion of me – my mind is not so well regulated – I am much weaker, much sillier, than you imagine – than you can conceive," said Belinda.

Lady Anne soothed her with the most affectionate expressions, and concluded with saying: "Mr Vincent has promised not to return from Harrowgate, to torment you with his addresses, if you be absolutely determined against him. He is of too generous, and perhaps too proud a temper, to persecute you with vain solicitations; and however Mr Percival and I may wish that he could obtain such a wife, we shall have the common, or uncommon, sense and good nature to allow our friends to be happy their own way."

"You are very good; too good. But am I then to be the cause of banishing Mr Vincent from all his friends – from Oakly-park?"

"Will he not do what is most prudent to avoid the charming Miss Portman," said Lady Anne smiling, "if he must not love her? This was at least the advice I gave him, when he consulted us yesterday evening. But I will not sign his writ of banishment lightly. Nothing but the assurance that the heart is engaged can be a sufficient cause for despair; nothing else could, in my eyes, justify you, my dear Belinda, from the charge of caprice."

"I can give you no such assurance, I hope – I believe," said Belinda in great confusion; "and yet I would not for the world deceive you; you have a right to my sincerity." She paused; and Lady Anne said with a smile, "Perhaps I can spare you the trouble of telling me in words what a blush told me, or at least made me suspect, yesterday evening, when we were standing by the river-side, when little Charles asked you – "

"Yes. I remember – I saw you look at me."

"Undesignedly, believe me."

"Undesignedly, I am sure; but I was afraid you would think – "

"The truth."

"No, but more than the truth. The truth you shall hear; and the rest I will leave to your judgment and your kindness."

Belinda gave a full account of her acquaintance with Clarence Hervey; of the variations in his manner towards her; of his excellent conduct with respect to Lady Delacour (of this, by the by, she spoke at large). But she was more concise when she touched upon the state of her own heart; and her voice almost failed when she came to the history of the lock of beautiful hair, the Windsor incognita, and the picture of Virginia. She concluded by expressing her conviction of the propriety of forgetting a man, who was in all probability attached to another, and she declared it to be her resolution, to banish him from her thoughts. Lady Anne said, "that nothing could be more prudent, or praiseworthy, than forming such a resolution – except keeping it." Lady Anne had a high opinion of Mr Hervey; but she had no doubt, from Belinda's account, and from her own observations on Mr Hervey, and from slight circumstances which had accidentally come to Mr Percival's knowledge, that he was, as Belinda suspected, attached to Virginia St Pierre. She wished, therefore, to confirm Miss Portman in this belief, and to turn her thoughts towards one who, beside being deserving of her esteem and love, felt for her the most sincere affection. She did not, however, press the subject farther at this time, but contented herself with requesting, that Belinda would take three days (the usual time given for deliberation in fairy tales) before she should decide against Mr Vincent.

The next day they went to look at a porter's lodge, which Mr Percival had just built; it was inhabited by an old man and woman, who had for many years been industrious tenants, but who, in their old age, had been reduced to poverty, not by imprudence, but by misfortune. Lady Anne was pleased to see them comfortably settled in their new habitation; and whilst she and Belinda were talking to the old couple, their granddaughter, a pretty-looking girl of about eighteen, came in with a basket of eggs in her hand. "Well, Lucy," said Lady Anne, "have you overcome your fear of poor Juba's black face?" The girl reddened, smiled, and looked at her grandmother, who answered for her in an arch tone, "O, yes, my lady! We are not afraid of Juba's black face *now*; we are grown very great friends. This pretty cane chair for my good man was his handiwork, and these baskets he made for me. Indeed, he's a most industrious, ingenious, good natured youth; and our Lucy takes no offence at his black face now, my lady, I can assure you. That necklace," added she in a half-whisper, pointing to a necklace of Angola pease which the girl wore — "that necklace is a present of his, which is never off her neck now, my lady. So I tell him he need not be discouraged, though so be she did not take to him at the first; for she's a good girl, and a sensible girl, I say it, though she's my own: and the eyes are used to a face after a time, and then it's nothing. They say, fancy's all in all in love. Now, in my judgment, fancy's little or nothing with girls that have sense. But I beg pardon for prating at this rate, more especially when I am so old as to have forgot all the little I ever knew about such things."

"But you have the best right in the world to speak about such things, and your granddaughter has the best reason in the world to listen to you," said Lady Anne, "because, in spite of all the crosses of fortune, you have been an excellent and happy wife, at least ever since I can remember."

"And ever since I can remember, that's more; no offence to your ladyship," said the old man, striking his crutch against the ground. "Ever since I can remember, she has made me the happiest man in the whole world, in the whole parish, as every body knows, and I best of all!" cried he with a degree of enthusiasm, that lighted up his aged countenance, and animated his feeble voice.

"And yet," said the honest dame, "if I had followed my fancy, and taken up with my first love, it would not ha' been with *he*, Lucy. I had a sort of a fancy (since my lady's so good as to let me speak), I had a sort of a fancy for an idle young man; but he, very luckily for me, took it into his head to fall in love with another young woman, and then I had leisure enough left me to think of your grandfather, who was not so much to my taste like at first. But when I found out his goodness and cleverness, and, joined to all, his great tenderness for me, I thought better of it, Lucy (as who knows but you may do, though there shall not be a word said on my part to press you, for poor Juba?); and my thinking better is the cause why I have been so happy ever since, and am so still in my old age. Ah, Lucy, dear! what a many years that same old age lasts, after all! But young folks, for the most part, never think what's to come after thirty or forty at furthest. But I don't say this for you, Lucy; for you are a good girl, and a sensible girl, though my own, as I said before, and therefore won't be run away with by fancy, which is soon past and gone – but make a prudent choice, that you won't never have cause to repent of. But I'll not say a word more; I'll leave it all to yourself and poor Juba, who, I hope, won't be long away at Harrowgate, my lady."

"I hope not," said Lady Anne; "but that depends neither on you nor me. Good morning to you! Farewell, Lucy! That's a pretty necklace, and is very becoming to you – fare ye well!"

And she hurried out of the cottage with Belinda, apprehensive that the talkative old dame might weaken the effect of her good sense and experience by a further profusion of words.

"One would think," said Belinda with an ingenuous smile, "that this lesson upon the dangers of *fancy* was intended for me: at any rate, I may turn it to my own advantage."

"Happy those who can turn all the experience of others to their own advantage!" said Lady Anne. "This would be a more valuable privilege, than the power of turning every thing that is touched to gold."

They walked on in silence for a few minutes; and then Miss Portman, pursuing the train of her own thoughts, and unconscious that she had not explained them to Lady Anne, abruptly exclaimed, "But if I should be entangled, so as not to be able to retract! – and if it should not be in my power to love him at last, he will think me a coquette, a jilt perhaps; he will have reason to complain of me, if I waste his time, and trifle with his affections. Then is it not better that I should avoid, by a decided refusal, all possibility of injury to Mr Vincent, and of blame to myself?"

"There is no danger of Mr Vincent's misunderstanding or misrepresenting you. The risk that he runs is by his voluntary choice; and I am sure that, if after further acquaintance with him you find it impossible to return his affection, he will not consider himself as ill-used by your refusal."

"But after a certain time – after the world suspects that two people are engaged to each other, it is scarcely possible for the woman to recede: when they come within a certain distance, they are pressed to unite, by the irresistible force of external circumstances. A woman is too often reduced to this dilemma – Either she must marry a man she does not love, or she must be blamed by the world – either she must sacrifice a portion of her reputation, or the whole of her happiness."

"The world is indeed often too curious, and too rash in these affairs," said Lady Anne. "A young woman is not in this respect allowed sufficient time for freedom of deliberation. She sees, as Mr Percival once said, 'the drawn sword of tyrant custom suspended over her head by a single hair'."

"And yet, not withstanding you are so well aware of the danger, your ladyship would expose me to it," said Belinda.

"Yes. For I think the chance of happiness, in this instance, overbalances the risk," said Lady Anne. "As we cannot alter the common law of custom, and as we cannot render the world less gossiping, or less censorious, we must not expect always to avoid censure; all we can do is never to deserve it – and it would be absurd to enslave ourselves to the opinion of the idle and ignorant. To a certain point, respect for the opinion of the world is prudence; beyond that point, it is weakness. You should also consider that *the world* at Oakly-park and in London are two different worlds. In London if you and Mr Vincent were seen often in each other's company, it would be immediately buzzed about, that Miss Portman and Mr Vincent were going to be married; and if the match did not take place, a thousand foolish stories might be told to account for its being broken off. But here you are not surrounded by busy eyes and busy tongues. The butchers, bakers, ploughmen, and spinsters, who compose our world, have all affairs of their own to mind. Besides, their comments can have no very extensive circulation; they are used to see Mr Vincent continually here; and his staying with us the remainder of the autumn will not appear to them any thing wonderful, or portentous."

Lady Anne's arguments and raillery had such an effect upon Miss Portman, that no writ of banishment was issued against Mr Vincent. He returned to Oakly-park – but upon the express condition, that he should not make his attachment public by any particular attentions, and that he should draw no conclusions in his favour from Belinda's consenting to converse with him freely upon every common subject. To this treaty of amity Lady Anne Percival was guarantee.

CHAPTER XIX

A Wedding

Belinda and Mr Vincent could never agree in their definition of the word *flattery*; so that there were continual complaints on the one hand of a breach of treaty, and, on the other, solemn protestations of the most scrupulous adherence to his compact. However this might be, it is certain that the gentleman gained so much either by truth or fiction, that, in the course of some weeks, he got the lady as far as – "gratitude and esteem".

One evening, Belinda was playing with little Charles Percival at jackstraws. Mr Vincent, who found pleasure in every thing which amused Belinda, and Mr Percival, who took an interest in every thing which entertained his children, were looking on at this simple game.

"Mr Percival," said Belinda, "condescending to look at a game of jackstraws!"

"Yes," said Lady Anne; "for he is of Dryden's opinion, that, if a straw can be made the instrument of happiness, he is a wise man who does not despise it."

"Ah! Miss Portman, take care!" cried Charles, who was anxious that she should win, though he was playing against her. "Take care! don't touch that knave!"

"I would lay a hundred guineas upon the steadiness of Miss Portman's hand," cried Mr Vincent.

"I'll lay you sixpence though," cried Charles eagerly, "that she'll stir the king, if she touches that knave – I'll lay you a shilling."

"Done! done!" cried Mr Vincent.

"Done! done!" cried the boy, stretching out his hand, but his father caught it.

"Softly! softly, Charles! – No betting, if you please, my dear. – Done! and done! – sometimes ends in – Undone."

"It was my fault – it was I who was in the wrong," cried Vincent immediately, with that candour which he showed in trifles as well as in matters of consequence.

"I am sure you are in the right now," said Mr Percival; "and, what is better than my saying so, Miss Portman thinks so, as her smile tells me."

"You moved, Miss Portman!" cried Charles, "Oh, indeed! the king's head stirred the very instant papa spoke. I knew it was impossible that you could get that knave clear off without shaking the king. Now, papa, only look how they were balanced."

"I grant you," said Mr Vincent, "I should have made an imprudent bet. So it is well I made none; for now I see the chances were ten to one, twenty to one, a hundred to one against me."

"It does not appear to me to be a matter of chance," said Mr Percival. "This is a game of address, not chance, and that is the reason I like it."

"O papa! O Miss Portman! look how nicely these are balanced. There! my breath has set them in motion. – Look! they shake, shake, shake, like the great rocking stones at Brimham Crags."

"That is comparing small things to great, indeed!" said Mr Percival.

"By the by," cried Mr Vincent, "Miss Portman has never seen those wonderful rocking stones – Suppose we were to ride to see them tomorrow?"

The proposal was warmly seconded by the children, and agreed to by every one. It was settled, that after they had seen Brimham Crags they should spend the remainder of the day at Lord — 's, a beautiful place in the neighbourhood.

The next morning was neither too hot nor too cold, and they set out on their little party of pleasure: the children went with their mother, to their great delight, in the *sociable*;* and Mr Vincent, to his great delight, rode with Belinda. When they came within sight of the Crags, Mr Percival, who was riding with them, exclaimed – "What is that yonder on the top of one of the great rocking stones?"

"It looks like a statue," said Vincent. "It has been put up since we were here last."

"I fancy it has got up of itself," said Belinda, "for it seems to be getting down of itself. I think I saw it stoop. – O! I see now, it is a man who has got up there, and he seems to have a gun in his hand, has not he? He is going through his manual exercise for his diversion – For the diverson of the spectators below, I perceive – There is a party of people looking at him."

"Him!" said Mr Percival.

"I protest it is a woman!" said Vincent.

"No, surely," said Belinda: "It cannot be a woman!"

"Not unless it be Mrs Freke," replied Mr Percival.

In fact, it was Mrs Freke, who had been out shooting with a party of gentlemen, and who had scrambled upon this rocking stone, on the summit of which she went through the manual exercise at the word of command from her officer. As they rode nearer to the scene of action, Belinda heard the shrill screams of a female voice, and they descried amongst the gentlemen a slight figure in a riding-habit.

"Miss Moreton I suppose?" said Mr Vincent.

"Poor girl! what are they doing with her?" cried Belinda. "They seem to be forcing her up to the top of that place, where she has no mind to go. – Look how Mrs Freke drags her up by the arm!"

As they drew nearer, they heard Mrs Freke laughing loud as she rocked this frightened girl upon the top of the stone.

"We had better keep out of the way, I think," said Belinda; "for perhaps, as she has vowed vengeance against me, she might take a fancy to setting me upon that pinnacle of glory."

"She dare not," cried Vincent, his eyes flashing with anger: "you may trust to us to defend you."

"Certainly! – But I will not run into danger on purpose to give you the pleasure of defending me," said Belinda; and as she spoke, she turned her horse another way.

"You won't turn back, Miss Portman?" cried Vincent eagerly, laying his hand on her bridle. – "Good God, ma'am! we can't run away! – We came here to look at these rocking stones! We have not half seen them. Lady Anne and the children will be here immediately. You would not deprive them of the pleasure of seeing these things!"

"I doubt whether they would have much pleasure in seeing *some of these things*; and, as to the rest, if I disappoint the children now, Mr Percival will, perhaps, have the goodness to bring them some other day."

"Certainly," said Mr Percival: "Miss Portman shows her usual prudence."

"The children are so good tempered, that I am sure they will forgive me," continued Belinda; "and Mr Vincent will be ashamed not to follow their example, though he seems to be rather angry with me at present for obliging him to turn back – out of the path of danger."

"You must not be surprised at that," said Mr Percival, laughing; "for Mr Vincent is a lover and a hero. You know it is a ruled case, in all romances, that, when a lover and his mistress go out riding together, some adventure must befall them. The horse must run away with the lady, and the gentleman must catch her in his arms just as her neck is about to be broken. If the horse have been too ill trained for the heroine's purpose, 'some footpad, bandit fierce, or mountaineer,' some jealous rival must make his appearance quite unexpectedly at the turn of a road, and the lady must be carried off, robes flying! hair streaming! like Buerger's Leonora.* Then her lover must come to her rescue just in the proper moment. – But, if the damsel cannot conveniently be run away with, she must, as the last resource, tumble into a river to make herself interesting, and the hero must be at least half drowned in dragging her out, that she may be under eternal obligations to him, and at last be forced to marry him out of pure gratitude."

"Gratitude!" interrupted Mr Vincent: "He is no hero to my mind, who would be content with gratitude, instead of love."

"You need not alarm yourself: Miss Portman does not seem inclined to put you to the trial, you see," said Mr Percival, smiling. "Now it is really to be regretted, that she deprived you of an opportunity of fighting some of the gentlemen in Mrs Freke's train, or of delivering her from the perilous height of one of those rocking stones. – It would have been a new incident in a novel."

"How that poor girl screamed!" said Belinda. "Was her terror real or affected?"

"Partly real, partly affected, I fancy," said Mr Percival.

"I pity her," said Mr Vincent; "for Mrs Freke leads her a weary life."

"She is certainly to be pitied, but also to be blamed," said Mr Percival. "You do not know her history. Miss Moreton ran away from her friends to live with this Mrs Freke, who has led her into all kinds of mischief and absurdity. The girl is weak and vain, and believes that every thing becomes her, which Mrs Freke assures her is becoming. At one time she was persuaded to go to a public ball with her arms as bare as Juno's, and her feet as naked as Madame Tallien's.* At another time Miss Moreton (who unfortunately had never heard the Greek proverb, that half is better than the whole) was persuaded by Mrs Freke to lay aside her half boots, and to equip herself in men's whole boots; and thus she rode about the country, to the amazement of all the world. – These are trifles: but women who love to set the world at defiance in trifles, seldom respect its opinion in matters of consequence. Miss Moreton's whole boots in the morning, and her bare feet in the evening, were talked of by every body, till she gave them more to talk of about her attachment to a young officer. Mrs Freke, whose philosophy is professedly latitudinarian in morals, laughed at the girl's prejudice in favour of the ceremony of marriage. So did the officer; for Miss Moreton had no fortune. It is suspected, that the young lady did not feel the difficulty, which philosophers are sometimes said to find in suiting their practice to their theory. The *unenlightened* world reprobated the theory much, and the practice more. I am inclined, in spite of scandal, to think the poor girl was only imprudent: at all events, she repents her folly too late. She has now no friend upon earth but Mrs Freke, who is, in fact, her worst enemy, and who tyrannises over her without mercy. Imagine what it is to be the butt of a buffoon!"

"What a lesson to young ladies in the choice of female friends!" said Belinda. "But had Miss Moreton no relations, who could interfere to get her out of Mrs Freke's hands?"

"Her father amd mother were old, and, what is more contemptible, old-fashioned: she would not listen to their advice, she ran away from them. Some of her relations were, I believe, willing that she should stay with Mrs Freke, because she was a dashing fashionable woman, and they thought it might be what is called *an advantage* to her. She had one relation, indeed, who was quite of a different opinion, who saw the danger of her situation, and remonstrated in the strongest manner – but to no purpose. This was a cousin of Miss Moreton's, a respectable clergyman. Mrs Freke was so much incensed by his *insolent interference* as she was pleased to call it, that she made an effigy of Mr Moreton dressed in his canonicals, and hung the figure up as a scarecrow in a garden close by the high road. He was so much beloved and respected for his benevolence and unaffected piety, that Mrs Freke totally failed in her design of making him ridiculous; her scarecrow was torn to pieces by his parishioners; and though, in the true spirit of charity, he did all he could to moderate their indignation against his enemy, the lady became such an object of detestation, that she was followed with hisses and groans whenever she appeared, and she dared not venture within ten miles of the village.

"Mrs Freke now changed the mode of her persecution; she was

acquainted with a nobleman from whom our clergyman expected a living, and she worked upon his lordship so successfully, that he insisted upon having an apology made to the lady. Mr Moreton had as much dignity of mind as gentleness of character; his forbearance was that of principle, and so was his firmness: he refused to make the concessions that were required. His noble patron bullied. Though he had a large family to provide for, this clergyman would not degrade himself by any improper submission. The incumbent died, and the living was given to a more compliant friend. – So ends the history of one of Mrs Freke's numerous frolics."

"This was the story," said Mr Vincent, "which effectually changed my opinion of her. Till I heard it, I always looked upon her as one of those thoughtless, good natured people, who, as the common saying is, do nobody any harm but themselves."

"It is difficult in society," said Mr Percival, "especially for women, to do harm to themselves, without doing harm to others. They may begin in frolic, but they must end in malice. They defy the world – the world in return excommunicates them – the female outlaws become desperate, and make it the business and pride of their lives to disturb the peace of their sober neighbours. Women who have lowered themselves in the public opinion cannot rest without attempting to bring others to their own level."

"Mrs Freke, notwithstanding the blustering merriment that she affects, is obviously unhappy," said Belinda; "and since we cannot do her any good, either by our blame or our pity, we had better think of something else."

"Scandal," said Mr Vincent, "does not seem to give you much pleasure, Miss Portman. You will be glad to hear, that Mrs Freke's malice against poor Mr Moreton has not ruined him. Do you know, Mr Percival, that he has just been presented to a good living by a generous young man, who heard of his excellent conduct."

"I am extremely glad of it," said Mr Percival. "Who is this generous young man? I should like to be acquainted with him."

"So should I," said Mr Vincent; "he is a Mr Hervey."

"Clarence Hervey, perhaps?"

"Yes, Clarence was his name."

"No man more likely to do a generous action than Clarence Hervey," said Mr Percival.

"Nobody more likely to do a generous action than Mr Hervey," repeated Belinda in rather a lower tone. She could now praise Clarence Hervey without blushing, and she could think even of his generosity without enthusiasm, though not without pleasure. By strength of mind, and timely exertion, she had prevented her prepossession from growing into a passion that might have made her miserable. Proud of this conquest over herself, she was now disposed to treat Mr Vincent with more favour than usual. Self-complacency generally puts us in good humour with our friends.

After spending some pleasant hours in Lord C — 's beautiful grounds, where the children explored to their satisfaction every dingle and bushy dell, they returned home in the cool of the evening. – Mr Vincent thought it the most delightful evening he had ever felt.

"What! as charming as a West-Indian evening?" said Mr Percival. "This is more than I expected ever to hear you acknowledge in favour of England. Do you remember how you used to rave of the climate and of the prospects of Jamaica?"

"Yes, but my taste has quite changed."

"I remember the time," said Mr Percival, "when you thought it impossible that your taste should ever change; when you told me that taste, whether for the beauties of animate or inanimate nature, was immutable."

"You and Miss Portman have taught me better sense. First loves are generally silly things," added he, colouring a little. Belinda coloured also.

"First loves," continued Mr Percival, "are not necessarily more foolish than others; but the chances are certainly against them. Proximity of time or place, a variety of accidental circumstances more than the essential merits of the object, often produce what is called first love. From poetry or romance young people usually form their early ideas of love, before they have actually felt the passion; and the image which they have in their own minds of the *beau ideal* is cast upon the first objects they afterward behold. This, if I may be allowed the expression, is Cupid's Fata Morgana. Deluded mortals are in ecstasy whilst the illusion lasts, and in despair when it vanishes."

Mr Percival appeared to be unconscious, that what he was saying was any way applicable to Belinda. He addressed himself to Mr Vincent solely, and she listened at her ease.

"But," said she, "do not you think that this prejudice, as I am willing to allow it to be, in favour of first loves, may *in our sex* be advantageous? Even when a woman may be convinced that she ought not to indulge a *first* love, should she not be prevented by delicacy from thinking of a second?"

"Delicacy, my dear Miss Portman, is a charming word, and a still more charming thing, and Mrs Freke has probably increased our affection for it; but even delicacy, like all other virtues, must be judged by the test of utility. We should run into romance, and error, and misery, if we did not constantly refer to this standard. Our reasonings as to the conduct of life, as far as moral prudence is concerned, must depend ultimately upon facts. Now, of the numbers of people in this world how many do you think have married their *first loves*? Probably not one out of ten. – Then, would you have nine out of ten pine all their lives in celibacy, or fret in matrimony, because they cannot have the persons who first struck their *fancy*?"

"I acknowledge this would not add to the happiness of society," said Belinda.

"Nor to its virtue," said Mr Percival. "I scarcely know an idea more dangerous to domestic happiness, than this belief in the unextinguishable nature of a first flame. There are people who would persuade us, that, though it may be smothered for years, it must break out at last, and blaze with destructive fury. – Pernicious doctrine! false as it is pernicious! – The struggles between duty and passion may be the charm of romance, but must be the misery of real life. The woman who marries one man, and loves another, who, in spite of all that an amiable and estimable husband can do to win her confidence and affection, nourishes in secret a *fatal* prepossession for her first love, may perhaps, by the eloquence of a fine writer, be made an interesting heroine; but would any man of sense or feeling choose to be troubled with such a wife? – Would not even the idea that women admired such conduct necessarily tend to diminish our confidence, if not in their virtue, at least in their sincerity? And would not this suspicion destroy our happiness? Husbands may sometimes have delicate feelings as well as their wives, though they are seldom allowed to have any by these unjust novel writers. – Now could a husband who has any delicacy be content, to possess the person without the mind? – The duty without the love? – Could he be perfectly happy, if, in the fondest moments, he might doubt whether he were an object of disgust or affection? whether the smiles of apparent joy were only the efforts of a suffering martyr? – Thank Heaven! I am not married to one of these charming martyrs. Let those live with them, who admire them. For my part, I admire and love the wife, who not only seems but is happy – as I," added Mr Percival smiling, "have the fond credulity to believe. If I have spoken too long or too warmly upon the chapter of *first loves*, I have at least been a perfectly disinterested declaimer; for I can assure you, Miss Portman, that I do not suspect Lady Anne Percival of sighing in secret for some vision of perfection, any more than she suspects me of pining for the charming Lady Delacour, who, perhaps, you may have heard was my *first love*. In these days, however, so few people marry with even the pretence to love of any sort, that you will think I might have spared this tirade. – No; there are ingenuous minds which will never be enslaved by fashion or interest, though they may be exposed to be deceived by romance, or by the *delicacy* of their own imaginations."

"I hear," said Belinda smiling, "I hear and understand the emphasis, with which you pronounce that word *delicacy*. I see you have not forgotten, that I used it improperly half an hour ago, as you have convinced me."

"Happy they," said Mr Percival, "who can be convinced in half an hour! There are some people who cannot be convinced in a whole life, and who end where they began, with saying – 'This is my opinion – I always thought so, and always shall.'"

Mr Vincent at all times loved Mr Percival; but he never felt so much affection for him as he did this evening, and his arguments appeared to him unanswerable. – Though Belinda had never mentioned to Mr Vincent the name of Clarence Hervey till this day; and though he did not in the least suspect from her manner, that this gentleman ever possessed any interest in her heart; yet with her accustomed sincerity she had confessed to him, that an impression had been made upon her mind before she came to Oakly-park.

After this conversation with Mr Percival, Mr Vincent perceived that he gained ground more rapidly in her favour; she became accustomed to consider him as a lover, and his company grew every day more agreeable to her taste; he was convinced that, as he possessed her esteem, he should in time secure her affections.

"In time," repeated Lady Anne Percival: "you must allow her time, or you will spoil all."

It was with some difficulty that Mr Vincent restrained his impatience, even though he was persuaded of the prudence of his friend's advice. Things went on in this happy, but as he thought slow, state of progression, till towards the latter end of September.

One fine morning Lady Anne Percival came into Belinda's room with a bridal favour in her hand – "Do you know," said she, "that we are to have a wedding today. This favour has just been sent to my maid. Lucy, the pretty girl whom you may remember to have seen some time ago in a necklace of Angola pease, is the bride, and Juba is the bridegroom. Mr Vincent has let them a very pretty little farm in the neighbourhood, and – hark! there's the sound of music."

They looked out of the window, and they saw a troop of villagers gaily dressed, going to the wedding. Lady Anne, who was always eager to promote innocent festivity, sent immediately to have a tent pitched in the park, and all the rural company were invited to a dance in the evening: it was a very cheerful spectacle. – Belinda heard from all sides praises of Mr Vincent's generosity; and she could not be insensible to the simple but enthusiastic testimony, which Juba bore to his master's goodness. Juba had composed, in his broken dialect, a little song in honour of his benefactor, which he sang to his banjore with the most touching expression of joyful gratitude. In some of the stanzas, Belinda could distinguish that her own name was frequently repeated. Lady Anne called him, and desired to have the words of this song. They were a mixture of English and of his native language; they described in the strongest manner what had been his feelings, whilst he was under the terror of Mrs Freke's fiery obeah-woman, then his joy on being relieved from these horrors, with the delightful sensations of returning health; and thence he suddenly passed to his gratitude to Belinda, the person to whom he owed his recovery. He concluded with wishing her all sorts of happiness, and, above all, that she might be fortunate in her love; which Juba thought the highest degree of felicity. He had no sooner finished his song, which particularly touched and pleased Miss Portman, than he begged his master to offer to her the little instrument, which he had made with much pains and ingenuity. She accepted the banjore with a smile that enchanted Mr Vincent;

but at this instant they were startled by the sound of a carriage driving rapidly into the park. Belinda looked up, and between the heads of the dancers she just caught a glimpse of a well-known livery. – "Good heavens!" she exclaimed, "Lady Delacour's carriage! – Can it be Lady Delacour?"

The carriage stopped, and Marriott hastily jumped out of it. Belinda pressed forward to meet her; poor Marriott was in great agitation: – "Oh, Miss Portman! my poor lady is very ill – very ill indeed. She has sent me for you – here's her letter. Dear Miss Portman, I hope you won't refuse to come? – She *has* been very ill, and *is* very ill; but she would be better, if she could see you again. But I'll tell every thing, ma'am, when we are by ourselves, and when you have read your letter."

Miss Portman immediately accompanied Marriott towards the house; and as they walked thither, she learned that Lady Delacour had applied to the quack in whom she had such implicit faith, and had in vain endeavoured to engage him to perform for her the operation, to which she had determined to submit. He was afraid to hazard it, and he prevailed upon her to give up the scheme, and to try some new external remedy from which he promised wonders. No one knew what his medicines were, but they affected her head in the most alarming manner.

In her delirium she called frequently upon Miss Portman, sometimes accusing her of the basest treachery, sometimes addressing her as if she were present, and pouring forth the warmest expressions of friendship. "In her lucid intervals, ma'am," continued Marriott, "she for some weeks scarcely ever mentioned your name, nor could bear to hear me mention it. One day, when I was saying how much I wished that you were with her again, she darted at me the most terrible look that ever I beheld.

"'When I am in my grave, Marriott,' cried my lady, 'it will be time enough for Miss Portman again to visit this house, and you may then express your attachment to her with more propriety than at present.' These were my lady's own words – I shall never forget them – They struck and astonished me, ma'am, so much, I stood like one stupefied, and then left the room to think them over again by myself, and make sense of them if I could. – Well, ma'am, to be sure, it then struck me like a flash of lightning, that my lady was jealous – and, begging your pardon, ma'am, of you. This seemed to me the most unnatural thing in the world, considering how easy my lady had always seemed to be about my lord; but it was now clear to me, that this was the cause of your leaving us so suddenly, ma'am. – Well, I was confident that Mr Champfort was at the bottom of the business from the first; and now that I knew what scent to go upon, I went to work with fresh spirit to find him out; which was a thing I was determined upon, and what I'm determined upon I generally do, ma'am. So I put together things about Miss Portman and my lord, that had dropped at odd times from Sir Philip Baddely's gentleman; and I, partly serious and partly flirting, which in a good cause is no sin, drew from him (for he pretends to be a little an admirer of mine, ma'am, though I never gave him the smallest encouragement) all he knew or suspected, or had heard reported, or whispered: – and out it came, ma'am, that Mr Champfort was the original of all; and that he had told a heap of lies about some banknotes that my lord had given you, and that you and my lord were to be married as soon as my lady was dead; and I don't know what, which he maliciously circulated through Sir Philip's gentleman to Sir Philip himself, and so round again to my lady. Now, Sir Philip's man behaved like a gentleman upon the occasion, which I shall ever be free to acknowledge and remember: and when I represented things properly, and made him sensible of the mischief, which he assured me was done purely with an eye to serve Sir Philip his master, he very candidly offered to assist me to unmask that villain Champfort, which he could easily do with the assistance of a few bottles of claret, and a few fair words; which, though I can't abide hypocrisy, I thought quite allowable upon such an occasion. So, ma'am, when Mr Champfort was thrown off his guard by the claret, Sir Philip's gentleman began to talk of my lord and my lady, and Miss Portman; and he observed that my lord and my lady were coming together more than they used to be since Miss Portman left the house. To which Champfort replied with an oath, like an unmannered reprobate as he is, and in his gibberish, French and English, which I can't speak; but the sense of it was this: – 'My lord and lady shall never come together if I can help it. It was to hinder this I got Miss Portman banished; for my lord was quite another man after she got Miss Helena into the house; and I don't doubt but he might have been brought to leave off his Burgundy, and set up for a sober regular man; which would not suit me at all. If my lady once was to get power over him again, I might go whistle – so (with another reprobate oath) my lord and my lady shall never come together again whilst I live.'

"Well, ma'am," continued Marriott, "as soon as I was in possession of this precious speech, I carried it, and a letter of Sir Philip Baddely's gentleman vouching it, to my lady. My lady was thunderstruck, and so vexed to have been, as she said, a dupe, that she sent for my lord directly, and insisted upon his giving up Mr Champfort. – My lord demurred, because my lady spoke so high, and said *insist*. He would have done it, I'm satisfied, of his own accord, with the greatest pleasure, if my lady had not as it were commanded it. But he answered at last, 'My Lady Delacour, I'm not a man to be governed by a wife – I shall keep or part with my own servants, in my own house, according to my own pleasure'; and saying so he left the room. I never saw my lady so angry as she was at this refusal of my lord's to part with him. The house was quite in a state of distraction for some days. I never would sit down to the same table, ma'am, with Mr Champfort, nor speak to him, nor look at him, and parties ran high above and below stairs. – And at last my lady, who had been getting better, took to her bed again with a nervous fever, which brought her almost to death's door; she having been so much weakened before by the quack medicines, and convulsions, and all her sufferings in secret. She would not see my lord on no account, and Champfort persuaded him her illness was pretence, to bring him to her purpose; which was the more readily believed, because nobody was ever let into my lady's bedchamber but myself. All this time she never mentioned your name, ma'am; but once, when I was sitting by her bedside, as she was asleep, she started suddenly, and cried out, – 'O, my dearest Belinda! are you come back to me?' – She wakened herself with the start; and raising herself quite up in her bed, she pulled back the curtains, and looked all round the room. I'm sure she expected to see you; and when she found it was a dream, she gave a heavy sigh, and sunk down upon her pillow. I then could not forbear to speak, and this time my lady was greatly touched when I mentioned your name: – she shed tears, ma'am, and you know it is not a little thing that can draw tears from my lady. But when I said something about sending for you, she answered, she was sure you would not return to her, and that she would never condescend to ask a favour in vain, even from you. Then I replied, that I was sure you loved her still, and as well as ever; and that the proof of that was, that Mrs Luttridge and Mrs Freke together, by all their wiles, could not draw you over to their party at Harrowgate, and that you had affronted Mrs Freke by defending her ladyship. My lady was all surprise at this, and eagerly asked how I came to know it. – Now, ma'am, I had it all by a post letter from Mrs Luttridge's maid, who is my cousin, and knows every thing that's going on. My lady from this moment forward could scarce rest an instant without wishing for you, and fretting for you, as I knew by her manner. One day my lord met me on the stairs as I was coming down from my poor lady's room, and he asked me how she was, and why she did not send for a physician. 'The best physician, my lord, she could send for,' said I, 'would be Miss Portman; for she'll never be well till that good young lady comes back again, in my humble opinion.'

"'And what should prevent that good young lady from coming back again? Not I, surely?' rejoined my lord, 'for I wish she was here with all my heart.'

"'It is not easy to suppose, my lord,'" said I, 'after all that has passed, that the young lady would choose to return, or that my lady could ask her whilst Mr Champfort remains paramount in the house.' – 'If that's all,' cried my lord, 'tell your lady I'll part with Champfort upon the spot; for the rascal has just had the insolence to insist upon it, that a pair of new boots are not too tight for me, when I said they were. I'll show him I can be master, and will, in my own house.' – Ma'am, my heart leaped for joy within me at hearing these words, and I ran up to my lady with them. I easily concluded in my own mind, that my lord was glad of the pretence of the boots, to give up handsomely after his standing out so long. To be sure, my lord's mightily jealous of being master, and mighty fond of his own way; but I forgive him every thing for doing as I would have him at last, and dismissing that prince of mischiefmakers Mr Champfort. My lady called for her writing-desk directly, and sat up in her bed, and with her trembling hand, as you see by the writing, ma'am, wrote a letter to you as fast as ever she could, and the chariot was ordered. I don't know what fancy seized her – but, if you remember, ma'am, the hammer-cloth to her new carriage had orange and black fringe at first. She would not use it, till this had been changed to blue and white. Well ma'am, she recollected this on a sudden, as I was getting ready to come for you; and she set the servants at work directly to take off the blue and white, and put on the black and orange fringe again, which she said must be done before your coming. But, ma'am, I won't keep you any longer from reading your letter, only to say that I hope to Heaven you will not refuse to return to my poor lady, if it be only to put her mind at ease before she dies. She cannot have long to live."

As Marriott finished these words they reached the house, and Belinda went to her own room to read Lady Delacour's letter. It contained none of her customary '*éloquence du billet*,' no sprightly wit, no real, no affected gaiety; her mind seemed to be exhausted by bodily suffering, and her high spirit subdued. She expressed the most poignant anguish for having indulged such unjust suspicions and intemperate passions. She lamented having forfeited the esteem and affection of the only real friend she had ever possessed – a friend of whose forbearance, tenderness, and fidelity, she had received such indisputable proofs. She concluded by saying, "I feel my end fast approaching; and perhaps, Belinda, your humanity will induce you to grant my last request, and to let me see you once more before I die."

Belinda immediately decided to return to Lady Delacour – though it was with real regret that she thought of leaving Lady Anne Percival, and the amiable and happy family to whom she had become so much attached. The children crowded round her when they heard that she was going, and Mr Vincent stood in silent sorrow – but we spare our readers this parting scene. Miss Portman promised to return to Oakly-park as soon as she possibly could. Mr Vincent anxiously requested permission to follow her to town: but this she positively refused; and he submitted with as good a grace as a lover can submit to any thing that crosses his passion.

CHAPTER XX

Reconciliation

Aware that her remaining in town at such an unusual season of the year would appear unaccountable to her fashionable acquaintance, Lady Delacour contrived for herself a characteristic excuse; she declared that there was no possibility of finding pleasure in any thing but novelty, and that the greatest novelty to her would be to remain a whole summer in town. Most of her friends, amongst whom she had successfully established a character for caprice, were satisfied that this was merely some new whim, practised to signalise herself by singularity. The real reason that detained her was her dependence upon the quack, who had repeatedly visited and constantly prescribed for her. Convinced however, by the dreadful situation to which his prescriptions had lately reduced her, that he was unworthy of her confidence, she determined to dismiss him; but she could not do this, as she had a considerable sum to pay him, till Marriott's return, because she could not trust anyone but Marriott to let him up the private staircase into the boudoir.

During Marriott's absence, her ladyship suffered no one to attend her but a maid who was remarkable for her stupidity. She thought that she could have nothing to fear from this girl's spirit of inquiry, for never was any human being so destitute of curiosity. It was about noon when Belinda and Marriott arrived. Lady Delacour, who had passed a restless night, was asleep. When she awoke, she found Marriott standing beside her bed –

"Then it is all in vain, I see?" cried her ladyship: "Miss Portman is not with you? – Give me my laudanum."

"Miss Portman is come, my lady," said Marriott: "she would not come in here with me, lest she should startle you."

"Belinda is come! do you say? Admirable Belinda!" cried Lady Delacour, and she clasped her hands with ecstasy.

"Shall I tell her, my lady, that you are awake?"

"Yes – No – Stay – Lord Delacour is at home. – I will get up

immediately. Let my lord be told that I wish to speak with him –
that I beg he will breakfast with me in my dressing-room half an
hour hence. I will dress immediately."

Marriott in vain represented that she ought not to hurry
herself in her present weak state. Intent upon her own thoughts,
she listened to nothing that was said, but frequently urged
Marriott to be expeditious. She put on an unusual quantity of
rouge; then looking at herself in the glass, she said with a forced
smile –

"Marriott, I look so charmingly, that Miss Portman, perhaps,
will be of Lord Delacour's opinion, and think that nothing is the
matter with me. – Ah, no! – She has been behind the scenes, she
knows the truth too well! – Marriott, pray did she ask you many
questions about me? – Was not she very sorry to leave Oakly-
park? – Were not they all extremely concerned to part with her?
– Did she ask after Helena? – Did you tell her that I insisted
upon my lord's parting with Champfort?"

At the word Champfort, Marriott's mouth opened eagerly,
and she began to answer with her usual volubility. Lady
Delacour waited not for any reply to the various questions which
in the hurry of her mind she had asked; but, passing swiftly by
Marriott, she threw open the door of her dressing-room. At the
sight of Belinda she stopped short; and, totally overpowered, she
would have sunk upon the floor, had not Miss Portman caught
her in her arms, and supported her to a sofa. When she came to
herself, and heard the soothing tone of Belinda's voice, she
looked up timidly in her face for a few moments without being
able to speak.

"And are you really here once more, my dear Belinda?" cried
she at last – "And may I still call you my friend? – And do you
forgive me? – Yes, I *see* you do – and from you I can endure the
humiliation of being forgiven. Enjoy the noble sense of your own
superiority."

"My dear Lady Delacour," said Belinda, "you see all this in
too strong a light – you have done me no injury – I have nothing
to forgive."

"I *cannot* see it in too strong a light – Nothing to forgive! –
Yes, you have; that which it is the most difficult to forgive –
injustice. – O! how you must have despised me for the folly, the
meanness of my suspicions! Of all tempers, that which appears
to me, and I am sure to you, the most despicable, the most

intolerable, is a suspicious temper. Mine was once open, generous as your own – You see how the best dispositions may be depraved! – What am I now? – Fit only

'To point a moral, or adorn a tale'–

A mismatched, misplaced, miserable perverted being."

"And now you have abused yourself till you are breathless, I may have some chance," said Belinda, "of being heard in your defence. I perfectly agree with you in thinking, that a suspicious temper is despicable and intolerable, but there is a vast difference between an acute fit of jealousy, as our friend Dr X — would say, and a chronic habit of suspicion. The noblest natures may be worked up to suspicion by designing villainy; and then a handkerchief, or a hammer-cloth, – 'trifles light as air' – "

"Oh my dear! you are too good. But my folly admits of no excuse, no palliation," interrupted Lady Delacour; "mine was jealousy without love."

"That indeed would admit of no excuse," said Belinda: "therefore you will pardon me if I think it incredible – especially as I have detected you in feeling something like affection for your little daughter, after you had done your best, I mean your worst, to make me believe that you were a monster of a mother."

"That was quite another affair, my dear. I did not know Helena was worth loving. I did not imagine my little daughter could love me. When I found my mistake I changed my tone. But there is no hope of mistake with my poor husband. Your own sense must show you, that Lord Delacour is not a man to be loved."

"That could not *always* have been your ladyship's opinion," said Belinda with an arch smile.

"Lord, my dear!" said Lady Delacour, a little embarrassed, "in the highest paroxysm of my madness, I never suspected that you could *love* Lord Delacour. I surely only hinted that you were in love with his coronet. That was absurd enough in all conscience. Don't make me more absurd than I am."

"Is it then the height of absurdity to love a husband?"

"Love! Nonsense! – Impossible! – Hush! – Here he comes with his odious creaking shoes. What man can ever expect to be loved who wears creaking shoes?" – pursued her ladyship as Lord Delacour entered the room, his shoes creaking at every step; and assuming an air of levity she welcomed him as a stranger to her dressing-room. "No speeches, my lord! no speeches, I beseech you," cried she, as he was beginning to speak to Miss Portman. "Believe me that explanations always make bad worse. Miss Portman is here, thank Heaven, and her! — And Champfort is gone – Thank you – or your boots. And now let us sit down to breakfast and forget as soon as possible everything that is disagreeable."

When Lady Delacour had a mind to banish painful recollections, it was scarcely possible to resist the magical influence of her conversation and manners; yet her lord's features never relaxed to a smile during this breakfast. He maintained an obstinate silence, and a profound solemnity – till at last, rising from table, he turned to Miss Portman, and said,

"Of all the caprices of fine ladies, that which surprises me the most is the whim of keeping their beds without being sick. Now, Miss Portman, you would hardly suppose that my Lady Delacour, who had been so lively this morning, has kept her bed, as I am informed, a fortnight – Is not this astonishing?"

"Prodigiously astonishing, that my Lord Delacour, like all the rest of the world, should be liable to be deceived by appearances," cried her ladyship. "Honour me with your attention for a few minutes, my lord, and perhaps I may increase your astonishment."

His lordship, struck by the sudden change of her voice from gaiety to gravity, fixed his eyes upon her, and returned to his seat. She paused – then addressing herself to Belinda: – "My incomparable friend," said she, "I will not give you a convincing proof of the unlimited power you have over my mind. My lord, Miss Portman has persuaded me to the step, which I am now going to take. She has prevailed upon me to make a decisive trial of your prudence and kindness. She has determined me to throw myself on your mercy."

"Mercy!" repeated Lord Delacour, and a confused idea, that she was now about to make a confession of the justice of some of his former suspicions, took possession of his mind: he looked aghast.

"I am going, my lord, to confide to you a secret of the utmost importance – a secret which is known to but three people in the world, Miss Portman, Marriott, and a man whose name I cannot reveal to you."

"Stop, Lady Delacour!" cried his lordship with a degree of

emotion and energy, which he had never shown till now. "Stop, I conjure, I command you, madam – I am not sufficiently master of myself – I once loved you too well to bear such a stroke. Trust me with no such secret – say no more – you have said enough, too much. I forgive you, that is all I can do; but we must part, Lady Delacour!" said he, breaking from her with agony expressed in his countenance.

"The man has a heart, a soul, I protest! – You knew him better than I did, Miss Portman. Nay, you are not gone yet, my lord! You really love me, I find."

"No, no, no," cried he vehemently. "Weak as you take me to be, Lady Delacour, I am incapable of loving a woman who has disgraced me, disgraced herself, her family, her station, her high endowments, her — "

His utterance failed – "O, Lady Delacour!" cried Belinda, "how can you trifle in this manner?"

"I meant not," said her ladyship, "to trifle. I am satisfied. My lord, it is time that you should be satisfied. I *can* give you the most irrefragable proof that, whatever may have been the apparent levity of my conduct, you have had no serious cause for jealousy. But the proof will shock – disgust you. – Have you courage to know more? – Then follow me."

He followed her. – Belinda heard the boudoir door unlock. – In a few minutes they returned. – Grief, and horror, and pity, were painted in Lord Delacour's countenance as he passed hastily through the room.

"My dearest friend, I have taken your advice; would to Heaven I had taken it sooner!" said Lady Delacour to Miss Portman. "I have revealed to Lord Delacour my real situation. Poor man! he was shocked beyond expression. He behaved incomparably well. I am convinced that he would, as he said, let his hand be cut off to save my life. The moment his foolish jealousy was extinguished, his love for me revived in full force. Would you believe it? he has promised me to break with odious Mrs Luttridge. Upon my charging him to keep my secret from her, he instantly, in the handsomest manner in the world, declared he would never see her more, rather than give me a moment's uneasiness. How I reproach myself for having been for years the torment of this man's life!"

"You may do better than reproach yourself, my dear Lady Delacour!" said Belinda: "you may yet live for years to be the blessing and pride of his life. I am persuaded, that nothing but your despair of obtaining domestic happiness has so long enslaved you to dissipation; and now that you find a friend in your husband, now that you know the affectionate temper of your little Helena, you will have fresh views and fresh hopes; you will have the courage to live for yourself, and not for what is called the world."

"The world!" cried Lady Delacour with a tone of disdain; "how long has that word enslaved a soul formed for higher purposes!" She paused, and looked up towards Heaven with an expression of fervent devotion, which Belinda had once, and but once before, seen in her countenance. Then, as if forgetful even that Belinda was present, she threw herself upon a sofa, and fell, or seemed to fall, into a profound reverie. She was roused by the entrance of Marriott, who came into the room to ask whether she would now take her laudanum. "I thought I had taken it," said she in a feeble voice; and as she raised her eyes and saw Belinda, she added, with a faint smile, "Miss Portman, I believe, has been laudanum to me this morning: but even that will not do long, you see; nothing will do for me now but *this*," and she stretched out her hand for the laudanum. "Is not it shocking to think," continued she, after she had swallowed it, "that laudanum alone I find the means of supporting existence?"

She put her hand to her head, as if partly conscious of the confusion of her own ideas; and ashamed that Belinda should witness it, she desired Marriott to assist her to rise, and to support her to her bedchamber. She made a sign to Miss Portman not to follow her. "Do not take it unkindly, but I am quite exhausted, and wish to be alone; for I am grown fond of being alone some hours in the day, and perhaps I shall sleep."

Marriott came out of her lady's room about a quarter of an hour afterward, and said that her lady seemed disposed to sleep, but that she desired to have her book left by her bed-side. Marriott searched amongst several which lay upon the table, for one in which a mark was put. Belinda looked over them along with Marriott, and she was surprised to find that they had almost all methodistical titles. Lady Delacour's mark was in the middle of Wesley's Admonitions. Several pages in other books of the same description Miss Portman found marked with a pencil, with reiterated lines, which she knew to be her ladyship's customary mode of distinguishing passages that she particularly liked. Some were highly oratorical, but most of them were of a mystical cast, and appeared to Belinda scarcely intelligible. She had reason to be astonished at meeting with such books in the dressing-room of a woman of Lady Delacour's character. During the solitude of her illness, her ladyship had first begun to think seriously on religious subjects, and the early impressions that had been made on her mind in her childhood, by a methodistical mother, recurred. Her understanding, weakened perhaps by disease, and never accustomed to reason, was incapable of distinguishing between truth and error; and her temper, naturally enthusiastic, hurried her from one extreme to the other – from thoughtless scepticism to visionary credulity. Her devotion was by no means steady or permanent; it came on by fits usually at the time when the effect of laudanum was exhausted, or before a fresh dose began to operate. In these intervals she was low-spirited – bitter reflections on the manner in which she had thrown away her talents and her life obtruded themselves; the idea of the untimely death of Colonel Lawless, of which she reproached herself as the cause, returned; and her mind, from being a prey to remorse, began to sink in these desponding moments under the most dreadful superstitious terrors – terrors the more powerful, as they were secret. Whilst the stimulus of laudanum lasted, the train of her ideas always changed, and she was amazed at the weak fears and strange notions by which she had been disturbed; yet it was not in her power entirely to chase away these visions of the night, and they gained gradually a dominion over her, of which she was heartily ashamed. She resolved to conceal this *weakness*, as in her gayer moments she thought it, from Belinda, from whose superior strength of understanding she dreaded ridicule or contempt. Her experience of Miss Portman's gentleness and friendship might reasonably have prevented or dispelled such apprehensions; but Lady Delacour was governed by pride, by sentiment, by whim, by enthusiasm, by passion – by anything but reason.

When she began to revive after her fit of languor, and had been refreshed by opium and sleep, she rang for Marriott, and inquired for Belinda. She was much provoked when Marriott, by way of proving to her that Miss Portman could not have been tired of being left alone, told her, that she had been in the dressing-room *rummaging over the books*.

"What books?" cried Lady Delacour. "I forgot that *they* were left there. Miss Portman is not reading them still, I suppose? Go for them, and let them be locked up in my own book-case, and bring me the key."

Her ladyship appeared in good spirits when she saw Belinda again. She rallied her upon the serious studies she had chosen for her morning's amusement. "Those methodistical books, with their strange quaint titles," said she, "are, however, diverting enough to those who, like myself, can find diversion in the height of human absurdity."

Deceived by the levity of her manner, Belinda concluded that the marks of approbation in these books were ironical, and she thought no more of the matter; for Lady Delacour suddenly gave a new turn to the conversation by exclaiming,

"Now we talk of the height of human absurdity, what are we to think of Clarence Harvey?"

"Why should we think of him at all?" said Belinda.

"For two excellent reasons, my dear! because we cannot help it, and because he deserves it. Yes, he deserves it, believe me, if it were only for having written me these charming letters," said Lady Delacour, opening a cabinet, and taking out a small packet of letters, which she put into Belinda's hands. "Pray read them, you will find them amazingly edifying, as well as entertaining. I protest I am only puzzled to know, whether I shall bind them up with Sterne's Sentimental Journey, or Fordyce's Sermons for Young Women. Here, my love, if you like description," continued her ladyship, opening one of the letters, "here is a Radcliffean* tour along the picturesque coasts of Dorset and Devonshire. Why he went this tour, unless for the pleasure and glory of describing it, Heaven knows! Clouds and darkness rest over the tourist's private history; but this, of course, renders his letters more *piquantes* and interesting. All who have a just taste either for literature or for gallantry, know how much we are indebted to the obscure for the sublime, and orators and lovers feel what felicity there is in the use of the fine figure of suspension."

"Very good description indeed!" said Belinda, without raising her eyes from the letter, or seeming to pay any attention to the latter part of Lady Delacour's speech, "very good description, certainly!"

"Well, my dear! But here is something better than *pure description*; here is sense for you: and pray mark the politeness of addressing sense to a woman – to a woman of sense, I mean – and which of us is not? Then here is sentiment for you," continued her ladyship, spreading another letter before Belinda; "a story of a Dorsetshire lady, who had the misfortune to be married to a man as *unlike* Mr Percival, and as like Lord Delacour, as possible; and yet, O, wonderful! they make as happy a couple as one's heart could wish. Now, I am truly candid and good natured to admire this letter; for every word of it is a lesson to me, and evidently was so intended. But I take it all in good part, because, to do Clarence justice, he describes the joys of domestic Paradise in such elegant language, that he does not make me sick. In short, my dear Belinda, to finish my panegyric, as it has been said of some other epistles, if ever there were letters calculated to make you fall in love with the writer of them, these are they."

"Then," said Miss Portman, folding up the letter which she was just going to read, "I will not run the hazard of reading them."

"Why, my dear!" said Lady Delacour with a look of mingled concern, reproach, and raillery, "have you actually given up my poor Clarence, merely on account of this mistress in the wood, this Virginia St Pierre? Nonsense! Begging your pardon, my dear, the man loves you. Some entanglement, some punctilio, some doubt, some delicacy, some folly, prevents him from being just at this moment where, I confess, he ought to be – at your feet – and you, out of patience, which a young lady ought never to be, if she can help it, will go and marry – I know you will – some stick of a rival purely to provoke him."

"If ever I marry," said Belinda with a look of proud humility, "I shall certainly marry to please myself, and not to provoke any body else – and at all events I hope I shall never marry *a stick*."

"Pardon me that word," said Lady Delacour, "I am convinced you never will – but one is apt to judge of others by one's self. I am willing to believe that Mr Vincent – "

"Mr Vincent! How did you know – " exclaimed Belinda.

"How did I know? Why, my dear, do you think I am so little interested about you, that I have not found out some of your secrets? And do you think that Marriott could refrain from telling me, in her most triumphant tone, that 'Miss Portman has not gone to Oakly-park for nothing; that she has made a conquest of a Mr Vincent, a West Indian, a ward, or lately a ward, of Mr Percival's, the handsomest man that ever was seen, and the richest, &c. &c. &c?' Now, simple I rejoiced at the news; for I took it for granted, you would never seriously think of marrying the man."

"Then why did your ladyship rejoice?"

"Why? O, you novice at Cupid's chess-board! do not you see the next move? Check with your new knight, and the game is your own. Now, if your aunt Stanhope saw your look at this instant she would give you up for ever – if she have not done that already. In plain, unmetaphorical prose, then, cannot you comprehend, my straightforward Belinda, that if you make Clarence Hervey heartily jealous, let the impediments to your union be what they may, he will acknowledge himself to be heartily in love with you? I should make no scruple of frightening him within an inch of his life, for his good. Sir Philip Baddely was not the man to frighten him; but this Mr Vincent, by all accounts, is just the thing."

"And do you imagine that I could use Mr Vincent so ill? – And can you think me capable of such double dealing?"

"O! in love and war, you know, all stratagems are allowable. – But you take the matter so seriously, and you redden with such virtuous indignation, that I dare not say a word more – Only – may I ask – are you absolutely engaged to Mr Vincent?"

"No. We have had the prudence to avoid all promises, all engagements."

"There's my good girl!" cried Lady Delacour, kissing her: "all may yet turn out well – Read those letters – Take them to your room, read them, read them; and depend upon it, my dearest Belinda! you are not the sort of woman that will, that can be happy, if you make a mere match of convenience. – Forgive me, I love you too well not to speak the truth, though it may offend for a moment."

"You do not offend, but you misunderstand me," said Belinda. "Have patience with me, and you shall find that I am incapable of making a mere match of convenience."

Then Miss Portman gave Lady Delacour a simple but full account of all that had passed at Oakly-park relative to Mr Vincent. She repeated the arguments by which Lady Anne Percival had first prevailed upon her to admit of Mr Vincent's addresses. She said, that she had been convinced by Mr Percival, that the omnipotence of a *first love* was an idea founded in folly, and realised only in romance; and that to believe that none could be happy in marriage, except with the first object of their fancy or their affections, would be an error pernicious to individuals and to society. When she detailed the arguments used by Mr Percival on this subject, Lady Delacour sighed, and observed that Mr Percival was certainly right, judging from *his own experience*, to declaim against the folly of *first loves*; "and for the same reason," added she, "perhaps I may be pardoned if I retain some prejudice in their favour." She turned aside her head to hide a starting tear, and here the conversation dropped. Belinda, recollecting the circumstances of her ladyship's early history, reproached herself for having touched on this tender subject, yet at the same time she felt with increased force, at this moment, the justice of Mr Percival's observations; for, evidently, the hold which this prejudice had kept in Lady Delacour's mind had materially injured her happiness, by making her neglect, after her marriage, all the means of content that were in her reach. Her incessant comparisons between her *first love* and her husband excited perpetual contempt and disgust in her mind for her wedded lord, and for many years precluded all perception of his good qualities, all desire to live with him upon good terms, and all idea of securing that share of domestic happiness that was actually in her power. Belinda resolved at some future moment, whenever she could with propriety and with effect to suggest these reflections to Lady Delacour, and in the mean time she was determined to turn them to her own advantage. She perceived that she should have need of all her steadiness to preserve her judgment unbiassed by her ladyship's wit and persuasive eloquence on the one hand, and on the other by her own high opinion of Lady Anne Percival's judgment, and the anxious desire she felt to secure her approbation. The letters from Clarence Hervey she read at night when she retired to her own room; and they certainly raised not only Belinda's opinion of his talents, but her esteem for his character. She saw that he had, with great address, made use of the influence he possessed over Lady Delacour, to turn her mind to everything that could make her amiable, estimable, and happy – she saw that Clarence, so far from attempting, for the sake of his own vanity, to retain his preeminence in her ladyship's imagination, used, on the contrary, "his utmost skill" to turn the tide of her affections toward her husband and her daughter. In one of his letters, and but in one, he mentioned Belinda. He expressed great regret at hearing from Lady Delacour, that her friend Miss Portman was no longer with her. He expatiated on the inestimable advantages and happiness of having such a friend – but this referred to Lady Delacour, not to himself. There was an air of much respect and some embarrassment in all he said of Belinda, but nothing like love. A few words at the end of this paragraph were cautiously obliterated, however; and, without any obvious link of connexion, the writer began a new sentence with a general reflection upon the folly and imprudence of forming romantic projects. Then he enumerated some of the various schemes he had formed in his early youth, and humourously recounted how they had failed, or how they had been abandoned. Afterward, changing his tone from playful wit to serious philosophy, he observed the changes which these experiments had made in his own character.

"My friend Dr X — ," said he, "divides mankind into three classes. – "Those, who learn from the experience of others – They are happy men. – Those who learn from their own experience – They are wise men. – And, lastly, those who learn neither from their own nor from other people's experience – They are fools. – This class is by far the largest. I am content," continued Clarence, "to be in the middle class – perhaps you will say, because I cannot be in the first. However, were it in my power to choose my own character, I should, forgive me the seeming vanity of the speech, still be content to remain in my present station upon this principle – The characters of those who are taught by their own experience must be progressive in knowledge and virtue. Those who learn from the experience of others may become stationary, because they must depend for their progress on the experiments that we brave volunteers, at whose expense they are to live and learn, are pleased to try. There may be much safety in thus snugly fighting, or rather seeing the battle of life, behind the broad shield of a stouter warrior. Yet it seems to me, to be rather an ignominious than an enviable situation. But I should not mingle the notions of military glory with my philosophy, or talk of broad shields and battles, to look grand in the eyes of a fair lady. Instead of an allusion, your ladyship then shall have – a theory. It is my theory, that vigorous, quick-shooting intellects, during the periods of their growth, are sometimes awkwardly and ridiculously out of all *moral proportion*. Injudicious attempts to reduce and rectify them only dwarf or deform the character.

"Our friend Dr X — would laugh at my theory, and still more at my insisting upon being amongst the class of learners by their own experience. He would ask me, whether it be the ultimate end of my philosophy to try experiments, or to be happy. And what answer should I make? I have none ready. Common sense stares me in the face, and my feelings even at this instant, alas! confute my system. I shall pay too dear yet for some of my experiments.

'Sois grand homme, et sois malheureux,'* is, I am afraid, the law of nature, or rather the decree of the world. Your ladyship will not read this without a smile; for you will immediately infer, that I think myself a great man; and as I detest hypocrisy yet more than vanity, I shall not deny the charge. At all events, I feel that I am at present – however gaily I talk of it – in as far a way to be unhappy for life, as if I were, in good earnest, the greatest man in Europe.

> Your ladyship's
> > most respectful admirer,
> > > and sincere friend,
> > > > CLARENCE HERVEY.

"P.S. Is there any hope that your friend Miss Portman may spend the winter in town?"

Though Lady Delacour had been much fatigued by the exertion of her spirits during the day, she sat up at night to write to Mr Hervey. Her love and gratitude to Miss Portman interested her most warmly for her happiness, and she was persuaded that the most effectual way to secure it would be to promote her union with her *first love*. Lady Delacour, who had also the best opinion of Clarence Hervey, and the most sincere friendship for him, thought she was likewise acting highly for his interest; and she felt that she had some merit in at once parting with him from the train of her admirers, and urging him to become a dull married man. Beside these generous motives, she was, perhaps, a little influenced by jealousy of the superior power, which Lady Anne Percival had in so short a time acquired over Belinda's mind. "Strange," thought she, "if love and I be not a match for Lady Anne Percival and reason!" To do Lady Delacour justice, it must be observed, that she took the utmost care in her letter not to *commit* her friend; she wrote with all the delicate address of which she was mistress. She began by rallying her correspondent on his indulging himself so charmingly in *the melancholy of genius*; and she prescribed as a cure to her *malheureux imaginaire*,* as she called him, those joys of domestic life which he so well knew how to paint.

"*Precepte commence, exemple acheve*,"* said her ladyship. "You will never see me *la femme comme il y en a peu*, till I see you *le bon mari.** Belinda Portman has this day returned to me from Oakly-park, fresh, blooming, wise, and gay, as country air, flattery, philosophy, and love, can make her. It seems that she has had full employment for her head and heart. Mr Percival and Lady Anne, by right of science and reason, have taken possession of the head, and a Mr Vincent, their ci-devant ward and declared favourite, has laid close siege to the heart, of which he is in a fair way, I think, to take possession by the right of conquest. As far as I can understand – for I have not yet seen *le futur** – he deserves my Belinda: for, beside being as handsome as any hero of romance, ancient or modern, he has a soul in which neither spot nor blemish can be found, except the amiable weakness of being desperately in love – a weakness which we ladies are apt to prefer to the most philosophic stoicism. – à propos to philosophy – We may presume, that notwithstanding Mr V — is a creole, he has been bred up by his guardian in the class of men who learn by the experience of others. As such, according to your system, he has a right to expect to be a *happy man*, has not he? According to Mrs Stanhope's system, I am sure that he has; for his thousands and tens of thousands, as I am credibly informed, pass the comprehension of the numeration table.

"But these will weigh not a grain in the estimation of her truly disinterested and noble-minded niece. Mrs Stanhope knows nothing of Vincent's proposal; and it is well for him she does not, for her worldly good word would mar the whole. – Not so as to Lady Anne and Mr Percival's approbation – Their opinion is all in all with my friend. How they have contrived it I know not, but they have gained over Belinda's mind a degree of power almost equal to parental authority. So you may guess that the doubtful beam will not much longer nod from side to side. Indeed, it seems to me scarcely necessary to throw in the sword of authority to turn the scale.

"If you can persuade yourself to finish your picturesque tour before the ides of the charming month of November, do, my dear Clarence! make haste and come back to us in time for Belinda's wedding – and do not forget my commission about the Dorsetshire angel; bring me one in your right hand with a gold ring upon her taper finger – So help you Cupid! – or never more expect a smile.

From your sincere friend
and admirer,
T.C.H. DELACOUR.

"P.S. Observe, my good sir! that I am not in such a desperate hurry to congratulate you on your marriage, that I should be satisfied with an ordinary Mrs Hervey. So do not, under pretence of obliging me, or for any other consideration, yoke yourself to some damsel that you will be ashamed to produce. For one woman worthy to be Clarence Hervey's wife, I have seen, at a moderate computation, a hundred fit to be his mistress. If he should, on this subject, mistake the *fitness of things or of persons*, he would, indeed, be *in a fair way to be unhappy for life*.

"The substance of a lady's letter, it has been said, always is comprised in the postscript."

After Lady Delacour had finished this letter, which she had no doubt would bring Clarence immediately to town, she left it with Marriott, with orders to have it sent by the next post. Much fatigued, she then retired to rest, and was not visible the next day till near dinner-time. When Miss Portman returned the packet of Mr Hervey's letters, her ladyship was dissatisfied with the measured terms of Belinda's approbation, and she said with a sarcastic smile,

"So, they have made a complete philosopher of you at Oakly-park! – You are perfect in the first lesson – not to admire. And is the torch of Cupid to be extinguished on the altar of Reason?"

"Rather to be lighted there, if possible," said Belinda; and she endeavoured to turn the conversation to what she thought must be more immediately interesting to Lady Delacour – her own health. She assured her, with perfect truth, that she was at present more intent upon her situation than upon Cupid or his torch.

"I believe you, my generous Belinda!" said Lady Delacour; "and for that very reason I am interested in your affairs, I am afraid, even to the verge of impertinence. May I ask why this *preux chevalier** of yours did not attend you, or follow you, to town?"

"Mr Vincent? – He knew that I came to attend your ladyship. I told him that you had been confined by a nervous fever, and that it would be impossible for me to see him at present; but I promised, when you could spare me, to return to Oakly-park."

Lady Delacour sighed, and opened Clarence Hervey's letters one after another, looking over them without speaking, and without seeming well to know what she was about. Lord Delacour came into the room whilst these letters were still in her hand. He had been absent since the preceding morning, and he now seemed as if he was just come home much fatigued. He began in a tone of great anxiety to inquire after Lady Delacour's health. She was piqued at his having left home at such a time, and, merely bowing her head at him, she went on reading. His eyes glanced upon the letters which she held in her hand; and when he saw the well-known writing of Clarence Hervey, his manner immediately altered, and, stammering out some commonplace phrases, he threw himself into an arm chair by the fireside, protesting that he was tired to death – that he was half dead – that he had been in a postchaise for three hours, which he hated – had ridden fifty miles since yesterday – and he muttered, that he was a fool for his pains: – an observation, which, though it reached her ladyship's ears, she did not think proper to contradict.

His lordship then had recourse to his watch, his never-failing friend in need, which he always pulled out with a particular jerk when he was vexed.

"It is time for me to be gone – I shall be late at Studley's."

"You dine with his lordship, then?" said Lady Delacour in a careless tone.

"Yes; and his good Burgundy, I hope, will wind me up again," said he, stretching himself, "for I am quite down."

"Quite down? – Then we may conclude that my friend Mrs Luttridge is not yet come to *Rantipole*? – Rantipole, my dear," continued Lady Delacour, turning to Miss Portman, "is the name of Harriet Freke's villa in Kent. However strange it may sound to your ears and mine, I can assure you the name has *made fortune* amongst a certain description of wits. And candour must allow, that, if not elegant, it is appropriate; it gives a just idea of the manners and way of life of the place, for every thing at Rantipole is rantipole.* But I am really concerned, my lord, you should have ridden yourself down in this way for nothing. Why did not you get better intelligence before you set out? I am afraid you feel the loss of Champfort. Why did not you contrive to learn for certain, my dear good lord, whether *the Luttridge* was at Rantipole before you set out on this wild goose chase?"

"My dear good lady," replied Lord Delacour, assuming a degree of spirit which startled her as much as it became him, "why do not you get better intelligence before you suspect me of being a brute and a liar! Did not I promise you yesterday, that I would break with *the Luttridge*, as you call her? and how could you imagine that the instant afterward, just as the time I was wrung to the soul, as you knew I was – how could you imagine I would leave you to go to Rantipole, or to any woman upon earth?"

"O, my lord! I beg your pardon, I beg your pardon a thousand times," cried Lady Delacour, rising with much emotion; and, going towards him with a sudden impulse, she kissed his forehead.

"And so you ought to beg my pardon," said Lord Delacour in a faltering voice, but without moving his posture.

"You will acknowledge you left me, however, my lord? That is clear."

"Left you! Yes, so I did; to ride all over the country in search of a house that would suit you. For what else did you think I *could* leave you at such a time as this?"

Lady Delacour again stopped, and leaned her arm upon his shoulder.

"I wish to Heaven, my dear," said his lordship, shrinking as he put away her hand, which still held Clarence Hervey's letters – "I wish to Heaven, my dear, you would not hold those abominable perfumed papers just under my very nose. You know I cannot stand perfumes."

"Are they perfumed? Ay; so every thing is that I keep in that cabinet of curiosities. Thank you, my dear Miss Portman," said her ladyship, as Belinda rose to take the letters from her hand. "Will you have the goodness to put them back into their cabinet, if you can endure to touch them, if the perfume have not overcome you, as well as my lord. After all, it is only attar of roses, to which few people's olfactory nerves have an antipathy."

"I have the honour to be one of the few," said his lordship, rising from his seat with so sudden a motion as to displace Lady Delacour's arm which leaned upon him. "For my part," continued he, taking down one of the Argand's lamps from the chimney piece, and trimming it, "I would rather a hundred to one snuff up the oil of this cursed lamp."

Whilst his lordship applied himself to trimming the lamp with great earnestness, Lady Delacour negligently walked away to the farthest end of the room, where stood the cabinet, which Belinda was trying to unlock.

"Stay, my love, it has a secret lock, which I alone can manage."

"O, my dear Lady Delacour!" whispered Belinda, holding her hand as she gave her the key, "I never can love or esteem you, if you use Lord Delacour ill now."

"Ill now? Ill how? This lock is spoilt, I do believe," said she aloud.

"Nay, you understand me, Lady Delacour! You see what is passing in his mind."

"To be sure. I am not a fool, though he is. I see he is jealous, though he has had such *damning proof* – that – all's right – The man's a fool, that's all. Are you sure this is the key I gave you, my dear?"

"And can you think him a fool," pursued Belinda in a still more earnest whisper, "for being more jealous of your mind than of your person? Fools have seldom so much penetration, or so much delicacy."

"But, Lord! what would you have me do? what would you have me say? That Lord Delacour writes better letters than these?"

"O No! – But show him these letters, and you will do justice to him, to yourself, to Cla — , to every body."

"I am sure I should be happy to do justice to *every body*."

"Then pray do this very instant, my dearest Lady Delacour! and I shall love you for it all my life."

"Done! – for who can withstand that offer? Done!" said her ladyship; then turning to Lord Delacour, "My lord, will you come here and tell us what can be the matter with this lock?"

"If the lock be spoiled, Lady Delacour, you had better send for a locksmith," replied his lordship, who was still employed about the wick of the Argand. "I am no locksmith – I do not pretend to understand locks – especially secret locks."

"But you will not desert us at our utmost need, I am sure, my lord;" said Belinda, approaching him with a conciliatory smile.

"You want the light, I believe, more than I do," said his lordship, advancing with the lamp to meet her. "Well! what is the matter with this confounded lock of yours, Lady Delacour? I know I should be at Studley's by this time – But how in the devil's name can you expect me to open a secret lock when I do not know the secret, Lady Delacour?"

"Then I will tell you the secret, Lord Delacour – that there is no secret at all in the lock; or in the letters. Here, if you can stand the odious smell of attar of roses, take these letters and read them, foolish man! and keep them till the shocking perfume is gone off."

Lord Delacour could scarcely believe his senses: he looked in Lady Delacour's eyes to see whether he had understood her rightly.

"But I am afraid," said she, smiling, "that you will find the perfume too overcoming."

"Not half so overcoming," cried he, seizing her hand, and kissing it often with eager tenderness – "not half so overcoming as this confidence, this kindness, this condescension from you."

"Miss Portman will think us both a couple of old fools," said her ladyship, making a slight effort to withdraw her hand. "But she is almost as great a simpleton herself, I think," continued she, observing that the tears stood in Belinda's eyes.

"My lord," said a footman who came in at this instant, "do you dress? The carriage is at the door, as you ordered, to go to Lord Studley's."

"I'd see Lord Studley at the devil, sir, and his burgundy along with him, before I'd go to him today; and you may tell him so, if you please," cried Lord Delacour.

"Very well, my lord!" said the footman.

"My lord dines at home. They may put up the carriage. That's all," said Lady Delacour. "Only let us have dinner directly," added she as the servant shut the door. "Miss Portman will be famished amongst us. There is no living upon sentiment."

"And there is no living with such belles, without being something more of a beau," said Lord Delacour, looking at his splashed boots. "I will be ready for dinner before dinner is ready for me." And with activity very unusual to him, he hurried out of the room to change his dress.

"O day of wonders!" exclaimed Lady Delacour: "And O night of wonders! If we can get him through the evening without the help of Lord Studley's wine. You must give us some music, my good Belinda, and make him accompany you with his flute. I can tell you he has really a very pretty taste for music, and knows fifty times more of the matter than half the dilettanti, who squeeze the human face divine into all manner of ridiculous shapes, by way of persuading you that they are in ecstasy! And, my dear, do not forget to show us the charming little portfolio of drawings that you have brought from Oakly-park. Lord Delacour was with me at Harrowgate in the days of his courtship; he knows all those charming views that you have been taking about Knaresborough and Fountain's Abbey, and all those places. I will answer for it, he remembers them all a hundred times better than I do. And, my love, I assure you he is a better judge of drawing than many whom we saw ogling Venus rising from the sea, in the Orleans' gallery. Lord Delacour has let his talents go to sleep in a shameless manner; but really he has talents, if they could be wakened. By the by, pray make him tell you the story of Lord Studley's original Titian: he tells that story with real humour. Perhaps you have not found it out, but Lord Delacour has a vast deal of drollery in his own way, and – "

"Dinner's ready, my lady!"

"That is a pity!' whispered Lady Delacour; "for, if they had let me go on, in my present humour, I should have found out that my lord has every accomplishment under the sun, and every requisite under the moon, to make the marriage state happy."

With the assistance of Belinda's portfolio and her harp, and the good humour and sprightliness of Lady Delacour's wit, his lordship got through the evening much to his own satisfaction. He played on the flute, he told the story of Studley's original Titian, and he detected a fault that had escaped Mr Percival in the perspective of Miss Portman's sketch of Fountain's Abbey. The perception that his talents were *called out*, and that he appeared to unusual advantage made him *excellent company*: he found that the spirits can be raised by self-complacency, even more agreeably than by burgundy.

CHAPTER XXI

Helena

Whilst they were at breakfast the next morning in Lady Delacour's dressing-room, Marriott knocked at the door, and, immediately opening it, exclaimed in a joyful tone, "Miss Portman, they're eating it! Ma'am, they're eating it as fast as ever they can!"

"Bring them in; your lady will give you leave, Marriott, I fancy," said Miss Portman. Marriott brought in her gold fishes; some green leaves were floating on the top of the water in the glass globe.

"See, my lady," said she, "what Miss Portman has been so good to bring from Oakly-park for my poor gold fish, who, I am sure, ought to be much obliged to her, as well as myself." Marriott set the globe beside her lady, and retired.

"From Oakly-park! And by what name impossible to pronounce must I call these green leaves, to please botanic ears?" said Lady Delacour.

"This," replied Belinda, "is what

'Th' unlearned, duckweed; learned, lemma, call,'

and it is to be found in any ditch or standing pool."

"And what possessed you, my dear, for the sake of Marriott and her gold fishes, to trouble yourself to bring such stuff a hundred and seventy miles?"

"To oblige little Charles Percival," said Miss Portman. "He was anxious to keep his promise of sending it to your Helena. She found out in some book that she was reading with him last summer, that gold fishes are fond of this plant, and I wish," added Belinda in a timid voice, "that she were here at this instant to see them eat it!"

Lady Delacour was silent for some minutes, and kept her eyes steadily upon the gold fishes. At length she said, "I never shall forget how well the poor little creature behaved about those gold fishes. I grew amazingly fond of her whilst she was with me. But you know, circumstanced as I was, after you left me I could not have her at home."

"But now I am here," said Belinda, "will she be any trouble to you? And will she not make your home more agreeable to you, and to Lord Delacour, who was evidently very fond of her?"

"Ah! my dear," said Lady Delacour, "you forget, and so do I at times, what I have to go through. It is in vain to talk, to think of making homes, or any place, or anything, or any person agreeable to me now. What am I? The outside rind is left – the sap is gone. The tree lasts from day to day by miracle – it cannot last long. You would not wonder to hear me talk in this way, if you knew the terrible night I had last night after we parted. But I have these nights constantly now. – Let us talk of something else. What have you there? A manuscript?"

"Yes, a little journal of Charles Percival's, which he sent for the entertainment of Helena."

Lady Delacour stretched out her hand for it. "The boy will write as like his father as possible," said she, turning over the leaves. "I wish to have this poor girl with me – but I have not spirits. And you know, whenever Lord Delacour can find a house that will suit us, we shall leave town, and I could not take Helena with me. But this may be the last opportunity I may ever have of seeing her; and I *can* refuse you nothing, my dear. So, will you go for her? She can stay with us a few days. Lady Boucher, that most convenient dowager, who likes going about, no matter where, all morning, will go with you to Mrs Dumont's academy in Sloane-street. I would as soon go to a bird fancier's as to a boarding-school for young ladies. Indeed, I am not well enough to go any where. So I will throw myself upon a sofa, and read this child's journal. I wonder how that or anything else can interest me now."

Belinda, who had been used to the variations of Lady Delacour's spirits, was not much alarmed by the despondent strain in which she now spoke, especially when she considered that the thoughts of the dreadful trial this unfortunate woman was soon to go through must naturally depress her courage. Rejoiced at the permission that she had obtained to go for Helena, Miss Portman sent immediately to Lady Boucher, who took her to Sloane-street.

"Now, my dear considerate Miss Portman," said Lady Boucher, "I must beg and request that you will hurry Miss Delacour into the carriage as fast as possible. I have not a moment to spare; for I am to be at a china auction at two, that I would not miss for the whole world. Well, what's the matter with the people? Why does not James knock at the door? Can't the man read? Can't the man see?" cried the purblind dowager. "Is not that Mrs Dumont's name on the door before his eyes?"

"No, ma'am, I believe this name is Ellicott," said Belinda.

"Ellicott, is it? Ay, true. But what's the man stopping for then? Mrs Dumont's is the next door, tell the blind dunce. Mercy on us! To waste one's time in this way! I shall, as sure as fate, be too late for the china auction. What upon earth stops us?"

"Nothing but a little covered cart, which stands at Mrs Dumont's door. There, now it is going; an old man is drawing it out of the way as fast as he can."

"Open the coach-door, James!" cried Lady Boucher the moment that they had drawn up. "Now, my dear considerate Miss Portman, remember the auction, and don't let Miss Delacour stay to change her dress or anything."

Belinda promised not to detain her ladyship a minute. The door at Mrs Dumont's was open, and a servant was assisting an old man to carry in some geraniums and balsams out of the covered cart which had stopped the way. In the hall a crowd of children were gathered round a high stand, on which they were eagerly arranging their flower-pots, and the busy hum of voices was so loud that, when Miss Portman first went in, she could neither hear the servant nor make him hear her name. Nothing was to be heard but "O, how beautiful! O, how sweet! That's mine! That's yours! The great rose geranium for Miss Jefferson! The white Provence rose for Miss Adderly! No, indeed, Miss Pococke, that's for Miss Delacour; the old man said so."

"*Silence, silence, mesdemoiselles!*" cried the voice of a French woman, and all was silence. The little crowd looked towards the hall-door; and from the midst of her companions, Helena Delacour, who now caught a glimpse of Belinda, sprang forward, throwing down her white Provence rose as she passed.

"Lady Boucher's compliments, ma'am," said the servant to Mrs Dumont, "she's in indispensable haste, and she begs you won't let Miss Delacour think of changing her dress."

It was the last thing of which Miss Delacour was likely to think at this instant. She was so much overjoyed, when she heard that Belinda was come by her mamma's desire to take her home, that she would scarcely stay whilst Mrs Dumont was tying on her straw hat, and exhorting her to let Lady Delacour know how it happened that she was "so far from fit to be seen."

"Yes, ma'am; yes, ma'am, I'll remember; I'll be sure to remember," said Helena tripping down the steps. But just as she was getting into the carriage, she stopped at the sight of the old man, and exclaimed,

"O, good old man! I must not forget you."

"Yes, indeed you must though, my dear Miss Delacour," said Lady Boucher, pulling her into the carriage. "'Tis no time to think of good old men now."

"But I must. Dear Miss Portman, will you speak for me? I must pay – I must settle – and I have a great deal to say."

Miss Portman desired the old man to call in Berkeley square at Lady Delacour's; and this satisfying all parties, they drove away.

When they arrived in Berkeley square, Marriott told them that her lady was just gone to lie down. Charles Percival's little journal, which she had been reading, was left on the sofa, and Belinda gave it to Helena, who eagerly began to look over it. "Thirteen pages! O, how good he has been to write so much for me!" said she; and she had almost finished reading it before her mother came into the room.

Lady Delacour shrunk back as her daughter ran towards her; for she recollected too well the agony she had once suffered from an embrace of Helena's. The little girl appeared more grieved than surprised at this; and after kissing her mother's hand; without speaking, she again looked down at the manuscript.

"Does that engross your attention so entirely, my dear," said Lady Delacour, "that you can neither spare one word nor one look for your mother?"

"O mamma! I only tried to read because I thought you were angry with me."

"An odd reason for trying to read, my dear!" said Lady Delacour with a smile: "have you any better reason for thinking I was angry with you?"

"Ah, I know you are not angry now, for you smile," said Helena; "but I thought at first that you were, mamma, because you gave me only your hand to kiss."

"Only my hand – The next time, simpleton! I'll give you only my foot to kiss," said her ladyship, sitting down and holding out her foot playfully.

Her daughter threw aside the book, and kneeling down kissed

her foot, saying in a low voice, "Dear mamma, I never was so happy in my life; for you never looked so very, *very* kindly at me before."

"Do not judge always of the kindness people feel for you, child, by their looks; and remember that it is *possible* a person might have felt more than you could guess by their looks. Pray now, Helena, you who are such a good judge of physiognomy, should you guess that I was dying, by my looks?"

The little girl laughed, and repeated "*Dying*? – O, no, mamma."

"O no! because I have such a fine colour in my cheeks – Hey?"

"Not for that reason, mamma," said Helena, withdrawing her eyes from her mother's face.

"What, then you know rouge already when you see it? – You perceive some difference, for instance, between Miss Portman's colour and mine? Upon my word, you are a nice observer. Such nice observers are sometimes dangerous to have near one."

"I hope, mother," said Helena, "that you do not think I would try to find out anything that you wish, or that I imagined you wished, I should not know?"

"I do not understand you, child," cried Lady Delacour, raising herself suddenly upon the sofa, and looking full in her daughter's face.

Helena's colour rose to her temples, but, with a firmness that surprised even Belinda, she repeated what she had said nearly in the same words.

"Do you understand her, Miss Portman?" said Lady Delacour.

"She expresses, I think," said Belinda, "a very honourable sentiment, and one that is easily understood."

"Ay, in general, certainly," said Lady Delacour, checking herself; "but I thought that she meant to allude to something in particular – *that* was what I did not understand. Undoubtedly, my dear, you have just expressed a very honourable sentiment, and one that I should scarcely have expected from a child of your age."

"Helena, my dear!" said her mother after a silence of some minutes, "did you ever read the Arabian Tales? – 'Yes, mamma,' I know must be the answer. But do you remember the story of Zobeide, who carried the porter home with her, on condition that, let him hear or see what he might, he would ask no questions?"

"Yes, mamma."

"On the same conditions should you like to stay with me for a few days?"

"Yes. On any conditions, mamma, I should like to stay with you."

"Agreed then, my dear!" said Lady Delacour. "And now let us go to the gold fishes, and see them eat lemma, or whatever you please to call it."

Whilst they were looking at the gold fishes, the old man who had been desired by Miss Portman to call, arrived. "Who is this fine grey haired old man?" said Lady Delacour. And Helena, who did not know the share which Belinda's aunt and her own mother had in the transaction, began with great eagerness to tell the history of the poor gardener, who had been cheated by some fine ladies out of his aloe, &c. She then related how kind Lady Anne Percival and her aunt Margaret had been to this old man; that they had gotten him a place as a gardener at Twickenham; and that he had pleased the family to whom he was recommended so much by his good behaviour, that, as they were leaving their house, and obliged to part with him, they had given him all the geraniums and balsams out of the green-house of which he had the care, and these he had been this day selling to the young ladies at Mrs Dumont's. "I received the money for him, and I was just going to pay him," said Helena, "when Miss Portman came; and that put everything else out of my head. May I go and give him his money now, mamma?"

"He can wait a few minutes," said Lady Delacour, who had listened to this story with much embarrassment and impatience. "Before you go, Helena, favour us with the names of *the fine ladies who cheated* this old gardener out of his aloe?"

"Indeed, mamma, I don't know their names."

"No! – Did you never ask Lady Anne Percival or your aunt Margaret? – Look in my face, child! Did they never inform you?"

"No, ma'am, never. I once asked Lady Anne, and she said that she did not choose to tell me; that it would be of no use to me to know."

"I give Lady Anne Percival more credit and more thanks for this," cried Lady Delacour, "than for all the rest. I see she has not attempted to lower me in my child's opinion. I am the fine lady, Helena – I was the cause of his being cheated – I was intent upon *the noble end* of outshining a certain Mrs Luttridge – the *noble means* I left to others, and the means have proved worthy of the end. I deserve to be brought to shame for my folly; yet my being ashamed will do nobody any good but myself. Restitution is in these cases the best proof of repentance. Go, Helena, my love! settle your little affairs with this old man, and bid him call here again to morrow. I will see what we can do for him."

Lord Delacour had this very morning sent home to her ladyship a handsome diamond ring, which had been intended as a present for Mrs Luttridge, and which he imagined would therefore be peculiarly acceptable to his lady. In the evening, when his lordship asked her how she liked the ring, which he desired the jeweller to have for her to look at, she answered, that it was a handsome ring, but that she hoped he had not purchased it for her.

"It is not actually bought, my dear," said his lordship; "but if it suits your fancy, I hope you will do me the honour to wear it for my sake."

"I will wear it for your sake, my lord," said Lady Delacour, "if you desire it; and as a mark of your regard it is agreeable – But as to the rest –

'My taste for diamonds now is o'er,
'The sparkling baubles please no more.'

If you wish to do me a kindness, I will tell you what I should like much better than diamonds, though I know it is rather ungracious to dictate the form and fashion of a favour. But as my dictatorship in all human probability cannot last much longer — "

"O, my dear Lady Delacour! I must not hear you talk in this manner: your dictatorship, as you call it, will I hope last many, many happy years. But to the point – What should you like better, my dear, than this foolish ring?"

Her ladyship then expressed her wish, that a small annuity might be settled upon a poor old man, whom she said she had unwittingly injured. She told the story of the rival galas and the aloe, and concluded by observing, that her lord was in some measure called upon to remedy part of the unnumbered ills which had sprung from her hatred of Mrs Luttridge, as he had originally been the cause of her unextinguishable ire. Lord Delacour was flattered by this hint, and the annuity was imediately promised to the old gardener.

In talking to this old man afterward, Lady Delacour found, that the family in whose service he lately lived had a house at Twickenham that would just answer her purpose. Lord

Delacour's inquiries had hitherto been unsuccessful; he was rejoiced to find what he wanted just as he was giving up the search. The house was taken, and the old man hired as gardener – a circumstance which seemed to give him almost as much pleasure as the annuity; for there was a morello cherry-tree in the garden which had succeeded the aloe in his affection: "it would have grieved him sorely," he said, "to leave his favourite tree to strangers, after all the pains he had been at in *netting* it to keep off the birds."

As the period approached when her fate was to be decided, lady Delacour's courage seemed to rise; and at the same time her anxiety, that her secret should not be discovered, appeared to increase.

"If I survive *this business*," said she, "it is my firm intention to appear in a new character, or rather to assert my real character. I will break through the spell of dissipation – I will at once cast off all the acquaintance that are unworthy of me – I will, in one word, go with you, my dear Belinda! to Mr Percival's. I can bear to be mortified for my good; and I am willing, since I find that Lady Anne Percival has behaved generously to me with regard to Helena's affections – I am willing that the recovery of my moral health should be attributed to the salubrious air of Oakly-park. But it would be inexpressible, intolerable mortification to me, to have it said or suspected in the world of fashion, that I retreated from the ranks disabled instead of disgusted. A voluntary retirement is graceful and dignified; a forced retreat is awkward and humiliating. You must be sensible that I could not endure to have it whispered – 'Lady Delacour now sets up for being a prude, because she can no longer be a coquette.' Lady Delacour would become the subject of witticism, epigrams, caricatures without end. It would just be the very thing for odious Mrs Luttridge; then she would revenge herself without mercy for *the ass and her panniers*. We should have 'Lord and Lady D —, or The Domestic Tête-à-Tête, or The reformed Amazon,' stuck up in a print-shop window! Oh, my dear! think of seeing such a thing! I should die with vexation, and of all deaths that is the death I should like the least."

Though Belinda could not entirely enter into those feelings, which thus made Lady Delacour invent wit against herself, and anticipate caricatures; yet she did everything in her power to calm her ladyship's apprehensions of a discovery.

"My dear," said Lady Delacour, "I have perfect confidence in Lord Delacour's promise, and in his good nature, of which he has within these few days given me proofs that are not lost upon my heart; but, he is not the most discreet man in the world. Whenever he is anxious about anything, you may read it a mile off in his eyes, nose, mouth, and chin. And to tell you all my fears in one word, Marriott informed me this morning, that *the Luttridge*, who came from Harrowgate to Rantipole to meet Lord Delacour, finding that there was no drawing him to her, has actually brought herself to town.

"To town! At this strange time of year! How will my lord resist this unequivocal, unprecedented proof of passion? – If she catch hold of him again, I am undone. Or, even suppose him firm as a rock, her surprise, her jealousy, her curiosity, will set all engines at work, to find out by what witchcraft I have taken my husband from her. Every precaution that prudence could devise against her malicious curiosity I have taken – Marriott, you know, is above all temptation. – That vile wretch (naming the person whose quack medicines had nearly destroyed her), that vile wretch will be silent from fear, for his own sake. He is yet to be paid and dismissed. That should have been done long ago, but I had not money both for him and Mrs Franks the milliner. She is now paid; and Lord Delacour – I am glad to tell his friend how well he deserves her good opinion – Lord Delacour in the handsomest manner supplied me with the means of satisfying this man. He is to be here at three o'clock to day; and this is the last interview he will ever have with Lady Delacour in *the mysterious boudoir*."

The fears which her ladyship expressed of Mrs Luttridge's malicious curiosity were not totally without foundation – Champfort was at work for her and for himself. The memorable night of Lady Delacour's overturn, and the bustle that Marriott made about the key of the boudoir, were still fresh in his memory; and he was in hopes that, if he could discover the mystery, he should at once regain his power over Lord Delacour, reinstate himself in his lucrative place, and obtain a handsome reward, or, more properly speaking, bribe, from Mrs Luttridge. The means of obtaining information of all that passed in Lady Delacour's family were, he thought, still in his power, though he was no longer an inmate of the house. The *stupid maid* was not so stupid as to be impenetrable to the voice of flattery, or, as Mr Champfort called it, the voice of love. He found it his interest to court, and she her pleasure to be courted. On these 'coquettes of the *second table*,' – on these underplots in the drama, much of the comedy and some of the tragedy of life depend. Under the unsuspected mask of stupidity this worthy mistress of our intriguing valet de chambre concealed the quick ears of a listener, and the demure eyes of a spy. Long however did she listen, and long did she spy in vain, till at last Mr Champfort gave her notice in writing, that his love would not last another week, unless she could within that time contrive to satisfy his curiosity; and that, in short, she *must* find out the reason why the boudoir was always locked, and why Mrs Marriott alone was to be trusted with the key. Now it happened that this billet-doux was received on the very day appointed for Lady Delacour's last interview with the quack surgeon in the mysterious boudoir. Marriott, as it was her custom upon such occasions, let the surgeon in, and showed him up the back stairs into the boudoir, locked the door, and bade him wait there till her lady came. The man had not been punctual to the hour appointed; and Lady Delacour, giving up all expectation of his coming till the next day, had retired to her bedchamber, where she of late usually at this hour secluded herself to read methodistical books, or to sleep. Marriott, when she went up to let her lady know that *the person*, as she always called him, was come, found her so fast asleep that she thought it a pity to waken her, as she had not slept at all the preceding night. She shut the door very softly, and left her lady to repose. At the bottom of the stairs she was met by *the stupid maid*, whom she immediately dispatched with orders to wash some lace – "Your lady's asleep," said she, "and pray let me have no running up and down stairs." The room into which the stupid maid went was directly underneath the boudoir; and whilst she was there she thought that she heard the steps of a man's foot walking over head. She listened more attentively – she heard them again. She armed herself with a glass of jelly in her hand, *for my lady*, and hurried up stairs instantly to *my lady's* room. She was much surprised to see my lady fast asleep. Her astonishment at finding that Mrs Marriott had told her the truth was such, as for a moment to bereave her of all presence of mind, and she stood with the door ajar in her hand. As thus she stood she was roused by the sound of some one clearing his throat very softly in the boudoir – *His* throat – for she recollected the footsteps she had heard before, and she was convinced it could be no other than a masculine throat. She listened again, and stooped down to try whether any feet could be seen under the door. As she was in this attitude, her lady suddenly turned on her bed, and the book which she had been reading fell from the pillow to the floor with a noise, that made the listener start up instantaneously in great terror. The noise, however, did not waken Lady Delacour, who was in that dead sleep which is sometimes the effect of laudanum. The noise was louder than what could have been made by a fall of a book alone, and the girl descried a key that had fallen along with the book. It occurred to her, that this might possibly be the key of the boudoir. From one of those irresistible impulses which some people make an excuse for doing whatever they please, she seized it, resolved at all hazards to open the mysterious door. She was cautiously putting the key into the key-hole, so as not to make the least noise, when she was suddenly startled by a voice behind her, which said, "Who gave you leave to open the door?"

She turned, and saw Helena standing at the half open bed-chamber door.

"Mercy, Miss Delacour! – Who thought of seeing you! – For God's sake, don't make a noise to waken my lady!"

"Did my mother desire you to go into that room?" repeated Helena.

"Dear me! No, miss," said the maid, putting on her stupid face. "But I only thought to open the door to let in a little air to freshen the room, which my lady always likes, and bids me to do – and I thought — "

Helena took the key gently from her hand without listening to any more of her thoughts, and the woman left the room muttering something about *jelly*, and *my lady*. Helena went to the side of her mother's bed, determined to wait there till she awakened, then to give her the key, and tell her the circumstance. Notwithstanding the real simplicity of this little girl's character, she was, as her mother had discovered, *a nice observer*, and she had remarked that her mother never let anyone but Marriott go into the boudoir. This remark did not excite her to dive into the mystery: on the contrary, she carefully repressed all curiosity, remembering the promise she had given to her mother when she talked of Zobeide and the porter. She had not been without temptation to break this promise; for the house-maid, who usually attended her toilette, had employed every art in her power to stimulate her curiosity. As she was dressing Helena this morning, she had said to her,

"The reason I was so late calling you, miss, this morning, was because I was so late myself last night – for I went to the play, miss, last night, which was Bluebeard – Lord bless us! I'm sure, if I had been Bluebeard's wife, I should have opened the door if I'd died for it: – for to have the notion of living all day long, and all night too, in a house in which there was a room that one was never to go into, is a thing I could not put up with." Then after a pause, and after waiting in vain for some reply from Helena, she added, –"Pray, Miss Delacour, did you ever go into that little room within my lady's bedchamber, that Mrs Marriott keeps the key of always?"

"No," said Helena.

"I've often wondered what's in it – but then that's only because I'm a simpleton. I thought, to be sure, *you* knew."

Observing that Helena looked much displeased, she here broke off her speech, hoping that what she had said would operate in due time, and that she should thus excite the young lady to get the secret from Marriott, which she had no doubt afterward of *worming* from Miss Delacour.

In all this she calculated ill; for what she had said only made Helena distrust and dislike her. It was the recollection of this conversation, that made her follow the maid to her mother's bedchamber, to see what detained her there so long. Helena had heard Marriott say, that "she ought not to run up and down stairs, because her lady was asleep," and it appeared extraordinary, that but a few minutes after this information she should have gone into the room with a glass of jelly in her hand.

"Ah mamma!" thought Helena, as she stood beside her mother's bed, "you did not understand, and perhaps you did not believe me, when I said that I would not try to find out anything that you wished me not to know. Now I hope you will *understand* me better."

Lady Delacour opened her eyes – "Helena!" cried she starting up, "how come you by that key?"

"O, mother! don't look as if you suspected me." She then told her mother how the key came into her hands.

"My dear child, you have done me an essential service," said Lady Delacour, "You know not its importance, at least in my estimation. But what gives me infinitely more satisfaction, you have proved yourself worthy of my esteem – my love."

Marriott came into the room and whispered a few words to her lady.

"You may speak out, Marriott, before my Helena," said Lady Delacour, rising from the bed as she spoke – "Child as she is, Helena has deserved my confidence; and she shall be convinced that, where her mother has once reason to confide, she is incapable of suspicion. Wait here for a few minutes, my dear."

She went to her boudoir, paid and dismissed the surgeon expeditiously – then returned – and taking her daughter by the hand, she said,

"You look all simplicity, my dear! I see you have no vulgar school-girl curiosity. You will have all your mother's strength of mind; may you never have any of her faults, or any of her misfortunes! – I speak to you not as to a child, Helena, for you have reason far above your years; and you will remember what I now say to you as long as you live. You will possess talents, beauty, fortune; you will be admired, followed, and flattered, as I have been: – but do not throw away your life as I have thrown away mine, to win the praise of fools. Had I used but half the talents I possess, as I hope you will use yours, I might have been an ornament to my sex, I might have been a Lady Anne Percival."

Here Lady Delacour's voice failed – but, commanding her emotion, she in a few moments went on speaking.

"Choose your friends well, my dear daughter! It was my misfortune, my folly, early in life to connect myself with a woman, who under the name of frolic led me into every species of mischief. You are too young, too innocent, to hear the particulars of my history now; but you will hear them all at a proper time from my best friend Miss Portman. I shall leave you to her care, my dear, when I die."

"When you die! – O, mother!" said Helena, "but why do you talk of dying?" and she threw her arms round her mother.

"Gently, my love!" said Lady Delacour, shrinking back; and she seized this moment to explain to her daughter why she shrunk in this manner from her caresses, and why she talked of dying.

Helena was excessively shocked.

"I wished, my dear," resumed her mother calmly, "I wished to have spared you the pain of knowing all this. I have given you but little pleasure in my life, it is unjust to give you so much pain. We shall go to Twickenham to morrow, and I will leave you with your aunt Margaret, my dear, till all is over. If I die, Belinda will take you with her immediately to Oakly-park – you shall have as little sorrow as possible. If you had shown me less of your affectionate temper, you would have spared yourself the anguish that you now feel, and you would have spared me — "

"My dear kind mother," interrupted Helena, throwing herself on her knees at her mother's feet, "do not send me way from you — I don't wish to go to my aunt Margaret — I don't wish to go to Oakly-park — I wish to stay with you. Do not send me away from you; for I shall suffer ten times more if I am not with you, though I know I can be of no use."

Overcome by her daughter's entreaties, Lady Delacour at last consented that she should remain with her, and that she should accompany her to Twickenham.

The remainder of this day was taken up in preparations for their departure. The *stupid maid* was immediately dismissed. No questions were asked, and no reasons for her dismissal assigned, except that Lady Delacour had no farther occasion for her services. Marriott alone was to attend her lady to Twickenham. Lord Delacour, it was settled, should stay in town, lest the unusual circumstance of his attending his lady should excite public curiosity. His lordship, who was naturally a good natured man, and who had been touched by the kindness his wife had lately shown him, was in extreme agitation during the whole of this day, which he thought might possibly be the last of her existence. She, on the contrary, was calm and collected; her courage seemed to rise with the necessity for its exertion.

In the morning when the carriage came to the door, as she parted with Lord Delacour, she put into his hand a paper that contained some directions and requests, with which she said she hoped that he would comply, if they should prove to be her *last requests*. The paper contained only some legacies to her servants, a provision for Marriott, and a bequest, to her excellent and beloved friend Belinda Portman, of the cabinet in which she kept Clarence Hervey's letters.

Interlined in this place, Lady Delacour had written these words: "My daughter is nobly provided for; and lest any doubt or difficulty should arise from the omission, I think it necessary to mention that the said cabinet contains the valuable jewels left to me by my late uncle, and that it is my intention that the said jewels should be part of my bequest to the said Belinda Portman. — If she marry a man of good fortune, she will wear them for my sake: if she do not marry an opulent husband, I hope she will sell the jewels without scruple, as they are intended for her convenience, and not as an ostentatious bequest. It is fit that she should be as independent in her circumstances, as she is in her mind."

Lord Delacour with much emotion looked over this paper, and assured her ladyship that she should be obeyed, if — He could say no more.

"Farewell, then, my lord!" said she: "Keep up your spirits, for I intend to live many years yet to try them."

CHAPTER XXII

A Spectre

The surgeon who was to attend Lady Delacour was prevented from going to her on the day appointed; he was one of the surgeons of the queen's household, and his attendance was required at the palace. This delay was extremely irksome to Lady Delacour, who had worked up her courage to the highest point, but who had not prepared herself to endure suspense. She spent nearly a week at Twickenham in this anxious state, and Belinda observed that she every day became more and more thoughtful and reserved. She seemed as if she had some secret subject of meditation, from which she could not bear to be distracted. When Helena was present, she exerted herself to converse in her usual sprightly strain; but as soon as she could escape, as she thought, unobserved, she would shut herself up in her own apartment, and remain there for hours.

"I wish to Heaven, Miss Portman!" said Marriott, coming one morning into her room with a portentous face. "I wish to Heaven, ma'am, that you could any way persuade my lady not to spend so many hours of the day and night as she does in reading those methodistical books that she keeps to herself! – I'm sure that they do her no good, but a great deal of harm, especially now her spirits should be kept up as much as possible. I am sensible, ma'am, that 'tis those books that have made my lady melancholy of a sudden. Ma'am, my lady has let drop very odd hints within these two or three days, and she speaks in a strange *disconnected* sort of style, and at times I do not think she is quite right in her head."

When Belinda questioned Marriott more particularly about the strange hints which her lady had let fall, she with looks of embarrassment and horror declined repeating the words that had been said to her; yet persisted in asserting that Lady Delacour had been very *strange* for these two or three days. "And I'm sure, ma'am, you'd be shocked if you were to see my lady in a morning when she wakens, or rather when I first go into the room – for, as to wakening, that's out of the question. I am certain she does not sleep during the whole night. You'll find, ma'am, it is as I tell you, those books will quite turn her poor head, and I wish they were burnt. I know the mischief that the same sort of things did to a poor cousin of my own, who was driven melancholy mad by a methodist preacher, and came to an untimely end. Oh, m'am! if you knew as much as I do, you'd be as much alarmed for my lady as I am."

It was impossible to prevail upon Marriott to explain herself more distinctly. The only circumstances that could be drawn from her, seemed to Belinda so trifling as to be scarcely worth mentioning. For instance, that Lady Delacour, contrary to Marriott's advice, had insisted on sleeping in a bedchamber upon the ground floor, and had refused to let a curtain be put up before a glass door that was at the foot of her bed. "When I offered to put up the curtain, ma'am," said Marriott, "my lady said she liked the moonlight, and that she would not have it put up till the fine nights were over. Now, Miss Portman, to hear my lady talk of the moon, and moonlights, and liking the moon, is rather extraordinary and unaccountable; for I never heard her say any thing of the sort in my life before; I question whether she ever knew there was a moon or not from one year's end to another. But they say the moon has a great deal to do with mad people; and, from my own experience, I'm perfectly sensible, ma'am, it had in my own cousin's case; for, before he came to the worst, he took a prodigious fancy to the moon, and was always for walking by moonlight, and talking to one of the beauty of the moon, and such melancholy nonsense, ma'am."

Belinda could not forbear smiling at this melancholy nonsense; though she was inclined to be of Marriott's opinion about the methodistical books, and she determined to talk to Lady Delacour on the subject. The moment that she made the attempt, her ladyship, commanding her countenance, with her usual ability replied only by cautious, cold monosyllables, and changed the conversation as soon as she could.

At night, when they were retiring to rest, Marriott, as she lighted them to their rooms, observed that she was afraid her lady would suffer from sleeping in so cold a bedchamber, and Belinda pressed her friend to change her apartment.

"No, my dear," replied Lady Delacour calmly. "I have chosen this for my bedchamber, because it is at a distance from the servants' rooms; and when *the operation*, which I have to go through, shall be performed, my cries, if I should utter any, will not be overheard. The surgeon will be here in a few days, and it is not worth while to make any change."

The next day, towards evening, the surgeon and Doctor X — arrived. Belinda's blood ran cold at the sight of them.

"Will you be so kind, Miss Portman," said Marriott, "as to let my lady know that they are come? for I am not well able to go, and you can speak more composed to her than I can."

Miss Portman went to Lady Delacour's bedchamber. The door was bolted. As she opened it, she fixed her eyes upon Belinda, and said to her with a mild voice, "You are come to tell me that the surgeon is arrived. I knew that by the manner in which you knocked at the door. I will see him this moment," continued she in a firm tone; and she deliberately put a mark in the book in which she had been reading, walked leisurely to the other end of the room, and locked it up in her book-case. There was an air of determined dignity in all her motions. "Shall we go? I am ready," said she, holding out her hand to Belinda, who had sunk upon a chair. "One would think that you were the person that was going to suffer. But drink this water, my dear, and do not tremble for me; you see that I do not tremble for myself. Listen to me, dearest Belinda! I owe it to your friendship not to torment you with unnecesary apprehensions. Your humanity shall be spared this dreadful scene."

"No," said Belinda, "Marriott is incapable of attending you. I must – I will – I am ready now. Forgive me one moment's weakness. I admire, and will imitate, your courage. I will keep my promise."

"Your promise was to be with me in my dying moments, and to let me breathe my last in your arms."

"I hope that I shall never be called upon to perform that promise."

Lady Delacour made no answer, but walked on before her with steady steps into the room where Dr X — and the surgeon were waiting. Without adverting in the least to the object of their visit, she paid her compliments to them, as if they came on a visit of mere civility. Without seeming to notice the serious countenances of her companions, she talked of indifferent subjects with the most perfect ease, occupying herself all the time with cleaning a seal, which she unhooked from her watch-chain. "This seal," said she, turning to Dr X — "is a fine onyx – it is a head of Esculapius.

I have a great value for it. It was given to me by your friend, Clarence Hervey; and I have left it in my will, doctor," continued she smiling, "to you, as no slight token of my regard. He is an excellent young man; and I request," said she, drawing Dr X — to a window, and lowering her voice, "I request, when you see him again, and when I am out of the way, that you will tell him such were my sentiments to the hour of my death. Here is a letter which you will have the goodness to put into his hands, sealed with my favourite seal. You need have no scruple to take charge of it; it relates not to myself. It expresses only my opinion concerning a lady who stands almost as high in your esteem, I believe, as she does in mine. My affection and my gratitude have not biassed my judgment in the advice which I have ventured to give to Mr Hervey."

"But he will soon be here," interrupted Dr X — , "and then – " "And then I shall be gone," said Lady Delacour coolly,

'To the undiscovered country,
'From whose bourn no traveller returns.' "

Dr X — was going to interrupt her, but she continued rapidly.

"And now, my dear doctor! tell me candidly, have you seen any symptoms of cowardice in my manner this evening?"

"None," replied he. "On the contrary, I have admired your calm self-possession."

"Then do not suspect me of want of fortitude, when I request that this operation may not be performed to day. I have changed my mind within these few hours. I have determined, for a reason which I am sure that you would feel to be sufficient, to postpone this affair till to morrow. Believe me, I do not act from caprice."

She saw Dr X — did not yield assent to her last assertion, and that he looked displeased.

"I will tell you my reason," said she, "and then you will have no right to be displeased if I persist, as I shall inflexibly, in my determination. It is my belief that I shall die this night. To submit to a painful operation to day would be only to sacrifice the last moments of my existence to no purpose. If I survive this night, manage me as you please. But I am the best judge of my own feelings. I shall die to night."

Dr X — looked at her with a mixture of astonishment and compassion. Her pulse was high, she was extremely feverish, and he thought that the best thing which he could do was to stay with her till the next day, and to endeavour to divert her mind from this fancy, which he considered as an insane idea. He prevailed upon the surgeon to stay with her till the next morning; and he communicated his intentions to Belinda, who joined with him in doing all that was possible to entertain and interest Lady Delacour by conversation during the remainder of the day. She had sufficient penetration to perceive, that they gave not the least faith to her prognostics, and she never said one word more upon the subject; but appeared willing to be amused by their attempts to divert her, and resolute to support her courage till the last moment. She did not affect trifling gaiety: on the contrary, there was in all she said more strength and less point than usual.

The evening passed away, and Lady Delacour seemed totally to have forgotten her own prophecy respecting the event of the ensuing night; so much so, that she spoke of several things that she intended to do the next day. Helena knew nothing of what had passed, and Belinda imagined that her friend put this constraint upon herself to avoid alarming her daughter. Yet, after Helena retired, her mother's manner continued to be so much the same, that Dr X — began to believe that her ladyship was actuated merely by caprice. In this opinion she confirmed him by bursting out a laughing when he proposed that someone should sit up with her during the night.

"My sage sir," said she, "have you lived to this time without ever having been duped by a woman before? I wanted a day's reprieve, and I have gained it – gained a day, spent in most agreeable conversation, for which I thank you. To morrow," said she, turning to the surgeon, "I must invent some new excuse for my cowardice; and though I give you notice of it beforehand, as Barrington did when he picked the man's pocket, yet, neverthe-less, I shall succeed. Good night!"

She hurried to her own apartment, leaving them all in astonishment and perplexity. Belinda was persuaded that she only affected this gaiety to prevent Dr X — from insisting upon sitting up in her room, as he had proposed. Dr X — , judging, as he said, from her ladyship's general character, attributed the whole to caprice; and the surgeon, judging, as he said, from human nature in general, was decided in his belief that she had been influenced, as she herself declared, by cowardice. After having all expressed their opinions, without making any impression upon one another, they retired to rest.

Belinda's bedchamber was next to Helena's; and after she
had been in bed about an hour, she fancied that she heard some
one walking softly in the next room. She rose, and found Lady
Delacour standing beside her daughter's bed. She started at the
sight of Belinda, but only said in a low voice, as she pointed to
her child, "Don't waken her." She then looked at her for some
moments in silence. The moon shone full upon her face. She
stooped over Helena, parted the ringlets of hair upon her forehead, and kissed her gently.

"You will be good to this poor girl when I am gone, Belinda!"
said she, turning away from her as she spoke: "I only came to
look at her for the last time."

"Are you then serious, my dear Lady Delacour?"

"Hush! Don't waken her," said Lady Delacour, putting her
finger on her lips; and, walking slowly out of the room, she
forbade Belinda to follow.

"If my fears be vain," said she, "why should I disturb you with
them? If they be just, you will hear my bell ring, and then come
to me."

For some time afterward all was perfectly silent in the house.
Belinda did not go to bed, but sat waiting and listening anxiously. The clock struck two; and as she heard no other sound,
she began to hope that she had suffered herself to be falsely
alarmed by a foolish imagination, and she lay down upon her
bed, resolving to compose herself to rest. She was just sinking to
sleep, when she thought she heard the faint sound of a bel!. She
was not sure whether she was dreaming or awake. She started up
and listened. All was silent. But in a few minutes Lady
Delacour's bell rang violently. Belinda flew to her room. The
surgeon was already there; he had been sitting up in the next
room to write letters, and he had heard the first sound of the bell.
Lady Delacour was senseless, supported in the surgeon's arms.
Belinda, by his directions, ran immediately for Dr X — , who
was at the other end of the house. Before she returned Lady
Delacour had recovered her senses. She begged that the surgeon
would leave the room, and that neither Dr X — nor Marriott
might yet be admitted, as she had something of importance to
communciate to Miss Portman. The surgeon withdrew, and she
beckoned to Belinda, who sat down upon the side of her bed.
Lady Delacour held out her hand to her; it was covered with a
cold dew.

"My dear friend," said she, "my prophecy is accomplishing – I know I must die."

"The surgeon said that you were not in the least danger, my dear Lady Delacour! that it was merely a fainting fit. Do not suffer a vain imagination thus to overpower your reason."

"It is no vain imagination – I must die," said Lady Delacour.

> "I hear a voice you cannot hear,
> "Which says I must not stay:
> "I see a hand you cannot see,
> "Which beckons me away."

"You perceive that I am in my perfect senses, my dear! or I could not quote poetry. – I am not insane – I am not delirious."

She paused. "I am ashamed to tell you what I know will expose me to your ridicule."

"Ridicule!" cried Belinda: "can you think me so cruel as to consider your sufferings as a subject for ridicule?"

Lady Delacour was overcome by the tenderness with which Belinda spoke.

"I will then speak to you," said she, "without reserve. Inconsistent as it is with the strength of mind which you might expect from me, I cannot resist the impression which has been made on my mind by – a vision."

"A vision!"

"Three times," continued Lady Delacour, "it has appeared to me about this hour. The first night after we came here I saw it; last night it returned; and tonight I have beheld it for the third time. I consider it as a warning to prepare for death. – You are surprised – You are incredulous. I know that this must appear to you extravagant; but, depend upon it that what I tell you is true. It is scarcely a quarter of an hour since I beheld the figure of — , that man for whose untimely death I am answerable. Whenever I close my eyes the same form appears before me."

"These visions," said Belinda, "are certainly the effects of opium."

"The forms that flit before my eyes when I am between sleeping and waking," said Lady Delacour, "I am willing to believe, are the effects of opium; but, Belinda, it is impossible I should be convinced that my senses have deceived me with respect to what I have beheld when I have been as broad awake, and in as perfect possession of my understanding, as I am at this instant. The habits of my life, and the natural gaiety, not to say levity, of my temper, have always inclined me rather to incredulity than to superstition. But there are things which no strength of mind, no temerity, can resist. I repeat it, – This is a warning to me to prepare for death. No human means, no human power, can save me!"

Here they were interrupted by Marriott, who could no longer be restrained from bursting into the room. Dr X — followed, and, going calmly to the side of Lady Delacour's bed, took her hand to feel her pulse.

"Mrs Marriott, you need not alarm yourself in this manner," said he: "your lady is at this instant in as little danger as I am."

"*You* think she'll live! O, my lady! why did you terrify us in this manner?"

Lady Delacour smiled, and calmly said, as Dr X — still continued to count her pulse,

"The pulse may deceive you, doctor, but I do not. – Marriott, you may – "

Belinda heard no more; for at this instant, as she was standing alone, near the glass door that was opposite to the bed, she saw at a distance in the garden the figure which Lady Delacour had described. Lady Delacour was now so intent upon speaking to Dr X — , that she saw nothing but him. Belinda had the presence of mind to be perfectly silent. The figure stood still for some moments. She advanced a few steps nearer to the window, and the figure vanished. She kept her eye steadily fixed upon the spot where it had disappeared, and she saw it rise again and glide quickly behind some bushes. Belinda beckoned to Dr X — , who perceived, by the eagerness of her manner, that she wished to speak to him immediately. He resigned his patient to Marriott, and followed Miss Portman out of the room. She told him what she had just seen, said that it was of the utmost consequence to Lady Delacour to have the truth ascertained, requested that Dr X — would go with some of the men servants and search the garden, to discover whether anyone was there concealed, or whether any footsteps could be traced. The doctor did not search long before he perceived footsteps in the borders opposite to the glass door of Lady Delacour's bedchamber; he was carefully following their track, when he heard a loud cry, which seemed to come from the other side of the garden wall. There was a breach in the wall, over which he scrambled with some difficulty. The screams continued with redoubled violence. As he was making his way to the spot from which they proceeded, he was met by the old gardener, who was crossing one of the walks with a lantern in his hand.

"Ho! ho!" cried the gardener, "I take it that we have the thief at last. I fancy that the fellow whose footsteps I traced, and who has been at my morello cherry-tree every night, has been caught in the trap. I hope his leg is not broke, though! – This way, sir! This way!"

The gardener led the doctor to the place, and there they found a man, whose leg had actually been caught in the spring trap which had been set for the defence of the cherry-tree. The man had by this time fallen into a swoon; they extricated him as fast as possible, and Dr X — had him brought to Lady Delacour's, in order that the surgeon, who was there, might see his leg.

As they were carrying him across the hall, Belinda met them. She poured out a glass of water for the man, who was just recovering from his swoon; but, as she went nearer to give it to him, she was struck with his wonderful resemblance to Harriet Freke.

"It must be Mrs Freke herself!" whispered she to Marriott, whose wide opening eyes, at this instant, fixed themselves upon her.

"It must be Mrs Freke herself, ma'am!" – repeated Marriott.

And so in fact it was.

There is a certain class of people, who are incapable of generous confidence in their equals, but who are disposed to yield implicit credit to the underhand information of mean emissaries. Through the medium of Champfort and the *stupid maid*, Mrs Freke had learned a confused story of a man's footsteps having been heard in Lady Delacour's boudoir, of his being let in by Marriott secretly, of his having remained locked up there for several hours, and of the maid's having been turned away, merely because she innocently went to open the door whilst the gentleman was in concealment. Mrs Freke was further informed, by the same unquestionable authority, that Lady Delacour had taken a house at Twickenham, for the express purpose of meeting her lover; that Miss Portman and Marriott were the only persons who were to be of this party of pleasure.

Upon the faith of this intelligence, Mrs Freke, who had accompanied Mrs Luttridge to town, immediately repaired to Twickenham, to pay a visit to a third cousin, that she might have an opportunity of detecting the intrigues, and afterward of publishing the disgrace, of her former friend. The desire of revenging herself upon Miss Portman, for having declined her civilities at Harrowgate, had also a powerful influence in stimulating her malicious activity. She knew, that if it were proved that Belinda was the confidante of Lady Delacour's intrigues, her reputation must be materially injured, and that the Percivals would then be as desirous to break off, as they now were anxious to promote, the match with Mr Vincent. Charmed with this hope of a double triumph, the vindictive lady commenced her operations; nor was she ashamed to descend to the character of a spy. The general and convenient name of *frolic*, she thought, would cover every species of meanness. She swore that "it was charming fun to equip herself at night in man's clothes, and to sally forth to reconnoitre the motions of the enemy."

By an unfrequented path, she used to gain the window that looked into Lady Delacour's bedchamber. This was the figure, which appeared at night at a certain hour, and which, to her ladyship's disturbed imagination, seemed to be the form of Colonel Lawless. There was, indeed, a resemblance in their size and persons, which favoured the delusion. For several nights Mrs Freke paid these visits without obtaining any satisfaction; but this night she thought herself overpaid for her exertions, by the charming discovery which she fancied she had made. She mistook the surgeon for a lover of Lady Delacour's; and she was hurrying home with the joyful intelligence, when she was caught in the gardener's trap. The agony that she suffered was at first intense; but in a few hours the pain somewhat subsided; and in this interval of rest she turned to Belinda, and with a malicious smile said, — "Miss Portman, 'tis fair I should pay for my peeping; but I shall not pay quite so dear for it as some of my friends."

Miss Portman did not in the least comprehend her, till she added, "I'm sure you'll allow that 'tis better for a lady to lose her leg, than her reputation — and for my part, I'd rather be caught in a man trap, than have a man caught in my bedchamber. My service to your friend Lady Delacour, and tell her so."

"And do you know who the gentleman was that you saw in her ladyship's room?"

"Not I — Not yet but I'll make it my business to find out. I give you fair notice: I'm a very devil when provoked. Why didn't you make me your friend when you could? — You'll not baffle me. I have seen all I wanted, and I am capable of painting all I saw. As to who the man might be, that's no matter. One Lothario is as good as another for my purpose."

Longer had Mrs Freke spoken with malignant triumph, had she not been interrupted by a burst of laughter from the surgeon. Her vexation was indescribable when he informed her, that he was the man whom she had seen in Lady Delacour's bedchamber, and whom she had mistaken for a favoured lover.

"Like the surgeon in Gil Blas," said Dr X —, "who was challenged for having had the honour of a surgical tête-à-tête with dame Sephora."

Mrs Freke's leg was much cut and bruised; and now that she was no longer supported by the hopes of revenge, she began to lament loudly and incessantly the injury that she had sustained. She impatiently inquired how long it was probable, that she should be confined by this accident; and she grew quite outrageous when it was hinted, that the beauty of her legs would be spoiled, and that she would never more be able to appear to advantage in man's apparel. The dread of being seen by Lady Delacour in the deplorable yet ludicrous situation, to which she had reduced herself, operated next upon her mind, and every time the door of her apartment opened, she looked with terror towards it, expecting to see her ladyship appear. But though Lady Delacour heard from Marriott immediately the news of Mrs Freke's disaster, she never disturbed the lady by her presence. She was too generous to insult a fallen foe.

Early in the morning, Mrs Freke was by her own desire conveyed to her cousin's house, where without regret we shall leave her to enjoy the consequences of her frolic.

"A false prophetess! – Notwithstanding all my vision I have outlived the night, you see," said Lady Delacour to Miss Portman when they met in the morning. "I have heard, my dear Belinda, and I believe, that the passion of love, which can endure caprice, vice, wrinkles, deformity, poverty, nay disease itself, is notwithstanding so squeamish as to be instantaneously disgusted by the perception of folly in the object beloved. I hope friendship, though akin to love, is of a more robust constitution, else what would become of me? My folly, and my visions, and my spectre – O that I had not exposed myself to you in this manner! – Harriet Freke herself is scarcely more contemptible. Spies and cowards are upon an equal footing. Her malice and her *frolic* are consistent with her character, but my fears and my superstition are totally inconsistent with mine. Forget the nonsense I talked to you last night, my dear, or fancy that I was then under the dominion of laudanum. This morning you shall see Lady Delacour *herself again.* Is Dr X — , is the surgeon ready? Where are they? I am prepared. My fortitude shall redeem me in your opinion, Belinda, and in my own.'

Dr X — and the surgeon immediately obeyed her summons.

Helena heard them go into Lady Delacour's room, and she saw by Marriott's countenance, who followed, that her mother was going to submit to the operation. She sat down trembling on the steps which led to her mother's room, and waited there a long time, as she thought, in the most painful suspense. At last she heard some one call Helena. She looked up, and saw her father close to her.

'Helena,' said he, 'how is your mother?'

'I don't know, – O papa, you cannot go in there *now*,' said Helena, stopping him as he was pressing forwards.

'Why did you not or Miss Portman write to me yesterday, as you promised?' said Lord Delacour in a voice that showed he was scarcely able to ask the question.

'Because, papa, we had nothing to tell you. Nothing was done yesterday. But the surgeon is now there,' said Helena, pointing towards her mother's room.

Lord Delacour stood motionless for an instant; then suddenly seizing his daughter's hand, 'Let us go,' said he: 'if we stay here we shall hear her screams;' and he was hurrying her away, when the door of Lady Delacour's apartment opened, and Belinda appeared, her countenance radiant with joy.

'Good news, dear Helena! – O, my lord! you are come in a happy moment – I give you joy.'

'Joy! Joy! Joy!' cried Marriott, following.

'Is it all over?' said Lord Delacour.

'And without a single shriek!' said Helena. 'What courage!'

'There's no need of shrieks, or courage either, thank God!' said Marriott. Dr X — says so, and the surgeon is not wanted. Dr X — says so, and he is the best man in the world, and the cleverest. And I was right from the first; I said it was impossible my Lady should have such a shocking complaint as she thought she had. There's no such thing at all in the case, my lord! I said so always till I was persuaded out of my senses by this villainous quack, who contradicted me for his own 'molument. And Dr X — says, if my lady will leave off the terrible quantities of laudanum she takes, he'll engage for her recovery. Now I'm morally certain Mr Champfort would die with vexation, if he could see the joy that's painted in my lord's face this minute. And we may thank Miss Portman for this, for 'twas she made every thing go right, and I never expected to live to see so happy a day."

Whilst Marriott ran on in this manner, with all the volubility of joy, Lord Delacour passed her with some difficulty, and Helena was in her mother's arms in an instant.

Lady Delacour, struck to the heart by their affectionate looks and words, burst into tears. "How little have I deserved this kindness from you, my lord! or from you, my child! But my feelings," added she, wiping away her tears, "shall not waste themselves in tears, nor in vain thanks. My actions, the whole course of my future life, shall show that I am not quite a brute. Even brutes are won by kindness. Observe, my lord," continued she smiling, "I said *won*, not *tamed*! – A tame Lady Delacour would be a sorry animal, not worth looking at. Were she even to become domesticated, she would fare the worse."

"How so? – How so, my dear?" said Lord Delacour and Belinda almost in the same breath.

"How so! – Why, if Lady Delacour were to wash off her rouge, and lay aside her airs, and be as gentle, good, and kind as Belinda Portman, for instance, her lord would certainly say to her,

'So altered are your face and mind,
''Twere perjury to love you now.'"

CHAPTER XXIII

The Chaplain

In some minds, emotions of joy are always connected with feelings of benevolence and generosity. Lady Delacour's heart expanded with the sensations of friendship and gratitude, now that she was relieved from those fears by which she had long been oppressed.

"My dear daughter," said she to Helena, "have you at this instant any wish that I can gratify – Ask anything you please, the fairy Goodwill shall contrive to get it to you in a trice. You have thought of a wish at this moment I know by your eyes, by your blush. Nay do not hesitate. Do you doubt me because I do not appear before you in the shape of a little ugly old woman, like Cinderella's godmother? or do you despise me because you do not see a wand waving in my hand? – 'Ah, little skilled of fairy lore!' know that I am in possession of a talisman that can command more than ever fairy granted. Behold my talisman," continued she, drawing out her purse, and showing the gold through the net-work. "Speak boldly, then," cried she to Helena, "and be obeyed."

"Ah, mamma," said Helena, "I was not thinking of what fairies or gold can give; but *you* can grant my wish, and if you will let me I will whisper it to you."

Lady Delacour stooped to hear her daughter's whisper.

"Your wish is granted, my own grateful charming girl!" said her mother.

Helena's wish was that her mother could be reconciled to her good aunt Margaret Delacour. Her ladyship sat down instantly, and wrote to Mrs Delacour. Helena was the bearer of this letter, and Lady Delacour promised to wait upon this excellent old lady as soon as she should return to town.

In the mean time her ladyship's health rapidly improved under the skilful care of Dr X — : it had been terribly injured by the ignorance and villainy of the wretch, to whom she had so long and so rashly trusted. The nostrums which he persuaded her to take, and the immoderate use of opium to which she accustomed herself, would have ruined her constitution, had it not been uncommonly strong. Dr X — recommended it to her ladyship to abstain gradually from opium, and this advice she had the resolution to follow with uninterrupted perseverance.

The change in Lady Delacour's manner of life, in the hours and the company that she kept, contributed much to her recovery. She was no longer in continual anxiety to conceal the state of her health from the world. She had no secret to keep – no part to act; her reconciliation with her husband and with his friends restored her mind to ease and self-complacency. Her little Helena was a source of daily pleasure; and no longer conscious of neglecting her daughter, she no longer feared that the affections of her child should be alienated. Dr X — , well aware that the passions have a powerful influence over the body, thought it full as necessary in some cases to attend to the mind as to the pulse. By conversing with Lady Delacour, and by combining hints and circumstances, he soon discovered what had lately been the course of her reading, and what impression it had made on her imagination. Mrs Marriott, indeed, assisted him with her opinion concerning *the methodistical books*; and when he recollected the forebodings of death which her ladyship had felt, and the terror with which she had been seized on the night of Mrs Freke's adventure, he was convinced that superstitious horrors hung upon his patient's spirits, and affected her health. To argue on religious subjects was not his province, much less his inclination; but he was acquainted with a person qualified by his profession and his character 'to minister to a mind diseased', and he resolved on the first favourable opportunity to introduce this gentleman to her ladyship.

One morning Lady Delacour was complaining to Belinda that the books in the library were in dreadful confusion. "My lord has really a very fine library," said she, "but I wish he had half as many books twice as well arranged; I never can find anything I want. Dr X — , I wish to Heaven you could recommend a librarian to my lord – Not a chaplain, observe."

"Why not a chaplain? may I ask your ladyship?" said the doctor.

"O, because we had once a chaplain, who gave me a surfeit of the whole tribe. The meanest sycophant, yet the most impertinent busybody – always cringing, yet always intriguing – wanting to govern the whole family, and at the same time every creature's humble servant – fawning to my lord the bishop, insolent to the poor curate – anathematising all who differed from him in opinion, yet without dignity to enforce the respect due to his faith or his profession – Greedy for preferment, yet without a thought of the duties of his profession. It was the common practice of this man to leap from his horse at the church door after following a pack of hounds, huddle on his surplice, and gabble over the service with the most indecent mockery of religion – Do I speak with acrimony? I have reason. It was this chaplain who first led my lord to Newmarket; it was he who first taught my lord to drink. Then he was *a wit* – an unsufferable wit! His conversation after he had drunk was such as no woman but Harriet Freke could understand, and such as few *gentlemen* could hear. I have never, alas! been thought a prude, but in the heyday of my youth and gaiety this man always disgusted me. In one word, he was a buck parson. I hope you have as great a horror for this species of animal as I have?"

"Full as great," replied Dr X — ; "but I consider them as monsters, which, belonging to no species, can disgrace none."

"They ought to be hunted by common consent out of civilised society," said Lady Delacour.

"They are by public opinion banished from all rational society; and your ladyship's just indignation proves, that they have no chance of being tolerated by fashion. But would it not allow such beings too much consequence, would it not extend their power to do mischief, if we perceived that one such parson could disgust Lady Delacour with the whole race of chaplains?"

"It is uncommon," replied her ladyship, "to hear a physician *earnest* in the defence of the clergy – and a literary philosophic physician too! Shall we have an eulogium upon bishops as well as chaplains?"

"We have had that already," replied Dr X — . "All ranks, persuasions, and descriptions of people, including I hope those stigmatised by the name of philosophers, have joined in admiration of the bishop of St Pol de Leon.* The conduct of the real martyrs to their faith amongst the French clergy not even the most witty or brutal sceptic could ridicule."

"You surprise me, doctor!" said Lady Delacour; "for I assure you that you have the character of being very liberal in your opinions."

"I hope I am liberal in my opinions," replied the doctor, "and that I give your ladyship a proof of it."

"You would not then persecute a man or woman with ridicule for believing more than you do?" said Lady Delacour.

"Those who persecute, to overturn religion, can scarcely pretend to more philosophy, or more liberality, than those who persecute to support it," said Dr X — .

"Perhaps, doctor, you are only speaking popularly?"

"I believe what I now say to be true," said Dr X , "and I always endeavour to make truth popular."

"But possibly these are only truths for ladies. Dr X — may be such an ungallant philosopher, as to think that some truths are not fit for ladies. He may hold a different language with gentlemen."

"I should not only be an ungallant but a weak philosopher," said Dr X — , "if I thought that truth was not the same for all the world who can understand it. And who can doubt Lady Delacour's being of that number?"

Lady Delacour, who at the beginning of this conversation had spoken guardedly, from the fear of lowering the doctor's opinion of her understanding, was put at her ease by the manner in which he now spoke; and, half laying aside the tone of raillery, she said to him,

"Well, doctor! seriously, I am not so *illiberal* as to condemn *all* chaplains for one, odious as he was. But where to find his contrast in these degenerate days? Can you, who are a defender of the faith, and so forth, assist me? Will you recommend a chaplain to my lord?"

"Willingly," said Dr X — ; "and that is what I would not say for a world of fees, unless I were sure of my man."

"What sort of a man is he?"

"Not a buck parson."

"And I hope not a pedant, not a dogmatist, for that would be almost as bad. Before we domesticate another chaplain, I wish to know all his qualities, and to have a full and true description of him."

"Shall I then give you a full and true description of him in the words of Chaucer?"

"In any words you please. But Chaucer's chaplain must be a little old-fashioned by this time, I should think."

"Pardon me. Some people, as well as some things, never grow old-fashioned. I should not be ashamed to produce Chaucer's parish priest at this day to the best company in England. I am not ashamed to produce him to your ladyship; and, if I can remember twenty lines in his favour, I hope you will give me credit for being a sincere friend to the worthy part of the clergy. Observe, you must take them as I can patch them together; I will not promise that I can recollect twenty lines *de suite*,* and without missing a word; that is what I would not swear to do for his grace the archbishop of Canterbury."

"His grace would probably excuse you from swearing, at least I will," said Lady Delacour, "on the present occasion. So now for your twenty lines in whatever order you please."

Dr X — with sundry intervals of recollection, which may be spared the reader, repeated the following lines:

> "Yet has his aspect nothing of severe,
> But such a face as promis'd him sincere.
> Nothing reserv'd or sullen was to see,
> But sweet regards, and pleasing sanctity,
> Mild was his accent, and his action free.
> With eloquence innate his tongue was arm'd,
> Though harsh the precept, yet the preacher charm'd;
> For, letting down the golden chain from high,
> He drew his audience upwards to the sky.
> He taught the Gospel rather than the law,
> And forc'd himself to drive, but lov'd to draw.
> The titles his parish freely paid, he took;
> But never sued, or curs'd with bell and book.
> Wide was his parish, not contracted close
> In streets – but here and there a straggling house.
> Yet still he was at hand, without request,
> To serve the sick, and succour the distrest.
> The proud he tam'd, the penitent he cheer'd,
> Nor to rebuke the rich offender fear'd.
> His preaching much, but more his practice wrought,
> A living sermon of the truths he taught."*

Lady Delacour wished tht she could find a chaplain who in any degree resembled this charming parish priest, and Dr X — promised that he would the next day introduce to her his friend Mr Moreton.

"Mr Moreton!" said Belinda, "the gentleman of whom Mr Percival spoke, Mrs Freke's Mr Moreton?"

"Yes," said Dr X— , "the clergyman whom Mrs Freke hanged in effigy, and to whom Clarence Hervey has given a small living."

These circumstances, even if he had not precisely resembled Chaucer's character of a benevolent clergyman, would have strongly interested Lady Delacour in his favour. She found him, upon farther acquaintance, a perfect contrast to her former chaplain; and he gradually acquired such salutary influence over her mind, that he relieved her from the terrors of methodism, and in their place substituted the consolations of mild and rational piety.

Her conscience was now at peace; her spirts were real and equable, and never was her conversation so agreeable. Animated with the new feelings of returning health, and the new hopes of domestic happiness, she seemed desirous to impart her felicity to all around her, but chiefly to Belinda, who had the strongest claims upon her gratitude, and the warmest place in her affections. Belinda never made her friend feel the weight of any obligation, and consequently Lady Delacour's gratitude was a voluntary pleasure – not an expected duty. Nothing could be more delightful to Miss Portman than thus to feel herself the object at once of esteem, affection, and respect; to see that she had not only been the means of saving her friend's life, but that the influence she had obtained over her mind was likely to be so permanently beneficial to her family and to herself.

Belinda did not take all the merit of this reformation to herself: she was most willing to share it in her own imagination not only with Dr X — and Mr Moreton, but with *poor Clarence Hervey*. She was pleased to observe that Lady Delacour never omitted any occasion of doing justice to his merit, and she loved her for that generosity, which sometimes passed the bounds of justice in her eulogiums. But Belinda was careful to preserve her consistency, and to guard her heart from the dangerous effect of these enthusiastic praises; and as Lady Delacour was now sufficiently reestablished in her health, she announced her intention of returning immediately to Oakly-park, according to her promise to Lady Anne Percival and to Mr Vincent.

"But my dear," said Lady Delacour, "one week more is all I ask from you – May not friendship ask such a sacrifice from love?"

"You expect, I know," said Miss Portman ingenuously, "that before the end of that time Mr Hervey will be here."

"True. And have you no friendship for him?" said Lady Delacour with an arch smile, "or is friendship for every man in the creation, one Augustus Vincent always expected, prohibited by the statutes of Oakly-park?"

"By the statutes of Oakly-park nothing is forbidden," said Belinda, "but what reason – "

"Reason! O, I have done if you go to reason. You are invulnerable to the light shafts of wit, I know, when you are cased in this heavy armour of reason; Cupid himself may strain his bow and exhaust his quiver upon you in vain. But have a care – you cannot live in armour all your life – lay it aside but for a moment, and the little bold urchin will make it his prize. Remember Raphael's picture of Cupid creeping into the armour of the conqueror of the world."

"I am sufficiently aware," said Belinda, smiling, "of the power of Cupid and of his wiles. I would not brave his malice, but I would fly from it."

"It is so cowardly to fly!"

"Surely, prudence, not courage, is the virtue of our sex; and seriously, my dear Lady Delacour, I entreat you not to use your influence over my mind, lest you should lessen my happiness, though you cannot alter my determination."

Moved by the earnest manner in which Belinda uttered these word, Lady Delacour rallied her no more, nor did she longer oppose her resolution of returning immediately to Oakly-park.

"May I remind you," said Miss Portman, – "though it is seldom either politic or polite to remind people of their promises, – but may I remind you of something like a promise you made to accompany me to Mr Percival's?"

"And would you have me behave so brutally to poor Lord Delacour, as to run away from him in this manner the moment I have strength to run?"

"Lord Delacour is included in this invitation," said Miss Portman, putting the last letter that she had received from Lady Anne Percival into her hands.

"When I recollect," said Lady Delacour, as she looked over the letter, "how well this Lady Anne of yours has behaved to me about Helena – when I recollect, that, though you have been with her so long, she has not supplanted me in your affections, nor attempted to detain you when I sent Marriott to Oakly-park – and when I consider how much for my own advantage it will be to accept this invitation, I really cannot bring myself from pride, or folly, or any other motive, to refuse it. So, my dear Belinda, prevail upon Lord Delacour to spend his Christmas at Oakly-park instead of at Studley-manor (Rantipole, thank Heaven! is out of the question), and prevail upon yourself to stay a few days for me, and you shall take us all with you in triumph."

Belinda was convinced that, when Lady Delacour had once tasted the pleasures of domestic life, she would not easily return to that dissipation which she had followed from habit, and into which she had first been driven by a mixture of vanity and despair. All the connexions which she had imprudently formed with numbers of fashionable, but extravagant and thoughtless women, would insensibly be broken off by this measure; for Lady Delacour, who was already weary of their company, would be so much struck with the difference between their insipid conversation and the animated and interesting society in Lady Anne Percival's family, that she would afterward think them not only burdensome, but intolerable. Lord Delacour's intimacy with Lord Studley was one of his chief inducements to that intemperance, which injured almost equally his constitution and his understanding: for some weeks past he had abstained from all excess, but Belinda was well aware, that, when the immediate motive of humanity to Lady Delacour ceased to act upon him, he would probably return to his former habits, if he continued to visit his former associates. It was therefore of importance, to break at once his connexion with Lord Studley, and to place him in a situation where he might form new habits, and where his dormant talents might be roused to exertion. She was convinced, that his understanding was not so much *below par*, as he had once been taught to think it: she perceived also, that, since their reconciliation, Lady Delacour was anxious to make him appear to advantage: whenever he said anything that was worth hearing she looked at Belinda with triumph; and whenever he happened to make *a mistake* in conversation, she either showed involuntary signs of uneasiness, or passed it off with that easy wit, by which she generally knew how "to make the worse appear the better reason." Miss Portman knew, that Mr Percival possessed the happy talent of drawing out all the abilities of those with whom he conversed, and that he did not value men merely for their erudition, science, or litereature; he was capable of estimating *the potential*, as well as *the actual range* of the mind. Of his generosity she could not doubt, and she was persuaded that he would take every possible means, which good nature, joined to good sense, could suggest, to raise Lord Delacour in his lady's esteem, and to make that union happy, which was indissoluble. All these reflections passed with the utmost rapidity in Belinda's mind, and the result of them was, that she consented to wait Lady Delacour's leisure for her journey.

VOLUME III

CHAPTER XXIV

Peu à Peu*

___

Things were in this situation when, one day, Marriott made her appearance at her lady's toilette, with a face, which at once proclaimed, that something had discomposed her; and that she was impatient to be asked what it was.

"What *is* the matter, Marriott?" said Lady Delacour; "for I know you want me to ask."

"Want you to ask! O dear, my lady, no! – for I'm sure, it's a thing that goes quite against me to tell; for I thought indeed, my lady, *superiorly* of the person in question; so much so, indeed, that I wished, what, I declare, I should now be ashamed to mention, especially in the presence of Miss Portman, who deserves the best that this world can afford of every denomination. Well, ma'am, in one word," continued she, addressing herself to Belinda, "I am extremely rejoiced, that things are as they are; though, I confess, that was not always my wish or opinion, for which I beg Mr Vincent's pardon and yours; but I hope to be forgiven, since I'm now come entirely round to my Lady Anne Percival's way of thinking, which I learnt, from good authority, at Oakly-park; and I am now convinced, and confident, Miss Portman, that every thing is for the best."

"Marriott will inform us, in due course of time, what has thus suddenly and happily converted her," said Lady Delacour to Belinda, who was thrown into some surprise and confusion by Marriott's address but Marriott went on with much warmth – "Dear me! I'm sure I thought we had got rid of all double-dealers, when the house was cleared of Mr Champfort; but, O mercy! there's not traps enough in the world for them all; I only wish they were all caught, as finely as some people were, in a trap t'other night – 'Tis what all double-dealers, and Champfort at the head of the whole regiment, deserves; that's certain."

"We must take patience, my dear Belinda," said Lady Delacour, calmly, "till Marriott has exhausted all the expletives in and out of the English language; and presently, when she has fought all her battles with Champfort over again, we may hope to get at the fact."

"Dear! my lady, it has nothing to do with Mr Champfort, nor any such style of personage, I can assure you; for, I'm positive, I'd rather think contemptibly of a hundred million Mr Champforts, than of one such gentleman as Mr Clarence Hervey."

"Clarence Hervey!" exclaimed Lady Delacour. Taking it for granted, that Belinda blushed, though in fact she did not, her ladyship, with superfluous address, instantly turned, so as to hide her friend's face from Mrs Marriott. "Well, Marriott, what of Mr Hervey?"

"O! my lady, something you'll be surprised to hear, and Miss Portman too. It is not, by any means, that I am more of a prude than is becoming, my lady; nor, that I take upon me to be so innocent, as not to know, that young gentlemen of fortune will, if it be only for fashion's sake, have such things as kept mistresses, (begging pardon for mentioning such trash). But no one, that has lived in the world, thinks anything of that; except," added she, catching a glimpse of Belinda's countenance, – "except, to be sure, ma'am, morally speaking, it's very wicked and shocking, and makes one blush before company, till one's used to it, and ought certainly to be put down by act of parliament, ma'am; but, my lady, you know, in point of surprising anybody, or being discreditable in a young gentleman of Mr Hervey's fortune and pretensions, it would be mere envy and scandal, to deem it anything – worth mentioning."

"Then, for mercy's sake, or mine," said Lady Delacour, "go on to something that *is* worth mentioning."

"Well, my lady, you must know, then, that yesterday I wanted some hempseed for my bullfinch – Miss Helena's bullfinch, I mean; for it was she found it by accident, you know, Miss Portman, the day after we came here; poor thing, it got itself so entangled in the net over the morello cherry-tree, in the garden, that it could neither get itself in nor out; but very luckily, Miss Helena saw it, and saved, and brought it in: it was almost dead, my lady."

"Was it? – I am very sorry for it: – I mean – that is what you expect me to say. – Now, go on – get us once past the bullfinch, and tell us what it has to do with Clarence Hervey."

"That is what I am aiming at, as fast as possible, my lady. – So, I sent for some hempseed for the bullfinch, and along with the hempseed they brought me, wrapped round it, as it were, a printed handbill, as it might be, or advertisement, which I threw off, disregardingly, taking it for granted, it might have been some of those advertisements for lozenges or razor-strops, that meet one wherever one goes; but Miss Delacour picked it up, and found it was a kind of hue and cry after a stolen or strayed bullfinch. Ma'am, I was so provoked, I could have cried, when I learnt it was the exact description of our little Bobby to a feather – grey upon the back, and red on – '

"O! spare me the description to a feather. – Well, you took the bird, bullfinch, or Bobby, as you call it, home to its rightful owner, I presume. – Let me get you so far on your way."

"No, I beg your pardon, my lady, that is not the thing."

"Then you did not take the bird home to its owner – and you are a bird-stealer? – With all my heart – be a dog-stealer, if you will – only go on."

"But, my lady, you hurry me so, it puts every thing topsyturvy in my head; I could tell it as fast as possible my own way."

"Do so, then."

"I was ready to cry, when I found our little Bobby was claimed from us, to be sure; but Miss Delacour observed, that those, with whom it had lived till it was grey, must be sorrier still to part with it, so I resolved to do the honest and genteel thing by the lady who advertised for it, and to take it back myself, and to refuse the five guineas reward offered. The lady's name, according to the advertisement, was Ormond."

"Ormond!" repeated Lady Delacour, looking eagerly at Belinda; "was that the name Sir Philip Baddely mentioned to us – you remember?" —

"Yes; Ormond was the name, as well as I recollect," said Belinda, with a degree of steady composure, that provoked her ladyship. – "Go on, Marriott."

"And the words were, to leave the bird at a perfumer's in Twickenham, opposite to — ; but that's no matter. – Well, my lady, to the perfumer's I went with the bird, this morning. Now, I had my reasons for wishing to see this Mrs Ormond myself, because, my lady, there was one thing rather remarkable about this bullfinch, that it sings a very particular tune, which I never heard any bullfinch, or any human creature sing any thing like before; so I determined, in my own cogitations, to ask this Mrs Ormond to name the tunes her bullfinch could sing, before I produced it; and if she made no mention of its knowing any one out of the common way, I resolved to keep my bird to myself, as I might very conscientiously and genteelly too. So, my lady, when I got to the perfumer's, I inquired where Mrs Ormond was to be found? I was told, that she received no visits from any, at least from the female sex; and that I must leave the bird there till called for. I was considering what to do, and the strangeness of the information made about the female sex, when in there came, into the shop, a gentleman, who saved me all the indelicacy of asking particulars. The bullfinch was at this time piping away at a fine rate, and, as luck would have it, that very remarkable strange tune that I mentioned to you. – Says the gentleman, as he came into the shop, fixing his eyes on the bullfinch as if they would have come fairly out of his head – 'How did that bird come here?' – 'I brought it here, sir,' said I. Then he began to offer me mountains of gold, in a very strange way, if I could tell him any tidings of the lady, to whom it belonged. The shopman, from behind the counter, now bent forward, and whispered the gentleman, that he could give him some information, if he would make it worth his while; and they both went together to a little parlour behind the shop, and I saw no more of them. But, my lady, very opportunely for me, that was dying with curiosity, out of the parlour they turned a young woman in, to attend the shop, who proved to be an acquaintance of mine, whom I had done some little favours to when in service in London. – And this young woman, when I told her my distress about the advertisement and the bullfinch, let me into the whole of the affair. – 'Ma'am,' said she, 'all that is known about Mrs Ormond, in this house, or any where else, is from me; so there was no occasion for turning me out of the parlour. I lived with Mrs Ormond, ma'am,' says she, 'for half a year, in the very house she now occupies, and consequently nobody can be better informed than I am': – to which I agreed. Then she told me, that the reason that Mrs Ormond never saw any company of any sort was, because she is not fit to see company – proper company – for she's not a proper woman. She has a most beautiful young creature there, shut up, who has been seduced, and is now deserted in a most cruel manner by a Mr Hervey. O, my lady! how the name struck upon my ear! – I hoped, however, it was not our Mr Hervey, but it was the identical Mr Clarence Hervey. I made the young woman describe him, for she had often and often seen him, when he visited the unfortunate creature; and the description could suit none but our Mr Hervey;

and besides, it put it beyond a doubt, she told me his linen was all marked C.H. – So our Mr Hervey, ma'am," added Marriott, turning to Belinda, "it certainly proved to be, to my utter dismay and confusion."

"O, Marriott! my poor head!" exclaimed Lady Delacour, starting from under her hands – "that cruel comb went at least half an inch into my head: heads have feeling as well as hearts, believe me." And, as she spoke, she snatched out the comb, with which Marriott had just fastened up her hair, and flung it on a sofa, at some yards distance. While Marriott went to fetch it, Lady Delacour thought that Belinda would have time to recover from that utter dismay and confusion, into which she hoped that she must now be thrown. Her ladyship was again disappointed, when she examined Belinda's countenance. – Come, Marriott, make haste, I have done at least *you* a great favour, for you have all this hair to perform upon again, and you will have leisure to finish this story of yours – which, at all events, if it is not in any other respects wonderful, we must allow, is wonderfully long."

"Well, my lady, to be short, then – I was more curious than ever, when I heard all this, to hear more; and asked my friend, how she could ever think of staying in a house with ladies of such a description? Upon which she justified herself, by assuring me, upon her honour, that at first she believed the young lady was married privately to Mr Hervey, for that a clergyman came in secret, and read prayers, and she verily believes, that the unfortunate young creature was deceived barbarously, and made to fancy herself married to all intents and purposes, till at once Mr Hervey threw off the mask, and left off visiting her, pretending a necessity to take a journey, and handing her over to that vile woman, that Mrs Ormond, who bid her be comforted, and all the things that are said by such women, on such occasions, by all accounts. But the poor deluded young thing saw how it was now too plain, and she was ready to break her heart; but not in a violent, common sort of way, ma'am, but in silent grief, pining and drooping. My friend could not stand the sight, nor endure to look upon Mrs Ormond, now she knew what she was, and so she left the house, without giving any reason, immediately. I forgot to mention, that the unfortunate girl's maiden name was St Pierre, my lady; but her christian name, which was rather an out o' the way name, I quite forget."

"No matter," said Lady Delacour, "we can live without it; or we can imagine it."

"To be sure, I beg pardon, such sort of people's names can't be of any consequence and, I'm sure, I blame myself now for going to the house, after all I had heard."

"You did go to the house, then?"

"To my shame be it spoken; my curiosity got the better of me, and I went – but only on account of the bullfinch, in the eyes of the world. It was a great while before I could get in; but I was so firm, that I would not give up the bird to no one but the lady herself, that I got in at last. O! never did my eyes light upon so beautiful a creature, nor so graceful, nor so innocent to look at!" – Belinda sighed – Marriott echoed the sigh, and continued: "She was by herself, and in tears, when I was shown in, ma'am, and she started as if she had never seen any body before in her life. But when she saw the bullfinch, ma'am, she clapped her hands, and, smiling through her tears like a child, she ran up to me, and thanked me again and again, kissing the bird between times, and putting it into her bosom. Well, I declare, if she had talked to all eternity, she could never have made me pity her half so much as all this did, for it looked so much like innocence. I'm sure, nobody that was not – or, at least, that did not think themselves innocent, could have such ways, and such an innocent affection for a little bird. Not but what I know, ladies of a certain description often have birds; but, then, their fondness is all affectation and fashion; but this poor thing was all nature. Ah! poor unfortunate girl, thought I – but it's no matter what I thought now," said Marriott, shutting her eyes, to hide the tears that came into them at this instant; "I was ashamed of myself, when I saw Mrs Ormond just then come into the room, which made me recollect what sort of company I was in. La! my lady, how I detested the sight of her! She looked at me, too, more like a dragon than anything else; though in a civil way, and as if she was frightened out of her wits, she asked Miss St Pierre, as she called her, how I had got in, (in a whisper)? and she made all sort of signs afterward to her, to go out of the room. Never having been in such a situation before, I was quite robbed of all fluency, and could not, – what with the anger I felt for the one, and sorrow for the other, -- get out a word of common sense, or even recollect what pretence brought me into the room, till the bird very luckily put it into my head, by beginning to sing: so, then, I asked, whether they could certify it to be theirs by any particular tune of its own? 'Oh! yes,' said Miss St Pierre; and she sung the very same tune. I never heard so sweet a voice; but, poor thing, something came across her mind in the middle of it, and she stopped; but she thanked me again for bringing back the bird, which, she said, had been hers for a great many years, and that she loved it dearly. I stood, I believe, like one stupefied, till I was roused by *the woman's* offering to put the five guineas reward, mentioned in the advertisement, into my hand. The touch of her gold made me start, as if it had been a snake, and I pushed it from me; and when she pressed it again, I threw it on the table, scarce knowing what I did; and just then, in her iniquitous hand, I saw a letter, directed to Clarence Hervey, esq. O! how I hated the sight of his name, and everything belonging to him, ma'am, at that minute. I'm sure, I could not have kept myself from saying something quite outrageous, if I had not taken myself out of the house, as I did, that instant.

"When there are women enough born and bred good for nothing – and ladies enough to flirt with, that would desire no better, that a gentleman like Mr Clarence Hervey, ma'am, should set his wits, as one may say, to be the ruin of such a sweet, innocent looking young creature; and then desert her in that barbarous way, after bringing a clergyman to deceive her with the mock ceremony, and all – O! there's no fashion, nor nothing can countenance such wickedness! 'tis the worst wickedness and cruelty – and I shall think and say so to the latest hour of my life."

"Well said, Marriott," cried Lady Delacour.

"I always thought, that Marriott had a great deal of true spirit and feeling," said Belinda.

"And now you know the reason, ma'am," added Marriott, "that I said, I was glad *things are as they are*. To be sure, I and everybody once thought – but that's all over now – and I am glad *things are as they are*."

Lady Delacour once more turned her quick eyes upon Belinda, and was much disappointed to see, by her countenance, that she approved of Marriott's philosophy, even more than she sympathised in her indignation.

"Not jealous!" thought her ladyship; "then it is all over with Clarence. If one latent spark of love for him had remained in her mind, anger, in spite of prudence, would have blown it to a flame – but she is not jealous, alas! – her love for Hervey has been smothered by cold philosophy – but I cannot yet think it possible, that it is utterly extinguished."

In the evening, when they were alone, Lady Delacour touched upon the subject again, and observed, that as they should now, in all probability, see Mr Hervey in a few days, they might be able to form a better judgment of this affair, which, she doubted not, had been exaggerated. "You should judge from the whole of Clarence's conduct and character, and not from any particular part," said her ladyship. "Do not his letters breathe a spirit of generosity?"

"But," interrupted Miss Portman, "I am not called upon to judge of Mr Hervey's whole conduct and character, nor of any part of it; his letters and his generosity are nothing — "

"To you?" said Lady Delacour, with a smile.

"This is no time, and no subect for raillery, my dear friend," said Belinda; "you assured me, and I believed you, that the idea of Mr Hervey's return was entirely out of the question, when you prevailed upon me to delay my journey to Oakly-park. As I now understand, that your ladyship has changed her mind, I must request your ladyship will permit me — "

"I will permit you to do what you please, dearest Belinda, except to *call me your ladyship*, twice in one minute. You shall go to Oakly-park, the day after to morrow: will that content you, my dear? I admire your strength of mind – you are much fitter to conduct yourself, than I am to conduct you. I have done with raillery – my first, my only, object is your happiness – I respect and esteem as much as I love you, and I love you better than anything upon earth – power excepted, you will say – power not excepted, believe me; and, if you are one of those strange people, that cannot believe without proof, you shall have proof positive upon the spot," added she, ringing the bell as she spoke. "I will no longer contend for power over your mind, with your friend at Oakly-park. I will give orders, in your presence, to Marriott, to prepare for our march – I did not call it retreat; but there is nothing shows so much generalship as a good retreat, unless it be a great victory. I am, I confess, rather prejudiced in favour of victory."

"So am I," said Belinda, with a smile. "I am so strongly prejudiced in favour of victory, that rather than obtain no other, I would even be content with a victory over myself."

Scarcely had Belinda pronounced these words, when Lord Delacour, who had dined in town, entered the room, accompanied by Mr Vincent.

"Give me leave, Lady Delacour, to introduce to you," said his lordship, "a young gentleman, who has a great, and, I am sure, a most disinterested desire to cultivate, your ladyship's further acquaintance."

"Lady Delacour received him with all the politeness imaginable; and even her prepossessions in favour of Clarence Hervey could not prevent her from being struck with his appearance. "Il a infiniment l'air d'un héros de roman,"* thought she, and Belinda is not quite so great a philosopher as I imagined. In due time her ladyship recollected, that she had orders to give to Marriott about her journey, that made it absolutely necessary she should leave Miss Portman to entertain Mr Vincent, "if possible, without her", for a few minutes; and Lord Delacour departed, contenting himself with the usual excuse of – *letters to write*.

"I ought to be delighted with your gallantry, Mr Vincent," said Belinda, "in travelling so many miles, to remind me of my promise about Oakly-park; but, on the contrary, I am sorry you have taken so much unnecessary trouble: Lady Delacour is, at this instant, preparing for our journey to Mr Percival's. We intend to set out the day after tomorrow."

"I am heartily glad of it – I shall be infinitely overpaid for my journey, by having the pleasure of going back with you."

"More gallantry! – But come," said Belinda, "tell me, seriously, the real motive of your visit; for I see, that something passes in your mind, which you have not told me."

"Nothing, dear Belinda, is so agreeable to me as perfect openness and sincerity. I admire it in you, and I am proud of it in myself; but may it not be carried too far? Is it wise, to say what must give pain, when it is not absolutely necessary? For instance, if you heard anything injurious to my character, would you think it kind to repeat it, when you were not in the least inclined to believe it?"

"Yes; I should think it not only kind; but, I should *now* consider it as absolutely incumbent upon me. You may, therefore, without hesitation, mention what you have heard of me."

Mr Vincent put into her hands the following anonymous letter.

"Rash young man! beware of connecting yourself with the lady, to whom you have lately been drawn in to pay your addresses. She is the most artful of women. She has been educated, as you may find upon inquiry, by one, whose successful trade it has been, to draw in young men of fortune for her nieces, whence she has obtained the appellation of *the match-maker general*. The only niece, whom she could not get rid of any other way, she sent to the most dissipated and unprincipled viscountess in town. The viscountess fell sick, and, as it was universally reported last winter, the young lady was, immediately upon her friend's death, to have been married to the viscount widower. But the viscountess detected the connexion, and the young lady, to escape from her friend's rage, and from public shame, was obliged to retreat to certain shades in the neighbourhood of Harrowgate; where she passed herself for a saint upon those, who were too honourable themselves to be suspicious of others.

"At length the quarrel between her and the viscountess was made up, by her address and boldness, in declaring, that if she was not recalled, she would divulge some secrets respecting a certain *mysterious boudoir* in her ladyship's house. This threat terrified the viscountess, who sent off express for her late discarded humble companion. The quarrel was hushed up, and the young lady is now with her noble friend at Twickenham. The person, who used to be let up the private stairs, into the boudoir, by Mrs Marriott, is now more conveniently received at Twickenham."

Much more was said by the letter-writer, in the same strain. The name of Clarence Hervey, in the last page, caught Belinda's eye; and with a trepidation, which she did not feel at the beginning of this epistle, she read the conclusion.

"The viscount is not supposed to have been unrivalled in the young lady's favour. A young gentleman, of large fortune, great talents, and uncommon powers of pleasing, has, for some months, been her secret object; but he has been prudent enough to escape her matrimonial snares, though he carries on a correspondence with her, through the means of her friend, the viscountess, to whom he privately writes. The noble lady has bargained to make over to her confidante all her interest in Hervey's heart. He is expected every day to return from his tour; and, if the schemes upon him can be brought to bear, the promised return to the neighbourhood of Harrowgate will never be thought of. Mr Vincent will be left in the lurch; he will not even have the lady's fair hand – her *fair* heart is Clarence Hervey's, at all events. Farther particulars shall be communicated to Mr Vincent, if he pays due attention to this warning from

"A SINCERE FRIEND."

As soon as Belinda had finished this curious production, she gave her hand to Mr Vincent, with more kindness than she had ever before shown him.

"I thank you, Mr Vincent, for showing me this attempt to injure my reputation. It was not only handsome, but wise. If ever we are united, this will lay a sure foundation for the confidence which supports domestic happiness. The mean author of this falsehood could never have foreseen, that I should have told you everything, which it concerns you to know, relative to my former life. It has, indeed, mentioned Mr Hervey's name, which I did not think myself at liberty to reveal, because I might, perhaps, have seemed to impute some blame to him. I am, however, glad of this discovery, because I am sure he must appear to you a man of worth and talents. His name excites no emotion in my mind, that could give you pain."

Vincent's answer must be supposed: the enraptured acknowledgments of a lover are scarcely interesting upon the stage, where action and the theatre support the sympathy of the audience. Narration feebly supports enthusiasm, without these advantages.

It is sufficient to say, that Mr Vincent thought himself at the summit of felicity: with the utmost alacrity, he consented to show the anonymous letter to Lady Delacour, though he had previously dreaded the effect, which it might have upon her ladyship's feelings.

Her first exclamation was — "This is one of Harriet Freke's frolics;" but as her ladyship's indignation against Mrs Freke had long since subsided into utter contempt, she did not waste another thought upon the writer of this horrible letter; but, instantly, the whole energy of her mind, and fire of her eloquence, burst forth in an eulogium upon her friend. Careless of all that concerned herself, she explained, without a moment's hesitation, everything that could exalt Belinda: she described all the difficult circumstances, in which her friend had been placed; she mentioned the secret, with which she had been entrusted; the honour with which, even at the hazard of her own reputation, she had kept her promise of secrecy inviolable, when Lord Delacour, in a fit of intoxication and jealousy, had endeavoured to wrest from Marriott the key of *the mysterious boudoir*. She confessed her own absurd jealousy, explained how it had been excited by the artifices of Champfort and Sir Philip Baddely, how slight circumstances had worked her mind up almost to frenzy. "The temper, the dignity, the gentleness, the humanity, with which Belinda bore with me, during this paroxysm of madness," said Lady Delacour, "I never can forget; nor the spirit with which she left my house, when she saw me unworthy of her esteem, and ungrateful for her kindness; nor the magnanimity with which she returned to me, when I thought myself upon my deathbed: all this has made an impression upon my soul, which never, while I have life and reason, can be effaced. She has saved my life. She has made my life worth saving. She has made me feel my own value. She has made me know my own happiness. She has reconciled me to my husband. She has united me with my child. She has been my guardian angel. – *She*, the confidante of my intrigues! – *she* leagued with me in vice! – No, I am bound to her by ties stronger than vice ever felt; than vice, even in the utmost ingenuity of its depravity, can devise."

Exhausted by the vehemence with which she had spoken, Lady Delacour paused; but Vincent, who sympathised in her enthusiasm, kept his eyes fixed upon her, in hopes that she had yet more to say. —

"I might, perhaps, you will think," continued she, smiling "have spared you this history of myself, and of my own affairs, Mr Vincent; but I thought it necessary to tell you the plain facts, which malice has distorted into the most odious form. This is the quarrel, this is the reconciliation, of which your anonymous friend has been so well informed. Now as to Clarence Hervey."

"I have explained to Mr Vincent," interrupted Belinda, "every thing that he could wish to know, with respect to him. I now wish you to tell him, that I faithfully remembered my promise to return to Oakly-park, and that we were actually preparing for the journey." —

"Look here, sir," cried Lady Delacour, opening the door of her dressing-room, in which Marriott was upon her knees, locking a trunk; "here's dreadful note of preparation."

Mr Vincent renewed his thanks to Belinda, and his protestations, that she was wasting her time, by endeavouring to make his assurance of her goodness 'doubly secure'.

"You are a happier man than you yet know, Mr Vincent," continued Lady Delacour, "for I can tell you, that some persuasion, some raillery, and some wit, I flatter myself, have been used, to detain Miss Portman from you."

"From Oakly-park," interrupted Belinda.

"From Oakly-park, &c. – a few days longer – Shall I be frank with you, Mr Vincent? – Yes, for I cannot help it. – I am not of the nature of anonymous letter-writers: I cannot, either secretly or publicly, sign or say myself a *sincere friend*, without being one to the utmost extent of my influence. I never give my vote without my interest, nor my interest without my vote. Now, Clarence Hervey is my friend. Start not at all, sir – you have no reason; for if he is mine, Miss Portman is yours. Which has the better bargain? – But as I was going to tell you, Mr Clarence Hervey is my friend, and I am his. My vote, interest, and influence, have consequently been all in his favour. I had reason to believe, that he has long admired *the dignity of* Miss Portman's *mind, and the simplicity of her character*," continued her ladyship, with an arch look at Belinda; "and though he was too much a man of genius, to begin with the present tense of the indicative mood, 'I love,' yet I was, and am convinced, that he does love her."

"Can you, dear Lady Delacour," cried Belinda, "speak in this manner, and recollect all we heard from Marriott yesterday? And to what purpose all this?"

"To what purpose, my dear? To convince your friend, Mr Vincent, that I am neither fool nor knave; but that I deal fairly by you, by him, and by all the world. Mr Hervey's conduct towards Miss Portman has, I acknowledge, sir, been undecided. Some circumstances have lately come to my knowledge, which throw doubts upon his honour and integrity: – doubts, which I firmly believe, he will clear up to *my* satisfaction at least, as soon as I see him, or as soon as it is in his power; with this conviction, and believing as I do, that no man upon earth is so well suited to my friend, pardon me, Mr Vincent, if my wishes differ from yours: though my sincerity may give you present, it may save you from future, pain."

"Your ladyship's sincerity, whatever pain it may give me, I admire," said Mr Vincent, with some pride in his manner; "but I see, that I must despair of the honour of your ladyship's congratulations."

"Pardon me," interrupted Lady Delacour; "there you are quite mistaken – the man of Belinda's choice *must* receive my congratulations – he must do more – he must become my friend. I would never rest till I had won his regard, nor should I in the least be apprehensive, that he would not have sufficient greatness of mind, to forgive my having treated him with a degree of sincerity, which the common forms of politeness cannot justify, and at which common souls would be scandalised, past recovery."

Mr Vincent's pride was entirely vanquished by this speech; and with that frankness, by which his manners were usually characterised, he thanked her for having distinguished him from *common souls*; and assured her, that such sincerity as hers was infinitely more to his taste, than that refined politeness, of which, he was aware, no one was more perfect mistress than Lady Delacour.

Here their conversation ended, and Mr Vincent, as it was now late, took his leave.

"Really, my dear Belinda," said Lady Delacour, when he was gone, "I am not surprised at your impatience to return to Oakly-park; I am not so partial to my knight, as to compare him, in personal accomplishments, with your hero. I acknowledge also, that there is something vastly prepossessing in the frankness of his manners; he has behaved admirably well, about this abominable letter; but, what is better than all in a lady's eyes, he is *éperdument amoureux*."*

"Not *éperdument*, I hope," said Belinda.

Then, as you do not think it necessary for your hero to be *éperdument amoureux*, I presume," said Lady Delacour, "you do not think it necessary, that a heroine should be in love at all. I hope Mr Vincent is of the same opinion."

"I hope so," said Belinda, "for we shall then agree perfectly."

"So love and marriage are to be separated by philosophy, as well as by fashion. This is Lady Anne Percival's doctrine? I give Mr Percival joy. I remember the time, when he fancied love essential to happiness."

"I believe, he not only fancies, but is sure of it now, from experience."

"Then he interdicts love only to his friends? He does not think it essential, that you should know anything about the matter. You may marry his ward, and welcome, without being in love with him."

"But not without loving him," said Belinda.

"Absolutely you blushed, my dear, as you pronounced those words. And you *can* blush about loving Mr Vincent?"

"I hope, and I believe, that I shall never have any reason to blush *for* loving him," said Belinda.

"A deeper crimson! – Good Heavens! – Can I believe my senses? Was it the blush of anger or of love?"

"Not of anger," said Belinda. Lady Delacour was silent some moments.

"And is it possible, that you are seriously attached to this man?"

"Where is the impossibility? You will see none, my dear friend, when you are as thoroughly acquainted with his good qualities as I am."

"Good qualities! but we don't fall in love with good qualities, my dear."

"But we love them, and that is better, I must be allowed to repeat, that there is a great deal of difference between loving and being in love."

"As you know from experience? Why, I protest, you do not change colour, *much*, at the recollection of Clarence Hervey! You have at length convinced me, that it is all over with him. We all know 'qu'un petit nez retroussé, peut renverser les loix d'un empire.'* But what is un petit nez retroussé compared with an aquiline nose?"

"It is a comparison that I never made," said Belinda.

"You confess, however, that you think him handsome: and I candidly acknowledge, as I told you at first, that Mr Vincent has much the advantage of Clarence Hervey, in personal accomplishments."

"Certainly. But were he an Adonis, he would not have made any impression upon me, instantly. We gradually acquire a knowledge of the good qualities of those, who endeavour to please us; and if they are really amiable, their persons become agreeable to us by degrees, we become accustomed to their address, and time – "

"Accustomed!" said Lady Delacour, laughing; "forgive me, my dear – but I cannot help laughing – you put me in mind of Mr Transfer, in Zeluco;* the merchant, who disliked his nephew, because he was *not* accustomed to him; and afterward, when he became accustomed to him, if I remember right, liked him vastly well. But you surpass Transfer: never before did I hear a woman talk of liking a lover, because she was accustomed to him."

"And did you never hear of anybody's liking *a husband* better from being accustomed to him?" said Belinda.

"One does grow accustomed to disagreeable things, certainly; and it is well one does," said Lady Delacour, a little embarrassed. "But at this rate, my dear, I do not doubt, but you might become accustomed to Caliban."

"My belief in the reconciling power of custom does not go quite so far," said Belinda laughing. "It does not extend to Caliban, or even to la belle et la bête.* Though you have seen a French audience applaud with raptures, and an English audience tolerate, Zemire and Azor."*

"Faites moi le plaisir ma chère d'orienter votre royaume d'habitude,"* said Lady Delacour.

"Do me the favour, previously, to define the boundaries of the realm of Novelty; you must allow, that Novelty has precedence; therefore, show me all her titles first."

"I acknowledge," said Lady Delacour, "that Novelty and Custom divide the world of fancy. The young are subject to the one, the old to the other. You see, that I myself yield to my proper sovereign, but the youthful Belinda should follow the enterprising standard of Novelty."

"If Novelty must at last abandon her conquest, it is surely prudent," said Belinda, "to attach ourselves to the permanent victor."

"My dear Belinda, there can be no custom without previous novelty; you therefore begin at the wrong end."

"I think not; for, saying that I begin to be accustomed to Mr Vincent, is in terms granting, that he has been new to me. Now, seriously I think, that beside religion, morality, honour, prudence, and all the satellites, which guard the virtue of our sex; the force of custom is not to be disregarded: I do not mean, merely the customs of the world, but those which prevent us from suddenly thinking of any person as a lover."

"You have been told so by your aunt Stanhope, I will answer for it. Yes; what her history may have been, I know not; but whenever her maxims do not revolt against my feelings, I am glad to learn by her experience. Your aunt Stanhope is not wrong for once. Even Harriet Freke allows, that, though new love is charming, there is something awkward in the reception of a new lover."

"You will permit me, then, my dear Lady Delacour, to say, without being laughed at, that I am accustomed to Mr Vincent; and that though I do not like him merely from habit, I could not like him as well as I do, without it.

"I am forced to acknowledge, that you are right, my dear," said Lady Delacour, "and I am sorry for it."

Belinda sat down playfully at her piano forte, and sang that beautiful French air, which concludes with,

"Un peu d'amour, un peu de soin,
"Menent souvent un coeur bien loin." *

CHAPTER XXV

Love Me, Love My Dog

The only interest, that honest people can take in the fate of rogues, is in their detection and punishment; the reader then will be so far interested in the fate of Mr Champfort, as to feel some satisfaction at his being safely lodged in gaol. The circumstance, which led to this desirable catastrophe, was the anonymous letter to Mr Vincent. From the first moment that Marriott saw or heard of this letter, she was convinced, she said, that "Mr Champfort *was at the bottom of it.*" Lady Delacour was equally convinced, that Harriet Freke was the author of the epistle; and she supported her opinion, by observing, that Champfort could neither write nor spell English. Marriott and her lady were both right. It was a joint, or rather a triplicate performance. Champfort, in conjunction with the stupid maid, furnished the intelligence, which Mrs Freke manufactured; and when she had put the whole into proper style and form, Mr Champfort got her rough draught fairly copied at his leisure, and transmitted his copy to Mr Vincent. Now, all this was discovered by a very slight circumstance. The letter was copied by Mr Champfort, upon a sheet of mourning paper, off which he thought that he had carefully cut the edges; but one bit of the black edge remained, which did not escape Marriott's scrutinising eye. "Lord bless my stars, my lady!" she exclaimed, "this must be the paper; I mean, may be the paper, that Mr Champfort was cutting a quire of, the very day before Miss Portman left town. It's a great while ago, but I remember it, as well as if it was yesterday; I saw a parcel of black jags of paper littering the place, and asked what had been going on? and was told, that it was only Mr Champfort, who had been cutting some paper, which, to be sure, I concluded, my lord had given to him, having no farther occasion for; as my lord, and you my lady, were just going out of mourning at that time, as you may remember."

Lord Delacour, when the paper was shown to him, recognised it immediately by a private mark, which he had put on the outside sheet of a division of letter paper, which, indeed, he had never given to Champfort, but which he had missed about the time Marriott mentioned. Between the leaves of this paper, his lordship had put, as it was often his practice, some bank notes. They were notes but of small value, and when he missed them, he was easily persuaded by Champfort, that, as he had been much intoxicated the preceding night, he had thrown them away with some useless papers. He rummaged through his writing-desk in vain, and then gave up the search. It was true, that, on this very occasion, he gave Champfort the remainder of some mourning paper, which he made no scruple, therefore, of producing openly. Certain that he could swear to his own private mark upon this paper, and that he could identify his notes, by their numbers, &c., of which he had luckily a memorandum, Lord Delacour, enraged to find himself both robbed and duped by a favourite servant, in whom he had placed implicit confidence, was effectually roused from his natural indolence: he took such active and successful measures, that Mr Champfort was committed to gaol, to take his trial for the robbery. To make peace for himself, he confessed that he had been instigated by Mrs Freke, to get the anonymous letter written. This lady was now suffering just punishment for her *frolics*, and Lady Delacour thought her fallen so much below indignation, that she advised Belinda to take no manner of notice of her conduct, except simply returning the letter to her, with "Miss Portman's, Mr Vincent's, and Lord and Lady Delacour's compliments and thanks, to *a sincere friend*, who had been the means of bringing villainy to justice."

So much for Mrs Freke and Mr Champfort, who, both together, scarcely deserve an episode of ten lines.

Now to return to Mr Vincent. He perceived the advantage, which he had gained with Belinda, and animated by fresh hope, he pressed his suit with all the ardour of his sanguine temper. Though little disposed to fear any future evil, especially in the midst of present felicity, yet he was aware of the danger that might ensue to him, from Clarence Hervey's arrival; he was therefore impatient for the intermediate day to pass, and it was with heartfelt joy, that he saw the carriages at last at the door, which were actually to convey them to Oakly-park. Mr Vincent, who had all the West Indian love for magnificence, had, upon this occasion, an extremely handsome equipage. Lady Delacour, though she was disappointed by Clarence Hervey's not ap-

pearing, did not attempt to delay their departure. She contented
herself with leaving a note, to be delivered to him on his arrival,
which, she still flattered herself, would induce him immediately to
go to Harrowgate. The trunks were fastened upon the carriages,
the imperial* was carrying out, Marriott was full of a world of
business, Lord Delacour was looking at his horses as usual,
Helena was patting Mr Vincent's great dog, and Belinda was
rallying her lover, upon his taste for "the pomp, pride, and
circumstance" of glorious travelling –

When an express arrived from Oakly-park. It was to delay their
journey for a few weeks. Mr Percival and Lady Anne wrote word,
that they were unexpectedly called from home, by — . Lady
Delacour did not stay to read by what, or by whom, she was so
much delighted by this reprieve. Mr Vincent bore the disappointment as well as could be expected; particularly, when Belinda
observed, to comfort him, that "the mind is its own place," and
that hers, she believed, would be the same at Twickenham as at
Oakly-park. Nor did *she* give him any reason to doubt her
steadiness, or to regret that she was not immediately under the
influence of his own friends. The dread of being unduly biassed by
Lady Delacour, and the strong desire Belinda felt to act honour-
ably by Mr Vincent, to show him that she was not trifling with his
happiness, and that she was incapable of the meanness of
retaining a lover as a *pis aller**; were motives, which acted more
powerfully in his favour, than all that even Lady Anne Percival
could have looked or said. The contrast between the openness and
decision of his conduct towards her and Clarence Hervey's
vaccillation and mystery; the belief, that Mr Hervey was, or ought
to be, attached to another woman; the conviction, that Mr
Vincent was strongly attached to her, and that he possessed many
of the good qualities essential to her happiness, operated every
day more and more strongly upon her inclinations. We shall spare
the reader a journal of a lady's doubts and scruples, and of a
lover's hopes and fears; it will be sufficient to relate, that the
lover's hopes at last rose to expectations; and that the scrupulous
lady acknowledged them to be reasonable.

Where was Clarence Hervey all this time? Lady Delacour, alas!
could not divine. She every morning was certain, that he would
appear that day, and every night she was forced to acknowledge
her mistake. No inquiries – and she had made all that could be
made, by address and perseverance – no inquiries could clear up

the mystery of Virginia and Mrs Ormond: and her impatience to see her friend Clarence every hour increased. She was divided between her confidence in him, and her affection for Belinda; unwilling to give him up, yet afraid to injure her happiness, or to offend her, by injudicious advice, and improper interference. One thing kept Lady Delacour for some time in spirits – Miss Portman's assurances, that she would not bind herself by any promise, or engagement, to Mr Vincent, even when decided in his favour; and that she should hold both him and herself perfectly free, till they were actually married. This was according to Lady Anne and Mr Percival's principles; and Lady Delacour was never tired of expressing directly, or indirectly, her admiration of the prudence and propriety of their doctrine. But what availed her reliance even upon this saving clause against previous promises? for at length, a consent – blushing consent – was given, to ratify the most solemn of all vows at the altar, and preparations were now going to be made for the marriage of Augustus Vincent and Belinda Portman.

Lady Delacour recollected her own promise; to give her *sincere congratulations to the victorious knight*; and she endeavoured to persuade Belinda and herself, that she was well satisfied with the approaching union; she was, however, somewhat less disposed to like Mr Vincent, from the discovery, which she accidentally made, of his being still upon good terms with *odious Mrs Luttridge*. Helena, one morning, was playing with a large dog of Mr Vincent, of which he was excessively fond; it was called Juba, after his faithful servant.

"Helena, my dear," said Lady Delacour "take care! don't trust your hand in that creature's monstrous mouth."

"I can assure your ladyship," cried Mr Vincent, "that he is the very quietest and best creature in the world."

"No doubt," said Belinda, smiling, "since he belongs to you; for you know, as Mr Percival tells you, everything, animate or inanimate, that is under your protection, you think, must be the best of its kind in the universe."

"But really, Juba *is* the best creature in the world," repeated Mr Vincent, with great eagerness – "Juba is, without exception, the best creature in the universe."

"Juba, the dog, or Juba, the man?" said Belinda, "you know, they cannot be both the best creatures in the universe."

"Well! Juba, the man, is the best man – and Juba, the dog, is the best dog, in the universe," said Mr Vincent, laughing, with his usual candour, at his own foible, when it was pointed out to him – "But, seriously, Lady Delacour, you need not be in the least afraid to trust Miss Delacour with this poor fellow; for, do you know, during a whole month, that I lent him to Mrs Luttridge, at Harrowgate, she used constantly to let him sleep in the room with her; and now, whenever he sees her, he licks her hand, as gently as if he were a lapdog; and it was but yesterday, when I had him there, she declared, he was more gentle than any lapdog in London."

At the name of Luttridge Lady Delacour changed countenance, and she continued silent for some time. Mr Vincent, attributing her sudden seriousness to dislike or fear of his dog, took him out of the room.

"My dear Lady Delacour," said Belinda, observing that she still retained an air of displeasure, "I hope your antipathy to *odious Mrs Luttridge* does not extend to everybody who visits her."

"Tout au contraire,"* cried Lady Delacour, starting from her reverie, and assuming a playful manner; "I have made a general gaol-delivery of all my old hatreds; and even odious Mrs Luttridge, though a hardened offender, must be included in this act of grace; so you need not fear that Mr Vincent should fall under my royal displeasure, for consorting with this state criminal. Though I can't sympathise with him, I forgive him, both for liking that great dog, and that little woman; especially as I shrewdly suspect, that he likes the lady's E O table better than the lady."

"E O table! Good Heavens! You do not imagine that Mr Vincent — "

"Nay, my dear, don't look so terribly alarmed! I assure you, I did not mean to hint, that there was any serious, *improper* attachment to the E O table; only a little flirtation, perhaps, to which his passion for you has, doubtless, put a stop."

"I'll ask him the moment I see him," cried Belinda, "if he is fond of play; I know, he used to play at billiards at Oakly-park, but merely as an amusement. Games of address, as Mr Percival says, are not to be put upon a footing with games of hazard."

"A man may, however, contrive to lose a good deal of money at billiards, as poor Lord Delacour can tell you. But I beseech you, my dear, do not betray me to Mr Vincent; ten to one I am mistaken, for his great dog put me out of humour – "

"But with such a doubt upon my mind, unsatisfied — "

"It shall be satisfied; Lord Delacour shall make inquiries for me. – Lord Delacour *shall* make inquiries, did I say? – *will*, I should have said. If Champfort had heard me, to what excellent account he might have turned that unlucky *shall*. What a nice grammarian a woman had need to be, who would live well with a husband inferior to her in understanding! With a superior or an equal, she might use *shall* and *will* as inaccurately as she pleases. Glorious privilege! How I shall envy it you, my dear Belinda! But how can you ever hope to enjoy it? Where is your superior? Where is your equal?"

Mr Vincent, who had by this time seen his dog fed, which was one of his daily pleasures, returned, and politely assured Lady Delacour, that Juba should not again intrude. To make her peace with Mr Vincent, and to drive the E O table from Belinda's thoughts, her ladyship now turned the conversation from Juba, the dog, to Juba, the man. She talked of Harriet Freke's phosphoric obeah-woman, of whom, she said, she had heard an account from Miss Portman. She spoke of Juba's marriage, and of his master's generosity to him. From thence she went on to the African slave trade, by way of contrast, and she finished precisely where she had intended, and where Mr Vincent could have wished, by praising a poem called "The dying Negro", which he had, the preceding evening, brought to read to Belinda. This praise was peculiarly agreeable, because he was not perfectly sure of his own critical judgment, and his knowledge of English literature was not as extensive as Clarence Hervey's; a circumstance, which Lady Delacour had discovered one morning, when they went to see Pope's famous villa at Twickenham. Flattered by her present confirmation of his taste, Mr Vincent readily complied with a request to read the poem to Belinda; they were all deeply engaged by the charms of poetry, when they were suddenly interrupted by the entrance of – Clarence Hervey!

The book dropped from Vincent's hand, the instant that he heard his name. Lady Delacour's eyes sparkled with joy. Belinda's colour rose, but her countenance maintained an expression of calm dignity. Mr Hervey, upon his first entrance, appeared prepared to support an air of philosophic composure, which forsook him before he had walked across the room. He seemed overpowered by the kindness, with which Lady Delacour received him – struck by the reserve of Belinda's manner – but not surprised, or displeased, at the sight of Mr Vincent. On the contrary, he desired immediately to be introduced to him, with the air of a man resolute to cultivate his friendship. Provoked and perplexed, Lady Delacour, in a tone of mingled reproach and astonishment exclaimed – "Though you have not done me the honour, Mr Hervey, to take any other notice of my last letter, I am to understand, I presume, by the manner in which you desired me to introduce you to our friend Mr Vincent, that it has been received."

"Received! Good Heavens! Have not you had my answer?" cried Clarence Hervey, with a voice and look of extreme surprise and emotion! "Has not your ladyship received a packet?"

"I have had no packet! – I have had no letter! – Mr Vincent, do me the favour to ring the bell," cried Lady Delacour, eagerly – "I'll know, this instant what's become of it."

"Your ladyship must have thought me — ," and, as he spoke, his eye involuntarily glanced towards Belinda.

"No matter what I thought you," cried Lady Delacour, who forgave him everything for this single glance – "if I did you a little injustice, Clarence, when I was angry, you must forgive me; for, I assure you, I do you a great deal of justice at other times."

"Did any letter, any packet, come here for me? Inquire, inquire," said she, impatiently, to the servant, who came in. No letter or packet was to be heard of. It had been directed, Mr Hervey now remembered, to her ladyship's house in town. She gave orders to have it immediately sent for; but scarcely had she given them, when, turning to Mr Hervey, she laughed and said —

"A very foolish compliment to you and your letter, for you certainly can speak as well as you can write; nay, better, I think – though you don't write ill, neither – but you can tell me, in two words, what in writing would take half a volume. Leave this gentleman and lady to – "The dying Negro"; and let me hear your two words, in Lord Delacour's dressing-room, if you please," said she, opening the door of an adjoining apartment. "Lord Delacour will not be jealous if he find you tête-à-tête with me, I promise you. But you shall not be compelled. You look — "

"I look," said Mr Hervey, affecting to laugh, "as if I felt the impossibility of putting half a volume into two words. It is a long story, and — "

"And I must wait for the packet, whether I will or no – well, be it so," said Lady Delacour. Struck with the extreme perturbation into which he was thrown, she pressed him with no farther raillery, but instantly attempted to change the conversation to general subjects.

Again she had recourse to 'The dying Negro'. Mr Vincent, to whom she now addressed herself, said, "for my part, I neither have, nor pretend to have, much critical taste; but I admire in this poem the manly, energetic spirit of virtue, which it breathes." From the poem, an easy transition was made to the author; and Clarence Hervey, exerting himself to join in the conversation, observed, "that this writer (Mr Day*) was an instance, that genuine eloquence must spring from the heart. Cicero was certainly right," continued he, addressing himself to Mr Vincent, in his definition of a great orator, "to make it one of the first requisites, that he should be a good man."

Mr Vincent coldly replied, "This definition would exclude too many men of superior talents, to be easily admitted."

"Perhaps the appearance of virtue," said Belinda, "might, on many occasions, succeed, as well as the reality."

"Yes, if the man be as good an actor as Mr Hervey," said Lady Delacour, "and if he suit 'the action to the word' – the word to the action'."

Belinda never raised her eyes whilst her ladyship uttered these words; Mr Vincent was, or seemed to be, so deeply engaged in looking for something in that book, which he held in his hand, that he could take no farther part in the conversation; and a dead silence ensued.

Lady Delacour, who was naturally impatient in the extreme, especially in the vindication of her friends, could not bear to see, as she did by Belinda's countenance, that she had not forgotten Marriott's story of Virginia St Pierre; and though her ladyship was convinced, that *the packet* would clear up all mysteries, yet she could not endure, that even in the interim 'poor Clarence' should be unjustly suspected; nor could she refrain from trying an expedient, which just occurred to her, to satisfy herself and everybody present. She was the first to break silence.

"To do ye justice, my friends, you are all good company this morning. Mr Vincent is excusable, because he is in love; and Belinda is excusable, because – because – Mr Hervey, pray help me to an excuse for Miss Portman's stupidity, for I am dreadfully afraid of blundering out the truth. But why do I ask *you* to help me? In your present condition, you seem totally unable to help yourself. – Not a word! – Run over the common places of conversation – whether fashion – scandal – duels – deaths – marriages – Will none of these do? Suppose, then, you were to entertain me with other people's thoughts, since you have none of your own unpacked – Forfeit to arbitrary power," continued her ladyship, playfully, seizing Mr Vincent's book. "I have always observed, that none submit with so good a grace to arbitrary power from our sex, as your true men of spirit, who would shed the last drop of their blood, to resist it from one of their own. Inconsistent creatures, the best of you! – So read this charming little poem to us, Mr Hervey, will you?"

He was going to begin immediately, but Lady Delacour put her hand upon the book, and stopped him.

"Stay; though I am tyrannical, I will not be treacherous. I warn you, then, that I have imposed upon you a difficult, a dangerous task. If you have any 'unwhipt of justice,' there are lines, which I defy you to read without faltering – Listen to the preface."

Her ladyship then began as follows:

"Mr Day, indeed, retained, during all the periods of his life, as might be expected from his character, a strong detestation of female seduction . . . Happening to see some verses, written by a young lady, on a recent event of this nature, which was succeeded by a fatal catastrophe – the unhappy young woman, who had been a victim to the perfidy of a lover, overpowered by her sensibility of shame, having died of a broken heart – he addressed the fair poetess, in whose sentiments he sympathised, in the following manner."

Lady Delacour paused, and fixed her eyes upon Clarence Hervey. He, with all the appearance of conscious innocence, received the book, without hesitation, from her hands, and read aloud the lines, to which she pointed.

> "Swear by the dread avengers of the tomb,
> "By all thy hopes, by death's tremendous gloom,
> "That, ne'er by thee deceiv'd, the tender maid
> "Shall mourn her easy confidence betray'd,
> "Nor weep in secret the triumphant art,
> "With bitter anguish rankling in her heart;
> "So may each blessing, which impartial fate
> "Throws on the good, but snatches from the great,
> "Adorn thy favour'd course with rays divine,
> "And Heaven's best gift, a virtuous love, be thine!"

Mr Hervey read these lines with so much unaffected, unembarrassed energy, that Lady Delacour could not help casting a triumphant look at Belinda, which said, or seemed to say –

"You see, I was right in my opinion of Clarence!"

Belinda's countenance openly expressed satisfaction; it seemed to say – "I am glad that Mr Hervey is worthy of our esteem, though he can no longer have any claim to my love." Her manner toward him distinctly marked the same sentiment. That reserve, which had been retained, as long as she had any suspicion of his having acted dishonourably, was now dissipated, and she addressed her conversation to him with that easy, friendly familiarity, which a man of his discernment could not misunderstand. Had Mr Vincent been left to his own observations, he would have seen the truth; but he was alarmed and deceived by Lady Delacour's imprudent expressions of joy, and by the significant looks, that she gave her friend, Miss Portman, which seemed to be *looks of mutual intelligence*. He scarcely dared to turn his eyes toward his mistress, or upon him, whom he thought his rival; but he kept them anxiously fixed upon her ladyship, in whose face, as in a glass, he seemed to study every thing that was passing.

"Pray, have you ever played at chess, since we saw you last?" said Lady Delacour to Clarence. "I hope you do not forget, that you are *my knight*. I do not forget it, I assure you – I own you as my knight to all the world, in public and private – do not I, Belinda?"

A dark cloud overspread Mr Vincent's brow – he listened not to Belinda's answer. Seized with a transport of jealousy, he darted at Mr Hervey a glance of mingled scorn and rage; and, after saying a few unintelligible words to Miss Portman and Lady Delacour, he left the room.

Clarence Hervey, who seemed afraid to trust himself longer with Belinda, withdrew a few minutes afterward.

"My dear Belinda!" – exclaimed Lady Delacour, the moment that he was out of the room – "how glad I am he is gone, that I may say all the good I think of him. In the first place; Clarence Hervey loves you. Never was I so fully convinced of it, as this day. – Why had not we that letter of his sooner? – That will explain all to us – but I ask for no explanation; I ask for no letter, to confirm my opinion, my conviction – that he *loves* you; on this point I *cannot* be mistaken; he fondly loves you."

"He fondly loves her! – Yes, to be sure, I could have told you that news long ago," cried the dowager Lady Boucher, who was in the room before they were aware of her entrance; they had both been so eager, the one listening, and the other speaking.

"Fondly loves her!" repeated the dowager – "Yes; and no secret, I promise you, Lady Delacour: – and then, turning to Belinda, she began a congratulatory speech, upon the report of her approaching marriage with Mr Vincent. – "I distress you, I see, and it's quite out of rule, I am sensible, to speak in this sort of way, Miss Portman; but, as I'm an old acquaintance, and an old friend, and an old woman, you'll excuse me. I can't help saying, I feel quite rejoiced at your meeting with such a match – every way eligible, and every way agreeable. – A charming young man, I hear, Lady Delacour!" I see I must only speak to you, or I shall make Miss Portman sink to the centre of the Earth, which I would not wish to do, especially at such a critical moment as this. A charming young man! I hear, with a noble West Indian fortune, and a noble spirit, and well connected, and passionately in love – no wonder – But I have done now, I promise you; I'll ask no questions – so, don't run away, Miss Portman; I'll ask no questions, I promise you."

To ensure the performance of this promise, Lady Delacour asked, "What news there was in the world?" This question, she knew, would keep the dowager in delightful employment. "I live quite out of the world here; but since Lady Boucher has the charity to come to see me, we shall hear all the 'secrets worth knowing,' from the best authority."

"Then, the first piece of news, I have for you, is, that my Lord and my Lady Delacour are absolutely reconciled; and that they are the happiest couple that ever lived."

"All very true," replied Lady Delacour.

"True!" repeated Lady Boucher, "Why, my dear Lady Delacour, you amaze me! – Are you in earnest? – Was there ever anything so provoking? – There have I been contradicting the report, wherever I went, for I was convinced, that the whole story was a mistake, and a fabrication."

"The history of the reformation might not be exact, but the reformation itself your ladyship may depend upon, since you hear it from my own lips."

"Well, how amazing! – How incredible! – Lord bless me – but your ladyship certainly is not in earnest? for you look just the same, and speak just in the same sort of way: I see no alteration, I confess."

"And what alteration, my good Lady Boucher, did you expect to see? Did you think, that, by way of being exemplarily virtuous, I should, like Lady Q — let my sentences come out of my mouth only at the rate of a word a minute?"

"Like – minute – drops – from – off – the – eaves."

"Or did you expect, that, in hopes of being a pattern for the rising generation, I should hold my features in penance, immoveably, thus – like some of the poor ladies of Antigua, who, after they have blistered their faces all over, to get a fine complexion, are forced, whilst the new skin is coming, to sit, without speaking, smiling, or moving muscle or feature, lest an indelible wrinkle should be the consequence."

Lady Boucher was impatient to have this speech finished, for she had a piece of news to tell. "Well!" cried she, "there's no knowing what to believe, or disbelieve, one hears so many stange reports; but I have a piece of news for you, that you may all depend upon. I have one secret worth knowing, I can tell your ladyship – and one, your ladyship and Miss Portman, I'm sure, will be rejoiced to hear. Your friend, Clarence Hervey, is going to be married."

"Married! – married!" cried Lady Delacour.

"Ay, ay, your ladyship may look as much astonished as you please, you cannot be more so than I was, when I heard it. Clarence Hervey! Miss Portman, that was looked upon so completely, you know, as not a marrying man; and now the last man upon earth, that your ladyship would suspect of marrying in this sort of way!"

"In what sort of way? – My dear Belinda, how can you stand this fire?" said Lady Delacour, placing a screen dexterously, to hide her face from the dowager's observation.

"I do not want – I do not wish for a screen, I thank you," said Belinda, putting it aside, with gentle composure.

"Now only guess, who he is going to marry?" continued Lady Boucher – "Who, do *you* guess, Miss Portman?"

"An amiable woman, I should guess, from Mr Hervey's general character," said Belinda.

"O an amiable woman, I take for granted; every woman is amiable of course, as the newspapers tell us, when she is going to be married," said the dowager: – "an amiable woman, to be sure;

but that means nothing. Guess again. And not from general character, my dear Belinda; for there is no judging, in these cases, from general character, of what people will like or dislike."

"Then I will leave it to your ladyship to guess, this time, if you please," said Belinda.

"You will neither of you guess, till doomsday!" cried the dowager, "I must tell you Mr Hervey's going to marry – in the strangest sort of way! – a girl that nobody knows – a daughter of a Mr Hartley. – The father can give her a good fortune, it is true; but one should not have supposed, that fortune was an object with Mr Hervey, who has such a noble one of his own. It's really difficult to believe it."

"So difficult, that I find it quite impossible," said Lady Delacour, with an incredulous smile.

"Depend upon it, my dear Lady Delacour," said the dowager, laying the convincing weight of her arm upon her ladyship's – "depend upon it, my dear Lady Delacour, that my information is correct. Guess whom I had it from."

"Willingly. But first let me tell you, that I have seen Mr Hervey within this half hour, and I never saw a man look less like a bridegroom."

"Indeed! well, I've heard too, that he didn't like the match: but what a pity, when you saw him yourself this morning, that you didn't get all the particulars out of him. But let him look like what he will, you'll find, that my information is perfectly correct. – Guess whom I had it from. Mrs Margaret Delacour: it was at her house, that Clarence Hervey first met Mr Hartley, who, as I mentioned, is the father of the young lady. There was a charming scene, and some romantic story, about his finding the girl in a cottage, and calling her Virginia something or other, but I didn't clearly understand about that. However, this much is certain, that the girl, as her father told Mrs Delacour, is desperately in love with Mr Hervey, and they are to be married immediately. Depend upon it, you'll find my information corret. Good morning to you. – Lord bless me! now I recollect, I once heard, that Mr Hervey was a great admirer of Miss Portman," said the dowager.

"Your ladyship's information upon that point, I can assure you, from the best authority, was *not* correct;" said Belinda.

"You have not the presumption, to call your own the *best* authority, I hope," said Lady Delacour.

The inquisitive dowager, whose curiosity was put upon a new

scent, immediately fastened her eyes upon Belinda's face; but from that she could make out nothing. – Was it because she had not the best eyes, or because there was nothing to be seen? To determine this question, she looked through her glass, to take a clearer view; but Lady Delacour drew off her attention, by suddenly exclaiming – "My dear Lady Boucher, when you go back to town, do send me a bottle of concentrated anima of quassia."

"Ah! ha! have I made a convert of you at last?" said the dowager, and, satisfied with the glory of this conversion, she departed.

"Admire my knowledge of human nature, my dear Belinda," said Lady Delacour. "Now she will talk, at the next place she goes to, of nothing, but of my faith in anima of quassia; and she will forget to make a gossiping story out of that most imprudent hint, I foolishly gave her, about Clarence Hervey's having been an admirer of yours.

"Do not leave the room, Belinda, I have a thousand things to say to you, my dear."

"Excuse me, at present, my dear Lady Delacour, I am impatient to write a few lines to Mr Vincent. He went away – "

"In a fit of jealousy, and I am glad of it."

"And I am sorry for it," said Belinda – "sorry that he should have so little confidence in me, as to feel jealousy without cause – without sufficient cause, I should say; for certainly, your ladyship gave pain, by the manner in which you received Mr Hervey."

"Lord, my dear, you would spoil any man upon Earth. You could not act more foolishly, if the man were your husband. – Are you privately married to him? – If you be not, – for my sake – for your own – for Mr Vincent's, – do not write till we see the contents of Clarence Hervey's packet."

"It *can* make no alteration in what I write," said Belinda.

"Well, my dear; write what you please; but I only hope, you will not send your letter, till the packet arrives."

"Pardon me; I shall send it as soon as I possibly can: – the 'dear delight of giving pain' does not suit my taste".

Lady Delacour, as soon as she was left alone, began to reconsider the dowager's story: notwithstanding her unbelieving smile, it alarmed her, for she could not refuse to give it some degree of credit, when she learnt that Mrs Margaret Delacour was the authority from whom it came. Mrs Delacour was a woman of scrupulous veracity, and rigid in her dislike to gossiping; so that it was scarcely probable, a report originating with her, however it might be altered by the way, should prove to be totally void of foundation. The name of Virginia coincided with Sir Philip Baddely's hints, and with Marriott's discoveries: these circumstances considered, Lady Delacour knew not what opinion to form; and her eagerness to receive Mr Hervey's packet every moment increased. She walked up and down the room – looked at her watch – fancied that it had stopped – held it to her ear – rang the bell every quarter of an hour, to inquire whether the messenger was not *yet* come back. At last, the long expected packet arrived. – She seized it, and hurried with it immediately to Belinda's room.

"Clarence Hervey's packet, my love! – Now, woe be to the person who interrupts us!" She bolted the door as she spoke – rolled an arm chair to the fire – "Now for it!" said she, seating herself. – "The devil upon two sticks, if he were looking down upon me from the house-top, or Champfort, who is the worse devil of the two, would, if he were peeping through the key hole, swear I was going to open a love letter – and so I hope I am. Now for it!" cried she, breaking the seal.

"My dear friend," said Belinda, laying her hand upon Lady Delacour's, "before we open this packet, let me speak to you, whilst our minds are calm."

"Calm! It is the strangest time for your mind to be calm. – But I must not affront you by my incredulity. Speak, then, but be quick, for I do not pretend to be calm; it not being, thank my stars – '*mon métier d'être philosophe.*'* – Crack goes the last seal – Speak now, or forever after hold your tongue, my *calm philosopher* of Oakly-park; but do you wish me to attend to what you are going to say?"

"Yes," replied Belinda, smiling, "that is the usual wish of those who speak."

"Very true; and I can listen tolerably well, when I don't know what people are going to say; but when I know it all before hand, I have an unfortunate habit of not being able to attend to one word. Now, my dear, let me anticipate your speech, and, if my anticipation be wrong, then you shall rise to explain; and I will," said she, (putting her finger on her lips) "listen to you, like Harpocrates*, without moving an eye-lash."

Belinda, as the most certain way of being heard, consented to hear, before she spoke.

"I will tell you," pursued Lady Delacour, "if not what you are going to say to me, at least what you say to yourself, which is full as much to the purpose. You say to yourself, 'Let this packet of Clarence Hervey contain what it may, it comes too late. Let him say, or let him do, 'tis all the same to me, – because – (now for the reasoning) – because things have gone so far with Mr Vincent, that Lady Anne Percival, and all the world, (at Oakly-park) will blame me, if I retract. Then I have actually written to my aunt Stanhope; and preparations are absolutely making for my wedding. In short, *things have gone so far*, that I cannot recede; because – *things have gone so far*.' – This is the rondeau of your argument. Nay, hear me out, then you shall have your turn, my dear, for an hour, if you please. Let things have gone ever so far, they can stop, and turn about again, cannot they? Lady Anne Percival is your friend, of course can wish only for your happiness. You think she is 'the thing that's most uncommon, a reasonable woman:' then she cannot be angry with you for being happy your own way. So I need not, as the orators say, *labour this point any more*. Now, as to your aunt, your writing to her so precipitately was certainly wrong; that is, contrary to my advice. But the fear of displeasing Mrs Stanhope a little more or less, is not to be put in competition with the hope of your happiness for life, especially as you have contrived to exist some months in a state of utter excommunication from her favour. After all, you know Mrs Stanhope will not grieve for any thing but the loss of Mr Vincent's fortune; and Mr Hervey's fortune might do as well, or almost as well: at least, she may compound with her pride for the difference, by considering, that an English member of parliament is, in the eyes of the world (the only eyes with which she sees) a better connexion, than the son of a West India planter, even though he may be a protégé of Lady Anne Percival.

"Spare me your indignation, my dear! – What a look was there! – Reasoning for Mrs Stanhope, must not I reason as Mrs Stanhope does? – Now, as to these preparations for the wedding, you are not a girl, to marry because your wedding gown is made up. Some few guineas are thrown away, perhaps; do not throw away your whole happiness after them; that would be sorry economy. Trust to me, my dear, as I have to you, in time of need. Or, if you fear to be obliged to one, who never was afraid of being obliged to you, then to one the preparations for *a* wedding, though not *the* wedding, may be necessary immediately. – No matter to Mrs Franks who the bridegroom may be; so that her bill be paid, she will not care the turning of a feather, whether it be paid by Mrs Vincent or Mrs Hervey. I hope I have convinced, I am sure I have made you blush, my dear, and that is some satisfaction. A blush at this moment is an earnest of victory. Io, triumphe! Now I will open my packet; my hand shall not be held an instant longer."

"I absolve you from the penance of hearing me for an hour, but I claim your promise to attend to me for a few minutes, my dear friend," said Belinda: "I thank you most sincerely for your kindness; I should not hesitate to accept from you any species of obligation."

"Thanks! thanks! – there's a dear good girl! – my own Belinda!"

"But indeed you totally misunderstand me; your reasoning— "

"Show me the fault of it; I challenge all the logic of all the Percivals."

"Your reasoning is excellent, if your facts were not taken for granted. – You have taken it for granted, that Mr Hervey is in love with me."

"No," said Lady Delacour; "I take nothing for granted, as you will find, when I open this packet."

"You have taken it for granted," continued Belinda, "that I am still secretly attached to him – I assure you that I am not."

"That I can tell, without opening the packet," said Lady Delacour.

"And you take it for granted," said Belinda, "that I am restrained only by fear of Lady Anne Percival, my aunt, and the world, from breaking off with Mr Vincent? If you will read this letter, which I was writing to him when you came into the room, perhaps you will be convinced of your mistake."

"Then you do really and *bona fide*, as my old uncle, the lawyer, used to say – really, and *bona fide*, *love* Mr Vincent?"

"Can you imagine, that I would consent to marry a man without loving him?" said Belinda, indignantly.

"No; but you might love him positively – not comparatively – or superlatively. – In short, my dear, you might not know your own mind – Mr Hervey's return might make a difference. I really am so much afraid of offending you, that I can hardly find words – but, in fact, you certainly did once like my poor Clarence, and in spite of all Mr Percival's cure for *first loves*, I am inclined— "

"You are inclined," said Belinda, "to consider love as a distemper that can be had but once."

"You could not be witty, my dear, if you felt the passion. Believe me, Belinda, you are deceiving yourself; you are not in love with Mr Vincent; if you marry him, you will repent it; you will be miserable."

"I do not pretend to be what is called in love with Mr Vincent; nor do I think it necessary to my happiness, or to his, that I should. – But I esteem, I love him — "

"Ay, ay," said Lady Delacour, "as half the world do when they marry."

"As it would be happy for half the world if they did," replied Belinda, mildly, but with a firmness of tone that her ladyship felt – "I should despise myself, and deserve no pity from any human being, if, after all I have seen, I could think of marrying from motives of convenience or interest."

"O, pardon me! I meant not to insinuate such an idea; I meant but to hint, my dearest Belinda, that a heart, such as yours, is formed for love, in its highest, purest, happiest state — "

"Such as can be secured only by a union with a man of sense and virtue; such as may be not merely the amusement of a few months, but the charm of years," said Belinda; "such as I hope to enjoy with Mr Vincent, without being in love with him. Mr Vincent has behaved toward me with honour and sincerity; he has given me proofs of the steadiness of his affection, and of his confidence in my integrity. I have had full leisure to consult my judgment and my feelings. The former is in his favour, the latter are not against him."

"Not against him! – Hum! May I ask, would you, if you discovered that Mr Vincent kept a Virginia, discard him for ever from your thoughts?"

"If I discovered that he had deceived, and behaved dishonourably to any woman, I certainly should banish him from my regard."

"With as much ease as you did Clarence Hervey?"

"With more, perhaps."

"Then you acknowledge – that's all I want – that you liked Clarence better than ever you did Vincent?"

"I do – but that time is entirely past, and I never look back to it."

"But if you were forced to look back to it, my dear, if Clarence

Hervey proposed for you, would not you cast a lingering look behind? Would this make no change?"

"None."

"You would refuse him?"

"Without hesitation."

"Then I will go and read my packet in my own room," cried Lady Delacour, rising hastily, with evident displeasure.

"Not even your displeasure, my dear friend," said Belinda, "can alter my determination; and I can bear your anger, for I know it arises from your regard for me."

"I never loved you so little as at this instant, Belinda."

"You will do me justice when you are cool!"

"Cool!" repeated Lady Delacour, as she left the room, "I never wish to be as cool as you are, Belinda!"

CHAPTER XXVI

Virginia

Clarence Hervey's packet contained a history of his connexion with Virginia St Pierre.

To save our hero from the charge of egotism, we shall relate the principal circumstances in the third person.

It was about a year before he had seen Belinda, that Clarence Hervey returned from his travels; he had been in France just before the revolution, when luxury and dissipation were at their height in Paris, and when a universal spirit of licentious gallantry prevailed. Some circumstances, in which he was personally interested, disgusted him strongly with the Parisian belles; he felt, that women, who were full of vanity, affectation, and artifice, whose tastes were perverted, and whose feelings were depraved, were equally incapable of conferring, or enjoying real happiness. Whilst this conviction was full in his mind, he read the works of Rousseau: this eloquent writer's sense made its full impression upon Clarence's understanding, and his declamations produced more than their just effect upon an imagination naturally ardent. He was charmed with the picture of Sophia, when contrasted with the characters of the women of the world, with whom he had been disgusted; and he formed the romantic project of educating a wife for himself. Full of this idea, he returned to England, determined to carry his scheme immediately into execution; but he was some time delayed, by the difficulty of finding a proper object for his purpose: it was easy to meet with beauty in distress, and ignorance in poverty; but it was difficult to find simplicity without vulgarity, ingenuity without cunning, or even ignorance without prejudice; it was difficult to meet with an understanding totally uncultivated, yet likely to reward the labour of late instruction; a heart wholly unpractised, yet full of sensibility, capable of all the enthusiasm of passion, the delicacy of sentiment, and the firmness of rational constancy. It is not wonderful, that Mr Hervey, with such high expectations, should not immediately find them gratified. Disappointed in his first search, he did not, however, relinquish his design, and at length, by accident, he discovered, or thought that he discovered, an object formed expressly for his purpose.

One fine evening in autumn, as he was riding through the New Forest, charmed with the picturesque beauties of the place, he turned out of the beaten road, and struck into a fresh track, which he pursued with increasing delight, till the setting sun reminded him, that it was necessary to postpone his further reflections on forest scenery, and that it was time to think of finding his way out of the wood. He was now in the most retired part of the forest, and he saw no path to direct him; but, as he stopped, to consider which way he should turn, a dog sprang from a thicket, barking furiously at his horse: his horse was high spirited, but he was master of him, and obliged the animal to stand quietly till the dog, having barked himself hoarse, retreated of its own accord. Clarence watched, to see which way it would go, and followed it, in hopes of meeting with the person to whom it belonged: he kept his guide in sight, till he came into a beautiful glade, in the midst of which was a neat, but very small cottage, with numerous bee-hives in the garden, surrounded by a profusion of rose trees, which were in full blow. This cultivated spot was strikingly contrasted with the wildness of the surrounding scenery. As he came nearer, Mr Hervey saw a young girl watering the rose trees, which grew round the cottage, and an old woman beside her, filling a basket with the flowers. The old woman was like most other old women, except, that she had a remarkably benevolent countenance, and an air, that had been acquired in better days; but the young girl did not appear to Clarence like any other young girl that he had ever seen. The setting sun shone upon her countenance, the wind blew aside the ringlets of her light hair, and the blush of modesty overspread her cheeks, when she looked up at the stranger. In her large blue eyes, there was an expression of artless sensibility, with which Mr Hervey was so powerfully struck, that he remained for some moments silent, totally forgetting, that he came to ask his way out of the forest. His horse had made so little noise upon the soft grass, that he was within a few yards of them, before he was perceived by the old woman. As soon as she saw him, she turned abruptly to the young girl, put the basket of roses into her hand, and bid her carry them into the house. As she passed him, the girl, with a sweet innocent smile, held up the basket to Clarence, and offered him one of the roses.

"Go in, Rachel! – go in, child," said the old woman, in so loud and severe a tone, that both Rachel and Mr Hervey started; the basket was overturned, and the roses all scattered upon the grass. Clarence, though he attempted some apology, was by no means concerned for the accident, as it detained Rachel some instants longer to collect her flowers, and gave him an opportunity of admiring her finely shaped hands and arms, and the ease and natural grace of her motions.

"Go in, Rachel," repeated the old woman, in a still more severe tone; "leave the roses there – I can pick them up, as well as you, child – go in."

The girl looked at the old woman with astonishment, her eyes filled with tears, and throwing down the roses, that she held in her hand, she said, " I *am* going, grandmother." The door closed after her, before Clarence recollected himself sufficiently, to tell the old lady how he had lost his way, &c. Her severity vanished, as soon as her granddaughter was safe in the house, and with much readiness she showed him the road for which he inquired.

As soon, however, as it was in his power, he returned thither, for he had taken such good note of the place, that he easily found his way to the spot, which appeared to him a terrestrial paradise. As he descended into the valley, he heard the humming of bees, but he saw no smoke rising from the cottage chimney – no dog barked – no living creature was to be seen – the house door was shut – the window shutters closed – all was still. The place looked as if it had been deserted by its inhabitants – the roses had not been watered, many of them had shed their leaves; and a basket, half full of dead flowers, was left in the middle of the garden. Clarence alighted, and tried the latch of the door, but it was fastened; he listened, but heard no sound; he walked round to the back of the house: a small lattice window was half open, and, as he went toward it, he thought he heard a low moaning voice; he gently pulled aside the curtain, and peeped in at the window. The room was darkened, his eyes had been dazzled by the sun, so that he could not, at first, see any object distinctly; but he heard the moaning repeated, at intervals, and a soft voice at last said –

"O, speak to me! – speak to me, once again – only once – only once again, speak to me!"

The voice came from a corner of the room, to which he had not yet turned his eyes; and as he drew aside more of the curtain, to let in more light, a figure started up from the side of a bed, at which she had been kneeling, and he saw the beautiful young girl, with her hair all dishevelled, and the strongest expression of grief in her countenance. He asked, if he could do her any service. She beckoned to him to come in, and then, pointing to the bed, on which the old woman was stretched, said –

"She cannot speak to me – she cannot move one side – she has been so these three days – but she is not dead – she is not dead!"

The poor creature had been struck with the palsy. As Clarence went close to the bed, she opened her eyes, and fixing them upon him, she stretched out her withered hand, caught fast hold of her granddaughter, and then raising herself, with a violent effort, she pronounced the word, "Begone!" – Her face grew black, her features convulsed, and she sunk down again in her bed, without power of utterance. Clarence left the house instantly, mounted his horse, and galloped to the next town for medical assistance. The poor woman was so far recovered by a skilful apothecary, that she could, in a few days, articulate so as to be understood. She knew, that her end was approaching fast, and seemed piously resigned to her fate. Mr Hervey went constantly to see her; but, though grateful to him for his humanity, and for the assistance he had procured for her, yet she appeared agitated when he was in the room, and frequently looked at him, and at her granddaughter, with uncommon anxiety. At last, she whispered something to the girl, who immediately left the room; and she then beckoned to him, to come closer to the arm chair, in which she was seated.

"May be, sir," said she, "you thought me out of my right mind, the day when I was lying on that bed, and said to you, in such a peremptory tone – Begone! – It was all I could say then – and, in truth, I cannot speak quite plain yet; nor ever shall again. But God's will be done. I had only one thing to say to you, sir, about that poor girl of mine — "

Clarence listened to her with eagerness. She paused, and then laying her cold hand upon his, she looked up earnestly in his face, and continued –

"You are a fine young gentleman, and you look like a good gentleman, but so did the man who broke the heart of her poor mother. Her mother was carried off from a boarding-school, when she was scarcely sixteen, by a wretch, who, after privately marrying her, would not own his marriage, staid with her but two years, then went abroad, left his wife and his infant, and has never been heard of since. My daughter died of a broken heart. – Rachel was then between three and four years old, a beautiful child. – God forgive her father! – God's will be done!" She paused, to subdue her emotion, and then, with some difficulty, proceeded. –

"My only comfort is, I have bred Rachel up in innocence; I never sent her to a boarding-school. – No, no; from the moment of her birth, till now, I have kept her under my own eye. In this cottage she has lived with me, away from all the world. You are the first man she ever spoke to; the first man who ever was within these doors. She is innocence itself! – O, sir! as you hope for mercy, when you are as I am now, spare the innocence of that poor child! – never come here after her, when I am dead and gone! Consider, she is but a child, sir. – God never made a better creature. – O, promise me you will not be the ruin of my sweet innocent girl, and I shall die in peace!"

Clarence Hervey was touched. He instantly made the promise required of him; and, as nothing less would satisfy the poor dying woman, confirmed it by a solemn oath.

"Now I am easy," said she – "quite easy – and may God bless you for it. In the village here, there is a Mrs Smith, a good farmer's wife, who knows us well; she will see to have me decently buried, and then has promised to sell all the little I have for my girl, and to take care of her. – And you'll never come near her more?"

"I did not promise that," said Hervey.

The old woman again looked much disturbed. –

"Ah, good young gentleman!" said she, "take my advice, it will be best for you both. If you see her again, you will love her, sir – you can't help it – and, if she sees you – poor thing, how innocently she smiled, when she gave you the rose! – O, sir, never come near her when I am gone! It is too late for me now to get her out of your way. – This night, I'm sure, will be my last in this world – O, promise me you will never come here again!"

"After the oath I have taken," replied Clarence, "that promise would be unnecessary. Trust to my honour." –

"Honour! O, that was the word the gentleman said, that betrayed her poor mother, and left her afterward to die! – O, sir! sir! — "

The violent emotion that she felt was too much for her – she fell back exhausted – never spoke more – and an hour afterward she expired in the arms of her granddaughter. The poor girl could not believe, that she had breathed her last. She made a sign to the surgeon, and to Clarence Hervey, who stood beside her, to be silent; and listened, fancying that the corpse would breathe again. Then, she kissed the cold lips, and the shrivelled cheeks, and the eyelids, that were closed for ever. She warmed the dead fingers with her breath – she raised the heavy arm, and, when it fell, she perceived there was no hope: she threw herself upon her knees: – "She is dead!" she exclaimed; "and she has died without giving me her blessing. She can never bless me again."

They took her into the air, and Clarence Hervey sprinkled water upon her face. It was a fine night, and the fresh air soon brought her to her senses. He then said, that he would leave her to the care of the surgeon, and ride to the village, in search of that Mrs Smith, who had promised to be her friend.

"And so *you* are going away from me too?" said she; and she burst into tears. At the sight of these tears Clarence turned away, and hurried from her. He sent the woman from the village, but returned no more that night.

Her simplicity, sensibility, and, perhaps more than he was aware, her beauty, had pleased and touched him extremely. The idea of attaching a perfectly pure, disinterested, unpractised heart, was delightful to his imagination: the cultivation of her understanding, he thought, would be an easy and a pleasing task: all difficulties vanished before his sanguine hopes.

"Sensibility," said he to himself, "is the parent of great talents, and great virtues; and evidently she posseses natural feeling in an uncommon degree; it shall be developed with skill, patience, and delicacy; and I will deserve, before I claim my reward."

The next day he returned to the cottage, accompanied by an elderly lady, a Mrs Ormond; the same lady, who afterward to Marriott's prejudiced eyes had appeared *more like a dragon than anything else*; but who, to this simple, unsuspicious girl, seemed like what she really was, a truly good natured benevolent woman. She consented, most readily, to put herself under the protection of Mrs Ormond, "provided Mrs Smith would give her leave." There was no difficulty in persuading Mrs Smith, that it was for her advantage. Mrs Smith, who was a plain farmer's wife, told all that she knew of Rachel's history, but all that she knew was little. She had heard only hints at odd times from the old woman: these agreed perfectly with what Mr Hervey had already heard.

"The *old gentlewoman*," said Mrs Smith, "as I believe I should call her by rights, has lived in the forest there, where you found her, these many a year – she earned her subsistance by tending bees and making rose-water – she was a good soul, but very particular, especially about her granddaughter, which, considering all things, one cannot blame her for. She often told me, she would never put Rachel to no boarding school, which I approved, seeing she had no fortune; and it is the ruin of girls, to my mind, to be bred above their means; as it was of her mother, sir. Then she would not never teach Rachel to write, for fear she should take to scrawling nonsense of love-letters, as her mother did before her. Now, sir, this I approved too, for I don't much mind about book-learning myself; and I even thought it would have been as well if the girl had not learnt to read; but that she did learn, and was always fond of, and I'm sure it was more plague than use too to her grandmother, for she was as particular about the books that the girl was to read, as about all the rest. I'm sure I saw her myself in as great a flurry about a bit of old newspaper, that was wrapped round a parcel of linen I took to the house – as great a fuss, sir, as if the whole world had been coming to pieces, lest Rachel should have laid her eyes upon it. 'Now,' observes I, 'there's the use of reading; I've carried the paper in my hand this hour, and never thought of any harm, and no harm could it do to me. Pray what is there in it, after all?"

"Was Rachel present – Did she see this paper?" interrupted Clarence.

"Lord! no sir, no; she was tending the bees out of hearing, and the old lady had it in the middle of the fire in a minute. I'm only mentioning it, to show her particularities. She went farther than all that, sir; for she would never let the girl so much as speak to a man – not a man ever went within the doors of the house."

"So she told me."

"And she told you true enough. But there, I thought, she was quite wrong; for, seeing the girl must, some time or another, speak to men, where was the use of her not learning how, properly? Well, sir, I won't tell you all the argufyings I held on this point with her, but all to no purpose; she was, I take it, on this matter not quite rational, and it was but good natured to humour her. Lord! madam," continued Mrs Smith, addressing herself to Mrs Ormond – "Lord! madam, though it is a sin, to be remembering so much the particularities of the dead, I must say, there never was an old lady, who had more scrupulosities than the deceased. I verily thought, one day, she'd have died, about the picture of a man that Rachel lit upon by accident; as if a picture had any sense to hurt a body. Now, if it had been one of your naked pictures, there might have been some decency in her dislike to it; but it was no such thing, but a very proper picture, Lord! I really could not but laugh; but I checked myself, when the poor old soul's eyes filled with tears, which made me know, she was thinking of her daughter that was dead. When I thought on the cause of her particularity about Rachel, I could not laugh any more at her strangeness. I promised the good lady, that day, in case of her death, to take care of her granddaughter; and I thought, in my own mind, that, in time to come, if one of my boys should take a fancy to her, I should make no objections, because she was always a good, modest behaved girl; and, I'm sure, would make a good wife, though too delicate for hard country work: but, as it pleases God, to send you, madam, and the good gentleman to take the charge of her off my hands, I am content it should be so, and I will sell everything here for her honestly, and bring it to you, madam, for poor Rachel."

There was nothing that Rachel was anxious to carry away with her but a little bullfinch, of which she was very fond. One, and but one, circumstance about Rachel stopped the current of Clarence Hervey's imagination, and this, consequently, was excessively disagreeable to him – her name – the name of Rachel he could not endure, and he thought it so unsuited to her, that he could scarcely believe it belonged to her. He consequently resolved to change it as soon as possible. The first time that he beheld her, he was struck with the idea, that she resembled the description of Virginia in M. de St Pierre's celebrated romance; and by this name he always called her, from the hour that she quitted her cottage.

Mrs Ormond, the lady whom he had engaged to take care of his Virginia, was a widow, the mother of a gentleman, who had been his tutor at college. Her son died, and left her in such narrow circumstances, that she was obliged to apply to her friends for pecuniary assistance.

Mr Hervey had been liberal in his contributions; from his childhood he had known her worth, and her attachment to him was blended with the most profound respect; she was not a woman of superior abilities, or of much information; but her exellent temper and gentle disposition won affection, though she had not any talents to excite admiration. Mr Hervey had perfect confidence in her integrity, he believed that she would exactly comply with his directions, and he thought that her want of literature and ingenuity could easily be supplied by his own care and instructions. He took a house for her and his fair pupil at Windsor, and he exacted a solemn promise, that she would neither receive nor pay any visits. Virginia was thus secluded from all intercourse with the world: she saw no one but Mrs Ormond, Clarence Hervey, and Mr Moreton, an elderly clergyman, whom Mr Hervey engaged to attend every Sunday, to read prayers for them at home. Virginia never expressed the slightest curiosity to see any other persons, or any thing beyond the walls of the garden that belonged to the house in which she lived; her present retirement was not greater than that, to which she had long been accustomed, and consequently she did not feel her seclusion from the world as any restraint: with the circumstnaces that were altered in her situation, she seemed neither to be dazzled nor charmed; the objects of convenience or luxury, that were new to her, she looked upon with indifference, but with any thing that reminded her of her former way of life, and of her grandmother's cottage, she was delighted.

One day Mr Hervey asked her, whether she should like better to return to that cottage, or to remain where she was? He trembled for her answer – She innocently replied – "I should like best to go back to the cottage, if you would go with me – but I would rather stay here with you, than live there without you."

Clarence was touched and flattered by this artless answer, and for some time he discovered every day fresh indications, as he thought, of virtue and abilities in his charming pupil. Her indifference to objects of show and ornament appeared to him an indisputable proof of her magnanimity, and of the superiority of her unprejudiced mind. – What a difference, thought he, between this child of nature and the frivolous sophisticated slaves of art!

To try and prove the simplicity of her taste, and the purity of her mind, he once presented to her a pair of diamond earrings, and a moss rose bud, and asked her to take whichever she liked the best. – She eagerly snatched the rose, crying – "O! it puts me in mind of the cottage: – how sweet it smells!"

She placed it in her bosom, and then looking at the diamonds, said – "They are pretty sparkling things – What are they? – Of what use are they?" – And she looked with more curiosity and admiration at the manner in which the earring shut and opened, than at the diamonds. Clarence was charmed with her. When

Mrs Ormond told her, that these things were to hang in her ears, she laughed, and said – "How! how can I make them hang?"

"Have you never observed, that I wear earrings?" said Mrs Ormond.

"Ay! but yours are not like these – And, let me look, I never saw how you fastened them – let me look? – O! you have holes in your ears, but I have none in mine."

Mrs Ormond told her, that holes could easily be made in her ears, by running a steel pin through them. She shrunk back, defending her ear with one hand, and pushing the diamonds from her with the other, exclaiming – "O, no, no! – unless," added she, changing her tone, and turning to Clarence, "unless you wish it: – if you bid me, I will."

Clarence was scarcely master of himself at this instant; and it was with the utmost difficulty, that he could reply to her with that dispassionate calmness, which became his situation and hers – And yet: there was more of ignorance and timidity, perhaps, than of sound sense or philosophy, in Virgina's indifference to diamonds; she did not consider them as ornaments, that would confer distinction upon their possessor, because she was ignorant of the value affixed to them by society. Isolated in the world, she had no excitements to the love of finery, no competition, no means of comparison, or opportunities of display; diamonds were consequently as useless to her, as guineas were to Robinson Crusoe, on his desert island. It would not justly be said, that he was free from avarice, because he set no value on the gold; or that she was free from vanity, because she rejected the diamonds. These reflections would not possibly have escaped a man of Clarence Hervey's abilities; had he not been engaged in defence of a favourite system of education, or if his pupil had not been quite so handsome. Virginia's absolute ignorance of the world frequently gave an air of originality to her most trivial observations, which made her appear at once interesting and entertaining. All her ideas of happiness were confined to the life she had led during her childhood; and as she had accidentally lived in a beautiful situation in the New Forest, she appeared to have an instinctive taste for the beauties of nature, and for what we call the picturesque. This taste Mr Hervey perceived, whenever she showed her prints and drawings, and it was a fresh source of delight and self-complacency to him. All that was amiable or estimable in Virginia had a double charm, from the secret sense of his penetration, in having discovered and appreciated the treasure. The affections of this innocent girl had no object but himself and Mrs Ormond, and they were strong, perhaps, in proportion as they were concentrated. The artless familiarity of her manner, and her unsuspicious confidence, amounting almost to credulity, had irresistible power over Mr Hervey's mind; he felt them as appeals at once to his tenderness and his generosity. He treated her with the utmost delicacy, and his oath was never absent from his mind: but he felt proudly convinced, that if he had not been bound by any such solemn engagement, no temptation could have made him deceive or betray confiding innocence.

Conscious that his views were honourable, anticipating the generous pleasure he should have in showing his superiority to all mercenary considerations, and worldly prejudices, in the choice of a wife, he indulged, with a species of pride, his increasing attachment to Virginia; but he was not sensible of the rapid progress of his passion, till he was suddenly awakened by a few simple observations of Mrs Ormond.

"This is Virginia's birthday – she tells me she is seventeen to day."

"Seventeen! – is she only seventeen?" cried Clarence with a mixture of surprise and disappointment in his countenance – "Only seventeen! – Why she is but a child still."

"Quite a child," said Mrs Ormond, "and so much the better."

"So much the worse, I think," said Clarence. "But are you sure she's only seventeen – she must be mistaken – she must be eighteen at least."

"God forbid!"

"God forbid! – Why Mrs Ormond?"

"Because, you know, we have a year more before us."

"That may be a very satisfactory prospect to you," said Mr Hervey, smiling.

– "And to you, surely," said Mrs Ormond; "for I suppose, you would be glad that your wife should, at least, know the common things that everybody knows."

"As to that," said Clarence, "I should be glad that my wife were ignorant of what *everybody knows*. Nothing is so tiresome to a man of any taste or abilities, as *what everybody knows*. I am rather desirous to have a wife who has an uncommon, than a common understanding."

"But you would choose, would not you?" – said Mrs Ormond,

hesitating, with an air of great deference – "that your wife should know how to write?"

"To be sure," replied Clarence, colouring – "Does not Virginia know how to write?"

"How should she?" said Mrs Ormond – "it is no fault of hers, poor girl – She was never taught, you know: it was her grandmother's notion that she should not learn to write lest she should write love-letters."

"But *you* promised that she should be taught to write, and I trusted to you, Mrs Ormond."

"She has been here only two months, and all that time, I am sure, I have done everything in my power; but when a person comes to be sixteen or seventeen, it is uphill work."

"I will teach her myself," cried Clarence – "I am sure she may be taught anything."

"By you," said Mrs Ormond, smiling; "but not my me."

"You have no doubts of her capacity, surely?"

"I am no judge of capacity, especially of the capacity of those I love, and I am grown very fond of Virginia; she is a charming, open hearted, simple, affectionate creature. I rather think it is from indolence, that she does not learn, and not from want of abilities."

"All indolence arises from want of excitement," said Clarence – "If she had proper motives, she would conquer her indolence."

"Why, I dare say, if I were to tell her, that she would never have a letter from Mr Hervey, till she is able to write an answer, she would learn to write very expeditiously; but I thought, that would not be a proper motive; because you forbid me to tell her your future views. And indeed it would be highly imprudent, on your account, as well as hers, to give her any hint of that kind; because you might change your mind, before she's old enough for you to think of her seriously, and then you would not know what to do with her; and after entertaining hopes of becoming your wife, she would be miserable, I am sure, with that affectionate tender heart of hers, if you were to leave her. Now that she knows nothing of the matter, we are all safe, and as we should be."

Though Clarence Hervey did not at this time foresee any great probability of his changing his mind, yet he felt the good sense and justice of Mrs Ormond's suggestions; and he was alarmed, to perceive that his mind had been so intoxicated, as to suffer such obvious reflections to escape his attention. Mrs Ormond, a woman whom he had been accustomed to consider as far his inferior in capacity, he now felt was superior to him in prudence, merely because she was undisturbed by passion. He resolved to master his own mind: to consider, that it was not a mistress, but a wife, he wanted in Virginia: – that a wife without capacity, or without literature, could never be a companion suited to him; let her beauty or sensibility be ever so exquisite and captivating. The happiness of his life and of hers were at stake, and every motive of prudence and delicacy called upon him to command his affections. He was, however, still sanguine in his expectations from Virginia's understanding, and from his own power of developing her capacity. He made several attempts, with the greatest skill and patience; and his fair pupil, though she did not by any means equal his hopes, astonished Mrs Ormond, by her comparatively rapid progress.

"I always believed, that *you* could make her anything you pleased," said she. "You are a tutor, who can work miracles with Virginia."

"I see no miracles," replied Clarence; "I am conscious of no such power – I should be sorry to possess any such influence, until I am sure that it would be for our mutual happiness."

– Mr Hervey then conjured Mrs Ormond, by all her attachment to him and to her pupil, never to give Virginia the most distant idea, that he had any intentions of making her his wife. She promised to do all that was in her power, to keep this secret, but she could not help observing, that it had already been betrayed, as plainly as looks could speak, by Mr Hervey himself. Clarence in vain endeavoured to exculpate himself from this charge: Mrs Ormond brought to his recollection so many instances of his indiscretion, that it was substantiated even in his own judgment, and he was amazed to find, that all the time he had put so much constraint upon his inclinations, he had, nevertheless, so obviously betrayed them. His surprise, however, was at this time unmixed with any painful regret; he did not foresee the probability that he should change his mind, and notwithstanding Mrs Ormond assured him, that Virginia's sensibility had increased, he was persuaded that she was mistaken, and that his pupil's heart and imagination were yet untouched. The innocent openness, with which she expressed her affection for him, confirmed him, he said, in his opinion. To do him justice, Clarence had none of the presumption, which too often characterises men, who have been successful, as it is called, with the fair sex. His acquaintance with women had increased his persuasion, that it is difficult to excite genuine love in the female heart; and with respect to himself, he was upon this subject astonishingly incredulous. It was scarcely possible to convince him, that he was beloved.

Mrs Ormond, piqued upon this subject, determined to ascertain more decisively her pupil's sentiments.

"My dear," said she, one day to Virginia, who was feeding her bullfinch – "I do believe you are fonder of that bird, than of anything in the world – fonder of it, I am sure, than of me?"

"O! you cannot think so," said Virginia, with an affectionate smile.

"Well! fonder than you are of Mr Hervey, you will allow, at least?"

"No indeed!" cried she, eagerly: "how can you think me so foolish, so childish, so ungrateful, as to prefer a little worthless bird to him – " (the bullfinch began to sing so loud at this instant, that her enthusiastic speech was stopped.) – "My pretty bird," said she, as it perched upon her hand, "I love you very much, but if Mr Hervey were to ask it, to wish it, I would open that window, and let you fly; yes, and bid you fly away far from me forever. Perhaps he does wish it? – Does he? – Did he tell you so?" cried she, looking earnestly in Mrs Ormond's face, as she moved toward the window.

Mrs Ormond put her hand upon the sash, as Virginia was going to throw it up —

"Gently, gently, my love – Whither is your imagination carrying you?"

"I thought *something* by your look," said Virginia, blushing.

"And I thought *something*, my dear Virginia," said Mrs Ormond, smiling.

"What did you think? – What *could* you think?"

"I cannot – I mean, I would rather not at present tell you. But do not look so grave, I will tell you some time or other, if you cannot guess."

Virginia was silent, and stood abashed.

"I am sure, my sweet girl," said Mrs Ormond, "I do not mean, by anything I said, to confuse or blame you. It is very natural, that you should be grateful to Mr Hervey, and that you should admire, and, *to a certain degree*, *love* him."

Virginia looked up delighted, yet with some hesitation in her manner.

"He is indeed," said Mrs Ormond, "one of the first of human beings: such even *I* have always thought him; and I am sure I like you the better, my dear," said she, kissing Virginia as she spoke; "only we must take care of it, or this tenderness might go too far."

"How so," said Virginia, returning her caresses with fondness; "can I love you and Mr Hervey too much?"

"Not me."

"Nor him, I'm sure – he is so good, so very good! – I am afraid that I do not love him *enough*," said she, sighing. "I love him enough when he is absent, but not when he is present. When he is near me, I feel a sort of fear, mixed with my love. I wish to please him very much, but I should not quite like, that he should show his love for me as you do – as you did just now."

"My dear, it would not be proper that he should; you are quite right not to wish it."

"Am I? I was afraid that it was a sign of my not liking him as much as I ought."

"Ah, my poor child! – You love him full as much as you ought."

"Do you think so? I am glad of it," said Virginia, with a look of such confiding simplicity, that her friend was touched to the heart.

"I do think so, my love," said Mrs Ormond, "and I hope I shall never be sorry for it, nor you either. But it is not proper, that we should say any more upon this subject now. Where are your drawings? Where is your writing? My dear, we must get forward with these things as fast as we can. That is the way to please Mr Hervey, I can tell you."

Confirmed by this conversation in her own opinion, Mrs Ormond was satisfied. From delicacy to her pupil, she did not repeat all that had passed to Mr Hervey, resolving to wait till the *proper* moment. "She is too young and too childish, for him to think of marrying yet, for a year or two," thought she, "and it is better to repress her sensibility, till her education is more finished, by that time Mr Hervey will find out his mistake."

In the mean time, she could not help thinking that he was blind, for he continued steady in his belief of Virginia's indifference.

To dissipate his own mind, and to give time for the development of hers, he now, according to his resolution, left his pupil to the care of Mrs Ormond, and mixed as much as possible in gay and fashionable company. It was at this period, that he renewed his acquaintance with Lady Delacour, whom he had seen and admired before he went abroad. He found that his gallantry, on the famous day of the battle between the turkies and pigs, was still remembered with gratitude by her ladyship; she received him with marked courtesy, and he soon become a constant visitor at her house. Her wit entertained, her eloquence charmed him, and he followed, admired and *gallanted* her, without scruple, for he considered her merely as *une franche coquette*, who preferred the glory of conquest to the security of reputation. With such a woman he thought he could amuse himself without danger, and he every where appeared the foremost in the public train of her ladyship's admirers. He soon discovered, however, that her talents were far superior to what are necessary for playing the part of a fine lady; his visits became more and more agreeable to him, and he was glad to feel, that, by dividing his attention, his passion for Virginia insensibly diminished, or as he said to himself, became more reasonable. In conversing with Lady Delacour, his faculties were always called into full play; in talking to Virginia, his understanding was passive; he perceived that a large proportion of his intellectual powers and of his knowledge was absolutely useless to him in her company, and this did not raise her either in his love or esteem. Her simplicity and naïveté, however, sometimes relieved him, and he had been fatigued by the extravagant gaiety and *glare* of her ladyship's manners; and he reflected, that the coquetry, which amused him in an acquaintance, would be odious in a wife: the perfect innocence of Virginia promised security to his domestic happiness, and he did not change his view, though he was less eager for the period of their accomplishment. "I cannot expect every thing that is desirable," said he, to himself: "a more brilliant character than Virginia's would excite my admiration, but could not command my confidence." It was whilst his mind was in this situation, that he became acquainted with Belinda. At first, the idea of her having been educated by the matchmaking Mrs Stanhope prejudiced him against her; but as he had opportunities of observing her conduct, this prepossession was conquered, and when she had secured his esteem, he could no longer resist her power over his heart. In comparison with Belinda, Virginia appeared to him but an insipid, though innocent child; the one he found was his equal, the other his inferior; the one he saw could be a companion, a friend to him for life; the other would merely be his pupil or his plaything. Belinda had cultivated tastes, an active understanding, a knowledge of literature, the power and the habit of conducting herself. Virginia was ignorant and indolent, she had few ideas, and no wish to extend her knowledge. She was so entirely unacquainted with the world, that it was absolutely impossible she could conduct herself with that discretion, which must be the combined result of reasoning and experience. Mr Hervey had felt gratuitous confidence in Virginia's innocence; but on Belinda's prudence, which he had opportunities of seeing tried, he gradually learned to feel a different, and a higher species of reliance, which is neither in our power to bestow nor to refuse. The virtues of Virginia sprang from sentiment; those of Belinda, from reason.

Clarence, whilst he made all these comparisons, became every day more wisely and more fondly attached to Belinda; and, at length, he became desirous to change the nature of his connexion with Virginia, and to appear to her only in the light of a friend or a benefactor. He thought of giving her two thousand pounds, and of leaving her under the care of Mrs Ormond, till some suitable method of establishing her in the world should occur. Unfortunately, just at the time when Mr Hervey formed this plan, and before it was communicated to Mrs Ormond, difficulties arose, which prevented him from putting it into execution.

Whilst he had been engaged in the gay world at Lady Delacour's, his pupil had necessarily been left much to the management of Mrs Ormond. This lady, with the best possible intentions, had not that reach of mind and variety of resource, necessary to direct the exquisite sensibility and ardent imagination of Virginia. The solitude, in which she lived, added to the difficulty of the task; without companions to interest her social affections, without real objects to occupy her senses and understanding, Virginia's mind was either perfectly indolent, or *exalted* by romantic views and visionary ideas of happiness. As she had never seen anything of society, all her notions were drawn from books; the severe restrictions, which her grandmother had early laid upon the choice of these, seemed to have awakened her curiosity, and to have increased her appetite for books – it was insatiable. Reading, indeed, was now almost her only pleasure; for Mrs Ormond's conversation was seldom entertaining, and Virginia had no longer those occupations, which filled a portion of her day at the cottage.

Mr Hervey had cautioned Mrs Ormond against putting *common* novels into her hands, but he made no objection to romances: these, he thought, breathed a spirit favourable to female virtue, exalted the respect for chastity, and inspired enthusiastic admiration of honour, generosity, truth, and all the noble qualities, which dignify human nature. Virginia devoured these romances with the greatest eagerness; and Mrs Ormond, who found her a prey to ennui, when her fancy was not amused, indulged her taste; yet she strongly suspected, that they contributed to increase her passion for the only man who could, in her imagination, represent a hero.

One night Virginia found, in Mrs Ormond's room, a volume of St Pierre's Paul and Virginia. She knew, that her own name had been taken from this romance; Mr Hervey had her picture painted in this character; and these circumstances strongly excited her curiosity to read the book. Mrs Ormond could not refuse to let her have it; for, though it was not an ancient romance, it did not exactly come under the description of a common novel, and Mr Hervey was not at hand, to give his advice. Virginia sat down instantly to her volume, and never stirred from the spot, till she had nearly finished it.

"What is it, that strikes your fancy so much? What are you considering so deeply, my love?" said Mrs Ormond, observing, that she seemed lost in thought. "Let us see, my dear," continued Mrs Ormond, offering to take the book, which hung from her hand. – Virginia started from her reverie, but held the volume fast. – "Will you not let me read over your shoulder, along with you?" said Mrs Ormond. "Won't you let me share your pleasure?"

"It is not pleasure, that I felt, I believe," said Virginia. "I would rather, you should not see just that particular part I was reading; and, yet, if you desire it," added she, resigning the book reluctantly —

"What can make you so much afraid of me, my sweet girl?"

"I am not afraid of you – but – of myself," said Virginia, sighing.

Mrs Ormond read the following passage:

"She thought of Paul's friendship, more pure than the waters of the fountain, stronger than the united palms, and sweeter than the perfume of flowers; and these images, in night and in solitude, gave double force to the passion, which she nourished in her heart. She suddenly left the dangerous shades, and went to her mother, to seek protection against herself. She wished to reveal her distress to her; she pressed her hands, and the name of Paul was on her lips; but the oppression of her heart took away all utterance, and, laying her hand upon her mother's bosom, she only wept."

"And am not I a mother to you, my beloved Virginia?" said Mrs Ormond. "Though I cannot express my affection in such charming language as this, yet, believe me, no mother was ever fonder of a child."

Virginia threw her arms round Mrs Ormond, and laid her head upon her friend's bosom, as if she wished to realise the illusion, and to be the Virginia of whom she had been reading.

"I know all you think, and all you feel: I know," whispered Mrs Ormond, "the name that is on *your* lips."

"No, indeed, you do not; you cannot," cried Virginia, suddenly raising her head, and looking up in Mrs Ormond's face, with surprise and timidity – "how could you possibly know *all* my thoughts and feelings? I never told them to you; for, indeed, I have only confused ideas, floating in my imagination, from the books I have been reading. I do not distinctly know my own feelings."

"This is all very natural, and a proof of your perfect innocence and simplicity, my child. But, why did the passage you were reading just now strike you so much?"

"I was only considering," said Virginia, "whether it was the description of – love."

"And your heart told you, that it was?"

"I don't know," said she, sighing. "But of this I am certain, that I had not the name, which you were thinking of, upon my lips."

"Ah!" thought Mrs Ormond, "she has not forgotten how I checked her sensibility some time ago. Poor girl! she is become afraid of me, and I have taught her to dissemble; but she betrays herself every moment."

"My dear," said Mrs Ormond, "you need not fear me – I cannot blame you – In your situation, it is impossible, that you could help loving Mr Hervey."

"Is it?"

"Yes; quite impossible. So do not blame yourself for it."

"No, I do not blame myself for that. I only blame myself, for not loving him *enough*, as I told you once before."

"Yes, my dear; and the oftener you tell me so, the more I am convinced of your affection. It is one of the strongest symptoms of love, that we are unconscious of its extent. We fancy, that we can never do too much for the beloved object."

"That is exactly what I feel about Mr Hervey."

"That we can never love him enough."

"Ah! that is precisely what I feel for Mr Hervey."

"And what you ought – I mean, what it is natural you should feel: and what he will himself, I hope, indeed, I dare say, some time or other wish, and be glad that you should feel."

"Some time or other! – Does not he wish it now?"

"I – he – My dear, what a question is that? And how shall I answer it? We must judge of what he feels by what he expresses: when he expresses love for you, it will then be the time to show yours for him."

"He has always expressed love for me, I think," said Virginia –"always, till lately," continued Virginia; "but lately he has been away so much, and when he comes home, he does not look so well pleased; so that I was afraid he was angry with me, and that he thought me ungrateful."

"O, my love, do not torment yourself with these vain fears! And yet I know that you cannot help it."

"Since you are so kind, so very kind to me," said Virginia, "I will tell you all my fears and doubts. – But it is late. – There! the clock struck one. – I will not keep you up."

"I am not at all sleepy," said the indulgent Mrs Ormond.

"Nor I," said Virginia.

"Now, then," said Mrs Ormond, "for these doubts and fears."

"I was afraid that, perhaps, Mr Hervey would be angry if he knew that I thought of any thing in the world but him."

"Of what else do you think? – Of nothing else from morning till night, that I can see."

"Ah, then you do not see into my mind. In the daytime I often think of those heroes, those charming heroes, that I read of in the books you have given me."

"To be sure you do."

"And is not that wrong? Would not Mr Hervey be displeased if he knew it?"

"Why should he?"

"Because they are not quite like him. I love some of them better than I do him, and he might think that *ungrateful*."

How naturally love inspires the idea of jealousy, thought Mrs Ormond. "My dear," said she, "you carry your ideas of delicacy and gratitude to an extreme; but it is very natural you should: however, you need not be afraid, Mr Hervey cannot be jealous of those charming heroes, that never existed, though they are not quite like him."

"I am very glad that he would not think me ungrateful! – but if he knew that I dream of them sometimes?"

"He would think you dreamed, as all people do, of what they think of in the daytime."

"And he would not be angry? I am very glad of it. – But I once saw a picture — "

"I know you did – well," said Mrs Ormond, "and your grandmother was frightened because it was the picture of a man – hey? If she was not your grandmother, I should say that she was a simpleton. I assure you, Mr Hervey is not like her, if that is what you mean to ask. He would not be angry at your having seen fifty pictures."

"I am glad of it – But I see it very often in my dreams."

"Well, if you had seen more pictures, you would not see this so often. It was the first you ever saw, and very naturally you remember it. Mr Hervey would not be angry at that," said Mrs Ormond, laughing.

"But sometimes, in my dreams, it speaks to me."

"And what does it say?"

"The same sort of things that those heroes I read of say to their mistresses."

"And do you never, in your dreams, hear Mr Hervey say these sort of things?"

"No."

"And do you never see Mr Hervey in these dreams?"

"Sometimes; but he does not speak to me; he does not look at me with the same sort of tenderness, and he does not throw himself at my feet."

"No; because he has never done all this in reality."

"No; and I wonder how I come to dream of such things."

"So do I; but you have read and thought of them, it is plain. Now go to sleep, there's my good girl; that is the best thing you can do at present – Go to sleep."

It was not long after this conversation, that Sir Philip Baddely and Mr Rochfort scaled the garden wall, to obtain a sight of

Clarence Hervey's mistress. Virginia was astonished, terrified, and disgusted, by their appearance; they seemed to her a species of animals, for which she had no name, and of which she had no prototype in her imagination. That they were men she saw; but they were clearly not *Clarence Herveys*; they bore still less resemblance to the courteous knights of chivalry. Their language was so different from any of the books she had read, and any of the conversation she had heard, that they were scarcely intelligible. After they had forced themselves into her presence, they did not scruple to address her in the most unceremonious manner. Amongst other rude things, they said, "Damme, my pretty dear, you cannot love the man that keeps you prisoner in this manner, hey? Damme, you'd better come and live with one of us. You can't love this tyrant of a fellow."

"He is not a tyrant – I *do* love him, as much as I detest you," cried Virginia, shrinking from him with looks of horror.

"Damme! Good actress! Put her on the stage when he is tired of her. – So, you won't come with us? – Goodbye till we see you again. You're right, my girl, to be upon your good behaviour, may be you may get him to marry you, child!"

Virginia, upon hearing this speech, turned from the man who insulted her, with a degree of haughty indignation, of which her gentle nature had never before appeared capable.

Mrs Ormond hoped, that after the alarm was over, the circumstance would pass away from her pupil's mind; but, on the contrary, it left the most forcible impression. Virginia became silent and melancholy, and whole hours were spent in reverie. Mrs Ormond imagined, that notwithstanding Virginia's entire ignorance of the world, she had acquired from books sufficient knowledge to be alarmed at the idea of being taken for Clarence Hervey's mistress. She touched upon this subject with much delicacy, and the answers that she received confirmed her opinion. Virginia had been inspired by romances with the most exalted notions of female delicacy and honour; but from her perfect ignorance, these were rather vague ideas than principles of conduct.

"We shall see Mr Hervey to morrow; he has written me word that he will come from town, and spend the day with us."

"I shall be ashamed to see him after what has passed," said Virginia.

"You have no cause for shame, my dear; Mr Hervey will try to

discover the persons who insulted you, and he will punish them.
They will never return here, you need not fear that. He is willing
and able to protect you."

"Yes, of that I am sure. But what did that strange man mean,
when he said — "

"What, my dear?"

"That, perhaps, Mr Hervey would marry me."

Virginia pronounced these words with difficulty. Mrs Ormond
was silent, for she was much embarrassed. Virginia having
conquered her first difficulty, seemed resolute to obtain an
answer.

"You do not speak to me! Will you not tell me, dear Mrs
Ormond," said she, hanging upon her fondly, "what did he
mean?"

"What he said, I suppose."

"But he said, that if I behaved well, I might get Mr Hervey to
marry me. What did he mean by that?" said Virginia, in an accent
of offended pride.

"He spoke very rudely and improperly, but it is not worth while
to think of what he said or what he meant."

"But, dear Mrs Ormond, do not go away from me now, I never
so much wished to speak to you in my whole life, and you turn
away from me."

"Well, my love, well, what would you say?"

"Tell me one thing, only one thing, and you will set my heart at
ease. Does Mr Hervey *wish* me to be his wife?"

"I cannot tell you that, my dearest Virginia. Time will show us.
Perhaps his heart has not yet decided."

"I wish it would decide," said Virginia, sighing deeply; "and I
wish that strange man had not told me any thing about the matter;
it has made me very unhappy."

She covered her eyes with her hand, but the tears trickled
between her fingers, and rolled fast down her arm. Mrs Ormond,
quite overcome by the sight of her distress, was no longer able to
keep the secret, with which she had been entrusted by Clarence
Hervey. — "And after all," thought she, "Virginia will hear it from
himself soon. I shall only spare her some unnecessary pain; it is
cruel to see her thus, and to keep her in suspense. Besides, her
weakness might be her ruin, in his opinion, if it were to extinguish
all her energy, and deprive her of the very power of pleasing. How
wan she looks, and how heavy are those sleepless eyes! She is not,

indeed, in a condition to meet him, when he comes to us tomorrow: if she had some hopes, she would revive, and appear with her natural ease and grace."

"My sweet child," said Mrs Ormond, "I cannot bear to see you so melancholy; consider, Mr Hervey will be with us to morrow, and it will give him a great deal of pain to see you so."

"Will it? Then I will try to be very gay."

Mrs Ormond was so delighted to see Virginia smile, that she could not forbear adding, "The strange man was not wrong in every thing he said; you *will*, one of these days, be Mr Hervey's wife."

"That I am sure," said Virginia, bursting again into tears – "that I am sure I do not wish, unless *he* does."

"He does, he does, my dear – do not let this delicacy of yours, which has been wound up too high, make you miserable. He thought of you, he loved you long and long ago."

"He is very good, too good," said Virginia, sobbing.

"Nay, what is more – for I can keep nothing from you – he has been educating you all this time on purpose for his wife, and he only waits till your education is finished, and till he is sure that you feel no repugnance for him."

"I should be very ungrateful if I felt any repugnance for him," said Virginia; "I feel none."

"O, that you need not assure me," said Mrs Ormond.

"But I do not wish to marry him – I do not wish to marry."

"You are a modest girl to say so, if you did; and this modesty will make you ten times more amiable, especially in Mr Hervey's eyes. Heaven forbid that I should lessen it!"

The next morning Virginia, who always slept in the same room with Mrs Ormond, wakened her, by crying out in her sleep with a voice of terror, "O, save him! – save Mr Hervey! – Mr Hervey! – forgive me! forgive me!" —

Mrs Ormond drew back the curtain, and saw Virginia lying fast asleep; her beautiful face convulsed with agony.

"He's dead! – Mr Hervey!" – cried she, in a voice of exquisite distress: then starting up, and stretching out her arms, she uttered a piercing cry, and awoke.

"My love, you have been dreaming frightfully," said Mrs Ormond.

"Is Mr Hervey alive? Where is he? Has he forgiven me? Is it all a dream?" cried Virginia, looking round fearfully.

"All a dream, my dear!" said Mrs Ormond, taking her hand.

"I am very, very glad of it! – Let me breathe. – It was, indeed, a frightful dream!"

"Your hand still trembles," said Mrs Ormond; "let me put back this hair from your poor face, and you will grow cool, and forget this foolish dream."

"No; I must tell it you. I ought to tell it you. But it was all so confused, I can recollect only some parts of it. First, I remember that I thought I was not myself, but the Virginia that we were reading of the other night; and I was somewhere in the Isle of France. I thought the place was something like the forest where my grandmother's cottage used to be, only there were high mountains and rocks, and cocoa-trees and plantains."

"Such as you saw in the prints of that book?"

"Yes; only beautiful, beautiful beyond description! And it was moonlight, brighter and clearer than any moonlight I ever before had seen; and the air was fresh, yet perfumed; and I was seated under the shade of a plane-tree, beside Virginia's fountain."

"Just as you are in your picture?"

"Yes; but Paul was seated beside me."

"Paul!" said Mrs Ormond, smiling; "that is Mr Hervey."

"No; not Mr Hervey's figure, though it spoke with his voice – this is what I thought that I must tell you. It was another figure: it seemed a real living person: it knelt at my feet, and spoke to me so kindly, so tenderly; and just as it was going to kiss my hand, Mr Hervey appeared, and I started terribly, for I was afraid he would be displeased, and that he would think me *ungrateful*; and he was displeased, and he called me ungrateful Virginia, and frowned; and then I gave him my hand, and then everything changed, I do not know how suddenly, and I was in a place like the great print of the cathedral, which Mr Hervey showed me; and there were crowds of people – I was almost stifled. *You* pulled me on, as I remember; and Mr Moreton was there, standing upon some steps, by what you called the altar; and then we knelt down before him, and Mr Hervey was putting a ring on my finger; but there came suddenly from the crowd that strange man, who was here the other day, and he dragged me along with him, I don't know how or where, swiftly down precipices, whilst I struggled, and at last fell. Then all changed again, and I was in a magnificent field, covered with cloth of gold, and there were beautiful ladies seated under canopies; and I thought it was a tournament, such as I have read of, only more splendid; and two knights, clad in complete armour, and mounted on fiery steeds, were engaged in single combat, and they fought furiously, and I thought they were fighting for me. One of the knights wore black plumes in his helmet, and the other white; and, as he was passing by me, the vizor of the knight of the white plumes was let down, and I saw it was — "

"Clarence Hervey?" said Mrs Ormond.

"No; still the same figure that knelt to me; and I wished him to be victorious. And he was victorious. And he unhorsed his adversary, and stood over him with his drawn sword; and then I saw that the knight in the black plumes was Mr Hervey, and I ran to save him, but I could not. I saw him weltering in his blood, and I heard him say, 'Perfidious, *ungrateful* Virginia! you are the cause of my death! – and I screamed, I believe, and that wakened me."

"Well, it is only a dream, my love," said Mrs Ormond; "Mr Hervey is safe; get up, and dress yourself, and you will soon see him."

"But was it not wrong and *ungrateful*, to wish that the knight in the white plumes should be victorious?"

"Your poor little head is full of nothing but these romances, and love for Mr Hervey. It is your love for him, that makes you fear that he will be jealous. But he is not so simple as you are. He will forgive you for wishing that the knight in the white plumes should be victorious, especially as you did not know that the other knight was Mr Hervey. Come, my love, dress yourself, and think no more of these foolish dreams, and all will go well."

CHAPTER XXVII

A Discovery

Instead of the open, childish, affectionate familiarity, with which Virginia used to meet Clarence Hervey, she now received him with reserved timid embarrassment. Struck by this change in her manner, and alarmed by the dejection of her spirits, which she vainly strove to conceal, he eagerly inquired, from Mrs Ormond, into the cause of this alteration.

Mrs Ormond's answers, and her account of all that had passed during his absence, increased his anxiety. His indignation was roused, by the insult which Virginia had been offered by the stranger who had scaled the garden-wall. All his endeavours, to discover who they were, proved ineffectual; but, lest they should venture to repeat their visit, he removed her from Windsor, and took her directly to Twickenham. Here he staid with her and Mrs Ormond some days, to determine, by his own observation, how far the representations, that had been made to him, were just. Till this period he had been persuaded, that Virginia's regard for him was rather that of gratitude, than of love; and with this opinion, he thought, that he had no reason seriously to reproach himself for the imprudence, with which he had betrayed the partiality that he felt for her, in the beginning of their acquaintance. He flattered himself, that, even should she have discerned his intentions, her heart would not repine at any alteration in his sentiments: and if her happiness were uninjured, his reason told him, that he was not in honour bound to constancy. The case was now altered. – Unwilling as he was to believe, he could no longer doubt. – Virginia could neither meet his eyes, nor speak to him without a degree of embarrassment, which she had not sufficient art to conceal: she trembled whenever he came near her, and if he looked grave, or forbore to take notice of her, she would burst into tears. At other times, contrary to the natural indolence of her character, she would exert herself to please him, with surprising energy; she learned every thing that he wished; her capacity seemed suddenly to unfold. For an instant, Clarence flattered himself, that both her fits of melancholy and of exertion might arise from a secret desire to see something of that world, from which she had been secluded. One day, he touched upon this subject, to see what effect it would produce; but, contrary to his expectations, she seemed to have no desire to quit her retirement: she did not wish, she said, for amusements such as he described; she did not wish to go into the world.

It was during the time of his passion for her, that Clarence had her picture painted in the character of St Pierre's Virginia. It happened to be in the room in which they were now conversing, and when she spoke of loving a life of retirement, Clarence accidentally cast his eyes upon the picture, and then upon Virginia. She turned away – sighed deeply; and when, in a tone of kindness, he asked her, if she were unhappy, she hid her face in her hands, and made no answer.

Mr Hervey could not be insensible to her distress, or to her delicacy. He saw her bloom fading daily, her spirits depressed, her existence a burden to her, and he feared, that his own imprudence had been the cause of all this misery.

"I have taken her out of a situation, in which she might have spent her life usefully and happily; I have excited false hopes in her mind, and now she is a wretched and useless being; I have won her affections; her happiness depends totally upon me; and can I forsake her? Mrs Ormond says, that she is convinced, Virginia would not survive the day of my marriage with another. I am not disposed to believe, that girls often die or destroy themselves for love; nor am I coxcomb enough to suppose, that love for me must be extraordinarily desperate. But here's a girl, who is of a melancholy temperament, who has a great deal of natural sensibility, whose affections have all been concentrated, who has lived in solitude, whose imagination has dwelled, for a length of time, upon a certain set of ideas, who has but one object of hope: in such a mind, and in such circumstances, passion may rise to a paroxysm of despair."

Pity, generosity, and honour, made him resolve not to abandon this unfortunate girl; though he felt, that every time he saw her, his love for Belinda increased. It was this struggle in his mind, betwixt love and honour, which produced all the apparent inconsistency and irresolution, that puzzled Lady Delacour, and perplexed Belinda. The lock of beautiful hair, which so unluckily fell at Belinda's feet, was Virginia's; he was going to take it to the painter, who had made the hair in her picture considerably too dark. How this picture got into the exhibition must now be explained.

Whilst Mr Hervey's mind was in that painful state of doubt, which has just been described, a circumstance happened, that promised him some relief from his embarrassment. Mr Moreton, the clergyman who used to read prayers every Sunday for Mrs Ormond and Virginia, did not come one Sunday at the usual time: the next morning he called on Mr Hervey, with a face that showed he had something of importance to communicate.

"I have hopes, my dear Clarence," said he, "that I have found out your Virginia's father. Yesterday, a musical friend of mine persuaded me to go with him, to hear the singing at the Asylum for children, in St George's Fields. There is a girl there, who has, indeed, a charming voice – but that's not to the present purpose. After church was over, I happened to be one of the last that staid; for I am too old, to love bustling through a crowd. Perhaps, as you are impatient, you think, that's nothing to the purpose; and yet it is, as you shall hear. When the congregation had almost left the church, I observed, that the children of the Asylum remained in their places, by order of one of the governors; and a middle aged gentleman went round amongst the elder girls, examined their countenances with care, and inquired, with much anxiety, their ages, and every particular relative to their parents. The stranger held a miniature picture in his hand, with which he compared each face. I was not near enough to him," continued Mr Moreton, "to see the miniature distinctly; but, from the glimpse I caught of it, I thought that it was like your Virginia, though it seemed to be the portrait of a child but four or five years old. I understand, that this gentleman will be at the Asylum again next Sunday; I heard him express a wish to see some of the girls, who happened last Sunday to be absent."

"Do you know this gentleman's name, or where he lives?" said Clarence.

"I know nothing of him," replied Mr Moreton, "except, that he seems fond of painting, for he told one of the directors, who was looking at his miniature, that it was remarkably well painted, and that, in his happier days, he had been something of a judge of the art."

Impatient to see the stranger, who, he did not doubt, was Virginia's father, Clarence Hervey went the next Sunday to the

Asylum; but no such gentleman appeared, and all that he could learn, respecting him, was, that he had applied to one of the directors of the institution, for leave to see and question the girls, in hopes of finding amongst them his lost daughter; that in the course of the week, he had seen all those who were not at church the last Sunday. None of the directors knew any thing more concerning him; but the porter remarked, that he came in a very handsome coach, and one of the girls of the Asylum said, that he gave her half a guinea, because she was a little like *his poor Rachel, who was dead*; but that he had added, with a sigh, "This cannot be my daughter, for she is only thirteen, and my girl, if she be now living, must be nearly eighteen."

The age, the name, every circumstance confirmed Mr Hervey in the belief, that this stranger was the father of Virginia, and he was disappointed and provoked by having missed the opportunity of seeing or speaking to him. It occurred to Clarence, that the gentleman might probably visit the Foundling Hospital, and thither he immediately went, to make inquiries. He was told that a person, such as he described, had been there about a month before, and had compared the faces of the oldest girls with a little picture of a child: that he gave money to several of the girls, but that they did not know his name, or any thing more about him.

Mr Hervey now inserted proper advertisements in all the papers, but without producing any effect. At last, recollecting what Mr Moreton told him of the stranger's love of pictures, he determined to put his portrait of Virginia into the exhibition, in hopes that the gentleman might go there and ask some questions about it, which might lead to a discovery. The young artist, who had painted this picture, was under particular obligations to Clarence, and he promised that he would faithfully comply with his request, to be at Somerset-house regularly every morning, as soon as the exhibition opened; that he would stay there till it closed, and watch whether any of the spectators were particularly struck with the portrait of Virginia. If any person should ask questions respecting the picture, he was to let Mr Hervey know immediately, and to give the inquirer his address.

Now it happened, that the very day, when Lady Delacour and Belinda were at the exhibition, the painter called Clarence aside and informed him, that a gentleman had just inquired from him very eagerly, whether the picture of Virginia was a portrait. This gentleman proved to be, not the stranger who had been at the

Asylum, but an eminent jeweller, who told Mr Hervey, that his curiosity about the picture arose merely from its striking likeness to a miniature, which had been lately left at his house to be new set. It belonged to a Mr Hartley, a gentleman who had made a considerable fortune in the West Indies, but who was prevented from enjoying his affluence by the loss of an only daughter, of whom the miniature was a portrait, taken when she was not more than four or five years old. When Clarence heard all this, he was extremely impatient to know where Mr Hartley was to be found; but the jeweller could only tell him, that the miniature had been called for the preceding day by Mr Hartley's servant, who said his master was leaving town in a great hurry to go to Portsmouth, to join the West India fleet, which was to sail with the first favourable wind.

Clarence determined immediately to follow him to Portsmouth; he had not a moment to spare, for the wind was actually favourable, and his only chance of seeing Mr Hartley was by reaching Portsmouth as soon as possible. This was the cause of his taking leave of Belinda in such an abrupt manner: painful indeed were his feelings at that moment, and great the difficulty he felt in parting with her, without giving any explanation of his conduct, which must have appeared to her capricious and mysterious. He was aware, that he had explicitly to Lady Delacour avowed his admiration of Miss Portman, and that in a thousand instances he had betrayed his passion. Yet of her love he dared not trust himself to think, whilst his affairs were in this doubtful state. He had, it is true, some faint hopes, that a change in Virginia's situation might produce an alteration in her sentiments, and he resolved to decide his own conduct by the manner in which she should behave, if her father should be found, and she should become heiress to a considerable fortune. New views might then open to her imagination; the world, the fashionable world in all its glory, would be before her; her beauty and fortune would attract a variety of admirers, and Clarence thought, that perhaps her partiality for him might become less exclusive, when she had more opportunities of choice. If her love arose merely from circumstances, with circumstances it would change; if it were only a disease of the imagination, induced by her seclusion from society, it might be cured by mixing with the world; and then he would be at liberty to follow the dictates of his own heart and declare his attachment to Belinda. But if he should find that change of situation made no alteration in Virginia's sentiments, if her happiness should absolutely depend upon the realisation of those hopes, which he had imprudently excited, he felt that he should be bound to her by all the laws of justice and honour; laws, which no passion could tempt him to break. Full of these ideas, he hurried to Portsmouth in pursuit of Virginia's father. The first question he asked, upon his arrival there, may easily be guessed.

"Has the West India fleet sailed?"

"No: it sails tomorrow at one o'clock," was the answer.

He hastened instantly to make inquiries for Mr Hartley. No such person could be found, no such gentleman was to be heard of any where. *Hartley*, he was sure, was the name which the jeweller mentioned to him, but it was in vain that he repeated it, no Mr Hartley was to be heard of at Portsmouth, except a pawnbroker. At last, a steward of one of the West Indiamen, recollected that a gentleman of that name came over with him in the Effingham, and that he talked of returning in the same vessel to the West Indies, if he should ever leave England again.

"But we have heard nothing of him since, sir," said the steward. "No passage is taken for him with us."

"And my life to a china orange," cried a sailor who was standing by, "he's gone to kingdom come, or more likely to Bedlam afore this, for he was plaguy crazy in his timbers, and his head wanted righting I take it, if it was he, Jack, who used to walk the deck, you know, with a bit of a picture, not so big as *a dead man's eye*, in his hand, to which he seemed to be mumbling his prayers from morning to night. There's no use in sounding for him, master, he's down in Davy's locker long ago, or stowed into the tight waistcoat before this time o'day."

Notwithstanding this knowing sailor's opinion, Clarence would not desist from his sounding, because, having so lately heard of him at different places, he could not believe that he was gone either into Davy's locker, or to Bedlam. He imagined, that by some accident, Mr Hartley had been detained upon the road to Portsmouth; and in the expectation that he would certainly arrive before the fleet should sail, Clarence waited with tolerable patience. He waited, however, in vain; he saw the Effingham and the whole fleet sail – no Mr Hartley arrived. As he hailed one of the boats of the Effingham, which was rowing out with some passengers, who had been too late to get on board, his friend, the sailor, answered:

"We've no crazy man here: I told you, master, he'd never go out no more in the Effingham. He's where I said, master, you'll find, or no where."

Mr Hervey remained some days at Portsmouth, after the fleet had sailed, in hopes that he might yet obtain some information; but none could be had: neither could any farther tidings be obtained from the jeweller, who had first mentioned Mr Hartley. Despairing of success in the object of his journey, he however determined to delay his return to town, for some time, in hopes that absence might efface the impression which had been made on the heart of Virginia. He made a tour along the picturesque coasts of Dorset and Devonshire, and it was during this excursion, that he wrote the letters to Lady Delacour, which have so often been mentioned. He endeavoured to dissipate his thoughts by new scenes and employments; but all his ideas involuntarily centred in Belinda. If he saw new characters, he compared them with hers, or considered how far she would approve or condemn them. The books that he read were perused with a constant reference to what she would think or feel; and during his whole journey he never beheld any beautiful prospect, without wishing that it could at the same instant be seen by Belinda. If her name were mentioned but once in his letters, it were because he dared not trust himself to speak of her; she was for ever present to his mind: but whilst he was writing to Lady Delacour, her idea pressed more strongly upon his heart; he recollected, that it was she who first gave him a just insight into her ladyship's real character; he recollected, that she had joined with him in the benevolent design of reconciling her to Lord Delacour, and of creating in her mind a taste for domestic happiness. This remembrance operated powerfully to excite him to fresh exertions, and the eloquence, which touched Lady Delacour so much in these "*edifying*" letters as she called them, was in fact inspired by Belinda.

Whenever he thought distinctly upon his future plans, Virginia's attachment, and the hopes which he had imprudently inspired, appeared insuperable obstacles to his union with Miss Portman; but, in more sanguine moments, he flattered himself with a confused notion, that these difficulties would vanish. Great were his surprise and alarm, when he received that letter of Lady Delacour's, in which she announced the probability of Belinda's marriage with Mr Vincent. By one of those small unfortunate accidents, which sometimes occur in the most important moments of our lives, he did not receive this letter, till nearly a fortnight after it should have come to his hands. The instant he received it, he set out on his way home; he travelled with all that expedition, which money can command in England: his first thought, and first wish, when he arrived in town, were to go to Lady Delacour's; but he checked his impatience, and proceeded immediately to Twickenham, to have his fate decided by Virginia. It was with the utmost painful sensations, that he saw her again. The accounts, which he received from Mrs Ormond, convinced him, that absence had produced none of the effects, which he expected on the mind of her pupil. Mrs Ormond was naturally both of an affectionate dispostion and a timid temper; she had become excessively fond of Virginia, and her anxiety was more than in proportion to her love; it sometimes balanced and even overbalanced her regard and respect for Clarence Hervey himself. When he spoke of his attachment to Belinda, and of his doubts respecting Virginia, she could no longer restrain her emotion.

"O! indeed! Mrs Hervey," said she, "this is no time for reasoning and doubting. No man in his senses — no man, who is not wilfully blind, could doubt her being distractedly fond of you."

"I am sorry for it," said Clarence.

"And why? O, why, Mr Hervey? Don't you recollect the time, when you were all impatience to call her yours — when you thought her the most charming creature in the whole world?"

"I had not seen Belinda Portman then."

"And I wish to Heaven you never had seen her; but O, surely, Mr Hervey, you will not desert my Virginia! — Must her health, her happiness, her reputation, all be the sacrifice?"

"Reputation, Mrs Ormond!"

"Reputation, Mr Hervey! — you do not know in what light she is considered here; nor did I till lately. But I tell you, her reputation is injured, fatally injured. It is whispered, and more than whispered everywhere, that she is your mistress. A woman came here the other day with the bullfinch, and she looked at me, and spoke in such an extraordinary way, that I was shocked more than I can express. I need not tell you all the particulars; it is enough that I have made inquiries, and am sure, too sure, of what I say, that nothing but your marriage with Virginia can save her reputation; or — "

Mrs Ormond stopped short, for at this instant Virginia entered the room, walking in her slow manner, as if she were in a deep reverie.

"Since my return," said Clarence, in an embarrassed voice, "I have scarcely heard a syllable from Miss St Pierre's lips."

"*Miss St Pierre*! – He used to call me Virginia," said she, turning to Mrs Ormond – "he is angry with me – He used to call me Virginia."

"But you were a child then, you know, my love," said Mrs Ormond.

"And I wish I was still a child," said Virginia – Then, after a long pause, she approached Mr Hervey with extreme timidity, and opening a port-folio, which lay on the table, she said to him:

"If you are at leisure – if I do not interrupt you – would you look at these drawings; though they are not worth your seeing, except as proofs, that *I can* conquer my natural indolence?"

The drawings were views, which she had painted from memory, of scenes in the New Forest, near her grandmother's cottage. That cottage was drawn with an exactness, that proved how fresh it was in her remembrance. Many recollections rushed forcibly into Clarence Hervey's mind, at the sight of this cottage. The charming image of Virginia, as it first struck his fancy; the smile, the innocent affectionate smile, with which she offered him the finest rose in her basket; the stern voice, in which her grandmother spoke to her; the prophetic fear of her protectress; the figure of the dying woman; the solemn promise he made to her; all recurred, in rapid succession, to his memory.

"You don't seem to like that," said Virginia; and then putting another drawing into his hands, "perhaps this may please you better."

"They are beautiful; they are surprisingly well done!" exclaimed he.

"I knew he would like them! I told you so!" cried Mrs Ormond, in a triumphant tone.

"You see," said Virginia, "that though you have heard scarcely a syllable from Miss St Pierre's lips, since your return, yet she has not been unmindful of your wishes in your absence. You told her, some time ago, that you wished she would try to improve in drawing. She has done her best. But do not trouble yourself to look at them any longer," said Virginia, taking one of her drawings from his hand; "I merely wanted to show you, that though I have no genius, I have some –"

Her voice faltered so, that she could not pronounce the word *gratitude*.

Mrs Ormond pronounced it for her; and added, "I can answer for it, that Virginia is not ungrateful."

"Ungrateful!" repeated Clarence; "Who ever thought her so! Why did you put these ideas into her mind?"

Virginia, resting her head on Mrs Ormond's shoulder, wept bitterly.

"You have worked upon her sensibility, till you have made her miserable," cried Clarence, angrily. "Virginia, listen to me; look at me," said he, affectionately taking her hand: but she pressed closer to Mrs Ormond, and would not raise her head. "Do not consider me as your master – your tyrant – do not imagine that I think you ungrateful!"

"O, I am – I am – I am ungrateful to you," cried she, sobbing; "but Mrs Ormond never told me so: do not blame her; she has never worked upon my sensibility. Do you think," said she, looking up, while a transient expression of indignation passed over her countenance – "do you think I cannot *feel* without having been taught?"

Clarence uttered a deep sigh.

"But if you feel too much, my dearest Virginia – if you give way to your feelings, in this manner," said Mrs Ormond, "you will make both yourself and Mr Hervey unhappy!"

"Heaven forbid! – The first wish of my soul is – " She paused – "I should be the most ungrateful wretch in the world, if I were to make him unhappy."

"But if he sees you miserable, Virginia?"

"Then he shall not see it," said she, wiping the tears from her face.

"To imagine that you were unhappy, and that you concealed it from us, would be still worse," said Clarence.

"But why should you imagine it?" replied Virginia; "you are too good, too kind: but do not fancy that I am not happy; I am sure I ought to be happy."

"Do you regret your cottage?" said Clarence: "these drawings show how well you remember it."

Virginia coloured; and with some hesitation answered: "Is it my fault, if I cannot forget?"

"You were happier then, Virginia, than you are now, you will confess," said Mrs Ormond, who was not a woman of refined delicacy, and who thought, that the best chance she had of working upon Mr Hervey's sense of honour, was, by making it plain to him, how much her pupil's affections were engaged.

Virginia made no answer to this question, and her silence touched Clarence more than any thing she could have said. When Mrs Ormond repeated her question, he relieved the trembling girl, by saying:

"My dear Mrs Ormond, confidence must be won, not demanded."

"I have no right to *insist* upon confessions, I know," said Mrs Ormond; "but – "

"Confessions – I do not wish to conceal anything; but I think, sincerity is not *always*, in our sex, consistent with – I mean – I don't know what I mean – what I say – or what I ought to say," cried Virginia; and she sunk down on a sofa, in extreme confusion.

"Why will you agitate her, Mrs Ormond, in this manner?" said Mr Hervey with an expression of sudden anger. It was succeeded by a look of such tender compassion for Virginia, that Mrs Ormond rejoiced to have excited his anger: at any price, she wished to serve her beloved pupil.

"Do not be in the least apprehensive, my dear Virginia, that we should take ungenerous advantage of the openness and simplicity of your character," said Mr Hervey.

"O, no, no; I cannot, do not apprehend anything ungenerous from you – you are – you ever have been my best, my most generous friend! But I fear that I have not the simplicity of character, the openness that you imagine: and yet I am sure – I wish, from the bottom of my heart – I wish to do right, if I knew how. But there is not one, no not one person in the whole world," continued she, her eyes moving from Mrs Ormond to Mr Hervey, and from him to Mrs Ormond again – "Not one person in the whole world I dare – I ought to lay my heart open to. I have, perhaps, said more than is proper already. But this I know," added she in a firm tone, rising, and addressing herself to Clarence: "*You* shall never be made unhappy by me. And do not think about my happiness much," said she, forcing a smile. "I am, I will be perfectly happy; only let me always know your wishes, your sentiments, your feelings, and by them I will, as I ought, regulate mine."

"Amiable, charming, generous girl!" cried Clarence.

"Take care," said Mrs Ormond; "take care, Virginia, lest you promise more than you can perform. Wishes, and feelings, and sentiments, are not to be so easily regulated."

"I did not, I believe, say it was easy; but I hope it is possible," replied Virginia; "I promise nothing but what I am able to perform."

"I doubt it," said Mrs Ormond, shaking her head; "you *are* — you *will* be perfectly happy. O, Virginia, my love, do not deceive yourself; do not deceive us so terribly. I am sorry to put you to the blush; but" —

"Not a word more, my dear madam; I beg — I insist," said Mr Hervey, in a commanding tone; but, for the first time in her life, regardless of him, she persisted.

"I only ask you to call to mind, my dearest Virginia," said she, taking her hand, "the morning that you screamed in your sleep, the morning when you told me the frightful dream — Were you perfectly happy then?"

"It is easy to force my thoughts from me," said Virginia, withdrawing her hand from Mrs Ormond; "but it is cruel to do so." And with an air of offended dignity she passed them, and quitted the room.

"I wish to Heaven!" exclaimed Mrs Ormond, "that Miss Portman was married, and out of the way — I shall never forgive myself! We have used this poor girl cruelly amongst us: she loves you to distraction, and I have encouraged her passion, and I have betrayed her — O, fool that I was! I told her, that she would certainly be your wife."

"You have told her so! — Did I not charge you, Mrs Ormond — "

"Yes but I could not help it; when I saw the sweet girl fading away — and, besides, I am sure she thought it, from your manner, long and long before I told it to her. Do you forget, how fond of her you were scarce one short year ago? And do you forget, how plainly you let her see your passion? O, how can you blame her, if she loves you, and if she is unhappy?"

"I blame no one but myself," cried Clarence. "I must abide by the consequences of my own folly. — Unhappy! — she shall not be unhappy; she does not deserve to be so."

He walked backward and forward, with hasty steps, for some minutes; then sat down, and wrote a letter to Virginia.

When he had finished it, he put it into Mrs Ormond's hands.

"Read it – seal it – give it to her – and let her answer be sent to town to me, at Dr X —'s, in Clifford street."

Mrs Ormond clasped her hands, in an ecstasy of joy, as she glanced her eye over the letter, for it contained an offer of his hand. –

"This is like yourself; like what I always knew you to be, dear Mr Hervey!" she exclaimed.

But her exclamation was lost upon him. When she looked up to repeat her praises, she perceived he was gone. After the effort which he had made, he wished for time to tranquillise his mind, before he should again see Virginia: what her answer to this letter would be, he could not doubt; his fate was now decided, and he determined immediately to write to Lady Delacour, to explain his situation: he felt, that he had not sufficient fortitude at this moment to make such an explanation in person. With all the strength of his mind, he endeavoured to exclude Belinda from his thoughts, but *curiosity* – (for he would suffer himself to call it by no other name) – curiosity to know whether she were actually engaged to Mr Vincent, obtruded itself with such force, that it could not be resisted.

From Dr X — he thought he could obtain full information, and he hastened immediately to town. When he got to Clifford street, he found that the doctor was not at home; his servant said, he might probably be met with at Mrs Margaret Delacour's, as he usually finished his morning rounds at her house. Thither Mr Hervey immediately went.

The first sound that he heard, as he went up her stairs, was the screaming of a macaw; and the first person he saw through the open door of the drawing-room, was Helena Delacour. She was standing with her back to him, leaning over the macaw's cage, and he heard her say, in a joyful tone,

"Yes; though you do scream so frightfully, my pretty macaw, I love you as well as Marriott ever did. When my dear, good Miss Portman sent this macaw – My dear aunt! here's Mr Hervey! – You were just wishing to see him."

"Mr Hervey," said the old lady, with a benevolent smile, "your little friend Helena tells you truth. We were just wishing for you. I am sure it will give you pleasure to hear, that I am at last a convert to your opinion of Lady Delacour. She has given up all those that I used to call her rantipole acquaintance. She has reconciled herself to her husband, and to his friends; and Helena is to go home to live with her. Here is a charming note, I have just received from her! Dine with me on Thursday next, and you will meet her ladyship, and see a happy family party. You have had some share in *the reformation*, I know, and that was the reason I wished that you should be with us on Thursday. You see, I am not an obstinate old woman, though I was cross the first day I saw you at Lady Anne Percival's – I found I was mistaken in your character, and I am glad of it. But this note of Lady Delacour's seems to have struck you dumb."

There were, indeed, a few words in this note, which deprived him, for some moments, of all power of utterance.

"The report you have heard (unlike most other reports) is perfectly well founded. Belinda Portman is going to be married to Mr Vincent. – I will bring him with us on Thursday."

Mr Hervey was relieved from the necessity of accounting to Mrs Delacour for his sudden embarrassment, by the entrance of Dr X — and another gentleman, of whom, in the confusion of his mind, he did not at first take any notice. Dr X — , with his usual mixture of benevolence and raillery, addressed himself to Clarence, whilst the stranger took out of his pocket some papers, and, in a low voice, entered earnestly into conversation with Mrs Delacour.

"Now tell me, if you can, Clarence," said Dr X — , which of your three mistresses you like best? I think I left you some months ago in great doubt upon this subject. – Are you still in that philosophic state?"

"No;" said Clarence, "all doubts are over – I am going to be married."

"Bravo! – But you look as if you were going to be hanged. May I, as it will so soon be in the newspaper – may I ask the name of the fair lady?"

"Virginia St Pierre – You shall know her history and mine when we are alone," said Mr Hervey, lowering his voice.

"You need not lower your voice," said Dr X — , "for Mrs Delacour is, as you see, so much taken up with her own affairs, that she has no curiosity for those of her neighbours; and Mr Hartley is as busy as – "

"Mr who? Mr Hartley! did you say," interrupted Clarence, eagerly, turning his eyes upon the stanger, who was a middle-aged gentleman, exactly answering the description of the person who had been at the Asylum in search of his daughter. —

"Mr Hartley! yes. What astonishes you so much?" said Dr X——, calmly. "He is a West Indian. I met him in Cambridgeshire last summer, at his friend Mr Horton's; he has been very generous to the poor people who suffered by the fire, and he is now consulting with Mrs Delacour, who has an estate adjoining to Mr Horton's, about her tenants, whose houses in the village were burnt. Now I have, in as few words and parenthesises as possible, told you all I know of Mr Hartley's history; but your curiosity still looks voracious."

"I want to know whether he have a miniature?" said Clarence, hastily. "Introduce me to him, for Heaven's sake, directly!"

"Mr Hartley," cried the doctor, raising his voice, "give me leave to introduce my friend Mr Hervey to you, and to your miniature picture, if you have one."

Mr Hartley sighed profoundly, as he drew from his bosom a small portrait, which he put into Hervey's hands, saying, "Alas! sir, you cannot, I fear, give me any tidings of the original; it is the picture of a daughter, whom I have never seen since she was an infant – whom I never shall see again."

Clarence instantly knew it to be Virginia; but as he was upon the point of making some joyful exclamation, he felt Dr X —— touch his shoulder, and looking up at Mr Hartley, he saw in his countenance such strong workings of passion, that he prudently repressed his own emotion, and calmly said – "It would be cruel, sir, to give you false hopes."

"It would kill me, it would kill me, sir! – or worse! – worse! a thousand times worse!" cried Mr Hartley, putting his hand to his forehead. "What," continued he, impatiently – "what was the meaning of the look you gave, when you first saw that picture? Speak, if you have any humanity! Did you ever see any one that resembles that picture?"

"I have seen, I think, a picture," said Clarence Hervey, "that has some resemblance to it."

"When? where? — "

"My good sir," said Dr X ——, "let me recommend it to you to consider, that there is scarcely any possibility of judging, from the features of children, of what their faces may be when they grow up. Nothing can be more fallacious than these accidental resemblances between the pictures of children and of grown up people."

Mr Hartley's countenance fell.

"But," added Clarence Hervey, "you will perhaps, sir, think it worth your while to see the picture of which I speak; you can see it at Mr F — 's,. the painter, in Newman-street; and I will accompany you thither whenever you please."

"This moment, if you would have the goodness! My carriage is at the door; and Mrs Delacour will be so kind to excuse — "

"O, make no apologies to me at such a time as this," said Mrs Delacour. — "Away with you, gentlemen, as soon as you please; upon condition, that if you have any good news to tell, some of you will remember, in the midst of your joy, that such an old woman as Mrs Margaret Delacour exists, who loves to hear *good* news of those who deserve it."

It was so late in the day, when they got to Newman-street, that they were obliged to light candles. Trembling with eagerness, Mr Hartley drew near, while Clarence held the light to the picture.

"It is so like," said he, looking at his miniature, "that I dare not believe my senses. Dr X — , said he, pray do you look. My head is so dizzy, and my eyes so — What do you think, sir? What do you say, doctor?"

"That the likeness is certainly striking – but this seems to be a fancy piece."

"A fancy piece!" repeated Mr Hartley, with terror; — "Why then did you bring me here? – A fancy piece!"

"No, sir; it is a portrait," said Clarence; "and if you will be calm, I will tell you more. — "

"I will be calm; – only – is she alive?"

"The lady, of whom this is the portait, is alive," replied Clarence Hervey, who was obliged to exert his utmost command over himself, to maintain that composure, which he saw was necessary; "the lady, of whom this is the portait, is alive, and you shall see her tomorrow."

"O, why not now? Cannot I see her now? I must see her to night: this instant, sir!"

"It is impossible," said Mr Hervey, "that you should see her this instant, for she is some miles off, at Twickenham."

"It is too late to go thither now; you cannot think of it, Mr Hartley," continued Dr X — , in a tone of command, to which he yielded more readily than to reason.

Clarence had the presence of mind to recollect, that it would be necessary to prepare poor Virginia for this meeting, and he sent a messenger immediately, to request that Mrs Ormond would communicate the intelligence with all the caution in her power.

The next morning, Mr Hartley and Mr Hervey set off together for Twickenham. In their way thither, Clarence gradually confirmed Mr Hartley in the belief, that Virginia was his daughter, by relating all the circumstances, that he had learned from her grandmother, and from Mrs Smith, the farmer's wife, with whom she had formerly been acquainted: the name, the age, every particular, as it was disclosed, heightened his security and his joy. There was one slight mark, however, which, he said, would identify his child more satisfactorily to his own mind, than any collateral proofs; he knew, that his daughter, when she was an infant, had a little mole just above her right temple.

"I looked for this," added he, "in her picture yesterday; but, probably, as the painter might think it a defect, he would have omitted it; and, besides, the hair shaded the spot where it should have been."

For some time Mr Hartley's mind was so intent upon this mole, that he could not listen to any thing, and Clarence could not satisfy him on this point; but, at last, he engaged his attention, and suspended his anxiety, by giving him a history of his own connexion with Virginia, from the day of his first discovering her in the New Forest, to the letter which he had just written, to offer her his hand. The partiality, which it was suspected Virginia felt for him, was the only circumstance which he suppressed, because, notwithstanding all Mrs Ormond had said, and all he had himself heard and seen, his obstinate incredulity required confirmation under her own hand, or positively from her own lips. He still fancied it was possible, that change of situation might alter her views and sentiments; and he earnestly entreated, that she might be left entirely to her own decision. It was necessary to make this stipulation with her father; for, in the excess of his gratitude for the kindness, which Clarence had shown to her, he protested, that he should look upon her as a monster if she did not love him: he added, that if Mr Hervey had not a farthing, he should prefer him to every man upon earth: he, however, promised, that he would conceal his wishes, and that his daughter should act entirely from the dictates of her own mind. In the fullness of his heart, he told Clarence all those circumstances of his conduct towards Virginia's mother, which had filled his soul with remorse. She was scarcely sixteen, when he ran away with her from a boarding-school; he was at that time a gay officer, she a sentimental girl, who had been spoiled by early novel-reading. Her father had a small place at court, lived beyond his fortune, educated his daughter, to whom he could give no portion, as if she were to be heiress to a large estate; then died, and left his widow absolutely in penury. This widow was the old lady, who lived in the cottage in the New Forest. It was just at the time of her husband's death, and of her own distress, that she heard of the elopement of her daughter from school. Mr Hartley's parents were so much incensed by the match, that he was prevailed upon to separate from his wife, and to go abroad, to push his fortune in the army. His marriage had been secret, his own friends disavowed it, notwithstanding the repeated, urgent entreaties of his wife, and of her mother, who was her only surviving relation. His wife, on her deathbed, wrote, to urge him to take charge of his daughter; and, to make the appeal stronger to his feelings, she sent him a picture of his little girl, who was then about four years old. Mr Hartley, however, was intent upon forming a new connexion with the rich widow of a planter in Jamaica. He married the widow, took possession of her fortune, and all his affections soon were fixed upon a son, for whom he formed, even from the moment of his birth, various schemes of aggrandisement: the boy lived till he was about ten years old, when he caught a fever, which at that time raged in Jamaica, and, after a few days illness, died. His mother was carried off by the same disease; and Mr Hartley, left alone in the midst of his wealth, felt how insufficient it was to happiness. Remorse now seized him: in the desertion of his daughter he could not rest, but returned to England in search of her. To this neglected child he now looked forward, for the peace and happiness of the remainder of his life. Disappointment in all his inquiries for some months preyed upon his spirits to such a degree, that his intellects were at times disordered: this derangement was the cause of his not sooner recovering his child. He was in confinement, during the time that Clarence Hervey's advertisements were inserted in the papers; and his illness was also the cause of his not going to Portsmouth, and sailing in the Effingham, as he had originally intended. So that the sailor's conjecture, after all, was right, or nearly so. The history of his connexion with Mr Horton would be uninteresting to the reader; it is enough to say, that he was prevailed upon, by that gentleman, to spend some time in the country with him, for the recovery of his health. And it was there, that he became acquainted with Dr X—, who introduced him, as we have seen, to Mrs Margaret Delacour, at whose house he met Clarence Hervey. This is the most succinct account, that we can give of him and his affairs. His own account was ten times as long; but we spare readers his incoherencies and reflections, because, perhaps, they are in a hurry to get to Twickenham, and to hear of his meeting with Virginia.

Mrs Ormond found it no easy task, to prepare Virginia for the sight of Mr Hartley. Virginia had scarcely ever spoken of her father; but the remembrance of things, which she had heard of him from her grandmother, was fresh in her mind; she had often pictured him in her fancy, and she had secretly nourished the hope, that she should not for ever be a *deserted child*. Mrs Ormond had observed, that in those romances, of which Virginia was so fond, every thing that related to children, who were deserted by their parents, or to their sudden discovery, affected her strongly.

The belief in what the French call *la force du sang** was suited to her affectionate temper and ardent imagination, and it had taken full possession of her mind. The eloquence of romance persuaded her, that she should not only discover, but love her father with intuitive filial piety, and she longed to experience those *yearnings* of affection, of which she had read so much.

The first moment that Mrs Ormond began to speak of Mr Clarence Hervey's hopes of discovering her father, she was transported with joy.

"My *father*! – How delightful that word *father* sounds! – My father! – May I say, *my* father? – And will he own me, and will he love me, and will he give me his blessing, and will he fold me in his arms, and call me his daughter, his dear daughter? – O, how I shall love him! I will make it the whole business of my life to please him!"

"The *whole* business?" said Mrs Ormond, smiling.

"Not the whole," said Virginia; "I hope my father will like Mr Hervey. Did not you say, that he is rich? I wish, that my father may be *very* rich."

"That is the last wish, that I should have expected to hear from you, my Virginia."

"But do not you know why I wish it? – That I may show my gratitude to Mr Hervey."

"My dear child," said Mrs Ormond, "these are most generous sentiments, and worthy of you; but do not let your imagination run away with you at this rate – Mr Hervey is rich enough."

"I wish he was poor," said Virginia, that I might make him rich."

"He would not love you the better, my dear," said Mrs Ormond, "if you had the wealth of the Indies. Perhaps, your father may not be rich; therefore, do not set your heart upon this idea."

Virginia sighed – fear succeeded to hope, and her imagination immediately reversed the bright picture, that it had drawn.

"But I am afraid," said she, "that this gentleman is not my father – how disappointed I shall be! I wish you had never told me all this, my dear Mrs Ormond."

"I would not have told it to you, if Mr Hervey had not desired that I should; and, you may be sure, he would not have desired it, unless he had good reason to believe, that you would not be disappointed."

"But he is not sure – he does not say, he is quite sure. And, even if I were quite certain of his being my father, how can I be certain, that he will not disown me – he, who has deserted me so long? My grandmother, I remember, often used to say, that he had no natural affection."

"Your grandmother was mistaken then, for he has been searching for his child all over England, Mr Hervey says; and he has almost lost his senses with grief, and with remorse."

"Remorse!"

"Yes; remorse – for, having so long deserted you, he fears, that you will hate him."

"Hate him! – Is it possible to hate a father?" said Virginia.

"He dreads, that you should never forgive him."

"Forgive him! – I have read of parents forgiving their children; but I never remember, to have read of a daughter forgiving her father. – *Forgive*! You should not have used that word. I cannot *forgive* my father; but I can love him, and I will make him quite forget all his sorrows – I mean, all his sorrows about me."

After this conversation, Virginia spent her time in imagining, what sort of person her father would be; whether he was like Mr Hervey; what words he would say; where he would sit; whether he would sit beside her; and, above all, whether he would give her his blessing.

"I am afraid," said she, "of liking my father better than *any body else*."

"No danger of that, my dear," said Mrs Ormond, smiling.

"I am glad of it; for it would be very wrong and *ungrateful*, to like anything in this world so well as Mr Hervey."

The carriage now came to the door: Mrs Ormond instantly ran to the window, but Virginia had not power to move – her heart beat violently.

"Is he come?" said she.

"Yes, he is getting out of the carriage this moment!"

Virginia stood with her eyes eagerly fixed upon the door – "Hark!" said she, laying her hand upon Mrs Ormond's arm to prevent her from moving – "Hush! that we may hear his voice."

She was breathless – No voice was to be heard – "They are not coming," said she, turning as pale as death. An instant afterward her colour returned – She heard the steps of two people coming up the stairs.

"His step! – Do you hear it? – Is it my father?"

Virginia's imagination was worked to the highest pitch, she could scarcely sustain herself: Mrs Ormond supported her. At this instant her father appeared.

"My child! – the image of her mother!" exclaimed he – stopping short – he sunk upon a chair.

"My father!" cried Virginia, springing forward, and throwing herself at his feet.

"The voice of her mother!" said Mr Hartley – "My daughter! – My long lost child!"

He tried to raise her, but could not; her arms were clasped round his knee, her face rested upon it, and when he stooped to kiss her cheek, he found it cold. – She had fainted.

When she came to her senses, and found herself in her father's arms, she could scarcely believe that it was not a dream.

He parted the ringlets of her fine hair, and found the mole on her forehead. The delighted father kissed it in a transport of joy and tenderness.

"Your blessing! – give me your blessing, and then I shall know that you are indeed my father!" cried Virgina, kneeling to him, and looking up with an enthusiastic expression of filial piety in her countenance.

"God bless you, my sweet child!" said he, laying his hand upon her – "and God forgive your father!"

"My grandmother died without giving me her blessing," said Virginia, "but now I have been blessed by my father! – Happy! happy moment! – O that she could look down from Heaven, and see us at this instant!"

It is sometimes prudent to draw a veil over the excess of joy, as well as of grief. There are scenes, which may be imagined, but which cannot be described.

Virginia was so much astonished and overpowered by this sudden discovery of a parent, and by the novelty of his first caresses, that after the first violent effervescence of her sensibility was over, she might, to an indifferent spectator, have appeared stupid and insensible. Mrs Ormond, though far from an indifferent spectator, was by no means a penetrating judge of the human heart; she seldom saw more than the external symptoms of feeling, and she was apt to be rather impatient with her friends, if theirs did not accord with her own.

"Virginia, my dear," said she, in rather a reproachful tone, "Mr Hervey, you see, has left the room, on purpose to leave you at full liberty to talk to your father; and I am going – but you are so silent?"

"I have so much to say, and my heart is so full!" – said Virginia.

"Yes, I know you told me of a thousand things, that you had to say to your father, before you saw him."

"But now I see him, I have forgotten them all. I can think of nothing but of him."

"Of him and Mr Hervey," said Mrs Ormond.

"I was not thinking of Mr Hervey at that moment," said Virginia, blushing.

"Well, my love, I will leave you to think and talk of what you please," said Mrs Ormond, smiling significantly as she left the room.

Mr Hartley folded his daughter in his arms with the fondest expressions of parental affection, and he was upon the point of telling her how much he approved of the choice of her heart; but he recollected his promise, and he determined to sound her inclinations farther, before he even mentioned the name of Clarence Hervey.

He began, by representing to her all that was in his power and his wish to bestow. He painted the pleasures of the world, that world, from which she had hitherto been secluded.

She heard him with simple indifference: not even her curiosity was excited.

He observed, that though she had no curiosity to see, it was natural that she must have some pleasure in the thoughts of being seen.

"What pleasure?" said Virginia.

"The pleasure of being admired and loved: beauty and grace such as yours, my child, cannot be seen without commanding admiration and love."

"I do not want to be admired," replied Virginia, "and I want to be loved by those only whom I love."

"My dearest daughter, you shall be entirely your own mistress, I will never interfere, directly or indirectly, in the disposal of your heart."

At these last words, Virginia, who had listened to all the rest unmoved, took her father's hand, and kissed it repeatedly.

"Now that I have found you, my darling child, let me at least make you happy, if I can – It is the only atonement in my power; it will be the only solace of my declining years. All that wealth can bestow — "

"Wealth!" interrupted Virginia – "Then you have wealth?"

"Yes, my child – may it make you happy! that is all the enjoyment I expect from it. – It shall all be yours."

"And may I do what I please with it? – O then it will indeed make me happy. I will give it all, all to Mr Hervey. How delightful to have something to *give* to Mr Hervey!"

"And had you never any thing to give to Mr Hervey till now?"

"Never! never! he has given me every thing: now – O joyful day! – I can prove to him that Virginia is not ungrateful!"

"Dear generous girl," said her father, wiping the tears from his eyes, "what a daughter have I found! But tell me, my child," continued he, smiling; "do you think Mr Hervey will be content if you give him only your fortune? Do you think that he would accept the fortune without the heart? – Nay, do not turn away that dear blushing face from me: remember it is *your father* who speaks to you.

"Mr Hervey will not take your fortune without yourself, I am afraid – What shall we do? Must I refuse him your hand?"

"Refuse him! do you think that I could refuse him any thing, who has given me every thing? – I should be a monster indeed! There is no sacrifice I would not make, no exertion of which I am not capable, for Mr Hervey's sake. But my dear father," said she, changing her tone, "he never asked for my hand, till yesterday."

"But he had won your heart long ago, I see," thought her father.

"I have written an answer to his letter; will you look at it, and tell me if you approve of it."

"I do approve of it, my darling child: – I will not read it – I know what it must be – he has a right to the preference he has so nobly earned."

"O, he has! he has indeed," cried Virginia with an expression of strong feeling, "and now is the time to show him that I am not ungrateful."

"How I love you for this, my child!" cried her father, fondly embracing her.

"This is exactly what I wished, though I did not dare to say so, till I was sure of your sentiments. Mr Hervey charged me to leave you entirely to yourself; he thought that your new situation might perhaps produce some change in your sentiments: I see he was mistaken, and I am heartily glad of it — But you are going to say something, my dear, do not let me interrupt you."

"I was only going to beg, that you would give this letter, my dear father, to Mr Hervey. It is an answer to one, which he wrote to me when I was poor" – *and deserted* – she was near saying, but she stopped herself.

"I wish," continued she, "Mr Hervey should know, that my sentiments are precisely the same now, that they have always been. Tell him," added she, proudly, "that he did me injustice, by imagining that my sentiments could alter with my situation. He little knows Virginia."

Clarence at this moment entered the room, and Mr Hartley eagerly led his daughter to meet him.

"Take her hand," cried he – "you have her heart – you deserve it – and she has just been very angry with me for doubting. – But read her letter, that will speak better for her, and more to your satisfaction, no doubt, than I can."

Virginia hastily put the letter into Mr Hervey's hand, and breaking from her father, retired to her own apartment.

With all the trepidation of a person, who feels that the happiness of his life is to be decided in a few moments, Clarence tore open Virginia's letter, and conscious that he was not able to command his emotion, he withdrew from her father's inquiring eyes. Mr Hartley, however, saw nothing in this agitation, but what he thought natural to a lover, and he was delighted to perceive, that his daughter had inspired so strong a passion.

Virginia's letter contained but these few lines.

"Most happy shall I be, if the whole of my future life can prove to you how deeply I feel your goodness."

"VIRGINIA ST PIERRE."

An acceptance so direct left Clarence no alternative: his fate was decided. He determined immediately to force himself to see Belinda and Mr Vincent, for he fancied, that his mind would be more at ease, when he had convinced himself by ocular demonstration, that she was absolutely engaged to another; that consequently, even if he were free, he could have no chance of gaining her affections. There are moments, when we desire the conviction, which at another time would overwhelm us with despair. It was in this temper, that Mr Hervey paid his visit to Lady Delacour; but we have seen, that he was unable to support, for many minutes, that philosophic composure, to which, at his first entrance into the room, he had worked up his mind. The tranquillity, which he had expected would be the consequence of this visit, he was farther than ever from obtaining. The extravagant joy, with which Lady Delacour received him, and an indescribable something in her manner, when she looked from him to Belinda, and from Belinda to Mr Vincent, persuaded him her ladyship wished that he were in Mr Vincent's place. The idea was so delightful, that his soul was entranced, and for a few minutes Virginia, and everything that related to her, vanished from his remembrance. It was whilst he was in this state, that Lady Delacour (as the reader may recollect) invited him into her lord's dressing-room, to tell her the contents of the packet, which had not then reached her hands. The request suddenly recalled him to his senses, but he felt that he was not at this moment able to trust himself to her ladyship's penetration; he therefore referred her to his letter for that explanation, which he dreaded to make in person, and he escaped from Belinda's presence, resolving never more to expose himself to such danger.

What effect this packet produced on Lady Delacour's mind, and whether she forgave Belinda for the steadiness of her attachment to Mr Vincent, we shall not at present stop to inquire; but having brought up Clarence Hervey's affairs to the present day, we shall continue his history.

CHAPTER XXVIII

E O

Though Clarence Hervey was not much disposed to see either Virginia or her father, whilst he was in the state of perturbation, into which he had been thrown by his interview with Belinda; yet he did not delay to send his servant home, with a note to Mrs Ormond, to say that he would meet Mr Hartley, whenever he pleased, at his lawyer's, to make whatever arrangements might be necessary for proper settlements.

As he saw no possibility of receding with honour, he, with becoming resolution, desired to urge things forward as fast as possible, and to strengthen in his mind the sense of the *necessity* of the sacrifice, that he was bound to make. His passions were naturally impetuous; but he had, by persevering efforts, brought them under the subjection of his reason. His power over himself was now to be put to a severe trial.

As he was going to town, he met Lord Delacour, who was riding in the park: he was extremely intent upon his own thoughts, and was anxious to pass unnoticed. In former times, this would have been the most feasible thing imaginable; for Lord Delacour used to detest the sight of Clarence Hervey, whom he considered as the successor of Colonel Lawless in his lady's favour; but his opinion and his feelings had been entirely changed by the perusal of those letters, which were perfumed with attar of roses: even that perfume had from agreeable association become agreeable to him. He now accosted Clarence, with a warmth and cordiality in his manner, that at any other moment must have pleased, as much as it surprised him. But Clarence was not in a humour to enter into conversation.

"You seem to be in haste, Mr Hervey," said his lordship, observing his impatience; "but, as I know your good nature, I shall make no scruple to detain you a quarter of an hour."

As he spoke, he turned his horse, and rode with Clarence, who looked as if he wished that his lordship had been more scrupulous, and that he had not such a reputation for good nature.

"You will not refuse me this quarter of an hour, I am sure," continued Lord Delacour, "when you hear that, by favouring me with your attention, you may perhaps materially serve an old – or rather a young friend of yours, and one whom, I once fancied, was a particular favourite – I mean, Miss Belinda Portman."

At the name of Belinda Portman Clarence Hervey became all attention: he assured his lordship, that he was in no haste; and all his difficulty now was, to moderate the eagerness of his curiosity.

"We can take a turn or two in the park, as well as any where," said his lordship. "Nobody will overhear us; and the sooner you know what I have to say, the better."

"Certainly," said Clarence.

The most malevolent person upon earth could not have tried poor Clarence's patience, more than good natured Lord Delacour contrived to do, with the best intentions possible, by his habitual circumlocution.

He descanted at length upon the difficulties, as the world goes, of meeting with a confidential friend, whom it is prudent to trust, in an affair that demands delicacy, honour, and address. Men of talents were often, he observed, devoid of integrity, and men of integrity devoid of talents. When he had obtained Hervey's assent to this proposition, he next paid him sundry handsome, but longwinded compliments: then he complimented himself, for having just thought of Mr Hervey as the fittest person he could apply to: then he congratulated himself upon his good luck, in meeting with the very man he was just thinking of. At last, after Clarence had returned thanks for all his kindness, and had given assent to all his lordship's truisms, the substanace of the business came out.

Lord Delacour informed Mr Hervey, "that he had been lately commissioned, by Lady Delacour, to discover what attractions drew *a* Mr Vincent so constantly to Mrs Luttridge's — "

Here he was going to explain who Mr Vincent was; but Clarence assured him, that he knew perfectly well that he had been a ward of Mr Percival's; that he was a West Indian of large fortune, &c.

"And a lover of Miss Portman's – that is the most material part of the story to *me*," continued Lord Delacour; "for otherwise, you know, Mr Vincent would be no more to me than any other gentleman. But, in that point of view – I mean, as a lover of Belinda Portman, and, I may say, on the very eve of marriage with her – he is highly interesting to my Lady Delacour, and to me, and to you, as Miss Portman's wellwisher, doubtless."

"Doubtless!" was all Mr Hervey could reply.

"Now, you must know," continued his lordship, "that Lady Delacour has, for a woman, an uncommon share of penetration, and can put things together in a wonderful way: in short, it has come to her – (my Lady Delacour's) – knowledge, that, before Miss Portman was at Oakly-park last summer, and after she left it this autumn, Mr Vincent was a constant visitor at Mrs Luttridge's, whilst at Harrowgate, and used to play high (though unknown to the Percivals of course) at billiards, with Mr Luttridge – a *man*, I confess, I disliked *always*, even when I carried the election for them. — But no matter: it is not from enmity I speak now. But it is very well known, that Luttridge has but a small fortune, and yet lives as if he had a large one; and all the young men, who like high play, are sure to be well received at his house. – Now, I hope Mr Vincent is not well received on that footing.

"Since my Lady Delacour and I have been such good friends," continued his lordship, "I have dropped all connexion with the Luttridges, so cannot go there myself; moreover, I do not wish to be tempted to lose any more thousands to the lady: but you never play, and you are not likely to be tempted to it now; so you will oblige me and Lady Delacour, if you will go to Luttridge's to night; she is always charmed to see you, and you will easily discover how the land lies. Mr Vincent is certainly a very agreeable, open-hearted young man; but, if he game, God forbid that Miss Portman should ever be his wife!"

"God forbid!" said Clarence Hervey.

"The man," resumed Lord Delacour, "must, in my opinion, be very superior indeed, who is deserving of Belinda Portman. O! Mr Hervey, you do not – you cannot know her merit, as I do. It is one thing, sir, to see a fine girl in a ballroom, and another – quite another – to live in the house with her for months, and to see her, as I have seen Belinda Portman, in every-day-life, as one may call it. *Then* it is one can judge of the real temper, manners, and character; and never woman had so sweet a temper, such charming manners, such a fair, open, generous, decided, yet gentle character, as this Miss Portman."

"Your lordship speaks *con amore*,"* said Clarence.

"I speak, Mr Hervey, from the bottom of my soul," cried Lord

Delacour, pulling in his horse, and stopping short. "I should be an unfeeling, ungrateful brute, if I were not sensible of the obligations – yes, the obligations – which my Lady Delacour and I have received from Belinda Portman. Why, sir, she has been the peacemaker between us — But we will not talk of that now. Let us think of her affairs. If Mr Vincent once get into Mrs Luttrdige's cursed set, there's no knowing where it will end. I speak from my own experience, for I really never was fond of high play; and yet, when I got into that set, I would not withstand it. I lost by hundreds and thousands; and so will he, before he is aware of it, no doubt. Mrs Luttridge will look upon him as her dupe, and make him such. I always – but this is between ourselves – suspected, that I did not lose my last thousand to her fairly. Now, Hervey, you know the whole, do try and save Mr Vincent, for Belinda Portman's sake."

Clarence Hervey shook hands with Lord Delacour, with a sentiment of real gratitude and affection; and assured him, that his confidence was not misplaced. His lordship little suspected, that he had been soliciting him to save his rival; yet his confidence, as Mr Hervey assured him, was not misplaced. Clarence's love was not of that selfish sort, which, the moment that it is deprived of hope, sinks to indifference, or is converted into hatred. Belinda could not be his; but, in the midst of the bitterest regret, he was supported by the consciousness of his own honour and generosity: he felt a noble species of delight, in the prospect of promoting the happiness of the woman, upon whom his fondest affections had been fixed; and he rejoiced to feel, that he had sufficient magnanimity to save a rival from ruin. He was even determined to make that rival his friend, notwithstanding the prepossession which, he clearly perceived, Mr Vincent felt against him.

"His jealousy will be extinguished, the moment he knows my real situation," said Clarence to himself. "He will be convinced, that I have a soul incapable of envy; and, if he suspect my love for Belinda, he will respect the strength of mind with which I can command my passions. I take it for granted, that Mr Vincent must possess a heart and understanding, such as I should desire in a friend, or could never be – what he is to Belinda."

Full of these generous sentiments, Clarence waited, with impatience, for the hour when he might present himself at Mrs Luttridge's. He went there so early in the evening, that he found the drawing-room quite empty; the company, who had been invited to dine, had not yet left the parlour, and the servants had but just set the card-tables, and lighted the candles. Mr Hervey desired, that nobody should be disturbed by his coming so early; and, fortunately, Mrs Luttridge was detained some minutes by Lady Newland's lingering glass of Madeira. In the mean time, Clarence executed his design. From his former observations, and from the hints that Lord Delacour had let fall, he suspected, that there was sometimes in this house not only high play, but foul play: he recollected, that once, when he played there at billiards, he had perceived that the table was not perfectly horizontal; and it occurred to him that, perhaps, the E O table might be so contrived, as to put the fortunes of all who played at it in the power of the proprietor. Clarence had sufficient ingenuity to invent the method by which this might be done; and he had the infallible means in his possession of detecting the fraud. The E O table was in an apartment adjoining to the drawing-room: he found his way to it; and he discovered, beyond a possibility of doubt, that it was constructed for the purposes of fraud. His first impulse was, to tell this immediately to Mr Vincent, to put him on his guard; but, upon reflection, he determined to keep his discovery to himself, till he was satisfied whether that gentleman had, or had not, any passion for play.

"If he have," thought Clarence, "it is of the utmost consequence to Miss Portman, that he should early in life receive a shock, that may leave an indelible impression upon his mind. To save him a few hours of remorse, I will not give up the power of doing him the most essential service. I will let him go on – if he be so inclined – to the very verge of ruin and despair; I will let him feel all the horrors of gamester's fate, before I tell him, that I have the means to save him. Mrs Luttridge must, when I call upon her, refund whatever he may lose: she will not brave public shame – she cannot stand a public prosecution."

Scarcely had Clarence arranged his scheme, when he heard the voices of the ladies, who were coming from the parlour.

Mrs Luttridge made her appearance, accompanied by a very pretty, modish, affected young lady, Miss Annabella Luttridge, her niece. Her little coquettish airs were lost upon Clarence Hervey, whose eye was intently fixed upon the door, watching for the entrance of Mr Vincent. He was one of the dinner party, and he came upstairs soon after the ladies. He seemed prepared for the sight of Mr Hervey, to whom he bowed with a cold, haughty air; and then addressed himself to Miss Annabella Luttride, who showed the most obvious desire to attract his attention.

From all that passed this evening, Mr Hervey was led to suspect, notwithstanding the reasons which made it apparently improbable, that the fair Annabella was the secret cause of Mr Vincent's frequent visits at her aunt's. It was natural that Clarence should be disposed to this opinion, from the circumstances of his own situation. During three hours, that he staid at Mrs Luttridge's, Mr Vincent never joined any of the parties at play; but, just as he was going away, he heard some one say – "How comes it, Vincent, that you've been idle all night?" This question revived Mr Hervey's suspicions; and, uncertain what report he should make to Lord Delacour, he resolved to defer making any, till he had farther opportunities of judging.

When Mr Hervey asked himself, how it was possible that the pupil of Mr Percival could become a gamester, he forgot that Mr Vincent had not been educated by his guardian; that he had lived in the West Indies, till he was eighteen; and that he had only been under the care of Mr Percival for a few years, after his habits and character were in a great measure formed. The taste for gambling he had acquired whilst he was a child; but, as it was then confined to trifles, it had been passed over, as a thing of no consequence, a boyish folly, that would never grow up with him: his father used to see him, day after day, playing with eagerness, at games of chance, with his negroes, or with the sons of neighbouring planters; yet he was never alarmed; he was too intent upon making a fortune for his family, to consider how they would spend it; and he did not foresee, that this boyish fault might be the means of his son's losing, in a few hours, the wealth which he had been years amassing. When young Vincent came over to England, Mr Percival had not immediate opportunities of discovering this particular foible in his ward; but he perceived, that in his mind there was that presumptuous belief in his special good fortune, which naturally leads to the love of gambling. Instead of lecturing him, his guardian appealed to his understanding, and took opportunities of showing him the ruinous effect of high play in real life. Yong Vincent was touched, and, as he thought, convinced; but his emotion was stronger than his conviction; his feelings were always more powerful than his reason. His detestation of the selfish character of a gamester was felt and expressed

with enthusiasm and eloquence; and his indignation rose afterward, at the slightest hint that *he* might ever in future be tempted,
to become what he abhorred. Unfortunately, he disdained
prudence, as the factitious virtue of inferior minds; he thought,
that the *feelings* of a man of honour were to be his guide, in the
first and last appeal; and for his conduct through life, as a man
and as a gentleman, he proudly professed to trust to the sublime
instinct of a good heart. His guardian's doubts of the infallibility,
and even of the existence, of this moral instinct, wounded Mr
Vincent's pride, instead of alarming his understanding; and he
was rather eager, than averse, to expose himself to the danger,
that he might prove his superiority to the temptation. – How
different are the feelings in different situations! Yet, often as this
has been repeated, how difficult it is to impress the truth upon
inexperienced, sanguine minds! – Whilst young Vincent was
immediately under his guardian's eye at Oakly-park, his safety
from vice appeared to him inglorious; he was impatient to sally
forth into the world, confident rather of his innate than acquired
virtue.

When he first became acquainted with Mrs Luttridge at
Harrowgate, he knew that she was a professed gambler, and he
despised the character; yet, without reflecting on the danger, or
perhaps for the pleasure of convincing Mr Percival that he was
superior to it, he continued his visits. For some time he was a
passive spectator. Billiards, however, was a game of address, not
chance; there was a billiard-table at Oakly-park, as well as at Mr
Luttridge's, and he had played with his guardian. Why then
should he not play with Mr Luttridge? He did play: his skill was
admired; he betted and his bets were successful: but he did not call
this gaming, for the bets were not to any great amount, and it was
only playing at billiards. Mr Percival was delayed in town some
weeks longer than usual, and he knew nothing of the manner in
which his young friend spent his time. As soon as Mr Vincent
heard of his arrival at Oakly-park, he left half finished his game at
billiards; and, fortunately for him, the charms of Belinda made
him forget for some months, that such a thing as a billiard-table
existed. All that had happened at Mr Luttridge's passed from his
mind as a dream; and whilst his heart was agitated by his new
passion, he could scarcely believe, that he had ever been interested
by any other feelings. He was surprised, when he accidentally
recollected the eagerness, with which he used to *amuse* himself in

Mr Luttridge's company; but he was certain, that all this was past
for ever; and precisely because he was under the dominion of one
strong passion, he thought he could never be under the dominion
of another. Thus persisting in his disdain of reason as a moral
guide, Mr Vincent thought, acted, and suffered as a man of
feeling. Scarcely had Belinda left Oakly-park for one week, when
the ennui consequent to violent passion became insupportable;
and to console himself for her absence, he flew to the billiard-
table. Emotion of some kind or other was become necessary to
him; he said that not to feel, was not to live; and soon the
suspense, the anxiety, the hopes, the fears, the perpetual vicissi-
tudes of a gamester's life, appeared to him almost as delightful as
those of a lover's. Deceived by these appearances, Mrs Luttridge
thought that his affection for Belinda either was, or might be
conquered, and her hopes of obtaining his fortune for her niece
Annabella revived. As Mr Vincent could not endure Mrs Freke,
she abstained, at her friend's particular desire, from appearing at
her house whilst he was there, and Mrs Luttridge interested him
much in her own favour, by representing her indignation at
Harriet's conduct to be such, that it had occasioned a total breach
in their friendship. Mrs Freke's sudden departure from
Harrowgate confirmed the probability of this quarrel; yet these
two ladies were secretly leagued together in a design of breaking
off Mr Vincent's match with Belinda, against whom Mrs Freke
had vowed revenge. The anonymous letter, which she hoped
would work her purpose, produced, however, an effect totally
unexpected upon his generous mind – he did not guess the writer;
but his indignation against such base accusations burst forth with
a violence that astounded Mrs Luttridge: his love for Belinda
appeared ten times more enthusiastic than before – the moment
she was accused, he felt himself her defender, as well as her lover.
He was dispossessed of the evil spirit of gambling as if by a
miracle; and the billiard-table, and Mrs Luttridge, and Miss
Annabella vanished from his view. He breathed nothing but love;
he would ask no permission; he would wait for none from
Belinda; he declared that instant he would set out in search of her,
and he would tear that infamous letter to atoms in her presence;
he would show her how impossible suspicion was to his nature.
The first violence of the hurricane Mrs Luttridge could not stand,
and thought not of opposing; but whilst his horses and curricle
were getting ready, she took such an affectionate leave of his dog

Juba, and she protested so much, that she and Annabella should not know how to live without poor Juba, that Mr Vincent, who was excessively fond of his dog, could not help sympathising in their sorrow: reasoning just as well as they wished, he extended his belief in their affection for this animal to friendship, if not love, for his master. He could not grant Mrs Luttridge's earnest supplication to leave the dog behind him, under her protection; but he promised – and laid his hand upon his heart, when he promised – that Juba should wait upon Mrs Luttridge as soon as she went to town. This appointment being made, Miss Annabella permitted herself to be somewhat consoled. It would be injustice to omit, that she did all that could be done by a cambric handkerchief, to evince delicate sensibility in this parting scene. Mrs Luttridge also deserves her share of praise, for the manner in which she reproved her niece for giving way to her feelings, and for the address, with which she wished to heaven, "that poor Annabella had the calm, philosophic temper, of which Miss Portman was, she understood, a most uncommon example."

As Mr Vincent drove toward London, he reflected upon these last words; and he could not help thinking, that if Belinda had more faults she would be more amiable. Her affection for him, he feared, would never be such as what he felt for her – never sufficiently tender, or ardent, to constitute his felicity, or to equal his idea of the passion of love.

These thoughts were however driven from his mind, and scarcely left a trace behind them, when he once more saw and conversed with her. The dignity, sincerity, and kindness, which she showed the evening that he put the anonymous letter into her hands, charmed and touched him; and his real feelings and his enthusiasm conspired to make him believe, that his whole happiness depended on her smiles. The confession, which she made to him of her former attachment to Clarence Hervey, as it raised in Vincent's mind strong emotions of jealousy, increased his passion as much as it piqued his pride, and she appeared in a new and highly interesting light, when he discovered that the coldness of manner, which he had attributed to want of sensibility, arose probably from its excess – that her heart should have been preoccupied, was more tolerable to him than the belief of her settled indifference. He was so intent upon these delightful varieties in his love for Belinda, that it was not, till he had received a reproachful note from Mrs Luttridge, to remind him of his promised visit from Juba, that he could prevail upon himself to leave Twickenham, even for a few hours. Lady Delacour's hatred or fear of Juba, which he accidentally mentioned to Miss Annabella, appeared to her and to her aunt "the most extraordinary thing upon Earth;" and when it was contrasted with their excessive fondness, it seeed to him indeed unaccountable. From pure consideration for her ladyship's nerves, Mrs Luttridge petitioned Vincent to leave the dog with her, that Helena might not be in such imminent danger from "the animal's monstrous jaws." – The petition was granted; and as the petitioners foresaw, Juba became to them a most useful auxiliary. Juba's master called daily to see him, and sometimes when he came in the morning Mrs Luttridge was not at home, so that his visits were repeated in the evening, and the evening in London is what, in other places, is called the night. – Mrs Luttridge's nights could not be passed without deep play. The sight of the E O table at first shocked Mr Vincent: he thought of Mr Percival, and he turned away from it: but to his active social disposition it was extremely irksome, to stand idle and uninterested, where all were busy and eager in one common pursuit; to his generous temper it seemed ungentlemanlike to stand by, the silent censor of the rest of the company; and when he considered, of how little importance a few hundreds, or even thousands, could be to a man of his large fortune, he *could not help feeling*, that it was sordid, selfish, avaricious, to dread their possible loss; and thus social spirit, courage, generosity, all conspired to carry our man of feeling to the gaming-table. Once there, his ruin was inevitable. Mrs Luttridge, whilst she held his doom in her power, hesitated only whether it would be more her interest to marry him to her niece, or to content herself with his fortune. His passion for Belinda, which she saw had been by some means or other increased, in spite of the anonymous letter, gave her little hopes of Annabella's succeeding, even with the assistance of Juba, and delicate sensibility. So the aunt, careless of her niece's disappointment, determined that Mr Vincent should be *her* victim; and sensible that she must not give him time for reflection, she hurried him on, till in the course of a few evenings spent at the E O table, he lost, not only thousands, but tens of thousands. – One lucky night, she assured him, would set all to rights; the run could not always be against him, and Fortune must change in his favour, if he tried her with sufficient perseverance.

The horror, the agony of mind, which he endured at this sudden

ruin, which seemed impending over him, the recollection of
Belinda, of Mr Percival, almost drove him to distraction – He
retreated from the E O table one night, swearing that he never
would hazard another guinea. But his ruin was not yet complete –
he had thousands yet to lose, and Mrs Luttridge would not thus
relinquish her prey. She persuaded him to try his fortune *once*
more. She now suffered him to regain courage, by winning back
some of his own fortune. His mind was relieved from the sense of
immediate danger; he rejoiced to be saved from the humiliation of
confessing his losses to Mr Percival and Belinda. The next day he
saw her with unusual pleasure, and this was the very morning
when Clarence Hervey paid his visit. The imprudence of Lady
Delacour, joined perhaps to his own consciousness, that he had a
secret fault, which ought to lower him in the esteem of his
mistress, made him misinterpret everything that passed – his
jealousy was excited in the most sudden and violent manner. He
flew from Lady Delacour's to Mrs Luttridge's – he was soothed
and flattered by the apparent kindness, with which he was
received by Annabella and her aunt; but after dinner, when one of
the servants whispered to Mrs Luttridge, who sat next to him, that
Mr Clarence Hervey was above stairs, he gave such a start, that
part of the bumper of wine, which he was going to drink to her
health, did not escape the fair Annabella's lap. In the confusion
and apologies, which this accident occasioned, Mrs Luttridge had
time to consider what might be the cause of the start, and she
combined her suspicions so quickly and so judiciously, that she
guessed the truth – that he feared to be seen at the E O table by a
person, who might find it for his interest to tell the truth to Belinda
Portman. – "Mr Vincent," said she, in a low voice, "I have such a
terrible headache, that I am fit for nothing – I am not *up to* E O to
night, so you must wait for your revenge till to morrow."

Mr Vincent was heartily glad to be relieved from his engagement, and he endeavoured to escape Clarence's suspicions, by
devoting his whole time this evening to Annabella, not in the least
apprehensive that Mr Hervey would return the next night. Mr
Vincent was at the E O table at the usual hour, for he was
excessively anxious to regain what he had lost, not so much for
the sake of the money, which he could afford to lose, but lest the
defalcation in his fortune should lead Mr Percival to the
knowledge of the means which had occasioned it. He could not
endure, after his high vaunts, to see himself humbled by his rash

confidence in himself, and he secretly vowed, that if he could but reinstate himself, by one night's good luck, he would for ever quit the society of gamblers. A few months before this time, he would have scorned the idea of concealing any part of his conduct, any one of his actions, from his best friend, Mr Percival; but his pride now reconciled him to the meanness of concealment; and here, the acuteness of his feelings was to his own mind an excuse for dissimulation: so fallacious is moral instinct, unenlightened or uncontrolled by reason or religion.

Mr Vincent was disappointed in his hopes of regaining what he had lost. This was not the fortunate night, which Mrs Luttridge's prognostics had vainly taught him to expect: he played on, however, with all the impetuosity of his natural temper; his judgment forsook him; he scarcely knew what he said or did; and, in the course of a few hours, he was worked up to such a pitch of insanity, that, in one desperate moment, he betted nearly all that he was worth in the world – and lost! – He stood like one stupefied – the hum of voices scarcely reached his ear – he saw figures moving before him, but he did not distinguish who, or what, they were.

Supper was announced, and the room emptied fast, while he remained motionless, leaning on the E O table. He was roused by Mrs Luttridge's saying, as she passed – "Don't you sup to night, Mr Hervey?" – Vincent looked up, and saw Clarence Hervey opposite to him. His countenance instantly changed, and the lightning of anger flashed through the gloom of despair: he uttered not a syllable; but his looks said – "How is this, sir? Here again to night, to watch me? – to enjoy my ruin? – to be ready to carry the first news of it to Belinda?"

At this last thought, Vincent struck his closed hand with violence against his forehead; and rushing by Mr Hervey, who in vain attempted to speak to him, he pressed into the midst of the crowd on the stairs, and let himself be carried along with them into the supper-room. At supper he took his usual seat between Mrs Luttridge and the fair Annabella; and, as if determined to brave the observing eyes of Clarence Hervey, who was at the same table, he affected extravagant gaiety; he ate, drank, talked, and laughed, more than any of the company. Toward the end of the supper, his dog, who was an inmate at Mrs Luttridge's, licked his hand, to put him in mind, that he had given him nothing to eat.

"Drink, Juba! – drink, and never have done, boy!" cried Vincent, holding a bumper of wine to the dog's mouth: "he's the only *dog* I ever saw taste wine." Then snatching up some of the flowers, which ornamented the table, he swore that Juba should henceforward be called Anacreon, and that he deserved to be crowned with roses by the hand of Beauty. The fair Annabella instantly took a hot-house rose from her bosom, and assisted in making the garland, with which she crowned the new Anacreon. Insensible to his honours, the dog, who was extremely hungry, turned suddenly to Mrs Luttridge, by whom he had, till this night, regularly been fed with the choicest morsels; and, lifting up his huge paw, laid it, as he had been wont to do, upon her arm. She shook it off: he, knowing nothing of the change in his master's affairs, laid the paw again upon her arm; and, with that familiarity, to which he had long been encouraged, raised his head almost close to the lady's cheek.

"Down, Juba! – down, sir, down!" cried Mrs Luttridge, in a sharp voice.

"Down, Juba! – down, sir!" repeated Mr Vincent, in a tone of bitter feeling, all his assumed gaiety forsaking him at this instant. "Down, Juba! – down, sir – down! – as low as your master!" thought he; and, pushing back his chair, he rose from table, and precipitately left the room.

Little notice was taken of his retreat; the chairs closed in; and the gap, which his vacant place left, was visible but for a moment: the company were as gay as before; the fair Annabella smiled with a grace as attractive; and Mrs Luttridge exulted in the success of her schemes – whilst her victim was in the agonies of despair.

Clarence Hervey, who had watched every change of Vincent's countenance, saw the agony of soul, with which he rose from the table, and quitted the room: he suspected his purpose, and followed him immediately. But Mr Vincent had got out of the house before he could overtake him: which way he was gone, no one could tell, for no one had seen him: the only information he could gain was, that he might possibly be heard of at Nerot's Hotel, or at Governor Montford's, in Portland-place. The hotel was but a few yards from Mrs Luttridge's. Clarence went there directly. He asked for Mr Vincent. One of the waiters said, that he was not yet come in; but another called out – "Mr Vincent, sir, did you say? I have just shown him up to his room."

"Which is his room? – I must see him instantly," cried Hervey.

"Not tonight – you can't see him now, sir. Mr Vincent won't let you in, I can assure you, sir. I went up myself, three minutes ago, with some letters, that came whilst he was away, but he would not let me in. I heard him double-lock the door, and he swore terribly. I can't go up again, at this time o'night – for my life I dare not, sir."

"Where is his own man? – Has Mr Vincent any servant here? – Mr Vincent's man!" cried Clarence; "let me see him!"

"You can't, sir. Mr Vincent has just sent his black, the only servant he has here, out on some message. – Indeed, sir, there's no use in going up," continued the waiter, as Clarence sprang up two or three stairs at once: "Mr Vincent has desired nobody may disturb him. I give you my word, sir, he'll be very angry; and, besides, 'twould be to no purpose, for he'll not unlock the door."

"Is there but one door to the room?" said Mr Hervey; and, as he asked the question, he pulled a guinea out of his pocket, and touched the waiter's hand with it.

"Oh – now I recollect – yes, sir, there's a private door through a closet – may be, that mayn't be fastened."

Clarence put the guinea into the waiter's hand, who instantly showed him the way up the back stair-case to the door, that opened into Mr Vincent's bedchamber.

"Leave me now," whispered he, "and make no noise."

The man withdrew; and as Mr Hervey went close to the concealed door, to try if it was fastened, he distinctly heard a pistol cocked. The door was not fastened: he pushed it softly open, and saw this unfortunate man upon his knees, the pistol at his temple, his eyes looking up to Heaven. Clarence was in one moment behind him; and, seizing hold of the pistol, he snatched it from Vincent's grasp with so much calm presence of mind and dexterity, that, although the pistol was cocked, it did not go off.

"Mr Hervey!" exclaimed Vincent, starting up. Astonishment overpowered all other sensations. But the next instant his eyes flashed anger. "Is this the conduct of a gentleman, Mr Hervey? – of a man of honour!" cried he, "thus to intrude upon my privacy; to be a spy upon my actions; to triumph in my ruin; to witness my despair; to rob me of the only – "

He looked wildly at the pistol, which Clarence held in his hand; then snatching up another which lay upon the table, he continued – "You are my enemy – I know it – you are my rival – I know it – Belinda loves you – Nay, affect not to start – this is no time for dissimulation – Belinda loves you – you know it – for her sake, for your own, put me out of the world – put me out of torture. It shall not be called murder; it shall be called a duel. You have been a spy upon my actions – I demand satisfaction. If you have one spark of honour or of courage within you, Mr Hervey, show it now – fight me, sir, openly as man to man, rival to rival, enemy to enemy – fire."

"If you fire upon me you will repent it," replied Clarence, calmly, "for I am not your enemy; I am not your rival."

"You *are*," interrupted Vincent, raising his voice to the highest pitch of indignation; "you are my rival, though you dare not avow it; the denial is base, false, unmanly. – O, Belinda, is this the being you prefer to *me*? Gamester! – wretch as I am, my soul never stooped to falsehood; treachery I abhor; courage, honour, and a heart worthy of Belinda, I posses. I beseech you, sir," continued he, addressing himself, in a tremulous tone of contempt to Mr Hervey – "I beseech you, sir, to leave me to my own feelings – and to myself."

"You are not yourself at this moment, and I cannot leave you to such mistaken feelings," replied Hervey; "command yourself for a moment, and hear me: use your reason, and you will soon be convinced that I am your friend."

"My friend!"

"Your friend – For what purpose did I come here, to snatch this pistol from your hand? If it were my interest, my wish, that you were out of the world, why did I prevent you from destroying yourself? Do you think *that* the action of an enemy? Use your reason."

"I cannot," said Vincent, striking his forehead; "I know not what to think; – I am not master of myself! – I conjure you, sir, for your own sake, to leave me."

"For my *own* sake!" repeated Hervey, disdainfully; "I am not thinking of myself; nor can any thing you have said provoke me from my purpose. My purpose is to save you from ruin, for the sake of a woman, whom, though I am no longer your rival, I have loved longer, if not better, than you have."

There was something so open in Hervey's countenance; such a strong expression of truth in his manner, that it could not be resisted, and Vincent, in an altered voice, exclaimed:

"You acknowledge that you have loved Belinda – and could you cease to love her? Impossible! – And, loving her, must you not detest me?"

"No," said Clarence, holding out his hand to him; "I wish to be your friend; I have not the baseness to wish to deprive others of happiness, because I cannot enjoy it myself. In one word, to put you at ease with me for ever, I have no pretentions, I can have none, to Miss Portman. I am engaged to another woman – in a few days you will hear of my marriage."

Mr Vincent threw the pistol from him, and gave his hand to Hervey.

"Pardon what I said to you just now," cried he; "I knew not what I said – I spoke in the agony of despair – your purpose is most generous – but it is in vain – you came too late – I am ruined, past all hope."

He folded his arms, and his eyes reverted involuntarily to his pistols. There was a pause of awful silence.

"The misery that you have this night experienced," said Mr Hervey, "was necessary to the security of your future happiness."

"Happiness!" repeated Vincent – "happiness – there is no happiness left for me. My doom is fixed – fixed by my own folly – my own rash headstrong folly. Madman that I was, what could tempt me to the gaming table? O! if I could recall but a few days, a few hours of my existence! – but remorse is vain; prudence comes too late. Do you know," said he, fixing his eyes upon Hervey, "do you know that I am a beggar? that I have not a farthing left upon earth. Go to Belinda; tell her so: tell her, that if she had ever the slightest regard for me, I deserve it no longer. Tell her to forget, despise, detest me. Give her joy, that she has escaped having a gamester for a husband."

"I will," said Clarence, "I will, if you please, tell her what I believe to be true, that the agony you have felt this night, the dear-bought experience you have had, will be for ever a warning."

"A warning!" interrupted Vincent – "O, that it could yet be useful to me! – But I tell you, it comes too late – Nothing can save me."

"*I* can," said Mr Hervey. "Swear to me, for Belinda's sake – solemnly swear to me, that you will never more trust your happiness and hers to the hazard of a die – swear that you will never more, directly or indirectly, play at any game of chance, and I will restore to you the fortune, the happiness that you have lost."

Mr Vincent stood, as if suspended between ecstasy and despair; he dared not trust his senses: with a fervent and solemn adjuration he made the vow that was required of him; and Clarence then revealed to him the secret of the E O table.

"When she knows that I have it in my power to expose her to public shame, she will instantly refund all that she has iniquitously won from you. Even among gamblers she would be blasted, for ever, by this discovery: she knows it, and if she dared to brave public opinion, we have then a sure resource in the law – prosecute her. The laws of honour, as well as the laws of the land will support the prosecution. But she will never let the affair go into a court of justice. I will see her early, as early as I can tomorrow, and put you out of suspense."

"Most generous of human beings!" exclaimed Vincent; "I cannot express to you what I feel; but your own heart, your own approbation – "

"Farewell, good night," interrupted Clarence, with a benevolent smile; "I see that I have made a friend; I was determined that Belinda's husband should be my friend – I have succeeded beyond my hopes. And now I will *intrude* no longer," said he, as he closed the door after him. His sensations, at this instant, were more delightful, even than those of the man he had relieved from the depth of despair. How wisely has Providence made the benevolent and generous passions the most pleasurable!

CHAPTER XXIX

A Jew

In the silence of the night, when the hurry of action was over, and the enthusiasm of generosity began to subside, the words, which had escaped from Mr Vincent, in the paroxysm of despair and rage – the words – "*Belinda loves you*" – recurred to Clarence Hervey; and it required all his power over himself, to banish the sound from his ear, and the idea from his mind. He endeavoured to persuade himself, that these words were dictated merely by sudden jealousy; and that there could be no real foundation for the assertion: perhaps this belief was a necessary support to his integrity. He reflected, that, at all events, his engagement with Virginia could not be violated; his proffered services to Mr Vincent could not be withdrawn: he was firm and consistent. Before two o'clock the next day, Vincent received from Clarence this short note:

"Enclosed is Mrs Luttridge's acknowledgment, that she has no claims upon you, in consequence of what passed last night. I said nothing about the money she had previously won, as I understand you have paid it.

"The lady fell into fits; but it would not do. The husband attempted to bully me. I told him, I should be at his service, after he had made the whole affair public, by calling you out.

"I would have seen you myself this morning, but that I am engaged with lawyers and marriage settlements.
                          "Yours sincerely,
                                    "CLARENCE HERVEY"

Overjoyed at the sight of Mrs Luttridge's acknowledgment, Vincent repeated his vow, never more to hazard himself in her dangerous society. He was impatient to see Belinda; and full of generous and grateful sentiments, in this first moment of joy, he determined to conceal nothing from her; to make at once the confession of his own imprudence and the eulogium of Clarence Hervey's generosity. He was just setting out for Twickenham, when he was sent for by his uncle, Governor Montford, who had business to settle with him, relative to his West India estates. He spent the remainder of the morning with his uncle; and there he received a charming letter from Belinda; – that letter, which she had written and sent, whilst Lady Delacour was reading Clarence Hervey's packet. It would have cured Vincent of jealousy, even if he had not, in the interim, seen Mr Hervey, and learnt from him the news of his approaching marriage. Miss Portman, at the conclusion of her letter, informed him, that Lady Delacour purposed being in Berkeley-square the next day; that they were to spend a week in town, on account of Mrs Margaret Delacour, who had promised her ladyship a visit: and to go to Twickenham would be a formidable journey to an infirm old lady, who seldom stirred out of her house.

Whatever displeasure Lady Delacour felt towards her friend Belinda, on account of her *coldness* to Mr Hervey, and her steadiness to Mr Vincent, had by this time subsided. Angry people, who express their passion, as it has been justly said, always speak worse than they think. This was usually the case with her ladyship.

The morning after they arrived in town, she came into Belinda's room, with an air of more than usual sprightliness and satisfaction. – "Great new! – Great news! – Extraordinary news! – But it is very imprudent to excite your expectations, my dear Belinda. Pray, did you hear a wonderful noise in the square a little while ago?"

"Yes; I thought I heard a great bustle; but Marriott appeased my curiosity, by saying, that it was only a battle between two dogs."

"It is well, if this battle between two dogs do not end in a duel between two men," said Lady Delacour.

"This prospect of mischief seems to have put your ladyship in wonderfully good spirits," said Belinda, smiling. "But what have you heard of Mr Vincent?"

"That Miss Annabella Luttridge is dying for love of him – or of his fortune. Knowing, as I do, the vanity of mankind, I suppose, that your Mr Vincent, all perfect as he is, was flattered by the little coquette; and perhaps he condescends to repay her in the same coin. I take it for granted – for I always fill up the gaps in a story my own way – I take it for granted, that Mr Vincent got into some entanglement with her; and that this has been the cause of the quarrel with the aunt. That there has been a quarrel is certain: for your friend Juba told Marriott so. His massa swore, that he would never go to Mrs Luttridge's again; and this morning he took the decisive measure of sending to request, that his dog might be returned. Juba went for his namesake. Miss Annabella Luttridge was the person, who delivered up the dog; and she desired the black to tell his master, with her compliments, that Juba's collar was rather too tight; and she begged, that he would not fail to take if off as soon as he could. Perhaps, my dear, you are as simple as the poor negro, and suspect no *finesse* in this message. Miss Luttridge, aware that the faithful fellow was too much in your interests, to be either persuaded or bribed to carry a billet-doux from any other lady to his master, did not dare to trust him upon this occasion; but she had the art to make him carry her letter, without his knowing it. *Colin maillard*, vulgarly called *blind man's buff*, was, some time ago, a favourite play amongst the Parisian ladies: now, *hide and seek* will be brought into fashion, I suppose, by the fair Annabella. Judge of her talents for the game by this instance: – She hid her billet-doux within the lining of Juba's collar. The dog, unconscious of his dignity as an ambassador, or rather as a chargé d'affaires, set out on his way home. As he was crossing Berkely square, he was met by Sir Philip Baddely and his dog. The baronet's insolent favourite bit the black's heels. Juba, the dog, resented the injury immediately, and a furious combat ensued. In the height of the battle Juba's collar fell off. Sir Philip Baddely espied the paper, that was sewed to the lining, and seized upon it immediately: the negro caught hold of it at the same instant: the baronet knocked him down. The great dog left his canine antagonist that moment, flew at your baronet, and would have eaten him up at three mouthfuls, if Sir Philip had not made good his retreat to Dangerfield's circulating library. The negro's head was terribly cut by the sharp point of a stone, and his ankle was sprained; but, as he has just told me, he did not feel this till afterward. He started up, and pursued his master's enemy. Sir Philip was actually reading Miss Luttridge's billet-doux aloud, when the black entered the library. He reclaimed his master's property, with great intrepidity; and a gentleman, who was present, took his part immediately.

"In the mean time, Lord Delacour, who had been looking at the battle from our breakfast-room window, declared he would go over to Dangerfield's, to see what was the matter, and how all this would end. He entered the library, just as the gentleman, who had volunteered in favour of poor Juba, was disputing with Sir Philip. The bleeding negro told my lord, in as plain words as he could, the cause of the dispute; and Lord Delacour, who, to do him justice, is a man of honour, joined instantly in his defence. The baronet thought proper, at length, to submit; and he left the field of battle, without having any thing to say for himself, but – 'Damme! – very extraordinary, damme!' – *or words to that effect.*

"Now, Lord Delacour, beside being a man of honour, is also a man of humanity. I know, that I cannot oblige you more, my dear Belinda, than by seasoning my discourse with a little conjugal flattery. My lord was concerned to see the poor black writhing in pain; and, with the assistance of the gentleman, who had joined in his defence, he brought Juba across the square to our house. Guess for what: – to try upon the strained ankle an infallible quack balsam recommended to him by the dowager Lady Boucher. I was in the hall, when they brought the poor fellow in. Marriott was called. 'Mrs Marriott,' cried my lord, 'pray let us have Lady Boucher's infallible balsam this instant!' Had you but seen the eagerness of face, or heard the emphasis, with which he said, '*infallible* balsam' – you must let me laugh at the recollection. One human smile must pass, and be forgiven."

"The smile may be the more readily forgiven," said Belinda, "since, I am sure, you are conscious, that it reflected almost as much upon yourself as upon Lord Delacour."

"Why, yes: belief in a quack doctor is full as bad as belief in a quack balsam, I allow. Your observation is so malicious, because so just, that, to punish you for it, I will not tell you the remainder of my story for a week to come; and I assure you, that the best part of it I have left untold. To return to our friend, Mr Vincent: – Could you but know, what reasons I have, at this instant, for wishing him in Jamaica, you would acknowledge, that I am truly candid in confession, that I believe my suspicions about E O were unfounded; and I am truly generous in admitting, that you are right to treat him with justice."

This last enigmatical sentence Belinda could not prevail upon Lady Delacour to explain.

In the evening Mr Vincent made his appearance. Lady Delacour immediately attacked him with raillery, on the subject of the fair Annabella. He was rejoiced to perceive, that her suspicions took this turn; and that nothing relative to the transaction, in which Clarence Hervey had been engaged, had transpired. Vincent wavered in his resolution to confess the truth to Belinda. Though he had determined upon this in the first moment of joyful enthusiasm, yet the delay of four-and-twenty hours had made a material change in his feelings: his dread of losing Belinda by his sincerity increased, the more time he had for reflection. Indeed, his most virtuous resolves were always rather the effect of sudden impulse, than of steady principle. But when the tide of passion had swept away the landmarks, he had no method of ascertaining the boundaries of right and wrong. Upon the present occasion, his love for Belinda confounded all his moral calculations: one moment, his feelings as a man of honour forbade him to condescend to the meanness of dissimulation, but the next instant, his feelings as the lover prevailed, and he satisfied his conscience by the idea that, as his vow must preclude all danger of his return to the gaming-table in future, it would be only creating an unnecessary alarm in Belinda's mind, to speak to her of his past imprudence. His generosity at first revolted from the thought of suppressing those praises of Clarence Hervey, which had been so well deserved; but his jealousy returned, to combat his first virtuous impulse. He considered, that his own inferiority must by comparison appear more striking to his mistress; that it would be for her happiness to conceal the merits of a rival, to whom she could never be united. In this vacillating state of mind he continued during the greatest part of the evening. About half an hour before he took his leave, Lady Delacour was called out of the room by Mrs Marriott. Left alone with Belinda, his embarrassment increased, and the unsuspecting kindness of her manner was to him the most bitter reproach. He stood in a silent agony, whilst in a playful tone she smiled and said,

"Where are your thoughts? If I were of a jealous temper, I should say with the fair Annabella — "

"You would say wrong then," replied Mr Vincent, in a constrained voice. He was upon the point of telling the truth; but to gain a reprieve of a few minutes, he entered into a defence of his conduct toward Miss Luttridge.

"I have not interrupted you," said Belinda, when he paused; "and I do not, from false generosity or politeness, preclude you from the opportunity of proving your integrity, by assuring you, that it was not suspected, and that your defence is totally unnecessary. I follow my own maxims, you see: this was the justice that I requested from you, when you treated me so generously about the anonymous letter. Believe me, I have not – I never shall, forget your handsome conduct upon that occasion."

She held out her hand to him as she spoke, with much sweetness in her countenance, and an air of perfect sincerity. He pressed it to his lips, and exclaimed, "Could I deceive such confidence as you repose in me?"

"Whether you could or could not, I am sure you *would* not," said Belinda; "and I trust myself with more pleasure to those who have not the will, than to those who have not the power, to deceive me."

But observing the excessive agitation of his whole frame at this instant, her gaiety forsook her.

"Are you not well? What is the matter? How long," said Belinda, "will you keep me in suspense? Have I no right to share your uneasiness? You are in some doubt, some difficulty, some distress! Do not persist in this painful silence; speak to me as to your friend, at least with all your accustomed sincerity!"

"Sincerity! – O, Belinda! – but if this sincerity should be fatal to me! – if it should cost me the whole happiness of my life – if it should by one word deprive me of your love – too well am I aware, that your affection for me has not that enthusiasm, which sustains the blast of adversity."

"This is poetry – almost blank verse," said Belinda, smiling.

"I am in earnest, believe me," continued Vincent; "I have something to communicate, something to confess to you."

"To confess!" repeated Belinda, with a look of sudden terror.

"Yes, something to confess, which I fear may deprive me of your affection."

"Is it a misfortune, or is it a crime?"

"It is *not* a crime," replied Vincent.

"Then how," said Belinda, "can you do me the injustice to fear that any misfortune should deprive you of my affection? Though I have never felt, or pretended to feel for you, that species of enthusiasm on which you set so high a value, yet, perhaps, my conduct will convince you, that without being in love like Clelia or Cleopatra, a woman may deserve the affection of a man of sense and honour."

"You are an angel!" cried Vincent.

"I have heard that so often, that I cannot help believing it," said Belinda; "but now, without farther hesitation, communicate, impart, or confess this dreadful misfortune."

"I suffer, at this instant, more than the utmost stretch of your imagination can conceive. Must I tell you, that the day before yesterday I was deprived by the fraud and villainy of one in whom I placed confidence, of almost my whole fortune? Can you, who have been accustomed to all the elegancies of affluence; you, who are formed to shine in the highest circles of society, consent to live with me in obscurity, in poverty?"

"I am not so romantic as to imagine, that I could be happy with you or you with me, if we were in absolute want of the common comforts of life; but if your word *poverty* be only a figure of speech; if between us there yet remain what prudence, not what the cant of fashion and affectation would allow to be, *a competence*, I can easily part with useless luxuries," said Belinda: – "to be more explicit, I can live without an equipage, and in the country. You know, that when your splendid equipage was ready to carry us to Oakly-park, I told you, that show could add nothing to my happiness, and I told you truly – Nor do I now feel, as Dr Johnson says, that 'It is misery to want what it is not happiness to have."

Mr Vincent burst into the most rapturous expressions of admiration and gratitude.

You rather offend, than gratify me, by these praises," said Belinda, "Are you surprised, that I should act as you would do in my place? You surely could not imagine, that I would desert you in adversity? You have lost your wealth by the fraud and villainy of one, in whom you had confidence; you shall not lose your happiness by the inconstancy or meanness of another, in whom you have placed yet greater confidence," said Belinda, with more tenderness, than she had ever before spoken to Mr Vincent. "Compose yourself, then," continued she, "and let us look into your affairs at our leisure, and explain to me how all this has happened."

"My generous, charming, adorable, Belinda! My fortune is not lost. All stratagems, you know, the poet says, are allowable in love and war. This was only a stratagem to excite your compassion."

"You have not done wisely," said Belinda, rising with a look of such serious displeasure as struck him speechless; "you have shown me, that I never stood as high in your esteem as I believed, and as I deserved."

Mr Vincent now thought that this was not the happy moment for any farther confessions. He had not the courage to increase her displeasure.

The sudden entrance of Lady Delacour relieved him from his embarrassment, and they conversed only on general subjects during the remainder of the evening: and he at last departed, secretly rejoicing that he was, as he fancied, under the necessity of postponing his explanation; he even thought of suppressing the history of his transactions with Mrs Luttridge. His former nice sense of honour had been considerably deadened at the gaming-table; and he could *now* stoop to that dissimulation, at which he would have shuddered but a few months before. He knew that his secret was safe with Clarence Hervey: Mrs Luttridge would be silent, for her own sake; and neither Lady Delacour nor Belinda had any connexion with her society. The next day, Miss Portman observed, that Mr Vincent looked extremely ill; and softened by the sorrow, that he expressed at having incurred her displeasure, she blamed herself for the harshness, with which she had spoken the preceding day. She forgave an error, which she thought had been more than sufficiently punished, and Mr Vincent was reinstated in her favour. He hurried forward the preparation for their nuptials with indescribable anxiety; still he postponed his explanation from day to day. And now he actually approached the completion of his hopes.

The very morning before that, which was fixed for their marriage, Mr Vincent went to Gray, the jeweller, for some trinkets, which he had bespoke for Belinda. Lord Delacour was there, speaking about the diamond ring, which Gray had promised to dispose of for him. Whilst his lordship and Mr Vincent were busy about their own affairs, Sir Philip Baddely and Mr Rochfort came into the shop. Sir Philip and Mr Vincent had never before met. Lord Delacour, to prevent him from getting into a quarrel about a lady, who was so little worth fighting for as Miss Annabella Luttridge, had positively refused to tell Mr Vincent what he knew of the affair, or to let him know the name of the gentleman who was concerned in it.

The shopman addressed Mr Vincent by his name, and immediately Sir Philip whispered to Rochfort, that Mr Vincent was "*the master of the black*". Vincent, who unluckily overheard him, instantly asked Lord Delacour, if that was the gentleman who had behaved so ill to his servant? Lord Delacour told him, that it was now of no consequence to inquire, and that he hoped he was too prudent, on the very eve of his marriage, to go in quest of a quarrel. "If," said his lordship, "any of these gentlemen choose to accost you, I shall think you do rightly to retort; but for Heaven's sake do not begin the attack!"

Vincent's impetuosity was not to be restrained; he demanded from Sir Philip, whether he was the person who had beaten his servant? Sir Philip readily obliged him with an answer in the affirmative; and the consequence was, the loss of a finger to the baronet, and a wound in the side to Mr Vincent, which, though it did not endanger his life, yet confined him to his room for several days. The impatience of his mind increased his fever, and retarded his recovery and his marriage.

Lady Delacour did not affect to conceal her satisfaction at this delay, though humanity made her wish, that it had been caused by any other means. When Belinda's first alarm for Mr Vincent's safety was over, she anxiously questioned Lord Delacour as to the particulars of all that had passed between Mr Vincent and Sir Philip, that she might judge of the manner, in which her lover had conducted himself. Lord Delacour, who was a man of strict truth, was compelled to confess, that Mr Vincent had shown more spirit than temper, and more courage than prudence. Lady Delacour rejoiced to perceive, that this account made Belinda uncommonly serious.

Mr Vincent now thought himself sufficiently recovered, to leave his room: his physicians, indeed, would have kept him prisoner a few days longer, but he was too impatient of restraint, to listen to their counsels.

"Juba, tell the doctor, when he comes, that you could not keep me at home; and that is all that is necessary to be said."

He had now summoned courage, to acknowledge to Belinda all that had happened, and was proceeding, without difficulty, down stairs, when he was suddenly struck by the sound of a voice, which he little expected at this moment; a voice he had formerly been accustomed to hear with pleasure, but now it smote him to the heart: – it was the voice of Mr Percival. For the first time in his life, he wished to deny himself to his friend. The recollection of the

E O table, of Mr Luttridge, of Mr Percival as his guardian, and of all the advice he had heard from him as his friend, rushed upon his mind at this instant; conscious and ashamed, he shrunk back, precipitately returned to his own room, and threw himself into a chair, breathless with agitation. He listened, expecting to hear Mr Percival coming upstairs, and endeavoured to compose himself, that he might not betray, by his own agitation, all that he wished most anxiously to conceal. After waiting for some time, he rang the bell, to make inquiries. The waiter told him, that a Mr Percival had asked for him; but, having been told by his black that he was just gone out, the gentleman being, as he said, much hurried, had left a note; for an answer to which he would call at 8 o'clock in the evening. Vincent was glad of this short reprieve. "Alas!" thought he, "how changed am I, when I fear to meet my best friend! To what has this one fatal propensity reduced me!"

He was little aware of the new difficulties that awaited him.

Mr Percival's note was as follows:

"My dear *friend*!

"Am not I a happy man, to find a friend in my ci-devant ward? But I have no time for sentiment; nor does it become the character, in which I am now writing to you – that of a D U N. – You are so rich, and so prudent, that the word in capital letters cannot frighten you. Lady Anne's cousin, poor Mr Carysfort, is dead. I am guardian to his boys; they are but ill provided for. I have fortunately obtained a partnership in a good house for the second son. Fifteen thousand pounds are wanting to establish him – we cannot raise the money amongst us, without dunning poor Mr Vincent. Enclosed is your bond for the purchase-money of the little estate you bought from me last summer. I know, that you have double the sum we want in ready money – so I make no ceremony. Let me have the ten thousand this evening, if you can, as I wish to leave town as soon as possible.

"Yours, most sincerely,

"HENRY PERCIVAL."

Now, Mr Vincent had lost, and had actually paid to Mrs Luttridge, the ready money, which had been destined to discharge his debt to Mr Percival: he expected fresh remittances from the West Indies in the course of a few weeks; but, in the mean time, he must raise this money immediately: this he could only do by having recourse to Jews – a desperate expedient. The Jew, to whom he applied, no sooner discovered, that Mr Vincent was under a necessity of having this sum before eight o'clock in the evening, than he became exorbitant in his demands; and the more impatient this unfortunate young man became, the more difficulties he raised. At last a bargain was concluded between them, in which Vincent knew, that he was grossly imposed upon; but to this he submitted, for he had no alternative. The Jew promised to bring him ten thousand pounds at five o'clock in the evening, but it was half after seven before he made his appearance; and then, he was so dilatory and circumspect, in reading over and signing the bonds, and in completing the formalities of the transaction, that before the money was actually in Vincent's possession, one of the waiters of the hotel knocked at the door, to let him know that Mr Percival was coming up stairs. Vincent hurried the Jew into an adjoining apartment, and bid him wait there, till he should come to finish the business. Though totally unsuspicious, Mr Percival could not help being struck with the perturbation, in which he found his young friend. Vincent immediately began to talk of the duel, which had delayed his marriage, and his friend was led to conclude, that his anxiety arose from this affair. He endeavoured to put him at ease, by changing the conversation. He spoke of the business, which brought him to town, and of the young man, whom he was going to place with a banker.

"I hope," said he, observing that Vincent grew more embarrassed, "that my *dunning* you for this money is not really inconvenient."

"Not in the least — not in the least. I have the money ready — in a few moments — if you'll be so good as to wait here — I have the money ready in the next room."

At this instant a loud noise was heard — the raised voices of two people quarrelling. It was Juba, the black, and Solomon, the Jew. Mr Vincent had sent Juba out of the way, on some errand, whilst he had been transacting his affairs with the Jew; but the black, having executed the commission on which he had been sent, returned, and went into his master's bedchamber, to read at his leisure a letter, which he had just received from his wife. He did not at first see the Jew, and he was spelling out the words of his wife's letter.

"My dear Juba,

"I take this op-por-tu — "

— *nity* he would have said; but the Jew, who had held his breath in, to avoid discovery, till he could hold it no longer, now drew it so loud, that Juba started, looked round and saw the feet of a man, which appeared beneath the bottom of the window curtain. Where fears of supernatural appearances were out of the question, our negro was a man of courage: he had no doubt, that the man who was concealed behind the curtain was a robber, but the idea of a robber did not unnerve him like that of an obeah-woman. With presence of mind worthy of a greater danger, Juba took down his master's pistols, which hung over the chimneypiece, and marching deliberately up to the enemy, he seized the Jew by the throat, exclaiming –

"You rob my massa? – You dead man, if you rob my massa."

Terrifed at the sight of the pistol, the Jew instantly explained who he was, and producing his large purse, assured Juba, that he was come to lend money, and not to take it from his master; but this appeared highly improbable to Juba, who believed his master to be the richest man in the world; besides, the Jew's language was scarcely intelligible to him, and he saw secret terror in Solomon's countenance. Solomon had an antipathy to the sight of a black, and he shrunk from the negro with strong signs of aversion. Juba would not relinquish his hold; each went on talking in their own angry gibberish as loud as they could, till at last the negro fairly dragged the Jew into the presence of his master and Mr Percival.

It is impossible to describe Mr Vincent's confusion, or Mr Percival's astonishment. The Jew's explanation was perfectly intelligible to him; he saw at once all the truth. Vincent, overwhelmed with shame, stood the picture of despair, incapable of uttering a single syllable.

"There is no necessity to borrow this money on my account," said Mr Percival calmly; "and if there were, we could probably have it on more reasonble terms than this gentleman proposes."

"I care not on what terms I have it – I care not what becomes of me – I am undone!" cried Vincent.

Mr Percival coolly dismissed the Jew, made a sign to Juba to leave the room, and then, addressing himself to Vincent, said – "I can borrow the money that I want elsewhere – Fear no reproaches from me – I foresaw all this – you have lost this sum at play – It is well, that it was not your whole fortune. I have only one question to ask you, on which depends my esteem – Have you informed Miss Portman of this affair?"

"I have not yet told her, but I was actually half downstairs in my way to tell her."

"Then, Mr Vincent, you are still my friend. I know the difficulty of such an avowal – but it is necessary."

"Cannot you, dear Mr Percival, save me the intolerable shame of confessing my own folly? – Spare me this mortification – Be yourself the bearer of this intelligence, and the mediator in my favour."

"I will with pleasure," said Mr Percival – "I will go this instant – but I cannot say, that I have any hope of persuading Belinda, to believe in your being irrevocably reclaimed from the charms of play."

"Indeed, my excellent friend, she may rely upon me: I feel such horror at the past, such heartfelt resolution against all future temptation, that you may pledge yourself for my total reformation."

Mr Percival promised, that he would exert all his influence, except by pledging his own honour: to this he could not consent. – "If I have any good news for you, I will return as soon as possible – but I will not be the bearer of any painful intelligence," said he: and he departed, leaving Mr Vincent in a state of anxiety, which, to his temper, was a punishment sufficient for almost any imprudence he could have committed.

Mr Percival returned no more that night. The next morning Mr Vincent received the following letter from Belinda. – He guessed his fate – he had scarcely power to read the words.

"You have frequently lamented, that my affection for you was not of the enthusiatic sort, which constitutes your idea of the passion of love. Instead of lamenting, we have now reason to rejoice at this, since it will save us from much useless pain. It spares me the difficulty of conquering a passion, that might be fatal to my happiness; and it will diminish the regret, which you may feel at our separation.

"From a person of your honourable character, I need not claim the terms of the agreement, that left each of us at liberty to recede, without reproach, whenever we should think proper; I am now obliged to say, that circumstances have made me certain we could not add to our felicity by that union, which, but a few days ago, appeared to me so desirable. The hopes of enjoying domestic happiness with a person whose manners, temper, and tastes, were suited to my own, induced me to listen to your addresses. Your unfortunate propensity to a dangerous amusement, which is now, for the first time, made known to me, puts an end to these hopes for ever.

"For my own sake, as well as for yours, I rejoice that your fortune has not been materially injured; as this relieves me from the fear, that my present conduct should be imputed to interested motives. Indeed, such is the generosity of your own temper, that in any situation I should scarcely have reason to apprehend from you such a suspicion.

"The absolute impossibility of my forming at present *another connexion*, will prevent you from imagining, that I am secretly influenced by sentiments different from those which I avow: nor can any weak doubts on this subject expose me to my own reproaches.

"You perceive, sir, that I am not willing, utterly to lose your esteem, even when I renounce, in the most unequivocal manner, all claim upon your affections. If anything should appear to you harsh in this letter, I beg you to impute it to the real cause – my desire to spare you all painful suspense, by convincing you at once, that my determination is irrevocable. I am persuaded, that love cannot long exist without hope. With sincere wishes for your happiness, and gratitude for your past attachment, I bid you farewell.

"Belinda Portman."

A few hours after Mr Vincent had read this letter, he threw himself into a postchaise, and set out for Germany. He saw that all hopes of being united to Belinda were over, and he hurried as far from her as possible. Her letter rather soothed than irritated his temper; her praises of his generosity were highly gratifying, and they had so powerful an effect upon his mind, that he was determined to prove that they were deserved. His conscience reproached him with not having made sufficiently honourable mention of Clarence Hervey's conduct, on the night when he was on the point of destroying himself. Before he left London he wrote a full account of this whole transaction, to be given to Miss Portman after his departure. It was delivered to Belinda by poor Juba, who would willingly have accompanied his unfortunate master in his voluntary exile, but Mr Vincent would not permit him to give this proof of attachment.

"Go," said he, "to your wife, and to your happy home."

The poor fellow put his master's letter into Miss Portman's hand, without being able to utter one syllable; the big tears rolled down his black cheeks, when she kindly said to him –

"I shall see you again, Juba, soon, at your cottage."

"But massa will not be there – massa is gone! – When shall we see massa again? – Never – never!"

He sobbed like an infant.

No torments, in the power of human cruelty to inflict, could in all probability have extorted from this negro one of the tears, which affection wrung from him so plentifully.

Belinda was deeply touched by this faithful creature's sensibility. He recalled to her mind some of the most amiable traits in his master's character, some of the happy days that she had spent in Mr Vincent's company. His letter – his farewell letter – she could not read without great emotion. It was written with true feeling, but in a manly style, without one word of vain lamentation. His generosity, in speaking of Clarence Hervey, was not lost upon her.

"What a pity," thought Belinda, "that with so many good and great qualities, I should be forced to bid him adieu for ever!"

Though she strongly felt the pain of this separation, yet she could not recede from her decision: nothing could tempt her to connect herself with a man, who had the fatal taste for play. Even Mr Percival, much as he loved his ward, much as he wished for his union with Belinda, dared not pledge his honour for Mr Vincent on this point. Reason and prudence then forbade her to trust the happiness of her life to a vain promise. She trembled at the thoughts of having been so near forming an indissoluble connexion with one, who had such a dangerous, and as she firmly believed, incurable taste. Even her sense of escape was attended with many painful feelings: not that she had ever loved him with passion, but she had been habituated to think of him with much kindness, esteem, and affection. Her thoughts had now for some months been fixed upon him, and she could not suddenly change their course, or console herself for his loss. She was soothed, however, by a most kind and sensible letter from Lady Anne Percival, who expressed the highest approbation of her conduct, the most friendly concern for her disappointment, and the most polite and sincere hopes, that Belinda would still continue to think of her with affection and esteem; though she had been so rash in her advice, and though her friendship had been apparently so selfish.

Belinda was conscious, that whatever might be her present regret, she had acted prudently in breaking off her connexion with Mr Vincent; she endeavoured to tranquillise her mind, and she occupied herself without ceasing, for she found employment the best relief from painful recollections.

CHAPTER XXX

News

"Do not expect that I should pretend to be sorry for Mr Vincent," said Lady Delacour. "Let him be as generous and as penitent as he pleases, I am heartily glad that he is on his way to Germany. I dare say he will find in the upper or *lower* circles of the empire, some heroine in the Kotzebue* taste, who will alternately make him miserable, till he is happy; and happy, till he is miserable. He is one of those men, who require great emotions. – Fine lovers these make for stage effect! – but the worst husbands in the world!

"I hope, Belinda, you give me credit, for having judged better of Mr Vincent than Lady Anne Percival did?"

"For having judged worse of him, you mean? Lady Anne always judges *as well* as possible of everybody."

"I will allow you to play upon words in a friend's defence but do not be alarmed for the reputation of Lady Anne's judgment. If it will be any satisfaction to you, I can with thorough sincerity assure you, that I never liked her so well in my life, as since I have detected her in a mistake. It saves her, in my imagination, from the odium of being a perfect character."

"And there was something so handsome in her manner of writing to me, when she found out her error," said Belinda —

"Very true, and my friend Mr Percival behaved handsomely. Where friendships clash, it is not every man who has clearness of head sufficient to know his duty to his neighbour. Mr Percival said no more, than just the thing he ought, for his ward. You have reason to be obliged to him; and as we are returning thanks to all persons concerned in our deliverance from this imminent danger, Juba the black, and Solomon the Jew, ought to come in for their share; for without that wrestling match of theirs, the truth might never have been dragged to light, and Mr Vincent would have been this day your lord and master. But the danger is over; you need not look so terrified – Do not be like the man who dropped down dead with terror, when he was shown by day light the broken bridge, which he had galloped over in the dark."

Lady Delacour was in such high spirits, that, without regard to connexion, she ran on from one subject to another.

"You have proved to me, my dear," said she, "that you are not a girl to marry, because your wedding-gown was sent home, or because the day was fixed, or because *things had gone so far*. I give you infinite credit for your *civil courage*, as Dr X — calls it: military courage, as he said to me yesterday — military courage, that seeks the bubble reputation even in the cannon's mouth, may be had for sixpence a day. But civil courage, such as enabled the Princess Parizade, in the Arabian Tales, to go straight up the hill to her object, though the magical multitude of advising and abusive voices continually called to her to turn back, is one of the rarest qualities in man or woman, and not to be had for love, money, or admiration."

"You place admiration not only above money, but above love, in your climax, I perceive," said Belinda, smiling.

"I will give you leave to be as philosophically sarcastic as you please, my dear, if you will only smile, and if you will not look as pale as Seneca's Paulina, whose story we heard — from whom?"

"From Mr Hervey, I believe."

"His name was ready upon your lips; I hope he was not far from your thoughts?"

"No one could be farther from my thoughts," said Belinda.

"Well, very likely — I believe it, because you say it; and because it is impossible."

"Rally me as much as you please, my dear Lady Delacour, I assure you, that I speak the simple truth."

"I cannot suspect you of affectation, my dear. Therefore honestly tell me, if Clarence Hervey were at your feet this instant, would you spurn him from you?"

"Spurn him! no — I would neither spurn him, nor *motion him from me*; but without using any of the terms in the heroine's dictionary — "

"You would refuse him?" interrupted Lady Delacour, with a look of indignation — "you would refuse him?"

"I did not say so, I *believe*."

"You would accept him?"

"I did not say so, I *am sure*."

"O, you would tell him that you were not *accustomed* to him?"

"Not exactly in these words, perhaps."

"Well, we shall not quarrel about words," said Lady Delacour; "I only beg you to remember your own principles; and if ever you are put to the trial, be consistent. The first thing in a philosopher is to be consistent."

"Fortunately, for the credit of my philosophy, there is no immediate danger of its being put to the test."

"Unfortunately, you surely mean; unless you are afraid that it might not stand the test. But I was going, when I spoke of consistency, to remind you, that all your own and Mr Percival's arguments about *first loves* may now, with equal propriety, be turned against you."

"How *against* me?"

"They are evidently as applicable to second as to first loves, I think."

"Perhaps they are," said Belinda; "but I really and truly am not inclined to think of love at present; particularly as there is no necessity that I should."

Belinda took up a book, and Lady Delacour for one half hour abstained from any farther raillery. But longer than half an hour she could not be silent on the subject uppermost in her thoughts.

"If Clarence Hervey," cried she, "were not the most honourable of blockheads, he might be the most happy of men. This Virginia! – O, how I hate her! – I am sure poor Clarence cannot love her."

"Because you hate her – or because you hate her without having ever seen her?" said Belinda.

"O, I know what she must be," replied Lady Delacour – "a soft, sighing, dying damsel, who puts bullfinches in her bosom. Smile, smile, my dear; you cannot help it: in spite of all your generosity, I know you must think as I do, and wish as I do, that she were at the bottom of the Black-sea this instant." Lady Delacour stood for some minutes musing, and then exclaimed, "I will move Heaven and Earth to break off this absurd match."

"Good Heavens, my dear Lady Delacour, what do you mean?"

"Mean! my dear, I mean what I say, which very few people do: no wonder I should surprise you!"

"I conjure you," cried Belinda, "if you have the least regard for my honour and happiness – "

"I have not the least, but the greatest; and depend upon it, my dear, I will do nothing that shall injure *that dignity of mind, and delicacy of character*, which I admire and love, as much as

Clarence Hervey did, and does. Trust to me – not Lady Anne Percival herself can be more delicate in her notions of propriety, than I am for my friends, and since my reformation, I hope I may add, for myself. – Fear nothing." – As she finished these words, she rang for her carriage. "I don't ask you to go out with me, my dear Belinda; I give you leave to sit in this arm chair, till I come back again, with your feet upon the fender, a book in your hand, and this little table beside you, like Lady S — 's picture of Comfort."

Lady Delacour spent the rest of the morning abroad, and when she returned home, she gave no account of what she had been doing, or of what or whom she had seen. This was so unusual, that Belinda could not avoid taking notice of it. Notwithstanding her ladyship's eulogium upon her own delicate sense of propriety, Miss Portman could not confide, with perfect resignation, in her prudence.

"Your ladyship reproached me once," said she, in a playful tone, "for my provoking want of curiosity: you have completely cured me of this defect, for never was woman more curious than I am, at this instant, to know the secret scheme that you have in agitation."

"Have patience a little longer, and the mystery will be unravelled. In the mean time, trust that everything I do is for the best. However, as you have behaved pretty well, I will give you one leading hint, when you have explained to me what you meant by saying, that your heart is not at present inclined to love? Pray have you quarrelled with love for ever?"

"No; but I can exist without it."

"Have you a heart?"

"I hope so."

"And it can exist without love? I now understand what was once said to me by a foolish lordling: – 'Of what use is the sun to the dial?'"[1]

Company came in, and relieved Belinda from any farther raillery. Lady Boucher and Mrs Margaret Delacour were, amongst a large party, to dine at Lady Delacour's. At dinner, the dowager seized the first auspicious moment of silence to announce a piece of intelligence, which she flattered herself would fix the eyes of all the world upon her.

1. A fact!

"So Mr Clarence Hervey is married at last!"

"Married!" cried Lady Delacour – she had sufficient presence of mind not to look directly at Belinda; but she fixed the dowager's eyes, by repeating – "married! are you sure of it?"

"Positive – positive! he was privately married yesterday at his aunt, Lady Almeria's apartments, at Windsor, to Miss Hartley. I told you it was to be, and now it is over; and a very extraordinary match Mr Hervey has made of it, after all. Think of his going, at last, and marrying a girl, who has been his mistress for years! No body will visit her, to be sure. Lady Almeria is excessively distressed; she did all she could to prevail on her brother, the bishop, to marry his nephew, but he very properly refused, giving it as a reason, that the girl's character was too well known."

"I thought my lord the bishop was at Spa," interposed a gentleman, whilst the dowager drew breath.

"O dear, no, sir; you have been misinformed," resumed she. "My lord the bishop has been returned from Spa this great while, and he has refused to see his nephew, to my certain knowledge. After all, I cannot but pity poor Clarence for being driven into this match. Mr Hartley has a prodigious fine fortune, to be sure, and he hurried things forward at an amazing rate, to patch up his daughter's reputation. He said, as I am credibly informed, yesterday morning, that if Clarence did not marry the girl before night, he would carry her and her fortune off the next day to the West Indies. Now the fortune was certainly an object."

"My dear Lady Boucher," interrupted Lord Delacour; "you must be misinformed in that particular: fortune is no object to Clarence Hervey; he is too generous a fellow to marry for fortune. What do you think – what do you say, Lady Delacour?"

"I say, and think, and feel, as you do, my lord," said Lady Delacour.

"You say, and think, and feel the same as my lord. Very extraordinary, indeed!" said the dowager. "Then if it were not for the sake of the fortune, pray why did Mr Hervey marry at all? Can anybody guess?"

"I should guess, because he was in love," said Lord Delacour, "for I remember, that was the reason I married myself."

"My dear good lord – but when I tell you the girl had been his mistress, till he was tired of her – "

"My Lady Boucher," said Mrs Margaret Delacour, who had hitherto listened in silence – "my Lady Boucher, you have been misinformed; Miss Hartley never was Clarence Hervey's mistress."

"I'm mighty glad you think so, Mrs Delacour; but I assure you, nobody else is so *charitable*. Those who live in the world hear a great deal more than those who live out of the world. I can promise you nobody will visit the bride, and that is the thing by which we are to judge."

Then the dowager and the rest of the company continued to descant upon the folly of the match. Those who wished to pay their court to Lady Delacour were the loudest in their astonishment, at his throwing himself away in this manner. Her ladyship smiled, and kept them in play by her address, on purpose to withdraw all eyes from Miss Portman, whilst, from time to time, she stole a glance at Belinda, to observe how she was affected by what passed: she was provoked by Belinda's self-possession. At last, when it had been settled that all the Herveys were *odd*, but that this match of Clarence's was the *oddest* of all the odd things, that any of the family had done for many generations, Mrs Delacour calmly said:

"Are you sure, Lady Boucher, that Mr Hervey is married?"

"Positive! as I said before, positive! Madam, my woman had it from Lady Newland's Swiss, who had it from Lady Singleton's Frenchwoman, who had it from Longueville, the hair-dresser, who had it from Lady Almeria's own woman, who was present at the ceremony, and must know, if anybody does."

"The report has come to us zigzag as quick as lightning, yet it does not flash conviction upon me," said Lady Delacour.

"Nor upon me," said Mrs Delacour, "for this simple reason. I have seen Miss Hartley, within these two hours, and I *had it* from her, that she is not married."

"Not married!" cried the dowager, with terror.

"I rather think not; she is now with her father, at my house, at dinner, I believe, and Clarence Hervey is at Lady Almeria's, at Windsor: her ladyship is confined by a fit of the gout, and sent for her nephew yesterday. If people who live out of the world hear less, they sometimes hear more correctly than those who live in it."

"Pray when does Mr Hervey return from Windsor?" said the incorrigible dowager.

"To morrow, madam," said Mrs Delacour. "As your ladyship is going to several parties this evening, I think it but *charitable* to set you right in these particulars, and I hope you will be so *charitable*, as to contradict the report of Miss Hartley's having been Clarence's mistress."

"Why, as to that, if the young lady is not married, we must presume there are good reasons for it," said the dowager. "Pray, on which side was the match broken off?"

"On neither side," answered Mrs Delacour.

"The thing goes on then? and what day is the marriage to take place?" said Lady Boucher.

"On Monday – or Tuesday – or Wednesday – or Thursday – or Friday – or Saturday – or Sunday, I believe," replied Mrs Delacour, who had the prudent art of giving answers effectually baffling to the curiosity of gossips.

The dowager consoled herself in her utmost need with a full plate of brandy cherries, and spoke not a word more during the second course. When the ladies retired after the dessert, she again commenced hostilities: she dared not come to open war with Mrs Delacour; but in a by-battle, in a corner, she carried every thing before her; and she triumphantly whispered, "We shall see, ma'am, that it will turn out, as I told you, that Miss Rachel, or Virginia, or whatever he pleased to call her, has been what I said; and, as I said, *nobody* will visit her, not a soul: fifty people I can count, who have declared to me they've made up their minds; and my own's made up, I candidly confess; and Lady Delacour, I am sure by her silence and looks, is of my way of thinking, and has no opinion of the young lady: as to Miss Portman, she is, poor thing! of course so wrapped up in her own affairs, no wonder she says nothing. That was a sad business of Mr Vincent's; I am surprised to see her look even as well as she does after it. Mr Percival, I am told," – said the well informed dowager, lowering her voice so much, that the lovers of scandal were obliged to close their heads round her – "Mr Percival, I am informed, refused his consent to his ward, (who is not of age) on account of an anonymous letter, and it is supposed Mr Vincent desired it for an excuse to get off handsomely. Fighting that duel, about her, with Sir Philip Baddely, settled his love – so he is gone to Germany, and she is left to wear the willow, which, you see, becomes her, as well as everything else. Did she eat any dinner, ma'am – you sat next her?'

"Yes – more than I did, I am sure."

"Very extraordinary! Then perhaps Sir Philip Baddely's *on* again – Lord bless me, what a match would that be for her! Why, Mrs Stanhope might then, indeed, deserve to be called the match-maker general. The seventh of her nieces this – But look, there's Mrs Delacour, leading Miss Portman off into the trictrac cabinet, with a face full of business – her hands in hers – Lord, I did not know they were on that footing! I wonder what's going forward –suppose old Hartley was to propose for Miss Portman – there would be a dénouement! – and cut his daughter off with a shilling! Nothing's impossible, you know. Did he ever see Miss Portman? I must go, and find out, positively."

In the mean time, Mrs Delacour, unconscious of the curiosity she had excited, was speaking to Belinda in the trictrac cabinet.

"My dear Miss Portman," said she; "you have a great deal of good nature, else I should not venture to apply to you on the present occasion. Will you oblige me, and serve a friend of mine – a gentleman who, as I once imagined, was an admirer of yours?"

"I will do anything in my power to oblige any friend of yours, madam" said Belinda; "but of whom are you speaking?"

"Of Mr Hervey, my dear young lady."

"He was never an admirer of mine," said Belinda; "but that does not make me the less disposed to serve him, as a friend – tell me, how it can possibly be in my power?"

"That you shall know immediately," said Mrs Delacour, rummaging and rustling for a considerable time amongst a heap of letters, which she had pulled out of the largest pockets that ever woman wore, even in the last century.

"O, here it is," continued she, opening and looking to them. "May I trouble you just to look over this letter? It is from poor Mr Hartley; he is, as you will see, excessively fond of this daughter, whom he has so fortunately discovered after his long search: he is dreadfully nervous, and has been terribly alarmed by these idle gossiping stories. You find, by what Lady Boucher said at dinner, that they have settled it amongst them; that Virginia is not a fit person to be visited; that she has been Clarence's mistress, instead of his pupil. Mr Hartley, you see by this letter, is almost out of his senses with the apprehension, that his daughter's reputation is ruined. I sent my carriage to Twickenham, the moment I received this letter, for the poor girl, and her gouvernante. They came to me this morning; but what can I do? – I am only one old woman against a confederacy of veteran gossips; but if I could gain you and Lady Delacour for my allies, I should fear no adversaries. Virginia is to stay with me for some days; and Lady Delacour, I see, has a great mind to come to see her; but she does not like to come without you, and she says, that she does not like to ask you to accompany her. I don't understand her delicacy about the matter; I have none, believing, as I do, that there is no foundation whatever for these malicious reports, which, *entre nous*, originated, I fancy, with Mrs Marriott. Now, will you oblige me? If you and Lady Delacour will come, and see Virginia tomorrow, all the world would follow your example the next day. It's often cowardice that makes people ill natured; have you the courage, my good Miss Portman, to be the first to do a benevolent action? I do assure you," continued Mrs Delacour with great earnestness – "I do assure you, I would as soon put my hand into that fire, this moment, as ask you to do anything that I thought improper – But forgive me for pressing this point; I am anxious to have your suffrage in her favour: Miss Belinda Portman's character for prudence and propriety stands so high, and is fixed so firmly, that she may venture to let us cling to it; and I am as firmly convinced of the poor girl's innocence, as I am of yours, and when you see her, you will be of my opinion."

"And I assure you, Mrs Delacour," said Belinda, "that you have wasted a great deal of eloquence upon this occasion, for – "

"I am sorry for it," interrupted Mrs Delacour, rising from her seat, with a look of some displeasure; "I meant not to distress or offend you, Miss Portman, by *my eloquence* – I am only concerned, that I should have so far mistaken your character as to expose myself to this refusal."

"I have given no refusal," said Belinda, mildly, "you did not let me finish my sentence."

"I beg pardon, that is a foolish old trick of mine."

"Mrs Delacour, I was going to say, has wasted a great deal of eloquence: for I am entirely of her opinion, and I shall with the greatest readiness comply with her request."

"You are a charming generous girl, and I am a passionate old fool – thank you a thousand times."

"You are not at all obliged to me," said Belinda. "When I first heard this story, I believed it, as Lady Boucher now does – but I have had reason to alter my opinion, and perhaps the same means of information would have changed hers; once convinced, it is impossible to relapse into suspicion."

"Impossible to *you* – the most truly virtuous women are always the least suspicious and uncharitable in their opinion of their own

sex. Lady Anne Percival inspired me with this belief, and Miss
Portman confirms it. – I admire your courage in daring to come
forward in the defence of innocence. I am very rude, alas! for
praising you so much."

"I have not a right to your admiration," said Belinda, "for I
must honestly confess to you, that I should not have this courage,
if there were any danger in the case; I do not think, that, in
doubtful cases, it is the business of a young woman to hazard her
own reputation, by an attempt to preserve another's: I do not
imagine, at least, that I am of sufficient consequence, in the world,
for this purpose; therefore I should never attempt it. It is the duty
of such women as Mrs Delacour, whose reputations are beyond
the power of scandal, to come forward in the defence of injured
innocence: but this would not be courage in Belinda Portman, it
would be presumption and temerity."

"Well, if you will not let me admire your courage, or your
generosity, or your prudence," said Mrs Delacour, laughing,
"you must positively let me admire *you* altogether, and love you
too, for I cannot help it. Farewell."

After the company was gone, Lady Delacour, was much
surprised, by the earnestness with which Belinda pressed the
request, that they might the next morning pay a visit to Virginia.

"My dear," said Lady Delacour, "to tell you the truth, I am full
of curiosity, and excessively anxious to go. I hesitated, merely on
your account; I fancied that you would not like the visit, and that
if I went without you, it might be taken notice of. – But I am
delighted to find that you will come with me; I can only say, that
you have more generosity, than I should have in the same
situation."

The next morning they went together to Mrs Delacour's. In
their way thither, Belinda, to divert her own thoughts, and to
rouse Lady Delacour from the profound and unnatural silence,
into which she had fallen, petitioned her to finish the history of Sir
Philip Baddely, the dog, Miss Annabella Luttridge, and her billet-
doux.

"For some of my high crimes and misdemeanours, you vowed
that you would not tell me the remainder of the story, till the
whole week had elapsed; now will you satisfy my curiosity? You
recollect, that you left off just where you said, that you were come
to the best part of the story."

"Was I? did I? – Very true, we shall have time enough to finish it by and by, my dear," said Lady Delacour; "at present my poor head is running upon something else, and I have left off being an accomplished actress, or I could talk of one subject, and think of another, as well as the best of you. Stop the carriage, my dear, I am afraid they have forgot my orders."

"Did you carry what I desired this morning to Mrs Delacour's?" said her ladyship to one of her footmen.

"I did, my lady."

"And did you say from me, that it was not to be opened, till I came?"

"Yes, my lady."

"Where did you leave it?"

"In Mrs Delacour's dressing-room, my lady: – she desired me to take it up there, and she locked the door, and said, no one should go in, till you came."

"Very well – go on. Belinda – My dear, I hope that I have worked up your curiosity to the highest pitch."

CHAPTER XXXI

The Denouement

Curiosity was not, at this instant, the strongest passion in Belinda's mind. When the carriage stopped at Mrs Delacour's door, her heart almost ceased to beat; but she summoned resolution to go through, with firmness and dignity, the task she had undertaken.

Clarence Hervey was not in the room when they entered, nor was Virginia: Mrs Ormond said, that she had been extremely feverish during the night, and that she had advised her not to get up, till late in the day. But Mrs Delacour immediately went for her, and in a few minutes she made her appearance.

Belinda and Lady Delacour exchanged a glance of surprise and admiration. There was a grace and simplicity in her manner, joined to an air of naïveté, that made an irresistible impression in her favour. Lady Delacour, however, after the first surprise was over, seemed to relapse into her former opinion; and the piercing looks, which her ladyship from time to time cast upon Virginia as she spoke, produced their effect. She was abashed and silent. Belinda endeavoured to engage her in conversation, and to her she talked with ease, and even with freedom. Virginia examined Miss Portman's countenance with a species of artless curiosity and interest, that was not restrained by factitious politeness. This examination was not peculiarly agreeable to Belinda, yet it was made with so much apparent simplicity, that she could not be displeased.

On the first pause in the conversation, Mrs Delacour said, "Pray, my dear Lady Delacour, what is this wonderful present that you sent to me this morning, which you desire that no one should see, till you came?"

"I cannot satisfy your curiosity yet," replied Lady Delacour. "I must wait till Clarence Hervey comes, for the present is intended for him."

An air of solemn mystery in her ladyship's manner, as she pronounced these words, excited general attention. There was a dead silence, which lasted several minutes: some feeble attempts were then made by each of the company, to start a fresh subject of conversation; but it would not do – all relapsed into the silence of expectation. At last, Clarence Hervey arrived. Belinda rejoiced that the universal curiosity, which Lady Delacour had inspired, prevented any one's observing the sudden change in Mr Hervey's countenance, when he beheld her.

"A pretty set of curious children you are!" cried Lady Delacour, laughing. "Do you know, Clarence, that they are all dying with impatience, to see *un gage d'amitié** that I have brought for you; and the reason that they are so curious is simply, because I had the address to say, in a solemn voice, 'I cannot satisfy your curiosity, till Clarence Hervey arrives.' Now, follow me, my friends; and if you be disappointed, lay the blame not to me, but to your own imaginations."

She led the way to Mrs Delacour's dressing-room, and all the company followed.

"Now, what do you expect to see?" said she, putting the key into the door.

After waiting some moments for a reply, but in vain, she threw open the door, and they saw, hung before the wall opposite to them, a green curtain.

"I thought, my dear Clarence," resumed Lady Delacour, "that no present could be more agreeable to you, than a companion for your Virginia. Does this figure," continued she, drawing back the curtain – "does this figure give you the idea of Paul?"

At these words Virginia turned her eyes upon the picture – uttered a piercing shriek, and fell senseless upon the floor.

"Take it coolly," said Lady Delacour, "and she will come to her senses presently. Young ladies must shriek and faint upon certain occasions; but men, (looking at Clarence Hervey) need not always be dupes. This is only a *scene*; consider it as such, and admire the actress as I do."

"Actress! O, she is no actress!" cried Mrs Ormond.

Clarence Hervey raised her from the ground, and Belinda sprinkled water over her face.

"She's dead! – she's dead! O, my sweet child! she's dead!" exclaimed Mrs Ormond, trembling so violently, that she could not sustain Virginia's weight.

"She is no actress, indeed," said Clarence Hervey; "her pulse is gone!"

Lady Delacour looked at Virginia's pale lips, touched her cold hands, and, with a look of horror, cried out, "Good Heavens! what have I done? What shall we do with her?"

"Give her air – give her air, air, air!" cried Belinda.

"You keep the air from her, Mrs Ormond," said Mrs Delacour. "Let us leave her to Miss Portman; she has more presence of mind than any of us." And as she spoke, she forced Mrs Ormond away with her out of the room.

"If Mr Hartley should come, keep him with you, Mrs Delacour," said Clarence Hervey. "Is her pulse quite gone?"

"No; it beats stronger and stronger," said Belinda.

"Her colour is returning," said Lady Delacour. "There! raise her a little, dear Belinda; she is coming to herself."

"Had not you better draw the curtain again before that picture," said Miss Portman; "lest she should see it, the moment that she opens her eyes?"

Virginia came slowly to her recollection, saw Lady Delacour drawing the curtain before the picture, then fixed her eyes upon Clarence Hervey, without uttering a word.

"Are you better now?" said he, in a gentle tone.

"O, do not speak – do not look so kindly!" cried Virginia. "I am well – quite well – better than I deserve to be" – and she pressed Belinda's hand, as if to thank her for assisting and supporting her.

"We may safely leave her now," whispered Belinda to Lady Delacour; "we are strangers, and our presence only distresses her."

They withdrew. But the moment Virginia found herself alone with Mr Hervey, she was seized with an universal tremor; she tried to speak, but could not articulate. At last, she burst into a flood of tears; and when this had in some measure relieved her, she threw herself upon her knees, and clasping her hands, exclaimed, as she looked up to Heaven –

"O, if I knew what I ought to do! – if I knew what I ought to say! — "

"Shall I tell you, Virginia? And will you believe me?"

"Yes, yes, yes!"

"You ought to say – the truth – whatever it may be."

"But you will think me the most ungrateful of human beings?"

"How often must I assure you, Virginia, that I make no claim upon your gratitude. Speak to me – I conjure you, as you value your happiness and mine – speak to me without disguise! What is all this mystery? Why should you fear to let me know what passes in your heart? Why did you shriek at the sight of that picture?"

"O, forgive me! forgive me!" cried Virginia; and she would have sunk at his feet, if he had not prevented her.

"I will – I can forgive anything, but deceit. Do not look at me with so much terror, Virginia – I have not deserved it – my wish is to make you happy – I would sacrifice even my own happiness, to secure yours – but do not mislead me, or you ruin us both. Cannot you give me a distinct answer to this simple question? – Why did you shriek at the sight of that picture?"

"Because – but you will call me '*perfidious, ungrateful Virginia*!' – because I have seen that figure – he has knelt to me – he has kissed my hand – and I – "

Clarence Hervey withdrew his arms, which had supported her, and placing her upon a sofa, left her, whilst he walked up and down the room for some minutes, in silence.

"And why, Virginia," said he, stopping short, "was it necessary to conceal all this from me? Why was it necessary to persuade me that I was beloved? Why was it necessary that my happiness should be the sacrifice?"

"It shall not! – it shall not! Your happiness shall not be the sacrifice. Heaven is my witness, that there is no sacrifice *I* would not make for you. Forgive me that shriek! I could not help fainting indeed! But I will be yours; I *ought* to be yours; and I am not perfidious, I am not ungrateful; do not look upon me as you did in my dream!"

"Do not talk to me in dreams, my dear Virginia; this is no time for trifling; I ask no sacrifice from you, I ask nothing but truth."

"Truth! Mrs Ormond knows all the truth. I have concealed nothing from her."

"But she has concealed every thing from me," cried Clarence; and, with a sudden impulse of indignation, he was going to summon her: but when his hand was upon the lock of the door, he paused, returned to Virginia, and said, "Let me hear the truth from *your* lips; it is all I shall ever ask from you. How! – when! – where did you see this man?"

"What man?" said Virginia, looking up, with the simple expression of innocence in her countenance.

Clarence pointed to the picture.

"At the village in the New Forest, at Mrs Smith's house," said Virginia, "one evening when I walked with her from my grandmother's cottage."

"And your grandmother knew of this?"

"Yes," said Virginia, blushing, "and she was very much displeased."

"And Mrs Ormond knew of this?" pursued Clarence.

"Yes; but she told me that you would not be displeased at it."

Mr Hervey made another hasty step toward the door, but restraining his impetuous temper, he again stopped, and, leaning over the back of a chair, opposite to Virginia, waited in silence for her to proceed. – He waited in vain.

"I do not mean to distress you, Miss Hartley," said he.

She burst into tears. – "I knew, I knew," cried she, "that you *would* be displeased; I told Mrs Ormond so. I knew you would never forgive me."

"In that you were mistaken," said Clarence, mildly; " I forgive you without difficulty, as I hope you may forgive yourself; nor can it be my wish to extort from you any mortifying confessions. But, perhaps, it may yet be in my power to serve you, if you will trust to me. I will myself speak to your father. I will do every thing to secure to you the object of your affections, if you will, in this last moment of our connexion, treat me with sincerity, and suffer me to be your friend."

Virginia sobbed so violently for some time, that she could not speak – at last she said –

"You are – you are – the most generous of men! You have always been my *best* friend! I am the most ungrateful of human beings! But I am sure I never wished, I never intended, to deceive you. Mrs Ormond told me — "

"Do not speak of her at present, or perhaps I may lose my temper," interrupted Clarence, in an altered voice; "only tell me, I conjure you – tell me, in one word, who is this man? and where is he to be found?"

"I do not know. I do not understand you," said Virginia.

"You do not know! – You will not trust me – Then I must leave you to – to Mr Hartley."

"Do not leave me – O, do not leave me in anger!" cried Virginia, clinging to him – "Not trust you! – I! – not trust you! – O, what *can* you mean? I have no confessions to make! Mrs Ormond knows every thought of my mind, and so shall you, if you will only hear me. I do not know who this man is, I assure you; nor where he is to be found."

"And yet you love him? Can you love a man whom you do not know, Virginia?"

"I only love his figure, I believe," said Virginia.

"His figure!"

"Indeed I am quite bewildered," said Virginia, looking round wildly; "I know not what I feel."

"If you permitted this man to kneel to you, to kiss your hand, surely you must know that you love him, Virginia?"

"But that was only in a dream; and Mrs Ormond said — "

"Only a dream! But you met him at Mrs Smith's, in the New Forest?"

"That was only a picture."

"Only a picture! – but you have seen the original?"

"Never – never in my life; and I wish to Heaven I had never, never seen that fatal picture! The image haunts me day and night. When I read of heroes in the day, that figure rises to my view, instead of yours. When I go to sleep at night I see it, instead of yours, in my dreams; it speaks to me, it kneels to me. I long ago told Mrs Ormond this, but she laughed at me. I told her of that frightful dream. I saw you weltering in your blood; I tried to save you, but could not. I heard you say, 'Perfidious, ungrateful Virginia! you are the cause of my death!' O, it was the most dreadful night I ever passed! Still this figure, this picture, was before me; and he was the knight of the white plumes; and it was he who stabbed you: but when I wished him to be victorious, I did not know that he was fighting against you. So Mrs Ormond told me, that I need not blame myself; and she said, that you were not so foolish as to be jealous of a picture; but I knew you would be displeased – I knew you would think me ungrateful – I knew you would never forgive me."

Whilst Virginia rapidly uttered all this, Clarence marked the wild animation of her eyes, the sudden changes of her countenace; he recollected her father's insanity; every feeling of his mind gave way to terror and pity; he approached her with all the calmness that he could assume, took both her hands, and holding them in his, said, in a soothing voice –

"My dear Virginia! you are not ungrateful. I do not think you so. I am not displeased with you. You have done nothing to displease me. Compose yourself, dear Virginia."

"I am quite composed, now you again call me dear Virginia. Only I am afraid, as I always told Mrs Ormond, that I do not love you *enough*; but she said, that I did, and that my thinking so was the strongest proof of my affection."

Virginia now spoke in so consistent a manner, that Clarence could not doubt, that she was in the clear possession of her understanding. She repeated to him all that she had said to Mrs Ormond; and he began to hope, that, without any intention to deceive, Mrs Ormond's ignorance of the human heart led her into a belief, that Virginia was in love with him; whilst, in fact, her imagination, exalted by solitude and romance, embodied and became enamoured of a phantom.

"I always told Mrs Ormond, that she was mistaken," said Clarence. "I never believed, that you loved me, Virginia, till — (he paused, and carefully examined her countenance) — till you yourself gave me reason to think so. Was it only a principle of gratitude, then, that dictated your answer to my letter?"

She looked irresolute; and at last, in a low voice, said —

"If I could see, if I could speak to Mrs Ormond — "

"She cannot tell what are the secret feelings of your heart, Virginia. Consult no Mrs Ormond. Consult no human creature but yourself."

"But Mrs Ormond told me, that you loved me, and that you had educated me to be your wife."

Mr Hervey made an involuntary exclamation against Mrs Ormond's folly.

"How, then, can you be happy," continued Virginia, "if I am so ungrateful as to say I do not love you? That I do not *love* you! — Oh! *that* I cannot say; for I do love you, better than any one living, except my father, and with the same sort of affection that I feel for him. You ask me to tell you the secret feelings of my heart. — The only secret feeling, of which I am conscious, is — a wish not to marry, unless I could see in reality such a person as — But that I knew was only a picture, a dream; and I thought, that I ought at least to sacrifice my foolish imaginations to you, who have done so much for me. I knew that it would be the height of ingratitude to refuse you; and besides, my father told me, that you would not accept of my fortune without my hand, so I consented to marry you: forgive me, if these were wrong motives, I thought them right. Only tell me what I can do to make you happy, as I am sure I wish to do; to that wish I would sacrific every other feeling."

Sacrifice nothing, dear Virginia. We may both be happy without making any sacrifice of our feelings," cried Clarence. And, transported at regaining his own freedom, Virginia's simplicity never appeared to him so charming as at this moment. – "Dearest Virginia, forgive me for suspecting you for one instant of any thing unhandsome. Mrs Ormond, with the best intentions possible, has led us both to the brink of misery. But I find you such as I always thought you, ingenuous, affectionate, innocent."

"And you are not angry with me?" interrupted Virginia, with joyful eagerness, "and you will not think me ungrateful? And you will not be unhappy? And Mrs Ormond was mistaken? And you do not wish, that I should *love* you, that I should be your wife I mean? O, don't deceive me, for I cannot help believing whatever you say."

Clarence Hervey, to give her a convincing proof, that Mrs Ormond had misled her as to his sentiments, immediately avowed his passion for Belinda.

"You have relieved me from all doubt, all fear, all anxiety," said Virginia, with the sweetest expression of innocent affection in her countenance. "May you be as happy as you deserve to be! May Belinda – is not that her name? – May Belinda — "

At this moment Lady Delacour half opened the door, exclaiming –

"Human patience can wait no longer!"

"Will you trust me to explain for you, dear Virginia?" said Clarence.

"Most willingly," said Virginia, retiring as Lady Delacour advanced. "Pray leave me here alone, whilst you, who are used to talk before strangers, speak for me."

"Dare you venture, Clarence," said her ladyship, as she closed the door, "to leave her alone with that picture? You are no lover, if you be not jealous."

"I am not jealous," said Clarence, "yet I am a lover – a passionate lover."

"A passionate lover!" cried Lady Delacour, stopping short as they were crossing the antichamber; – "then I have done nothing but mischief. In love with Virginia? – I will not – cannot believe it."

"In love with Belinda! – Cannot you, will not you believe it?"

"My dear Clarence, I never doubted it for an instant. But are you at liberty to own it to any body but me?"

"I am at liberty to declare it to all the world."

"You transport me with joy! I will not keep you from her a second. But stay – I am sorry to tell you, that, as she informed me this morning, *her heart is not at present inclined to love*. And here are half a dozen poor wretches in this room dying with curiosity. Curiosity is as strong a passion as love, and has as good a right to compassion."

As he entered the room, Clarence Hervey's first glance was at Belinda, and rapid as it was, it explained his whole heart.

"What is become of Mr Hartley?" said Clarence, looking round – "I do not see him."

"No: for I have hid him," said Lady Delacour: "he shall be forthcoming presently."

"Dear Mr Clarence Hervey, what have you done with my Virginia?" said Mrs Ormond.

"Dear Mrs Ormond, what have *you* done with her?" replied Clarence. "By your mistaken kindness, by insisting upon doing us both good against our wills, you were very near making us both miserable for life. But I blame nobody, I have no right to blame any one so much as myself. All this has arisen from my own presumption and imprudence. Nothing could be more absurd than my scheme of educating a woman in solitude, to make her fit for society. I might have foreseen what must happen, that Virginia would consider me as her tutor, her father, not as her lover, or her husband; that, with the most affectionate of hearts, she could for me feel nothing but *gratitude*."

"Nothing but gratitude!" repeated Mrs Ormond, with a degree of amazement in her countenance, which made everybody present smile: "I am sure, I thought she was dying for love of you."

"My dear Belinda," whispered Lady Delacour, "if I might judge by the colour of this cheek, which has been for some moments permanent crimson, I should guess, that you were beginning to find out *of what use the sun is to the dial*."

"You will not let me hear what Mr Hervey is saying," replied Belinda; "I am very curious."

"Curiosity is a stronger passion than love, as I told him just now," said Lady Delacour.

In spite of all his explanations, Mrs Ormond could not be made to comprehend Virginia's feelings. She continually repeated —

"But it is impossible for Virginia, or for any body, to be in love with a picture."

"It is not said that she is in love with a picture," replied Mrs Delacour, "though even for that I could find you a precedent."

"My dear Lady Delacour," said Mrs Ormond, "will you explain to us how that picture came into your possession, and how it came here, and, in short, all that is to be known about it?"

"Ay, explain! explain! my dear Lady Delacour," cried Mrs Delacour — "I am afraid, I am grown almost as curious as my Lady Boucher. Explain! explain!"

"Most willingly," said Lady Delacour.

"To Marriott's ruling passion for birds you are all of you indebted for this discovery. A few weeks ago, whilst we were at Twickenham, as Marriott was waiting at a stationer's, to bid her last adieus to a bullfinch, a gentleman came into the shop where she and Bobby (as she calls this bird) were coquetting, and the gentleman was struck even more than Marriott with the bullfinch. He went almost distracted on hearing a particular tune, which this bird sung. I suspected, from the symptoms, that the gentleman must be, or must have been, in love with the bullfinch's mistress. Now the bullfinch was traced home to the ci-devant Virginia St Pierre, the present Miss Hartley. I had my reasons for being curious about her loves and lovers, and as soon as I learned the story from Marriott, I determined, if possible, to find out who this stranger, with the strange passion for bullfinches, might be. I questioned and cross-questioned all those people at the stationer's who were present, when he fell into extasies; and from the shopman, who had been bribed to secrecy, I learned that our gentleman returned to the stationer's the day after he met Marriott, and watched till he obtained a sight of Virginia, as she came to her window. Now it was believed by the girl of this shop, who had lived for some time with Mrs Ormond — Forgive me, Mr Hervey, for what I am going to say – forgive me, Mrs Ormond – scandal, like death, is common to all. — It was believed that Virginia was Mr Hervey's mistress. My stranger no sooner learnt this, than he swore that he would think of her no more, and after bestowing a variety of seaman's execrations upon the villain who had seduced his heavenly creature, he departed from Twickenham, and was no more seen or heard of. My inquiries after him were indefatigable, but for some time unsuccessful. And so they might have continued, and we might have been all making one another miserable at this moment, if it had not been for Mr Vincent's great dog Juba — Miss Annabella Luttridge's billet-doux

– Sir Philip Baddely's insolence – my Lord Delacour's belief in a quack balsam – and Captain Sunderland's humanity."

"Captain Sunderland! who is Captain Sunderland? we never heard of him before," cried Mrs Ormond.

"You shall hear of him just as I did, if you please," said Lady Delacour, "and if Belinda will submit to hear me tell the same story twice."

Here her ladyship repeated the history of the battle of the dogs; and of Sir Philip Baddely's knocking down Juba the man, for struggling in defence of Juba the dog.

"Now the gentleman, who assisted my Lord Delacour in bringing the disabled negro across the square to our house, was Captain Sunderland. My lord summoned Marriott to produce Lady Boucher's infallible balsam, that it might be tried upon Juba's sprained ankle. Whilst my lord was intent upon the balsam, Marriott was intent upon Captain Sunderland. She recollected, that she had met him some where before, and the moment he spoke, she knew him to be the gentleman, who had fallen into extasies, in the shop at Twickenham, about the bullfinch. Marriott hastened to me with the news; I hastened to my lord, made him introduce Captain Sunderland to me, and I never rested, till he had told me all that I wanted to know. Some years ago, just before he went to sea, he paid a visit to his mother, who then lodged with a widow Smith, in the New Forest. Whilst he was there, he heard of the young beauty who lived in the Forest, with a grandmother, who was *not a little particular*; and who would not permit any body to see her.

"My captain's curiosity was excited; he took out his spyglass one day, and unseen by the duenna, obtained a distinct view of Virginia, watering her roses and tending her bees. Struck with her uncommon beauty, he approached carefully to the thicket, in which the cottage was inclosed, and found a *lair*, where he concealed himself, day after day, and contemplated at leisure the budding charms of the fair woodnymph. In short, he became so enamoured, that he was determined to gain admittance at the cottage, and declare his passion.

"For ought I know, he is the first knight or squire upon record, who ever fell in love with his mistress through a telescope. But Virginia, who, according to your account, Clarence, is better read in romances than any of us, can set me right, if I am incorrect. At all events, I hope the novelty and delicacy of this mode of

courtship will recommend him to her favour. To his honour be it
told, that when the history of the poor girl's mother, the situation
and fears of the old lady, who was her only friend, were known to
him, in consideration of the extreme youth of the ward, and the
extreme age of her guardian, he determined to defer his addresses,
till his return from the West Indies, whither he was shortly to sail,
and where he had hopes of making a fortune, that might put him
in a situation to render the object of his affections independent.
He left a bullfinch with Mrs Smith, who gave it to Virginia, without telling to whom it had belonged, lest her grandmother might
be displeased.

"I really thought, that all this showed too nice a moral sense for
a young dashing lieutenant in the navy, and I was persuaded, that
my gentleman was only keeping his mistress's secret like a man of
honour. With this belief, I regretted, that Clarence Hervey should
throw himself away upon a girl, who was unworthy of him."

"I hope," interrupted Clarence, "you are perfectly convinced of
your mistake."

"Perfectly! perfectly! – I am convinced that Virginia is only half
mad. But let me go on with my story. I was determined to discover
whether she had any remains of affection for this captain. It was in
vain he assured me, that she had never seen him. I prevailed upon
him to let me go on my own way, and I required nothing from
him, but to sit for his picture in the character of Paul, in St Pierre's
romance. 'If,' thought I, 'he speak truth, Virginia will see this
picture without emotion, and it will only seem to be a present for
Clarence. But if she had ever seen him before, or had any secret to
conceal, she will betray herself on the sudden appearance of this
picture.' Things have turned out contrary to all my expectations,
and yet better. — And now, Clarence, I must beg you will prevail
on Miss Hartley to appear, I can go on no farther without her."

Lady Delacour took Virginia by the hand the moment she
entered the room.

"Will you trust yourself with me, Miss Hartley?" said she; "I
have made you faint once to day by the sight of a picture, will you
promise me not to faint again, when I produce the original?"

"The original!" said Virginia – "I will trust myself with you, for
I am sure you cannot mean to laugh at me – though, perhaps, I
deserve to be laughed at."

Lady Delacour threw open the door of another apartment. Mr
Hartley appeared, and with him Captain Sunderland.

"My dear daughter," said Mr Hartley, "give me leave to introduce to you a friend, to whom I owe more obligations than to any man living, except to Mr Hervey. This gentleman was stationed some years ago at Jamaica, and in a rebellion of the negroes on my plantation he saved my life. Fortune has accidentally thrown my benefactor in my way. To show my sense of my obligations is out of my power."

Virginia's surprise was extreme; her vivid dreams, the fond wishes of her waking fancy, were at once accomplished. For the first moment, she gazed as on an animated picture, and all the ideas of love and romance, associated with this image, rushed upon her mind.

But when the realities, by which she was surrounded, dispelled the illusion, she suddenly withdrew her eyes, and blushed deeply, with such timid and graceful modesty as charmed every body present.

"To prevent all difficulties and embarrassments, I must inform you, Miss Hartley," said Lady Delacour, "that Captain Sunderland will not insist upon prompt payment of your father's debt of gratitude; he has but one quarter of an hour to spend with us, he is actually under sailing orders, and he must be absent for some weeks, so that you will have time to become accustomed to the idea of a new lover, before his return. Clarence, I advise you to accompany Captain Sunderland on this cruise, don't you, Belinda?"

"And now, my good friends," continued Lady Delacour, "shall I finish the novel for you?"

"If your ladyship pleases; nobody can do it better."

"But I hope you will remember, dear Lady Delacour," said Belinda, "that there is nothing in which novelists are so apt to err, as in hurrying things toward the conclusion. In not allowing *time* enough for that change of feeling, which change of situation cannot instantly produce."

"That's right, my dear Belinda, true to your principles to the last gasp. Fear nothing – you shall have *time* enough to become accustomed to Clarence. Would you choose that I should draw out the story to five volumes more? With your advice and assistance, I can, with the greatest ease, my dear. – A declaration of love, you know, is only the beginning of things; there may be blushes, and sighs, and doubts, and fears, and misunderstandings, and jealousies without end or common sense, to fill up the necessary space, and to gain the necessary *time*; but if I might conclude the business in two lines, I should say,

> 'Ye Gods, annihilate both space and time,
> 'And make four lovers happy.'"

"O, that would be cutting matters too short," said Mrs Margaret Delacour. "I am of the old school, and though I could dispense with the description of Miss Harriet Byron's* worked chairs and fine china, yet I own, I like to hear something of the preparation for a marriage, as well as of the mere wedding. I like to hear *how* people become happy in a rational manner, better than to be told in the huddled style of an old fairy tale – *and so they were all married, and they lived very happily all the rest of their days*."

"We are not in much danger of hearing such an account of modern marriages," said Lady Delacour. – "But how shall I please you all ? – Some people cry – 'Tell me everything' – Others say, that,

> 'Le secret d'ennuyer est celui de tout dire.'*

"Something must be left to the imagination. Positively I will not describe wedding dresses, or a procession to church. I have no objection to saying, that the happy couples were united by the worthy Mr Moreton; that Mr Percival gave Belinda away; and that immediately after the ceremony, he took the whole party down with him to Oakly-park. – Will this do? – Or, we may conclude, if you like it better, with a characteristic letter of congratulation from Mrs Stanhope to her *dearest* niece, Belinda, acknowledging that she was wrong to quarrel with her, for refusing Sir Philip Baddely, and giving her infinite credit for that admirable *management* of Clarence Hervey, which she hopes will continue through life."

"Well, I have no objection to ending with a letter," said Mrs Delacour, "for last speeches are always tiresome."

"Yes," said her ladyship; "it is so difficult, as the critic says, to get lovers off upon their knees. Now I think of it, let me place you all in proper attitudes for stage effect. What signifies being happy, unless we appear so? – Captain Sunderland – kneeling with Virginia, if you please, sir, at her father's feet – You in the act of giving them your blessing, Mr Hartley – Mrs Ormond clasps her hands with joy – Nothing can be better than that, madam – I give you infinite credit for the attitude – Clarence, you have a right to

Belinda's hand, and may kiss it too – Nay, Miss Portman, it is the rule of the stage – Now, where's my Lord Delacour? – He should be embracing me, to show that we are reconciled – Ha! here he comes – Enter Lord Delacour, with little Helena in his hand – Very well! a good start of surprise, my lord – Stand still, pray, you cannot be better than you are – Helena, my love, do not let go your father's hand – There! quite pretty and natural! – Now, Lady Delacour, to show that she is reformed, comes forward to address the audience with a moral – a moral! – yes,

> 'Our *tale* contains a *moral*, and, no doubt,
> 'You all have wit enough to find it out.'

NOTES

VOLUME I

p.8 **birthnight** evening of a royal birthday.

p.13 **Duchesse de Brinvilliers** Marie-Madeleine d'Aubray, executed 1676, famous poisoner.

p.14 **Garrick between tragedy and comedy** critics disputed whether David Garrick (1717–79), the famous actor, was more at home in tragedy or comedy.

p.17 **Fuseli** Henry Fuseli (1741–1825) Anglo–Swiss painter, illustrator of Milton, friend of Blake and of ME's publisher, Joseph Johnson.

p.19 **School for Scandal** comedy (1777) by Richard Brinsley Sheridan (1751–1816).

p.23 **Anacharsis Cloots** member of the National Convention which governed France during the Reign of Terror, executed in 1794.

Orateur du genre humain spokesman of the human race.

p.25 **celebrated character** Francis Blake Delaval (1727–71), friend of Maria Edgeworth's father, Richard Lovell Edgeworth. See sketch of *Belinda*.

p.29 **l'éloquence du billet** eloquence in writing familiar letters.

Amazons legendary race of female warriors who, in order to shoot better with the bow, cauterised one breast to prevent its developing.

p.30 **Mrs Bellamy** eighteenth-century actress (1731–88), published her *Apology* in 1788.

Gil Blas picaresque novel by Alain-René le Sage (1668–1747), published Paris 1715–35.

p.32 **the torpedo** the torpedo-fish.

p.33 **in petto** in reserve.

p.37 **à plus forte raison** for the same reason even more strongly applied.

tracasseries trouble-making.

p.40 **Sheridan's speech** the Irish dramatist Richard Brinsley Sheridan was also a noted parliamentary orator at Westminster.

p.41 **Sir Bertrand** *Sir Bertram*, (1773) novel by Anna Letitia Aikin, later Barbauld (1743–1825).

p.50 **toute éplorée** all in tears.

p.57 au fin fond right to the depths.

p.59 les dessous des cartes literally, the undersides of the cards.

p.64 Camilla *Camilla* (1796), novel by Frances Burney (1752–1840).

p.65 Zara quotation from *Zaire* (1732), tragedy by Voltaire (1684–1778).

   Hervey's Meditations *Meditations among the tombs, in a letter to a lady* (1746), by James Hervey (1714–58).

p.67 Linnaeus Swedish botanist (1707–78), first to create a system of naming species and genera of plants.

   émigrée female royalist who fled France at the revolution of 1789.

   Madame de Sevigné; Madame de Grignan Madame de Sevigné (1626–96) wrote a famous series of letters from the court of Louis XIV to her daughter Madame de Grignan.

   belle chevelure beautiful tresses.

p.68 Rape of the Lock poem (1714) by Alexander Pope (1688–1744) in which a lock of hair is stolen from a heroine named Belinda.

p.69 de part et d'autre on either side.

p.70 cela est selon that depends.

   forming a country novice a hint of the subplot of chapters 26–31.

p.79 malheureusement unfortunately.

p.82 Dr Franklin Benjamin Franklin (1706–90), American author and revolutionary politician.

p.84 Dr X — based on the novelist Dr John Moore – see the sketch of *Belinda*.

p.85 bloody bad hand the bloody hand is the heraldic designation of the baronet (ME's note in later editions).

p.88 Griselda heroine of Chaucer's *Clerk's Tale*, who unprotestingly complies when her husband pretends to make away with her children and repudiate herself. Maria Edgeworth's *The Modern Griselda* (1805) parodies this tale.

p.89 exigeante demanding.

p.90 Abbé Nollet French physician and scientist (1700–70).

p.93 Savage and Lady Macclesfield the poet Richard Savage (1697–1742) claimed to be the illegitimate son of Lady Macclesfield who rejected the claim.

p.95 la femme comme il y en a peu the woman like few others: heroine of a tale by Marmontel (see note to p.162).

   la bonne mère the good mother.

   bonne bouche morsel eaten at the end of a meal to clear the palate.

p.96 sulphurs 'sulphur impressions', impressions of a seal or medal in a mixture of sulphur and wax.

   Vertumnus and Pomona Pomona, goddess of tree fruit, wooed by Vertumnus, god of the seasons.

p.103 Twiss Richard Twiss (1747–1821), author of *Travels through Portugal and Spain* (1775).

Vida Marco Girolamo Vida (1480–1566) wrote *De ludo scacchorum* (1527), a poem on the game of chess.

Irwin Eyles Irwin (1748–1817), poet and traveller in India.

Sir William Jones Orientalist (1746–94), author of a poem on chess, published 1763.

p.108 tant pis/tant mieux so much the better/so much the worse.

p.129 Zimmerman Johann Georg Zimmermann (1728–95) in 1756 wrote *Solitude considered with respect to its influence on the mind and heart* (Title of the English translation, 1791).

Would Chloe know . . . (ME's note; the quotation is from Pope's *Of the Characters of Women* (1735), 11.177–8)

p.131 n'a pas une ame de boue has not a soul of mud.

p.133 gouvernante chaperone.

p.135 stadtholder title of the chief magistrate in the Dutch republic, hereditary from 1747 in the house of Orange.

p.136 Virginia St Pierre name based on the French romance, *Paul et Virginie* (1787) by Bernardin de St Pierre (1737–1814).

p.137 d'aller votre train continue on your way.

p.139 d'avance in advance.

p.144 en attendant meanwhile.

VOLUME II

p.153 ci-devant former (often used to designate French aristocrats whose titles had been abolished by the revolutionary government).

note The reference is to Charles Johnstone's *Chrysal: or the adventures of a guinea*, (1765).

qui sait donner mais qui ne sait pas vivre 'Who knows how to give, but not how to live'.

p.157 en conscience in all conscience.

Ninon de l'Enclos celebrated Parisian beauty and wit (1620–1705).

au juste exactly.

p.162 Sortes Virgilianæ telling fortunes by opening a copy of Virgil's poems at random.

Marmontel French writer of novels, plays and moral tales (1723–99); member of the group called the *Philosophes*. Richard Lovell Edgeworth may have met him in France in 1772–3.

p.163 me dire des vérités tell me truths.

la femme comme il n'y en a point the woman like *no* others.

p.164 vous parlez avec . . . you speak with a great deal of unction.

comédie larmoyante sentimental comedy.

p.169 Volto sciolto pensieri stretti face open, thoughts hidden (Italian proverb).

p.175 hammer-cloth cloth covering the coachman's seat.

p.181 Westal Richard Westall (1765–1836), painter, engraver and illustrator.

p.183 moralité à la glace ice-cold morality.

Et puis? and then?

p.188 ce n'est que le premier mot . . . only the first word is difficult. Parody of 'il n'y a que le premier pas qui coute', only the first step is difficult, remark attributed to Mme du Deffand (1697–1780) on hearing the legend that the martyr St Denis walked from Paris to the town of St Denis carrying his head after his martyrdom.

p.190 chevalier d'Eon (1728–1810) famous French transvestite and secret agent for Louis XV.

p.208 obeah-woman West Indian witch.

p.211 unicorn carriage drawn by three horses, two abreast and one in front.

p.217 Lacedæmonian ladies men and women exercised naked together in ancient Sparta.

Honi soit qui mal y pense motto of the Order of the Garter: 'Shame to him who thinks ill.'

p.227 Ithuriel's spear in Milton's *Paradise Lost*, IV, 810.

p.235 sociable carriage with two facing side seats.

p.237 Buerger's Leonora heroine of the ballad 'Lenore', written in 1773 by Gottfried August Bürger (1743–1825).

Madame Tallien wife of a French revolutionary politician, she caused a sensation by appearing in Grecian costume in public in the late 1790s, and made it fashionable.

p.256 Radcliffean reminiscent of the Gothic novels of Anne Radcliffe (1764–1823) and their characteristic scenery.

p.261 Sois grand homme . . . 'Be a great man and be unhappy.'

malheureux imaginaire imaginary sufferer.

Precepte commence . . . instruction begins, example completes.

le bon mari the good husband.

p.262 le futur the intended husband.

p.263 preux chevalier chivalrous knight.

p.264 rantipole wild, careless, disorderly.

p.299 the bishop of St Pol de Leon Jean-François de la Marche (1729–1809). Having refused in 1791 to conform to the revolutionary government's regulations for the French church, he fled to London where he worked on behalf of the French political refugees.

p.301 de suite in sequence.

Yet has his aspect . . . A much modernised version of the description of the parson in Chaucer's *Prologue to the Canterbury Tales*, 11.477–528.

VOLUME III

p.307 Peu à peu little by little.

p.315 Il a infiniment l'air d'un héros de roman He has just the air of the hero of a novel.

p.320 éperdument amoureux desperately in love.

p.321 un petit nez retroussé A little turned-up nose can overturn the laws of an empire.

    Zeluco novel (1786) by Dr John Moore.

p.322 la belle et la bête Beauty and the Beast.

    Zemire and Azor comic opera by Marmontel.

    Faites moi le plaisir Do me the favour, my dear, of fixing the position of your kingdom of habit.

p.323 Un peu d'amour . . . A little love, a little care/often bring a heart a long way.

p.326 imperial trunk designed for the roof of a coach.

    pis aller second-best.

p.328 Tout au contraire Quite on the contrary.

p.331 Mr Day Richard Lovell Edgeworth's friend Thomas Day (1748–89). See Introduction.

p.338 mon métier d'être philosophe my profession to be a philosopher.

    Harpocrates Egyptian god, depicted with a finger to his lips.

p.387 la force du sang the power of blood-relationship.

p.396 con amore lovingly (a musical term).

p.426 Kotzebue German dramatist (1761–1819).

p.438 un gage d'amitié a pledge of friendship.

p.450 Harriet Byron heroine of *Sir Charles Grandison* (1754) by Samuel Richardson (1689–1761).

    Le secret d'ennuyer . . . The secret of being boring is to tell everything.

Sketch of *Belinda* from *A Memoir of Maria Edgeworth*, Mrs Frances Edgeworth, *1867*.

Several of the sketches which Maria made for her stories have been preserved, and as they show the pains she took with her design, and are curious from the alterations which occurred in the writing out of the story, I subjoin a specimen of them. They were written in small, narrow, books shaped like a cheque-book, and, indeed, often sewed into the empty cover of a cheque or stamped receipt-book.

"ORIGINAL SKETCH of BELINDA.

Abroad and at Home.

May 10, 1800.

"*Characters.* — Mrs Stanhope: a politic, well-bred, catch-match-making Aunt, who has succeeded in marrying half-a-dozen nieces to men superior to them in fortune, on which she prides herself extremely. She has only one niece left upon hand, Belinda Portman, whom she is determined to get rid of as soon as possible; and for this purpose she documents her in the art of showing herself off. Mrs Stanhope's character must be shown in a letter of advice to Belinda. She is at Bath with one of her married daughters, who is ill. She has been for some time plotting to get her into the society of Lady Delacour: succeeds.

"Belinda Portman, a young lady of about seventeen, very handsome and accomplished, fond of dress and public amusements, merely because she has tasted no other pleasure. She has good abilities, but she has never yet thought for herself; has been merely a puppet in the hands of her manoeuvring aunt. She is charmed with the idea of her visit to Lady Delacour.

"Lady Delacour, a woman of wit and fashion, who married with the hope of managing her husband and his large fortune, and of distinguishing herself by every species of fashionable folly and extravagance. Dashing, harum-scarum manners happen to be the mode, and she endeavours to exceed all her predecessors and competitors, not only in all that woman, but 'all that man dare do'. Her ambition is to be odd. She thinks that women are

> 'Ne'er so sure the passions to create,
> As when they touch the brink of all we hate.'

She goes so near the brink, that her husband thinks she has gone beyond. They quarrel, hate one another, do not separate, because they cannot afford it; but live miserably together, each following their own pleasures: one of the chief of these pleasures is tormenting each other. Lord Delacour is excessively apprehensive of appearing to be led or governed by his wife. He is a drunkard of the highest fashion, a gambler, and a jockey.

"The contrast between the apparent prosperity and real misery of Lady Delacour must be strongly marked. At home she is wretched; abroad she assumes the air of exuberant gaiety, like the man who wept behind the mask which made others laugh. She has acquaintance in abundance, but no friends. Her manners abroad elegant and fascinating, at home negligent and irascible.

"In a short time after her arrival at Lady Delacour's, Belinda begins to see through this thin veil with which politeness covers domestic misery. She is astonished at the discovery that Lady Delacour, who had appeared to her the most enviable of human beings, is in reality the most wretched. She begins to reflect upon Mrs Stanhope's theories of happiness. *Good* matches, she finds, are not always happy matches. She overhears at Ranelagh, while she is waiting with Lady Delacour for her carriage, a conversation between some young gentlemen about her sisters, her aunt, Lady Delacour, and herself; she is shocked at the manner in which female fortune-hunters are spoken of. She finds that the people who seem most to admire Lady Delacour are the first to abuse her when out of sight: she defends her.

"Lady Delacour finds her with colour raised, in great agitation: begs to know the cause: extorts from Belinda the truth: affects to laugh at the abuse which so much hurt Belinda, but is really vexed by the treachery of her acquaintance and admirers. As she is going home in the carriage she hears her ladyship give a deep sigh: 'If I had served myself with half the zeal that I have served my acquaintance, they would not now forsake me. I have sacrificed reputation and happiness to the love of frolic. I am dying; I shall die unlamented by any human being. If I were to live my life over again, what a different person I would be!'

"Belinda's astonishment at hearing that Lady Delacour is dying! She seems in perfect health and spirits. Lady Delacour repeats, 'I am dying—I know I am dying', and then continues silent till they arrive at home. Invites Belinda for the first time to her toilette. There had always been a great mystery about this toilette. Belinda at first imagined that the mystery was, that her ladyship used cosmetics— yet this she could not long imagine, as she hears her speak of painting, rouge, etc, without hestitation or disguise.

"When she goes into Lady Delacour's dressing-room she finds her ladyship without paint, but still in the dress she wore at Ranelagh — contrast of pale emaciated sallow countenance and gay dress shocks Belinda. Lady Delacour uncovers her bosom and shows her the hideous spectacle of a cancer.

"'My mind is eaten away by an incurable disease like my body. You shall know how I myself caused this cancer; I will tell you my history to-morrow; now I am exhausted. Leave me.'

"Lady Delacour's history: Her account of her feelings when she was acting the various parts of a fine lady's character, gaming without loving gambling — being a dasher, a jockey, her coquetting with a man she did not like, to excite her husband's jealousy — a politician, an electioneerer, and a woman of spirit, affronted by a Mrs Luttridge, who was of an opposite party at an election; quarrel on the hustings — challenge one another, go out in men's clothes; fight a duel, Lady Delacour's pistol recoiled, blow on her breast brought on a cancer.

"This melancholy history makes a great impression on Belinda. So that the very means her aunt had taken to form her for a fine lady had a directly contrary effect. The same objects appear very differently on a distant and a near view. It is safer for young people to see than to hear of certain things.

"Character of Clarence Hervey, one of the young men of fashion who are in the train of Lady Delacour; he has a large fortune: aims at excelling in everything, and ambitious of praise from all descriptions of people; his character, or at least his conduct, varies with every new company or new situation into which he happens to be thrown. He admires Belinda, when he first sees her, because his companions pronounce her to be beautiful. Her Aunt Stanhope extremely anxious that Belinda should spread a net and provide a cage for this young heir.

"Character of Doctor Sane, the physician who attends Lady Delacour in her illness; like Doctor Moore, if you can draw him like the idea that may be found of Doctor Moore from his works; a benevolent man who knows human nature and what is called the world, perfectly: who has polite manners and talents for conversation in a high degree. He is interested for Belinda, a young girl who he thinks is in Lady Delacour's house on the verge of ruin and misery; make use of him to open her eyes to the real characters of all who frequent Lady Delacour's house. He warns her against Clarence Hervey. She is disposed to admire this dashing genius, but her eyes are opened to his real views, (which are not matrimonial), by the conversation she overhears at Ranelagh, and by the prudence and penetration of Doctor Sane, who makes him show off the worst parts of his character. Her reflections upon the miseries of Lady Delacour's apparently happy and really wretched marriage give her sufficient force of mind to conquer her incipient passion for Clarence Hervey; contrary to her Aunt Stanhope's peremptory advice, she discourages instead of attempting to attract him. He considers this as an artifice to draw him on to marriage and trots off.

"Mrs Stanhope quarrels with Belinda for her disobedience and rashness. Illness of Lady Delacour; rapid progress of her disease. Commissions Belinda to go to see her daughter who is at a school in London: she has seen her only for a few weeks at holidays for some years. After having once settled her at a fashionable boarding school she took it for granted that her education would go on in the usual course, and that she should send for her home, and bring her out into the best company at the proper age. When her health so rapidly declines she dreads an interview with her daughter, and she defers it till it is no longer possible.

"The last whimsical ambition with which Lady Delacour is seized is to conceal from all the world that she has a cancer: the secret kept for a considerable time, but her maid Marriott, whom she has indulged partly from vanity and partly from convenience, is incensed at Belinda's being admitted to the secrets of her lady's toilette: she detests Belinda for refusing Clarence Hervey, because he would have bribed her highly if Belinda would have trusted her, and would have encouraged him. Marriott betrays the cancer secret to Mrs Luttridge, the whisper circulates — reaches Lady Delacour the day she has undergone the dreadful operation of having her breast cut off — her vexation brings on fever — gaming debts: her husband refuses to pay. Doctor Sane attends her from humanity, but takes high fees – when he has accumulated a sufficient sum he restores it to her to pay, not her gaming, but her tradesmen's debts. Her death.

"Lord Delacour's brutal insensibility: Belinda endeavours to rouse him to some recollection of his daughter, but that is impossible: he takes a fancy to Belinda – she refuses him: his astonishment. The refusal reaches Clarence Hervey's ears: his opinion of Belinda changed.

"Mrs Stanhope's rage at her niece's refusal of Lord Delacour. Belinda goes to see Helena Delacour: it is during the midsummer holidays: she is on a visit in Kent at the house of a Mrs Piercefield, a cousin of Lady Delacour's, a most amiable woman.

"Upon second thoughts I believe it will be best that Belinda should go to see Lady Delacour's daughter and find her at Mrs Piercefield's during her ladyship's last illness: the contrast between the domestic agonies of Lady Delacour and the domestic happiness of Mrs Piercefield will be more striking.

"Mrs Piercefield was first struck with compassion for the child, seeing that it was so totally neglected by its mother, – pictures of domestic happiness at Mrs Piercefield's, she invites Belinda to her house, who gladly accepts this invitation.

"Whilst all this has been going on Clarence Hervey's character has been undergoing various changes. Doctor Sane's conversations with him during an illness – madness – brought on by drinking for a wager. Anecdotes of Sir Francis Delaval related by Doctor Sane, – Clarence becomes sensible that he has superior abilities, – this consciousness makes him disdain his former associates. He is deeply in debt; has the courage to stop short in the career of dissipation and applies himself to the cultivation of his talents, goes into Parliament, distinguishes himself. Belinda meets with a newspaper with his first speech in it at Mrs Piercefield's; thinks it must be some other Mr Hervey; meets him there; each astonished at the change in the other.

"An uncle of Belinda's dies and she comes unexpectedly into the possession of a large fortune; Mrs Stanhope's affection for her returns, and contrary to her former advice, she now counsels her not to throw herself away upon Hervey: says he admires her judgment in having formerly refused him: he is an eccentric young man, she observes, who with great abilities will not make them useful to himself or any of his connections: he has to her certain knowledge refused the most advantageous offers from ministry upon the old fashioned romantic notion of never acting or speaking contrary to his conscience. Mrs Stanhope's advice and information produces an effect diametrically opposite to her intentions: she marries Hervey, preferring happiness at Home to happiness Abroad.

Review of the first edition of *Belinda* in *Monthly Review*, April 1802, Olyett Woodhouse

The name of Miss Edgeworth does not now require any introduction to our readers; and the account which we gave to her elaborate treatise on Education (Rev. vols. xxx and xxxi. N. S.) will, in particular, have produced considerable respect for her talents. We are here called to notice a production apparently of a different nature, but which may in reality be considered as designed to answer purposes somewhat similar, since the author offers it as 'a Moral Tale'. The spirit and vivacity conspicuous in the first part of it, and the high colouring and boldness of outline which it exhibits in the drawing of some of its characters at the commencement of their action, are in unison with the reputation which Miss E. has already acquired; since they mark this work as the production of no common pen, and evince powers capable of superior productions. We must acknowledge, however, that the imagination of the fair writer seems to have been fatigued and exhausted by the vigour of its first exertions; or, having too highly excited the feelings of the reader by the brilliancy of its first flashes, a tameness and insipidity of effect are hence conceived to prevail in its subsequent efforts. The character of the heroine herself creates so little interest, that she appears to have usurped the superior right of Lady Delacour to give the title to the work: for it is to the character and agency of the latter, in our opinion, that the tale owes its principal attractions. Yet even here the rule of Horace is violated,

> "Servetur ad imum
> Qualis ab incoepto processerit, et sibi constet."

Lady Delacour, while she continues to appear as the votary of vanity and fashion, and heroic under excruciating corporeal suffering, is a Being who interests and even commands some respect: but Lady Delacour reformed, (however favourable to the moral effect of the work this reformation may be), and unexpectedly rescued from bodily pain, is a comparatively flat and vapid creature.

We must confess, also, that there is one circumstance in the conduct of the intended heroine, Belinda Portman, which does not altogether meet with our approbation. Old as we are, and cold too, perhaps, as critics ought to be, we have still so much romance within us, as to deem the virgin's first love an almost sacred bond; to regard with reverence and respect an inviolable constancy to its object; and to feel a kind of repugnance at the admission of a second attachment. We do not mean to deny the justice of the author's arguments against a belief in the unextinguishable nature of a first flame; they may be occasionally introduced into the pages of a novel, or form the subject in a moral essay, with great propriety; we only object to the exemplification of them by the conduct of the present heroine. According to our ideas, (we have pleaded guilty to a little romance), it lessens her amiability; and we should have been better pleased to have seen her in the weeds of widowed affection, than in the gay attire of a second courtship. To enforce the observance of a moral duty by the example of an amiable object is certainly very proper: but then the duty ought to be unequivocal, and the conduct by which it is exemplified should be unambiguously laudable; and neither of these circumstances, we apprehend, exists in the instance to which we are alluding, since celibacy (even volutary celibacy) is no sin, and a want of constancy is no virtue. For these reasons, therefore, as Miss Belinda Portman was once in love with Mr Clarence Hervey, and afterward admitted and encouraged the addresses of Mr Vincent; though we may allow her to be a good reasoner, a great philosopher, and a very proper example for some of our outrageously romantic ladies of the present day; yet she has not called forth in us a great portion of interest in her behalf, nor entitled herself to our highest love and admiration, as a perfect model of the female character.

After these remarks on the principal personages of this work, we shall present our readers with a specimen of its execution in the following extract: which we do not select as the best that we could have chosen, but as containing the most *novel* circumstance, a female duel . . .

The drawing of the character of Lady Delacour certainly possesses great merit, in several respects; and that of Clarence Harvey claims praise for a considerable degree of novelty and force. To speak in detail of the other persons introduced would carry us too far. The good Dr X — is a counterpart of Miss Burney's Dr Lister in *Cecilia*: but we are too much pleased with such a man, to murmur at a second introduction to his acquaintance. Merit, of various kinds, is undoubtedly displayed in the different parts of this work: but, if we describe it generally, and consider it relatively to Miss Edgeworth's former productions, we shall rather be inclined to give the opinion that here she is *sibi dispar*. [unequal to herself].

A second edition of these volumes has appeared, which is said in the title page of be 'corrected and improved'; but, as no particular alterations are specified, and as we had read the former impression, we could not discover the corrections and improvements without perusing the work a second time; and this our leisure will seldom permit, even where our inclination would prompt.

Some other publications by Miss Edgeworth, on the subject of education, are on our table, and will call for our future attention.

Extract from a Review of *Miss Edgeworth's Tales and Novels* [a collected edition] in *Fraser's Magazine*, November 1832

Miss Edgeworth has likewise been very successful in delineating English manners. Her *Modern Griselda, Leonora, Belinda*, and *Patronage*, are great works, consider them as we will. Their ethical merit is not to be doubted, and the spirit of their characteristic sketches not to be exceeded. They contain, it is true, but few full-length portraits; but this is a defect amply compensated by the variety which distinguishes her picture gallery, and the general *vraisemblance* of the likenesses of which it is composed . . .

Belinda is a work of length, though called only a moral tale – "the author not wishing to acknowledge a novel." An incident in *Belinda* gives rise to a point of criticism, which Miss Edgeworth has, however, anticipated. The story of Viginia and Clarence

Harvey was suggested by the circumstance of Mr Day's educating[1] Sabrina for his wife; and many other hints for invention were furnished to Miss Edgeworth by the incidents and characters which her father had met with in his youth, and which he related to her. But, in many cases, she adds, the attempt to join truth and fiction did not succeed; and, in her opinion, the story of Virginia was a failure. To avoid representing the real character of Mr Day, which she did not think it right to draw, she used the incident, with the fictitious characters, which she made as unlike the real persons as she possibly could. Her father observed to her afterwards, that in this and other instances, the very circumstances that were taken from real life are those that have been objected to as improbable or impossible. For this, as he showed her, there were good and sufficient reasons. In the first place, anxiety to avoid drawing the *characters* that were to be blamable or ridiculous from any individuals in real life, led her to apply whatever *circumstances* were taken from reality to characters quite different from those to whom the facts had occurred; and, consequently, when so applied, they were unsuitable and improbable: besides, as her father remarked, the circumstances which in real life fix the attention, because they are out of the common course of events, are for this very reason unfit for the moral purposes, as well as for the dramatic effect of fiction. The interest we take in hearing an uncommon fact, often depends on our belief in its truth. Introduce it into fiction, and this interest ceases – the reader stops to question the truth or probability of the narrative – the illusion and the dramatic effect are destroyed; and as to the moral, no safe conclusion for conduct can be drawn from any circumstances which have not frequently happened, and which are not likely often to recur. In proportion as events are extraordinary, they are useless or unsafe as foundations for prudential reasoning. Besides all this, there are usually, as Miss Edgeworth judiciously remarks, some small concurrent circumstances connected with extraordinary facts, which we like, and admit as evidences of the truth, which the rules of composition and taste forbid the introducing into fiction; so that the writer is reduced to the difficulty either of omitting the evidence on which the belief of reality rests, or of introducing what may be contrary to good taste, incongruous, out of proportion to the rest of the story, delaying its progress or destructive of its unity. In short, it is dangerous to put a patch of truth into a fiction, for the truth is too strong for the fiction, and on all sides pulls it asunder.

1. Mr Day, the author of *Sandford and Merton*, a pleasing poem called the *Dying Negro*. He was a singular character. At the time of Mr Edgeworth's first acquaintance with him, he lived with his parents at Barehill, in Berkshire. He visited at Hare-hatch, during an Oxford vacation: his exterior was not prepossessing; he seldom combed his raven locks, though he was remarkably fond of bathing and he was of a grave and melancholy temperament. Suspicious of the female sex, and averse to risk his happiness with them, he delighted, even in their company, to descant on the evils brought upon mankind by love. Yet he expected that, with a person neither formed by nature nor cultivated by art to please, he should win some female wiser than the rest of women, who should moreover feel for him the most romantic and everlasting attachment. He was perfectly moral, incalculably generous, and enthusiastically patriotic. He conversed on literature of all sorts, but principally on metaphysics; his reasoning was profound and logical – stated with eloquence.

This eccentric individual determined to breed up two girls, as equally as possible, under his own eye; hoping that they might be companions to each other while they were children, and that before they grew up to be women, he might be able to decide which of them would be most agreeable to himself for a wife. From a number of orphans he selected one girl, to whom he gave the name of Sabrina Sydney, and in a few days after went to the Foundling Hospital in London, and chose another, whom he called Lucretia. He took them with him to France, and resided a considerable time at Avignon, where he excited much surprise by his mode of life and by his opinions; but his simplicity of conduct, strict morality, uncommon generosity, and excellent understanding, soon made him respected. He took care that his pupils should not learn French, leaving thus their minds open to such ideas and sentiments only as he desired to implant. Fashion he permitted not, and was not desirous of cultivating their understandings. Their ignorance was, with him, a security for their innocence. He taught them by slow degrees to read and write; by continually talking to them, by reasoning, and by ridicule, he endeavoured to imbue them with a deep hatred for dress, and luxury, and fine people, and fashion, and titles. One of his pupils, being invincibly stupid, he disposed of to a husband with a fortune of three or four hundred pounds. His other pupil, Sabrina Sydney, was, at Mr Day's return from France, a very pleasing girl of thirteen. Her countenance was engaging. She had fine auburn hair, that hung in natural ringlets on her neck; a beauty which was then more striking, because other people wore enormous quantities of powder and pomatum. Her long eyelashes, and eyes expressive of sweetness, interested all who saw her, and the uncommon melody of her voice made a favourable impression upon every person to whom she spoke.

How ended this philosophic romance?

In a pleasant house at Star Hill, close to Lichfield, Mr Day pursued his plan of education with Sabrina, until she was too old to remain in his house without a protectress, when he removed her to a boarding-school at Sutton Colefield. During the early part of the year 1771, however, her guardian conceived an attachment for Miss Honoria Sneyd (afterwards Mrs Honoria Edgeworth), and was in a fair way of acceptance, when he proposed such hard terms as the conditions of his marriage, that the lady was compelled to decline the offer of his hand, and transferred him over to her sister, Miss Elizabeth Sneyd, who succeeded in converting the cynic to some of the assiduities of social life, but could not reward him for his exertions with her heart.

SUGGESTIONS FOR FURTHER READING

There is a large body of biographical information about Maria Edgeworth and her family. The standard modern biography is Marylin Butler's *Maria Edgeworth: A Literary Biography* (Oxford, 1972). This is scholarly and readable, and has some interesting things to say about *Belinda*, including a balanced account of Richard Lovell Edgeworth's influence on the composition of this and other novels. An appendix gives a summary of the post-publication history of *Belinda*.

The original sources for the Edgeworths' lives are also highly readable. They are Richard Lovell Edgeworth's *Memoirs*, published in 1820 in two volumes, of which he wrote the first and Maria the second after his death. In 1867 her family published *A Memoir of Maria Edgeworth*, written by her stepmother Frances Edgeworth, with a selection of her letters. More letters have been published in the twentieth century, in particular *Letters from England* edited by Christian Colvin, 1971.

The following critics write on Maria Edgeworth's fiction generally, tending to stress the Irish novels. Donald Davie, *The Heyday of Sir Walter Scott*; Thomas Flanagan, *The Irish Novelists, 1800–1850*; W.J. McCormack, *Ascendancy and Tradition in Anglo–Irish Literary History from 1789 to 1939*.

On *Belinda* as a novel on the theme of upper-class women's lives and their problem of excess leisure and forced inaction, see Eiléan Ní Chuilleanáin, 'Women as Writers: *Dánta Grá* to Maria Edgeworth', in Eiléan Ní Chuilleanáin ed., *Irish Women: Image and Achievement* (Dublin, 1985) pp.111–26.

Beth Kowaleski-Wallace, 'Home Economics' in *The Eighteenth Century: Theory and Interpretation* (1988) pp.242–62, is interesting on Lady Delacour's supposed breast cancer and contemporary medical writing.

TEXT SUMMARY

Delacour tells Lord Delacour all. She is reconciled both with her husband and Belinda.

XXI *Helena*
Helena returns to her mother and the family move to Twickenham.

XXII *A Spectre*
Lady Delacour is plagued by a 'vision' at night, outside her window. Dr X— informs her she has no need of an operation; her illness is due to the drugs she was taking.

XXIII *The Chaplain*
Dr X— finds a chaplain, Mr Moreton, to minister to Lady Delacour.

VOLUME III

XXIV *Peu à Peu*
Marriott tells Belinda and Lady Delacour of her discoveries about Clarence Hervey. Lady Delacour is introduced to Mr Vincent.

XXV *Love Me, Love My Dog*
Clarence Hervey arrives at Lady Delacour's and meets Mr Vincent and Belinda. Lady Delacour and Belinda are informed by Lady Boucher that Clarence is to be married. Lady Delacour urgently awaits Clarence's packet.

XXVI *Virginia*
Clarence Hervey's packet contains an explanation of his connection with Virginia St Pierre.

XXVII *A Discovery*
Virginia and her long-lost father are reunited.

XXVIII *E O*
Mr Vincent loses his fortune at Mrs Luttridge's E O table but is (temporarily) saved from ruin by Clarence Hervey.

XXIX *A Jew*
Mr Vincent seeks urgent help from a moneylender; a fracas ensues and Mr Vincent's past is revealed. When Belinda hears, she ends their relationship.

xxx *News*
Rumours abound as to whether Clarence Hervey has or has not married Virginia St Pierre.

xxxi *The Denouement*
Belinda and Lady Delacour visit Virginia St Pierre and Lady Delacour executes her plan by which all ends happily.

CLASSIC FICTION
IN EVERYMAN

A SELECTION

Frankenstein
MARY SHELLEY
A masterpiece of Gothic terror in its original 1818 version **£3.99**

Dracula
BRAM STOKER
One of the best known horror stories in the world **£3.99**

The Diary of A Nobody
GEORGE AND WEEDON GROSSMITH
A hilarious account of suburban life in Edwardian London **£4.99**

Some Experiences and Further Experiences of an Irish R. M.
SOMERVILLE AND ROSS
Gems of comic exuberance and improvisation **£4.50**

Three Men in a Boat
JEROME K. JEROME
English humour at its best **£2.99**

Twenty Thousand Leagues under the Sea
JULES VERNE
Scientific fact combines with fantasy in this prophetic tale of underwater adventure **£4.99**

The Best of Father Brown
G. K. CHESTERTON
An irresistible selection of crime stories – unique to Everyman **£3.99**

The Collected Raffles
E. W. HORNUNG
Dashing exploits from the most glamorous figure in crime fiction **£4.99**

£2.99

£5.99

£5.99

AVAILABILITY

All books are available from your local bookshop or direct from
Littlehampton Book Services Cash Sales, 14 Eldon Way, LinesideEstate, Littlehampton, West Sussex BN17 7HE. PRICES ARE SUBJECT TO CHANGE.

To order any of the books, please enclose a cheque (in £ sterling) made payable to Littlehampton Book Services, or phone your order through with credit card details (Access, Visa or Mastercard) on 0903 721596 (24 hour answering service) stating card number and expiry date. Please add £1.25 for package and postage to the total value of your order.

WOMEN'S WRITING IN EVERYMAN

A SELECTION

Female Playwrights of the Restoration
FIVE COMEDIES
Rediscovered literary treasures in a unique selection **£5.99**

The Secret Self
SHORT STORIES BY WOMEN
'A superb collection' *Guardian* **£4.99**

Short Stories
KATHERINE MANSFIELD
An excellent selection displaying the remarkable range of Mansfield's talent **£3.99**

Women Romantic Poets 1780-1830: An Anthology
Hidden talent from the Romantic era, rediscovered for the first time **£5.99**

Selected Poems
ELIZABETH BARRETT BROWNING
A major contribution to our appreciation of this inspiring and innovative poet **£5.99**

Frankenstein
MARY SHELLEY
A masterpiece of Gothic terror in its original 1818 version **£3.99**

The Life of Charlotte Brontë
MRS GASKELL
A moving and perceptive tribute by one writer to another **£4.99**

Vindication of the Rights of Woman and The Subjection of Women
MARY WOLLSTONECRAFT
AND J. S. MILL
Two pioneering works of early feminist thought **£4.99**

The Pastor's Wife
ELIZABETH VON ARNIM
A funny and accomplished novel by the author of *Elizabeth and Her German Garden* **£5.99**

£4.99

£2.99

£5.99

AVAILABILITY
All books are available from your local bookshop or direct from
Littlehampton Book Services Cash Sales, 14 Eldon Way, LinesideEstate, Littlehampton, West Sussex BN17 7HE. PRICES ARE SUBJECT TO CHANGE.

To order any of the books, please enclose a cheque (in £ sterling) made payable to Littlehampton Book Services, or phone your order through with credit card details (Access, Visa or Mastercard) on 0903 721596 (24 hour answering service) stating card number and expiry date. Please add £1.25 for package and postage to the total value of your order.

AMERICAN LITERATURE IN EVERYMAN

A SELECTION

Selected Poems
HENRY LONGFELLOW
A new selection spanning the whole of Longfellow's literary career **£7.99**

Typee
HERMAN MELVILLE
Melville's stirring debut, drawing directly on his own adventures in the South Sea **£4.99**

Billy Budd and Other Stories
HERMAN MELVILLE
The compelling parable of innocence destroyed by a fallen world **£4.99**

The Scarlet Letter
NATHANIEL HAWTHORNE
The compelling tale of an independent woman's struggle against a crushing moral code **£3.99**

The Last of The Mohicans
JAMES FENIMORE COOPER
The classic tale of old America, full of romantic adventure **£5.99**

The Red Badge of Courage
STEPHEN CRANE
A vivid portrayal of a young soldier's experience of the American Civil War **£2.99**

Essays and Poems
RALPH WALDO EMERSON
An indispensable edition celebrating one of the most influential American writers **£5.99**

The Federalist
HAMILTON, MADISON, AND JAY
Classics of political science, these essays helped to found the American Constitution **£6.99**

Leaves of Grass and Selected Prose
WALT WHITMAN
The best of Whitman in one volume **£6.99**

£5.99

£4.99

£4.99

AVAILABILITY

All books are available from your local bookshop or direct from
Littlehampton Book Services Cash Sales, 14 Eldon Way, LinesideEstate, Littlehampton, West Sussex BN17 7HE. PRICES ARE SUBJECT TO CHANGE.

To order any of the books, please enclose a cheque (in £ sterling) made payable to Littlehampton Book Services, or phone your order through with credit card details (Access, Visa or Mastercard) on 0903 721596 (24 hour answering service) stating card number and expiry date. Please add £1.25 for package and postage to the total value of your order.

ESSAYS, CRITICISM AND HISTORY IN EVERYMAN

A SELECTION

The Embassy to Constantinople and Other Writings
LIUDPRAND OF CREMONA
An insider's view of political machinations in medieval Europe
£5.99

The Rights of Man
THOMAS PAINE
One of the great masterpieces of English radicalism **£4.99**

Speeches and Letters
ABRAHAM LINCOLN
A key document of the American Civil War **£4.99**

Essays
FRANCIS BACON
An excellent introduction to Bacon's incisive wit and moral outlook **£3.99**

Puritanism and Liberty: Being the Army Debates (1647-49) from the Clarke Manuscripts
A fascinating revelation of Puritan minds in action **£7.99**

History of His Own Time
BISHOP GILBERT BURNET
A highly readable contemporary account of the Glorious Revolution of 1688 **£7.99**

Biographia Literaria
SAMUEL TAYLOR COLERIDGE
A masterpiece of criticism, marrying the study of literature with philosophy **£4.99**

Essays on Literature and Art
WALTER PATER
Insights on culture and literature from a major voice of the 1890s **£3.99**

Chesterton on Dickens: Criticisms and Appreciations
A landmark in Dickens criticism, rarely surpassed **£4.99**

Essays and Poems
R. L. STEVENSON
Stevenson's hidden treasures in a new selection **£4.99**

£3.99

£4.99

AVAILABILITY

All books are available from your local bookshop or direct from
Littlehampton Book Services Cash Sales, 14 Eldon Way, LinesideEstate, Littlehampton, West Sussex BN17 7HE. PRICES ARE SUBJECT TO CHANGE.

To order any of the books, please enclose a cheque (in £ sterling) made payable to Littlehampton Book Services, or phone your order through with credit card details (Access, Visa or Mastercard) on 0903 721596 (24 hour answering service) stating card number and expiry date. Please add £1.25 for package and postage to the total value of your order.

POETRY
IN EVERYMAN

A SELECTION

Silver Poets of the Sixteenth Century

EDITED BY
DOUGLAS BROOKS-DAVIES
A new edition of this famous
Everyman collection **£6.99**

Complete Poems

JOHN DONNE
The father of metaphysical verse in
this highly-acclaimed edition **£4.99**

Complete English Poems, Of Education, Areopagitica

JOHN MILTON
An excellent introduction to
Milton's poetry and prose **£6.99**

Selected Poems

JOHN DRYDEN
A poet's portrait of Restoration
England **£4.99**

Selected Poems

PERCY BYSSHE SHELLEY
'The essential Shelley' in one
volume **£3.50**

Women Romantic Poets 1780-1830: An Anthology

Hidden talent from the Romantic era,
rediscovered for the first time **£5.99**

Poems in Scots and English

ROBERT BURNS
The best of Scotland's greatest lyric
poet **£4.99**

Selected Poems

D. H. LAWRENCE
A newly-edited selection spanning
the whole of Lawrence's literary
career **£4.99**

The Poems

W. B. YEATS
Ireland's greatest lyric poet
surveyed in this ground-breaking
edition **£6.50**

£5.99

£4.99

£3.50

AVAILABILITY

All books are available from your local bookshop or direct from
Littlehampton Book Services Cash Sales, 14 Eldon Way, LinesideEstate, Littlehampton, West Sussex BN17 7HE. PRICES ARE SUBJECT TO CHANGE.

To order any of the books, please enclose a cheque (in £ sterling) made payable to
Littlehampton Book Services, or phone your order through with credit card details (Access,
Visa or Mastercard) on 0903 721596 (24 hour answering service) stating card number and
expiry date. Please add £1.25 for package and postage to the total value of your order.

SHORT STORY COLLECTIONS
IN EVERYMAN

A SELECTION

**The Secret Self
Short Stories by Women**
'A superb collection' *Guardian* **£4.99**

**Selected Short Stories
and Poems**
THOMAS HARDY
The best of Hardy's Wessex in a
unique selection **£4.99**

**The Best of
Sherlock Holmes**
ARTHUR CONAN DOYLE
All the favourite adventures in one
volume **£4.99**

**Great Tales of Detection
Nineteen Stories**
Chosen by Dorothy L. Sayers **£3.99**

Short Stories
KATHERINE MANSFIELD
A selection displaying the
remarkable range of Mansfield's
writing **£3.99**

Selected Stories
RUDYARD KIPLING
Includes stories chosen to reveal the
'other' Kipling **£4.50**

**The Strange Case of
Dr Jekyll and Mr Hyde
and Other Stories**
R. L. STEVENSON
An exciting selection of gripping
tales from a master of suspense **£3.99**

**Modern Short Stories 2:
1940-1980**
Thirty-one stories from the greatest
modern writers **£3.50**

**The Day of Silence and
Other Stories**
GEORGE GISSING
Gissing's finest stories, available for
the first time in one volume **£4.99**

Selected Tales
HENRY JAMES
Stories portraying the tensions
between private life and the outside
world **£5.99**

£4.99

£6.99

AVAILABILITY

All books are available from your local bookshop or direct from
**Littlehampton Book Services Cash Sales, 14 Eldon Way, LinesideEstate,
Littlehampton, West Sussex BN17 7HE.** PRICES ARE SUBJECT TO CHANGE.

To order any of the books, please enclose a cheque (in £ sterling) made payable to
Littlehampton Book Services, or phone your order through with credit card details (Access,
Visa or Mastercard) on 0903 721596 (24 hour answering service) stating card number and
expiry date. Please add £1.25 for package and postage to the total value of your order.

DRAMA
IN EVERYMAN

A SELECTION

Everyman and Medieval Miracle Plays

EDITED BY A. C. CAWLEY
A selection of the most popular
medieval plays **£3.99**

Complete Plays and Poems

CHRISTOPHER MARLOWE
The complete works of this
fascinating Elizabethan in one
volume **£5.99**

Complete Poems and Plays

ROCHESTER
The most sexually explicit – and
strikingly modern – writing of the
seventeenth century **£5.99**

Restoration Plays

Five comedies and two tragedies
representing the best of the
Restoration stage **£7.99**

Female Playwrights of the Restoration: Five Comedies

Rediscovered literary treasures in a
unique selection **£5.99**

Poems and Plays

OLIVER GOLDSMITH
The most complete edition of
Goldsmith available **£4.99**

Plays, Poems and Prose

J. M. SYNGE
The most complete edition of Synge
available **£6.99**

Plays, Prose Writings and Poems

OSCAR WILDE
The full force of Wilde's wit in one
volume **£4.99**

A Doll's House/The Lady from the Sea/The Wild Duck

HENRIK IBSEN
A popular selection of Ibsen's major
plays **£3.99**

£2.99

£2.99

£2.99

AVAILABILITY

All books are available from your local bookshop or direct from
**Littlehampton Book Services Cash Sales, 14 Eldon Way, LinesideEstate,
Littlehampton, West Sussex BN17 7HE.** PRICES ARE SUBJECT TO CHANGE.

To order any of the books, please enclose a cheque (in £ sterling) made payable to
Littlehampton Book Services, or phone your order through with credit card details (Access,
Visa or Mastercard) on 0903 721596 (24 hour answering service) stating card number and
expiry date. Please add £1.25 for package and postage to the total value of your order.